PERCY JACKSON

DEMIGOD COLLECTION

THE LIGHTNING THIEF

THE LOST HERO

THE HIDDEN ORACLE

ALSO BY RICK RIORDAN

PERCY JACKSON AND THE OLYMPIANS
Book One: *The Lightning Thief*
Book Two: *The Sea of Monsters*
Book Three: *The Titan's Curse*
Book Four: *The Battle of the Labyrinth*
Book Five: *The Last Olympian*
The Demigod Files
The Lightning Thief: The Graphic Novel
The Sea of Monsters: The Graphic Novel
The Titan's Curse: The Graphic Novel
The Battle of the Labyrinth: The Graphic Novel
The Last Olympian: The Graphic Novel
Percy Jackson's Greek Gods
Percy Jackson's Greek Heroes
From Percy Jackson: Camp Half-Blood Confidential

THE KANE CHRONICLES
Book One: *The Red Pyramid*
Book Two: *The Throne of Fire*
Book Three: *The Serpent's Shadow*
The Red Pyramid: The Graphic Novel
The Throne of Fire: The Graphic Novel
The Serpent's Shadow: The Graphic Novel
From the Kane Chronicles: Brooklyn House Magicians' Manual

THE HEROES OF OLYMPUS
Book One: *The Lost Hero*
Book Two: *The Son of Neptune*
Book Three: *The Mark of Athena*
Book Four: *The House of Hades*
Book Five: *The Blood of Olympus*
The Demigod Diaries
The Lost Hero: The Graphic Novel
The Son of Neptune: The Graphic Novel
Demigods & Magicians

MAGNUS CHASE AND THE GODS OF ASGARD
Book One: *The Sword of Summer*
Book Two: *The Hammer of Thor*
Book Three: *The Ship of the Dead*
For Magnus Chase: Hotel Valhalla Guide to the Norse Worlds
9 from the Nine Worlds

THE TRIALS OF APOLLO
Book One: *The Hidden Oracle*
Book Two: *The Dark Prophecy*
Book Three: *The Burning Maze*
Book Four: *The Tyrant's Tomb*

RICK RIORDAN

PERCY JACKSON
DEMIGOD COLLECTION

PERCY JACKSON AND THE OLYMPIANS, BOOK ONE
THE LIGHTNING THIEF

THE HEROES OF OLYMPUS, BOOK ONE
THE LOST HERO

THE TRIALS OF APOLLO, BOOK ONE
THE HIDDEN ORACLE

DISNEP • HYPERION
LOS ANGELES   NEW YORK

First Bind-Up Edition, September 2019
10 9 8 7 6 5 4 3 2 1
FAC-025438-19221
Printed in the United States of America
Designed by Joann Hill
Text is set in Adobe Caslon Pro, Danton, Gauthier FY, Goudy, Goudy Oldstyle,
Trajan Pro 3, Questal/Fontspring; Centaur MT, Sabon/Monotype

Library of Congress Control Number for *The Lightning Thief* Hardcover Edition:
2005299400
Library of Congress Control Number for *The Lost Hero* Hardcover Edition:
2010015469
Library of Congress Control Number for *The Hidden Oracle* Hardcover Edition:
2015045235
ISBN 978-1-368-05748-6

Visit www.DisneyBooks.com
Follow @ReadRiordan

RICK RIORDAN

PERCY JACKSON

AND THE OLYMPIANS

I

THE LIGHTNING THIEF

DISNEP·HYPERION
Los Angeles New York

To Haley,
who heard the story first

CONTENTS

1. I Accidentally Vaporize My Pre-algebra Teacher / 1

2. Three Old Ladies Knit the Socks of Death / 16

3. Grover Unexpectedly Loses His Pants / 29

4. My Mother Teaches Me Bullfighting / 44

5. I Play Pinochle with a Horse / 57

6. I Become Supreme Lord of the Bathroom / 75

7. My Dinner Goes Up in Smoke / 93

8. We Capture a Flag / 107

9. I Am Offered a Quest / 127

10. I Ruin a Perfectly Good Bus / 149

11. We Visit the Garden Gnome Emporium / 168

12. We Get Advice from a Poodle / 188

13. I Plunge to My Death / 197

14. I Become a Known Fugitive / 212

15. A God Buys Us Cheeseburgers / 219

16. We Take a Zebra to Vegas / 242

17. We Shop for Water Beds / 266

18. Annabeth Does Obedience School / 283

19. We Find Out the Truth, Sort Of / 300

20. I Battle My Jerk Relative / 320

21. I Settle My Tab / 334

22. The Prophecy Comes True / 354

I ACCIDENTALLY VAPORIZE MY PRE-ALGEBRA TEACHER

Look, I didn't want to be a half-blood.

If you're reading this because you think you might be one, my advice is: close this book right now. Believe whatever lie your mom or dad told you about your birth, and try to lead a normal life.

Being a half-blood is dangerous. It's scary. Most of the time, it gets you killed in painful, nasty ways.

If you're a normal kid, reading this because you think it's fiction, great. Read on. I envy you for being able to believe that none of this ever happened.

But if you recognize yourself in these pages—if you feel something stirring inside—stop reading immediately. You might be one of us. And once you know that, it's only a matter of time before *they* sense it too, and they'll come for you.

Don't say I didn't warn you.

My name is Percy Jackson.

I'm twelve years old. Until a few months ago, I was a boarding student at Yancy Academy, a private school for troubled kids in upstate New York.

Am I a troubled kid?

Yeah. You could say that.

I could start at any point in my short miserable life to prove it, but things really started going bad last May, when our sixth-grade class took a field trip to Manhattan—twenty-eight mental-case kids and two teachers on a yellow school bus, heading to the Metropolitan Museum of Art to look at ancient Greek and Roman stuff.

I know—it sounds like torture. Most Yancy field trips were.

But Mr. Brunner, our Latin teacher, was leading this trip, so I had hopes.

Mr. Brunner was this middle-aged guy in a motorized wheelchair. He had thinning hair and a scruffy beard and a frayed tweed jacket, which always smelled like coffee. You wouldn't think he'd be cool, but he told stories and jokes and let us play games in class. He also had this awesome collection of Roman armor and weapons, so he was the only teacher whose class didn't put me to sleep.

I hoped the trip would be okay. At least, I hoped that for once I wouldn't get in trouble.

Boy, was I wrong.

See, bad things happen to me on field trips. Like at my fifth-grade school, when we went to the Saratoga battlefield, I had this accident with a Revolutionary War cannon. I wasn't aiming for the school bus, but of course I got expelled anyway. And before that, at my fourth-grade school, when we took a behind-the-scenes tour of the Marine World shark pool, I sort of hit the wrong lever on the catwalk and our class took an unplanned swim. And the time before that . . . Well, you get the idea.

This trip, I was determined to be good.

All the way into the city, I put up with Nancy Bobofit, the freckly, redheaded kleptomaniac girl, hitting my best friend Grover in the back of the head with chunks of peanut butter-and-ketchup sandwich.

Grover was an easy target. He was scrawny. He cried when he got frustrated. He must've been held back several grades, because he was the only sixth grader with acne and the start of a wispy beard on his chin. On top of all that, he was crippled. He had a note excusing him from PE for the rest of his life because he had some kind of muscular disease in his legs. He walked funny, like every step hurt him, but don't let that fool you. You should've seen him run when it was enchilada day in the cafeteria.

Anyway, Nancy Bobofit was throwing wads of sandwich that stuck in his curly brown hair, and she knew I couldn't do anything back to her because I was already on probation. The headmaster had threatened me with death by in-school suspension if anything bad, embarrassing, or even mildly entertaining happened on this trip.

"I'm going to kill her," I mumbled.

Grover tried to calm me down. "It's okay. I like peanut butter."

He dodged another piece of Nancy's lunch.

"That's it." I started to get up, but Grover pulled me back to my seat.

"You're already on probation," he reminded me. "You know who'll get blamed if anything happens."

Looking back on it, I wish I'd decked Nancy Bobofit

right then and there. In-school suspension would've been nothing compared to the mess I was about to get myself into.

Mr. Brunner led the museum tour.

He rode up front in his wheelchair, guiding us through the big echoey galleries, past marble statues and glass cases full of really old black-and-orange pottery.

It blew my mind that this stuff had survived for two thousand, three thousand years.

He gathered us around a thirteen-foot-tall stone column with a big sphinx on the top, and started telling us how it was a grave marker, a *stele*, for a girl about our age. He told us about the carvings on the sides. I was trying to listen to what he had to say, because it was kind of interesting, but everybody around me was talking, and every time I told them to shut up, the other teacher chaperone, Mrs. Dodds, would give me the evil eye.

Mrs. Dodds was this little math teacher from Georgia who always wore a black leather jacket, even though she was fifty years old. She looked mean enough to ride a Harley right into your locker. She had come to Yancy halfway through the year, when our last math teacher had a nervous breakdown.

From her first day, Mrs. Dodds loved Nancy Bobofit and figured I was devil spawn. She would point her crooked finger at me and say, "Now, honey," real sweet, and I knew I was going to get after-school detention for a month.

One time, after she'd made me erase answers out of old math workbooks until midnight, I told Grover I didn't think Mrs. Dodds was human. He looked at me, real serious, and said, "You're absolutely right."

Mr. Brunner kept talking about Greek funeral art.

Finally, Nancy Bobofit snickered something about the naked guy on the stele, and I turned around and said, "Will you *shut up?*"

It came out louder than I meant it to.

The whole group laughed. Mr. Brunner stopped his story.

"Mr. Jackson," he said, "did you have a comment?"

My face was totally red. I said, "No, sir."

Mr. Brunner pointed to one of the pictures on the stele. "Perhaps you'll tell us what this picture represents?"

I looked at the carving, and felt a flush of relief, because I actually recognized it. "That's Kronos eating his kids, right?"

"Yes," Mr. Brunner said, obviously not satisfied. "And he did this because . . ."

"Well . . ." I racked my brain to remember. "Kronos was the king god, and—"

"God?" Mr. Brunner asked.

"Titan," I corrected myself. "And . . . he didn't trust his kids, who were the gods. So, um, Kronos ate them, right? But his wife hid baby Zeus, and gave Kronos a rock to eat instead. And later, when Zeus grew up, he tricked his dad, Kronos, into barfing up his brothers and sisters—"

"Eeew!" said one of the girls behind me.

"—and so there was this big fight between the gods and the Titans," I continued, "and the gods won."

Some snickers from the group.

Behind me, Nancy Bobofit mumbled to a friend, "Like we're going to use this in real life. Like it's going to say on our job applications, 'Please explain why Kronos ate his kids.'"

"And why, Mr. Jackson," Brunner said, "to paraphrase Miss Bobofit's excellent question, does this matter in real life?"

"Busted," Grover muttered.

"Shut up," Nancy hissed, her face even brighter red than her hair.

At least Nancy got packed, too. Mr. Brunner was the only one who ever caught her saying anything wrong. He had radar ears.

I thought about his question, and shrugged. "I don't know, sir."

"I see." Mr. Brunner looked disappointed. "Well, half credit, Mr. Jackson. Zeus did indeed feed Kronos a mixture of mustard and wine, which made him disgorge his other five children, who, of course, being immortal gods, had been living and growing up completely undigested in the Titan's stomach. The gods defeated their father, sliced him to pieces with his own scythe, and scattered his remains in Tartarus, the darkest part of the Underworld. On that happy note, it's time for lunch. Mrs. Dodds, would you lead us back outside?"

The class drifted off, the girls holding their stomachs, the guys pushing each other around and acting like doofuses.

Grover and I were about to follow when Mr. Brunner said, "Mr. Jackson."

I knew that was coming.

I told Grover to keep going. Then I turned toward Mr. Brunner. "Sir?"

Mr. Brunner had this look that wouldn't let you go— intense brown eyes that could've been a thousand years old and had seen everything.

"You must learn the answer to my question," Mr. Brunner told me.

"About the Titans?"

"About real life. And how your studies apply to it."

"Oh."

"What you learn from me," he said, "is vitally important. I expect you to treat it as such. I will accept only the best from you, Percy Jackson."

I wanted to get angry, this guy pushed me so hard.

I mean, sure, it was kind of cool on tournament days, when he dressed up in a suit of Roman armor and shouted: "What ho!" and challenged us, sword-point against chalk, to run to the board and name every Greek and Roman person who had ever lived, and their mother, and what god they worshipped. But Mr. Brunner expected me to be as good as everybody else, despite the fact that I have dyslexia and attention deficit disorder and I had never made above a C— in my life. No—he didn't expect me to be *as good*; he expected me to be *better*. And I just couldn't learn all those names and facts, much less spell them correctly.

I mumbled something about trying harder, while Mr.

Brunner took one long sad look at the stele, like he'd been at this girl's funeral.

He told me to go outside and eat my lunch.

The class gathered on the front steps of the museum, where we could watch the foot traffic along Fifth Avenue.

Overhead, a huge storm was brewing, with clouds blacker than I'd ever seen over the city. I figured maybe it was global warming or something, because the weather all across New York state had been weird since Christmas. We'd had massive snow storms, flooding, wildfires from lightning strikes. I wouldn't have been surprised if this was a hurricane blowing in.

Nobody else seemed to notice. Some of the guys were pelting pigeons with Lunchables crackers. Nancy Bobofit was trying to pickpocket something from a lady's purse, and, of course, Mrs. Dodds wasn't seeing a thing.

Grover and I sat on the edge of the fountain, away from the others. We thought that maybe if we did that, everybody wouldn't know we were from *that* school—the school for loser freaks who couldn't make it elsewhere.

"Detention?" Grover asked.

"Nah," I said. "Not from Brunner. I just wish he'd lay off me sometimes. I mean—I'm not a genius."

Grover didn't say anything for a while. Then, when I thought he was going to give me some deep philosophical comment to make me feel better, he said, "Can I have your apple?"

I didn't have much of an appetite, so I let him take it.

I watched the stream of cabs going down Fifth Avenue, and thought about my mom's apartment, only a little ways uptown from where we sat. I hadn't seen her since Christmas. I wanted so bad to jump in a taxi and head home. She'd hug me and be glad to see me, but she'd be disappointed, too. She'd send me right back to Yancy, remind me that I had to try harder, even if this was my sixth school in six years and I was probably going to be kicked out again. I wouldn't be able to stand that sad look she'd give me.

Mr. Brunner parked his wheelchair at the base of the handicapped ramp. He ate celery while he read a paperback novel. A red umbrella stuck up from the back of his chair, making it look like a motorized café table.

I was about to unwrap my sandwich when Nancy Bobofit appeared in front of me with her ugly friends—I guess she'd gotten tired of stealing from the tourists—and dumped her half-eaten lunch in Grover's lap.

"Oops." She grinned at me with her crooked teeth. Her freckles were orange, as if somebody had spray-painted her face with liquid Cheetos.

I tried to stay cool. The school counselor had told me a million times, "Count to ten, get control of your temper." But I was so mad my mind went blank. A wave roared in my ears.

I don't remember touching her, but the next thing I knew, Nancy was sitting on her butt in the fountain, screaming, "Percy pushed me!"

Mrs. Dodds materialized next to us.

Some of the kids were whispering: "Did you see—"

"—the water—"

"—like it grabbed her—"

I didn't know what they were talking about. All I knew was that I was in trouble again.

As soon as Mrs. Dodds was sure poor little Nancy was okay, promising to get her a new shirt at the museum gift shop, etc., etc., Mrs. Dodds turned on me. There was a triumphant fire in her eyes, as if I'd done something she'd been waiting for all semester. "Now, honey—"

"I know," I grumbled. "A month erasing workbooks."

That wasn't the right thing to say.

"Come with me," Mrs. Dodds said.

"Wait!" Grover yelped. "It was me. *I* pushed her."

I stared at him, stunned. I couldn't believe he was trying to cover for me. Mrs. Dodds scared Grover to death.

She glared at him so hard his whiskery chin trembled.

"I don't think so, Mr. Underwood," she said.

"But—"

"You—*will*—stay—here."

Grover looked at me desperately.

"It's okay, man," I told him. "Thanks for trying."

"Honey," Mrs. Dodds barked at me. *"Now."*

Nancy Bobofit smirked.

I gave her my deluxe I'll-kill-you-later stare. Then I turned to face Mrs. Dodds, but she wasn't there. She was standing at the museum entrance, way at the top of the steps, gesturing impatiently at me to come on.

How'd she get there so fast?

I have moments like that a lot, when my brain falls asleep or something, and the next thing I know I've missed something, as if a puzzle piece fell out of the universe and left me staring at the blank place behind it. The school counselor told me this was part of the ADHD, my brain misinterpreting things.

I wasn't so sure.

I went after Mrs. Dodds.

Halfway up the steps, I glanced back at Grover. He was looking pale, cutting his eyes between me and Mr. Brunner, like he wanted Mr. Brunner to notice what was going on, but Mr. Brunner was absorbed in his novel.

I looked back up. Mrs. Dodds had disappeared again. She was now inside the building, at the end of the entrance hall.

Okay, I thought. She's going to make me buy a new shirt for Nancy at the gift shop.

But apparently that wasn't the plan.

I followed her deeper into the museum. When I finally caught up to her, we were back in the Greek and Roman section.

Except for us, the gallery was empty.

Mrs. Dodds stood with her arms crossed in front of a big marble frieze of the Greek gods. She was making this weird noise in her throat, like growling.

Even without the noise, I would've been nervous. It's weird being alone with a teacher, especially Mrs. Dodds. Something about the way she looked at the frieze, as if she wanted to pulverize it . . .

"You've been giving us problems, honey," she said.

I did the safe thing. I said, "Yes, ma'am."

She tugged on the cuffs of her leather jacket. "Did you really think you would get away with it?"

The look in her eyes was beyond mad. It was evil.

She's a teacher, I thought nervously. It's not like she's going to hurt me.

I said, "I'll—I'll try harder, ma'am."

Thunder shook the building.

"We are not fools, Percy Jackson," Mrs. Dodds said. "It was only a matter of time before we found you out. Confess, and you will suffer less pain."

I didn't know what she was talking about.

All I could think of was that the teachers must've found the illegal stash of candy I'd been selling out of my dorm room. Or maybe they'd realized I got my essay on *Tom Sawyer* from the Internet without ever reading the book and now they were going to take away my grade. Or worse, they were going to make me read the book.

"Well?" she demanded.

"Ma'am, I don't . . ."

"Your time is up," she hissed.

Then the weirdest thing happened. Her eyes began to glow like barbecue coals. Her fingers stretched, turning into talons. Her jacket melted into large, leathery wings. She wasn't human. She was a shriveled hag with bat wings and claws and a mouth full of yellow fangs, and she was about to slice me to ribbons.

Then things got even stranger.

Mr. Brunner, who'd been out in front of the museum a minute before, wheeled his chair into the doorway of the gallery, holding a pen in his hand.

"What ho, Percy!" he shouted, and tossed the pen through the air.

Mrs. Dodds lunged at me.

With a yelp, I dodged and felt talons slash the air next to my ear. I snatched the ballpoint pen out of the air, but when it hit my hand, it wasn't a pen anymore. It was a sword—Mr. Brunner's bronze sword, which he always used on tournament day.

Mrs. Dodds spun toward me with a murderous look in her eyes.

My knees were jelly. My hands were shaking so bad I almost dropped the sword.

She snarled, "Die, honey!"

And she flew straight at me.

Absolute terror ran through my body. I did the only thing that came naturally: I swung the sword.

The metal blade hit her shoulder and passed clean through her body as if she were made of water. *Hisss!*

Mrs. Dodds was a sand castle in a power fan. She exploded into yellow powder, vaporized on the spot, leaving nothing but the smell of sulfur and a dying screech and a chill of evil in the air, as if those two glowing red eyes were still watching me.

I was alone.

There was a ballpoint pen in my hand.

Mr. Brunner wasn't there. Nobody was there but me.

My hands were still trembling. My lunch must've been contaminated with magic mushrooms or something.

Had I imagined the whole thing?

I went back outside.

It had started to rain.

Grover was sitting by the fountain, a museum map tented over his head. Nancy Bobofit was still standing there, soaked from her swim in the fountain, grumbling to her ugly friends. When she saw me, she said, "I hope Mrs. Kerr whipped your butt."

I said, "Who?"

"Our *teacher*. Duh!"

I blinked. We had no teacher named Mrs. Kerr. I asked Nancy what she was talking about.

She just rolled her eyes and turned away.

I asked Grover where Mrs. Dodds was.

He said, "Who?"

But he paused first, and he wouldn't look at me, so I thought he was messing with me.

"Not funny, man," I told him. "This is serious."

Thunder boomed overhead.

I saw Mr. Brunner sitting under his red umbrella, reading his book, as if he'd never moved.

I went over to him.

He looked up, a little distracted. "Ah, that would be my pen. Please bring your own writing utensil in the future, Mr. Jackson."

I handed Mr. Brunner his pen. I hadn't even realized I

was still holding it.

"Sir," I said, "where's Mrs. Dodds?"

He stared at me blankly. "Who?"

"The other chaperone. Mrs. Dodds. The pre-algebra teacher."

He frowned and sat forward, looking mildly concerned. "Percy, there is no Mrs. Dodds on this trip. As far as I know, there has never been a Mrs. Dodds at Yancy Academy. Are you feeling all right?"

TWO

THREE OLD LADIES KNIT THE SOCKS OF DEATH

I was used to the occasional weird experience, but usually they were over quickly. This twenty-four/seven hallucination was more than I could handle. For the rest of the school year, the entire campus seemed to be playing some kind of trick on me. The students acted as if they were completely and totally convinced that Mrs. Kerr—a perky blond woman whom I'd never seen in my life until she got on our bus at the end of the field trip—had been our pre-algebra teacher since Christmas.

Every so often I would spring a Mrs. Dodds reference on somebody, just to see if I could trip them up, but they would stare at me like I was psycho.

It got so I almost believed them—Mrs. Dodds had never existed.

Almost.

But Grover couldn't fool me. When I mentioned the name Dodds to him, he would hesitate, then claim she didn't exist. But I knew he was lying.

Something was going on. Something *had* happened at the museum.

I didn't have much time to think about it during the days, but at night, visions of Mrs. Dodds with talons and leathery wings would wake me up in a cold sweat.

The freak weather continued, which didn't help my mood. One night, a thunderstorm blew out the windows in my dorm room. A few days later, the biggest tornado ever spotted in the Hudson Valley touched down only fifty miles from Yancy Academy. One of the current events we studied in social studies class was the unusual number of small planes that had gone down in sudden squalls in the Atlantic that year.

I started feeling cranky and irritable most of the time. My grades slipped from Ds to Fs. I got into more fights with Nancy Bobofit and her friends. I was sent out into the hallway in almost every class.

Finally, when our English teacher, Mr. Nicoll, asked me for the millionth time why I was too lazy to study for spelling tests, I snapped. I called him an old sot. I wasn't even sure what it meant, but it sounded good.

The headmaster sent my mom a letter the following week, making it official: I would not be invited back next year to Yancy Academy.

Fine, I told myself. Just fine.

I was homesick.

I wanted to be with my mom in our little apartment on the Upper East Side, even if I had to go to public school and put up with my obnoxious stepfather and his stupid poker parties.

And yet . . . there were things I'd miss at Yancy. The view of the woods out my dorm window, the Hudson River in the distance, the smell of pine trees. I'd miss Grover, who'd been a good friend, even if he was a little strange. I worried how he'd survive next year without me.

I'd miss Latin class, too—Mr. Brunner's crazy tournament days and his faith that I could do well.

As exam week got closer, Latin was the only test I studied for. I hadn't forgotten what Mr. Brunner had told me about this subject being life-and-death for me. I wasn't sure why, but I'd started to believe him.

The evening before my final, I got so frustrated I threw the *Cambridge Guide to Greek Mythology* across my dorm room. Words had started swimming off the page, circling my head, the letters doing one-eighties as if they were riding skateboards. There was no way I was going to remember the difference between Chiron and Charon, or Polydictes and Polydeuces. And conjugating those Latin verbs? Forget it.

I paced the room, feeling like ants were crawling around inside my shirt.

I remembered Mr. Brunner's serious expression, his thousand-year-old eyes. *I will accept only the best from you, Percy Jackson.*

I took a deep breath. I picked up the mythology book.

I'd never asked a teacher for help before. Maybe if I talked to Mr. Brunner, he could give me some pointers. At least I could apologize for the big fat F I was about to score on his exam. I didn't want to leave Yancy Academy with him thinking I hadn't tried.

I walked downstairs to the faculty offices. Most of them were dark and empty, but Mr. Brunner's door was ajar, light from his window stretching across the hallway floor.

I was three steps from the door handle when I heard voices inside the office. Mr. Brunner asked a question. A voice that was definitely Grover's said ". . . worried about Percy, sir."

I froze.

I'm not usually an eavesdropper, but I dare you to try not listening if you hear your best friend talking about you to an adult.

I inched closer.

". . . alone this summer," Grover was saying. "I mean, a Kindly One in the *school*! Now that we know for sure, and *they* know too—"

"We would only make matters worse by rushing him," Mr. Brunner said. "We need the boy to mature more."

"But he may not have time. The summer solstice deadline—"

"Will have to be resolved without him, Grover. Let him enjoy his ignorance while he still can."

"Sir, he *saw* her. . . ."

"His imagination," Mr. Brunner insisted. "The Mist over the students and staff will be enough to convince him of that."

"Sir, I . . . I can't fail in my duties again." Grover's voice was choked with emotion. "You know what that would mean."

"You haven't failed, Grover," Mr. Brunner said kindly. "I should have seen her for what she was. Now let's just worry about keeping Percy alive until next fall—"

The mythology book dropped out of my hand and hit the floor with a thud.

Mr. Brunner went silent.

My heart hammering, I picked up the book and backed down the hall.

A shadow slid across the lighted glass of Brunner's office door, the shadow of something much taller than my wheelchair-bound teacher, holding something that looked suspiciously like an archer's bow.

I opened the nearest door and slipped inside.

A few seconds later I heard a slow *clop-clop-clop*, like muffled wood blocks, then a sound like an animal snuffling right outside my door. A large, dark shape paused in front of the glass, then moved on.

A bead of sweat trickled down my neck.

Somewhere in the hallway, Mr. Brunner spoke. "Nothing," he murmured. "My nerves haven't been right since the winter solstice."

"Mine neither," Grover said. "But I could have sworn . . ."

"Go back to the dorm," Mr. Brunner told him. "You've got a long day of exams tomorrow."

"Don't remind me."

The lights went out in Mr. Brunner's office.

I waited in the dark for what seemed like forever.

Finally, I slipped out into the hallway and made my way back up to the dorm.

Grover was lying on his bed, studying his Latin exam notes like he'd been there all night.

"Hey," he said, bleary-eyed. "You going to be ready for this test?"

I didn't answer.

"You look awful." He frowned. "Is everything okay?"

"Just . . . tired."

I turned so he couldn't read my expression, and started getting ready for bed.

I didn't understand what I'd heard downstairs. I wanted to believe I'd imagined the whole thing.

But one thing was clear: Grover and Mr. Brunner were talking about me behind my back. They thought I was in some kind of danger.

The next afternoon, as I was leaving the three-hour Latin exam, my eyes swimming with all the Greek and Roman names I'd misspelled, Mr. Brunner called me back inside.

For a moment, I was worried he'd found out about my eavesdropping the night before, but that didn't seem to be the problem.

"Percy," he said. "Don't be discouraged about leaving Yancy. It's . . . it's for the best."

His tone was kind, but the words still embarrassed me. Even though he was speaking quietly, the other kids finishing the test could hear. Nancy Bobofit smirked at me and made sarcastic little kissing motions with her lips.

I mumbled, "Okay, sir."

"I mean . . ." Mr. Brunner wheeled his chair back and forth, like he wasn't sure what to say. "This isn't the right place for you. It was only a matter of time."

My eyes stung.

Here was my favorite teacher, in front of the class, telling me I couldn't handle it. After saying he believed in me all year, now he was telling me I was destined to get kicked out.

"Right," I said, trembling.

"No, no," Mr. Brunner said. "Oh, confound it all. What I'm trying to say . . . you're not normal, Percy. That's nothing to be—"

"Thanks," I blurted. "Thanks a lot, sir, for reminding me."

"Percy—"

But I was already gone.

On the last day of the term, I shoved my clothes into my suitcase.

The other guys were joking around, talking about their vacation plans. One of them was going on a hiking trip to Switzerland. Another was cruising the Caribbean for a month. They were juvenile delinquents, like me, but they were *rich* juvenile delinquents. Their daddies were executives, or ambassadors, or celebrities. I was a nobody, from a family of nobodies.

They asked me what I'd be doing this summer and I told them I was going back to the city.

What I didn't tell them was that I'd have to get a summer job walking dogs or selling magazine subscriptions, and spend my free time worrying about where I'd go to school in the fall.

"Oh," one of the guys said. "That's cool."

They went back to their conversation as if I'd never existed.

The only person I dreaded saying good-bye to was Grover, but as it turned out, I didn't have to. He'd booked a ticket to Manhattan on the same Greyhound as I had, so there we were, together again, heading into the city.

During the whole bus ride, Grover kept glancing nervously down the aisle, watching the other passengers. It occurred to me that he'd always acted nervous and fidgety when we left Yancy, as if he expected something bad to happen. Before, I'd always assumed he was worried about getting teased. But there was nobody to tease him on the Greyhound.

Finally I couldn't stand it anymore.

I said, "Looking for Kindly Ones?"

Grover nearly jumped out of his seat. "Wha—what do you mean?"

I confessed about eavesdropping on him and Mr. Brunner the night before the exam.

Grover's eye twitched. "How much did you hear?"

"Oh . . . not much. What's the summer solstice deadline?"

He winced. "Look, Percy . . . I was just worried for you, see? I mean, hallucinating about demon math teachers . . ."

"Grover—"

"And I was telling Mr. Brunner that maybe you were overstressed or something, because there was no such person as Mrs. Dodds, and . . ."

"Grover, you're a really, really bad liar."

His ears turned pink.

From his shirt pocket, he fished out a grubby business card. "Just take this, okay? In case you need me this summer."

The card was in fancy script, which was murder on my dyslexic eyes, but I finally made out something like:

Grover Underwood
Keeper

Half-Blood Hill
Long Island, New York
(800) 009-0009

"What's Half—"

"Don't say it aloud!" he yelped. "That's my, um . . . summer address."

My heart sank. Grover had a summer home. I'd never considered that his family might be as rich as the others at Yancy.

"Okay," I said glumly. "So, like, if I want to come visit your mansion."

He nodded. "Or . . . or if you need me."

"Why would I need you?"

It came out harsher than I meant it to.

Grover blushed right down to his Adam's apple. "Look, Percy, the truth is, I—I kind of have to protect you."

I stared at him.

All year long, I'd gotten in fights, keeping bullies away

from him. I'd lost sleep worrying that he'd get beaten up next year without me. And here he was acting like he was the one who defended *me*.

"Grover," I said, "what exactly are you protecting me from?"

There was a huge grinding noise under our feet. Black smoke poured from the dashboard and the whole bus filled with a smell like rotten eggs. The driver cursed and limped the Greyhound over to the side of the highway.

After a few minutes clanking around in the engine compartment, the driver announced that we'd all have to get off. Grover and I filed outside with everybody else.

We were on a stretch of country road—no place you'd notice if you didn't break down there. On our side of the highway was nothing but maple trees and litter from passing cars. On the other side, across four lanes of asphalt shimmering with afternoon heat, was an old-fashioned fruit stand.

The stuff on sale looked really good: heaping boxes of bloodred cherries and apples, walnuts and apricots, jugs of cider in a claw-foot tub full of ice. There were no customers, just three old ladies sitting in rocking chairs in the shade of a maple tree, knitting the biggest pair of socks I'd ever seen.

I mean these socks were the size of sweaters, but they were clearly socks. The lady on the right knitted one of them. The lady on the left knitted the other. The lady in the middle held an enormous basket of electric-blue yarn.

All three women looked ancient, with pale faces

wrinkled like fruit leather, silver hair tied back in white bandannas, bony arms sticking out of bleached cotton dresses.

The weirdest thing was, they seemed to be looking right at me.

I looked over at Grover to say something about this and saw that the blood had drained from his face. His nose was twitching.

"Grover?" I said. "Hey, man—"

"Tell me they're not looking at you. They are, aren't they?"

"Yeah. Weird, huh? You think those socks would fit me?"

"Not funny, Percy. Not funny at all."

The old lady in the middle took out a huge pair of scissors—gold and silver, long-bladed, like shears. I heard Grover catch his breath.

"We're getting on the bus," he told me. "Come on."

"What?" I said. "It's a thousand degrees in there."

"Come on!" He pried open the door and climbed inside, but I stayed back.

Across the road, the old ladies were still watching me. The middle one cut the yarn, and I swear I could hear that *snip* across four lanes of traffic. Her two friends balled up the electric-blue socks, leaving me wondering who they could possibly be for—Sasquatch or Godzilla.

At the rear of the bus, the driver wrenched a big chunk of smoking metal out of the engine compartment. The bus shuddered, and the engine roared back to life.

The passengers cheered.

"Darn right!" yelled the driver. He slapped the bus with his hat. "Everybody back on board!"

Once we got going, I started feeling feverish, as if I'd caught the flu.

Grover didn't look much better. He was shivering and his teeth were chattering.

"Grover?"

"Yeah?"

"What are you not telling me?"

He dabbed his forehead with his shirt sleeve. "Percy, what did you see back at the fruit stand?"

"You mean the old ladies? What is it about them, man? They're not like . . . Mrs. Dodds, are they?"

His expression was hard to read, but I got the feeling that the fruit-stand ladies were something much, much worse than Mrs. Dodds. He said, "Just tell me what you saw."

"The middle one took out her scissors, and she cut the yarn."

He closed his eyes and made a gesture with his fingers that might've been crossing himself, but it wasn't. It was something else, something almost—older.

He said, "You saw her snip the cord."

"Yeah. So?" But even as I said it, I knew it was a big deal.

"This is not happening," Grover mumbled. He started chewing at his thumb. "I don't want this to be like the last time."

"What last time?"

"Always sixth grade. They never get past sixth."

"Grover," I said, because he was really starting to scare me. "What are you talking about?"

"Let me walk you home from the bus station. Promise me."

This seemed like a strange request to me, but I promised he could.

"Is this like a superstition or something?" I asked.

No answer.

"Grover—that snipping of the yarn. Does that mean somebody is going to die?"

He looked at me mournfully, like he was already picking the kind of flowers I'd like best on my coffin.

THREE

GROVER UNEXPECTEDLY LOSES HIS PANTS

Confession time: I ditched Grover as soon as we got to the bus terminal.

I know, I know. It was rude. But Grover was freaking me out, looking at me like I was a dead man, muttering "Why does this always happen?" and "Why does it always have to be sixth grade?"

Whenever he got upset, Grover's bladder acted up, so I wasn't surprised when, as soon as we got off the bus, he made me promise to wait for him, then made a beeline for the restroom. Instead of waiting, I got my suitcase, slipped outside, and caught the first taxi uptown.

"East One-hundred-and-fourth and First," I told the driver.

A word about my mother, before you meet her.

Her name is Sally Jackson and she's the best person in the world, which just proves my theory that the best people have the rottenest luck. Her own parents died in a plane crash when she was five, and she was raised by an uncle who didn't care much about her. She wanted to be a novelist, so she spent high school working to save enough money for a college with a good creative-writing program. Then her uncle got cancer, and she had to quit school her senior year to take care of him. After he died, she was left with no money, no family, and no diploma.

The only good break she ever got was meeting my dad.

I don't have any memories of him, just this sort of warm glow, maybe the barest trace of his smile. My mom doesn't like to talk about him because it makes her sad. She has no pictures.

See, they weren't married. She told me he was rich and important, and their relationship was a secret. Then one day, he set sail across the Atlantic on some important journey, and he never came back.

Lost at sea, my mom told me. Not dead. Lost at sea.

She worked odd jobs, took night classes to get her high school diploma, and raised me on her own. She never complained or got mad. Not even once. But I knew I wasn't an easy kid.

Finally, she married Gabe Ugliano, who was nice the first thirty seconds we knew him, then showed his true colors as a world-class jerk. When I was young, I nicknamed him Smelly Gabe. I'm sorry, but it's the truth. The guy reeked like moldy garlic pizza wrapped in gym shorts.

Between the two of us, we made my mom's life pretty hard. The way Smelly Gabe treated her, the way he and I got along . . . well, when I came home is a good example.

I walked into our little apartment, hoping my mom would be home from work. Instead, Smelly Gabe was in the living room, playing poker with his buddies. The television blared ESPN. Chips and beer cans were strewn all over the carpet.

Hardly looking up, he said around his cigar, "So, you're home."

"Where's my mom?"

"Working," he said. "You got any cash?"

That was it. No *Welcome back. Good to see you. How has your life been the last six months?*

Gabe had put on weight. He looked like a tuskless walrus in thrift-store clothes. He had about three hairs on his head, all combed over his bald scalp, as if that made him handsome or something.

He managed the Electronics Mega-Mart in Queens, but he stayed home most of the time. I don't know why he hadn't been fired long before. He just kept on collecting paychecks, spending the money on cigars that made me nauseous, and on beer, of course. Always beer. Whenever I was home, he expected me to provide his gambling funds. He called that our "guy secret." Meaning, if I told my mom, he would punch my lights out.

"I don't have any cash," I told him.

He raised a greasy eyebrow.

Gabe could sniff out money like a bloodhound, which was surprising, since his own smell should've covered up everything else.

"You took a taxi from the bus station," he said. "Probably paid with a twenty. Got six, seven bucks in change. Somebody expects to live under this roof, he ought to carry his own weight. Am I right, Eddie?"

Eddie, the super of the apartment building, looked at me with a twinge of sympathy. "Come on, Gabe," he said. "The kid just got here."

"Am I *right*?" Gabe repeated.

Eddie scowled into his bowl of pretzels. The other two guys passed gas in harmony.

"Fine," I said. I dug a wad of dollars out of my pocket and threw the money on the table. "I hope you lose."

"Your report card came, brain boy!" he shouted after me. "I wouldn't act so snooty!"

I slammed the door to my room, which really wasn't my room. During school months, it was Gabe's "study." He didn't study anything in there except old car magazines, but he loved shoving my stuff in the closet, leaving his muddy boots on my windowsill, and doing his best to make the place smell like his nasty cologne and cigars and stale beer.

I dropped my suitcase on the bed. Home sweet home.

Gabe's smell was almost worse than the nightmares about Mrs. Dodds, or the sound of that old fruit lady's shears snipping the yarn.

But as soon as I thought that, my legs felt weak. I remembered Grover's look of panic—how he'd made me promise I wouldn't go home without him. A sudden chill rolled through me. I felt like someone—something—was looking for me right now, maybe pounding its way up the stairs, growing long, horrible talons.

Then I heard my mom's voice. "Percy?"

She opened the bedroom door, and my fears melted.

My mother can make me feel good just by walking into

the room. Her eyes sparkle and change color in the light. Her smile is as warm as a quilt. She's got a few gray streaks mixed in with her long brown hair, but I never think of her as old. When she looks at me, it's like she's seeing all the good things about me, none of the bad. I've never heard her raise her voice or say an unkind word to anyone, not even me or Gabe.

"Oh, Percy." She hugged me tight. "I can't believe it. You've grown since Christmas!"

Her red-white-and-blue Sweet on America uniform smelled like the best things in the world: chocolate, licorice, and all the other stuff she sold at the candy shop in Grand Central. She'd brought me a huge bag of "free samples," the way she always did when I came home.

We sat together on the edge of the bed. While I attacked the blueberry sour strings, she ran her hand through my hair and demanded to know everything I hadn't put in my letters. She didn't mention anything about my getting expelled. She didn't seem to care about that. But was I okay? Was her little boy doing all right?

I told her she was smothering me, and to lay off and all that, but secretly, I was really, really glad to see her.

From the other room, Gabe yelled, "Hey, Sally—how about some bean dip, huh?"

I gritted my teeth.

My mom is the nicest lady in the world. She should've been married to a millionaire, not to some jerk like Gabe.

For her sake, I tried to sound upbeat about my last days at Yancy Academy. I told her I wasn't too down about the expulsion. I'd lasted almost the whole year this time. I'd made some new friends. I'd done pretty well in Latin. And honestly, the fights hadn't been as bad as the headmaster said. I liked Yancy Academy. I really did. I put such a good spin on the year, I almost convinced myself. I started choking up, thinking about Grover and Mr. Brunner. Even Nancy Bobofit suddenly didn't seem so bad.

Until that trip to the museum . . .

"What?" my mom asked. Her eyes tugged at my conscience, trying to pull out the secrets. "Did something scare you?"

"No, Mom."

I felt bad lying. I wanted to tell her about Mrs. Dodds and the three old ladies with the yarn, but I thought it would sound stupid.

She pursed her lips. She knew I was holding back, but she didn't push me.

"I have a surprise for you," she said. "We're going to the beach."

My eyes widened. "Montauk?"

"Three nights—same cabin."

"When?"

She smiled. "As soon as I get changed."

I couldn't believe it. My mom and I hadn't been to Montauk the last two summers, because Gabe said there wasn't enough money.

Gabe appeared in the doorway and growled, "Bean dip, Sally? Didn't you hear me?"

I wanted to punch him, but I met my mom's eyes and I understood she was offering me a deal: be nice to Gabe for a little while. Just until she was ready to leave for Montauk. Then we would get out of here.

"I was on my way, honey," she told Gabe. "We were just talking about the trip."

Gabe's eyes got small. "The trip? You mean you were serious about that?"

"I knew it," I muttered. "He won't let us go."

"Of course he will," my mom said evenly. "Your step-father is just worried about money. That's all. Besides," she added, "Gabriel won't have to settle for bean dip. I'll make him enough seven-layer dip for the whole weekend. Guacamole. Sour cream. The works."

Gabe softened a bit. "So this money for your trip . . . it comes out of your clothes budget, right?"

"Yes, honey," my mother said.

"And you won't take my car anywhere but there and back."

"We'll be very careful."

Gabe scratched his double chin. "Maybe if you hurry with that seven-layer dip . . . And maybe if the kid apologizes for interrupting my poker game."

Maybe if I kick you in your soft spot, I thought. And make you sing soprano for a week.

But my mom's eyes warned me not to make him mad.

Why did she put up with this guy? I wanted to scream. Why did she care what he thought?

"I'm sorry," I muttered. "I'm really sorry I interrupted your incredibly important poker game. Please go back to it right now."

Gabe's eyes narrowed. His tiny brain was probably trying to detect sarcasm in my statement.

"Yeah, whatever," he decided.

He went back to his game.

"Thank you, Percy," my mom said. "Once we get to Montauk, we'll talk more about . . . whatever you've forgotten to tell me, okay?"

For a moment, I thought I saw anxiety in her eyes—the same fear I'd seen in Grover during the bus ride—as if my mom too felt an odd chill in the air.

But then her smile returned, and I figured I must have been mistaken. She ruffled my hair and went to make Gabe his seven-layer dip.

An hour later we were ready to leave.

Gabe took a break from his poker game long enough to watch me lug my mom's bags to the car. He kept griping and groaning about losing her cooking—and more important, his '78 Camaro—for the whole weekend.

"Not a scratch on this car, brain boy," he warned me as I loaded the last bag. "Not one little scratch."

Like I'd be the one driving. I was twelve. But that didn't matter to Gabe. If a seagull so much as pooped on his paint job, he'd find a way to blame me.

Watching him lumber back toward the apartment building, I got so mad I did something I can't explain. As Gabe reached the doorway, I made the hand gesture I'd seen Grover make on the bus, a sort of warding-off-evil gesture, a clawed hand over my heart, then a shoving movement toward Gabe. The screen door slammed shut so hard it whacked him in the butt and sent him flying up the staircase as if he'd been shot from a cannon. Maybe it was just the wind, or some freak accident with the hinges, but I didn't stay long enough to find out.

I got in the Camaro and told my mom to step on it.

Our rental cabin was on the south shore, way out at the tip of Long Island. It was a little pastel box with faded curtains, half sunken into the dunes. There was always sand in the sheets and spiders in the cabinets, and most of the time the sea was too cold to swim in.

I loved the place.

We'd been going there since I was a baby. My mom had been going even longer. She never exactly said, but I knew why the beach was special to her. It was the place where she'd met my dad.

As we got closer to Montauk, she seemed to grow younger, years of worry and work disappearing from her face. Her eyes turned the color of the sea.

We got there at sunset, opened all the cabin's windows, and went through our usual cleaning routine. We walked on the beach, fed blue corn chips to the seagulls, and munched on blue jelly beans, blue saltwater taffy, and all the other free samples my mom had brought from work.

I guess I should explain the blue food.

See, Gabe had once told my mom there was no such thing. They had this fight, which seemed like a really small thing at the time. But ever since, my mom went out of her way to eat blue. She baked blue birthday cakes. She mixed blueberry smoothies. She bought blue-corn tortilla chips and brought home blue candy from the shop. This—along with keeping her maiden name, Jackson, rather than calling herself Mrs. Ugliano—was proof that she wasn't totally suckered by Gabe. She did have a rebellious streak, like me.

When it got dark, we made a fire. We roasted hot dogs and marshmallows. Mom told me stories about when she was a kid, back before her parents died in the plane crash. She told me about the books she wanted to write someday, when she had enough money to quit the candy shop.

Eventually, I got up the nerve to ask about what was always on my mind whenever we came to Montauk—my father. Mom's eyes went all misty. I figured she would tell me the same things she always did, but I never got tired of hearing them.

"He was kind, Percy," she said. "Tall, handsome, and powerful. But gentle, too. You have his black hair, you know, and his green eyes."

Mom fished a blue jelly bean out of her candy bag. "I wish he could see you, Percy. He would be so proud."

I wondered how she could say that. What was so great about me? A dyslexic, hyperactive boy with a D+ report card, kicked out of school for the sixth time in six years.

"How old was I?" I asked. "I mean . . . when he left?"

She watched the flames. "He was only with me for one summer, Percy. Right here at this beach. This cabin."

"But . . . he knew me as a baby."

"No, honey. He knew I was expecting a baby, but he never saw you. He had to leave before you were born."

I tried to square that with the fact that I seemed to remember . . . something about my father. A warm glow. A smile.

I had always assumed he knew me as a baby. My mom had never said it outright, but still, I'd felt it must be true. Now, to be told that he'd never even seen me . . .

I felt angry at my father. Maybe it was stupid, but I resented him for going on that ocean voyage, for not having the guts to marry my mom. He'd left us, and now we were stuck with Smelly Gabe.

"Are you going to send me away again?" I asked her. "To another boarding school?"

She pulled a marshmallow from the fire.

"I don't know, honey." Her voice was heavy. "I think . . . I think we'll have to do something."

"Because you don't want me around?" I regretted the words as soon as they were out.

My mom's eyes welled with tears. She took my hand, squeezed it tight. "Oh, Percy, no. I—I *have* to, honey. For your own good. I have to send you away."

Her words reminded me of what Mr. Brunner had said—that it was best for me to leave Yancy.

"Because I'm not normal," I said.

"You say that as if it's a bad thing, Percy. But you don't realize how important you are. I thought Yancy Academy would be far enough away. I thought you'd finally be safe."

"Safe from what?"

She met my eyes, and a flood of memories came back to me—all the weird, scary things that had ever happened to me, some of which I'd tried to forget.

During third grade, a man in a black trench coat had stalked me on the playground. When the teachers threatened to call the police, he went away growling, but no one believed me when I told them that under his broad-brimmed hat, the man only had one eye, right in the middle of his head.

Before that—a really early memory. I was in preschool, and a teacher accidentally put me down for a nap in a cot that a snake had slithered into. My mom screamed when she came to pick me up and found me playing with a limp, scaly rope I'd somehow managed to strangle to death with my meaty toddler hands.

In every single school, something creepy had happened, something unsafe, and I was forced to move.

I knew I should tell my mom about the old ladies at the fruit stand, and Mrs. Dodds at the art museum, about my weird hallucination that I had sliced my math teacher into dust with a sword. But I couldn't make myself tell her. I had a strange feeling the news would end our trip to Montauk, and I didn't want that.

"I've tried to keep you as close to me as I could," my mom said. "They told me that was a mistake. But there's only one other option, Percy—the place your father wanted to send you. And I just . . . I just can't stand to do it."

"My father wanted me to go to a special school?"

"Not a school," she said softly. "A summer camp."

My head was spinning. Why would my dad—who

hadn't even stayed around long enough to see me born—talk to my mom about a summer camp? And if it was so important, why hadn't she ever mentioned it before?

"I'm sorry, Percy," she said, seeing the look in my eyes. "But I can't talk about it. I—I couldn't send you to that place. It might mean saying good-bye to you for good."

"For good? But if it's only a summer camp . . ."

She turned toward the fire, and I knew from her expression that if I asked her any more questions she would start to cry.

That night I had a vivid dream.

It was storming on the beach, and two beautiful animals, a white horse and a golden eagle, were trying to kill each other at the edge of the surf. The eagle swooped down and slashed the horse's muzzle with its huge talons. The horse reared up and kicked at the eagle's wings. As they fought, the ground rumbled, and a monstrous voice chuckled somewhere beneath the earth, goading the animals to fight harder.

I ran toward them, knowing I had to stop them from killing each other, but I was running in slow motion. I knew I would be too late. I saw the eagle dive down, its beak aimed at the horse's wide eyes, and I screamed, *No!*

I woke with a start.

Outside, it really was storming, the kind of storm that cracks trees and blows down houses. There was no horse or eagle on the beach, just lightning making false daylight, and twenty-foot waves pounding the dunes like artillery.

With the next thunderclap, my mom woke. She sat up, eyes wide, and said, "Hurricane."

I knew that was crazy. Long Island never sees hurricanes this early in the summer. But the ocean seemed to have forgotten. Over the roar of the wind, I heard a distant bellow, an angry, tortured sound that made my hair stand on end.

Then a much closer noise, like mallets in the sand. A desperate voice—someone yelling, pounding on our cabin door.

My mother sprang out of bed in her nightgown and threw open the lock.

Grover stood framed in the doorway against a backdrop of pouring rain. But he wasn't . . . he wasn't exactly Grover.

"Searching all night," he gasped. "What were you thinking?"

My mother looked at me in terror—not scared of Grover, but of why he'd come.

"Percy," she said, shouting to be heard over the rain. "What happened at school? What didn't you tell me?"

I was frozen, looking at Grover. I couldn't understand what I was seeing.

"*O Zeu kai alloi theoi!*" he yelled. "It's right behind me! Didn't you *tell* her?"

I was too shocked to register that he'd just cursed in Ancient Greek, and I'd understood him perfectly. I was too shocked to wonder how Grover had gotten here by himself in the middle of the night. Because Grover didn't have his pants on—and where his legs should be . . . where his legs should be . . .

My mom looked at me sternly and talked in a tone she'd never used before: "*Percy*. Tell me *now!*"

I stammered something about the old ladies at the fruit stand, and Mrs. Dodds, and my mom stared at me, her face deathly pale in the flashes of lightning.

She grabbed her purse, tossed me my rain jacket, and said, "Get to the car. Both of you. *Go!*"

Grover ran for the Camaro—but he wasn't running, exactly. He was trotting, shaking his shaggy hindquarters, and suddenly his story about a muscular disorder in his legs made sense to me. I understood how he could run so fast and still limp when he walked.

Because where his feet should be, there were no feet. There were cloven hooves.

FOUR

MY MOTHER TEACHES ME BULLFIGHTING

We tore through the night along dark country roads. Wind slammed against the Camaro. Rain lashed the windshield. I didn't know how my mom could see anything, but she kept her foot on the gas.

Every time there was a flash of lightning, I looked at Grover sitting next to me in the backseat and I wondered if I'd gone insane, or if he was wearing some kind of shag-carpet pants. But, no, the smell was one I remembered from kindergarten field trips to the petting zoo—lanolin, like from wool. The smell of a wet barnyard animal.

All I could think to say was, "So, you and my mom . . . know each other?"

Grover's eyes flitted to the rearview mirror, though there were no cars behind us. "Not exactly," he said. "I mean, we've never met in person. But she knew I was watching you."

"Watching me?"

"Keeping tabs on you. Making sure you were okay. But I wasn't faking being your friend," he added hastily. "I *am* your friend."

"Um . . . what *are* you, exactly?"

"That doesn't matter right now."

"It doesn't matter? From the waist down, my best friend is a donkey—"

Grover let out a sharp, throaty *"Blaa-ha-ha!"*

I'd heard him make that sound before, but I'd always assumed it was a nervous laugh. Now I realized it was more of an irritated bleat.

"Goat!" he cried.

"What?"

"I'm a *goat* from the waist down."

"You just said it didn't matter."

"Blaa-ha-ha! There are satyrs who would trample you underhoof for such an insult!"

"Whoa. Wait. Satyrs. You mean like . . . Mr. Brunner's myths?"

"Were those old ladies at the fruit stand a *myth*, Percy? Was Mrs. Dodds a myth?"

"So you *admit* there was a Mrs. Dodds!"

"Of course."

"Then why—"

"The less you knew, the fewer monsters you'd attract," Grover said, like that should be perfectly obvious. "We put Mist over the humans' eyes. We hoped you'd think the Kindly One was a hallucination. But it was no good. You started to realize who you are."

"Who I—wait a minute, what do you mean?"

The weird bellowing noise rose up again somewhere behind us, closer than before. Whatever was chasing us was still on our trail.

"Percy," my mom said, "there's too much to explain and not enough time. We have to get you to safety."

"Safety from what? Who's after me?"

"Oh, nobody much," Grover said, obviously still miffed about the donkey comment. "Just the Lord of the Dead and a few of his blood-thirstiest minions."

"Grover!"

"Sorry, Mrs. Jackson. Could you drive faster, please?"

I tried to wrap my mind around what was happening, but I couldn't do it. I knew this wasn't a dream. I had no imagination. I could never dream up something this weird.

My mom made a hard left. We swerved onto a narrower road, racing past darkened farmhouses and wooded hills and PICK YOUR OWN STRAWBERRIES signs on white picket fences.

"Where are we going?" I asked.

"The summer camp I told you about." My mother's voice was tight; she was trying for my sake not to be scared. "The place your father wanted to send you."

"The place you didn't want me to go."

"Please, dear," my mother begged. "This is hard enough. Try to understand. You're in danger."

"Because some old ladies cut yarn."

"Those weren't old ladies," Grover said. "Those were the Fates. Do you know what it means—the fact they appeared in front of you? They only do that when you're about to . . . when someone's about to die."

"Whoa. You said 'you.'"

"No I didn't. I said 'someone.'"

"You meant 'you.' As in *me*."

"I meant *you*, like 'someone.' Not you, *you*."

"Boys!" my mom said.

She pulled the wheel hard to the right, and I got a glimpse of a figure she'd swerved to avoid—a dark fluttering shape now lost behind us in the storm.

"What was that?" I asked.

"We're almost there," my mother said, ignoring my question. "Another mile. Please. Please. Please."

I didn't know where *there* was, but I found myself leaning forward in the car, anticipating, wanting us to arrive.

Outside, nothing but rain and darkness—the kind of empty countryside you get way out on the tip of Long Island. I thought about Mrs. Dodds and the moment when she'd changed into the thing with pointed teeth and leathery wings. My limbs went numb from delayed shock. She really *hadn't* been human. She'd meant to kill me.

Then I thought about Mr. Brunner . . . and the sword he had thrown me. Before I could ask Grover about that, the hair rose on the back of my neck. There was a blinding flash, a jaw-rattling *boom!*, and our car exploded.

I remember feeling weightless, like I was being crushed, fried, and hosed down all at the same time.

I peeled my forehead off the back of the driver's seat and said, "Ow."

"Percy!" my mom shouted.

"I'm okay. . . ."

I tried to shake off the daze. I wasn't dead. The car hadn't really exploded. We'd swerved into a ditch. Our driver's-side doors were wedged in the mud. The roof had cracked open like an eggshell and rain was pouring in.

Lightning. That was the only explanation. We'd been blasted right off the road. Next to me in the backseat was a big motionless lump. "Grover!"

He was slumped over, blood trickling from the side of his mouth. I shook his furry hip, thinking, No! Even if you are half barnyard animal, you're my best friend and I don't want you to die!

Then he groaned "Food," and I knew there was hope.

"Percy," my mother said, "we have to . . ." Her voice faltered.

I looked back. In a flash of lightning, through the mud-spattered rear windshield, I saw a figure lumbering toward us on the shoulder of the road. The sight of it made my skin crawl. It was a dark silhouette of a huge guy, like a football player. He seemed to be holding a blanket over his head. His top half was bulky and fuzzy. His upraised hands made it look like he had horns.

I swallowed hard. "Who is——"

"Percy," my mother said, deadly serious. "Get out of the car."

My mother threw herself against the driver's-side door. It was jammed shut in the mud. I tried mine. Stuck too. I looked up desperately at the hole in the roof. It might've been an exit, but the edges were sizzling and smoking.

"Climb out the passenger's side!" my mother told me. "Percy—you have to run. Do you see that big tree?"

"*What?*"

Another flash of lightning, and through the smoking hole in the roof I saw the tree she meant: a huge, White House Christmas tree–sized pine at the crest of the nearest hill.

"That's the property line," my mom said. "Get over that hill and you'll see a big farmhouse down in the valley. Run and don't look back. Yell for help. Don't stop until you reach the door."

"Mom, you're coming too."

Her face was pale, her eyes as sad as when she looked at the ocean.

"No!" I shouted. "You *are* coming with me. Help me carry Grover."

"Food!" Grover moaned, a little louder.

The man with the blanket on his head kept coming toward us, making his grunting, snorting noises. As he got closer, I realized he *couldn't* be holding a blanket over his head, because his hands—huge meaty hands—were swinging at his sides. There was no blanket. Meaning the bulky, fuzzy mass that was too big to be his head . . . was his head. And the points that looked like horns . . .

"He doesn't want *us*," my mother told me. "He wants you. Besides, I can't cross the property line."

"But . . ."

"We don't have time, Percy. Go. Please."

I got mad, then—mad at my mother, at Grover the goat, at the thing with horns that was lumbering toward us slowly and deliberately like, like a bull.

I climbed across Grover and pushed the door open into the rain. "We're going together. Come on, Mom."

"I told you—"

"Mom! I am not leaving you. Help me with Grover."

I didn't wait for her answer. I scrambled outside, dragging Grover from the car. He was surprisingly light, but I couldn't have carried him very far if my mom hadn't come to my aid.

Together, we draped Grover's arms over our shoulders and started stumbling uphill through wet waist-high grass.

Glancing back, I got my first clear look at the monster. He was seven feet tall, easy, his arms and legs like something from the cover of *Muscle Man* magazine—bulging biceps and triceps and a bunch of other 'ceps, all stuffed like baseballs under vein-webbed skin. He wore no clothes except underwear—I mean, bright white Fruit of the Looms—which would've looked funny, except that the top half of his body was so scary. Coarse brown hair started at about his belly button and got thicker as it reached his shoulders.

His neck was a mass of muscle and fur leading up to his enormous head, which had a snout as long as my arm, snotty nostrils with a gleaming brass ring, cruel black eyes, and horns—enormous black-and-white horns with points you just couldn't get from an electric sharpener.

I recognized the monster, all right. He had been in one of the first stories Mr. Brunner told us. But he couldn't be real.

I blinked the rain out of my eyes. "That's—"

"Pasiphae's son," my mother said. "I wish I'd known how badly they want to kill you."

"But he's the Min—"

"Don't say his name," she warned. "Names have power."

The pine tree was still way too far—a hundred yards uphill at least.

I glanced behind me again.

The bull-man hunched over our car, looking in the windows—or not looking, exactly. More like snuffling, nuzzling. I wasn't sure why he bothered, since we were only about fifty feet away.

"Food?" Grover moaned.

"Shhh," I told him. "Mom, what's he doing? Doesn't he see us?"

"His sight and hearing are terrible," she said. "He goes by smell. But he'll figure out where we are soon enough."

As if on cue, the bull-man bellowed in rage. He picked up Gabe's Camaro by the torn roof, the chassis creaking and groaning. He raised the car over his head and threw it down the road. It slammed into the wet asphalt and skidded in a shower of sparks for about half a mile before coming to a stop. The gas tank exploded.

Not a scratch, I remembered Gabe saying.

Oops.

"Percy," my mom said. "When he sees us, he'll charge. Wait until the last second, then jump out of the way—directly sideways. He can't change directions very well once he's charging. Do you understand?"

"How do you know all this?"

"I've been worried about an attack for a long time. I should have expected this. I was selfish, keeping you near me."

"Keeping me near you? But——"

Another bellow of rage, and the bull-man started tromping uphill.

He'd smelled us.

The pine tree was only a few more yards, but the hill was getting steeper and slicker, and Grover wasn't getting any lighter.

The bull-man closed in. Another few seconds and he'd be on top of us.

My mother must've been exhausted, but she shouldered Grover. "Go, Percy! Separate! Remember what I said."

I didn't want to split up, but I had the feeling she was right—it was our only chance. I sprinted to the left, turned, and saw the creature bearing down on me. His black eyes glowed with hate. He reeked like rotten meat.

He lowered his head and charged, those razor-sharp horns aimed straight at my chest.

The fear in my stomach made me want to bolt, but that wouldn't work. I could never outrun this thing. So I held my ground, and at the last moment, I jumped to the side.

The bull-man stormed past like a freight train, then bellowed with frustration and turned, but not toward me this time, toward my mother, who was setting Grover down in the grass.

We'd reached the crest of the hill. Down the other side I could see a valley, just as my mother had said, and the lights of a farmhouse glowing yellow through the rain. But that was half a mile away. We'd never make it.

The bull-man grunted, pawing the ground. He kept

eyeing my mother, who was now retreating slowly downhill, back toward the road, trying to lead the monster away from Grover.

"Run, Percy!" she told me. "I can't go any farther. Run!"

But I just stood there, frozen in fear, as the monster charged her. She tried to sidestep, as she'd told me to do, but the monster had learned his lesson. His hand shot out and grabbed her by the neck as she tried to get away. He lifted her as she struggled, kicking and pummeling the air.

"Mom!"

She caught my eyes, managed to choke out one last word: "Go!"

Then, with an angry roar, the monster closed his fists around my mother's neck, and she dissolved before my eyes, melting into light, a shimmering golden form, as if she were a holographic projection. A blinding flash, and she was simply . . . gone.

"No!"

Anger replaced my fear. Newfound strength burned in my limbs—the same rush of energy I'd gotten when Mrs. Dodds grew talons.

The bull-man bore down on Grover, who lay helpless in the grass. The monster hunched over, snuffling my best friend, as if he were about to lift Grover up and make him dissolve too.

I couldn't allow that.

I stripped off my red rain jacket.

"Hey!" I screamed, waving the jacket, running to one side of the monster. "Hey, stupid! Ground beef!"

"Raaaarrrrr!" The monster turned toward me, shaking his meaty fists.

I had an idea—a stupid idea, but better than no idea at all. I put my back to the big pine tree and waved my red jacket in front of the bull-man, thinking I'd jump out of the way at the last moment.

But it didn't happen like that.

The bull-man charged too fast, his arms out to grab me whichever way I tried to dodge.

Time slowed down.

My legs tensed. I couldn't jump sideways, so I leaped straight up, kicking off from the creature's head, using it as a springboard, turning in midair, and landing on his neck.

How did I do that? I didn't have time to figure it out. A millisecond later, the monster's head slammed into the tree and the impact nearly knocked my teeth out.

The bull-man staggered around, trying to shake me. I locked my arms around his horns to keep from being thrown. Thunder and lightning were still going strong. The rain was in my eyes. The smell of rotten meat burned my nostrils.

The monster shook himself around and bucked like a rodeo bull. He should have just backed up into the tree and smashed me flat, but I was starting to realize that this thing had only one gear: forward.

Meanwhile, Grover started groaning in the grass. I wanted to yell at him to shut up, but the way I was getting tossed around, if I opened my mouth I'd bite my own tongue off.

"Food!" Grover moaned.

The bull-man wheeled toward him, pawed the ground again, and got ready to charge. I thought about how he had squeezed the life out of my mother, made her disappear in a flash of light, and rage filled me like high-octane fuel. I got both hands around one horn and I pulled backward with all my might. The monster tensed, gave a surprised grunt, then—*snap!*

The bull-man screamed and flung me through the air. I landed flat on my back in the grass. My head smacked against a rock. When I sat up, my vision was blurry, but I had a horn in my hands, a ragged bone weapon the size of a knife.

The monster charged.

Without thinking, I rolled to one side and came up kneeling. As the monster barreled past, I drove the broken horn straight into his side, right up under his furry rib cage.

The bull-man roared in agony. He flailed, clawing at his chest, then began to disintegrate—not like my mother, in a flash of golden light, but like crumbling sand, blown away in chunks by the wind, the same way Mrs. Dodds had burst apart.

The monster was gone.

The rain had stopped. The storm still rumbled, but only in the distance. I smelled like livestock and my knees were shaking. My head felt like it was splitting open. I was weak and scared and trembling with grief. I'd just seen my mother vanish. I wanted to lie down and cry, but there was Grover, needing my help, so I managed to haul him up and stagger down into the valley, toward the lights of the farm-house. I was crying, calling for my mother, but I held on to Grover—I wasn't going to let him go.

The last thing I remember is collapsing on a wooden porch, looking up at a ceiling fan circling above me, moths flying around a yellow light, and the stern faces of a familiar-looking bearded man and a pretty girl, her blond hair curled like a princess's. They both looked down at me, and the girl said, "He's the one. He must be."

"Silence, Annabeth," the man said. "He's still conscious. Bring him inside."

FIVE

I PLAY PINOCHLE
WITH A HORSE

I had weird dreams full of barnyard animals. Most of them wanted to kill me. The rest wanted food.

I must've woken up several times, but what I heard and saw made no sense, so I just passed out again. I remember lying in a soft bed, being spoon-fed something that tasted like buttered popcorn, only it was pudding. The girl with curly blond hair hovered over me, smirking as she scraped drips off my chin with the spoon.

When she saw my eyes open, she asked, "What will happen at the summer solstice?"

I managed to croak, "What?"

She looked around, as if afraid someone would overhear. "What's going on? What was stolen? We've only got a few weeks!"

"I'm sorry," I mumbled, "I don't . . ."

Somebody knocked on the door, and the girl quickly filled my mouth with pudding.

The next time I woke up, the girl was gone.

A husky blond dude, like a surfer, stood in the corner of the bedroom keeping watch over me. He had blue eyes— at least a dozen of them—on his cheeks, his forehead, the backs of his hands.

When I finally came around for good, there was nothing weird about my surroundings, except that they were nicer than I was used to. I was sitting in a deck chair on a huge porch, gazing across a meadow at green hills in the distance. The breeze smelled like strawberries. There was a blanket over my legs, a pillow behind my neck. All that was great, but my mouth felt like a scorpion had been using it for a nest. My tongue was dry and nasty and every one of my teeth hurt.

On the table next to me was a tall drink. It looked like iced apple juice, with a green straw and a paper parasol stuck through a maraschino cherry.

My hand was so weak I almost dropped the glass once I got my fingers around it.

"Careful," a familiar voice said.

Grover was leaning against the porch railing, looking like he hadn't slept in a week. Under one arm, he cradled a shoe box. He was wearing blue jeans, Converse hi-tops and a bright orange T-shirt that said CAMP HALF-BLOOD. Just plain old Grover. Not the goat boy.

So maybe I'd had a nightmare. Maybe my mom was okay. We were still on vacation, and we'd stopped here at this big house for some reason. And . . .

"You saved my life," Grover said. "I . . . well, the least I could do . . . I went back to the hill. I thought you might want this."

Reverently, he placed the shoe box in my lap.

Inside was a black-and-white bull's horn, the base jagged

from being broken off, the tip splattered with dried blood. It hadn't been a nightmare.

"The Minotaur," I said.

"Um, Percy, it isn't a good idea—"

"That's what they call him in the Greek myths, isn't it?" I demanded. "The Minotaur. Half man, half bull."

Grover shifted uncomfortably. "You've been out for two days. How much do you remember?"

"My mom. Is she really . . ."

He looked down.

I stared across the meadow. There were groves of trees, a winding stream, acres of strawberries spread out under the blue sky. The valley was surrounded by rolling hills, and the tallest one, directly in front of us, was the one with the huge pine tree on top. Even that looked beautiful in the sunlight.

My mother was gone. The whole world should be black and cold. Nothing should look beautiful.

"I'm sorry," Grover sniffled. "I'm a failure. I'm—I'm the worst satyr in the world."

He moaned, stomping his foot so hard it came off. I mean, the Converse hi-top came off. The inside was filled with Styrofoam, except for a hoof-shaped hole.

"Oh, Styx!" he mumbled.

Thunder rolled across the clear sky.

As he struggled to get his hoof back in the fake foot, I thought, Well, that settles it.

Grover was a satyr. I was ready to bet that if I shaved his curly brown hair, I'd find tiny horns on his head. But I was too miserable to care that satyrs existed, or even minotaurs.

All that meant was my mom really had been squeezed into nothingness, dissolved into yellow light.

I was alone. An orphan. I would have to live with . . . Smelly Gabe? No. That would never happen. I would live on the streets first. I would pretend I was seventeen and join the army. I'd do something.

Grover was still sniffling. The poor kid—poor goat, satyr, whatever—looked as if he expected to be hit.

I said, "It wasn't your fault."

"Yes, it was. I was supposed to *protect* you."

"Did my mother ask you to protect me?"

"No. But that's my job. I'm a keeper. At least . . . I was."

"But why . . ." I suddenly felt dizzy, my vision swimming.

"Don't strain yourself," Grover said. "Here."

He helped me hold my glass and put the straw to my lips.

I recoiled at the taste, because I was expecting apple juice. It wasn't that at all. It was chocolate-chip cookies. Liquid cookies. And not just any cookies—my mom's homemade blue chocolate-chip cookies, buttery and hot, with the chips still melting. Drinking it, my whole body felt warm and good, full of energy. My grief didn't go away, but I felt as if my mom had just brushed her hand against my cheek, given me a cookie the way she used to when I was small, and told me everything was going to be okay.

Before I knew it, I'd drained the glass. I stared into it, sure I'd just had a warm drink, but the ice cubes hadn't even melted.

"Was it good?" Grover asked.

I nodded.

"What did it taste like?" He sounded so wistful, I felt guilty.

"Sorry," I said. "I should've let you taste."

His eyes got wide. "No! That's not what I meant. I just . . . wondered."

"Chocolate-chip cookies," I said. "My mom's. Home-made."

He sighed. "And how do you feel?"

"Like I could throw Nancy Bobofit a hundred yards."

"That's good," he said. "That's good. I don't think you could risk drinking any more of that stuff."

"What do you mean?"

He took the empty glass from me gingerly, as if it were dynamite, and set it back on the table. "Come on. Chiron and Mr. D are waiting."

The porch wrapped all the way around the farmhouse.

My legs felt wobbly, trying to walk that far. Grover offered to carry the Minotaur horn, but I held on to it. I'd paid for that souvenir the hard way. I wasn't going to let it go.

As we came around the opposite end of the house, I caught my breath.

We must've been on the north shore of Long Island, because on this side of the house, the valley marched all the way up to the water, which glittered about a mile in the distance. Between here and there, I simply couldn't process everything I was seeing. The landscape was dotted with buildings that looked like ancient Greek architecture—an open-air pavilion, an amphitheater, a circular arena—except that they all looked brand new, their white marble columns sparkling in the sun. In a nearby sandpit, a dozen high school–age kids and satyrs played volleyball. Canoes glided across a small lake. Kids in bright orange T-shirts like Grover's were chasing each other around a cluster of cabins nestled in the woods. Some shot targets at an archery range. Others rode horses down a wooded trail, and, unless I was hallucinating, some of their horses had wings.

Down at the end of the porch, two men sat across from each other at a card table. The blond-haired girl who'd spoon-fed me popcorn-flavored pudding was leaning on the porch rail next to them.

The man facing me was small, but porky. He had a red nose, big watery eyes, and curly hair so black it was almost purple. He looked like those paintings of baby angels—what do you call them, hubbubs? No, cherubs. That's it. He looked like a cherub who'd turned middle-aged in a trailer park. He wore a tiger-pattern Hawaiian shirt, and he would've fit right in at one of Gabe's poker parties, except I got the feeling this guy could've out-gambled even my step-father.

"That's Mr. D," Grover murmured to me. "He's the camp director. Be polite. The girl, that's Annabeth Chase. She's just a camper, but she's been here longer than just about anybody. And you already know Chiron. . . ."

He pointed at the guy whose back was to me.

First, I realized he was sitting in the wheelchair. Then I

recognized the tweed jacket, the thinning brown hair, the scraggly beard.

"Mr. Brunner!" I cried.

The Latin teacher turned and smiled at me. His eyes had that mischievous glint they sometimes got in class when he pulled a pop quiz and made all the multiple choice answers *B*.

"Ah, good, Percy," he said. "Now we have four for pinochle."

He offered me a chair to the right of Mr. D, who looked at me with bloodshot eyes and heaved a great sigh. "Oh, I suppose I must say it. Welcome to Camp Half-Blood. There. Now, don't expect me to be glad to see you."

"Uh, thanks." I scooted a little farther away from him because, if there was one thing I had learned from living with Gabe, it was how to tell when an adult has been hitting the happy juice. If Mr. D was a stranger to alcohol, I was a satyr.

"Annabeth?" Mr. Brunner called to the blond girl.

She came forward and Mr. Brunner introduced us. "This young lady nursed you back to health, Percy. Annabeth, my dear, why don't you go check on Percy's bunk? We'll be putting him in cabin eleven for now."

Annabeth said, "Sure, Chiron."

She was probably my age, maybe a couple of inches taller, and a whole lot more athletic looking. With her deep tan and her curly blond hair, she was almost exactly what I thought a stereotypical California girl would look like, except her eyes ruined the image. They were startling gray, like storm clouds; pretty, but intimidating, too, as if she were analyzing the best way to take me down in a fight.

She glanced at the minotaur horn in my hands, then back at me. I imagined she was going to say, *You killed a minotaur!* or *Wow, you're so awesome!* or something like that.

Instead she said, "You drool when you sleep."

Then she sprinted off down the lawn, her blond hair flying behind her.

"So," I said, anxious to change the subject. "You, uh, work here, Mr. Brunner?"

"Not Mr. Brunner," the ex–Mr. Brunner said. "I'm afraid that was a pseudonym. You may call me Chiron."

"Okay." Totally confused, I looked at the director. "And Mr. D . . . does that stand for something?"

Mr. D stopped shuffling the cards. He looked at me like I'd just belched loudly. "Young man, names are powerful things. You don't just go around using them for no reason."

"Oh. Right. Sorry."

"I must say, Percy," Chiron-Brunner broke in, "I'm glad to see you alive. It's been a long time since I've made a house call to a potential camper. I'd hate to think I've wasted my time."

"House call?"

"My year at Yancy Academy, to instruct you. We have satyrs at most schools, of course, keeping a lookout. But Grover alerted me as soon as he met you. He sensed you were something special, so I decided to come upstate. I convinced the other Latin teacher to . . . ah, take a leave of absence."

I tried to remember the beginning of the school year. It seemed like so long ago, but I did have a fuzzy memory of there being another Latin teacher my first week at Yancy. Then, without explanation, he had disappeared and Mr. Brunner had taken the class.

"You came to Yancy just to teach me?" I asked.

Chiron nodded. "Honestly, I wasn't sure about you at first. We contacted your mother, let her know we were keeping an eye on you in case you were ready for Camp Half-Blood. But you still had so much to learn. Nevertheless, you made it here alive, and that's always the first test."

"Grover," Mr. D said impatiently, "are you playing or not?"

"Yes, sir!" Grover trembled as he took the fourth chair, though I didn't know why he should be so afraid of a pudgy little man in a tiger-print Hawaiian shirt.

"You *do* know how to play pinochle?" Mr. D eyed me suspiciously.

"I'm afraid not," I said.

"I'm afraid not, *sir*," he said.

"Sir," I repeated. I was liking the camp director less and less.

"Well," he told me, "it is, along with gladiator fighting and Pac-Man, one of the greatest games ever invented by humans. I would expect all *civilized* young men to know the rules."

"I'm sure the boy can learn," Chiron said.

"Please," I said, "what is this place? What am I doing here? Mr. Brun—Chiron—why would you go to Yancy Academy just to teach me?"

Mr. D snorted. "I asked the same question."

The camp director dealt the cards. Grover flinched every time one landed in his pile.

Chiron smiled at me sympathetically, the way he used to in Latin class, as if to let me know that no matter what my average was, *I* was his star student. He expected *me* to have the right answer.

"Percy," he said. "Did your mother tell you nothing?"

"She said . . ." I remembered her sad eyes, looking out over the sea. "She told me she was afraid to send me here, even though my father had wanted her to. She said that once I was here, I probably couldn't leave. She wanted to keep me close to her."

"Typical," Mr. D said. "That's how they usually get killed. Young man, are you bidding or not?"

"What?" I asked.

He explained, impatiently, how you bid in pinochle, and so I did.

"I'm afraid there's too much to tell," Chiron said. "I'm afraid our usual orientation film won't be sufficient."

"Orientation film?" I asked.

"No," Chiron decided. "Well, Percy. You know your friend Grover is a satyr. You know"—he pointed to the horn in the shoe box—"that you have killed the Minotaur. No small feat, either, lad. What you may not know is that great powers are at work in your life. Gods—the forces you call the Greek gods—are very much alive."

I stared at the others around the table.

I waited for somebody to yell, *Not!* But all I got was Mr. D yelling, "Oh, a royal marriage. Trick! Trick!" He cackled as he tallied up his points.

"Mr. D," Grover asked timidly, "if you're not going to eat it, could I have your Diet Coke can?"

"Eh? Oh, all right."

Grover bit a huge shard out of the empty aluminum can and chewed it mournfully.

"Wait," I told Chiron. "You're telling me there's such a thing as God."

"Well, now," Chiron said. "God—capital G, God. That's a different matter altogether. We shan't deal with the metaphysical."

"Metaphysical? But you were just talking about—"

"Ah, gods, plural, as in, great beings that control the forces of nature and human endeavors: the immortal gods of Olympus. That's a smaller matter."

"Smaller?"

"Yes, quite. The gods we discussed in Latin class."

"Zeus," I said. "Hera. Apollo. You mean them."

And there it was again—distant thunder on a cloudless day.

"Young man," said Mr. D, "I would really be less casual about throwing those names around, if I were you."

"But they're stories," I said. "They're—myths, to explain

lightning and the seasons and stuff. They're what people believed before there was science."

"Science!" Mr. D scoffed. "And tell me, Perseus Jackson"—I flinched when he said my real name, which I never told anybody—"what will people think of your 'science' two thousand years from now?" Mr. D continued. "Hmm? They will call it primitive mumbo jumbo. That's what. Oh, I love mortals—they have absolutely no sense of perspective. They think they've come so-o-o far. And have they, Chiron? Look at this boy and tell me."

I wasn't liking Mr. D much, but there was something about the way he called me mortal, as if . . . he wasn't. It was enough to put a lump in my throat, to suggest why Grover was dutifully minding his cards, chewing his soda can, and keeping his mouth shut.

"Percy," Chiron said, "you may choose to believe or not, but the fact is that *immortal* means immortal. Can you imagine that for a moment, never dying? Never fading? Existing, just as you are, for all time?"

I was about to answer, off the top of my head, that it sounded like a pretty good deal, but the tone of Chiron's voice made me hesitate.

"You mean, whether people believed in you or not," I said.

"Exactly," Chiron agreed. "If you were a god, how would you like being called a myth, an old story to explain lightning? What if I told you, Perseus Jackson, that someday people would call *you* a myth, just created to explain how little boys can get over losing their mothers?"

My heart pounded. He was trying to make me angry for some reason, but I wasn't going to let him. I said, "I wouldn't like it. But I don't believe in gods."

"Oh, you'd better," Mr. D murmured. "Before one of them incinerates you."

Grover said, "P-please, sir. He's just lost his mother. He's in shock."

"A lucky thing, too," Mr. D grumbled, playing a card. "Bad enough I'm confined to this miserable job, working with boys who don't even believe!"

He waved his hand and a goblet appeared on the table, as if the sunlight had bent, momentarily, and woven the air into glass. The goblet filled itself with red wine.

My jaw dropped, but Chiron hardly looked up.

"Mr. D," he warned, "your restrictions."

Mr. D looked at the wine and feigned surprise.

"Dear me." He looked at the sky and yelled, "Old habits! Sorry!"

More thunder.

Mr. D waved his hand again, and the wineglass changed into a fresh can of Diet Coke. He sighed unhappily, popped the top of the soda, and went back to his card game.

Chiron winked at me. "Mr. D offended his father a while back, took a fancy to a wood nymph who had been declared off-limits."

"A wood nymph," I repeated, still staring at the Diet Coke can like it was from outer space.

"Yes," Mr. D confessed. "Father loves to punish me. The first time, Prohibition. Ghastly! Absolutely horrid ten years! The second time—well, she really was pretty, and I couldn't stay away—the second time, he sent me here. Half-Blood Hill. Summer camp for brats like you. 'Be a better influence,' he told me. 'Work with youths rather than tearing them down.' Ha! Absolutely unfair."

Mr. D sounded about six years old, like a pouting little kid.

"And . . ." I stammered, "your father is . . ."

"*Di immortales*, Chiron," Mr. D said. "I thought you taught this boy the basics. My father is Zeus, of course."

I ran through D names from Greek mythology. Wine. The skin of a tiger. The satyrs that all seemed to work here. The way Grover cringed, as if Mr. D were his master.

"You're Dionysus," I said. "The god of wine."

Mr. D rolled his eyes. "What do they say, these days, Grover? Do the children say, 'Well, duh!'?"

"Y-yes, Mr. D."

"Then, well, duh! Percy Jackson. Did you think I was Aphrodite, perhaps?"

"You're a god."

"Yes, child."

"A god. You."

He turned to look at me straight on, and I saw a kind of purplish fire in his eyes, a hint that this whiny, plump little man was only showing me the tiniest bit of his true nature. I saw visions of grape vines choking unbelievers to death, drunken warriors insane with battle lust, sailors screaming as their hands turned to flippers, their faces elongating into dolphin snouts. I knew that if I pushed him,

Mr. D would show me worse things. He would plant a disease in my brain that would leave me wearing a strait-jacket in a rubber room for the rest of my life.

"Would you like to test me, child?" he said quietly.

"No. No, sir."

The fire died a little. He turned back to his card game. "I believe I win."

"Not quite, Mr. D," Chiron said. He set down a straight, tallied the points, and said, "The game goes to me."

I thought Mr. D was going to vaporize Chiron right out of his wheelchair, but he just sighed through his nose, as if he were used to being beaten by the Latin teacher. He got up, and Grover rose, too.

"I'm tired," Mr. D said. "I believe I'll take a nap before the sing-along tonight. But first, Grover, we need to talk, *again,* about your less-than-perfect performance on this assignment."

Grover's face beaded with sweat. "Y-yes, sir."

Mr. D turned to me. "Cabin eleven, Percy Jackson. And mind your manners."

He swept into the farmhouse, Grover following miserably.

"Will Grover be okay?" I asked Chiron.

Chiron nodded, though he looked a bit troubled. "Old Dionysus isn't really mad. He just hates his job. He's been . . . ah, grounded, I guess you would say, and he can't stand waiting another century before he's allowed to go back to Olympus."

"Mount Olympus," I said. "You're telling me there really is a palace there?"

"Well now, there's Mount Olympus in Greece. And then there's the home of the gods, the convergence point of their powers, which did indeed used to be on Mount Olympus. It's still called Mount Olympus, out of respect to the old ways, but the palace moves, Percy, just as the gods do."

"You mean the Greek gods are here? Like . . . in *America*?"

"Well, certainly. The gods move with the heart of the West."

"The what?"

"Come now, Percy. What you call 'Western civilization.' Do you think it's just an abstract concept? No, it's a living force. A collective consciousness that has burned bright for thousands of years. The gods are part of it. You might even say they are the source of it, or at least, they are tied so tightly to it that they couldn't possibly fade, not unless all of Western civilization were obliterated. The fire started in Greece. Then, as you well know—or as I hope you know, since you passed my course—the heart of the fire moved to Rome, and so did the gods. Oh, different names, perhaps—Jupiter for Zeus, Venus for Aphrodite, and so on—but the same forces, the same gods."

"And then they died."

"Died? No. Did the West die? The gods simply moved, to Germany, to France, to Spain, for a while. Wherever the flame was brightest, the gods were there. They spent several centuries in England. All you need to do is look at the architecture. People do not forget the gods. Every place they've ruled, for the last three thousand years, you can see them in paintings, in statues, on the most important buildings. And yes, Percy, of course they are now in your United States. Look at your symbol, the eagle of Zeus. Look at the statue of Prometheus in Rockefeller Center, the Greek facades of your government buildings in Washington. I defy you to find any American city where the Olympians are not prominently displayed in multiple places. Like it or not—and believe me, plenty of people weren't very fond of Rome, either—America is now the heart of the flame. It is the great power of the West. And so Olympus is here. And we are here."

It was all too much, especially the fact that *I* seemed to be included in Chiron's *we*, as if I were part of some club.

"Who are you, Chiron? Who . . . who am I?"

Chiron smiled. He shifted his weight as if he were going to get up out of his wheelchair, but I knew that was impossible. He was paralyzed from the waist down.

"Who are you?" he mused. "Well, that's the question we all want answered, isn't it? But for now, we should get you a bunk in cabin eleven. There will be new friends to meet. And plenty of time for lessons tomorrow. Besides, there will be s'mores at the campfire tonight, and I simply adore chocolate."

And then he did rise from his wheelchair. But there was something odd about the way he did it. His blanket fell away from his legs, but the legs didn't move. His waist kept getting longer, rising above his belt. At first, I thought he was wearing very long, white velvet underwear, but as he kept rising out of the chair, taller than any man, I realized that the velvet underwear wasn't underwear; it was the front of an animal, muscle and sinew under coarse white fur. And the wheelchair wasn't a chair. It was some kind of container, an enormous box on wheels, and it must've been magic, because there's no way it could've held all of him. A leg came out, long and knobby-kneed, with a huge polished hoof. Then another front leg, then hindquarters, and then the box was empty, nothing but a metal shell with a couple of fake human legs attached.

I stared at the horse who had just sprung from the wheelchair: a huge white stallion. But where its neck should be was the upper body of my Latin teacher, smoothly grafted to the horse's trunk.

"What a relief," the centaur said. "I'd been cooped up in there so long, my fetlocks had fallen asleep. Now, come, Percy Jackson. Let's meet the other campers."

SIX

⚷

I BECOME SUPREME LORD
OF THE BATHROOM

Once I got over the fact that my Latin teacher was a horse, we had a nice tour, though I was careful not to walk behind him. I'd done pooper-scooper patrol in the Macy's Thanksgiving Day Parade a few times, and, I'm sorry, I did not trust Chiron's back end the way I trusted his front.

We passed the volleyball pit. Several of the campers nudged each other. One pointed to the minotaur horn I was carrying. Another said, "That's *him.*"

Most of the campers were older than me. Their satyr friends were bigger than Grover, all of them trotting around in orange CAMP HALF-BLOOD T-shirts, with nothing else to cover their bare shaggy hindquarters. I wasn't normally shy, but the way they stared at me made me uncomfortable. I felt like they were expecting me to do a flip or something.

I looked back at the farmhouse. It was a lot bigger than I'd realized—four stories tall, sky blue with white trim, like an upscale seaside resort. I was checking out the brass eagle weather vane on top when something caught my eye, a shadow in the uppermost window of the attic gable. Something had moved the curtain, just for a second, and I got the distinct impression I was being watched.

"What's up there?" I asked Chiron.

He looked where I was pointing, and his smile faded. "Just the attic."

"Somebody lives there?"

"No," he said with finality. "Not a single living thing."

I got the feeling he was being truthful. But I was also sure something had moved that curtain.

"Come along, Percy," Chiron said, his lighthearted tone now a little forced. "Lots to see."

We walked through the strawberry fields, where campers were picking bushels of berries while a satyr played a tune on a reed pipe.

Chiron told me the camp grew a nice crop for export to New York restaurants and Mount Olympus. "It pays our expenses," he explained. "And the strawberries take almost no effort."

He said Mr. D had this effect on fruit-bearing plants: they just went crazy when he was around. It worked best with wine grapes, but Mr. D was restricted from growing those, so they grew strawberries instead.

I watched the satyr playing his pipe. His music was causing lines of bugs to leave the strawberry patch in every direction, like refugees fleeing a fire. I wondered if Grover could work that kind of magic with music. I wondered if he was still inside the farmhouse, getting chewed out by Mr. D.

"Grover won't get in too much trouble, will he?" I asked Chiron. "I mean . . . he was a good protector. Really."

Chiron sighed. He shed his tweed jacket and draped it over his horse's back like a saddle. "Grover has big dreams,

Percy. Perhaps bigger than are reasonable. To reach his goal, he must first demonstrate great courage by succeeding as a keeper, finding a new camper and bringing him safely to Half-Blood Hill."

"But he did that!"

"I might agree with you," Chiron said. "But it is not my place to judge. Dionysus and the Council of Cloven Elders must decide. I'm afraid they might not see this assignment as a success. After all, Grover lost you in New York. Then there's the unfortunate . . . ah . . . fate of your mother. And the fact that Grover was unconscious when you dragged him over the property line. The council might question whether this shows any courage on Grover's part."

I wanted to protest. None of what happened was Grover's fault. I also felt really, really guilty. If I hadn't given Grover the slip at the bus station, he might not have gotten in trouble.

"He'll get a second chance, won't he?"

Chiron winced. "I'm afraid that *was* Grover's second chance, Percy. The council was not anxious to give him another, either, after what happened the first time, five years ago. Olympus knows, I advised him to wait longer before trying again. He's still so small for his age. . . ."

"How old is he?"

"Oh, twenty-eight."

"What! And he's in sixth grade?"

"Satyrs mature half as fast as humans, Percy. Grover has been the equivalent of a middle school student for the past six years."

"That's horrible."

"Quite," Chiron agreed. "At any rate, Grover is a late bloomer, even by satyr standards, and not yet very accomplished at woodland magic. Alas, he was anxious to pursue his dream. Perhaps now he will find some other career. . . ."

"That's not fair," I said. "What happened the first time? Was it really so bad?"

Chiron looked away quickly. "Let's move along, shall we?"

But I wasn't quite ready to let the subject drop. Something had occurred to me when Chiron talked about my mother's fate, as if he were intentionally avoiding the word *death*. The beginnings of an idea—a tiny, hopeful fire—started forming in my mind.

"Chiron," I said. "If the gods and Olympus and all that are real . . ."

"Yes, child?"

"Does that mean the Underworld is real, too?"

Chiron's expression darkened.

"Yes, child." He paused, as if choosing his words carefully. "There is a place where spirits go after death. But for now . . . until we know more . . . I would urge you to put that out of your mind."

"What do you mean, 'until we know more'?"

"Come, Percy. Let's see the woods."

As we got closer, I realized how huge the forest was. It took up at least a quarter of the valley, with trees so tall and thick, you could imagine nobody had been in there since the Native Americans.

Chiron said, "The woods are stocked, if you care to try your luck, but go armed."

"Stocked with what?" I asked. "Armed with what?"

"You'll see. Capture the flag is Friday night. Do you have your own sword and shield?"

"My own——?"

"No," Chiron said. "I don't suppose you do. I think a size five will do. I'll visit the armory later."

I wanted to ask what kind of summer camp had an armory, but there was too much else to think about, so the tour continued. We saw the archery range, the canoeing lake, the stables (which Chiron didn't seem to like very much), the javelin range, the sing-along amphitheater, and the arena where Chiron said they held sword and spear fights.

"Sword and spear fights?" I asked.

"Cabin challenges and all that," he explained. "Not lethal. Usually. Oh, yes, and there's the mess hall."

Chiron pointed to an outdoor pavilion framed in white Grecian columns on a hill overlooking the sea. There were a dozen stone picnic tables. No roof. No walls.

"What do you do when it rains?" I asked.

Chiron looked at me as if I'd gone a little weird. "We still have to eat, don't we?" I decided to drop the subject.

Finally, he showed me the cabins. There were twelve of them, nestled in the woods by the lake. They were arranged in a U, with two at the base and five in a row on either side. And they were without doubt the most bizarre collection of buildings I'd ever seen.

Except for the fact that each had a large brass number above the door (odds on the left side, evens on the right), they looked absolutely nothing alike. Number nine had smokestacks, like a tiny factory. Number four had tomato vines on the walls and a roof made out of real grass. Seven seemed to be made of solid gold, which gleamed so much in the sunlight it was almost impossible to look at. They all faced a commons area about the size of a soccer field, dotted with Greek statues, fountains, flower beds, and a couple of basketball hoops (which were more my speed).

In the center of the field was a huge stone-lined firepit. Even though it was a warm afternoon, the hearth smoldered. A girl about nine years old was tending the flames, poking the coals with a stick.

The pair of cabins at the head of the field, numbers one and two, looked like his-and-hers mausoleums, big white marble boxes with heavy columns in front. Cabin one was the biggest and bulkiest of the twelve. Its polished bronze doors shimmered like a hologram, so that from different angles lightning bolts seemed to streak across them. Cabin two was more graceful somehow, with slimmer columns garlanded with pomegranates and flowers. The walls were carved with images of peacocks.

"Zeus and Hera?" I guessed.

"Correct," Chiron said.

"Their cabins look empty."

"Several of the cabins are. That's true. No one ever stays in one or two."

Okay. So each cabin had a different god, like a mascot.

Twelve cabins for the twelve Olympians. But why would some be empty?

I stopped in front of the first cabin on the left, cabin three.

It wasn't high and mighty like cabin one, but long and low and solid. The outer walls were of rough gray stone studded with pieces of seashell and coral, as if the slabs had been hewn straight from the bottom of the ocean floor. I peeked inside the open doorway and Chiron said, "Oh, I wouldn't do that!"

Before he could pull me back, I caught the salty scent of the interior, like the wind on the shore at Montauk. The interior walls glowed like abalone. There were six empty bunk beds with silk sheets turned down. But there was no sign anyone had ever slept there. The place felt so sad and lonely, I was glad when Chiron put his hand on my shoulder and said, "Come along, Percy."

Most of the other cabins were crowded with campers.

Number five was bright red—a real nasty paint job, as if the color had been splashed on with buckets and fists. The roof was lined with barbed wire. A stuffed wild boar's head hung over the doorway, and its eyes seemed to follow me. Inside I could see a bunch of mean-looking kids, both girls and boys, arm wrestling and arguing with each other while rock music blared. The loudest was a girl maybe thirteen or fourteen. She wore a size XXXL CAMP HALF-BLOOD T-shirt under a camouflage jacket. She zeroed in on me and gave me an evil sneer. She reminded me of Nancy Bobofit, though the camper girl was much bigger and tougher looking, and her hair was long and stringy, and brown instead of red.

I kept walking, trying to stay clear of Chiron's hooves. "We haven't seen any other centaurs," I observed.

"No," said Chiron sadly. "My kinsmen are a wild and barbaric folk, I'm afraid. You might encounter them in the wilderness, or at major sporting events. But you won't see any here."

"You said your name was Chiron. Are you really . . ."

He smiled down at me. "*The* Chiron from the stories? Trainer of Hercules and all that? Yes, Percy, I am."

"But, shouldn't you be dead?"

Chiron paused, as if the question intrigued him. "I honestly don't know about *should* be. The truth is, I *can't* be dead. You see, eons ago the gods granted my wish. I could continue the work I loved. I could be a teacher of heroes as long as humanity needed me. I gained much from that wish . . . and I gave up much. But I'm still here, so I can only assume I'm still needed."

I thought about being a teacher for three thousand years. It wouldn't have made my Top Ten Things to Wish For list.

"Doesn't it ever get boring?"

"No, no," he said. "Horribly depressing, at times, but never boring."

"Why depressing?"

Chiron seemed to turn hard of hearing again.

"Oh, look," he said. "Annabeth is waiting for us."

* * *

The blond girl I'd met at the Big House was reading a book in front of the last cabin on the left, number eleven.

When we reached her, she looked me over critically, like she was still thinking about how much I drooled.

I tried to see what she was reading, but I couldn't make out the title. I thought my dyslexia was acting up. Then I realized the title wasn't even English. The letters looked Greek to me. I mean, literally Greek. There were pictures of temples and statues and different kinds of columns, like those in an architecture book.

"Annabeth," Chiron said, "I have masters' archery class at noon. Would you take Percy from here?"

"Yes, sir."

"Cabin eleven," Chiron told me, gesturing toward the doorway. "Make yourself at home."

Out of all the cabins, eleven looked the most like a regular old summer camp cabin, with the emphasis on *old*. The threshold was worn down, the brown paint peeling. Over the doorway was one of those doctor's symbols, a winged pole with two snakes wrapped around it. What did they call it . . . ? A caduceus.

Inside, it was packed with people, both boys and girls, way more than the number of bunk beds. Sleeping bags were spread all over on the floor. It looked like a gym where the Red Cross had set up an evacuation center.

Chiron didn't go in. The door was too low for him. But when the campers saw him they all stood and bowed respectfully.

"Well, then," Chiron said. "Good luck, Percy. I'll see you at dinner."

He galloped away toward the archery range.

I stood in the doorway, looking at the kids. They weren't bowing anymore. They were staring at me, sizing me up. I knew this routine. I'd gone through it at enough schools.

"Well?" Annabeth prompted. "Go on."

So naturally I tripped coming in the door and made a total fool of myself. There were some snickers from the campers, but none of them said anything.

Annabeth announced, "Percy Jackson, meet cabin eleven."

"Regular or undetermined?" somebody asked.

I didn't know what to say, but Annabeth said, "Undetermined."

Everybody groaned.

A guy who was a little older than the rest came forward. "Now, now, campers. That's what we're here for. Welcome, Percy. You can have that spot on the floor, right over there."

The guy was about nineteen, and he looked pretty cool. He was tall and muscular, with short-cropped sandy hair and a friendly smile. He wore an orange tank top, cutoffs, sandals, and a leather necklace with five different-colored clay beads. The only thing unsettling about his appearance was a thick white scar that ran from just beneath his right eye to his jaw, like an old knife slash.

"This is Luke," Annabeth said, and her voice sounded different somehow. I glanced over and could've sworn she was blushing. She saw me looking, and her expression hardened again. "He's your counselor for now."

"For now?" I asked.

"You're undetermined," Luke explained patiently. "They don't know what cabin to put you in, so you're here. Cabin eleven takes all newcomers, all visitors. Naturally, we would. Hermes, our patron, is the god of travelers."

I looked at the tiny section of floor they'd given me. I had nothing to put there to mark it as my own, no luggage, no clothes, no sleeping bag. Just the Minotaur's horn. I thought about setting that down, but then I remembered that Hermes was also the god of thieves.

I looked around at the campers' faces, some sullen and suspicious, some grinning stupidly, some eyeing me as if they were waiting for a chance to pick my pockets.

"How long will I be here?" I asked.

"Good question," Luke said. "Until you're determined."

"How long will that take?"

The campers all laughed.

"Come on," Annabeth told me. "I'll show you the volleyball court."

"I've already seen it."

"Come on."

She grabbed my wrist and dragged me outside. I could hear the kids of cabin eleven laughing behind me.

When we were a few feet away, Annabeth said, "Jackson, you have to do better than that."

"What?"

She rolled her eyes and mumbled under her breath, "I can't believe I thought you were the one."

"What's your problem?" I was getting angry now. "All I know is, I kill some bull guy——"

"Don't talk like that!" Annabeth told me. "You know how many kids at this camp wish they'd had your chance?"

"To get killed?"

"To fight the Minotaur! What do you think we train for?"

I shook my head. "Look, if the thing I fought really was *the* Minotaur, the same one in the stories . . ."

"Yes."

"Then there's only one."

"Yes."

"And he died, like, a gajillion years ago, right? Theseus killed him in the labyrinth. So . . ."

"Monsters don't die, Percy. They can be killed. But they don't die."

"Oh, thanks. That clears it up."

"They don't have souls, like you and me. You can dispel them for a while, maybe even for a whole lifetime if you're lucky. But they are primal forces. Chiron calls them archetypes. Eventually, they re-form."

I thought about Mrs. Dodds. "You mean if I killed one, accidentally, with a sword——"

"The Fur . . . I mean, your math teacher. That's right. She's still out there. You just made her very, very mad."

"How did you know about Mrs. Dodds?"

"You talk in your sleep."

"You almost called her something. A Fury? They're Hades' torturers, right?"

Annabeth glanced nervously at the ground, as if she expected it to open up and swallow her. "You shouldn't call them by name, even here. We call them the Kindly Ones, if we have to speak of them at all."

"Look, is there anything we *can* say without it thundering?" I sounded whiny, even to myself, but right then I didn't care. "Why do I have to stay in cabin eleven, anyway? Why is everybody so crowded together? There are plenty of empty bunks right over there."

I pointed to the first few cabins, and Annabeth turned pale. "You don't just choose a cabin, Percy. It depends on who your parents are. Or . . . your parent."

She stared at me, waiting for me to get it.

"My mom is Sally Jackson," I said. "She works at the candy store in Grand Central Station. At least, she used to."

"I'm sorry about your mom, Percy. But that's not what I mean. I'm talking about your other parent. Your dad."

"He's dead. I never knew him."

Annabeth sighed. Clearly, she'd had this conversation before with other kids. "Your father's not dead, Percy."

"How can you say that? You know him?"

"No, of course not."

"Then how can you say—"

"Because I know *you.* You wouldn't be here if you weren't one of us."

"You don't know anything about me."

"No?" She raised an eyebrow. "I bet you moved around

from school to school. I bet you were kicked out of a lot of them."

"How——"

"Diagnosed with dyslexia. Probably ADHD, too."

I tried to swallow my embarrassment. "What does that have to do with anything?"

"Taken together, it's almost a sure sign. The letters float off the page when you read, right? That's because your mind is hardwired for ancient Greek. And the ADHD—you're impulsive, can't sit still in the classroom. That's your battle-field reflexes. In a real fight, they'd keep you alive. As for the attention problems, that's because you see too much, Percy, not too little. Your senses are better than a regular mortal's. Of course the teachers want you medicated. Most of them are monsters. They don't want you seeing them for what they are."

"You sound like . . . you went through the same thing?"

"Most of the kids here did. If you weren't like us, you couldn't have survived the Minotaur, much less the ambrosia and nectar."

"Ambrosia and nectar."

"The food and drink we were giving you to make you better. That stuff would've killed a normal kid. It would've turned your blood to fire and your bones to sand and you'd be dead. Face it. You're a half-blood."

A half-blood.

I was reeling with so many questions I didn't know where to start.

Then a husky voice yelled, "Well! A newbie!"

I looked over. The big girl from the ugly red cabin was sauntering toward us. She had three other girls behind her, all big and ugly and mean looking like her, all wearing camo jackets.

"Clarisse," Annabeth sighed. "Why don't you go polish your spear or something?"

"Sure, Miss Princess," the big girl said. "So I can run you through with it Friday night."

"Erre es korakas!" Annabeth said, which I somehow understood was Greek for 'Go to the crows!' though I had a feeling it was a worse curse than it sounded. "You don't stand a chance."

"We'll pulverize you," Clarisse said, but her eye twitched. Perhaps she wasn't sure she could follow through on the threat. She turned toward me. "Who's this little runt?"

"Percy Jackson," Annabeth said, "meet Clarisse, Daughter of Ares."

I blinked. "Like . . . the war god?"

Clarisse sneered. "You got a problem with that?"

"No," I said, recovering my wits. "It explains the bad smell."

Clarisse growled. "We got an initiation ceremony for newbies, Prissy."

"Percy."

"Whatever. Come on, I'll show you."

"Clarisse—" Annabeth tried to say.

"Stay out of it, wise girl."

Annabeth looked pained, but she did stay out of it, and

I didn't really want her help. I was the new kid. I had to earn my own rep.

I handed Annabeth my minotaur horn and got ready to fight, but before I knew it, Clarisse had me by the neck and was dragging me toward a cinder-block building that I knew immediately was the bathroom.

I was kicking and punching. I'd been in plenty of fights before, but this big girl Clarisse had hands like iron. She dragged me into the girls' bathroom. There was a line of toilets on one side and a line of shower stalls down the other. It smelled just like any public bathroom, and I was thinking—as much as I *could* think with Clarisse ripping my hair out—that if this place belonged to the gods, they should've been able to afford classier johns.

Clarisse's friends were all laughing, and I was trying to find the strength I'd used to fight the Minotaur, but it just wasn't there.

"Like he's 'Big Three' material," Clarisse said as she pushed me toward one of the toilets. "Yeah, right. Minotaur probably fell over laughing, he was so stupid looking."

Her friends snickered.

Annabeth stood in the corner, watching through her fingers.

Clarisse bent me over on my knees and started pushing my head toward the toilet bowl. It reeked like rusted pipes and, well, like what goes into toilets. I strained to keep my head up. I was looking at the scummy water, thinking, I will not go into that. I won't.

Then something happened. I felt a tug in the pit of my stomach. I heard the plumbing rumble, the pipes shudder. Clarisse's grip on my hair loosened. Water shot out of the toilet, making an arc straight over my head, and the next thing I knew, I was sprawled on the bathroom tiles with Clarisse screaming behind me.

I turned just as water blasted out of the toilet again, hitting Clarisse straight in the face so hard it pushed her down onto her butt. The water stayed on her like the spray from a fire hose, pushing her backward into a shower stall.

She struggled, gasping, and her friends started coming toward her. But then the other toilets exploded, too, and six more streams of toilet water blasted them back. The showers acted up, too, and together all the fixtures sprayed the camouflage girls right out of the bathroom, spinning them around like pieces of garbage being washed away.

As soon as they were out the door, I felt the tug in my gut lessen, and the water shut off as quickly as it had started.

The entire bathroom was flooded. Annabeth hadn't been spared. She was dripping wet, but she hadn't been pushed out the door. She was standing in exactly the same place, staring at me in shock.

I looked down and realized I was sitting in the only dry spot in the whole room. There was a circle of dry floor around me. I didn't have one drop of water on my clothes. Nothing.

I stood up, my legs shaky.

Annabeth said, "How did you . . ."

"I don't know."

We walked to the door. Outside, Clarisse and her friends were sprawled in the mud, and a bunch of other campers had gathered around to gawk. Clarisse's hair was flattened across her face. Her camouflage jacket was sopping and she smelled like sewage. She gave me a look of absolute hatred. "You are dead, new boy. You are totally dead."

I probably should have let it go, but I said, "You want to gargle with toilet water again, Clarisse? Close your mouth."

Her friends had to hold her back. They dragged her toward cabin five, while the other campers made way to avoid her flailing feet.

Annabeth stared at me. I couldn't tell whether she was just grossed out or angry at me for dousing her.

"What?" I demanded. "What are you thinking?"

"I'm thinking," she said, "that I want you on my team for capture the flag."

SEVEN

MY DINNER GOES UP
IN SMOKE

Word of the bathroom incident spread immediately. Wherever I went, campers pointed at me and murmured something about toilet water. Or maybe they were just staring at Annabeth, who was still pretty much dripping wet.

She showed me a few more places: the metal shop (where kids were forging their own swords), the arts-and-crafts room (where satyrs were sandblasting a giant marble statue of a goat-man), and the climbing wall, which actually consisted of two facing walls that shook violently, dropped boulders, sprayed lava, and clashed together if you didn't get to the top fast enough.

Finally we returned to the canoeing lake, where the trail led back to the cabins.

"I've got training to do," Annabeth said flatly. "Dinner's at seven-thirty. Just follow your cabin to the mess hall."

"Annabeth, I'm sorry about the toilets."

"Whatever."

"It wasn't my fault."

She looked at me skeptically, and I realized it *was* my fault. I'd made water shoot out of the bathroom fixtures. I didn't understand how. But the toilets had responded to me. I had become one with the plumbing.

"You need to talk to the Oracle," Annabeth said.

"Who?"

"Not who. What. The Oracle. I'll ask Chiron."

I stared into the lake, wishing somebody would give me a straight answer for once.

I wasn't expecting anybody to be looking back at me from the bottom, so my heart skipped a beat when I noticed two teenage girls sitting cross-legged at the base of the pier, about twenty feet below. They wore blue jeans and shimmering green T-shirts, and their brown hair floated loose around their shoulders as minnows darted in and out. They smiled and waved as if I were a long-lost friend.

I didn't know what else to do. I waved back.

"Don't encourage them," Annabeth warned. "Naiads are terrible flirts."

"Naiads," I repeated, feeling completely overwhelmed. "That's it. I want to go home now."

Annabeth frowned. "Don't you get it, Percy? You *are* home. This is the only safe place on earth for kids like us."

"You mean, mentally disturbed kids?"

"I mean *not human*. Not totally human, anyway. Half-human."

"Half-human and half-what?"

"I think you know."

I didn't want to admit it, but I was afraid I did. I felt a tingling in my limbs, a sensation I sometimes felt when my mom talked about my dad.

"God," I said. "Half-god."

Annabeth nodded. "Your father isn't dead, Percy. He's one of the Olympians."

"That's . . . crazy."

"Is it? What's the most common thing gods did in the old stories? They ran around falling in love with humans and having kids with them. Do you think they've changed their habits in the last few millennia?"

"But those are just——" I almost said *myths* again. Then I remembered Chiron's warning that in two thousand years, *I* might be considered a myth. "But if all the kids here are half-gods——"

"Demigods," Annabeth said. "That's the official term. Or half-bloods."

"Then who's your dad?"

Her hands tightened around the pier railing. I got the feeling I'd just trespassed on a sensitive subject.

"My dad is a professor at West Point," she said. "I haven't seen him since I was very small. He teaches American history."

"He's human."

"What? You assume it has to be a male god who finds a human female attractive? How sexist is that?"

"Who's your mom, then?"

"Cabin six."

"Meaning?"

Annabeth straightened. "Athena. Goddess of wisdom and battle."

Okay, I thought. Why not?

"And my dad?"

"Undetermined," Annabeth said, "like I told you before. Nobody knows."

"Except my mother. She knew."

"Maybe not, Percy. Gods don't always reveal their identities."

"My dad would have. He loved her."

Annabeth gave me a cautious look. She didn't want to burst my bubble. "Maybe you're right. Maybe he'll send a sign. That's the only way to know for sure: your father has to send you a sign claiming you as his son. Sometimes it happens."

"You mean sometimes it doesn't?"

Annabeth ran her palm along the rail. "The gods are busy. They have a lot of kids and they don't always . . . Well, sometimes they don't care about us, Percy. They ignore us."

I thought about some of the kids I'd seen in the Hermes cabin, teenagers who looked sullen and depressed, as if they were waiting for a call that would never come. I'd known kids like that at Yancy Academy, shuffled off to boarding school by rich parents who didn't have the time to deal with them. But gods should behave better.

"So I'm stuck here," I said. "That's it? For the rest of my life?"

"It depends," Annabeth said. "Some campers only stay the summer. If you're a child of Aphrodite or Demeter, you're probably not a real powerful force. The monsters might ignore you, so you can get by with a few months of summer training and live in the mortal world the rest of the year. But for some of us, it's too dangerous to leave. We're year-rounders. In the mortal world, we attract monsters. They sense us. They come to challenge us. Most of the time, they'll ignore us until we're old enough to cause trouble—about ten or eleven years old, but after that, most demigods either make their way here, or they get killed off. A few manage to survive in the outside world and become famous. Believe me, if I told you the names, you'd know them. Some don't even realize they're demigods. But very, very few are like that."

"So monsters can't get in here?"

Annabeth shook her head. "Not unless they're intentionally stocked in the woods or specially summoned by somebody on the inside."

"Why would anybody want to summon a monster?"

"Practice fights. Practical jokes."

"Practical jokes?"

"The point is, the borders are sealed to keep mortals and monsters out. From the outside, mortals look into the valley and see nothing unusual, just a strawberry farm."

"So . . . you're a year-rounder?"

Annabeth nodded. From under the collar of her T-shirt she pulled a leather necklace with five clay beads of different colors. It was just like Luke's, except Annabeth's also had a big gold ring strung on it, like a college ring.

"I've been here since I was seven," she said. "Every August, on the last day of summer session, you get a bead for surviving another year. I've been here longer than most of the counselors, and they're all in college."

"Why did you come so young?"

She twisted the ring on her necklace. "None of your business."

"Oh." I stood there for a minute in uncomfortable silence. "So . . . I could just walk out of here right now if I wanted to?"

"It would be suicide, but you could, with Mr. D's or Chiron's permission. But they wouldn't give permission until the end of the summer session unless . . ."

"Unless?"

"You were granted a quest. But that hardly ever happens. The last time . . ."

Her voice trailed off. I could tell from her tone that the last time hadn't gone well.

"Back in the sick room," I said, "when you were feeding me that stuff—"

"Ambrosia."

"Yeah. You asked me something about the summer solstice."

Annabeth's shoulders tensed. "So you *do* know something?"

"Well . . . no. Back at my old school, I overheard Grover and Chiron talking about it. Grover mentioned the summer solstice. He said something like we didn't have much time, because of the deadline. What did that mean?"

She clenched her fists. "I wish I knew. Chiron and the satyrs, they know, but they won't tell me. Something is wrong in Olympus, something pretty major. Last time I was there, everything seemed so *normal*."

"You've been to Olympus?"

"Some of us year-rounders—Luke and Clarisse and I and a few others—we took a field trip during winter solstice. That's when the gods have their big annual council."

"But . . . how did you get there?"

"The Long Island Railroad, of course. You get off at Penn Station. Empire State Building, special elevator to the six hundredth floor." She looked at me like she was sure I must know this already. "You *are* a New Yorker, right?"

"Oh, sure." As far as I knew, there were only a hundred and two floors in the Empire State Building, but I decided not to point that out.

"Right after we visited," Annabeth continued, "the weather got weird, as if the gods had started fighting. A couple of times since, I've overheard satyrs talking. The best I can figure out is that something important was stolen. And if it isn't returned by summer solstice, there's going to be trouble. When you came, I was hoping . . . I mean— Athena can get along with just about anybody, except for Ares. And of course she's got the rivalry with Poseidon. But, I mean, aside from that, I thought we could work together. I thought you might know something."

I shook my head. I wished I could help her, but I felt too hungry and tired and mentally overloaded to ask any more questions.

"I've got to get a quest," Annabeth muttered to herself. "I'm *not* too young. If they would just tell me the problem . . ."

I could smell barbecue smoke coming from somewhere

nearby. Annabeth must've heard my stomach growl. She told me to go on, she'd catch me later. I left her on the pier, tracing her finger across the rail as if drawing a battle plan.

Back at cabin eleven, everybody was talking and horsing around, waiting for dinner. For the first time, I noticed that a lot of the campers had similar features: sharp noses, upturned eyebrows, mischievous smiles. They were the kind of kids that teachers would peg as troublemakers. Thankfully, nobody paid much attention to me as I walked over to my spot on the floor and plopped down with my minotaur horn.

The counselor, Luke, came over. He had the Hermes family resemblance, too. It was marred by that scar on his right cheek, but his smile was intact.

"Found you a sleeping bag," he said. "And here, I stole you some toiletries from the camp store."

I couldn't tell if he was kidding about the stealing part. I said, "Thanks."

"No prob." Luke sat next to me, pushed his back against the wall. "Tough first day?"

"I don't belong here," I said. "I don't even believe in gods."

"Yeah," he said. "That's how we all started. Once you start believing in them? It doesn't get any easier."

The bitterness in his voice surprised me, because Luke seemed like a pretty easygoing guy. He looked like he could handle just about anything.

"So your dad is Hermes?" I asked.

He pulled a switchblade out of his back pocket, and for a second I thought he was going to gut me, but he just scraped the mud off the sole of his sandal. "Yeah. Hermes."

"The wing-footed messenger guy."

"That's him. Messengers. Medicine. Travelers, merchants, thieves. Anybody who uses the roads. That's why you're here, enjoying cabin eleven's hospitality. Hermes isn't picky about who he sponsors."

I figured Luke didn't mean to call me a nobody. He just had a lot on his mind.

"You ever meet your dad?" I asked.

"Once."

I waited, thinking that if he wanted to tell me, he'd tell me. Apparently, he didn't. I wondered if the story had anything to do with how he got his scar.

Luke looked up and managed a smile. "Don't worry about it, Percy. The campers here, they're mostly good people. After all, we're extended family, right? We take care of each other."

He seemed to understand how lost I felt, and I was grateful for that, because an older guy like him—even if he was a counselor—should've steered clear of an uncool middle-schooler like me. But Luke had welcomed me into the cabin. He'd even stolen me some toiletries, which was the nicest thing anybody had done for me all day.

I decided to ask him my last big question, the one that had been bothering me all afternoon. "Clarisse, from Ares, was joking about me being 'Big Three' material. Then

Annabeth . . . twice, she said I might be 'the one.' She said I should talk to the Oracle. What was that all about?"

Luke folded his knife. "I hate prophecies."

"What do you mean?"

His face twitched around the scar. "Let's just say I messed things up for everybody else. The last two years, ever since my trip to the Garden of the Hesperides went sour, Chiron hasn't allowed any more quests. Annabeth's been dying to get out into the world. She pestered Chiron so much he finally told her he already knew her fate. He'd had a prophecy from the Oracle. He wouldn't tell her the whole thing, but he said Annabeth wasn't destined to go on a quest yet. She had to wait until . . . somebody special came to the camp."

"Somebody special?"

"Don't worry about it, kid," Luke said. "Annabeth wants to think every new camper who comes through here is the omen she's been waiting for. Now, come on, it's dinnertime."

The moment he said it, a horn blew in the distance. Somehow, I knew it was a conch shell, even though I'd never heard one before.

Luke yelled, "Eleven, fall in!"

The whole cabin, about twenty of us, filed into the commons yard. We lined up in order of seniority, so of course I was dead last. Campers came from the other cabins, too, except for the three empty cabins at the end, and cabin eight, which had looked normal in the daytime, but was now starting to glow silver as the sun went down.

We marched up the hill to the mess hall pavilion. Satyrs joined us from the meadow. Naiads emerged from the canoeing lake. A few other girls came out of the woods—and when I say out of the woods, I mean *straight* out of the woods. I saw one girl, about nine or ten years old, melt from the side of a maple tree and come skipping up the hill.

In all, there were maybe a hundred campers, a few dozen satyrs, and a dozen assorted wood nymphs and naiads.

At the pavilion, torches blazed around the marble columns. A central fire burned in a bronze brazier the size of a bathtub. Each cabin had its own table, covered in white cloth trimmed in purple. Four of the tables were empty, but cabin eleven's was way overcrowded. I had to squeeze on to the edge of a bench with half my butt hanging off.

I saw Grover sitting at table twelve with Mr. D, a few satyrs, and a couple of plump blond boys who looked just like Mr. D. Chiron stood to one side, the picnic table being way too small for a centaur.

Annabeth sat at table six with a bunch of serious-looking athletic kids, all with her gray eyes and honey-blond hair.

Clarisse sat behind me at Ares's table. She'd apparently gotten over being hosed down, because she was laughing and belching right alongside her friends.

Finally, Chiron pounded his hoof against the marble floor of the pavilion, and everybody fell silent. He raised a glass. "To the gods!"

Everybody else raised their glasses. "To the gods!"

Wood nymphs came forward with platters of food:

grapes, apples, strawberries, cheese, fresh bread, and yes, barbecue! My glass was empty, but Luke said, "Speak to it. Whatever you want—nonalcoholic, of course."

I said, "Cherry Coke."

The glass filled with sparkling caramel liquid.

Then I had an idea. "*Blue* Cherry Coke."

The soda turned a violent shade of cobalt.

I took a cautious sip. Perfect.

I drank a toast to my mother.

She's not gone, I told myself. Not permanently, anyway. She's in the Underworld. And if that's a real place, then someday . . .

"Here you go, Percy," Luke said, handing me a platter of smoked brisket.

I loaded my plate and was about to take a big bite when I noticed everybody getting up, carrying their plates toward the fire in the center of the pavilion. I wondered if they were going for dessert or something.

"Come on," Luke told me.

As I got closer, I saw that everyone was taking a portion of their meal and dropping it into the fire, the ripest strawberry, the juiciest slice of beef, the warmest, most buttery roll.

Luke murmured in my ear, "Burnt offerings for the gods. They like the smell."

"You're kidding."

His look warned me not to take this lightly, but I couldn't help wondering why an immortal, all-powerful being would like the smell of burning food.

Luke approached the fire, bowed his head, and tossed in a cluster of fat red grapes. "Hermes."

I was next.

I wished I knew what god's name to say.

Finally, I made a silent plea. *Whoever you are, tell me. Please.*

I scraped a big slice of brisket into the flames.

When I caught a whiff of the smoke, I didn't gag.

It smelled nothing like burning food. It smelled of hot chocolate and fresh-baked brownies, hamburgers on the grill and wildflowers, and a hundred other good things that shouldn't have gone well together, but did. I could almost believe the gods could live off that smoke.

When everybody had returned to their seats and finished eating their meals, Chiron pounded his hoof again for our attention.

Mr. D got up with a huge sigh. "Yes, I suppose I'd better say hello to all you brats. Well, hello. Our activities director, Chiron, says the next capture the flag is Friday. Cabin five presently holds the laurels."

A bunch of ugly cheering rose from the Ares table.

"Personally," Mr. D continued, "I couldn't care less, but congratulations. Also, I should tell you that we have a new camper today. Peter Johnson."

Chiron murmured something.

"Er, Percy Jackson," Mr. D corrected. "That's right. Hurrah, and all that. Now run along to your silly campfire. Go on."

Everybody cheered. We all headed down toward the amphitheater, where Apollo's cabin led a sing-along. We sang camp songs about the gods and ate s'mores and joked around, and the funny thing was, I didn't feel that anyone was staring at me anymore. I felt that I was home.

Later in the evening, when the sparks from the campfire were curling into a starry sky, the conch horn blew again, and we all filed back to our cabins. I didn't realize how exhausted I was until I collapsed on my borrowed sleeping bag.

My fingers curled around the Minotaur's horn. I thought about my mom, but I had good thoughts: her smile, the bedtime stories she would read me when I was a kid, the way she would tell me not to let the bedbugs bite.

When I closed my eyes, I fell asleep instantly.

That was my first day at Camp Half-Blood.

I wish I'd known how briefly I would get to enjoy my new home.

EIGHT

WE CAPTURE A FLAG

The next few days I settled into a routine that felt almost normal, if you don't count the fact that I was getting lessons from satyrs, nymphs, and a centaur.

Each morning I took Ancient Greek from Annabeth, and we talked about the gods and goddesses in the present tense, which was kind of weird. I discovered Annabeth was right about my dyslexia: Ancient Greek wasn't that hard for me to read. At least, no harder than English. After a couple of mornings, I could stumble through a few lines of Homer without too much headache.

The rest of the day, I'd rotate through outdoor activities, looking for something I was good at. Chiron tried to teach me archery, but we found out pretty quick I wasn't any good with a bow and arrow. He didn't complain, even when he had to desnag a stray arrow out of his tail.

Foot racing? No good either. The wood-nymph instructors left me in the dust. They told me not to worry about it. They'd had centuries of practice running away from lovesick gods. But still, it was a little humiliating to be slower than a tree.

And wrestling? Forget it. Every time I got on the mat, Clarisse would pulverize me.

"There's more where that came from, punk," she'd mumble in my ear.

The only thing I really excelled at was canoeing, and that wasn't the kind of heroic skill people expected to see from the kid who had beaten the Minotaur.

I knew the senior campers and counselors were watching me, trying to decide who my dad was, but they weren't having an easy time of it. I wasn't as strong as the Ares kids, or as good at archery as the Apollo kids. I didn't have Hephaestus's skill with metalwork or—gods forbid—Dionysus's way with vine plants. Luke told me I might be a child of Hermes, a kind of jack-of-all-trades, master of none. But I got the feeling he was just trying to make me feel better. He really didn't know what to make of me either.

Despite all that, I liked camp. I got used to the morning fog over the beach, the smell of hot strawberry fields in the afternoon, even the weird noises of monsters in the woods at night. I would eat dinner with cabin eleven, scrape part of my meal into the fire, and try to feel some connection to my real dad. Nothing came. Just that warm feeling I'd always had, like the memory of his smile. I tried not to think too much about my mom, but I kept wondering: if gods and monsters were real, if all this magical stuff was possible, surely there was some way to save her, to bring her back. . . .

I started to understand Luke's bitterness and how he seemed to resent his father, Hermes. So okay, maybe gods had important things to do. But couldn't they call once in a while, or thunder, or something? Dionysus could make Diet Coke appear out of thin air. Why couldn't my dad, who-ever he was, make a phone appear?

Thursday afternoon, three days after I'd arrived at Camp Half-Blood, I had my first sword-fighting lesson. Every-body from cabin eleven gathered in the big circular arena, where Luke would be our instructor.

We started with basic stabbing and slashing, using some straw-stuffed dummies in Greek armor. I guess I did okay. At least, I understood what I was supposed to do and my reflexes were good.

The problem was, I couldn't find a blade that felt right in my hands. Either they were too heavy, or too light, or too long. Luke tried his best to fix me up, but he agreed that none of the practice blades seemed to work for me.

We moved on to dueling in pairs. Luke announced he would be my partner, since this was my first time.

"Good luck," one of the campers told me. "Luke's the best swordsman in the last three hundred years."

"Maybe he'll go easy on me," I said.

The camper snorted.

Luke showed me thrusts and parries and shield blocks the hard way. With every swipe, I got a little more battered and bruised. "Keep your guard up, Percy," he'd say, then whap me in the ribs with the flat of his blade. "No, not that far up!" *Whap!* "Lunge!" *Whap!* "Now, back!" *Whap!*

By the time he called a break, I was soaked in sweat. Everybody swarmed the drinks cooler. Luke poured ice water on his head, which looked like such a good idea, I did the same.

Instantly, I felt better. Strength surged back into my arms. The sword didn't feel so awkward.

"Okay, everybody circle up!" Luke ordered. "If Percy doesn't mind, I want to give you a little demo."

Great, I thought. Let's all watch Percy get pounded.

The Hermes guys gathered around. They were suppressing smiles. I figured they'd been in my shoes before and couldn't wait to see how Luke used me for a punching bag. He told everybody he was going to demonstrate a disarming technique: how to twist the enemy's blade with the flat of your own sword so that he had no choice but to drop his weapon.

"This is difficult," he stressed. "I've had it used against me. No laughing at Percy, now. Most swordsmen have to work years to master this technique."

He demonstrated the move on me in slow motion. Sure enough, the sword clattered out of my hand.

"Now in real time," he said, after I'd retrieved my weapon. "We keep sparring until one of us pulls it off. Ready, Percy?"

I nodded, and Luke came after me. Somehow, I kept him from getting a shot at the hilt of my sword. My senses opened up. I saw his attacks coming. I countered. I stepped forward and tried a thrust of my own. Luke deflected it easily, but I saw a change in his face. His eyes narrowed, and he started to press me with more force.

The sword grew heavy in my hand. The balance wasn't

right. I knew it was only a matter of seconds before Luke took me down, so I figured, What the heck?

I tried the disarming maneuver.

My blade hit the base of Luke's and I twisted, putting my whole weight into a downward thrust.

Clang.

Luke's sword rattled against the stones. The tip of my blade was an inch from his undefended chest.

The other campers were silent.

I lowered my sword. "Um, sorry."

For a moment, Luke was too stunned to speak.

"Sorry?" His scarred face broke into a grin. "By the gods, Percy, why are you sorry? Show me that again!"

I didn't want to. The short burst of manic energy had completely abandoned me. But Luke insisted.

This time, there was no contest. The moment our swords connected, Luke hit my hilt and sent my weapon skidding across the floor.

After a long pause, somebody in the audience said, "Beginner's luck?"

Luke wiped the sweat off his brow. He appraised at me with an entirely new interest. "Maybe," he said. "But I wonder what Percy could do with a balanced sword. . . ."

Friday afternoon, I was sitting with Grover at the lake, resting from a near-death experience on the climbing wall. Grover had scampered to the top like a mountain goat, but the lava had almost gotten me. My shirt had smoking holes in it. The hairs had been singed off my forearms.

We sat on the pier, watching the naiads do underwater basket-weaving, until I got up the nerve to ask Grover how his conversation had gone with Mr. D.

His face turned a sickly shade of yellow.

"Fine," he said. "Just great."

"So your career's still on track?"

He glanced at me nervously. "Chiron t-told you I want a searcher's license?"

"Well . . . no." I had no idea what a searcher's license was, but it didn't seem like the right time to ask. "He just said you had big plans, you know . . . and that you needed credit for completing a keeper's assignment. So did you get it?"

Grover looked down at the naiads. "Mr. D suspended judgment. He said I hadn't failed or succeeded with you yet, so our fates were still tied together. If you got a quest and I went along to protect you, and we both came back alive, then maybe he'd consider the job complete."

My spirits lifted. "Well, that's not so bad, right?"

"*Blaa-ha-ha!* He might as well have transferred me to stable-cleaning duty. The chances of you getting a quest . . . and even if you did, why would you want *me* along?"

"Of course I'd want you along!"

Grover stared glumly into the water. "Basket-weaving . . . Must be nice to have a useful skill."

I tried to reassure him that he had lots of talents, but that just made him look more miserable. We talked about canoeing and swordplay for a while, then debated the pros and cons of the different gods. Finally, I asked him about the four empty cabins.

"Number eight, the silver one, belongs to Artemis," he said. "She vowed to be a maiden forever. So of course, no kids. The cabin is, you know, honorary. If she didn't have one, she'd be mad."

"Yeah, okay. But the other three, the ones at the end. Are those the Big Three?"

Grover tensed. We were getting close to a touchy subject. "No. One of them, number two, is Hera's," he said. "That's another honorary thing. She's the goddess of marriage, so of course she wouldn't go around having affairs with mortals. That's her husband's job. When we say the Big Three, we mean the three powerful brothers, the sons of Kronos."

"Zeus, Poseidon, Hades."

"Right. You know. After the great battle with the Titans, they took over the world from their dad and drew lots to decide who got what."

"Zeus got the sky," I remembered. "Poseidon the sea, Hades the Underworld."

"Uh-huh."

"But Hades doesn't have a cabin here."

"No. He doesn't have a throne on Olympus, either. He sort of does his own thing down in the Underworld. If he did have a cabin here . . ." Grover shuddered. "Well, it wouldn't be pleasant. Let's leave it at that."

"But Zeus and Poseidon—they both had, like, a bazillion kids in the myths. Why are their cabins empty?"

Grover shifted his hooves uncomfortably. "About sixty years ago, after World War II, the Big Three agreed they wouldn't sire any more heroes. Their children were just too powerful. They were affecting the course of human events too much, causing too much carnage. World War II, you know, that was basically a fight between the sons of Zeus and Poseidon on one side, and the sons of Hades on the other. The winning side, Zeus and Poseidon, made Hades swear an oath with them: no more affairs with mortal women. They all swore on the River Styx."

Thunder boomed.

I said, "That's the most serious oath you can make."

Grover nodded.

"And the brothers kept their word—no kids?"

Grover's face darkened. "Seventeen years ago, Zeus fell off the wagon. There was this TV starlet with a big fluffy eighties hairdo—he just couldn't help himself. When their child was born, a little girl named Thalia . . . well, the River Styx is serious about promises. Zeus himself got off easy because he's immortal, but he brought a terrible fate on his daughter."

"But that isn't fair! It wasn't the little girl's fault."

Grover hesitated. "Percy, children of the Big Three have powers greater than other half-bloods. They have a strong aura, a scent that attracts monsters. When Hades found out about the girl, he wasn't too happy about Zeus breaking his oath. Hades let the worst monsters out of Tartarus to torment Thalia. A satyr was assigned to be her keeper when she was twelve, but there was nothing he could do. He tried to escort her here with a couple of other half-bloods she'd befriended. They almost made it. They got all the way to the top of that hill."

He pointed across the valley, to the pine tree where I'd fought the minotaur. "All three Kindly Ones were after them, along with a hoard of hellhounds. They were about to be overrun when Thalia told her satyr to take the other two half-bloods to safety while she held off the monsters. She was wounded and tired, and she didn't want to live like a hunted animal. The satyr didn't want to leave her, but he couldn't change her mind, and he had to protect the others. So Thalia made her final stand alone, at the top of that hill. As she died, Zeus took pity on her. He turned her into that pine tree. Her spirit still helps protect the borders of the valley. That's why the hill is called Half-Blood Hill."

I stared at the pine in the distance.

The story made me feel hollow, and guilty too. A girl my age had sacrificed herself to save her friends. She had faced a whole army of monsters. Next to that, my victory over the Minotaur didn't seem like much. I wondered, if I'd acted differently, could I have saved my mother?

"Grover," I said, "have heroes really gone on quests to the Underworld?"

"Sometimes," he said. "Orpheus. Hercules. Houdini."

"And have they ever returned somebody from the dead?"

"No. Never. Orpheus came close. . . . Percy, you're not seriously thinking—"

"No," I lied. "I was just wondering. So . . . a satyr is always assigned to guard a demigod?"

Grover studied me warily. I hadn't persuaded him that I'd really dropped the Underworld idea. "Not always. We go undercover to a lot of schools. We try to sniff out the half-bloods who have the makings of great heroes. If we find one with a very strong aura, like a child of the Big Three, we alert Chiron. He tries to keep an eye on them, since they could cause really huge problems."

"And you found me. Chiron said you thought I might be something special."

Grover looked as if I'd just led him into a trap. "I didn't . . . Oh, listen, don't think like that. If you *were*—you know—you'd never *ever* be allowed a quest, and I'd never get my license. You're probably a child of Hermes. Or maybe even one of the minor gods, like Nemesis, the god of revenge. Don't worry, okay?"

I got the idea he was reassuring himself more than me.

That night after dinner, there was a lot more excitement than usual.

At last, it was time for capture the flag.

When the plates were cleared away, the conch horn sounded and we all stood at our tables.

Campers yelled and cheered as Annabeth and two of her siblings ran into the pavilion carrying a silk banner. It was about ten feet long, glistening gray, with a painting of a barn owl above an olive tree. From the opposite side of the pavilion, Clarisse and her buddies ran in with another banner, of identical size, but gaudy red, painted with a bloody spear and a boar's head.

I turned to Luke and yelled over the noise, "Those are the flags?"

"Yeah."

"Ares and Athena always lead the teams?"

"Not always," he said. "But often."

"So, if another cabin captures one, what do you do—repaint the flag?"

He grinned. "You'll see. First we have to get one."

"Whose side are we on?"

He gave me a sly look, as if he knew something I didn't. The scar on his face made him look almost evil in the torchlight. "We've made a temporary alliance with Athena. Tonight, we get the flag from Ares. And *you* are going to help."

The teams were announced. Athena had made an alliance with Apollo and Hermes, the two biggest cabins. Apparently, privileges had been traded—shower times, chore schedules, the best slots for activities—in order to win support.

Ares had allied themselves with everybody else: Dionysus, Demeter, Aphrodite, and Hephaestus. From what I'd seen, Dionysus's kids were actually good athletes, but there were only two of them. Demeter's kids had the edge with nature skills and outdoor stuff, but they weren't very aggressive. Aphrodite's sons and daughters I wasn't too worried about. They mostly sat out every activity and checked their reflections in the lake and did their hair and gossiped. Hephaestus's kids weren't pretty, and there were only four of them, but they were big and burly from working in the metal shop all day. They might be a problem. That, of course, left Ares's cabin: a dozen of the biggest, ugliest, meanest kids on Long Island, or anywhere else on the planet.

Chiron hammered his hoof on the marble.

"Heroes!" he announced. "You know the rules. The creek is the boundary line. The entire forest is fair game. All magic items are allowed. The banner must be prominently displayed, and have no more than two guards. Prisoners may be disarmed, but may not be bound or gagged. No killing or maiming is allowed. I will serve as referee and battlefield medic. Arm yourselves!"

He spread his hands, and the tables were suddenly covered with equipment: helmets, bronze swords, spears, oxhide shields coated in metal.

"Whoa," I said. "We're really supposed to use these?"

Luke looked at me as if I were crazy. "Unless you want to get skewered by your friends in cabin five. Here—Chiron thought these would fit. You'll be on border patrol."

My shield was the size of an NBA backboard, with a big caduceus in the middle. It weighed about a million pounds. I could have snowboarded on it fine, but I hoped nobody seriously expected me to run fast. My helmet, like all the helmets on Athena's side, had a blue horsehair plume on top. Ares and their allies had red plumes.

Annabeth yelled, "Blue team, forward!"

We cheered and shook our swords and followed her down the path to the south woods. The red team yelled taunts at us as they headed off toward the north.

I managed to catch up with Annabeth without tripping over my equipment. "Hey."

She kept marching.

"So what's the plan?" I asked. "Got any magic items you can loan me?"

Her hand drifted toward her pocket, as if she were afraid I'd stolen something.

"Just watch Clarisse's spear," she said. "You don't want that thing touching you. Otherwise, don't worry. We'll take the banner from Ares. Has Luke given you your job?"

"Border patrol, whatever that means."

"It's easy. Stand by the creek, keep the reds away. Leave the rest to me. Athena always has a plan."

She pushed ahead, leaving me in the dust.

"Okay," I mumbled. "Glad you wanted me on your team."

It was a warm, sticky night. The woods were dark, with fireflies popping in and out of view. Annabeth stationed me next to a little creek that gurgled over some rocks, then she and the rest of the team scattered into the trees.

Standing there alone, with my big blue-feathered helmet and my huge shield, I felt like an idiot. The bronze sword, like all the swords I'd tried so far, seemed balanced wrong. The leather grip pulled on my hand like a bowling ball.

There was no way anybody would actually attack me, would they? I mean, Olympus had to have liability issues, right?

Far away, the conch horn blew. I heard whoops and yells in the woods, the clanking of metal, kids fighting. A blue-plumed ally from Apollo raced past me like a deer, leaped through the creek, and disappeared into enemy territory.

Great, I thought. I'll miss all the fun, as usual.

Then I heard a sound that sent a chill up my spine, a low canine growl, somewhere close by.

I raised my shield instinctively; I had the feeling something was stalking me.

Then the growling stopped. I felt the presence retreating.

On the other side of the creek, the underbrush exploded. Five Ares warriors came yelling and screaming out of the dark.

"Cream the punk!" Clarisse screamed.

Her ugly pig eyes glared through the slits of her helmet. She brandished a five-foot-long spear, its barbed metal tip flickering with red light. Her siblings had only the standard-issue bronze swords—not that that made me feel any better.

They charged across the stream. There was no help in sight. I could run. Or I could defend myself against half the Ares cabin.

I managed to sidestep the first kid's swing, but these guys were not as stupid as the Minotaur. They surrounded me, and Clarisse thrust at me with her spear. My shield deflected the point, but I felt a painful tingling all over my body. My hair stood on end. My shield arm went numb, and the air burned.

Electricity. Her stupid spear was electric. I fell back.

Another Ares guy slammed me in the chest with the butt of his sword and I hit the dirt.

They could've kicked me into jelly, but they were too busy laughing.

"Give him a haircut," Clarisse said. "Grab his hair."

I managed to get to my feet. I raised my sword, but Clarisse slammed it aside with her spear as sparks flew. Now both my arms felt numb.

"Oh, wow," Clarisse said. "I'm scared of this guy. Really scared."

"The flag is that way," I told her. I wanted to sound angry, but I was afraid it didn't come out that way.

"Yeah," one of her siblings said. "But see, we don't care about the flag. We care about a guy who made our cabin look stupid."

"You do that without my help," I told them. It probably wasn't the smartest thing to say.

Two of them came at me. I backed up toward the creek, tried to raise my shield, but Clarisse was too fast. Her spear stuck me straight in the ribs. If I hadn't been wearing an armored breastplate, I would've been shish-ke-babbed. As it was, the electric point just about shocked my teeth out of my mouth. One of her cabinmates slashed his sword across my arm, leaving a good-size cut.

Seeing my own blood made me dizzy—warm and cold at the same time.

"No maiming," I managed to say.

"Oops," the guy said. "Guess I lost my dessert privilege."

He pushed me into the creek and I landed with a splash. They all laughed. I figured as soon as they were through being amused, I would die. But then something happened. The water seemed to wake up my senses, as if I'd just had a bag of my mom's double-espresso jelly beans.

Clarisse and her cabinmates came into the creek to get me, but I stood to meet them. I knew what to do. I swung the flat of my sword against the first guy's head and knocked his helmet clean off. I hit him so hard I could see his eyes vibrating as he crumpled into the water.

Ugly Number Two and Ugly Number Three came at me. I slammed one in the face with my shield and used my sword to shear off the other guy's horsehair plume. Both of them backed up quick. Ugly Number Four didn't look really anxious to attack, but Clarisse kept coming, the point of her spear crackling with energy. As soon as she thrust, I caught the shaft between the edge of my shield and my sword, and I snapped it like a twig.

"Ah!" she screamed. "You idiot! You corpse-breath worm!"

She probably would've said worse, but I smacked her between the eyes with my sword-butt and sent her stumbling backward out of the creek.

Then I heard yelling, elated screams, and I saw Luke racing toward the boundary line with the red team's banner lifted high. He was flanked by a couple of Hermes guys covering his retreat, and a few Apollos behind them, fighting off the Hephaestus kids. The Ares folks got up, and Clarisse muttered a dazed curse.

"A trick!" she shouted. "It was a trick."

They staggered after Luke, but it was too late. Everybody converged on the creek as Luke ran across into friendly territory. Our side exploded into cheers. The red banner shimmered and turned to silver. The boar and spear were replaced with a huge caduceus, the symbol of cabin eleven. Everybody on the blue team picked up Luke and started carrying him around on their shoulders. Chiron cantered out from the woods and blew the conch horn.

The game was over. We'd won.

I was about to join the celebration when Annabeth's voice, right next to me in the creek, said, "Not bad, hero."

I looked, but she wasn't there.

"Where the heck did you learn to fight like that?" she asked. The air shimmered, and she materialized, holding a Yankees baseball cap as if she'd just taken it off her head.

I felt myself getting angry. I wasn't even fazed by the fact that she'd just been invisible. "You set me up," I said. "You put me here because you knew Clarisse would come after me, while you sent Luke around the flank. You had it all figured out."

Annabeth shrugged. "I told you. Athena always, always has a plan."

"A plan to get me pulverized."

"I came as fast as I could. I was about to jump in, but . . ." She shrugged. "You didn't need help."

Then she noticed my wounded arm. "How did you do that?"

"Sword cut," I said. "What do you think?"

"No. It *was* a sword cut. Look at it."

The blood was gone. Where the huge cut had been, there was a long white scratch, and even that was fading. As I watched, it turned into a small scar, and disappeared.

"I—I don't get it," I said.

Annabeth was thinking hard. I could almost see the gears turning. She looked down at my feet, then at Clarisse's broken spear, and said, "Step out of the water, Percy."

"What—"

"Just do it."

I came out of the creek and immediately felt bone tired. My arms started to go numb again. My adrenaline rush left me. I almost fell over, but Annabeth steadied me.

"Oh, Styx," she cursed. "This is *not* good. I didn't want . . . I assumed it would be Zeus. . . ."

Before I could ask what she meant, I heard that canine growl again, but much closer than before. A howl ripped through the forest.

The campers' cheering died instantly. Chiron shouted something in Ancient Greek, which I would realize, only later, I had understood perfectly: *"Stand ready! My bow!"*

Annabeth drew her sword.

There on the rocks just above us was a black hound the size of a rhino, with lava-red eyes and fangs like daggers.

It was looking straight at me.

Nobody moved except Annabeth, who yelled, "Percy, run!"

She tried to step in front of me, but the hound was too fast. It leaped over her—an enormous shadow with teeth—and just as it hit me, as I stumbled backward and felt its razor-sharp claws ripping through my armor, there was a cascade of thwacking sounds, like forty pieces of paper being ripped one after the other. From the hound's neck sprouted a cluster of arrows. The monster fell dead at my feet.

By some miracle, I was still alive. I didn't want to look underneath the ruins of my shredded armor. My chest felt warm and wet, and I knew I was badly cut. Another second, and the monster would've turned me into a hundred pounds of delicatessen meat.

Chiron trotted up next to us, a bow in his hand, his face grim.

"Di immortales!" Annabeth said. "That's a hellhound from the Fields of Punishment. They don't . . . they're not supposed to . . ."

"Someone summoned it," Chiron said. "Someone inside the camp."

Luke came over, the banner in his hand forgotten, his moment of glory gone.

Clarisse yelled, "It's all Percy's fault! Percy summoned it!"

"Be quiet, child," Chiron told her.

We watched the body of the hellhound melt into shadow, soaking into the ground until it disappeared.

"You're wounded," Annabeth told me. "Quick, Percy, get in the water."

"I'm okay."

"No, you're not," she said. "Chiron, watch this."

I was too tired to argue. I stepped back into the creek, the whole camp gathering around me.

Instantly, I felt better. I could feel the cuts on my chest closing up. Some of the campers gasped.

"Look, I—I don't know why," I said, trying to apologize. "I'm sorry. . . ."

But they weren't watching my wounds heal. They were staring at something above my head.

"Percy," Annabeth said, pointing. "Um . . ."

By the time I looked up, the sign was already fading, but I could still make out the hologram of green light, spinning and gleaming. A three-tipped spear: a trident.

"Your father," Annabeth murmured. "This is *really* not good."

"It is determined," Chiron announced.

All around me, campers started kneeling, even the Ares cabin, though they didn't look happy about it.

"My father?" I asked, completely bewildered.

"Poseidon," said Chiron. "Earthshaker, Stormbringer, Father of Horses. Hail, Perseus Jackson, Son of the Sea God."

NINE

I AM OFFERED A QUEST

The next morning, Chiron moved me to cabin three.

I didn't have to share with anybody. I had plenty of room for all my stuff: the Minotaur's horn, one set of spare clothes, and a toiletry bag. I got to sit at my own dinner table, pick all my own activities, call "lights out" whenever I felt like it, and not listen to anybody else.

And I was absolutely miserable.

Just when I'd started to feel accepted, to feel I had a home in cabin eleven and I might be a normal kid—or as normal as you can be when you're a half-blood—I'd been separated out as if I had some rare disease.

Nobody mentioned the hellhound, but I got the feeling they were all talking about it behind my back. The attack had scared everybody. It sent two messages: one, that I was the son of the Sea God; and two, monsters would stop at nothing to kill me. They could even invade a camp that had always been considered safe.

The other campers steered clear of me as much as possible. Cabin eleven was too nervous to have sword class with me after what I'd done to the Ares folks in the woods, so my lessons with Luke became one-on-one. He pushed me harder than ever, and wasn't afraid to bruise me up in the process.

"You're going to need all the training you can get," he promised, as we were working with swords and flaming torches. "Now let's try that viper-beheading strike again. Fifty more repetitions."

Annabeth still taught me Greek in the mornings, but she seemed distracted. Every time I said something, she scowled at me, as if I'd just poked her between the eyes.

After lessons, she would walk away muttering to herself: "Quest . . . Poseidon? . . . Dirty rotten . . . Got to make a plan . . ."

Even Clarisse kept her distance, though her venomous looks made it clear she wanted to kill me for breaking her magic spear. I wished she would just yell or punch me or something. I'd rather get into fights every day than be ignored.

I knew somebody at camp resented me, because one night I came into my cabin and found a mortal newspaper dropped inside the doorway, a copy of the *New York Daily News*, opened to the Metro page. The article took me almost an hour to read, because the angrier I got, the more the words floated around on the page.

BOY AND MOTHER STILL MISSING AFTER FREAK CAR ACCIDENT
BY EILEEN SMYTHE

Sally Jackson and son Percy are still missing one week after their mysterious disappearance. The family's badly burned '78 Camaro was discovered last Saturday on a north Long Island road with the roof ripped off and the front axle broken. The car had flipped and skidded for several hundred feet before exploding.

Mother and son had gone for a weekend vacation to Montauk, but left hastily, under mysterious circumstances. Small traces of blood were found in the car and near the scene of the wreck, but there were no other signs of the missing Jacksons. Residents in the rural area reported seeing nothing unusual around the time of the accident.

Ms. Jackson's husband, Gabe Ugliano, claims that his stepson, Percy Jackson, is a troubled child who has been kicked out of numerous boarding schools and has expressed violent tendencies in the past.

Police would not say whether son Percy is a suspect in his mother's disappearance, but they have not ruled out foul play. Below are recent pictures of Sally Jackson and Percy. Police urge anyone with information to call the following toll-free crime-stoppers hotline.

The phone number was circled in black marker.

I wadded up the paper and threw it away, then flopped down in my bunk bed in the middle of my empty cabin.

"Lights out," I told myself miserably.

That night, I had my worst dream yet.

I was running along the beach in a storm. This time,

there was a city behind me. Not New York. The sprawl was different: buildings spread farther apart, palm trees and low hills in the distance.

About a hundred yards down the surf, two men were fighting. They looked like TV wrestlers, muscular, with beards and long hair. Both wore flowing Greek tunics, one trimmed in blue, the other in green. They grappled with each other, wrestled, kicked and head-butted, and every time they connected, lightning flashed, the sky grew darker, and the wind rose.

I had to stop them. I didn't know why. But the harder I ran, the more the wind blew me back, until I was running in place, my heels digging uselessly in the sand.

Over the roar of the storm, I could hear the blue-robed one yelling at the green-robed one, *Give it back! Give it back!* Like a kindergartner fighting over a toy.

The waves got bigger, crashing into the beach, spraying me with salt.

I yelled, *Stop it! Stop fighting!*

The ground shook. Laughter came from somewhere under the earth, and a voice so deep and evil it turned my blood to ice.

Come down, little hero, the voice crooned. *Come down!*

The sand split beneath me, opening up a crevice straight down to the center of the earth. My feet slipped, and darkness swallowed me.

I woke up, sure I was falling.

I was still in bed in cabin three. My body told me it was morning, but it was dark outside, and thunder rolled across the hills. A storm was brewing. I hadn't dreamed that.

I heard a clopping sound at the door, a hoof knocking on the threshold.

"Come in?"

Grover trotted inside, looking worried. "Mr. D wants to see you."

"Why?"

"He wants to kill . . . I mean, I'd better let him tell you."

Nervously, I got dressed and followed, sure that I was in huge trouble.

For days, I'd been half expecting a summons to the Big House. Now that I was declared a son of Poseidon, one of the Big Three gods who weren't supposed to have kids, I figured it was a crime for me just to be alive. The other gods had probably been debating the best way to punish me for existing, and now Mr. D was ready to deliver their verdict.

Over Long Island Sound, the sky looked like ink soup coming to a boil. A hazy curtain of rain was coming in our direction. I asked Grover if we needed an umbrella.

"No," he said. "It never rains here unless we want it to."

I pointed at the storm. "What the heck is that, then?"

He glanced uneasily at the sky. "It'll pass around us. Bad weather always does."

I realized he was right. In the week I'd been here, it had never even been overcast. The few rain clouds I'd seen had skirted right around the edges of the valley.

But this storm . . . this one was huge.

At the volleyball pit, the kids from Apollo's cabin were playing a morning game against the satyrs. Dionysus's twins were walking around in the strawberry fields, making the plants grow. Everybody was going about their normal business, but they looked tense. They kept their eyes on the storm.

Grover and I walked up to the front porch of the Big House. Dionysus sat at the pinochle table in his tiger-striped Hawaiian shirt with his Diet Coke, just as he had on my first day. Chiron sat across the table in his fake wheelchair. They were playing against invisible opponents—two sets of cards hovering in the air.

"Well, well," Mr. D said without looking up. "Our little celebrity."

I waited.

"Come closer," Mr. D said. "And don't expect me to kowtow to you, mortal, just because old Barnacle-Beard is your father."

A net of lightning flashed across the clouds. Thunder shook the windows of the house.

"Blah, blah, blah," Dionysus said.

Chiron feigned interest in his pinochle cards. Grover cowered by the railing, his hooves clopping back and forth.

"If I had my way," Dionysus said, "I would cause your molecules to erupt in flames. We'd sweep up the ashes and be done with a lot of trouble. But Chiron seems to feel this would be against my mission at this cursed camp: to keep you little brats safe from harm."

"Spontaneous combustion *is* a form of harm, Mr. D," Chiron put in.

"Nonsense," Dionysus said. "Boy wouldn't feel a thing.

[132]

Nevertheless, I've agreed to restrain myself. I'm thinking of turning you into a dolphin instead, sending you back to your father."

"Mr. D——" Chiron warned.

"Oh, all right," Dionysus relented. "There's one more option. But it's deadly foolishness." Dionysus rose, and the invisible players' cards dropped to the table. "I'm off to Olympus for the emergency meeting. If the boy is still here when I get back, I'll turn him into an Atlantic bottlenose. Do you understand? And Perseus Jackson, if you're at all smart, you'll see that's a much more sensible choice than what Chiron feels you must do."

Dionysus picked up a playing card, twisted it, and it became a plastic rectangle. A credit card? No. A security pass.

He snapped his fingers.

The air seemed to fold and bend around him. He became a hologram, then a wind, then he was gone, leaving only the smell of fresh-pressed grapes lingering behind.

Chiron smiled at me, but he looked tired and strained. "Sit, Percy, please. And Grover."

We did.

Chiron laid his cards on the table, a winning hand he hadn't gotten to use.

"Tell me, Percy," he said. "What did you make of the hellhound?"

Just hearing the name made me shudder.

Chiron probably wanted me to say, *Heck, it was nothing. I eat hellhounds for breakfast.* But I didn't feel like lying.

"It scared me," I said. "If you hadn't shot it, I'd be dead."

"You'll meet worse, Percy. Far worse, before you're done."

"Done . . . with what?"

"Your quest, of course. Will you accept it?"

I glanced at Grover, who was crossing his fingers.

"Um, sir," I said, "you haven't told me what it is yet."

Chiron grimaced. "Well, that's the hard part, the details."

Thunder rumbled across the valley. The storm clouds had now reached the edge of the beach. As far as I could see, the sky and the sea were boiling together.

"Poseidon and Zeus," I said. "They're fighting over something valuable . . . something that was stolen, aren't they?"

Chiron and Grover exchanged looks.

Chiron sat forward in his wheelchair. "How did you know that?"

My face felt hot. I wished I hadn't opened my big mouth. "The weather since Christmas has been weird, like the sea and the sky are fighting. Then I talked to Annabeth, and she'd overheard something about a theft. And . . . I've also been having these dreams."

"I knew it," Grover said.

"Hush, satyr," Chiron ordered.

"But it is his quest!" Grover's eyes were bright with excitement. "It must be!"

"Only the Oracle can determine." Chiron stroked his bristly beard. "Nevertheless, Percy, you are correct. Your father and Zeus are having their worst quarrel in centuries.

They are fighting over something valuable that was stolen. To be precise: a lightning bolt."

I laughed nervously. "A *what?*"

"Do not take this lightly," Chiron warned. "I'm not talking about some tinfoil-covered zigzag you'd see in a second-grade play. I'm talking about a two-foot-long cylinder of high-grade celestial bronze, capped on both ends with god-level explosives."

"Oh."

"Zeus's master bolt," Chiron said, getting worked up now. "The symbol of his power, from which all other lightning bolts are patterned. The first weapon made by the Cyclopes for the war against the Titans, the bolt that sheered the top off Mount Etna and hurled Kronos from his throne; the master bolt, which packs enough power to make mortal hydrogen bombs look like firecrackers."

"And it's missing?"

"Stolen," Chiron said.

"By who?"

"By *whom*," Chiron corrected. Once a teacher, always a teacher. "By you."

My mouth fell open.

"At least"—Chiron held up a hand—"that's what Zeus thinks. During the winter solstice, at the last council of the gods, Zeus and Poseidon had an argument. The usual nonsense: 'Mother Rhea always liked you best,' 'Air disasters are more spectacular than sea disasters,' et cetera. Afterward, Zeus realized his master bolt was missing, taken from the throne room under his very nose. He immediately blamed Poseidon. Now, a god cannot usurp another god's symbol of power directly—that is forbidden by the most ancient of divine laws. But Zeus believes your father convinced a human hero to take it."

"But I didn't—"

"Patience and listen, child," Chiron said. "Zeus has good reason to be suspicious. The forges of the Cyclopes are under the ocean, which gives Poseidon some influence over the makers of his brother's lightning. Zeus believes Poseidon has taken the master bolt, and is now secretly having the Cyclopes build an arsenal of illegal copies, which might be used to topple Zeus from his throne. The only thing Zeus wasn't sure about was which hero Poseidon used to steal the bolt. Now Poseidon has openly claimed you as his son. You were in New York over the winter holidays. You could easily have snuck into Olympus. Zeus believes he has found his thief."

"But I've never even been to Olympus! Zeus is crazy!"

Chiron and Grover glanced nervously at the sky. The clouds didn't seem to be parting around us, as Grover had promised. They were rolling straight over our valley, sealing us in like a coffin lid.

"Er, Percy . . . ?" Grover said. "We don't use the *c*-word to describe the Lord of the Sky."

"Perhaps *paranoid*," Chiron suggested. "Then again, Poseidon has tried to unseat Zeus before. I believe that was question thirty-eight on your final exam. . . ." He looked at me as if he actually expected me to remember question thirty-eight.

How could anyone accuse me of stealing a god's weapon? I couldn't even steal a slice of pizza from Gabe's poker party without getting busted. Chiron was waiting for an answer.

"Something about a golden net?" I guessed. "Poseidon and Hera and a few other gods . . . they, like, trapped Zeus and wouldn't let him out until he promised to be a better ruler, right?"

"Correct," Chiron said. "And Zeus has never trusted Poseidon since. Of course, Poseidon denies stealing the master bolt. He took great offense at the accusation. The two have been arguing back and forth for months, threatening war. And now, you've come along—the proverbial last straw."

"But I'm just a kid!"

"Percy," Grover cut in, "if you were Zeus, and you already thought your brother was plotting to overthrow you, then your brother suddenly admitted he had broken the sacred oath he took after World War II, that he's fathered a new mortal hero who might be used as a weapon against you. . . . Wouldn't that put a twist in your toga?"

"But I didn't do anything. Poseidon—my dad—he didn't really have this master bolt stolen, did he?"

Chiron sighed. "Most thinking observers would agree that thievery is not Poseidon's style. But the Sea God is too proud to try convincing Zeus of that. Zeus has demanded that Poseidon return the bolt by the summer solstice. That's June twenty-first, ten days from now. Poseidon wants an apology for being called a thief by the same date. I hoped that diplomacy might prevail, that Hera or Demeter or Hestia would make the two brothers see sense. But your arrival has inflamed Zeus's temper. Now neither god will back down. Unless someone intervenes, unless the master bolt is found and returned to Zeus before the solstice, there will be war. And do you know what a full-fledged war would look like, Percy?"

"Bad?" I guessed.

"Imagine the world in chaos. Nature at war with itself. Olympians forced to choose sides between Zeus and Poseidon. Destruction. Carnage. Millions dead. Western civilization turned into a battleground so big it will make the Trojan War look like a water-balloon fight."

"Bad," I repeated.

"And you, Percy Jackson, would be the first to feel Zeus's wrath."

It started to rain. Volleyball players stopped their game and stared in stunned silence at the sky.

I had brought this storm to Half-Blood Hill. Zeus was punishing the whole camp because of me. I was furious.

"So I have to find the stupid bolt," I said. "And return it to Zeus."

"What better peace offering," Chiron said, "than to have the son of Poseidon return Zeus's property?"

"If Poseidon doesn't have it, where is the thing?"

"I believe I know." Chiron's expression was grim. "Part of a prophecy I had years ago . . . well, some of the lines make sense to me, now. But before I can say more, you must officially take up the quest. You must seek the counsel of the Oracle."

"Why can't you tell me where the bolt is beforehand?"

"Because if I did, you would be too afraid to accept the challenge."

I swallowed. "Good reason."

"You agree then?"

I looked at Grover, who nodded encouragingly.

Easy for him. I was the one Zeus wanted to kill.

"All right," I said. "It's better than being turned into a dolphin."

"Then it's time you consulted the Oracle," Chiron said. "Go upstairs, Percy Jackson, to the attic. When you come back down, assuming you're still sane, we will talk more."

Four flights up, the stairs ended under a green trap-door.

I pulled the cord. The door swung down, and a wooden ladder clattered into place.

The warm air from above smelled like mildew and rotten wood and something else . . . a smell I remembered from biology class. Reptiles. The smell of snakes.

I held my breath and climbed.

The attic was filled with Greek hero junk: armor stands covered in cobwebs; once-bright shields pitted with rust; old leather steamer trunks plastered with stickers saying ITHAKA, CIRCE'S ISLE, and LAND OF THE AMAZONS. One long table was stacked with glass jars filled with pickled *things*—severed hairy claws, huge yellow eyes, various other parts of monsters. A dusty mounted trophy on the wall looked like a giant snake's head, but with horns and a full set of shark's teeth. The plaque read, HYDRA HEAD #1, WOODSTOCK, N.Y., 1969.

By the window, sitting on a wooden tripod stool, was the most gruesome memento of all: a mummy. Not the wrapped-in-cloth kind, but a human female body shriveled to a husk. She wore a tie-dyed sundress, lots of beaded necklaces, and a headband over long black hair. The skin of her face was thin and leathery over her skull, and her eyes were glassy white slits, as if the real eyes had been replaced by marbles; she'd been dead a long, long time.

Looking at her sent chills up my back. And that was before she sat up on her stool and opened her mouth. A green mist poured from the mummy's mouth, coiling over the floor in thick tendrils, hissing like twenty thousand snakes. I stumbled over myself trying to get to the trapdoor, but it slammed shut. Inside my head, I heard a voice, slithering into one ear and coiling around my brain: *I am the spirit of Delphi, speaker of the prophecies of Phoebus Apollo, slayer of the mighty Python. Approach, seeker, and ask.*

I wanted to say, *No thanks, wrong door, just looking for the bathroom.* But I forced myself to take a deep breath.

The mummy wasn't alive. She was some kind of gruesome receptacle for something else, the power that was now swirling around me in the green mist. But its presence didn't feel evil, like my demonic math teacher Mrs. Dodds or the Minotaur. It felt more like the Three Fates I'd seen knitting the yarn outside the highway fruit stand: ancient, powerful, and definitely *not* human. But not particularly interested in killing me, either.

I got up the courage to ask, "What is my destiny?"

The mist swirled more thickly, collecting right in front of me and around the table with the pickled monster-part jars. Suddenly there were four men sitting around the table, playing cards. Their faces became clearer. It was Smelly Gabe and his buddies.

My fists clenched, though I knew this poker party couldn't be real. It was an illusion, made out of mist.

Gabe turned toward me and spoke in the rasping voice of the Oracle: *You shall go west, and face the god who has turned.*

His buddy on the right looked up and said in the same voice: *You shall find what was stolen, and see it safely returned.*

The guy on the left threw in two poker chips, then said: *You shall be betrayed by one who calls you a friend.*

Finally, Eddie, our building super, delivered the worst line of all: *And you shall fail to save what matters most, in the end.*

The figures began to dissolve. At first I was too stunned to say anything, but as the mist retreated, coiling into a huge green serpent and slithering back into the mouth of the mummy, I cried, "Wait! What do you mean? What friend? What will I fail to save?"

The tail of the mist snake disappeared into the mummy's mouth. She reclined back against the wall. Her mouth closed tight, as if it hadn't been open in a hundred years. The attic was silent again, abandoned, nothing but a room full of mementos.

I got the feeling that I could stand here until I had cobwebs, too, and I wouldn't learn anything else.

My audience with the Oracle was over.

"Well?" Chiron asked me.

I slumped into a chair at the pinochle table. "She said I would retrieve what was stolen."

Grover sat forward, chewing excitedly on the remains of a Diet Coke can. "That's great!"

"What did the Oracle say *exactly*?" Chiron pressed. "This is important."

My ears were still tingling from the reptilian voice. "She . . . she said I would go west and face a god who had turned. I would retrieve what was stolen and see it safely returned."

"I knew it," Grover said.

Chiron didn't look satisfied. "Anything else?"

I didn't want to tell him.

What friend would betray me? I didn't have that many.

And the last line—I would fail to save what mattered most. What kind of Oracle would send me on a quest and tell me, *Oh, by the way, you'll fail.*

How could I confess that?

"No," I said. "That's about it."

He studied my face. "Very well, Percy. But know this: the Oracle's words often have double meanings. Don't dwell on them too much. The truth is not always clear until events come to pass."

I got the feeling he knew I was holding back something bad, and he was trying to make me feel better.

"Okay," I said, anxious to change topics. "So where do I go? Who's this god in the west?"

"Ah, think, Percy," Chiron said. "If Zeus and Poseidon weaken each other in a war, who stands to gain?"

"Somebody else who wants to take over?" I guessed.

"Yes, quite. Someone who harbors a grudge, who has been unhappy with his lot since the world was divided eons ago, whose kingdom would grow powerful with the deaths of millions. Someone who hates his brothers for forcing him into an oath to have no more children, an oath that both of them have now broken."

I thought about my dreams, the evil voice that had spoken from under the ground. "Hades."

Chiron nodded. "The Lord of the Dead is the only possibility."

A scrap of aluminum dribbled out of Grover's mouth. "Whoa, wait. Wh-what?"

"A Fury came after Percy," Chiron reminded him. "She watched the young man until she was sure of his identity, then tried to kill him. Furies obey only one lord: Hades."

"Yes, but—but Hades hates *all* heroes," Grover protested. "Especially if he has found out Percy is a son of Poseidon. . . ."

"A hellhound got into the forest," Chiron continued. "Those can only be summoned from the Fields of Punishment, and it had to be summoned by someone within the camp. Hades must have a spy here. He must suspect Poseidon will try to use Percy to clear his name. Hades would very much like to kill this young half-blood before he can take on the quest."

"Great," I muttered. "That's two major gods who want to kill me."

"But a quest to . . ." Grover swallowed. "I mean, couldn't the master bolt be in some place like Maine? Maine's very nice this time of year."

"Hades sent a minion to steal the master bolt," Chiron insisted. "He hid it in the Underworld, knowing full well that Zeus would blame Poseidon. I don't pretend to understand the Lord of the Dead's motives perfectly, or why he chose this time to start a war, but one thing is certain. Percy must go to the Underworld, find the master bolt, and reveal the truth."

A strange fire burned in my stomach. The weirdest thing was: it wasn't fear. It was anticipation. The desire for revenge. Hades had tried to kill me three times so far, with the Fury, the Minotaur, and the hellhound. It was his fault my mother had disappeared in a flash of light. Now he was trying to frame me and my dad for a theft we hadn't committed.

I was ready to take him on.

Besides, if my mother was in the Underworld . . .

Whoa, boy, said the small part of my brain that was still sane. You're a kid. Hades is a god.

Grover was trembling. He'd started eating pinochle cards like potato chips.

The poor guy needed to complete a quest with me so he could get his searcher's license, whatever that was, but how could I ask him to do this quest, especially when the Oracle said I was destined to fail? This was suicide.

"Look, if we know it's Hades," I told Chiron, "why can't we just tell the other gods? Zeus or Poseidon could go down to the Underworld and bust some heads."

"Suspecting and knowing are not the same," Chiron said. "Besides, even if the other gods suspect Hades—and I imagine Poseidon does—they couldn't retrieve the bolt themselves. Gods cannot cross each other's territories except by invitation. That is another ancient rule. Heroes, on the other hand, have certain privileges. They can go anywhere, challenge anyone, as long as they're bold enough and strong enough to do it. No god can be held responsible for a hero's actions. Why do you think the gods always operate through humans?"

"You're saying I'm being used."

"I'm saying it's no accident Poseidon has claimed you now. It's a very risky gamble, but he's in a desperate situation. He needs you."

My dad needs me.

Emotions rolled around inside me like bits of glass in a kaleidoscope. I didn't know whether to feel resentful or grateful or happy or angry. Poseidon had ignored me for twelve years. Now suddenly he needed me.

I looked at Chiron. "You've known I was Poseidon's son all along, haven't you?"

"I had my suspicions. As I said . . . I've spoken to the Oracle, too."

I got the feeling there was a lot he wasn't telling me about his prophecy, but I decided I couldn't worry about that right now. After all, I was holding back information too.

"So let me get this straight," I said. "I'm supposed go to the Underworld and confront the Lord of the Dead."

"Check," Chiron said.

"Find the most powerful weapon in the universe."

"Check."

"And get it back to Olympus before the summer solstice, in ten days."

"That's about right."

I looked at Grover, who gulped down the ace of hearts.

"Did I mention that Maine is very nice this time of year?" he asked weakly.

"You don't have to go," I told him. "I can't ask that of you."

"Oh . . ." He shifted his hooves. "No . . . it's just that satyrs and underground places . . . well . . ."

He took a deep breath, then stood, brushing the shredded cards and aluminum bits off his T-shirt. "You saved my life, Percy. If . . . if you're serious about wanting me along, I won't let you down."

I felt so relieved I wanted to cry, though I didn't think that would be very heroic. Grover was the only friend I'd ever had for longer than a few months. I wasn't sure what good a satyr could do against the forces of the dead, but I felt better knowing he'd be with me.

"All the way, G-man." I turned to Chiron. "So where do we go? The Oracle just said to go west."

"The entrance to the Underworld is always in the west. It moves from age to age, just like Olympus. Right now, of course, it's in America."

"Where?"

Chiron looked surprised. "I thought that would be obvious enough. The entrance to the Underworld is in Los Angeles."

"Oh," I said. "Naturally. So we just get on a plane—"

"No!" Grover shrieked. "Percy, what are you thinking? Have you ever been on a plane in your life?"

I shook my head, feeling embarrassed. My mom had never taken me anywhere by plane. She'd always said we didn't have the money. Besides, her parents had died in a plane crash.

"Percy, think," Chiron said. "You are the son of the Sea God. Your father's bitterest rival is Zeus, Lord of the Sky. Your mother knew better than to trust you in an airplane. You would be in Zeus's domain. You would never come down again alive."

Overhead, lightning crackled. Thunder boomed.

"Okay," I said, determined not to look at the storm. "So, I'll travel overland."

"That's right," Chiron said. "Two companions may accompany you. Grover is one. The other has already volunteered, if you will accept her help."

"Gee," I said, feigning surprise. "Who else would be stupid enough to volunteer for a quest like this?"

The air shimmered behind Chiron.

Annabeth became visible, stuffing her Yankees cap into her back pocket.

"I've been waiting a long time for a quest, seaweed brain," she said. "Athena is no fan of Poseidon, but if you're going to save the world, I'm the best person to keep you from messing up."

"If you do say so yourself," I said. "I suppose you have a plan, wise girl?"

Her cheeks colored. "Do you want my help or not?"

The truth was, I did. I needed all the help I could get.

"A trio," I said. "That'll work."

"Excellent," Chiron said. "This afternoon, we can take you as far as the bus terminal in Manhattan. After that, you are on your own."

Lightning flashed. Rain poured down on the meadows that were never supposed to have violent weather.

"No time to waste," Chiron said. "I think you should all get packing."

TEN

𐤀

I RUIN A PERFECTLY GOOD BUS

It didn't take me long to pack. I decided to leave the Minotaur horn in my cabin, which left me only an extra change of clothes and a toothbrush to stuff in a backpack Grover had found for me.

The camp store loaned me one hundred dollars in mortal money and twenty golden drachmas. These coins were as big as Girl Scout cookies and had images of various Greek gods stamped on one side and the Empire State Building on the other. The ancient mortal drachmas had been silver, Chiron told us, but Olympians never used less than pure gold. Chiron said the coins might come in handy for nonmortal transactions—whatever that meant. He gave Annabeth and me each a canteen of nectar and a Ziploc bag full of ambrosia squares, to be used only in emergencies, if we were seriously hurt. It was god food, Chiron reminded us. It would cure us of almost any injury, but it was lethal to mortals. Too much of it would make a half-blood very, very feverish. An overdose would burn us up, literally.

Annabeth was bringing her magic Yankees cap, which she told me had been a twelfth-birthday present from her mom. She carried a book on famous classical architecture, written in Ancient Greek, to read when she got bored, and a long bronze knife, hidden in her shirt sleeve. I was sure the knife would get us busted the first time we went through a metal detector.

Grover wore his fake feet and his pants to pass as human. He wore a green rasta-style cap, because when it rained his curly hair flattened and you could just see the tips of his horns. His bright orange backpack was full of scrap metal and apples to snack on. In his pocket was a set of reed pipes his daddy goat had carved for him, even though he only knew two songs: Mozart's Piano Concerto no. 12 and Hilary Duff's "So Yesterday," both of which sounded pretty bad on reed pipes.

We waved good-bye to the other campers, took one last look at the strawberry fields, the ocean, and the Big House, then hiked up Half-Blood Hill to the tall pine tree that used to be Thalia, daughter of Zeus.

Chiron was waiting for us in his wheelchair. Next to him stood the surfer dude I'd seen when I was recovering in the sick room. According to Grover, the guy was the camp's head of security. He supposedly had eyes all over his body so he could never be surprised. Today, though, he was wearing a chauffeur's uniform, so I could only see extra peepers on his hands, face and neck.

"This is Argus," Chiron told me. "He will drive you into the city, and, er, well, keep an eye on things."

I heard footsteps behind us.

Luke came running up the hill, carrying a pair of basketball shoes.

"Hey!" he panted. "Glad I caught you."

Annabeth blushed, the way she always did when Luke was around.

"Just wanted to say good luck," Luke told me. "And I thought . . . um, maybe you could use these."

He handed me the sneakers, which looked pretty normal. They even smelled kind of normal.

Luke said, *"Maia!"*

White bird's wings sprouted out of the heels, startling me so much, I dropped them. The shoes flapped around on the ground until the wings folded up and disappeared.

"Awesome!" Grover said.

Luke smiled. "Those served me well when I was on my quest. Gift from Dad. Of course, I don't use them much these days. . . ." His expression turned sad.

I didn't know what to say. It was cool enough that Luke had come to say good-bye. I'd been afraid he might resent me for getting so much attention the last few days. But here he was giving me a magic gift. . . . It made me blush almost as much as Annabeth.

"Hey, man," I said. "Thanks."

"Listen, Percy . . ." Luke looked uncomfortable. "A lot of hopes are riding on you. So just . . . kill some monsters for me, okay?"

We shook hands. Luke patted Grover's head between his horns, then gave a good-bye hug to Annabeth, who looked like she might pass out.

After Luke was gone, I told her, "You're hyperventilating."

"Am not."

"You let him capture the flag instead of you, didn't you?"

"Oh . . . why do I want to go anywhere with you, Percy?"

She stomped down the other side of the hill, where a white SUV waited on the shoulder of the road. Argus followed, jingling his car keys.

I picked up the flying shoes and had a sudden bad feeling. I looked at Chiron. "I won't be able to use these, will I?"

He shook his head. "Luke meant well, Percy. But taking to the air . . . that would not be wise for you."

I nodded, disappointed, but then I got an idea. "Hey, Grover. You want a magic item?"

His eyes lit up. "Me?"

Pretty soon we'd laced the sneakers over his fake feet, and the world's first flying goat boy was ready for launch.

"*Maia!*" he shouted.

He got off the ground okay, but then fell over sideways so his backpack dragged through the grass. The winged shoes kept bucking up and down like tiny broncos.

"Practice," Chiron called after him. "You just need practice!"

"Aaaaa!" Grover went flying sideways down the hill like a possessed lawn mower, heading toward the van.

Before I could follow, Chiron caught my arm. "I should have trained you better, Percy," he said. "If only I had more time. Hercules, Jason—they all got more training."

"That's okay. I just wish—"

I stopped myself because I was about to sound like a

brat. I was wishing my dad had given me a cool magic item to help on the quest, something as good as Luke's flying shoes, or Annabeth's invisible cap.

"What am I thinking?" Chiron cried. "I can't let you get away without this."

He pulled a pen from his coat pocket and handed it to me. It was an ordinary disposable ballpoint, black ink, removable cap. Probably cost thirty cents.

"Gee," I said. "Thanks."

"Percy, that's a gift from your father. I've kept it for years, not knowing you were who I was waiting for. But the prophecy is clear to me now. You are the one."

I remembered the field trip to the Metropolitan Museum of Art, when I'd vaporized Mrs. Dodds. Chiron had thrown me a pen that turned into a sword. Could this be . . . ?

I took off the cap, and the pen grew longer and heavier in my hand. In half a second, I held a shimmering bronze sword with a double-edged blade, a leather-wrapped grip, and a flat hilt riveted with gold studs. It was the first weapon that actually felt balanced in my hand.

"The sword has a long and tragic history that we need not go into," Chiron told me. "Its name is Anaklusmos."

"'Riptide,'" I translated, surprised the Ancient Greek came so easily.

"Use it only for emergencies," Chiron said, "and only against monsters. No hero should harm mortals unless absolutely necessary, of course, but this sword wouldn't harm them in any case."

I looked at the wickedly sharp blade. "What do you mean it wouldn't harm mortals? How could it not?"

"The sword is celestial bronze. Forged by the Cyclopes, tempered in the heart of Mount Etna, cooled in the River Lethe. It's deadly to monsters, to any creature from the Underworld, provided they don't kill you first. But the blade will pass through mortals like an illusion. They simply are not important enough for the blade to kill. And I should warn you: as a demigod, you can be killed by either celestial or normal weapons. You are twice as vulnerable."

"Good to know."

"Now recap the pen."

I touched the pen cap to the sword tip and instantly Riptide shrank to a ballpoint pen again. I tucked it in my pocket, a little nervous, because I was famous for losing pens at school.

"You can't," Chiron said.

"Can't what?"

"Lose the pen," he said. "It is enchanted. It will always reappear in your pocket. Try it."

I was wary, but I threw the pen as far as I could down the hill and watched it disappear in the grass.

"It may take a few moments," Chiron told me. "Now check your pocket."

Sure enough, the pen was there.

"Okay, that's *extremely* cool," I admitted. "But what if a mortal sees me pulling out a sword?"

Chiron smiled. "Mist is a powerful thing, Percy."

"Mist?"

"Yes. Read *The Iliad*. It's full of references to the stuff. Whenever divine or monstrous elements mix with the mortal world, they generate Mist, which obscures the vision of humans. You will see things just as they are, being a half-blood, but humans will interpret things quite differently. Remarkable, really, the lengths to which humans will go to fit things into their version of reality."

I put Riptide back in my pocket.

For the first time, the quest felt real. I was actually leaving Half-Blood Hill. I was heading west with no adult supervision, no backup plan, not even a cell phone. (Chiron said cell phones were traceable by monsters; if we used one, it would be worse than sending up a flare.) I had no weapon stronger than a sword to fight off monsters and reach the Land of the Dead.

"Chiron . . ." I said. "When you say the gods are immortal . . . I mean, there was a time *before* them, right?"

"Four ages before them, actually. The Time of the Titans was the Fourth Age, sometimes called the Golden Age, which is definitely a misnomer. This, the time of Western civilization and the rule of Zeus, is the Fifth Age."

"So what was it like . . . before the gods?"

Chiron pursed his lips. "Even I am not old enough to remember that, child, but I know it was a time of darkness and savagery for mortals. Kronos, the lord of the Titans, called his reign the Golden Age because men lived innocent and free of all knowledge. But that was mere propaganda. The Titan king cared nothing for your kind except as appetizers or a source of cheap entertainment. It was only in the early reign of Lord Zeus, when Prometheus the good Titan brought fire to mankind, that your species began to progress, and even then Prometheus was branded a radical thinker. Zeus punished him severely, as you may recall. Of course, eventually the gods warmed to humans, and Western civilization was born."

"But the gods can't die now, right? I mean, as long as Western civilization is alive, they're alive. So . . . even if I failed, nothing could happen so bad it would mess up *everything*, right?"

Chiron gave me a melancholy smile. "No one knows how long the Age of the West will last, Percy. The gods are immortal, yes. But then, so were the Titans. *They* still exist, locked away in their various prisons, forced to endure endless pain and punishment, reduced in power, but still very much alive. May the Fates forbid that the gods should ever suffer such a doom, or that we should ever return to the darkness and chaos of the past. All we can do, child, is follow our destiny."

"Our destiny . . . assuming we know what that is."

"Relax," Chiron told me. "Keep a clear head. And remember, you may be about to prevent the biggest war in human history."

"Relax," I said. "I'm very relaxed."

When I got to the bottom of the hill, I looked back. Under the pine tree that used to be Thalia, daughter of Zeus, Chiron was now standing in full horse-man form, holding his bow high in salute. Just your typical summer-camp send-off by your typical centaur.

Argus drove us out of the countryside and into western Long Island. It felt weird to be on a highway again, Annabeth and Grover sitting next to me as if we were normal carpoolers. After two weeks at Half-Blood Hill, the real world seemed like a fantasy. I found myself staring at every McDonald's, every kid in the back of his parents' car, every billboard and shopping mall.

"So far so good," I told Annabeth. "Ten miles and not a single monster."

She gave me an irritated look. "It's bad luck to talk that way, seaweed brain."

"Remind me again—why do you hate me so much?"

"I don't hate you."

"Could've fooled me."

She folded her cap of invisibility. "Look . . . we're just not supposed to get along, okay? Our parents are rivals."

"Why?"

She sighed. "How many reasons do you want? One time my mom caught Poseidon with his girlfriend in Athena's temple, which is *hugely* disrespectful. Another time, Athena and Poseidon competed to be the patron god for the city of Athens. Your dad created some stupid saltwater spring for his gift. My mom created the olive tree. The people saw that her gift was better, so they named the city after her."

"They must really like olives."

"Oh, forget it."

"Now, if she'd invented pizza—*that* I could understand."

"I said, forget it!"

In the front seat, Argus smiled. He didn't say anything, but one blue eye on the back of his neck winked at me.

Traffic slowed us down in Queens. By the time we got into Manhattan it was sunset and starting to rain.

Argus dropped us at the Greyhound Station on the Upper East Side, not far from my mom and Gabe's apartment. Taped to a mailbox was a soggy flyer with my picture on it: HAVE YOU SEEN THIS BOY?

I ripped it down before Annabeth and Grover could notice.

Argus unloaded our bags, made sure we got our bus tickets, then drove away, the eye on the back of his hand opening to watch us as he pulled out of the parking lot.

I thought about how close I was to my old apartment. On a normal day, my mom would be home from the candy store by now. Smelly Gabe was probably up there right now, playing poker, not even missing her.

Grover shouldered his backpack. He gazed down the street in the direction I was looking. "You want to know why she married him, Percy?"

I stared at him. "Were you reading my mind or something?"

"Just your emotions." He shrugged. "Guess I forgot to tell you satyrs can do that. You were thinking about your mom and your stepdad, right?"

I nodded, wondering what else Grover might've forgotten to tell me.

"Your mom married Gabe for *you*," Grover told me. "You call him 'Smelly,' but you've got no idea. The guy has

[158]

this aura. . . . Yuck. I can smell him from here. I can smell traces of him on you, and you haven't been near him for a week."

"Thanks," I said. "Where's the nearest shower?"

"You should be grateful, Percy. Your stepfather smells so repulsively human he could mask the presence of any demigod. As soon as I took a whiff inside his Camaro, I knew: Gabe has been covering your scent for years. If you hadn't lived with him every summer, you probably would've been found by monsters a long time ago. Your mom stayed with him to protect you. She was a smart lady. She must've loved you a lot to put up with that guy—if that makes you feel any better."

It didn't, but I forced myself not to show it. I'll see her again, I thought. She isn't gone.

I wondered if Grover could still read my emotions, mixed up as they were. I was glad he and Annabeth were with me, but I felt guilty that I hadn't been straight with them. I hadn't told them the real reason I'd said yes to this crazy quest.

The truth was, I didn't care about retrieving Zeus's lightning bolt, or saving the world, or even helping my father out of trouble. The more I thought about it, I resented Poseidon for never visiting me, never helping my mom, never even sending a lousy child-support check. He'd only claimed me because he needed a job done.

All I cared about was my mom. Hades had taken her unfairly, and Hades was going to give her back.

You will be betrayed by one who calls you a friend, the Oracle whispered in my mind. *You will fail to save what matters most in the end.*

Shut up, I told it.

The rain kept coming down.

We got restless waiting for the bus and decided to play some Hacky Sack with one of Grover's apples. Annabeth was unbelievable. She could bounce the apple off her knee, her elbow, her shoulder, whatever. I wasn't too bad myself.

The game ended when I tossed the apple toward Grover and it got too close to his mouth. In one mega goat bitc, our Hacky Sack disappeared—core, stem, and all.

Grover blushed. He tried to apologize, but Annabeth and I were too busy cracking up.

Finally the bus came. As we stood in line to board, Grover started looking around, sniffing the air like he smelled his favorite school cafeteria delicacy—enchiladas.

"What is it?" I asked.

"I don't know," he said tensely. "Maybe it's nothing."

But I could tell it wasn't nothing. I started looking over my shoulder, too.

I was relieved when we finally got on board and found seats together in the back of the bus. We stowed our backpacks. Annabeth kept slapping her Yankees cap nervously against her thigh.

As the last passengers got on, Annabeth clamped her hand onto my knee. "Percy."

An old lady had just boarded the bus. She wore a crumpled velvet dress, lace gloves, and a shapeless orange-knit hat that shadowed her face, and she carried a big paisley purse. When she tilted her head up, her black eyes glittered, and my heart skipped a beat.

It was Mrs. Dodds. Older, more withered, but definitely the same evil face.

I scrunched down in my seat.

Behind her came two more old ladies: one in a green hat, one in a purple hat. Otherwise they looked exactly like Mrs. Dodds—same gnarled hands, paisley handbags, wrinkled velvet dresses. Triplet demon grandmothers.

They sat in the front row, right behind the driver. The two on the aisle crossed their legs over the walkway, making an X. It was casual enough, but it sent a clear message: nobody leaves.

The bus pulled out of the station, and we headed through the slick streets of Manhattan. "She didn't stay dead long," I said, trying to keep my voice from quivering. "I thought you said they could be dispelled for a lifetime."

"I said if you're *lucky*," Annabeth said. "You're obviously not."

"All three of them," Grover whimpered. *"Di immortales!"*

"It's okay," Annabeth said, obviously thinking hard. "The Furies. The three worst monsters from the Underworld. No problem. No problem. We'll just slip out the windows."

"They don't open," Grover moaned.

"A back exit?" she suggested.

There wasn't one. Even if there had been, it wouldn't

have helped. By that time, we were on Ninth Avenue, heading for the Lincoln Tunnel.

"They won't attack us with witnesses around," I said. "Will they?"

"Mortals don't have good eyes," Annabeth reminded me. "Their brains can only process what they see through the Mist."

"They'll see three old ladies killing us, won't they?"

She thought about it. "Hard to say. But we can't count on mortals for help. Maybe an emergency exit in the roof . . . ?"

We hit the Lincoln Tunnel, and the bus went dark except for the running lights down the aisle. It was eerily quiet without the sound of the rain.

Mrs. Dodds got up. In a flat voice, as if she'd rehearsed it, she announced to the whole bus: "I need to use the restroom."

"So do I," said the second sister.

"So do I," said the third sister.

They all started coming down the aisle.

"I've got it," Annabeth said. "Percy, take my hat."

"What?"

"You're the one they want. Turn invisible and go up the aisle. Let them pass you. Maybe you can get to the front and get away."

"But you guys—"

"There's an outside chance they might not notice us," Annabeth said. "You're a son of one of the Big Three. Your smell might be overpowering."

"I can't just leave you."

"Don't worry about us," Grover said. "Go!"

My hands trembled. I felt like a coward, but I took the Yankees cap and put it on.

When I looked down, my body wasn't there anymore.

I started creeping up the aisle. I managed to get up ten rows, then duck into an empty seat just as the Furies walked past.

Mrs. Dodds stopped, sniffing, and looked straight at me. My heart was pounding.

Apparently she didn't see anything. She and her sisters kept going.

I was free. I made it to the front of the bus. We were almost through the Lincoln Tunnel now. I was about to press the emergency stop button when I heard hideous wailing from the back row.

The old ladies were not old ladies anymore. Their faces were still the same—I guess those couldn't get any uglier—but their bodies had shriveled into leathery brown hag bodies with bat's wings and hands and feet like gargoyle claws. Their handbags had turned into fiery whips.

The Furies surrounded Grover and Annabeth, lashing their whips, hissing: "Where is it? Where?"

The other people on the bus were screaming, cowering in their seats. They saw *something*, all right.

"He's not here!" Annabeth yelled. "He's gone!"

The Furies raised their whips.

Annabeth drew her bronze knife. Grover grabbed a tin can from his snack bag and prepared to throw it.

What I did next was so impulsive and dangerous I should've been named ADHD poster child of the year.

The bus driver was distracted, trying to see what was going on in his rearview mirror.

Still invisible, I grabbed the wheel from him and jerked it to the left. Everybody howled as they were thrown to the right, and I heard what I hoped was the sound of three Furies smashing against the windows.

"Hey!" the driver yelled. "Hey—whoa!"

We wrestled for the wheel. The bus slammed against the side of the tunnel, grinding metal, throwing sparks a mile behind us.

We careened out of the Lincoln Tunnel and back into the rainstorm, people and monsters tossed around the bus, cars plowed aside like bowling pins.

Somehow the driver found an exit. We shot off the highway, through half a dozen traffic lights, and ended up barreling down one of those New Jersey rural roads where you can't believe there's so much nothing right across the river from New York. There were woods to our left, the Hudson River to our right, and the driver seemed to be veering toward the river.

Another great idea: I hit the emergency brake.

The bus wailed, spun a full circle on the wet asphalt, and crashed into the trees. The emergency lights came on. The door flew open. The bus driver was the first one out, the passengers yelling as they stampeded after him. I stepped into the driver's seat and let them pass.

The Furies regained their balance. They lashed their

whips at Annabeth while she waved her knife and yelled in Ancient Greek, telling them to back off. Grover threw tin cans.

I looked at the open doorway. I was free to go, but I couldn't leave my friends. I took off the invisible cap. "Hey!"

The Furies turned, baring their yellow fangs at me, and the exit suddenly seemed like an excellent idea. Mrs. Dodds stalked up the aisle, just as she used to do in class, about to deliver my F— math test. Every time she flicked her whip, red flames danced along the barbed leather.

Her two ugly sisters hopped on top of the seats on either side of her and crawled toward me like huge nasty lizards.

"Perseus Jackson," Mrs. Dodds said, in an accent that was definitely from somewhere farther south than Georgia. "You have offended the gods. You shall die."

"I liked you better as a math teacher," I told her.

She growled.

Annabeth and Grover moved up behind the Furies cautiously, looking for an opening.

I took the ballpoint pen out of my pocket and uncapped it. Riptide elongated into a shimmering double-edged sword.

The Furies hesitated.

Mrs. Dodds had felt Riptide's blade before. She obviously didn't like seeing it again.

"Submit now," she hissed. "And you will not suffer eternal torment."

"Nice try," I told her.

"Percy, look out!" Annabeth cried.

Mrs. Dodds lashed her whip around my sword hand while the Furies on the either side lunged at me.

My hand felt like it was wrapped in molten lead, but I managed not to drop Riptide. I stuck the Fury on the left with its hilt, sending her toppling backward into a seat. I turned and sliced the Fury on the right. As soon as the blade connected with her neck, she screamed and exploded into dust. Annabeth got Mrs. Dodds in a wrestler's hold and yanked her backward while Grover ripped the whip out of her hands.

"Ow!" he yelled. "Ow! Hot! Hot!"

The Fury I'd hilt-slammed came at me again, talons ready, but I swung Riptide and she broke open like a piñata.

Mrs. Dodds was trying to get Annabeth off her back. She kicked, clawed, hissed and bit, but Annabeth held on while Grover got Mrs. Dodds's legs tied up in her own whip. Finally they both shoved her backward into the aisle. Mrs. Dodds tried to get up, but she didn't have room to flap her bat wings, so she kept falling down.

"Zeus will destroy you!" she promised. "Hades will have your soul!"

"Braccas meas vescimini!" I yelled.

I wasn't sure where the Latin came from. I think it meant "Eat my pants!"

Thunder shook the bus. The hair rose on the back of my neck.

"Get out!" Annabeth yelled at me. "Now!" I didn't need any encouragement.

We rushed outside and found the other passengers wandering around in a daze, arguing with the driver, or running around in circles yelling, "We're going to die!" A Hawaiian-shirted tourist with a camera snapped my photograph before I could recap my sword.

"Our bags!" Grover realized. "We left our—"

BOOOOOM!

The windows of the bus exploded as the passengers ran for cover. Lightning shredded a huge crater in the roof, but an angry wail from inside told me Mrs. Dodds was not yet dead.

"Run!" Annabeth said. "She's calling for reinforcements! We have to get out of here!"

We plunged into the woods as the rain poured down, the bus in flames behind us, and nothing but darkness ahead.

ELEVEN

WE VISIT THE GARDEN GNOME EMPORIUM

In a way, it's nice to know there are Greek gods out there, because you have somebody to blame when things go wrong. For instance, when you're walking away from a bus that's just been attacked by monster hags and blown up by lightning, and it's raining on top of everything else, most people might think that's just really bad luck; when you're a half-blood, you understand that some divine force really is trying to mess up your day.

So there we were, Annabeth and Grover and I, walking through the woods along the New Jersey riverbank, the glow of New York City making the night sky yellow behind us, and the smell of the Hudson reeking in our noses.

Grover was shivering and braying, his big goat eyes turned slit-pupiled and full of terror. "Three Kindly Ones. All three at once."

I was pretty much in shock myself. The explosion of bus windows still rang in my ears. But Annabeth kept pulling us along, saying: "Come on! The farther away we get, the better."

"All our money was back there," I reminded her. "Our food and clothes. Everything."

"Well, maybe if you hadn't decided to jump into the fight—"

"What did you want me to do? Let you get killed?"

"You didn't need to protect me, Percy. I would've been fine."

"Sliced like sandwich bread," Grover put in, "but fine."

"Shut up, goat boy," said Annabeth.

Grover brayed mournfully. "Tin cans . . . a perfectly good bag of tin cans."

We sloshed across mushy ground, through nasty twisted trees that smelled like sour laundry.

After a few minutes, Annabeth fell into line next to me. "Look, I . . ." Her voice faltered. "I appreciate your coming back for us, okay? That was really brave."

"We're a team, right?"

She was silent for a few more steps. "It's just that if you died . . . aside from the fact that it would really suck for you, it would mean the quest was over. This may be my only chance to see the real world."

The thunderstorm had finally let up. The city glow faded behind us, leaving us in almost total darkness. I couldn't see anything of Annabeth except a glint of her blond hair.

"You haven't left Camp Half-Blood since you were seven?" I asked her.

"No . . . only short field trips. My dad—"

"The history professor."

"Yeah. It didn't work out for me living at home. I mean, Camp Half-Blood *is* my home." She was rushing her words out now, as if she were afraid somebody might try to stop her. "At camp you train and train. And that's all cool and everything, but the real world is where the monsters are. That's where you learn whether you're any good or not."

If I didn't know better, I could've sworn I heard doubt in her voice.

"You're pretty good with that knife," I said.

"You think so?"

"Anybody who can piggyback-ride a Fury is okay by me."

I couldn't really see, but I thought she might've smiled.

"You know," she said, "maybe I should tell you . . . Something funny back on the bus . . ."

Whatever she wanted to say was interrupted by a shrill *toot-toot-toot*, like the sound of an owl being tortured.

"Hey, my reed pipes still work!" Grover cried. "If I could just remember a 'find path' song, we could get out of these woods!"

He puffed out a few notes, but the tune still sounded suspiciously like Hilary Duff.

Instead of finding a path, I immediately slammed into a tree and got a nice-size knot on my head.

Add to the list of superpowers I did *not* have: infrared vision.

After tripping and cursing and generally feeling miserable for another mile or so, I started to see light up ahead: the colors of a neon sign. I could smell food. Fried, greasy, excellent food. I realized I hadn't eaten anything unhealthy since I'd arrived at Half-Blood Hill, where we lived on grapes, bread, cheese, and extra-lean-cut nymph-prepared barbecue. This boy needed a double cheeseburger.

We kept walking until I saw a deserted two-lane road through the trees. On the other side was a closed-down gas station, a tattered billboard for a 1990s movie, and one open business, which was the source of the neon light and the good smell.

It wasn't a fast-food restaurant like I'd hoped. It was one of those weird roadside curio shops that sell lawn flamingos and wooden Indians and cement grizzly bears and stuff like that. The main building was a long, low warehouse, surrounded by acres of statuary. The neon sign above the gate was impossible for me to read, because if there's anything worse for my dyslexia than regular English, it's red cursive neon English.

To me, it looked like: *ATNYU MES GDERAN GOMEN MEPROUIM.*

"What the heck does that say?" I asked.

"I don't know," Annabeth said.

She loved reading so much, I'd forgotten she was dyslexic, too.

Grover translated: "Aunty Em's Garden Gnome Emporium."

Flanking the entrance, as advertised, were two cement garden gnomes, ugly bearded little runts, smiling and waving, as if they were about to get their picture taken.

I crossed the street, following the smell of the hamburgers.

"Hey . . ." Grover warned.

"The lights are on inside," Annabeth said. "Maybe it's open."

"Snack bar," I said wistfully.

"Snack bar," she agreed.

"Are you two crazy?" Grover said. "This place is weird."

We ignored him.

The front lot was a forest of statues: cement animals, cement children, even a cement satyr playing the pipes, which gave Grover the creeps.

"*Bla-ha-ha!*" he bleated. "Looks like my Uncle Ferdinand!"

We stopped at the warehouse door.

"Don't knock," Grover pleaded. "I smell monsters."

"Your nose is clogged up from the Furies," Annabeth told him. "All I smell is burgers. Aren't you hungry?"

"Meat!" he said scornfully. "I'm a vegetarian."

"You eat cheese enchiladas and aluminum cans," I reminded him.

"Those are vegetables. Come on. Let's leave. These statues are . . . looking at me."

Then the door creaked open, and standing in front of us was a tall Middle Eastern woman—at least, I assumed she was Middle Eastern, because she wore a long black gown that covered everything but her hands, and her head was completely veiled. Her eyes glinted behind a curtain of black gauze, but that was about all I could make out. Her coffee-colored hands looked old, but well-manicured and elegant, so I imagined she was a grandmother who had once been a beautiful lady.

Her accent sounded vaguely Middle Eastern, too. She

said, "Children, it is too late to be out all alone. Where are your parents?"

"They're . . . um . . ." Annabeth started to say.

"We're orphans," I said.

"Orphans?" the woman said. The word sounded alien in her mouth. "But, my dears! Surely not!"

"We got separated from our caravan," I said. "Our circus caravan. The ringmaster told us to meet him at the gas station if we got lost, but he may have forgotten, or maybe he meant a different gas station. Anyway, we're lost. Is that food I smell?"

"Oh, my dears," the woman said. "You must come in, poor children. I am Aunty Em. Go straight through to the back of the warehouse, please. There is a dining area."

We thanked her and went inside.

Annabeth muttered to me, "Circus caravan?"

"Always have a strategy, right?"

"Your head is full of kelp."

The warehouse was filled with more statues—people in all different poses, wearing all different outfits and with different expressions on their faces. I was thinking you'd have to have a pretty huge garden to fit even one of these statues, because they were all life-size. But mostly, I was thinking about food.

Go ahead, call me an idiot for walking into a strange lady's shop like that just because I was hungry, but I do impulsive stuff sometimes. Plus, you've never smelled Aunty Em's burgers. The aroma was like laughing gas in the dentist's chair—it made everything else go away. I barely noticed Grover's nervous whimpers, or the way the statues' eyes seemed to follow me, or the fact that Aunty Em had locked the door behind us.

All I cared about was finding the dining area. And sure enough, there it was at the back of the warehouse, a fast-food counter with a grill, a soda fountain, a pretzel heater, and a nacho cheese dispenser. Everything you could want, plus a few steel picnic tables out front.

"Please, sit down," Aunty Em said.

"Awesome," I said.

"Um," Grover said reluctantly, "we don't have any money, ma'am."

Before I could jab him in the ribs, Aunty Em said, "No, no, children. No money. This is a special case, yes? It is my treat, for such nice orphans."

"Thank you, ma'am," Annabeth said.

Aunty Em stiffened, as if Annabeth had done something wrong, but then the old woman relaxed just as quickly, so I figured it must've been my imagination.

"Quite all right, Annabeth," she said. "You have such beautiful gray eyes, child." Only later did I wonder how she knew Annabeth's name, even though we had never introduced ourselves.

Our hostess disappeared behind the snack counter and started cooking. Before we knew it, she'd brought us plastic trays heaped with double cheeseburgers, vanilla shakes, and XXL servings of French fries.

I was halfway through my burger before I remembered to breathe.

Annabeth slurped her shake.

Grover picked at the fries, and eyed the tray's waxed paper liner as if he might go for that, but he still looked too nervous to eat.

"What's that hissing noise?" he asked.

I listened, but didn't hear anything. Annabeth shook her head.

"Hissing?" Aunty Em asked. "Perhaps you hear the deep-fryer oil. You have keen ears, Grover."

"I take vitamins. For my ears."

"That's admirable," she said. "But please, relax."

Aunty Em ate nothing. She hadn't taken off her head-dress, even to cook, and now she sat forward and interlaced her fingers and watched us eat. It was a little unsettling, having someone stare at me when I couldn't see her face, but I was feeling satisfied after the burger, and a little sleepy, and I figured the least I could do was try to make small talk with our hostess.

"So, you sell gnomes," I said, trying to sound interested.

"Oh, yes," Aunty Em said. "And animals. And people. Anything for the garden. Custom orders. Statuary is very popular, you know."

"A lot of business on this road?"

"Not so much, no. Since the highway was built . . . most cars, they do not go this way now. I must cherish every customer I get."

My neck tingled, as if somebody else was looking at me. I turned, but it was just a statue of a young girl holding an Easter basket. The detail was incredible, much better than you see in most garden statues. But something was wrong with her face. It looked as if she were startled, or even terrified.

"Ah," Aunty Em said sadly. "You notice some of my creations do not turn out well. They are marred. They do not sell. The face is the hardest to get right. Always the face."

"You make these statues yourself?" I asked.

"Oh, yes. Once upon a time, I had two sisters to help me in the business, but they have passed on, and Aunty Em is alone. I have only my statues. This is why I make them, you see. They are my company." The sadness in her voice sounded so deep and so real that I couldn't help feeling sorry for her.

Annabeth had stopped eating. She sat forward and said, "Two sisters?"

"It's a terrible story," Aunty Em said. "Not one for children, really. You see, Annabeth, a bad woman was jealous of me, long ago, when I was young. I had a . . . a boyfriend, you know, and this bad woman was determined to break us apart. She caused a terrible accident. My sisters stayed by me. They shared my bad fortune as long as they could, but eventually they passed on. They faded away. I alone have survived, but at a price. Such a price."

I wasn't sure what she meant, but I felt bad for her. My eyelids kept getting heavier, my full stomach making me sleepy. Poor old lady. Who would want to hurt somebody so nice?

"Percy?" Annabeth was shaking me to get my attention.

"Maybe we should go. I mean, the ringmaster will be waiting."

She sounded tense. I wasn't sure why. Grover was eating the waxed paper off the tray now, but if Aunty Em found that strange, she didn't say anything.

"Such beautiful gray eyes," Aunty Em told Annabeth again. "My, yes, it has been a long time since I've seen gray eyes like those."

She reached out as if to stroke Annabeth's cheek, but Annabeth stood up abruptly.

"We really should go."

"Yes!" Grover swallowed his waxed paper and stood up. "The ringmaster is waiting! Right!"

I didn't want to leave. I felt full and content. Aunty Em was so nice. I wanted to stay with her a while.

"Please, dears," Aunty Em pleaded. "I so rarely get to be with children. Before you go, won't you at least sit for a pose?"

"A pose?" Annabeth asked warily.

"A photograph. I will use it to model a new statue set. Children are so popular, you see. Everyone loves children."

Annabeth shifted her weight from foot to foot. "I don't think we can, ma'am. Come on, Percy—"

"Sure we can," I said. I was irritated with Annabeth for being so bossy, so rude to an old lady who'd just fed us for free. "It's just a photo, Annabeth. What's the harm?"

"Yes, Annabeth," the woman purred. "No harm."

I could tell Annabeth didn't like it, but she allowed

Aunty Em to lead us back out the front door, into the garden of statues.

Aunty Em directed us to a park bench next to the stone satyr. "Now," she said, "I'll just position you correctly. The young girl in the middle, I think, and the two young gentlemen on either side."

"Not much light for a photo," I remarked.

"Oh, enough," Aunty Em said. "Enough for us to see each other, yes?"

"Where's your camera?" Grover asked.

Aunty Em stepped back, as if to admire the shot. "Now, the face is the most difficult. Can you smile for me please, everyone? A large smile?"

Grover glanced at the cement satyr next to him, and mumbled, "That sure does look like Uncle Ferdinand."

"Grover," Aunty Em chastised, "look this way, dear."

She still had no camera in her hands.

"Percy—" Annabeth said.

Some instinct warned me to listen to Annabeth, but I was fighting the sleepy feeling, the comfortable lull that came from the food and the old lady's voice.

"I will just be a moment," Aunty Em said. "You know, I can't see you very well in this cursed veil. . . ."

"Percy, something's wrong," Annabeth insisted.

"Wrong?" Aunty Em said, reaching up to undo the wrap around her head. "Not at all, dear. I have such noble company tonight. What could be wrong?"

"That *is* Uncle Ferdinand!" Grover gasped.

"Look away from her!" Annabeth shouted. She whipped

her Yankees cap onto her head and vanished. Her invisible hands pushed Grover and me both off the bench.

I was on the ground, looking at Aunt Em's sandaled feet.

I could hear Grover scrambling off in one direction, Annabeth in another. But I was too dazed to move.

Then I heard a strange, rasping sound above me. My eyes rose to Aunty Em's hands, which had turned gnarled and warty, with sharp bronze talons for fingernails.

I almost looked higher, but somewhere off to my left Annabeth screamed, "No! Don't!"

More rasping—the sound of tiny snakes, right above me, from . . . from about where Aunty Em's head would be.

"Run!" Grover bleated. I heard him racing across the gravel, yelling, *"Maia!"* to kick-start his flying sneakers.

I couldn't move. I stared at Aunty Em's gnarled claws, and tried to fight the groggy trance the old woman had put me in.

"Such a pity to destroy a handsome young face," she told me soothingly. "Stay with me, Percy. All you have to do is look up."

I fought the urge to obey. Instead I looked to one side and saw one of those glass spheres people put in gardens— a gazing ball. I could see Aunty Em's dark reflection in the orange glass; her headdress was gone, revealing her face as a shimmering pale circle. Her hair was moving, writhing like serpents.

Aunty Em.

Aunty "M."

How could I have been so stupid?

Think, I told myself. How did Medusa die in the myth?

But I couldn't think. Something told me that in the myth Medusa had been asleep when she was attacked by my namesake, Perseus. She wasn't anywhere near asleep now. If she wanted, she could take those talons right now and rake open my face.

"The Gray-Eyed One did this to me, Percy," Medusa said, and she didn't sound anything like a monster. Her voice invited me to look up, to sympathize with a poor old grandmother. "Annabeth's mother, the cursed Athena, turned me from a beautiful woman into this."

"Don't listen to her!" Annabeth's voice shouted, somewhere in the statuary. "Run, Percy!"

"Silence!" Medusa snarled. Then her voice modulated back to a comforting purr. "You see why I must destroy the girl, Percy. She is my enemy's daughter. I shall crush her statue to dust. But you, dear Percy, you need not suffer."

"No," I muttered. I tried to make my legs move.

"Do you really want to help the gods?" Medusa asked. "Do you understand what awaits you on this foolish quest, Percy? What will happen if you reach the Underworld? Do not be a pawn of the Olympians, my dear. You would be better off as a statue. Less pain. Less pain."

"Percy!" Behind me, I heard a buzzing sound, like a two-hundred-pound hummingbird in a nosedive. Grover yelled, "Duck!"

I turned, and there he was in the night sky, flying in from twelve o'clock with his winged shoes fluttering,

Grover, holding a tree branch the size of a baseball bat. His eyes were shut tight, his head twitched from side to side. He was navigating by ears and nose alone.

"Duck!" he yelled again. "I'll get her!"

That finally jolted me into action. Knowing Grover, I was sure he'd miss Medusa and nail me. I dove to one side.

Thwack!

At first I figured it was the sound of Grover hitting a tree. Then Medusa roared with rage.

"You miserable satyr," she snarled. "I'll add you to my collection!"

"That was for Uncle Ferdinand!" Grover yelled back.

I scrambled away and hid in the statuary while Grover swooped down for another pass.

Ker-whack!

"Arrgh!" Medusa yelled, her snake-hair hissing and spitting.

Right next to me, Annabeth's voice said, "Percy!"

I jumped so high my feet nearly cleared a garden gnome. "Jeez! Don't do that!"

Annabeth took off her Yankees cap and became visible. "You have to cut her head off."

"What? Are you crazy? Let's get out of here."

"Medusa is a menace. She's evil. I'd kill her myself, but . . ." Annabeth swallowed, as if she were about to make a difficult admission. "But you've got the better weapon. Besides, I'd never get close to her. She'd slice me to bits because of my mother. You—you've got a chance."

"What? I can't—"

"Look, do you want her turning more innocent people into statues?"

She pointed to a pair of statue lovers, a man and a woman with their arms around each other, turned to stone by the monster.

Annabeth grabbed a green gazing ball from a nearby pedestal. "A polished shield would be better." She studied the sphere critically. "The convexity will cause some distortion. The reflection's size should be off by a factor of—"

"Would you speak English?"

"I *am*!" She tossed me the glass ball. "Just look at her in the glass. *Never* look at her directly."

"Hey, guys!" Grover yelled somewhere above us. "I think she's unconscious!"

"*Roooaaarrr!*"

"Maybe not," Grover corrected. He went in for another pass with the tree branch.

"Hurry," Annabeth told me. "Grover's got a great nose, but he'll eventually crash."

I took out my pen and uncapped it. The bronze blade of Riptide elongated in my hand.

I followed the hissing and spitting sounds of Medusa's hair.

I kept my eyes locked on the gazing ball so I would only glimpse Medusa's reflection, not the real thing. Then, in the green tinted glass, I saw her.

Grover was coming in for another turn at bat, but this time he flew a little too low. Medusa grabbed the stick and pulled him off course. He tumbled through the air and crashed into the arms of a stone grizzly bear with a painful "Ummphh!"

Medusa was about to lunge at him when I yelled, "Hey!"

I advanced on her, which wasn't easy, holding a sword and a glass ball. If she charged, I'd have a hard time defending myself.

But she let me approach—twenty feet, ten feet.

I could see the reflection of her face now. Surely it wasn't really *that* ugly. The green swirls of the gazing ball must be distorting it, making it look worse.

"You wouldn't harm an old woman, Percy," she crooned. "I know you wouldn't."

I hesitated, fascinated by the face I saw reflected in the glass—the eyes that seemed to burn straight through the green tint, making my arms go weak.

From the cement grizzly, Grover moaned, "Percy, don't listen to her!"

Medusa cackled. "Too late."

She lunged at me with her talons.

I slashed up with my sword, heard a sickening *shlock!*, then a hiss like wind rushing out of a cavern—the sound of a monster disintegrating.

Something fell to the ground next to my foot. It took all my willpower not to look. I could feel warm ooze soaking into my sock, little dying snake heads tugging at my shoelaces.

"Oh, yuck," Grover said. His eyes were still tightly closed, but I guess he could hear the thing gurgling and steaming. "Mega-yuck."

Annabeth came up next to me, her eyes fixed on the sky. She was holding Medusa's black veil. She said, "Don't move."

Very, very carefully, without looking down, she knelt and draped the monster's head in black cloth, then picked it up. It was still dripping green juice.

"Are you okay?" she asked me, her voice trembling.

"Yeah," I decided, though I felt like throwing up my double cheeseburger. "Why didn't . . . why didn't the head evaporate?"

"Once you sever it, it becomes a spoil of war," she said. "Same as your minotaur horn. But don't unwrap the head. It can still petrify you."

Grover moaned as he climbed down from the grizzly statue. He had a big welt on his forehead. His green rasta cap hung from one of his little goat horns, and his fake feet had been knocked off his hooves. The magic sneakers were flying aimlessly around his head.

"The Red Baron," I said. "Good job, man."

He managed a bashful grin. "That really was *not* fun, though. Well, the hitting-her-with-a-stick part, that was fun. But crashing into a concrete bear? *Not* fun."

He snatched his shoes out of the air. I recapped my sword. Together, the three of us stumbled back to the warehouse.

We found some old plastic grocery bags behind the snack counter and double-wrapped Medusa's head. We plopped it on the table where we'd eaten dinner and sat around it, too exhausted to speak.

Finally I said, "So we have Athena to thank for this monster?"

Annabeth flashed me an irritated look. "Your dad, actually. Don't you remember? Medusa was Poseidon's girlfriend. They decided to meet in my mother's temple. That's why Athena turned her into a monster. Medusa and her two sisters who had helped her get into the temple, they became the three gorgons. That's why Medusa wanted to slice me up, but she wanted to preserve you as a nice statue. She's still sweet on your dad. You probably reminded her of him."

My face was burning. "Oh, so now it's *my* fault we met Medusa."

Annabeth straightened. In a bad imitation of my voice, she said: "'It's just a photo, Annabeth. What's the harm?'"

"Forget it," I said. "You're impossible."

"You're insufferable."

"You're—"

"Hey!" Grover interrupted. "You two are giving me a migraine, and satyrs don't even *get* migraines. What are we going to do with the head?"

I stared at the thing. One little snake was hanging out of a hole in the plastic. The words printed on the side of the bag said: WE APPRECIATE YOUR BUSINESS!

I was angry, not just with Annabeth or her mom, but with all the gods for this whole quest, for getting us blown off the road and in two major fights the very first day out from camp. At this rate, we'd never make it to L.A. alive, much less before the summer solstice.

What had Medusa said?

Do not be a pawn of the Olympians, my dear. You would be better off as a statue.

I got up. "I'll be back."

"Percy," Annabeth called after me. "What are you—"

I searched the back of the warehouse until I found Medusa's office. Her account book showed her six most recent sales, all shipments to the Underworld to decorate Hades and Persephone's garden. According to one freight bill, the Underworld's billing address was DOA Recording Studios, West Hollywood, California. I folded up the bill and stuffed it in my pocket.

In the cash register I found twenty dollars, a few golden drachmas, and some packing slips for Hermes Overnight Express, each with a little leather bag attached for coins. I rummaged around the rest of the office until I found the right-size box.

I went back to the picnic table, packed up Medusa's head, and filled out a delivery slip:

The Gods
Mount Olympus
600th Floor,
Empire State Building
New York, NY

With best wishes,
PERCY JACKSON

"They're not going to like that," Grover warned. "They'll think you're impertinent."

I poured some golden drachmas in the pouch. As soon as I closed it, there was a sound like a cash register. The package floated off the table and disappeared with a *pop!*

"I *am* impertinent," I said.

I looked at Annabeth, daring her to criticize.

She didn't. She seemed resigned to the fact that I had a major talent for ticking off the gods. "Come on," she muttered. "We need a new plan."

TWELVE

WE GET ADVICE
FROM A POODLE

We were pretty miserable that night.

We camped out in the woods, a hundred yards from the main road, in a marshy clearing that local kids had obviously been using for parties. The ground was littered with flattened soda cans and fast-food wrappers.

We'd taken some food and blankets from Aunty Em's, but we didn't dare light a fire to dry our damp clothes. The Furies and Medusa had provided enough excitement for one day. We didn't want to attract anything else.

We decided to sleep in shifts. I volunteered to take first watch.

Annabeth curled up on the blankets and was snoring as soon as her head hit the ground. Grover fluttered with his flying shoes to the lowest bough of a tree, put his back to the trunk, and stared at the night sky.

"Go ahead and sleep," I told him. "I'll wake you if there's trouble."

He nodded, but still didn't close his eyes. "It makes me sad, Percy."

"What does? The fact that you signed up for this stupid quest?"

"No. *This* makes me sad." He pointed at all the garbage

on the ground. "And the sky. You can't even see the stars. They've polluted the sky. This is a terrible time to be a satyr."

"Oh, yeah. I guess you'd be an environmentalist."

He glared at me. "Only a human wouldn't be. Your species is clogging up the world so fast . . . ah, never mind. It's useless to lecture a human. At the rate things are going, I'll never find Pan."

"Pam? Like the cooking spray?"

"Pan!" he cried indignantly. "P-A-N. The great god Pan! What do you think I want a searcher's license for?"

A strange breeze rustled through the clearing, temporarily overpowering the stink of trash and muck. It brought the smell of berries and wildflowers and clean rainwater, things that might've once been in these woods. Suddenly I was nostalgic for something I'd never known.

"Tell me about the search," I said.

Grover looked at me cautiously, as if he were afraid I was just making fun.

"The God of Wild Places disappeared two thousand years ago," he told me. "A sailor off the coast of Ephesos heard a mysterious voice crying out from the shore, 'Tell them that the great god Pan has died!' When humans heard the news, they believed it. They've been pillaging Pan's kingdom ever since. But for the satyrs, Pan was our lord and master. He protected us and the wild places of the earth. We refuse to believe that he died. In every generation, the bravest satyrs pledge their lives to finding Pan. They search the earth, exploring all the wildest places, hoping to find where he is hidden, and wake him from his sleep."

"And you want to be a searcher."

"It's my life's dream," he said. "My father was a searcher. And my Uncle Ferdinand . . . the statue you saw back there—"

"Oh, right, sorry."

Grover shook his head. "Uncle Ferdinand knew the risks. So did my dad. But I'll succeed. I'll be the first searcher to return alive."

"Hang on—*the first?*"

Grover took his reed pipes out of his pocket. "No searcher has ever come back. Once they set out, they disappear. They're never seen alive again."

"Not once in two thousand years?"

"No."

"And your dad? You have no idea what happened to him?"

"None."

"But you still want to go," I said, amazed. "I mean, you really think you'll be the one to find Pan?"

"I have to believe that, Percy. Every searcher does. It's the only thing that keeps us from despair when we look at what humans have done to the world. I have to believe Pan can still be awakened."

I stared at the orange haze of the sky and tried to understand how Grover could pursue a dream that seemed so hopeless. Then again, was I any better?

"How are we going to get into the Underworld?" I asked him. "I mean, what chance do we have against a god?"

"I don't know," he admitted. "But back at Medusa's,

when you were searching her office? Annabeth was telling me—"

"Oh, I forgot. Annabeth will have a plan all figured out."

"Don't be so hard on her, Percy. She's had a tough life, but she's a good person. After all, she forgave me. . . ." His voice faltered.

"What do you mean?" I asked. "Forgave you for what?"

Suddenly, Grover seemed very interested in playing notes on his pipes.

"Wait a minute," I said. "Your first keeper job was five years ago. Annabeth has been at camp five years. She wasn't . . . I mean, your first assignment that went wrong—"

"I can't talk about it," Grover said, and his quivering lower lip suggested he'd start crying if I pressed him. "But as I was saying, back at Medusa's, Annabeth and I agreed there's something strange going on with this quest. Something isn't what it seems."

"Well, duh. I'm getting blamed for stealing a thunderbolt that Hades took."

"That's not what I mean," Grover said. "The Fur—The Kindly Ones were sort of holding back. Like Mrs. Dodds at Yancy Academy . . . why did she wait so long to try to kill you? Then on the bus, they just weren't as aggressive as they could've been."

"They seemed plenty aggressive to me."

Grover shook his head. "They were screeching at us: 'Where is it? Where?'"

"Asking about me," I said.

"Maybe . . . but Annabeth and I, we both got the feeling they weren't asking about a person. They said 'Where is *it*?' They seemed to be asking about an object."

"That doesn't make sense."

"I know. But if we've misunderstood something about this quest, and we only have nine days to find the master bolt. . . ." He looked at me like he was hoping for answers, but I didn't have any.

I thought about what Medusa had said: I was being used by the gods. What lay ahead of me was worse than petrification. "I haven't been straight with you," I told Grover. "I don't care about the master bolt. I agreed to go to the Underworld so I could bring back my mother."

Grover blew a soft note on his pipes. "I know that, Percy. But are you sure that's the only reason?"

"I'm not doing it to help my father. He doesn't care about me. I don't care about him."

Grover gazed down from his tree branch. "Look, Percy, I'm not as smart as Annabeth. I'm not as brave as you. But I'm pretty good at reading emotions. You're glad your dad is alive. You feel good that he's claimed you, and part of you wants to make him proud. That's why you mailed Medusa's head to Olympus. You wanted him to notice what you'd done."

"Yeah? Well maybe satyr emotions work differently than human emotions. Because you're wrong. I don't care what he thinks."

Grover pulled his feet up onto the branch. "Okay, Percy. Whatever."

"Besides, I haven't done anything worth bragging about. We barely got out of New York and we're stuck here with no money and no way west."

Grover looked at the night sky, like he was thinking about that problem. "How about *I* take first watch, huh? You get some sleep."

I wanted to protest, but he started to play Mozart, soft and sweet, and I turned away, my eyes stinging. After a few bars of Piano Concerto no. 12, I was asleep.

In my dreams, I stood in a dark cavern before a gaping pit. Gray mist creatures churned all around me, whispering rags of smoke that I somehow knew were the spirits of the dead.

They tugged at my clothes, trying to pull me back, but I felt compelled to walk forward to the very edge of the chasm.

Looking down made me dizzy.

The pit yawned so wide and was so completely black, I knew it must be bottomless. Yet I had a feeling that something was trying to rise from the abyss, something huge and evil.

The little hero, an amused voice echoed far down in the darkness. *Too weak, too young, but perhaps you will do.*

The voice felt ancient—cold and heavy. It wrapped around me like sheets of lead.

They have misled you, boy, it said. *Barter with me. I will give you what you want.*

A shimmering image hovered over the void: my mother, frozen at the moment she'd dissolved in a shower of gold.

Her face was distorted with pain, as if the Minotaur were still squeezing her neck. Her eyes looked directly at me, pleading: *Go!*

I tried to cry out, but my voice wouldn't work.

Cold laughter echoed from the chasm.

An invisible force pulled me forward. It would drag me into the pit unless I stood firm.

Help me rise, boy. The voice became hungrier. *Bring me the bolt. Strike a blow against the treacherous gods!*

The spirits of the dead whispered around me, *No! Wake!*

The image of my mother began to fade. The thing in the pit tightened its unseen grip around me.

I realized it wasn't interested in pulling me in. It was using me to pull itself *out*.

Good, it murmured. *Good.*

Wake! the dead whispered. *Wake!*

Someone was shaking me.

My eyes opened, and it was daylight.

"Well," Annabeth said, "the zombie lives."

I was trembling from the dream. I could still feel the grip of the chasm monster around my chest. "How long was I asleep?"

"Long enough for me to cook breakfast." Annabeth tossed me a bag of nacho-flavored corn chips from Aunty Em's snack bar. "And Grover went exploring. Look, he found a friend."

My eyes had trouble focusing.

Grover was sitting cross-legged on a blanket with

something fuzzy in his lap, a dirty, unnaturally pink stuffed animal.

No. It wasn't a stuffed animal. It was a pink poodle.

The poodle yapped at me suspiciously. Grover said, "No, he's not."

I blinked. "Are you . . . talking to that thing?"

The poodle growled.

"This *thing*," Grover warned, "is our ticket west. Be nice to him."

"You can talk to animals?"

Grover ignored the question. "Percy, meet Gladiola. Gladiola, Percy."

I stared at Annabeth, figuring she'd crack up at this practical joke they were playing on me, but she looked deadly serious.

"I'm not saying hello to a pink poodle," I said. "Forget it."

"Percy," Annabeth said. "I said hello to the poodle. You say hello to the poodle."

The poodle growled.

I said hello to the poodle.

Grover explained that he'd come across Gladiola in the woods and they'd struck up a conversation. The poodle had run away from a rich local family, who'd posted a $200 reward for his return. Gladiola didn't really want to go back to his family, but he was willing to if it meant helping Grover.

"How does Gladiola know about the reward?" I asked.

"He read the signs," Grover said. "Duh."

"Of course," I said. "Silly me."

"So we turn in Gladiola," Annabeth explained in her best strategy voice, "we get money, and we buy tickets to Los Angeles. Simple."

I thought about my dream—the whispering voices of the dead, the thing in the chasm, and my mother's face, shimmering as it dissolved into gold. All that might be waiting for me in the West.

"Not another bus," I said warily.

"No," Annabeth agreed.

She pointed downhill, toward train tracks I hadn't been able to see last night in the dark. "There's an Amtrack station half a mile that way. According to Gladiola, the westbound train leaves at noon."

THIRTEEN

I PLUNGE TO
MY DEATH

We spent two days on the Amtrak train, heading west through hills, over rivers, past amber waves of grain.

We weren't attacked once, but I didn't relax. I felt that we were traveling around in a display case, being watched from above and maybe from below, that something was waiting for the right opportunity.

I tried to keep a low profile because my name and picture were splattered over the front pages of several East Coast newspapers. The *Trenton Register-News* showed a photo taken by a tourist as I got off the Greyhound bus. I had a wild look in my eyes. My sword was a metallic blur in my hands. It might've been a baseball bat or a lacrosse stick.

The picture's caption read:

Twelve-year-old Percy Jackson, wanted for questioning in the Long Island disappearance of his mother two weeks ago, is shown here fleeing from the bus where he accosted several elderly female passengers. The bus exploded on an east New Jersey roadside shortly after Jackson fled the scene. Based on eyewitness accounts, police believe the boy may be traveling with two teenage accomplices. His stepfather, Gabe Ugliano, has offered a cash reward for information leading to his capture.

"Don't worry," Annabeth told me. "Mortal police could never find us." But she didn't sound so sure.

The rest of the day I spent alternately pacing the length of the train (because I had a really hard time sitting still) or looking out the windows.

Once, I spotted a family of centaurs galloping across a wheat field, bows at the ready, as they hunted lunch. The little boy centaur, who was the size of a second-grader on a pony, caught my eye and waved. I looked around the passenger car, but nobody else had noticed. The adult riders all had their faces buried in laptop computers or magazines.

Another time, toward evening, I saw something huge moving through the woods. I could've sworn it was a lion, except that lions don't live wild in America, and this thing was the size of a Hummer. Its fur glinted gold in the evening light. Then it leaped through the trees and was gone.

Our reward money for returning Gladiola the poodle had only been enough to purchase tickets as far as Denver. We couldn't get berths in the sleeper car, so we dozed in our seats. My neck got stiff. I tried not to drool in my sleep, since Annabeth was sitting right next to me.

Grover kept snoring and bleating and waking me up. Once, he shuffled around and his fake foot fell off. Annabeth and I had to stick it back on before any of the other passengers noticed.

"So," Annabeth asked me, once we'd gotten Grover's sneaker readjusted. "Who wants your help?"

"What do you mean?"

"When you were asleep just now, you mumbled, 'I won't help you.' Who were you dreaming about?"

I was reluctant to say anything. It was the second time I'd dreamed about the evil voice from the pit. But it bothered me so much I finally told her.

Annabeth was quiet for a long time. "That doesn't sound like Hades. He always appears on a black throne, and he never laughs."

"He offered my mother in trade. Who else could do that?"

"I guess . . . if he meant, 'Help me rise from the Underworld.' If he wants war with the Olympians. But why ask you to bring him the master bolt if he already has it?"

I shook my head, wishing I knew the answer. I thought about what Grover had told me, that the Furies on the bus seemed to have been looking for something.

Where is it? Where?

Maybe Grover sensed my emotions. He snorted in his sleep, muttered something about vegetables, and turned his head.

Annabeth readjusted his cap so it covered his horns. "Percy, you can't barter with Hades. You know that, right? He's deceitful, heartless, and greedy. I don't care if his Kindly Ones weren't as aggressive this time—"

"This time?" I asked. "You mean you've run into them before?"

Her hand crept up to her necklace. She fingered a glazed white bead painted with the image of a pine tree, one of her clay end-of-summer tokens. "Let's just say I've got no love for the Lord of the Dead. You can't be tempted to make a deal for your mom."

"What would you do if it was your dad?"

"That's easy," she said. "I'd leave him to rot."

"You're not serious?"

Annabeth's gray eyes fixed on me. She wore the same expression she'd worn in the woods at camp, the moment she drew her sword against the hellhound. "My dad's resented me since the day I was born, Percy," she said. "He never wanted a baby. When he got me, he asked Athena to take me back and raise me on Olympus because he was too busy with his work. She wasn't happy about that. She told him heroes had to be raised by their mortal parent."

"But how . . . I mean, I guess you weren't born in a hospital. . . ."

"I appeared on my father's doorstep, in a golden cradle, carried down from Olympus by Zephyr the West Wind. You'd think my dad would remember that as a miracle, right? Like, maybe he'd take some digital photos or something. But he always talked about my arrival as if it were the most inconvenient thing that had ever happened to him. When I was five he got married and totally forgot about Athena. He got a 'regular' mortal wife, and had two 'regular' mortal kids, and tried to pretend I didn't exist."

I stared out the train window. The lights of a sleeping town were drifting by. I wanted to make Annabeth feel better, but I didn't know how.

"My mom married a really awful guy," I told her. "Grover said she did it to protect me, to hide me in the scent of a human family. Maybe that's what your dad was thinking."

Annabeth kept worrying at her necklace. She was pinching the gold college ring that hung with the beads. It occurred to me that the ring must be her father's. I wondered why she wore it if she hated him so much.

"He doesn't care about me," she said. "His wife—my stepmom—treated me like a freak. She wouldn't let me play with her children. My dad went along with her. Whenever something dangerous happened—you know, something with monsters—they would both look at me resentfully, like, 'How dare you put our family at risk.' Finally, I took the hint. I wasn't wanted. I ran away."

"How old were you?"

"Same age as when I started camp. Seven."

"But . . . you couldn't have gotten all the way to Half-Blood Hill by yourself."

"Not alone, no. Athena watched over me, guided me toward help. I made a couple of unexpected friends who took care of me, for a short time, anyway."

I wanted to ask what happened, but Annabeth seemed lost in sad memories. So I listened to the sound of Grover snoring and gazed out the train windows as the dark fields of Ohio raced by.

Toward the end of our second day on the train, June 13, eight days before the summer solstice, we passed through some golden hills and over the Mississippi River into St. Louis.

Annabeth craned her neck to see the Gateway Arch, which looked to me like a huge shopping bag handle stuck on the city.

"I want to do that," she sighed.

"What?" I asked.

"Build something like that. You ever see the Parthenon, Percy?"

"Only in pictures."

"Someday, I'm going to see it in person. I'm going to build the greatest monument to the gods, ever. Something that'll last a thousand years."

I laughed. "You? An architect?"

I don't know why, but I found it funny. Just the idea of Annabeth trying to sit quietly and draw all day.

Her cheeks flushed. "Yes, an architect. Athena expects her children to create things, not just tear them down, like a certain god of earthquakes I could mention."

I watched the churning brown water of the Mississippi below.

"Sorry," Annabeth said. "That was mean."

"Can't we work together a little?" I pleaded. "I mean, didn't Athena and Poseidon ever cooperate?"

Annabeth had to think about it. "I guess . . . the chariot," she said tentatively. "My mom invented it, but Poseidon created horses out of the crests of waves. So they had to work together to make it complete."

"Then we can cooperate, too. Right?"

We rode into the city, Annabeth watching as the Arch disappeared behind a hotel.

"I suppose," she said at last.

We pulled into the Amtrak station downtown. The intercom told us we'd have a three-hour layover before departing for Denver.

Grover stretched. Before he was even fully awake, he said, "Food."

"Come on, goat boy," Annabeth said. "Sightseeing."

"Sightseeing?"

"The Gateway Arch," she said. "This may be my only chance to ride to the top. Are you coming or not?"

Grover and I exchanged looks.

I wanted to say no, but I figured that if Annabeth was going, we couldn't very well let her go alone.

Grover shrugged. "As long as there's a snack bar without monsters."

The Arch was about a mile from the train station. Late in the day the lines to get in weren't that long. We threaded our way through the underground museum, looking at covered wagons and other junk from the 1800s. It wasn't all that thrilling, but Annabeth kept telling us interesting facts about how the Arch was built, and Grover kept passing me jelly beans, so I was okay.

I kept looking around, though, at the other people in line. "You smell anything?" I murmured to Grover.

He took his nose out of the jelly-bean bag long enough to sniff. "Underground," he said distastefully. "Underground air always smells like monsters. Probably doesn't mean anything."

But something felt wrong to me. I had a feeling we shouldn't be here.

"Guys," I said. "You know the gods' symbols of power?"

Annabeth had been in the middle of reading about the construction equipment used to build the Arch, but she looked over. "Yeah?"

"Well, Hade—"

Grover cleared his throat. "We're in a public place. . . . You mean, our friend downstairs?"

"Um, right," I said. "Our friend *way* downstairs. Doesn't he have a hat like Annabeth's?"

"You mean the Helm of Darkness," Annabeth said. "Yeah, that's his symbol of power. I saw it next to his seat during the winter solstice council meeting."

"He was there?" I asked.

She nodded. "It's the only time he's allowed to visit Olympus—the darkest day of the year. But his helm is a lot more powerful than my invisibility hat, if what I've heard is true. . . ."

"It allows him to become darkness," Grover confirmed. "He can melt into shadow or pass through walls. He can't be touched, or seen, or heard. And he can radiate fear so intense it can drive you insane or stop your heart. Why do you think all rational creatures fear the dark?"

"But then . . . how do we know he's not here right now, watching us?" I asked.

Annabeth and Grover exchanged looks.

"We don't," Grover said.

"Thanks, that makes me feel a lot better," I said. "Got any blue jelly beans left?"

I'd almost mastered my jumpy nerves when I saw the tiny little elevator car we were going to ride to the top of the Arch, and I knew I was in trouble. I hate confined places. They make me nuts.

We got shoehorned into the car with this big fat lady and her dog, a Chihuahua with a rhinestone collar. I figured maybe the dog was a seeing-eye Chihuahua, because none of the guards said a word about it.

We started going up, inside the Arch. I'd never been in an elevator that went in a curve, and my stomach wasn't too happy about it.

"No parents?" the fat lady asked us.

She had beady eyes; pointy, coffee-stained teeth; a floppy denim hat, and a denim dress that bulged so much, she looked like a blue-jean blimp.

"They're below," Annabeth told her. "Scared of heights."

"Oh, the poor darlings."

The Chihuahua growled. The woman said, "Now, now, sonny. Behave." The dog had beady eyes like its owner, intelligent and vicious.

I said, "Sonny. Is that his name?"

"No," the lady told me.

She smiled, as if that cleared everything up.

At the top of the Arch, the observation deck reminded me of a tin can with carpeting. Rows of tiny windows looked out over the city on one side and the river on the other. The view was okay, but if there's anything I like less than a confined space, it's a confined space six hundred feet in the air. I was ready to go pretty quick.

Annabeth kept talking about structural supports, and how she would've made the windows bigger, and designed a see-through floor. She probably could've stayed up there for hours, but luckily for me the park ranger announced that the observation deck would be closing in a few minutes.

I steered Grover and Annabeth toward the exit, loaded them into the elevator, and I was about to get in myself when I realized there were already two other tourists inside. No room for me.

The park ranger said, "Next car, sir."

"We'll get out," Annabeth said. "We'll wait with you."

But that was going to mess everybody up and take even more time, so I said, "Naw, it's okay. I'll see you guys at the bottom."

Grover and Annabeth both looked nervous, but they let the elevator door slide shut. Their car disappeared down the ramp.

Now the only people left on the observation deck were me, a little boy with his parents, the park ranger, and the fat lady with her Chihuahua.

I smiled uneasily at the fat lady. She smiled back, her forked tongue flickering between her teeth.

Wait a minute.

Forked tongue?

Before I could decide if I'd really seen that, her Chihuahua jumped down and started yapping at me.

"Now, now, sonny," the lady said. "Does this look like a good time? We have all these nice people here."

"Doggie!" said the little boy. "Look, a doggie!"

His parents pulled him back.

The Chihuahua bared his teeth at me, foam dripping from his black lips.

"Well, son," the fat lady sighed. "If you insist."

Ice started forming in my stomach. "Um, did you just call that Chihuahua your son?"

"*Chimera*, dear," the fat lady corrected. "Not a Chihuahua. It's an easy mistake to make."

She rolled up her denim sleeves, revealing that the skin of her arms was scaly and green. When she smiled, I saw that her teeth were fangs. The pupils of her eyes were sideways slits, like a reptile's.

The Chihuahua barked louder, and with each bark, it grew. First to the size of a Doberman, then to a lion. The bark became a roar.

The little boy screamed. His parents pulled him back toward the exit, straight into the park ranger, who stood, paralyzed, gaping at the monster.

The Chimera was now so tall its back rubbed against the roof. It had the head of a lion with a blood-caked mane, the body and hooves of a giant goat, and a serpent for a tail, a ten-foot-long diamondback growing right out of its shaggy behind. The rhinestone dog collar still hung around its neck, and the plate-sized dog tag was now easy to read: CHIMERA—RABID, FIRE-BREATHING, POISONOUS—IF FOUND, PLEASE CALL TARTARUS—EXT. 954.

I realized I hadn't even uncapped my sword. My hands were numb. I was ten feet away from the Chimera's bloody maw, and I knew that as soon as I moved, the creature would lunge.

The snake lady made a hissing noise that might've been laughter. "Be honored, Percy Jackson. Lord Zeus rarely allows me to test a hero with one of my brood. For I am the Mother of Monsters, the terrible Echidna!"

I stared at her. All I could think to say was: "Isn't that a kind of anteater?"

She howled, her reptilian face turning brown and green with rage. "I hate it when people say that! I hate Australia! Naming that ridiculous animal after me. For that, Percy Jackson, my son shall destroy you!"

The Chimera charged, its lion teeth gnashing. I managed to leap aside and dodge the bite.

I ended up next to the family and the park ranger, who were all screaming now, trying to pry open the emergency exit doors.

I couldn't let them get hurt. I uncapped my sword, ran to the other side of the deck, and yelled, "Hey, Chihuahua!"

The Chimera turned faster than I would've thought possible.

Before I could swing my sword, it opened its mouth, emitting a stench like the world's largest barbecue pit, and shot a column of flame straight at me.

I dove through the explosion. The carpet burst into flames; the heat was so intense, it nearly seared off my eyebrows.

Where I had been standing a moment before was a ragged hole in the side of the Arch, with melted metal steaming around the edges.

Great, I thought. We just blowtorched a national monument.

Riptide was now a shining bronze blade in my hands, and as the Chimera turned, I slashed at its neck.

That was my fatal mistake. The blade sparked harmlessly off the dog collar. I tried to regain my balance, but I was so worried about defending myself against the fiery lion's mouth, I completely forgot about the serpent tail until it whipped around and sank its fangs into my calf.

My whole leg was on fire. I tried to jab Riptide into the Chimera's mouth, but the serpent tail wrapped around my ankles and pulled me off balance, and my blade flew out of my hand, spinning out of the hole in the Arch and down toward the Mississippi River.

I managed to get to my feet, but I knew I had lost. I was weaponless. I could feel deadly poison racing up to my chest. I remembered Chiron saying that Anaklusmos would always return to me, but there was no pen in my pocket. Maybe it had fallen too far away. Maybe it only returned when it was in pen form. I didn't know, and I wasn't going to live long enough to figure it out.

I backed into the hole in the wall. The Chimera advanced, growling, smoke curling from its lips. The snake lady, Echidna, cackled. "They don't make heroes like they used to, eh, son?"

The monster growled. It seemed in no hurry to finish

me off now that I was beaten.

I glanced at the park ranger and the family. The little boy was hiding behind his father's legs. I had to protect these people. I couldn't just . . . die. I tried to think, but my whole body was on fire. My head felt dizzy. I had no sword. I was facing a massive, fire-breathing monster and its mother. And I was scared.

There was no place else to go, so I stepped to the edge of the hole. Far, far below, the river glittered.

If I died, would the monsters go away? Would they leave the humans alone?

"If you are the son of Poseidon," Echidna hissed, "you would not fear water. Jump, Percy Jackson. Show me that water will not harm you. Jump and retrieve your sword. Prove your bloodline."

Yeah, right, I thought. I'd read somewhere that jumping into water from a couple of stories up was like jumping onto solid asphalt. From here, I'd splatter on impact.

The Chimera's mouth glowed red, heating up for another blast.

"You have no faith," Echidna told me. "You do not trust the gods. I cannot blame you, little coward. Better you die now. The gods are faithless. The poison is in your heart."

She was right: I was dying. I could feel my breath slowing down. Nobody could save me, not even the gods.

I backed up and looked down at the water. I remembered the warm glow of my father's smile when I was a baby. He must have seen me. He must have visited me when I was in my cradle.

I remembered the swirling green trident that had appeared above my head the night of capture the flag, when Poseidon had claimed me as his son.

But this wasn't the sea. This was the Mississippi, dead center of the USA. There was no Sea God here.

"Die, faithless one," Echidna rasped, and the Chimera sent a column of flame toward my face.

"Father, help me," I prayed.

I turned and jumped. My clothes on fire, poison coursing through my veins, I plummeted toward the river.

FOURTEEN

I BECOME A
KNOWN FUGITIVE

I'd love to tell you I had some deep revelation on my way down, that I came to terms with my own mortality, laughed in the face of death, et cetera.

The truth? My only thought was: Aaaaggghhhhh!

The river raced toward me at the speed of a truck. Wind ripped the breath from my lungs. Steeples and skyscrapers and bridges tumbled in and out of my vision.

And then: *Flaaa-boooom!*

A whiteout of bubbles. I sank through the murk, sure that I was about to end up embedded in a hundred feet of mud and lost forever.

But my impact with the water hadn't hurt. I was falling slowly now, bubbles trickling up through my fingers. I settled on the river bottom soundlessly. A catfish the size of my stepfather lurched away into the gloom. Clouds of silt and disgusting garbage—beer bottles, old shoes, plastic bags—swirled up all around me.

At that point, I realized a few things: first, I had not been flattened into a pancake. I had not been barbecued. I couldn't even feel the Chimera poison boiling in my veins anymore. I was alive, which was good.

Second realization: I wasn't wet. I mean, I could feel the

coolness of the water. I could see where the fire on my clothes had been quenched. But when I touched my own shirt, it felt perfectly dry.

I looked at the garbage floating by and snatched an old cigarette lighter.

No way, I thought.

I flicked the lighter. It sparked. A tiny flame appeared, right there at the bottom of the Mississippi.

I grabbed a soggy hamburger wrapper out of the current and immediately the paper turned dry. I lit it with no problem. As soon as I let it go, the flames sputtered out. The wrapper turned back into a slimy rag. Weird.

But the strangest thought occurred to me only last: I was breathing. I was underwater, and I was breathing normally.

I stood up, thigh-deep in mud. My legs felt shaky. My hands trembled. I should've been dead. The fact that I wasn't seemed like . . . well, a miracle. I imagined a woman's voice, a voice that sounded a bit like my mother: *Percy, what do you say?*

"Um . . . thanks." Underwater, I sounded like I did on recordings, like a much older kid. "Thank you . . . Father."

No response. Just the dark drift of garbage downriver, the enormous catfish gliding by, the flash of sunset on the water's surface far above, turning everything the color of butterscotch.

Why had Poseidon saved me? The more I thought about it, the more ashamed I felt. So I'd gotten lucky a few times before. Against a thing like the Chimera, I had never stood a chance. Those poor people in the Arch were probably toast. I couldn't protect them. I was no hero. Maybe I should just stay down here with the catfish, join the bottom feeders.

Fump-fump-fump. A riverboat's paddlewheel churned above me, swirling the silt around.

There, not five feet in front of me, was my sword, its gleaming bronze hilt sticking up in the mud.

I heard that woman's voice again: *Percy, take the sword. Your father believes in you.* This time, I knew the voice wasn't in my head. I wasn't imagining it. Her words seemed to come from everywhere, rippling through the water like dolphin sonar.

"Where are you?" I called aloud.

Then, through the gloom, I saw her—a woman the color of the water, a ghost in the current, floating just above the sword. She had long billowing hair, and her eyes, barely visible, were green like mine.

A lump formed in my throat. I said, "Mom?"

No, child, only a messenger, though your mother's fate is not as hopeless as you believe. Go to the beach in Santa Monica.

"What?"

It is your father's will. Before you descend into the Underworld, you must go to Santa Monica. Please, Percy, I cannot stay long. The river here is too foul for my presence.

"But . . ." I was sure this woman was my mother, or a vision of her, anyway. "Who—how did you—"

There was so much I wanted to ask, the words jammed up in my throat.

I cannot stay, brave one, the woman said. She reached out, and I felt the current brush my face like a caress. *You must go to Santa Monica! And, Percy, do not trust the gifts. . . .*

Her voice faded.

"Gifts?" I asked. "What gifts? Wait!"

She made one more attempt to speak, but the sound was gone. Her image melted away. If it was my mother, I had lost her again.

I felt like drowning myself. The only problem: I was immune to drowning.

Your father believes in you, she had said.

She'd also called me brave . . . unless she was talking to the catfish.

I waded toward Riptide and grabbed it by the hilt. The Chimera might still be up there with its snaky, fat mother, waiting to finish me off. At the very least, the mortal police would be arriving, trying to figure out who had blown a hole in the Arch. If they found me, they'd have some questions.

I capped my sword, stuck the ballpoint pen in my pocket. "Thank you, Father," I said again to the dark water.

Then I kicked up through the muck and swam for the surface.

I came ashore next to a floating McDonald's.

A block away, every emergency vehicle in St. Louis was surrounding the Arch. Police helicopters circled overhead. The crowd of onlookers reminded me of Times Square on New Year's Eve.

A little girl said, "Mama! That boy walked out of the river."

"That's nice, dear," her mother said, craning her neck to watch the ambulances.

"But he's dry!"

"That's nice, dear."

A news lady was talking for the camera: "Probably not a terrorist attack, we're told, but it's still very early in the investigation. The damage, as you can see, is very serious. We're trying to get to some of the survivors, to question them about eyewitness reports of someone falling from the Arch."

Survivors. I felt a surge of relief. Maybe the park ranger and that family made it out safely. I hoped Annabeth and Grover were okay.

I tried to push through the crowd to see what was going on inside the police line.

". . . an adolescent boy," another reporter was saying. "Channel Five has learned that surveillance cameras show an adolescent boy going wild on the observation deck, somehow setting off this freak explosion. Hard to believe, John, but that's what we're hearing. Again, no confirmed fatalities . . ."

I backed away, trying to keep my head down. I had to go a long way around the police perimeter. Uniformed officers and news reporters were everywhere.

I'd almost lost hope of ever finding Annabeth and Grover when a familiar voice bleated, "Perrr-cy!"

I turned and got tackled by Grover's bear hug—or goat hug. He said, "We thought you'd gone to Hades the hard way!"

Annabeth stood behind him, trying to look angry, but even she seemed relieved to see me. "We can't leave you alone for five minutes! What happened?"

"I sort of fell."

"Percy! Six hundred and thirty feet?"

Behind us, a cop shouted, "Gangway!" The crowd parted, and a couple of paramedics hustled out, rolling a woman on a stretcher. I recognized her immediately as the mother of the little boy who'd been on the observation deck. She was saying, "And then this huge dog, this huge fire-breathing Chihuahua—"

"Okay, ma'am," the paramedic said. "Just calm down. Your family is fine. The medication is starting to kick in."

"I'm not crazy! This boy jumped out of the hole and the monster disappeared." Then she saw me. "There he is! That's the boy!"

I turned quickly and pulled Annabeth and Grover after me. We disappeared into the crowd.

"What's going on?" Annabeth demanded. "Was she talking about the Chihuahua on the elevator?"

I told them the whole story of the Chimera, Echidna, my high-dive act, and the underwater lady's message.

"Whoa," said Grover. "We've got to get you to Santa Monica! You can't ignore a summons from your dad."

Before Annabeth could respond, we passed another reporter doing a news break, and I almost froze in my tracks when he said, "Percy Jackson. That's right, Dan. Channel Twelve has learned that the boy who may have caused this explosion fits the description of a young man wanted by authorities for a serious New Jersey bus accident three days ago. *And* the boy is believed to be traveling west. For our viewers at home, here is a photo of Percy Jackson."

We ducked around the news van and slipped into an alley.

"First things first," I told Grover. "We've got to get out of town!"

Somehow, we made it back to the Amtrak station without getting spotted. We got on board the train just before it pulled out for Denver. The train trundled west as darkness fell, police lights still pulsing against the St. Louis skyline behind us.

FIFTEEN

A GOD BUYS US CHEESEBURGERS

The next afternoon, June 14, seven days before the solstice, our train rolled into Denver. We hadn't eaten since the night before in the dining car, somewhere in Kansas. We hadn't taken a shower since Half-Blood Hill, and I was sure that was obvious.

"Let's try to contact Chiron," Annabeth said. "I want to tell him about your talk with the river spirit."

"We can't use phones, right?"

"I'm not talking about phones."

We wandered through downtown for about half an hour, though I wasn't sure what Annabeth was looking for. The air was dry and hot, which felt weird after the humidity of St. Louis. Everywhere we turned, the Rocky Mountains seemed to be staring at me, like a tidal wave about to crash into the city.

Finally we found an empty do-it-yourself car wash. We veered toward the stall farthest from the street, keeping our eyes open for patrol cars. We were three adolescents hanging out at a car wash without a car; any cop worth his doughnuts would figure we were up to no good.

"What exactly are we doing?" I asked, as Grover took out the spray gun.

"It's seventy-five cents," he grumbled. "I've only got two quarters left. Annabeth?"

"Don't look at me," she said. "The dining car wiped me out."

I fished out my last bit of change and passed Grover a quarter, which left me two nickels and one drachma from Medusa's place.

"Excellent," Grover said. "We could do it with a spray bottle, of course, but the connection isn't as good, and my arm gets tired of pumping."

"What are you talking about?"

He fed in the quarters and set the knob to FINE MIST. "I-M'ing."

"Instant messaging?"

"*Iris*-messaging," Annabeth corrected. "The rainbow goddess Iris carries messages for the gods. If you know how to ask, and she's not too busy, she'll do the same for half-bloods."

"You summon the goddess with a spray gun?"

Grover pointed the nozzle in the air and water hissed out in a thick white mist. "Unless you know an easier way to make a rainbow."

Sure enough, late afternoon light filtered through the vapor and broke into colors.

Annabeth held her palm out to me. "Drachma, please."

I handed it over.

She raised the coin over her head. "O goddess, accept our offering."

She threw the drachma into the rainbow. It disappeared in a golden shimmer.

"Half-Blood Hill," Annabeth requested.

For a moment, nothing happened.

Then I was looking through the mist at strawberry fields, and the Long Island Sound in the distance. We seemed to be on the porch of the Big House. Standing with his back to us at the railing was a sandy-haired guy in shorts and an orange tank top. He was holding a bronze sword and seemed to be staring intently at something down in the meadow.

"Luke!" I called.

He turned, eyes wide. I could swear he was standing three feet in front of me through a screen of mist, except I could only see the part of him that appeared in the rainbow.

"Percy!" His scarred face broke into a grin. "Is that Annabeth, too? Thank the gods! Are you guys okay?"

"We're . . . uh . . . fine," Annabeth stammered. She was madly straightening her dirty T-shirt, trying to comb the loose hair out of her face. "We thought—Chiron—I mean—"

"He's down at the cabins." Luke's smile faded. "We're having some issues with the campers. Listen, is everything cool with you? Is Grover all right?"

"I'm right here," Grover called. He held the nozzle out to one side and stepped into Luke's line of vision. "What kind of issues?"

Just then a big Lincoln Continental pulled into the car wash with its stereo turned to maximum hip-hop. As the car slid into the next stall, the bass from the subwoofers vibrated so much, it shook the pavement.

"Chiron had to—what's that noise?" Luke yelled.

"I'll take care of it!" Annabeth yelled back, looking very relieved to have an excuse to get out of sight. "Grover, come on!"

"What?" Grover said. "But—"

"Give Percy the nozzle and come on!" she ordered.

Grover muttered something about girls being harder to understand than the Oracle at Delphi, then he handed me the spray gun and followed Annabeth.

I readjusted the hose so I could keep the rainbow going and still see Luke.

"Chiron had to break up a fight," Luke shouted to me over the music. "Things are pretty tense here, Percy. Word leaked out about the Zeus–Poseidon standoff. We're still not sure how—probably the same scumbag who summoned the hellhound. Now the campers are starting to take sides. It's shaping up like the Trojan War all over again. Aphrodite, Ares, and Apollo are backing Poseidon, more or less. Athena is backing Zeus."

I shuddered to think that Clarisse's cabin would ever be on my dad's side for anything. In the next stall, I heard Annabeth and some guy arguing with each other, then the music's volume decreased drastically.

"So what's your status?" Luke asked me. "Chiron will be sorry he missed you."

I told him pretty much everything, including my dreams. It felt so good to see him, to feel like I was back at camp even for a few minutes, that I didn't realize how long I had talked until the beeper went off on the spray machine, and I realized I only had one more minute before the water shut off.

"I wish I could be there," Luke told me. "We can't help much from here, I'm afraid, but listen . . . it had to be Hades who took the master bolt. He was there at Olympus at the winter solstice. I was chaperoning a field trip and we saw him."

"But Chiron said the gods can't take each other's magic items directly."

"That's true," Luke said, looking troubled. "Still . . . Hades has the helm of darkness. How could anybody else sneak into the throne room and steal the master bolt? You'd have to be invisible."

We were both silent, until Luke seemed to realize what he'd said.

"Oh, hey," he protested. "I didn't mean Annabeth. She and I have known each other forever. She would never . . . I mean, she's like a little sister to me."

I wondered if Annabeth would like that description. In the stall next to us, the music stopped completely. A man screamed in terror, car doors slammed, and the Lincoln peeled out of the car wash.

"You'd better go see what that was," Luke said. "Listen, are you wearing the flying shoes? I'll feel better if I know they've done you some good."

"Oh . . . uh, yeah!" I tried not to sound like a guilty liar. "Yeah, they've come in handy."

"Really?" He grinned. "They fit and everything?"

The water shut off. The mist started to evaporate.

"Well, take care of yourself out there in Denver," Luke

called, his voice getting fainter. "And tell Grover it'll be better this time! Nobody will get turned into a pine tree if he just—"

But the mist was gone, and Luke's image faded to nothing. I was alone in a wet, empty car wash stall.

Annabeth and Grover came around the corner, laughing, but stopped when they saw my face. Annabeth's smile faded. "What happened, Percy? What did Luke say?"

"Not much," I lied, my stomach feeling as empty as a Big Three cabin. "Come on, let's find some dinner."

A few minutes later, we were sitting at a booth in a gleaming chrome diner. All around us, families were eating burgers and drinking malts and sodas.

Finally the waitress came over. She raised her eyebrow skeptically. "Well?"

I said, "We, um, want to order dinner."

"You kids have money to pay for it?"

Grover's lower lip quivered. I was afraid he would start bleating, or worse, start eating the linoleum. Annabeth looked ready to pass out from hunger.

I was trying to think up a sob story for the waitress when a rumble shook the whole building; a motorcycle the size of a baby elephant had pulled up to the curb.

All conversation in the diner stopped. The motorcycle's headlight glared red. Its gas tank had flames painted on it, and a shotgun holster riveted to either side, complete with shotguns. The seat was leather—but leather that looked like . . . well, Caucasian human skin.

The guy on the bike would've made pro wrestlers run for Mama. He was dressed in a red muscle shirt and black jeans and a black leather duster, with a hunting knife strapped to his thigh. He wore red wraparound shades, and he had the cruelest, most brutal face I'd ever seen—handsome, I guess, but wicked—with an oily black crew cut and cheeks that were scarred from many, many fights. The weird thing was, I felt like I'd seen his face somewhere before.

As he walked into the diner, a hot, dry wind blew through the place. All the people rose, as if they were hypnotized, but the biker waved his hand dismissively and they all sat down again. Everybody went back to their conversations. The waitress blinked, as if somebody had just pressed the rewind button on her brain. She asked us again, "You kids have money to pay for it?"

The biker said, "It's on me." He slid into our booth, which was way too small for him, and crowded Annabeth against the window.

He looked up at the waitress, who was gaping at him, and said, "Are you still here?"

He pointed at her, and she stiffened. She turned as if she'd been spun around, then marched back toward the kitchen.

The biker looked at me. I couldn't see his eyes behind the red shades, but bad feelings started boiling in my stomach. Anger, resentment, bitterness. I wanted to hit a wall. I wanted to pick a fight with somebody. Who did this guy think he was?

He gave me a wicked grin. "So you're old Seaweed's kid, huh?"

I should've been surprised, or scared, but instead I felt like I was looking at my stepdad, Gabe. I wanted to rip this guy's head off. "What's it to you?"

Annabeth's eyes flashed me a warning. "Percy, this is—"

The biker raised his hand.

"S'okay," he said. "I don't mind a little attitude. Long as you remember who's the boss. You know who I am, little cousin?"

Then it struck me why this guy looked familiar. He had the same vicious sneer as some of the kids at Camp Half-Blood, the ones from cabin five.

"You're Clarisse's dad," I said. "Ares, god of war."

Ares grinned and took off his shades. Where his eyes should've been, there was only fire, empty sockets glowing with miniature nuclear explosions. "That's right, punk. I heard you broke Clarisse's spear."

"She was asking for it."

"Probably. That's cool. I don't fight my kids' fights, you know? What I'm here for—I heard you were in town. I got a little proposition for you."

The waitress came back with heaping trays of food—cheeseburgers, fries, onion rings, and chocolate shakes.

Ares handed her a few gold drachmas.

She looked nervously at the coins. "But, these aren't . . ."

Ares pulled out his huge knife and started cleaning his fingernails. "Problem, sweetheart?"

The waitress swallowed, then left with the gold.

"You can't do that," I told Ares. "You can't just threaten people with a knife."

Ares laughed. "Are you kidding? I love this country. Best place since Sparta. Don't you carry a weapon, punk? You should. Dangerous world out there. Which brings me to my proposition. I need you to do me a favor."

"What favor could I do for a god?"

"Something a god doesn't have time to do himself. It's nothing much. I left my shield at an abandoned water park here in town. I was going on a little . . . date with my girlfriend. We were interrupted. I left my shield behind. I want you to fetch it for me."

"Why don't you go back and get it yourself?"

The fire in his eye sockets glowed a little hotter.

"Why don't I turn you into prairie dog and run you over with my Harley? Because I don't feel like it. A god is giving you an opportunity to prove yourself, Percy Jackson. Will you prove yourself a coward?" He leaned forward. "Or maybe you only fight when there's a river to dive into, so your daddy can protect you."

I wanted to punch this guy, but somehow, I knew he was waiting for that. Ares's power was causing my anger. He'd love it if I attacked. I didn't want to give him the satisfaction.

"We're not interested," I said. "We've already got a quest."

Ares's fiery eyes made me see things I didn't want to see—blood and smoke and corpses on the battlefield. "I know all about your quest, punk. When that *item* was first stolen, Zeus sent his best out looking for it: Apollo, Athena, Artemis, and me, naturally. If I couldn't sniff out a weapon that powerful . . ." He licked his lips, as if the very thought of the master bolt made him hungry. "Well . . . if I couldn't find it, you got no hope. Nevertheless, I'm trying to give you the benefit of the doubt. Your dad and I go way back. After all, I'm the one who told him my suspicions about old Corpse Breath."

"You told him Hades stole the bolt?"

"Sure. Framing somebody to start a war. Oldest trick in the book. I recognized it immediately. In a way, you got me to thank for your little quest."

"Thanks," I grumbled.

"Hey, I'm a generous guy. Just do my little job, and I'll help you on your way. I'll arrange a ride west for you and your friends."

"We're doing fine on our own."

"Yeah, right. No money. No wheels. No clue what you're up against. Help me out, and maybe I'll tell you something you need to know. Something about your mom."

"My mom?"

He grinned. "That got your attention. The water park is a mile west on Delancy. You can't miss it. Look for the Tunnel of Love ride."

"What interrupted your date?" I asked. "Something scare you off?"

Ares bared his teeth, but I'd seen his threatening look before on Clarisse. There was something false about it, almost like he was nervous.

"You're lucky you met me, punk, and not one of the other Olympians. They're not as forgiving of rudeness as I am. I'll meet you back here when you're done. Don't disappoint me."

After that I must have fainted, or fallen into a trance, because when I opened my eyes again, Ares was gone. I might've thought the conversation had been a dream, but Annabeth and Grover's expressions told me otherwise.

"Not good," Grover said. "Ares sought you out, Percy. This is not good."

I stared out the window. The motorcycle had disappeared.

Did Ares really know something about my mom, or was he just playing with me? Now that he was gone, all the anger had drained out of me. I realized Ares must love to mess with people's emotions. That was his power—cranking up the passions so badly, they clouded your ability to think.

"It's probably some kind of trick," I said. "Forget Ares. Let's just go."

"We can't," Annabeth said. "Look, I hate Ares as much as anybody, but you don't ignore the gods unless you want serious bad fortune. He wasn't kidding about turning you into a rodent."

I looked down at my cheeseburger, which suddenly didn't seem so appetizing. "Why does he need us?"

"Maybe it's a problem that requires brains," Annabeth said. "Ares has strength. That's all he has. Even strength has to bow to wisdom sometimes."

"But this water park . . . he acted almost scared. What would make a war god run away like that?"

Annabeth and Grover glanced nervously at each other. Annabeth said, "I'm afraid we'll have to find out."

The sun was sinking behind the mountains by the time we found the water park. Judging from the sign, it once had been called WATERLAND, but now some of the letters were smashed out, so it read WAT R A D.

The main gate was padlocked and topped with barbed wire. Inside, huge dry waterslides and tubes and pipes curled everywhere, leading to empty pools. Old tickets and advertisements fluttered around the asphalt. With night coming on, the place looked sad and creepy.

"If Ares brings his girlfriend here for a date," I said, staring up at the barbed wire, "I'd hate to see what she looks like."

"Percy," Annabeth warned. "Be more respectful."

"Why? I thought you hated Ares."

"He's still a god. And his girlfriend is very temperamental."

"You don't want to insult her looks," Grover added.

"Who is she? Echidna?"

"No, Aphrodite," Grover said, a little dreamily. "Goddess of love."

"I thought she was married to somebody," I said. "Hephaestus."

"What's your point?" he asked.

"Oh." I suddenly felt the need to change the subject. "So how do we get in?"

"*Maia!*" Grover's shoes sprouted wings.

He flew over the fence, did an unintended somersault in midair, then stumbled to a landing on the opposite side. He dusted off his jeans, as if he'd planned the whole thing. "You guys coming?"

Annabeth and I had to climb the old-fashioned way, holding down the barbed wire for each other as we crawled over the top.

The shadows grew long as we walked through the park, checking out the attractions. There was Ankle Biter Island, Head Over Wedgie, and Dude, Where's My Swimsuit?

No monsters came to get us. Nothing made the slightest noise.

We found a souvenir shop that had been left open. Merchandise still lined the shelves: snow globes, pencils, postcards, and racks of—

"Clothes," Annabeth said. "Fresh clothes."

"Yeah," I said. "But you can't just—"

"Watch me."

She snatched an entire row of stuff of the racks and disappeared into the changing room. A few minutes later she came out in Waterland flower-print shorts, a big red Waterland T-shirt, and commemorative Waterland surf shoes. A Waterland backpack was slung over her shoulder, obviously stuffed with more goodies.

"What the heck." Grover shrugged. Soon, all three of us were decked out like walking advertisements for the defunct theme park.

We continued searching for the Tunnel of Love. I got

the feeling that the whole park was holding its breath. "So Ares and Aphrodite," I said, to keep my mind off the growing dark, "they have a thing going?"

"That's old gossip, Percy," Annabeth told me. "Three-thousand-year-old gossip."

"What about Aphrodite's husband?"

"Well, you know," she said. "Hephaestus. The blacksmith. He was crippled when he was a baby, thrown off Mount Olympus by Zeus. So he isn't exactly handsome. Clever with his hands, and all, but Aphrodite isn't into brains and talent, you know?"

"She likes bikers."

"Whatever."

"Hephaestus knows?"

"Oh sure," Annabeth said. "He caught them together once. I mean, literally caught them, in a golden net, and invited all the gods to come and laugh at them. Hephaestus is always trying to embarrass them. That's why they meet in out-of-the-way places, like . . ."

She stopped, looking straight ahead. "Like that."

In front of us was an empty pool that would've been awesome for skateboarding. It was at least fifty yards across and shaped like a bowl.

Around the rim, a dozen bronze statues of Cupid stood guard with wings spread and bows ready to fire. On the opposite side from us, a tunnel opened up, probably where the water flowed into when the pool was full. The sign above it read, THRILL RIDE O' LOVE: THIS IS NOT YOUR PARENTS' TUNNEL OF LOVE!

Grover crept toward the edge. "Guys, look."

Marooned at the bottom of the pool was a pink-and-white two-seater boat with a canopy over the top and little hearts painted all over it. In the left seat, glinting in the fading light, was Ares's shield, a polished circle of bronze.

"This is too easy," I said. "So we just walk down there and get it?"

Annabeth ran her fingers along the base of the nearest Cupid statue.

"There's a Greek letter carved here," she said. "Eta. I wonder . . ."

"Grover," I said, "you smell any monsters?"

He sniffed the wind. "Nothing."

"Nothing—like, in-the-Arch-and-you-didn't-smell-Echidna nothing, or really nothing?"

Grover looked hurt. "I told you, that was underground."

"Okay, I'm sorry." I took a deep breath. "I'm going down there."

"I'll go with you." Grover didn't sound too enthusiastic, but I got the feeling he was trying to make up for what had happened in St. Louis.

"No," I told him. "I want you to stay up top with the flying shoes. You're the Red Baron, a flying ace, remember? I'll be counting on you for backup, in case something goes wrong."

Grover puffed up his chest a little. "Sure. But what could go wrong?"

"I don't know. Just a feeling. Annabeth, come with me—"

"Are you kidding?" She looked at me as if I'd just dropped from the moon. Her cheeks were bright red.

"What's the problem now?" I demanded.

"Me, go with you to the . . . the 'Thrill Ride of Love'? How embarrassing is that? What if somebody saw me?"

"Who's going to see you?" But my face was burning now, too. Leave it to a girl to make everything complicated. "Fine," I told her. "I'll do it myself." But when I started down the side of the pool, she followed me, muttering about how boys always messed things up.

We reached the boat. The shield was propped on one seat, and next to it was a lady's silk scarf. I tried to imagine Ares and Aphrodite here, a couple of gods meeting in a junked-out amusement-park ride. Why? Then I noticed something I hadn't seen from up top: mirrors all the way around the rim of the pool, facing this spot. We could see ourselves no matter which direction we looked. That must be it. While Ares and Aphrodite were smooching with each other they could look at their favorite people: themselves.

I picked up the scarf. It shimmered pink, and the perfume was indescribable—rose, or mountain laurel. Something good. I smiled, a little dreamy, and was about to rub the scarf against my cheek when Annabeth ripped it out of my hand and stuffed it in her pocket. "Oh, no you don't. Stay away from that love magic."

"What?"

"Just get the shield, Seaweed Brain, and let's get out of here."

The moment I touched the shield, I knew we were in trouble. My hand broke through something that had been connecting it to the dashboard. A cobweb, I thought, but then I looked at a strand of it on my palm and saw it was some kind of metal filament, so fine it was almost invisible. A trip wire.

"Wait," Annabeth said.

"Too late."

"There's another Greek letter on the side of the boat, another Eta. This is a trap."

Noise erupted all around us, of a million gears grinding, as if the whole pool were turning into one giant machine.

Grover yelled, "Guys!"

Up on the rim, the Cupid statues were drawing their bows into firing position. Before I could suggest taking cover, they shot, but not at us. They fired at each other, across the rim of the pool. Silky cables trailed from the arrows, arcing over the pool and anchoring where they landed to form a huge golden asterisk. Then smaller metallic threads started weaving together magically between the main strands, making a net.

"We have to get out," I said.

"Duh!" Annabeth said.

I grabbed the shield and we ran, but going up the slope of the pool was not as easy as going down.

"Come on!" Grover shouted.

He was trying to hold open a section of the net for us, but wherever he touched it, the golden threads started to wrap around his hands.

The Cupids' heads popped open. Out came video cameras. Spotlights rose up all around the pool, blinding us with illumination, and a loudspeaker voice boomed: "Live to Olympus in one minute . . . Fifty-nine seconds, fifty-eight . . ."

"Hephaestus!" Annabeth screamed. "I'm so stupid! Eta is 'H.' He made this trap to catch his wife with Ares. Now we're going to be broadcast live to Olympus and look like absolute fools!"

We'd almost made it to the rim when the row of mirrors opened like hatches and thousands of tiny metallic . . . . things poured out.

Annabeth screamed.

It was an army of wind-up creepy-crawlies: bronze-gear bodies, spindly legs, little pincer mouths, all scuttling toward us in a wave of clacking, whirring metal.

"Spiders!" Annabeth said. "Sp—sp—aaaah!"

I'd never seen her like this before. She fell backward in terror and almost got overwhelmed by the spider robots before I pulled her up and dragged her back toward the boat.

The things were coming out from all around the rim now, millions of them, flooding toward the center of the pool, completely surrounding us. I told myself they probably weren't programmed to kill, just corral us and bite us and make us look stupid. Then again, this was a trap meant for gods. And we weren't gods.

Annabeth and I climbed into the boat. I started kicking away the spiders as they swarmed aboard. I yelled at

Annabeth to help me, but she was too paralyzed to do much more than scream.

"Thirty, twenty-nine," called the loudspeaker.

The spiders started spitting out strands of metal thread, trying to tie us down. The strands were easy enough to break at first, but there were so many of them, and the spiders just kept coming. I kicked one away from Annabeth's leg and its pincers took a chunk out of my new surf shoe.

Grover hovered above the pool in his flying sneakers, trying to pull the net loose, but it wouldn't budge.

Think, I told myself. Think.

The Tunnel of Love entrance was under the net. We could use it as an exit, except that it was blocked by a million robot spiders.

"Fifteen, fourteen," the loudspeaker called.

Water, I thought. Where does the ride's water come from?

Then I saw them: huge water pipes behind the mirrors, where the spiders had come from. And up above the net, next to one of the Cupids, a glass-windowed booth that must be the controller's station.

"Grover!" I yelled. "Get into that booth! Find the 'on' switch!"

"But—"

"Do it!" It was a crazy hope, but it was our only chance. The spiders were all over the prow of the boat now. Annabeth was screaming her head off. I had to get us out of there.

Grover was in the controller's booth now, slamming away at the buttons.

"Five, four—"

Grover looked up at me hopelessly, raising his hands. He was letting me know that he'd pushed every button, but still nothing was happening.

I closed my eyes and thought about waves, rushing water, the Mississippi River. I felt a familiar tug in my gut. I tried to imagine that I was dragging the ocean all the way to Denver.

"Two, one, *zero!*"

Water exploded out of the pipes. It roared into the pool, sweeping away the spiders. I pulled Annabeth into the seat next to me and fastened her seat belt just as the tidal wave slammed into our boat, over the top, whisking the spiders away and dousing us completely, but not capsizing us. The boat turned, lifted in the flood, and spun in circles around the whirlpool.

The water was full of short-circuiting spiders, some of them smashing against the pool's concrete wall with such force they burst.

Spotlights glared down at us. The Cupid-cams were rolling, live to Olympus.

But I could only concentrate on controlling the boat. I willed it to ride the current, to keep away from the wall. Maybe it was my imagination, but the boat seemed to respond. At least, it didn't break into a million pieces. We spun around one last time, the water level now almost high enough to shred us against the metal net. Then the boat's nose turned toward the tunnel and we rocketed through into the darkness.

Annabeth and I held tight, both of us screaming as the boat shot curls and hugged corners and took forty-five-degree plunges past pictures of Romeo and Juliet and a bunch of other Valentine's Day stuff.

Then we were out of the tunnel, the night air whistling through our hair as the boat barreled straight toward the exit.

If the ride had been in working order, we would've sailed off a ramp between the golden Gates of Love and splashed down safely in the exit pool. But there was a problem. The Gates of Love were chained. Two boats that had been washed out of the tunnel before us were now piled against the barricade—one submerged, the other cracked in half.

"Unfasten your seat belt," I yelled to Annabeth.

"Are you crazy?"

"Unless you want to get smashed to death." I strapped Ares's shield to my arm. "We're going to have to jump for it." My idea was simple and insane. As the boat struck, we would use its force like a springboard to jump the gate. I'd heard of people surviving car crashes that way, getting thrown thirty or forty feet away from an accident. With luck, we would land in the pool.

Annabeth seemed to understand. She gripped my hand as the gates got closer.

"On my mark," I said.

"No! On my mark!"

"What?"

"Simple physics!" she yelled. "Force times the trajectory angle—"

"Fine!" I shouted. "On *your* mark!"

She hesitated . . . hesitated . . . then yelled, "Now!"

Crack!

Annabeth was right. If we'd jumped when I thought we should've, we would've crashed into the gates. She got us maximum lift.

Unfortunately, that was a little more than we needed. Our boat smashed into the pileup and we were thrown into the air, straight over the gates, over the pool, and down toward solid asphalt.

Something grabbed me from behind.

Annabeth yelled, "Ouch!"

Grover!

In midair, he had grabbed me by the shirt, and Annabeth by the arm, and was trying to pull us out of a crash landing, but Annabeth and I had all the momentum.

"You're too heavy!" Grover said. "We're going down!"

We spiraled toward the ground, Grover doing his best to slow the fall.

We smashed into a photo-board, Grover's head going straight into the hole where tourists would put their faces, pretending to be Noo-Noo the Friendly Whale. Annabeth and I tumbled to the ground, banged up but alive. Ares's shield was still on my arm.

Once we caught our breath, Annabeth and I got Grover out of the photo-board and thanked him for saving our lives. I looked back at the Thrill Ride of Love. The water was subsiding. Our boat had been smashed to pieces against the gates.

A hundred yards away, at the entrance pool, the Cupids were still filming. The statues had swiveled so that their cameras were trained straight on us, the spotlights in our faces.

"Show's over!" I yelled. "Thank you! Good night!"

The Cupids turned back to their original positions. The lights shut off. The park went quiet and dark again, except for the gentle trickle of water into the Thrill Ride of Love's exit pool. I wondered if Olympus had gone to a commercial break, or if our ratings had been any good.

I hated being teased. I hated being tricked. And I had plenty of experience handling bullies who liked to do that stuff to me. I hefted the shield on my arm and turned to my friends. "We need to have a little talk with Ares."

SIXTEEN

WE TAKE A
ZEBRA TO VEGAS

The war god was waiting for us in the diner parking lot.

"Well, well," he said. "You didn't get yourself killed."

"You knew it was a trap," I said.

Ares gave me a wicked grin. "Bet that crippled black-smith was surprised when he netted a couple of stupid kids. You looked good on TV."

I shoved his shield at him. "You're a jerk."

Annabeth and Grover caught their breath.

Ares grabbed the shield and spun it in the air like pizza dough. It changed form, melting into a bulletproof vest. He slung it across his back.

"See that truck over there?" He pointed to an eighteen-wheeler parked across the street from the diner. "That's your ride. Take you straight to L.A., with one stop in Vegas."

The eighteen-wheeler had a sign on the back, which I could read only because it was reverse-printed white on black, a good combination for dyslexia: KINDNESS INTER-NATIONAL: HUMANE ZOO TRANSPORT. WARNING: LIVE WILD ANIMALS.

I said, "You're kidding."

Ares snapped his fingers. The back door of the truck

unlatched. "Free ride west, punk. Stop complaining. And here's a little something for doing the job."

He slung a blue nylon backpack off his handlebars and tossed it to me.

Inside were fresh clothes for all of us, twenty bucks in cash, a pouch full of golden drachmas, and a bag of Double Stuf Oreos.

I said, "I don't want your lousy—"

"Thank you, Lord Ares," Grover interrupted, giving me his best red-alert warning look. "Thanks a lot."

I gritted my teeth. It was probably a deadly insult to refuse something from a god, but I didn't want anything that Ares had touched. Reluctantly, I slung the backpack over my shoulder. I knew my anger was being caused by the war god's presence, but I was still itching to punch him in the nose. He reminded me of every bully I'd ever faced: Nancy Bobofit, Clarisse, Smelly Gabe, sarcastic teachers— every jerk who'd called me stupid in school or laughed at me when I'd gotten expelled.

I looked back at the diner, which had only a couple of customers now. The waitress who'd served us dinner was watching nervously out the window, like she was afraid Ares might hurt us. She dragged the fry cook out from the kitchen to see. She said something to him. He nodded, held up a little disposable camera and snapped a picture of us.

Great, I thought. We'll make the papers again tomorrow.

I imagined the headline: TWELVE-YEAR-OLD OUTLAW BEATS UP DEFENSELESS BIKER.

"You owe me one more thing," I told Ares, trying to

keep my voice level. "You promised me information about my mother."

"You sure you can handle the news?" He kick-started his motorcycle. "She's not dead."

The ground seemed to spin beneath me. "What do you mean?"

"I mean she was taken away from the Minotaur before she could die. She was turned into a shower of gold, right? That's metamorphosis. Not death. She's being kept."

"Kept. Why?"

"You need to study war, punk. Hostages. You take somebody to control somebody else."

"Nobody's controlling me."

He laughed. "Oh yeah? See you around, kid."

I balled up my fists. "You're pretty smug, Lord Ares, for a guy who runs from Cupid statues."

Behind his sunglasses, fire glowed. I felt a hot wind in my hair. "We'll meet again, Percy Jackson. Next time you're in a fight, watch your back."

He revved his Harley, then roared off down Delancy Street.

Annabeth said, "That was not smart, Percy."

"I don't care."

"You don't want a god as your enemy. Especially not that god."

"Hey, guys," Grover said. "I hate to interrupt, but . . ."

He pointed toward the diner. At the register, the last two customers were paying their check, two men in identical black coveralls, with a white logo on their backs that matched the one on the KINDNESS INTERNATIONAL truck.

"If we're taking the zoo express," Grover said, "we need to hurry."

I didn't like it, but we had no better option. Besides, I'd seen enough of Denver.

We ran across the street and climbed in the back of the big rig, closing the doors behind us.

The first thing that hit me was the smell. It was like the world's biggest pan of kitty litter.

The trailer was dark inside until I uncapped Anaklusmos. The blade cast a faint bronze light over a very sad scene. Sitting in a row of filthy metal cages were three of the most pathetic zoo animals I'd ever beheld: a zebra, a male albino lion, and some weird antelope thing I didn't know the name for.

Someone had thrown the lion a sack of turnips, which he obviously didn't want to eat. The zebra and the antelope had each gotten a Styrofoam tray of hamburger meat. The zebra's mane was matted with chewing gum, like somebody had been spitting on it in their spare time. The antelope had a stupid silver birthday balloon tied to one of his horns that read OVER THE HILL!

Apparently, nobody had wanted to get close enough to the lion to mess with him, but the poor thing was pacing around on soiled blankets, in a space way too small for him, panting from the stuffy heat of the trailer. He had flies buzzing around his pink eyes and his ribs showed through his white fur.

"This is kindness?" Grover yelled. "Humane zoo transport?"

He probably would've gone right back outside to beat up the truckers with his reed pipes, and I would've helped him, but just then the truck's engine roared to life, the trailer started shaking, and we were forced to sit down or fall down.

We huddled in the corner on some mildewed feed sacks, trying to ignore the smell and the heat and the flies. Grover talked to the animals in a series of goat bleats, but they just stared at him sadly. Annabeth was in favor of breaking the cages and freeing them on the spot, but I pointed out it wouldn't do much good until the truck stopped moving. Besides, I had a feeling we might look a lot better to the lion than those turnips.

I found a water jug and refilled their bowls, then used Anaklusmos to drag the mismatched food out of their cages. I gave the meat to the lion and the turnips to the zebra and the antelope.

Grover calmed the antelope down, while Annabeth used her knife to cut the balloon off his horn. She wanted to cut the gum out of the zebra's mane, too, but we decided that would be too risky with the truck bumping around. We told Grover to promise the animals we'd help them more in the morning, then we settled in for night.

Grover curled up on a turnip sack; Annabeth opened our bag of Double Stuf Oreos and nibbled on one half-heartedly; I tried to cheer myself up by concentrating on the fact that we were halfway to Los Angeles. Halfway to our destination. It was only June fourteenth. The solstice wasn't until the twenty-first. We could make it in plenty of time.

On the other hand, I had no idea what to expect next. The gods kept toying with me. At least Hephaestus had the decency to be honest about it—he'd put up cameras and advertised me as entertainment. But even when the cameras weren't rolling, I had a feeling my quest was being watched. I was a source of amusement for the gods.

"Hey," Annabeth said, "I'm sorry for freaking out back at the water park, Percy."

"That's okay."

"It's just . . ." She shuddered. "Spiders."

"Because of the Arachne story," I guessed. "She got turned into a spider for challenging your mom to a weaving contest, right?"

Annabeth nodded. "Arachne's children have been taking revenge on the children of Athena ever since. If there's a spider within a mile of me, it'll find me. I hate the creepy little things. Anyway, I owe you."

"We're a team, remember?" I said. "Besides, Grover did the fancy flying."

I thought he was asleep, but he mumbled from the corner, "I was pretty amazing, wasn't I?"

Annabeth and I laughed.

She pulled apart an Oreo, handed me half. "In the Iris message . . . did Luke really say nothing?"

I munched my cookie and thought about how to answer. The conversation via rainbow had bothered me all evening. "Luke said you and he go way back. He also said Grover wouldn't fail this time. Nobody would turn into a pine tree."

In the dim bronze light of the sword blade, it was hard to read their expressions.

Grover let out a mournful bray.

"I should've told you the truth from the beginning." His voice trembled. "I thought if you knew what a failure I was, you wouldn't want me along."

"You were the satyr who tried to rescue Thalia, the daughter of Zeus."

He nodded glumly.

"And the other two half-bloods Thalia befriended, the ones who got safely to camp . . ." I looked at Annabeth. "That was you and Luke, wasn't it?"

She put down her Oreo, uneaten. "Like you said, Percy, a seven-year-old half-blood wouldn't have made it very far alone. Athena guided me toward help. Thalia was twelve. Luke was fourteen. They'd both run away from home, like me. They were happy to take me with them. They were . . . amazing monster-fighters, even without training. We traveled north from Virginia without any real plans, fending off monsters for about two weeks before Grover found us."

"I was supposed to escort Thalia to camp," he said, sniffling. "Only Thalia. I had strict orders from Chiron: don't do anything that would slow down the rescue. We knew Hades was after her, see, but I couldn't just leave Luke and Annabeth by themselves. I thought . . . I thought I could lead all three of them to safety. It was my fault the Kindly Ones caught up with us. I froze. I got scared on the way back to camp and took some wrong turns. If I'd just been a little quicker . . ."

"Stop it," Annabeth said. "No one blames you. Thalia didn't blame you either."

"She sacrificed herself to save us," he said miserably. "Her death was my fault. The Council of Cloven Elders said so."

"Because you wouldn't leave two other half-bloods behind?" I said. "That's not fair."

"Percy's right," Annabeth said. "I wouldn't be here today if it weren't for you, Grover. Neither would Luke. We don't care what the council says."

Grover kept sniffling in the dark. "It's just my luck. I'm the lamest satyr ever, and I find the two most powerful half-bloods of the century, Thalia and Percy."

"You're not lame," Annabeth insisted. "You've got more courage than any satyr I've ever met. Name one other who would dare go to the Underworld. I bet Percy is really glad you're here right now."

She kicked me in the shin.

"Yeah," I said, which I would've done even without the kick. "It's not luck that you found Thalia and me, Grover. You've got the biggest heart of any satyr ever. You're a natural searcher. That's why you'll be the one who finds Pan."

I heard a deep, satisfied sigh. I waited for Grover to say something, but his breathing only got heavier. When the sound turned to snoring, I realized he'd fallen sleep.

"How does he do that?" I marveled.

"I don't know," Annabeth said. "But that was really a nice thing you told him."

"I meant it."

We rode in silence for a few miles, bumping around on the feed sacks. The zebra munched a turnip. The lion licked the last of the hamburger meat off his lips and looked at me hopefully.

Annabeth rubbed her necklace like she was thinking deep, strategic thoughts.

"That pine-tree bead," I said. "Is that from your first year?"

She looked. She hadn't realized what she was doing.

"Yeah," she said. "Every August, the counselors pick the most important event of the summer, and they paint it on that year's beads. I've got Thalia's pine tree, a Greek trireme on fire, a centaur in a prom dress—now *that* was a weird summer. . . ."

"And the college ring is your father's?"

"That's none of your—" She stopped herself. "Yeah. Yeah, it is."

"You don't have to tell me."

"No . . . it's okay." She took a shaky breath. "My dad sent it to me folded up in a letter, two summers ago. The ring was, like, his main keepsake from Athena. He wouldn't have gotten through his doctoral program at Harvard without her. . . . That's a long story. Anyway, he said he wanted me to have it. He apologized for being a jerk, said he loved me and missed me. He wanted me to come home and live with him."

"That doesn't sound so bad."

"Yeah, well . . . the problem was, I believed him. I tried

to go home for that school year, but my stepmom was the same as ever. She didn't want her kids put in danger by living with a freak. Monsters attacked. We argued. Monsters attacked. We argued. I didn't even make it through winter break. I called Chiron and came right back to Camp Half-Blood."

"You think you'll ever try living with your dad again?"

She wouldn't meet my eyes. "Please. I'm not into self-inflicted pain."

"You shouldn't give up," I told her. "You should write him a letter or something."

"Thanks for the advice," she said coldly, "but my father's made his choice about who he wants to live with."

We passed another few miles of silence.

"So if the gods fight," I said, "will things line up the way they did with the Trojan War? Will it be Athena versus Poseidon?"

She put her head against the backpack Ares had given us, and closed her eyes. "I don't know what my mom will do. I just know I'll fight next to you."

"Why?"

"Because you're my friend, Seaweed Brain. Any more stupid questions?"

I couldn't think of an answer for that. Fortunately I didn't have to. Annabeth was asleep.

I had trouble following her example, with Grover snoring and an albino lion staring hungrily at me, but eventually I closed my eyes.

My nightmare started out as something I'd dreamed a million times before: I was being forced to take a standardized test while wearing a straitjacket. All the other kids were going out to recess, and the teacher kept saying, *Come on, Percy. You're not stupid, are you? Pick up your pencil.*

Then the dream strayed from the usual.

I looked over at the next desk and saw a girl sitting there, also wearing a straitjacket. She was my age, with unruly black, punk-style hair, dark eyeliner around her stormy green eyes, and freckles across her nose. Somehow, I knew who she was. She was Thalia, daughter of Zeus.

She struggled against the straitjacket, glared at me in frustration, and snapped, *Well, Seaweed Brain? One of us has to get out of here.*

She's right, my dream-self thought. I'm going back to that cavern. I'm going to give Hades a piece of my mind.

The straitjacket melted off me. I fell through the classroom floor. The teacher's voice changed until it was cold and evil, echoing from the depths of a great chasm.

Percy Jackson, it said. *Yes, the exchange went well, I see.*

I was back in the dark cavern, spirits of the dead drifting around me. Unseen in the pit, the monstrous thing was speaking, but this time it wasn't addressing me. The numbing power of its voice seemed directed somewhere else.

And he suspects nothing? it asked.

Another voice, one I almost recognized, answered at my shoulder. *Nothing, my lord. He is as ignorant as the rest.*

I looked over, but no one was there. The speaker was invisible.

Deception upon deception, the thing in the pit mused aloud. *Excellent.*

Truly, my lord, said the voice next to me, *you are well-named the Crooked One. But was it really necessary? I could have brought you what I stole directly —*

You? the monster said in scorn. *You have already shown your limits. You would have failed me completely had I not intervened.*

But, my lord—

Peace, little servant. Our six months have bought us much. Zeus's anger has grown. Poseidon has played his most desperate card. Now we shall use it against him. Shortly you shall have the reward you wish, and your revenge. As soon as both items are delivered into my hands . . . but wait. He is here.

What? The invisible servant suddenly sounded tense. *You summoned him, my lord?*

No. The full force of the monster's attention was now pouring over me, freezing me in place. *Blast his father's blood—he is too changeable, too unpredictable. The boy brought himself hither.*

Impossible! the servant cried.

For a weakling such as you, perhaps, the voice snarled. Then its cold power turned back on me. *So . . . you wish to dream of your quest, young half-blood? Then I will oblige.*

The scene changed.

I was standing in a vast throne room with black marble walls and bronze floors. The empty, horrid throne was made from human bones fused together. Standing at the foot of the dais was my mother, frozen in shimmering golden light, her arms outstretched.

I tried to step toward her, but my legs wouldn't move. I reached for her, only to realize that my hands were withering to bones. Grinning skeletons in Greek armor crowded around me, draping me with silk robes, wreathing my head with laurels that smoked with Chimera poison, burning into my scalp.

The evil voice began to laugh. *Hail, the conquering hero!*

I woke with a start.

Grover was shaking my shoulder. "The truck's stopped," he said. "We think they're coming to check on the animals."

"Hide!" Annabeth hissed.

She had it easy. She just put on her magic cap and disappeared. Grover and I had to dive behind feed sacks and hope we looked like turnips.

The trailer doors creaked open. Sunlight and heat poured in.

"Man!" one of the truckers said, waving his hand in front of his ugly nose. "I wish I hauled appliances." He climbed inside and poured some water from a jug into the animals' dishes.

"You hot, big boy?" he asked the lion, then splashed the rest of the bucket right in the lion's face.

The lion roared in indignation.

"Yeah, yeah, yeah," the man said.

Next to me, under the turnip sacks, Grover tensed. For a peace-loving herbivore, he looked downright murderous.

The trucker threw the antelope a squashed-looking Happy Meal bag. He smirked at the zebra. "How ya doin', Stripes? Least we'll be getting rid of *you* this stop. You like magic shows? You're gonna love this one. They're gonna saw you in half!"

The zebra, wild-eyed with fear, looked straight at me.

There was no sound, but as clear as day, I heard it say: *Free me, lord. Please.*

I was too stunned to react.

There was a loud *knock, knock, knock* on the side of the trailer.

The trucker inside with us yelled, "What do you want, Eddie?"

A voice outside—it must've been Eddie's—shouted back, "Maurice? What'd ya say?"

"What are you banging for?"

Knock, knock, knock.

Outside, Eddie yelled, "What banging?"

Our guy Maurice rolled his eyes and went back outside, cursing at Eddie for being an idiot.

A second later, Annabeth appeared next to me. She must've done the banging to get Maurice out of the trailer. She said, "This transport business can't be legal."

"No kidding," Grover said. He paused, as if listening. "The lion says these guys are animal smugglers!"

That's right, the zebra's voice said in my mind.

"We've got to free them!" Grover said. He and Annabeth both looked at me, waiting for my lead.

I'd heard the zebra talk, but not the lion. Why? Maybe

it was another learning disability . . . I could only understand zebras? Then I thought: horses. What had Annabeth
said about Poseidon creating horses? Was a zebra close
enough to a horse? Was that why I could understand it?

The zebra said, *Open my cage, lord. Please. I'll be fine after that.*

Outside, Eddie and Maurice were still yelling at each
other, but I knew they'd be coming inside to torment the
animals again any minute. I grabbed Riptide and slashed the
lock off the zebra's cage.

The zebra burst out. It turned to me and bowed. *Thank
you, lord.*

Grover held up his hands and said something to the
zebra in goat talk, like a blessing.

Just as Maurice was poking his head back inside to check
out the noise, the zebra leaped over him and into the street.
There was yelling and screaming and cars honking. We
rushed to the doors of the trailer in time to see the zebra galloping down a wide boulevard lined with hotels and casinos
and neon signs. We'd just released a zebra in Las Vegas.

Maurice and Eddie ran after it, with a few policemen
running after them, shouting, "Hey! You need a permit for
that!"

"Now would be a good time to leave," Annabeth said.

"The other animals first," Grover said.

I cut the locks with my sword. Grover raised his hands
and spoke the same goat-blessing he'd used for the zebra.

"Good luck," I told the animals. The antelope and the
lion burst out of their cages and went off together into the
streets.

Some tourists screamed. Most just backed off and took pictures, probably thinking it was some kind of stunt by one of the casinos.

"Will the animals be okay?" I asked Grover. "I mean, the desert and all—"

"Don't worry," he said. "I placed a satyr's sanctuary on them."

"Meaning?"

"Meaning they'll reach the wild safely," he said. "They'll find water, food, shade, whatever they need until they find a safe place to live."

"Why can't you place a blessing like that on us?" I asked.

"It only works on wild animals."

"So it would only affect Percy," Annabeth reasoned.

"Hey!" I protested.

"Kidding," she said. "Come on. Let's get out of this filthy truck."

We stumbled out into the desert afternoon. It was a hundred and ten degrees, easy, and we must've looked like deep-fried vagrants, but everybody was too interested in the wild animals to pay us much attention.

We passed the Monte Carlo and the MGM. We passed pyramids, a pirate ship, and the Statue of Liberty, which was a pretty small replica, but still made me homesick.

I wasn't sure what we were looking for. Maybe just a place to get out of the heat for a few minutes, find a sand-wich and a glass of lemonade, make a new plan for getting west.

We must have taken a wrong turn, because we found

ourselves at a dead end, standing in front of the Lotus Hotel and Casino. The entrance was a huge neon flower, the petals lighting up and blinking. No one was going in or out, but the glittering chrome doors were open, spilling out air-conditioning that smelled like flowers—lotus blossom, maybe. I'd never smelled one, so I wasn't sure.

The doorman smiled at us. "Hey, kids. You look tired. You want to come in and sit down?"

I'd learned to be suspicious, the last week or so. I figured anybody might be a monster or a god. You just couldn't tell. But this guy was normal. One look at him, and I could see. Besides, I was so relieved to hear somebody who sounded sympathetic that I nodded and said we'd love to come in. Inside, we took one look around, and Grover said, "Whoa."

The whole lobby was a giant game room. And I'm not talking about cheesy old Pac-Man games or slot machines. There was an indoor waterslide snaking around the glass elevator, which went straight up at least forty floors. There was a climbing wall on the side of one building, and an indoor bungee-jumping bridge. There were virtual-reality suits with working laser guns. And hundreds of video games, each one the size of a widescreen TV. Basically, you name it, this place had it. There were a few other kids playing, but not that many. No waiting for any of the games. There were waitresses and snack bars all around, serving every kind of food you can imagine.

"Hey!" a bellhop said. At least I guessed he was a bell-hop. He wore a white-and-yellow Hawaiian shirt with lotus designs, shorts, and flip-flops. "Welcome to the Lotus Casino. Here's your room key."

I stammered, "Um, but . . ."

"No, no," he said, laughing. "The bill's taken care of. No extra charges, no tips. Just go on up to the top floor, room 4001. If you need anything, like extra bubbles for the hot tub, or skeet targets for the shooting range, or whatever, just call the front desk. Here are your LotusCash cards. They work in the restaurants and on all the games and rides."

He handed us each a green plastic credit card.

I knew there must be some mistake. Obviously he thought we were some millionaire's kids. But I took the card and said, "How much is on here?"

His eyebrows knit together. "What do you mean?"

"I mean, when does it run out of cash?"

He laughed. "Oh, you're making a joke. Hey, that's cool. Enjoy your stay."

We took the elevator upstairs and checked out our room. It was a suite with three separate bedrooms and a bar stocked with candy, sodas, and chips. A hotline to room service. Fluffy towels and water beds with feather pillows. A big-screen television with satellite and high-speed Internet. The balcony had its own hot tub, and sure enough, there was a skeet-shooting machine and a shotgun, so you could launch clay pigeons right out over the Las Vegas skyline and plug them with your gun. I didn't see how that could be legal, but I thought it was pretty cool. The view over the Strip and the desert was amazing, though I doubted we'd ever find time to look at the view with a room like this.

"Oh, goodness," Annabeth said. "This place is . . ."

"Sweet," Grover said. "Absolutely sweet."

There were clothes in the closet, and they fit me. I frowned, thinking that this was a little strange.

I threw Ares's backpack in the trash can. Wouldn't need that anymore. When we left, I could just charge a new one at the hotel store.

I took a shower, which felt awesome after a week of grimy travel. I changed clothes, ate a bag of chips, drank three Cokes, and came out feeling better than I had in a long time. In the back of my mind, some small problem kept nagging me. I'd had a dream or something . . . I needed to talk to my friends. But I was sure it could wait.

I came out of the bedroom and found that Annabeth and Grover had also showered and changed clothes. Grover was eating potato chips to his heart's content, while Annabeth cranked up the National Geographic Channel.

"All those stations," I told her, "and you turn on National Geographic. Are you insane?"

"It's interesting."

"I feel good," Grover said. "I love this place."

Without his even realizing it, the wings sprouted out of his shoes and lifted him a foot off the ground, then back down again.

"So what now?" Annabeth asked. "Sleep?"

Grover and I looked at each other and grinned. We both held up our green plastic LotusCash cards.

"Play time," I said.

I couldn't remember the last time I had so much fun. I came from a relatively poor family. Our idea of a splurge was eating out at Burger King and renting a video. A five-star Vegas hotel? Forget it.

I bungee-jumped the lobby five or six times, did the waterslide, snowboarded the artificial ski slope, and played virtual-reality laser tag and FBI sharpshooter. I saw Grover a few times, going from game to game. He really liked the reverse hunter thing—where the deer go out and shoot the rednecks. I saw Annabeth playing trivia games and other brainiac stuff. They had this huge 3-D sim game where you build your own city, and you could actually see the holographic buildings rise on the display board. I didn't think much of it, but Annabeth loved it.

I'm not sure when I first realized something was wrong.

Probably, it was when I noticed the guy standing next to me at VR sharpshooters. He was about thirteen, I guess, but his clothes were weird. I thought he was some Elvis imper-sonator's son. He wore bell-bottom jeans and a red T-shirt with black piping, and his hair was permed and gelled like a New Jersey girl's on homecoming night.

We played a game of sharpshooters together and he said, "Groovy, man. Been here two weeks, and the games keep getting better and better."

Groovy?

Later, while we were talking, I said something was "sick," and he looked at me kind of startled, as if he'd never heard the word used that way before.

He said his name was Darrin, but as soon as I started asking him questions he got bored with me and started to go back to the computer screen.

I said, "Hey, Darrin?"

"What?"

"What year is it?"

He frowned at me. "In the game?"

"No. In real life."

He had to think about it. "1977."

"No," I said, getting a little scared. "Really."

"Hey, man. Bad vibes. I got a game happening."

After that he totally ignored me.

I started talking to people, and I found it wasn't easy. They were glued to the TV screen, or the video game, or their food, or whatever. I found a guy who told me it was 1985. Another guy told me it was 1993. They all claimed they hadn't been in here very long, a few days, a few weeks at most. They didn't really know and they didn't care.

Then it occurred to me: how long had I been here? It seemed like only a couple of hours, but was it?

I tried to remember why we were here. We were going to Los Angeles. We were supposed to find the entrance to the Underworld. My mother . . . for a scary second, I had trouble remembering her name. Sally. Sally Jackson. I had to find her. I had to stop Hades from causing World War III.

I found Annabeth still building her city.

"Come on," I told her. "We've got to get out of here."

No response.

I shook her. "Annabeth?"

She looked up, annoyed. "What?"

"We need to leave."

"Leave? What are you talking about? I've just got the towers—"

"This place is a trap."

She didn't respond until I shook her again. "What?"

"Listen. The Underworld. Our quest!"

"Oh, come on, Percy. Just a few more minutes."

"Annabeth, there are people here from 1977. Kids who have never aged. You check in, and you stay forever."

"So?" she asked. "Can you imagine a better place?"

I grabbed her wrist and yanked her away from the game.

"Hey!" She screamed and hit me, but nobody else even bothered looking at us. They were too busy.

I made her look directly in my eyes. I said, "Spiders. Large, hairy spiders."

That jarred her. Her vision cleared. "Oh my gods," she said. "How long have we—"

"I don't know, but we've got to find Grover."

We went searching, and found him still playing Virtual Deer Hunter.

"Grover!" we both shouted.

He said, "Die, human! Die, silly polluting nasty person!"

"Grover!"

He turned the plastic gun on me and started clicking, as if I were just another image from the screen.

I looked at Annabeth, and together we took Grover by the arms and dragged him away. His flying shoes sprang to life and started tugging his legs in the other direction as he shouted, "No! I just got to a new level! No!"

The Lotus bellhop hurried up to us. "Well, now, are you ready for your platinum cards?"

"We're leaving," I told him.

"Such a shame," he said, and I got the feeling that he really meant it, that we'd be breaking his heart if we went. "We just added an entire new floor full of games for platinum-card members."

He held out the cards, and I wanted one. I knew that if I took one, I'd never leave. I'd stay here, happy forever, playing games forever, and soon I'd forget my mom, and my quest, and maybe even my own name. I'd be playing virtual rifleman with groovy Disco Darrin forever.

Grover reached for the card, but Annabeth yanked back his arm and said, "No, thanks."

We walked toward the door, and as we did, the smell of the food and the sounds of the games seemed to get more and more inviting. I thought about our room upstairs. We could just stay the night, sleep in a real bed for once. . . .

Then we burst through the doors of the Lotus Casino and ran down the sidewalk. It felt like afternoon, about the same time of day we'd gone into the casino, but something was wrong. The weather had completely changed. It was stormy, with heat lightning flashing out in the desert.

Ares's backpack was slung over my shoulder, which was odd, because I was sure I had thrown it in the trash can in room 4001, but at the moment I had other problems to worry about.

I ran to the nearest newspaper stand and read the year first. Thank the gods, it was the same year it had been when we went in. Then I noticed the date: June twentieth.

We had been in the Lotus Casino for five days.

We had only one day left until the summer solstice. One day to complete our quest.

SEVENTEEN

WE SHOP FOR WATER BEDS

It was Annabeth's idea.

She loaded us into the back of a Vegas taxi as if we actually had money, and told the driver, "Los Angeles, please."

The cabbie chewed his cigar and sized us up. "That's three hundred miles. For that, you gotta pay up front."

"You accept casino debit cards?" Annabeth asked.

He shrugged. "Some of 'em. Same as credit cards. I gotta swipe 'em through first."

Annabeth handed him her green LotusCash card.

He looked at it skeptically.

"Swipe it," Annabeth invited.

He did.

His meter machine started rattling. The lights flashed. Finally an infinity symbol came up next to the dollar sign.

The cigar fell out of the driver's mouth. He looked back at us, his eyes wide. "Where to in Los Angeles. . . uh, Your Highness?"

"The Santa Monica Pier." Annabeth sat up a little straighter. I could tell she liked the "Your Highness" thing. "Get us there fast, and you can keep the change."

Maybe she shouldn't have told him that.

The cab's speedometer never dipped below ninety-five the whole way through the Mojave Desert.

On the road, we had plenty of time to talk. I told Annabeth and Grover about my latest dream, but the details got sketchier the more I tried to remember them. The Lotus Casino seemed to have short-circuited my memory. I couldn't recall what the invisible servant's voice had sounded like, though I was sure it was somebody I knew. The servant had called the monster in the pit something other than "my lord" . . . some special name or title. . . .

"The Silent One?" Annabeth suggested. "The Rich One? Both of those are nicknames for Hades."

"Maybe . . ." I said, though neither sounded quite right.

"That throne room sounds like Hades's," Grover said. "That's the way it's usually described."

I shook my head. "Something's wrong. The throne room wasn't the main part of the dream. And that voice from the pit . . . I don't know. It just didn't feel like a god's voice."

Annabeth's eyes widened.

"What?" I asked.

"Oh . . . nothing. I was just—No, it *has* to be Hades. Maybe he sent this thief, this invisible person, to get the master bolt, and something went wrong—"

"Like what?"

"I—I don't know," she said. "But if he stole Zeus's symbol of power from Olympus, and the gods were hunting him, I mean, a lot of things could go wrong. So this thief had to hide the bolt, or he lost it somehow. Anyway, he failed to bring it to Hades. That's what the voice said in your dream, right? The guy failed. That would explain what the Furies were searching for when they came after us on the bus. Maybe they thought we had retrieved the bolt."

I wasn't sure what was wrong with her. She looked pale.

"But if I'd already retrieved the bolt," I said, "why would I be traveling to the Underworld?"

"To threaten Hades," Grover suggested. "To bribe or blackmail him into getting your mom back."

I whistled. "You have evil thoughts for a goat."

"Why, thank you."

"But the thing in the pit said it was waiting for *two* items," I said. "If the master bolt is one, what's the other?"

Grover shook his head, clearly mystified.

Annabeth was looking at me as if she knew my next question, and was silently willing me not to ask it.

"You have an idea what might be in that pit, don't you?" I asked her. "I mean, if it isn't Hades?"

"Percy . . . let's not talk about it. Because if it isn't Hades . . . No. It has to be Hades."

Wasteland rolled by. We passed a sign that said CALI-FORNIA STATE LINE, 12 MILES.

I got the feeling I was missing one simple, critical piece of information. It was like when I stared at a common word I should know, but I couldn't make sense of it because one or two letters were floating around. The more I thought about my quest, the more I was sure that confronting Hades wasn't the real answer. There was something else going on, something even more dangerous.

The problem was: we were hurtling toward the Underworld at ninety-five miles an hour, betting that Hades had the master bolt. If we got there and found out we were wrong, we wouldn't have time to correct ourselves. The solstice deadline would pass and war would begin.

"The answer is in the Underworld," Annabeth assured me. "You saw spirits of the dead, Percy. There's only one place that could be. We're doing the right thing."

She tried to boost our morale by suggesting clever strategies for getting into the Land of the Dead, but my heart wasn't in it. There were just too many unknown factors. It was like cramming for a test without knowing the subject. And believe me, I'd done *that* enough times.

The cab sped west. Every gust of wind through Death Valley sounded like a spirit of the dead. Every time the brakes hissed on an eighteen-wheeler, it reminded me of Echidna's reptilian voice.

At sunset, the taxi dropped us at the beach in Santa Monica. It looked exactly the way L.A. beaches do in the movies, only it smelled worse. There were carnival rides lining the Pier, palm trees lining the sidewalks, homeless guys sleeping in the sand dunes, and surfer dudes waiting for the perfect wave.

Grover, Annabeth, and I walked down to the edge of the surf.

"What now?" Annabeth asked.

The Pacific was turning gold in the setting sun. I thought about how long it had been since I'd stood on the beach at Montauk, on the opposite side of the country, looking out at a different sea.

How could there be a god who could control all that? What did my science teacher used to say—two-thirds of the earth's surface was covered in water? How could I be the son of someone that powerful?

I stepped into the surf.

"Percy?" Annabeth said. "What are you doing?"

I kept walking, up to my waist, then my chest.

She called after me, "You know how polluted that water is? There're all kinds of toxic—"

That's when my head went under.

I held my breath at first. It's difficult to intentionally inhale water. Finally I couldn't stand it anymore. I gasped. Sure enough, I could breathe normally.

I walked down into the shoals. I shouldn't have been able to see through the murk, but somehow I could tell where everything was. I could sense the rolling texture of the bottom. I could make out sand-dollar colonies dotting the sandbars. I could even see the currents, warm and cold streams swirling together.

I felt something rub against my leg. I looked down and almost shot out of the water like a ballistic missile. Sliding along beside me was a five-foot-long mako shark.

But the thing wasn't attacking. It was nuzzling me. Heeling like a dog. Tentatively, I touched its dorsal fin. It bucked a little, as if inviting me to hold tighter. I grabbed the fin with both hands. It took off, pulling me along. The shark carried me down into the darkness. It deposited me at the edge of the ocean proper, where the sand bank dropped off into a huge chasm. It was like standing on the rim of the Grand Canyon at midnight, not being able to see much, but knowing the void was right there.

The surface shimmered maybe a hundred and fifty feet above. I knew I should've been crushed by the pressure. Then again, I shouldn't have been able to breathe. I wondered if there was a limit to how deep I could go, if I could sink straight to the bottom of the Pacific.

Then I saw something glimmering in the darkness below, growing bigger and brighter as it rose toward me. A woman's voice, like my mother's, called: "Percy Jackson."

As she got closer, her shape became clearer. She had flowing black hair, a dress made of green silk. Light flickered around her, and her eyes were so distractingly beautiful I hardly noticed the stallion-sized sea horse she was riding.

She dismounted. The sea horse and the mako shark whisked off and started playing something that looked like tag. The underwater lady smiled at me. "You've come far, Percy Jackson. Well done."

I wasn't quite sure what to do, so I bowed. "You're the woman who spoke to me in the Mississippi River."

"Yes, child. I am a Nereid, a spirit of the sea. It was not easy to appear so far upriver, but the naiads, my freshwater cousins, helped sustain my life force. They honor Lord Poseidon, though they do not serve in his court."

"And . . . you serve in Poseidon's court?"

She nodded. "It has been many years since a child of the Sea God has been born. We have watched you with great interest."

Suddenly I remembered faces in the waves off Montauk Beach when I was a little boy, reflections of smiling women. Like so many of the weird things in my life, I'd never given it much thought before.

"If my father is so interested in me," I said, "why isn't he here? Why doesn't he speak to me?"

A cold current rose out of the depths.

"Do not judge the Lord of the Sea too harshly," the Nereid told me. "He stands at the brink of an unwanted war. He has much to occupy his time. Besides, he is forbidden to help you directly. The gods may not show such favoritism."

"Even to their own children?"

"Especially to them. The gods can work by indirect influence only. That is why I give you a warning, and a gift."

She held out her hand. Three white pearls flashed in her palm.

"I know you journey to Hades's realm," she said. "Few mortals have ever done this and survived: Orpheus, who had great music skill; Hercules, who had great strength; Houdini, who could escape even the depths of Tartarus. Do you have these talents?"

"Um . . . no, ma'am."

"Ah, but you have something else, Percy. You have gifts you have only begun to know. The oracles have foretold a great and terrible future for you, should you survive to man-hood. Poseidon would not have you die before your time. Therefore take these, and when you are in need, smash a pearl at your feet."

"What will happen?"

"That," she said, "depends on the need. But remember: what belongs to the sea will always return to the sea."

"What about the warning?"

Her eyes flickered with green light. "Go with what your heart tells you, or you will lose all. Hades feeds on doubt and hopelessness. He will trick you if he can, make you mis-trust your own judgment. Once you are in his realm, he will never willingly let you leave. Keep faith. Good luck, Percy Jackson."

She summoned her sea horse and rode toward the void.

"Wait!" I called. "At the river, you said not to trust the gifts. What gifts?"

"Good-bye, young hero," she called back, her voice fad-ing into the depths. "You must listen to your heart." She became a speck of glowing green, and then she was gone.

I wanted to follow her down into the darkness. I wanted to see the court of Poseidon. But I looked up at the sunset darkening on the surface. My friends were waiting. We had so little time. . . .

I kicked upward toward the shore.

When I reached the beach, my clothes dried instantly. I told Grover and Annabeth what had happened, and showed them the pearls.

Annabeth grimaced. "No gift comes without a price."

"They were free."

"No." She shook her head. "'There is no such thing as a free lunch.' That's an ancient Greek saying that translated pretty well into American. There will be a price. You wait."

On that happy thought, we turned our backs on the sea.

With some spare change from Ares's backpack, we took the bus into West Hollywood. I showed the driver the Underworld address slip I'd taken from Aunty Em's Garden Gnome Emporium, but he'd never heard of DOA Recording Studios.

"You remind me of somebody I saw on TV," he told me. "You a child actor or something?"

"Uh . . . I'm a stunt double . . . for a lot of child actors."

"Oh! That explains it."

We thanked him and got off quickly at the next stop.

We wandered for miles on foot, looking for DOA. Nobody seemed to know where it was. It didn't appear in the phone book.

Twice, we ducked into alleys to avoid cop cars.

I froze in front of an appliance-store window because a television was playing an interview with somebody who looked very familiar—my stepdad, Smelly Gabe. He was talking to Barbara Walters—I mean, as if he were some kind of huge celebrity. She was interviewing him in our apartment, in the middle of a poker game, and there was a young blond lady sitting next to him, patting his hand.

A fake tear glistened on his cheek. He was saying, "Honest, Ms. Walters, if it wasn't for Sugar here, my grief counselor, I'd be a wreck. My stepson took everything I cared about. My wife . . . my Camaro . . . I—I'm sorry. I have trouble talking about it."

"There you have it, America." Barbara Walters turned to the camera. "A man torn apart. An adolescent boy with serious issues. Let me show you, again, the last known photo of this troubled young fugitive, taken a week ago in Denver."

The screen cut to a grainy shot of me, Annabeth, and Grover standing outside the Colorado diner, talking to Ares.

"Who are the other children in this photo?" Barbara Walters asked dramatically. "Who is the man with them? Is Percy Jackson a delinquent, a terrorist, or perhaps the brainwashed victim of a frightening new cult? When we come back, we chat with a leading child psychologist. Stay tuned, America."

"C'mon," Grover told me. He hauled me away before I could punch a hole in the appliance-store window.

It got dark, and hungry-looking characters started coming out on the streets to play. Now, don't get me wrong. I'm a New Yorker. I don't scare easy. But L.A. had a totally different feel from New York. Back home, everything seemed close. It didn't matter how big the city was, you could get anywhere without getting lost. The street pattern and the subway made sense. There was a system to how things worked. A kid could be safe as long as he wasn't stupid.

L.A. wasn't like that. It was spread out, chaotic, hard to move around. It reminded me of Ares. It wasn't enough for

L.A. to be big; it had to prove it was big by being loud and strange and difficult to navigate, too. I didn't know how we were ever going to find the entrance to the Underworld by tomorrow, the summer solstice.

We walked past gangbangers, bums, and street hawkers, who looked at us like they were trying to figure if we were worth the trouble of mugging.

As we hurried passed the entrance of an alley, a voice from the darkness said, "Hey, you."

Like an idiot, I stopped.

Before I knew it, we were surrounded. A gang of kids had circled us. Six of them in all—white kids with expensive clothes and mean faces. Like the kids at Yancy Academy: rich brats playing at being bad boys.

Instinctively, I uncapped Riptide.

When the sword appeared out of nowhere, the kids backed off, but their leader was either really stupid or really brave, because he kept coming at me with a switchblade.

I made the mistake of swinging.

The kid yelped. But he must've been one hundred percent mortal, because the blade passed harmlessly right through his chest. He looked down. "What the . . ."

I figured I had about three seconds before his shock turned to anger. "Run!" I screamed at Annabeth and Grover.

We pushed two kids out of the way and raced down the street, not knowing where we were going. We turned a sharp corner.

"There!" Annabeth shouted.

Only one store on the block looked open, its windows glaring with neon. The sign above the door said something like CRSTUY'S WATRE BDE ALPACE.

"Crusty's Water Bed Palace?" Grover translated.

It didn't sound like a place I'd ever go except in an emergency, but this definitely qualified.

We burst through the doors, ran behind a water bed, and ducked. A split second later, the gang kids ran past outside.

"I think we lost them," Grover panted.

A voice behind us boomed, "Lost who?"

We all jumped.

Standing behind us was a guy who looked like a raptor in a leisure suit. He was at least seven feet tall, with absolutely no hair. He had gray, leathery skin, thick-lidded eyes, and a cold, reptilian smile. He moved toward us slowly, but I got the feeling he could move fast if he needed to.

His suit might've come from the Lotus Casino. It belonged back in the seventies, big-time. The shirt was silk paisley, unbuttoned halfway down his hairless chest. The lapels on his velvet jacket were as wide as landing strips. The silver chains around his neck—I couldn't even count them.

"I'm Crusty," he said, with a tartar-yellow smile.

I resisted the urge to say, *Yes, you are.*

"Sorry to barge in," I told him. "We were just, um, browsing."

"You mean hiding from those no-good kids," he grumbled. "They hang around every night. I get a lot of people in here, thanks to them. Say, you want to look at a water bed?"

I was about to say *No, thanks*, when he put a huge paw on my shoulder and steered me deeper into the showroom.

There was every kind of water bed you could imagine: different kinds of wood, different patterns of sheets; queen-size, king-size, emperor-of-the-universe-size.

"This is my most popular model." Crusty spread his hands proudly over a bed covered with black satin sheets, with built-in Lava Lamps on the headboard. The mattress vibrated, so it looked like oil-flavored Jell-O.

"Million-hand massage," Crusty told us. "Go on, try it out. Shoot, take a nap. I don't care. No business today, anyway."

"Um," I said, "I don't think . . ."

"Million-hand massage!" Grover cried, and dove in. "Oh, you guys! This is cool."

"Hmm," Crusty said, stroking his leathery chin. "Almost, almost."

"Almost what?" I asked.

He looked at Annabeth. "Do me a favor and try this one over here, honey. Might fit."

Annabeth said, "But what—"

He patted her reassuringly on the shoulder and led her over to the Safari Deluxe model with teakwood lions carved into the frame and a leopard-patterned comforter. When Annabeth didn't want to lie down, Crusty pushed her.

"Hey!" she protested.

Crusty snapped his fingers. *"Ergo!"*

Ropes sprang from the sides of the bed, lashing around Annabeth, holding her to the mattress.

Grover tried to get up, but ropes sprang from his black-satin bed, too, and lashed him down.

"N-not c-c-cool!" he yelled, his voice vibrating from the million-hand massage. "N-not c-cool a-at all!"

The giant looked at Annabeth, then turned toward me and grinned. "Almost, darn it."

I tried to step away, but his hand shot out and clamped around the back of my neck. "Whoa, kid. Don't worry. We'll find you one in a sec."

"Let my friends go."

"Oh, sure I will. But I got to make them fit, first."

"What do you mean?"

"All the beds are exactly six feet, see? Your friends are too short. Got to make them fit."

Annabeth and Grover kept struggling.

"Can't stand imperfect measurements," Crusty muttered. *"Ergo!"*

A new set of ropes leaped out from the top and bottom of the beds, wrapping around Grover and Annabeth's ankles, then around their armpits. The ropes started tightening, pulling my friends from both ends.

"Don't worry," Crusty told me. "These are stretching jobs. Maybe three extra inches on their spines. They might even live. Now why don't we find a bed you like, huh?"

"Percy!" Grover yelled.

My mind was racing. I knew I couldn't take on this giant water-bed salesman alone. He would snap my neck before I ever got my sword out.

"Your real name's not Crusty, is it?" I asked.

"Legally, it's Procrustes," he admitted.

"The Stretcher," I said. I remembered the story: the giant who'd tried to kill Theseus with excess hospitality on his way to Athens.

"Yeah," the salesman said. "But who can pronounce *Procrustes*? Bad for business. Now 'Crusty,' anybody can say that."

"You're right. It's got a good ring to it."

His eyes lit up. "You think so?"

"Oh, absolutely," I said. "And the workmanship on these beds? Fabulous!"

He grinned hugely, but his fingers didn't loosen on my neck. "I tell my customers that. Every time. Nobody bothers to look at the workmanship. How many built-in Lava Lamp headboards have you seen?"

"Not too many."

"That's right!"

"Percy!" Annabeth yelled. "What are you doing?"

"Don't mind her," I told Procrustes. "She's impossible."

The giant laughed. "All my customers are. Never six feet exactly. So inconsiderate. And then they complain about the fitting."

"What do you do if they're longer than six feet?"

"Oh, that happens all the time. It's a simple fix."

He let go of my neck, but before I could react, he reached behind a nearby sales desk and brought out a huge double-bladed brass axe. He said, "I just center the subject as best I can and lop off whatever hangs over on either end."

"Ah," I said, swallowing hard. "Sensible."

"I'm so glad to come across an intelligent customer!"

The ropes were really stretching my friends now. Annabeth was turning pale. Grover made gurgling sounds, like a strangled goose.

"So, Crusty . . ." I said, trying to keep my voice light. I glanced at the sales tag on the valentine-shaped Honeymoon Special. "Does this one really have dynamic stabilizers to stop wave motion?"

"Absolutely. Try it out."

"Yeah, maybe I will. But would it work even for a big guy like you? No waves at all?"

"Guaranteed."

"No way."

"Way."

"Show me."

He sat down eagerly on the bed, patted the mattress. "No waves. See?"

I snapped my fingers. *"Ergo."*

Ropes lashed around Crusty and flattened him against the mattress.

"Hey!" he yelled.

"Center him just right," I said.

The ropes readjusted themselves at my command. Crusty's whole head stuck out the top. His feet stuck out the bottom.

"No!" he said. "Wait! This is just a demo."

I uncapped Riptide. "A few simple adjustments . . ."

I had no qualms about what I was about to do. If

Crusty were human, I couldn't hurt him anyway. If he was a monster, he deserved to turn into dust for a while.

"You drive a hard bargain," he told me. "I'll give you thirty percent off on selected floor models!"

"I think I'll start with the top." I raised my sword.

"No money down! No interest for six months!"

I swung the sword. Crusty stopped making offers.

I cut the ropes on the other beds. Annabeth and Grover got to their feet, groaning and wincing and cursing me a lot.

"You look taller," I said.

"Very funny," Annabeth said. "Be faster next time."

I looked at the bulletin board behind Crusty's sales desk. There was an advertisement for Hermes Delivery Service, and another for the All-New Compendium of L.A. Area Monsters—"The only Monstrous Yellow Pages you'll ever need!" Under that, a bright orange flier for DOA Recording Studios, offering commissions for heroes' souls. "We are always looking for new talent!" DOA's address was right underneath with a map.

"Come on," I told my friends.

"Give us a minute," Grover complained. "We were almost stretched to death!"

"Then you're ready for the Underworld," I said. "It's only a block from here."

EIGHTEEN

ANNABETH DOES
OBEDIENCE SCHOOL

We stood in the shadows of Valencia Boulevard, looking up at gold letters etched in black marble: DOA RECORDING STUDIOS.

Underneath, stenciled on the glass doors: NO SOLICI-TORS. NO LOITERING. NO LIVING.

It was almost midnight, but the lobby was brightly lit and full of people. Behind the security desk sat a tough-looking guard with sunglasses and an earpiece.

I turned to my friends. "Okay. You remember the plan."

"The plan," Grover gulped. "Yeah. I love the plan."

Annabeth said, "What happens if the plan doesn't work?"

"Don't think negative."

"Right," she said. "We're entering the Land of the Dead, and I shouldn't think negative."

I took the pearls out of my pocket, the three milky spheres the Nereid had given me in Santa Monica. They didn't seem like much of a backup in case something went wrong.

Annabeth put her hand on my shoulder. "I'm sorry, Percy. You're right, we'll make it. It'll be fine."

She gave Grover a nudge.

"Oh, right!" he chimed in. "We got this far. We'll find the master bolt and save your mom. No problem."

I looked at them both, and felt really grateful. Only a few minutes before, I'd almost gotten them stretched to death on deluxe water beds, and now they were trying to be brave for my sake, trying to make me feel better.

I slipped the pearls back in my pocket. "Let's whup some Underworld butt."

We walked inside the DOA lobby.

Muzak played softly on hidden speakers. The carpet and walls were steel gray. Pencil cactuses grew in the corners like skeleton hands. The furniture was black leather, and every seat was taken. There were people sitting on couches, people standing up, people staring out the windows or waiting for the elevator. Nobody moved, or talked, or did much of anything. Out of the corner of my eye, I could see them all just fine, but if I focused on any one of them in particular, they started looking . . . transparent. I could see right through their bodies.

The security guard's desk was a raised podium, so we had to look up at him.

He was tall and elegant, with chocolate-colored skin and bleached-blond hair shaved military style. He wore tortoiseshell shades and a silk Italian suit that matched his hair. A black rose was pinned to his lapel under a silver name tag.

I read the name tag, then looked at him in bewilderment. "Your name is Chiron?"

He leaned across the desk. I couldn't see anything in his

glasses except my own reflection, but his smile was sweet and cold, like a python's, right before it eats you.

"What a precious young lad." He had a strange accent—British, maybe, but also as if he had learned English as a second language. "Tell me, mate, do I look like a centaur?"

"N-no."

"Sir," he added smoothly.

"Sir," I said.

He pinched the name tag and ran his finger under the letters. "Can you read this, mate? It says C-H-A-R-O-N. Say it with me: CARE-ON."

"Charon."

"Amazing! Now: *Mr.* Charon."

"Mr. Charon," I said.

"Well done." He sat back. "I *hate* being confused with that old horse-man. And now, how may I help you little dead ones?"

His question caught in my stomach like a fastball. I looked at Annabeth for support.

"We want to go the Underworld," she said.

Charon's mouth twitched. "Well, that's refreshing."

"It is?" she asked.

"Straightforward and honest. No screaming. No 'There must be a mistake, Mr. Charon.'" He looked us over. "How did you die, then?"

I nudged Grover.

"Oh," he said. "Um . . . drowned . . . in the bathtub."

"All three of you?" Charon asked.

We nodded.

"Big bathtub." Charon looked mildly impressed. "I don't suppose you have coins for passage. Normally, with adults, you see, I could charge your American Express, or add the ferry price to your last cable bill. But with children . . . alas, you never die prepared. Suppose you'll have to take a seat for a few centuries."

"Oh, but we have coins." I set three golden drachmas on the counter, part of the stash I'd found in Crusty's office desk.

"Well, now . . ." Charon moistened his lips. "Real drachmas. Real golden drachmas. I haven't seen these in . . ."

His fingers hovered greedily over the coins.

We were so close.

Then Charon looked at me. That cold stare behind his glasses seemed to bore a hole through my chest. "Here now," he said. "You couldn't read my name correctly. Are you dyslexic, lad?"

"No," I said. "I'm dead."

Charon leaned forward and took a sniff. "You're not dead. I should've known. You're a godling."

"We have to get to the Underworld," I insisted.

Charon made a growling sound deep in his throat.

Immediately, all the people in the waiting room got up and started pacing, agitated, lighting cigarettes, running hands through their hair, or checking their wristwatches.

"Leave while you can," Charon told us. "I'll just take these and forget I saw you."

He started to go for the coins, but I snatched them back.

"No service, no tip." I tried to sound braver than I felt.

Charon growled again—a deep, blood-chilling sound. The spirits of the dead started pounding on the elevator doors.

"It's a shame, too," I sighed. "We had more to offer."

I held up the entire bag from Crusty's stash. I took out a fistful of drachmas and let the coins spill through my fingers.

Charon's growl changed into something more like a lion's purr. "Do you think I can be bought, godling? Eh . . . just out of curiosity, how much have you got there?"

"A lot," I said. "I bet Hades doesn't pay you well enough for such hard work."

"Oh, you don't know the half of it. How would you like to babysit these spirits all day? Always 'Please don't let me be dead' or 'Please let me across for free.' I haven't had a pay raise in three thousand years. Do you imagine suits like this come cheap?"

"You deserve better," I agreed. "A little appreciation. Respect. Good pay."

With each word, I stacked another gold coin on the counter.

Charon glanced down at his silk Italian jacket, as if imagining himself in something even better. "I must say, lad, you're making some sense now. Just a little."

I stacked another few coins. "I could mention a pay raise while I'm talking to Hades."

He sighed. "The boat's almost full, anyway. I might as well add you three and be off."

He stood, scooped up our money, and said, "Come along."

We pushed through the crowd of waiting spirits, who started grabbing at our clothes like the wind, their voices whispering things I couldn't make out. Charon shoved them out of the way, grumbling, "Freeloaders."

He escorted us into the elevator, which was already crowded with souls of the dead, each one holding a green boarding pass. Charon grabbed two spirits who were trying to get on with us and pushed them back into the lobby.

"Right. Now, no one get any ideas while I'm gone," he announced to the waiting room. "And if anyone moves the dial off my easy-listening station again, I'll make sure you're here for another thousand years. Understand?"

He shut the doors. He put a key card into a slot in the elevator panel and we started to descend.

"What happens to the spirits waiting in the lobby?" Annabeth asked.

"Nothing," Charon said.

"For how long?"

"Forever, or until I'm feeling generous."

"Oh," she said. "That's . . . fair."

Charon raised an eyebrow. "Whoever said death was fair, young miss? Wait until it's your turn. You'll die soon enough, where you're going."

"We'll get out alive," I said.

"Ha."

I got a sudden dizzy feeling. We weren't going down

anymore, but forward. The air turned misty. Spirits around me started changing shape. Their modern clothes flickered, turning into gray hooded robes. The floor of the elevator began swaying.

I blinked hard. When I opened my eyes, Charon's creamy Italian suit had been replaced by a long black robe. His tortoiseshell glasses were gone. Where his eyes should've been were empty sockets—like Ares's eyes, except Charon's were totally dark, full of night and death and despair.

He saw me looking, and said, "Well?"

"Nothing," I managed.

I thought he was grinning, but that wasn't it. The flesh of his face was becoming transparent, letting me see straight through to his skull.

The floor kept swaying.

Grover said, "I think I'm getting seasick."

When I blinked again, the elevator wasn't an elevator anymore. We were standing in a wooden barge. Charon was poling us across a dark, oily river, swirling with bones, dead fish, and other, stranger things—plastic dolls, crushed carnations, soggy diplomas with gilt edges.

"The River Styx," Annabeth murmured. "It's so . . ."

"Polluted," Charon said. "For thousands of years, you humans have been throwing in everything as you come across—hopes, dreams, wishes that never came true. Irresponsible waste management, if you ask me."

Mist curled off the filthy water. Above us, almost lost in the gloom, was a ceiling of stalactites. Ahead, the far shore glimmered with greenish light, the color of poison.

Panic closed up my throat. What was I doing here? These people around me . . . they were dead.

Annabeth grabbed hold of my hand. Under normal circumstances, this would've embarrassed me, but I understood how she felt. She wanted reassurance that somebody else was alive on this boat.

I found myself muttering a prayer, though I wasn't quite sure who I was praying to. Down here, only one god mattered, and he was the one I had come to confront.

The shoreline of the Underworld came into view. Craggy rocks and black volcanic sand stretched inland about a hundred yards to the base of a high stone wall, which marched off in either direction as far as we could see. A sound came from somewhere nearby in the green gloom, echoing off the stones—the howl of a large animal.

"Old Three-Face is hungry," Charon said. His smile turned skeletal in the greenish light. "Bad luck for you, godlings."

The bottom of our boat slid onto the black sand. The dead began to disembark. A woman holding a little girl's hand. An old man and an old woman hobbling along arm in arm. A boy no older than I was, shuffling silently along in his gray robe.

Charon said, "I'd wish you luck, mate, but there isn't any down here. Mind you, don't forget to mention my pay raise."

He counted our golden coins into his pouch, then took

up his pole. He warbled something that sounded like a Barry Manilow song as he ferried the empty barge back across the river.

We followed the spirits up a well-worn path.

I'm not sure what I was expecting—Pearly Gates, or a big black portcullis, or something. But the entrance to the Underworld looked like a cross between airport security and the Jersey Turnpike.

There were three separate entrances under one huge black archway that said YOU ARE NOW ENTERING EREBUS. Each entrance had a pass-through metal detector with security cameras mounted on top. Beyond this were tollbooths manned by black-robed ghouls like Charon.

The howling of the hungry animal was really loud now, but I couldn't see where it was coming from. The three-headed dog, Cerberus, who was supposed to guard Hades's door, was nowhere to be seen.

The dead queued up in the three lines, two marked ATTENDANT ON DUTY, and one marked EZ DEATH. The EZ DEATH line was moving right along. The other two were crawling.

"What do you figure?" I asked Annabeth.

"The fast line must go straight to the Asphodel Fields," she said. "No contest. They don't want to risk judgment from the court, because it might go against them."

"There's a court for dead people?"

"Yeah. Three judges. They switch around who sits on the bench. King Minos, Thomas Jefferson, Shakespeare—

people like that. Sometimes they look at a life and decide that person needs a special reward—the Fields of Elysium. Sometimes they decide on punishment. But most people, well, they just lived. Nothing special, good or bad. So they go to the Asphodel Fields."

"And do what?"

Grover said, "Imagine standing in a wheat field in Kansas. Forever."

"Harsh," I said.

"Not as harsh as that," Grover muttered. "Look."

A couple of black-robbed ghouls had pulled aside one spirit and were frisking him at the security desk. The face of the dead man looked vaguely familiar.

"He's that preacher who made the news, remember?" Grover asked.

"Oh, yeah." I did remember now. We'd seen him on TV a couple of times at the Yancy Academy dorm. He was this annoying televangelist from upstate New York who'd raised millions of dollars for orphanages and then got caught spending the money on stuff for his mansion, like gold-plated toilet seats, and an indoor putt-putt golf course. He'd died in a police chase when his "Lamborghini for the Lord" went off a cliff.

I said, "What're they doing to him?"

"Special punishment from Hades," Grover guessed. "The really bad people get his personal attention as soon as they arrive. The Fur—the Kindly Ones will set up an eternal torture for him."

The thought of the Furies made me shudder. I realized

I was in their home territory now. Old Mrs. Dodds would be licking her lips with anticipation.

"But if he's a preacher," I said, "and he believes in a different hell. . . ."

Grover shrugged. "Who says he's seeing this place the way we're seeing it? Humans see what they want to see. You're very stubborn—er, persistent, that way."

We got closer to the gates. The howling was so loud now it shook the ground at my feet, but I still couldn't figure out where it was coming from.

Then, about fifty feet in front of us, the green mist shimmered. Standing just where the path split into three lanes was an enormous shadowy monster.

I hadn't seen it before because it was half transparent, like the dead. Until it moved, it blended with whatever was behind it. Only its eyes and teeth looked solid. And it was staring straight at me.

My jaw hung open. All I could think to say was, "He's a Rottweiler."

I'd always imagined Cerberus as a big black mastiff. But he was obviously a purebred Rottweiler, except of course that he was twice the size of a woolly mammoth, mostly invisible, and had three heads.

The dead walked right up to him—no fear at all. The ATTENDANT ON DUTY lines parted on either side of him. The EZ DEATH spirits walked right between his front paws and under his belly, which they could do without even crouching.

"I'm starting to see him better," I muttered. "Why is that?"

"I think . . ." Annabeth moistened her lips. "I'm afraid it's because we're getting closer to being dead."

The dog's middle head craned toward us. It sniffed the air and growled.

"It can smell the living," I said.

"But that's okay," Grover said, trembling next to me. "Because we have a plan."

"Right," Annabeth said. I'd never heard her voice sound quite so small. "A plan."

We moved toward the monster.

The middle head snarled at us, then barked so loud my eyeballs rattled.

"Can you understand it?" I asked Grover.

"Oh yeah," he said. "I can understand it."

"What's it saying?"

"I don't think humans have a four-letter word that translates, exactly."

I took the big stick out of my backpack—a bedpost I'd broken off Crusty's Safari Deluxe floor model. I held it up, and tried to channel happy dog thoughts toward Cerberus—Alpo commercials, cute little puppies, fire hydrants. I tried to smile, like I wasn't about to die.

"Hey, Big Fella," I called up. "I bet they don't play with you much."

"GROWWWLLLL!"

"Good boy," I said weakly.

I waved the stick. The dog's middle head followed the movement. The other two heads trained their eyes on

[294]

me, completely ignoring the spirits. I had Cerberus's undivided attention. I wasn't sure that was a good thing.

"Fetch!" I threw the stick into the gloom, a good solid throw. I heard it go *ker-sploosh* in the River Styx.

Cerberus glared at me, unimpressed. His eyes were baleful and cold.

So much for the plan.

Cerberus was now making a new kind of growl, deeper down in his three throats.

"Um," Grover said. "Percy?"

"Yeah?"

"I just thought you'd want to know."

"Yeah?"

"Cerberus? He's saying we've got ten seconds to pray to the god of our choice. After that . . . well . . . he's hungry."

"Wait!" Annabeth said. She started rifling through her pack.

Uh-oh, I thought.

"Five seconds," Grover said. "Do we run now?"

Annabeth produced a red rubber ball the size of a grapefruit. It was labeled WATERLAND, DENVER, CO. Before I could stop her, she raised the ball and marched straight up to Cerberus.

She shouted, "See the ball? You want the ball, Cerberus? Sit!"

Cerberus looked as stunned as we were.

All three of his heads cocked sideways. Six nostrils dilated.

"Sit!" Annabeth called again.

I was sure that any moment she would become the world's largest Milkbone dog biscuit.

But instead, Cerberus licked his three sets of lips, shifted on his haunches, and sat, immediately crushing a dozen spirits who'd been passing underneath him in the EZ DEATH line. The spirits made muffled hisses as they dissipated, like the air let out of tires.

Annabeth said, "Good boy!"

She threw Cerberus the ball.

He caught it in his middle mouth. It was barely big enough for him to chew, and the other heads started snapping at the middle, trying to get the new toy.

"Drop it!" Annabeth ordered.

Cerberus's heads stopped fighting and looked at her. The ball was wedged between two of his teeth like a tiny piece of gum. He made a loud, scary whimper, then dropped the ball, now slimy and bitten nearly in half, at Annabeth's feet.

"Good boy." She picked up the ball, ignoring the monster spit all over it.

She turned toward us. "Go now. EZ DEATH line—it's faster."

I said, "But—"

"Now!" She ordered, in the same tone she was using on the dog.

Grover and I inched forward warily.

Cerberus started to growl.

"Stay!" Annabeth ordered the monster. "If you want the ball, stay!"

Cerberus whimpered, but he stayed where he was.

"What about you?" I asked Annabeth as we passed her.

"I know what I'm doing, Percy," she muttered. "At least, I'm pretty sure. . . ."

Grover and I walked between the monster's legs.

Please, Annabeth, I prayed. Don't tell him to sit again.

We made it through. Cerberus wasn't any less scary-looking from the back.

Annabeth said, "Good dog!"

She held up the tattered red ball, and probably came to the same conclusion I did—if she rewarded Cerberus, there'd be nothing left for another trick.

She threw the ball anyway. The monster's left mouth immediately snatched it up, only to be attacked by the middle head, while the right head moaned in protest.

While the monster was distracted, Annabeth walked briskly under its belly and joined us at the metal detector.

"How did you do that?" I asked her, amazed.

"Obedience school," she said breathlessly, and I was surprised to see there were tears in her eyes. "When I was little, at my dad's house, we had a Doberman. . . ."

"Never mind that," Grover said, tugging at my shirt. "Come on!"

We were about to bolt through the EZ DEATH line when Cerberus moaned pitifully from all three mouths. Annabeth stopped.

She turned to face the dog, which had done a one-eighty to look at us.

Cerberus panted expectantly, the tiny red ball in pieces in a puddle of drool at its feet.

"Good boy," Annabeth said, but her voice sounded melancholy and uncertain.

The monster's heads turned sideways, as if worried about her.

"I'll bring you another ball soon," Annabeth promised faintly. "Would you like that?"

The monster whimpered. I didn't need to speak dog to know Cerberus was still waiting for the ball.

"Good dog. I'll come visit you soon. I—I promise." Annabeth turned to us. "Let's go."

Grover and I pushed through the metal detector, which immediately screamed and set off flashing red lights. "Unauthorized possessions! Magic detected!"

Cerberus started to bark.

We burst through the EZ DEATH gate, which started even more alarms blaring, and raced into the Underworld.

A few minutes later, we were hiding, out of breath, in the rotten trunk of an immense black tree as security ghouls scuttled past, yelling for backup from the Furies.

Grover murmured, "Well, Percy, what have we learned today?"

"That three-headed dogs prefer red rubber balls over sticks?"

"No," Grover told me. "We've learned that your plans really, really bite!"

I wasn't sure about that. I thought maybe Annabeth and I had both had the right idea. Even here in the Underworld, everybody—even monsters—needed a little attention once in a while.

I thought about that as we waited for the ghouls to pass. I pretended not to see Annabeth wipe a tear from her cheek as she listened to the mournful keening of Cerberus in the distance, longing for his new friend.

NINETEEN

WE FIND OUT THE TRUTH, SORT OF

Imagine the largest concert crowd you've ever seen, a football field packed with a million fans.

Now imagine a field a million times that big, packed with people, and imagine the electricity has gone out, and there is no noise, no light, no beach ball bouncing around over the crowd. Something tragic has happened backstage. Whispering masses of people are just milling around in the shadows, waiting for a concert that will never start.

If you can picture that, you have a pretty good idea what the Fields of Asphodel looked like. The black grass had been trampled by eons of dead feet. A warm, moist wind blew like the breath of a swamp. Black trees—Grover told me they were poplars—grew in clumps here and there.

The cavern ceiling was so high above us it might've been a bank of storm clouds, except for the stalactites, which glowed faint gray and looked wickedly pointed. I tried not to imagine they'd fall on us at any moment, but dotted around the fields were several that had fallen and impaled themselves in the black grass. I guess the dead didn't have to worry about little hazards like being speared by stalactites the size of booster rockets.

Annabeth, Grover, and I tried to blend into the crowd,

keeping an eye out for security ghouls. I couldn't help looking for familiar faces among the spirits of Asphodel, but the
dead are hard to look at. Their faces shimmer. They all look
slightly angry or confused. They will come up to you and
speak, but their voices sound like chatter, like bats twitter-
ing. Once they realize you can't understand them, they
frown and move away.

The dead aren't scary. They're just sad.

We crept along, following the line of new arrivals that
snaked from the main gates toward a black-tented pavilion
with a banner that read:

JUDGMENTS FOR ELYSIUM AND ETERNAL DAMNATION
Welcome, Newly Deceased!

Out the back of the tent came two much smaller lines.

To the left, spirits flanked by security ghouls were
marched down a rocky path toward the Fields of Punishment, which glowed and smoked in the distance, a vast,
cracked wasteland with rivers of lava and minefields and
miles of barbed wire separating the different torture areas.
Even from far away, I could see people being chased by
hellhounds, burned at the stake, forced to run naked
through cactus patches or listen to opera music. I could just
make out a tiny hill, with the ant-size figure of Sisyphus
struggling to move his boulder to the top. And I saw worse
tortures, too—things I don't want to describe.

The line coming from the right side of the judgment
pavilion was much better. This one led down toward a small
valley surrounded by walls—a gated community, which

seemed to be the only happy part of the Underworld. Beyond the security gate were neighborhoods of beautiful houses from every time period in history, Roman villas and medieval castles and Victorian mansions. Silver and gold flowers bloomed on the lawns. The grass rippled in rainbow colors. I could hear laughter and smell barbecue cooking.

Elysium.

In the middle of that valley was a glittering blue lake, with three small islands like a vacation resort in the Bahamas. The Isles of the Blest, for people who had chosen to be reborn three times, and three times achieved Elysium. Immediately I knew that's where I wanted to go when I died.

"That's what it's all about," Annabeth said, like she was reading my thoughts. "That's the place for heroes."

But I thought of how few people there were in Elysium, how tiny it was compared to the Fields of Asphodel or even the Fields of Punishment. So few people did good in their lives. It was depressing.

We left the judgment pavilion and moved deeper into the Asphodel Fields. It got darker. The colors faded from our clothes. The crowds of chattering spirits began to thin.

After a few miles of walking, we began to hear a familiar screech in the distance. Looming on the horizon was a palace of glittering black obsidian. Above the parapets swirled three dark batlike creatures: the Furies. I got the feeling they were waiting for us.

"I suppose it's too late to turn back," Grover said wistfully.

"We'll be okay." I tried to sound confident.

"Maybe we should search some of the other places first," Grover suggested. "Like, Elysium, for instance . . ."

"Come on, goat boy." Annabeth grabbed his arm.

Grover yelped. His sneakers sprouted wings and his legs shot forward, pulling him away from Annabeth. He landed flat on his back in the grass.

"Grover," Annabeth chided. "Stop messing around."

"But I didn't—"

He yelped again. His shoes were flapping like crazy now. They levitated off the ground and started dragging him away from us.

"Maia!" he yelled, but the magic word seemed to have no effect. *"Maia,* already! Nine-one-one! Help!"

I got over being stunned and made a grab for Grover's hand, but too late. He was picking up speed, skidding downhill like a bobsled.

We ran after him.

Annabeth shouted, "Untie the shoes!"

It was a smart idea, but I guess it's not so easy when your shoes are pulling you along feetfirst at full speed. Grover tried to sit up, but he couldn't get close to the laces.

We kept after him, trying to keep him in sight as he zipped between the legs of spirits who chattered at him in annoyance.

I was sure Grover was going to barrel straight through the gates of Hades's palace, but his shoes veered sharply to the right and dragged him in the opposite direction.

The slope got steeper. Grover picked up speed. Annabeth

and I had to sprint to keep up. The cavern walls narrowed on either side, and I realized we'd entered some kind of side tunnel. No black grass or trees now, just rock underfoot, and the dim light of the stalactites above.

"Grover!" I yelled, my voice echoing. "Hold on to something!"

"What?" he yelled back.

He was grabbing at gravel, but there was nothing big enough to slow him down.

The tunnel got darker and colder. The hairs on my arms bristled. It smelled evil down here. It made me think of things I shouldn't even know about—blood spilled on an ancient stone altar, the foul breath of a murderer.

Then I saw what was ahead of us, and I stopped dead in my tracks.

The tunnel widened into a huge dark cavern, and in the middle was a chasm the size of a city block.

Grover was sliding straight toward the edge.

"Come on, Percy!" Annabeth yelled, tugging at my wrist.

"But that's—"

"I know!" she shouted. "The place you described in your dream! But Grover's going to fall if we don't catch him." She was right, of course. Grover's predicament got me moving again.

He was yelling, clawing at the ground, but the winged shoes kept dragging him toward the pit, and it didn't look like we could possibly get to him in time.

What saved him were his hooves.

The flying sneakers had always been a loose fit on him,

and finally Grover hit a big rock and the left shoe came flying off. It sped into the darkness, down into the chasm. The right shoe kept tugging him along, but not as fast. Grover was able to slow himself down by grabbing on to the big rock and using it like an anchor.

He was ten feet from the edge of the pit when we caught him and hauled him back up the slope. The other winged shoe tugged itself off, circled around us angrily and kicked our heads in protest before flying off into the chasm to join its twin.

We all collapsed, exhausted, on the obsidian gravel. My limbs felt like lead. Even my backpack seemed heavier, as if somebody had filled it with rocks.

Grover was scratched up pretty bad. His hands were bleeding. His eyes had gone slit-pupiled, goat style, the way they did whenever he was terrified.

"I don't know how . . ." he panted. "I didn't . . ."

"Wait," I said. "Listen."

I heard something—a deep whisper in the darkness.

Another few seconds, and Annabeth said, "Percy, this place—"

"Shh." I stood.

The sound was getting louder, a muttering, evil voice from far, far below us. Coming from the pit.

Grover sat up. "Wh—what's that noise?"

Annabeth heard it too, now. I could see it in her eyes. "Tartarus. The entrance to Tartarus."

I uncapped Anaklusmos.

The bronze sword expanded, gleaming in the darkness,

and the evil voice seemed to falter, just for a moment, before resuming its chant.

I could almost make out words now, ancient, ancient words, older even than Greek. As if . . .

"Magic," I said.

"We have to get out of here," Annabeth said.

Together, we dragged Grover to his hooves and started back up the tunnel. My legs wouldn't move fast enough. My backpack weighed me down. The voice got louder and angrier behind us, and we broke into a run.

Not a moment too soon.

A cold blast of wind pulled at our backs, as if the entire pit were inhaling. For a terrifying moment, I lost ground, my feet slipping in the gravel. If we'd been any closer to the edge, we would've been sucked in.

We kept struggling forward, and finally reached the top of the tunnel, where the cavern widened out into the Fields of Asphodel. The wind died. A wail of outrage echoed from deep in the tunnel. Something was not happy we'd gotten away.

"What *was* that?" Grover panted, when we'd collapsed in the relative safety of a black poplar grove. "One of Hades's pets?"

Annabeth and I looked at each other. I could tell she was nursing an idea, probably the same one she'd gotten during the taxi ride to L.A., but she was too scared to share it. That was enough to terrify me.

I capped my sword, put the pen back in my pocket. "Let's keep going." I looked at Grover. "Can you walk?"

He swallowed. "Yeah, sure. I never liked those shoes, anyway."

He tried to sound brave about it, but he was trembling as badly as Annabeth and I were. Whatever was in that pit was nobody's pet. It was unspeakably old and powerful. Even Echidna hadn't given me that feeling. I was almost relieved to turn my back on that tunnel and head toward the palace of Hades.

Almost.

The Furies circled the parapets, high in the gloom. The outer walls of the fortress glittered black, and the two-story-tall bronze gates stood wide open.

Up close, I saw that the engravings on the gates were scenes of death. Some were from modern times—an atomic bomb exploding over a city, a trench filled with gas mask–wearing soldiers, a line of African famine victims waiting with empty bowls—but all of them looked as if they'd been etched into the bronze thousands of years ago. I wondered if I was looking at prophecies that had come true.

Inside the courtyard was the strangest garden I'd ever seen. Multicolored mushrooms, poisonous shrubs, and weird luminous plants grew without sunlight. Precious jewels made up for the lack of flowers, piles of rubies as big as my fist, clumps of raw diamonds. Standing here and there like frozen party guests were Medusa's garden statues—petrified children, satyrs, and centaurs—all smiling grotesquely.

In the center of the garden was an orchard of

pomegranate trees, their orange blooms neon bright in the dark. "The garden of Persephone," Annabeth said. "Keep walking."

I understood why she wanted to move on. The tart smell of those pomegranates was almost overwhelming. I had a sudden desire to eat them, but then I remembered the story of Persephone. One bite of Underworld food, and we would never be able to leave. I pulled Grover away to keep him from picking a big juicy one.

We walked up the steps of the palace, between black columns, through a black marble portico, and into the house of Hades. The entry hall had a polished bronze floor, which seemed to boil in the reflected torchlight. There was no ceiling, just the cavern roof, far above. I guess they never had to worry about rain down here.

Every side doorway was guarded by a skeleton in military gear. Some wore Greek armor, some British redcoat uniforms, some camouflage with tattered American flags on the shoulders. They carried spears or muskets or M-16s. None of them bothered us, but their hollow eye sockets followed us as we walked down the hall, toward the big set of doors at the opposite end.

Two U.S. Marine skeletons guarded the doors. They grinned down at us, rocket-propelled grenade launchers held across their chests.

"You know," Grover mumbled, "I bet Hades doesn't have trouble with door-to-door salesmen."

My backpack weighed a ton now. I couldn't figure out why. I wanted to open it, check to see if I had somehow picked up a stray bowling ball, but this wasn't the time.

"Well, guys," I said. "I suppose we should . . . knock?"

A hot wind blew down the corridor, and the doors swung open. The guards stepped aside.

"I guess that means *entrez-vous*," Annabeth said.

The room inside looked just like in my dream, except this time the throne of Hades was occupied.

He was the third god I'd met, but the first who really struck me as godlike.

He was at least ten feet tall, for one thing, and dressed in black silk robes and a crown of braided gold. His skin was albino white, his hair shoulder-length and jet black. He wasn't bulked up like Ares, but he radiated power. He lounged on his throne of fused human bones, looking lithe, graceful, and dangerous as a panther.

I immediately felt like he should be giving the orders. He knew more than I did. He should be my master. Then I told myself to snap out of it.

Hades's aura was affecting me, just as Ares's had. The Lord of the Dead resembled pictures I'd seen of Adolph Hitler, or Napoleon, or the terrorist leaders who direct suicide bombers. Hades had the same intense eyes, the same kind of mesmerizing, evil charisma.

"You are brave to come here, Son of Poseidon," he said in an oily voice. "After what you have done to me, very brave indeed. Or perhaps you are simply very foolish."

Numbness crept into my joints, tempting me to lie

down and just take a little nap at Hades's feet. Curl up here and sleep forever.

I fought the feeling and stepped forward. I knew what I had to say. "Lord and Uncle, I come with two requests."

Hades raised an eyebrow. When he sat forward in his throne, shadowy faces appeared in the folds of his black robes, faces of torment, as if the garment were stitched of trapped souls from the Fields of Punishment, trying to get out. The ADHD part of me wondered, off-task, whether the rest of his clothes were made the same way. What horrible things would you have to do in your life to get woven into Hades's underwear?

"Only two requests?" Hades said. "Arrogant child. As if you have not already taken enough. Speak, then. It amuses me not to strike you dead yet."

I swallowed. This was going about as well as I'd feared.

I glanced at the empty, smaller throne next to Hades's. It was shaped like a black flower, gilded with gold. I wished Queen Persephone were here. I recalled something in the myths about how she could calm her husband's moods. But it was summer. Of course, Persephone would be above in the world of light with her mother, the goddess of agriculture, Demeter. Her visits, not the tilt of the planet, create the seasons.

Annabeth cleared her throat. Her finger prodded me in the back.

"Lord Hades," I said. "Look, sir, there can't be a war among the gods. It would be . . . bad."

"Really bad," Grover added helpfully.

"Return Zeus's master bolt to me," I said. "Please, sir. Let me carry it to Olympus."

Hades's eyes grew dangerously bright. "You dare keep up this pretense, after what you have done?"

I glanced back at my friends. They looked as confused as I was.

"Um . . . Uncle," I said. "You keep saying 'after what you've done.' What exactly have I done?"

The throne room shook with a tremor so strong, they probably felt it upstairs in Los Angeles. Debris fell from the cavern ceiling. Doors burst open all along the walls, and skeletal warriors marched in, hundreds of them, from every time period and nation in Western civilization. They lined the perimeter of the room, blocking the exits.

Hades bellowed, "Do you think I *want* war, godling?"

I wanted to say, *Well, these guys don't look like peace activists.* But I thought that might be a dangerous answer.

"You are the Lord of the Dead," I said carefully. "A war would expand your kingdom, right?"

"A typical thing for my brothers to say! Do you think I need more subjects? Did you not see the sprawl of the Asphodel Fields?"

"Well . . ."

"Have you any idea how much my kingdom has swollen in this past century alone, how many subdivisions I've had to open?"

I opened my mouth to respond, but Hades was on a roll now.

"More security ghouls," he moaned. "Traffic problems

at the judgment pavilion. Double overtime for the staff. I used to be a rich god, Percy Jackson. I control all the precious metals under the earth. But my expenses!"

"Charon wants a pay raise," I blurted, just remembering the fact. As soon as I said it, I wished I could sew up my mouth.

"Don't get me started on Charon!" Hades yelled. "He's been impossible ever since he discovered Italian suits! Problems everywhere, and I've got to handle all of them personally. The commute time alone from the palace to the gates is enough to drive me insane! And the dead just keep arriving. *No*, godling. I need no help getting subjects! *I* did not ask for this war."

"But you took Zeus's master bolt."

"Lies!" More rumbling. Hades rose from his throne, towering to the height of a football goalpost. "Your father may fool Zeus, boy, but I am not so stupid. I see his plan."

"His plan?"

"*You* were the thief on the winter solstice," he said. "Your father thought to keep you his little secret. He directed you into the throne room on Olympus. You took the master bolt *and* my helm. Had I not sent my Fury to discover you at Yancy Academy, Poseidon might have succeeded in hiding his scheme to start a war. But now you have been forced into the open. You will be exposed as Poseidon's thief, and I will have my helm back!"

"But . . ." Annabeth spoke. I could tell her mind was going a million miles an hour. "Lord Hades, your helm of darkness is missing, too?"

"Do not play innocent with me, girl. You and the satyr have been helping this hero—coming here to threaten me in Poseidon's name, no doubt—to bring me an ultimatum. Does Poseidon think I can be blackmailed into supporting him?"

"No!" I said. "Poseidon didn't—I didn't—"

"I have said nothing of the helm's disappearance," Hades snarled, "because I had no illusions that anyone on Olympus would offer me the slightest justice, the slightest help. I can ill afford for word to get out that my most powerful weapon of fear is missing. So I searched for you myself, and when it was clear you were coming to me to deliver your threat, I did not try to stop you."

"You didn't try to stop us? But—"

"Return my helm now, or I will stop death," Hades threatened. "That is my counterproposal. I will open the earth and have the dead pour back into the world. I will make your lands a nightmare. And you, Percy Jackson—*your* skeleton will lead my army out of Hades."

The skeletal soldiers all took one step forward, making their weapons ready.

At that point, I probably should have been terrified. The strange thing was, I felt offended. Nothing gets me angrier than being accused of something I didn't do. I've had a lot of experience with that.

"You're as bad as Zeus," I said. "You think I stole from you? That's why you sent the Furies after me?"

"Of course," Hades said.

"And the other monsters?"

Hades curled his lip. "I had nothing to do with them. I

wanted no quick death for you—I wanted you brought before me alive so you might face every torture in the Fields of Punishment. Why do you think I let you enter my kingdom so easily?"

"Easily?"

"Return my property!"

"But I don't have your helm. I came for the master bolt."

"Which you already possess!" Hades shouted. "You came here with it, little fool, thinking you could you threaten me!"

"But I didn't!"

"Open your pack, then."

A horrible feeling struck me. The weight in my backpack, like a bowling ball. It couldn't be. . . .

I slung it off my shoulder and unzipped it. Inside was a two-foot-long metal cylinder, spiked on both ends, humming with energy.

"Percy," Annabeth said. "How—"

"I—I don't know. I don't understand."

"You heroes are always the same," Hades said. "Your pride makes you foolish, thinking you could bring such a weapon before me. I did not ask for Zeus's master bolt, but since it is here, you will yield it to me. I am sure it will make an excellent bargaining tool. And now . . . my helm. Where is it?"

I was speechless. I had no helm. I had no idea how the master bolt had gotten into my backpack. I wanted to think Hades was pulling some kind of trick. Hades was the bad guy. But suddenly the world turned sideways. I realized I'd been played with. Zeus, Poseidon, and Hades had been set at each other's throats by someone else. The master bolt had been in the backpack, and I'd gotten the backpack from . . .

"Lord Hades, wait," I said. "This is all a mistake."

"A mistake?" Hades roared.

The skeletons aimed their weapons. From high above, there was a fluttering of leathery wings, and the three Furies swooped down to perch on the back of their master's throne. The one with Mrs. Dodds's face grinned at me eagerly and flicked her whip.

"There is no mistake," Hades said. "I know why you have come—I know the *real* reason you brought the bolt. You came to bargain for *her*."

Hades loosed a ball of gold fire from his palm. It exploded on the steps in front of me, and there was my mother, frozen in a shower of gold, just as she was at the moment when the Minotaur began to squeeze her to death.

I couldn't speak. I reached out to touch her, but the light was as hot as a bonfire.

"Yes," Hades said with satisfaction. "I took her. I knew, Percy Jackson, that you would come to bargain with me eventually. Return my helm, and perhaps I will let her go. She is not dead, you know. Not yet. But if you displease me, that will change."

I thought about the pearls in my pocket. Maybe they could get me out of this. If I could just get my mom free . . .

"Ah, the pearls," Hades said, and my blood froze. "Yes, my brother and his little tricks. Bring them forth, Percy Jackson."

My hand moved against my will and brought out the pearls.

"Only three," Hades said. "What a shame. You do realize each only protects a single person. Try to take your mother, then, little godling. And which of your friends will you leave behind to spend eternity with me? Go on. Choose. Or give me the backpack and accept my terms."

I looked at Annabeth and Grover. Their faces were grim.

"We were tricked," I told them. "Set up."

"Yes, but why?" Annabeth asked. "And the voice in the pit—"

"I don't know yet," I said. "But I intend to ask."

"Decide, boy!" Hades yelled.

"Percy." Grover put his hand on my shoulder. "You can't give him the bolt."

"I know that."

"Leave me here," he said. "Use the third pearl on your mom."

"No!"

"I'm a satyr," Grover said. "We don't have souls like humans do. He can torture me until I die, but he won't get me forever. I'll just be reincarnated as a flower or something. It's the best way."

"No." Annabeth drew her bronze knife. "You two go on. Grover, you have to protect Percy. You have to get your searcher's license and start your quest for Pan. Get his mom out of here. I'll cover you. I plan to go down fighting."

"No way," Grover said. "I'm staying behind."

"Think again, goat boy," Annabeth said.

"Stop it, both of you!" I felt like my heart was being ripped in two. They had both been with me through so much. I remembered Grover dive-bombing Medusa in the statue garden, and Annabeth saving us from Cerberus; we'd survived Hephaestus's Waterland ride, the St. Louis Arch, the Lotus Casino. I had spent thousands of miles worried that I'd be betrayed by a friend, but these friends would never do that. They had done nothing but save me, over and over, and now they wanted to sacrifice their lives for my mom.

"I know what to do," I said. "Take these."

I handed them each a pearl.

Annabeth said, "But, Percy . . ."

I turned and faced my mother. I desperately wanted to sacrifice myself and use the last pearl on her, but I knew what she would say. She would never allow it. I had to get the bolt back to Olympus and tell Zeus the truth. I had to stop the war. She would never forgive me if I saved her instead. I thought about the prophecy made at Half-Blood Hill, what seemed like a million years ago. *You will fail to save what matters most in the end.*

"I'm sorry," I told her. "I'll be back. I'll find a way."

The smug look on Hades's face faded. He said, "Godling . . . ?"

"I'll find your helm, Uncle," I told him. "I'll return it. Remember about Charon's pay raise."

"Do not defy me—"

"And it wouldn't hurt to play with Cerberus once in a while. He likes red rubber balls."

"Percy Jackson, you will not—"

I shouted, "Now, guys!"

We smashed the pearls at our feet. For a scary moment, nothing happened.

Hades yelled, "Destroy them!"

The army of skeletons rushed forward, swords out, guns clicking to full automatic. The Furies lunged, their whips bursting into flame.

Just as the skeletons opened fire, the pearl fragments at my feet exploded with a burst of green light and a gust of fresh sea wind. I was encased in a milky white sphere, which was starting to float off the ground.

Annabeth and Grover were right behind me. Spears and bullets sparked harmlessly off the pearl bubbles as we floated up. Hades yelled with such rage, the entire fortress shook and I knew it was not going to be a peaceful night in L.A.

"Look up!" Grover yelled. "We're going to crash!"

Sure enough, we were racing right toward the stalactites, which I figured would pop our bubbles and skewer us.

"How do you control these things?" Annabeth shouted.

"I don't think you do!" I shouted back.

We screamed as the bubbles slammed into the ceiling and . . . Darkness.

Were we dead?

No, I could still feel the racing sensation. We were going up, right through solid rock as easily as an air bubble in water. That was the power of the pearls, I realized—*What belongs to the sea will always return to the sea.*

For a few moments, I couldn't see anything outside the

smooth walls of my sphere, then my pearl broke through on the ocean floor. The two other milky spheres, Annabeth and Grover, kept pace with me as we soared upward through the water. And—*ker-blam!*

We exploded on the surface, in the middle of the Santa Monica Bay, knocking a surfer off his board with an indignant, "Dude!"

I grabbed Grover and hauled him over to a life buoy. I caught Annabeth and dragged her over too. A curious shark was circling us, a great white about eleven feet long.

I said, "Beat it."

The shark turned and raced away.

The surfer screamed something about bad mushrooms and paddled away from us as fast as he could.

Somehow, I knew what time it was: early morning, June 21, the day of the summer solstice.

In the distance, Los Angeles was on fire, plumes of smoke rising from neighborhoods all over the city. There had been an earthquake, all right, and it was Hades's fault. He was probably sending an army of the dead after me right now.

But at the moment, the Underworld wasn't my biggest problem.

I had to get to shore. I had to get Zeus's thunderbolt back to Olympus. Most of all, I had to have a serious conversation with the god who'd tricked me.

I BATTLE MY
JERK RELATIVE

A Coast Guard boat picked us up, but they were too busy to keep us for long, or to wonder how three kids in street clothes had gotten out into the middle of the bay. There was a disaster to mop up. Their radios were jammed with distress calls.

They dropped us off at the Santa Monica Pier with towels around our shoulders and water bottles that said I'M A JUNIOR COAST GUARD! and sped off to save more people.

Our clothes were sopping wet, even mine. When the Coast Guard boat had appeared, I'd silently prayed they wouldn't pick me out of the water and find me perfectly dry, which might've raised some eyebrows. So I'd willed myself to get soaked. Sure enough, my usual waterproof magic had abandoned me. I was also barefoot, because I'd given my shoes to Grover. Better the Coast Guard wonder why one of us was barefoot than wonder why one of us had hooves.

After reaching dry land, we stumbled down the beach, watching the city burn against a beautiful sunrise. I felt as if I'd just come back from the dead—which I had. My backpack was heavy with Zeus's master bolt. My heart was even heavier from seeing my mother.

"I don't believe it," Annabeth said. "We went all that way—"

"It was a trick," I said. "A strategy worthy of Athena."

"Hey," she warned.

"You get it, don't you?"

She dropped her eyes, her anger fading. "Yeah. I get it."

"Well, I don't!" Grover complained. "Would somebody—"

"Percy . . ." Annabeth said. "I'm sorry about your mother. I'm so sorry. . . ."

I pretended not to hear her. If I talked about my mother, I was going to start crying like a little kid.

"The prophecy was right," I said. "'You shall go west and face the god who has turned.' But it wasn't Hades. Hades didn't want war among the Big Three. Someone else pulled off the theft. Someone stole Zeus's master bolt, and Hades's helm, and framed me because I'm Poseidon's kid. Poseidon will get blamed by both sides. By sundown today, there will be a three-way war. And I'll have caused it."

Grover shook his head, mystified. "But who would be that sneaky? Who would want war that bad?"

I stopped in my tracks, looking down the beach. "Gee, let me think."

There he was, waiting for us, in his black leather duster and his sunglasses, an aluminum baseball bat propped on his shoulder. His motorcycle rumbled beside him, its headlight turning the sand red.

"Hey, kid," Ares said, seeming genuinely pleased to see me. "You were supposed to die."

"You tricked me," I said. "*You* stole the helm and the master bolt."

Ares grinned. "Well, now, I didn't steal them personally. Gods taking each other's symbols of power—that's a big no-no. But you're not the only hero in the world who can run errands."

"Who did you use? Clarisse? She was there at the winter solstice."

The idea seemed to amuse him. "Doesn't matter. The point is, kid, you're impeding the war effort. See, you've got to die in the Underworld. Then Old Seaweed will be mad at Hades for killing you. Corpse Breath will have Zeus's master bolt, so Zeus'll be mad at *him*. And Hades is still looking for this . . ."

From his pocket he took out a ski cap—the kind bank robbers wear—and placed it between the handlebars of his bike. Immediately, the cap transformed into an elaborate bronze war helmet.

"The helm of darkness," Grover gasped.

"Exactly," Ares said. "Now where was I? Oh yeah, Hades will be mad at both Zeus and Poseidon, because he doesn't know who took this. Pretty soon, we got a nice little three-way slugfest going."

"But they're your family!" Annabeth protested.

Ares shrugged. "Best kind of war. Always the bloodiest. Nothing like watching your relatives fight, I always say."

"You gave me the backpack in Denver," I said. "The master bolt was in there the whole time."

"Yes and no," Ares said. "It's probably too complicated for your little mortal brain to follow, but the backpack is the master bolt's sheath, just morphed a bit. The bolt is connected to it, sort of like that sword you got, kid. It always returns to your pocket, right?"

I wasn't sure how Ares knew about that, but I guess a god of war had to make it his business to know about weapons.

"Anyway," Ares continued, "I tinkered with the magic a bit, so the bolt would only return to the sheath once you reached the Underworld. You get close to Hades. . . . Bingo, you got mail. If you died along the way—no loss. I still had the weapon."

"But why not just keep the master bolt for yourself?" I said. "Why send it to Hades?"

Ares got a twitch in his jaw. For a moment, it was almost as if he were listening to another voice, deep inside his head. "Why didn't I . . . yeah . . . with that kind of fire-power . . ."

He held the trance for one second . . . two seconds. . . .

I exchanged nervous looks with Annabeth.

Ares's face cleared. "I didn't want the trouble. Better to have you caught redhanded, holding the thing."

"You're lying," I said. "Sending the bolt to the Underworld wasn't your idea, was it?"

"Of course it was!" Smoke drifted up from his sunglasses, as if they were about to catch fire.

"You didn't order the theft," I guessed. "Someone else sent a hero to steal the two items. Then, when Zeus sent you to hunt him down, you caught the thief. But you didn't turn him over to Zeus. Something convinced you to let him go.

You kept the items until another hero could come along and complete the delivery. That thing in the pit is ordering you around."

"I am the god of war! I take orders from no one! I don't have dreams!"

I hesitated. "Who said anything about dreams?"

Ares looked agitated, but he tried to cover it with a smirk.

"Let's get back to the problem at hand, kid. You're alive. I can't have you taking that bolt to Olympus. You just might get those hardheaded idiots to listen to you. So I've got to kill you. Nothing personal."

He snapped his fingers. The sand exploded at his feet and out charged a wild boar, even larger and uglier than the one whose head hung above the door of cabin seven at Camp Half-Blood. The beast pawed the sand, glaring at me with beady eyes as it lowered its razor-sharp tusks and waited for the command to kill.

I stepped into the surf. "Fight me yourself, Ares."

He laughed, but I heard a little edge to his laughter . . . an uneasiness. "You've only got one talent, kid, running away. You ran from the Chimera. You ran from the Underworld. You don't have what it takes."

"Scared?"

"In your adolescent dreams." But his sunglasses were starting to melt from the heat of his eyes. "No direct involvement. Sorry, kid. You're not at my level."

Annabeth said, "Percy, run!"

The giant boar charged.

But I was done running from monsters. Or Hades, or Ares, or anybody.

As the boar rushed me, I uncapped my pen and side-stepped. Riptide appeared in my hands. I slashed upward. The boar's severed right tusk fell at my feet, while the disoriented animal charged into the sea.

I shouted, "Wave!"

Immediately, a wave surged up from nowhere and engulfed the boar, wrapping around it like a blanket. The beast squealed once in terror. Then it was gone, swallowed by the sea.

I turned back to Ares. "Are you going to fight me now?" I asked. "Or are you going to hide behind another pet pig?"

Ares's face was purple with rage. "Watch it, kid. I could turn you into—"

"A cockroach," I said. "Or a tapeworm. Yeah, I'm sure. That'd save you from getting your godly hide whipped, wouldn't it?"

Flames danced along the top of his glasses. "Oh, man, you are really asking to be smashed into a grease spot."

"If I lose, turn me into anything you want. Take the bolt. If I win, the helm and the bolt are mine and *you* have to go away."

Ares sneered.

He swung the baseball bat off his shoulder. "How would you like to get smashed: classic or modern?"

I showed him my sword.

"That's cool, dead boy," he said. "Classic it is." The

baseball bat changed into a huge, two-handed sword. The hilt was a large silver skull with a ruby in its mouth.

"Percy," Annabeth said. "Don't do this. He's a god."

"He's a coward," I told her.

She swallowed. "Wear this, at least. For luck."

She took off her necklace, with her five years' worth of camp beads and the ring from her father, and tied it around my neck.

"Reconciliation," she said. "Athena and Poseidon together."

My face felt a little warm, but I managed a smile. "Thanks."

"And take this," Grover said. He handed me a flattened tin can that he'd probably been saving in his pocket for a thousand miles. "The satyrs stand behind you."

"Grover . . . I don't know what to say."

He patted me on the shoulder. I stuffed the tin can in my back pocket.

"You all done saying good-bye?" Ares came toward me, his black leather duster trailing behind him, his sword glinting like fire in the sunrise. "I've been fighting for eternity, kid. My strength is unlimited and I cannot die. What have you got?"

A smaller ego, I thought, but I said nothing. I kept my feet in the surf, backing into the water up to my ankles. I thought back to what Annabeth had said at the Denver diner, so long ago: *Ares has strength. That's all he has. Even strength has to bow to wisdom sometimes.*

He cleaved downward at my head, but I wasn't there.

My body thought for me. The water seemed to push me into the air and I catapulted over him, slashing as I came down. But Ares was just as quick. He twisted, and the strike that should've caught him directly in the spine was deflected off the end of his sword hilt.

He grinned. "Not bad, not bad."

He slashed again and I was forced to jump onto dry land. I tried to sidestep, to get back to the water, but Ares seemed to know what I wanted. He outmaneuvered me, pressing so hard I had to put all my concentration on not getting sliced into pieces. I kept backing away from the surf. I couldn't find any openings to attack. His sword had a reach several feet longer than Anaklusmos.

Get in close, Luke had told me once, back in our sword class. *When you've got the shorter blade, get in close.*

I stepped inside with a thrust, but Ares was waiting for that. He knocked my blade out of my hands and kicked me in the chest. I went airborne—twenty, maybe thirty feet. I would've broken my back if I hadn't crashed into the soft sand of a dune.

"Percy!" Annabeth yelled. "Cops!"

I was seeing double. My chest felt like it had just been hit with a battering ram, but I managed to get to my feet.

I couldn't look away from Ares for fear he'd slice me in half, but out of the corner of my eye I saw red lights flashing on the shoreline boulevard. Car doors were slamming.

"There, officer!" somebody yelled. "See?"

A gruff cop voice: "Looks like that kid on TV . . . what the heck . . ."

"That guy's armed," another cop said. "Call for backup."

I rolled to one side as Ares's blade slashed the sand.

I ran for my sword, scooped it up, and launched a swipe at Ares's face, only to find my blade deflected again.

Ares seemed to know exactly what I was going to do the moment before I did it.

I stepped back toward the surf, forcing him to follow.

"Admit it, kid," Ares said. "You got no hope. I'm just toying with you."

My senses were working overtime. I now understood what Annabeth had said about ADHD keeping you alive in battle. I was wide awake, noticing every little detail.

I could see where Ares was tensing. I could tell which way he would strike. At the same time, I was aware of Annabeth and Grover, thirty feet to my left. I saw a second cop car pulling up, siren wailing. Spectators, people who had been wandering the streets because of the earthquake, were starting to gather. Among the crowd, I thought I saw a few who were walking with the strange, trotting gait of disguised satyrs. There were shimmering forms of spirits, too, as if the dead had risen from Hades to watch the battle. I heard the flap of leathery wings circling somewhere above.

More sirens.

I stepped farther into the water, but Ares was fast. The tip of his blade ripped my sleeve and grazed my forearm.

A police voice on a megaphone said, "Drop the guns! Set them on the ground. Now!"

Guns?

I looked at Ares's weapon, and it seemed to be flickering; sometimes it looked like a shotgun, sometimes a two-handed sword. I didn't know what the humans were seeing in my hands, but I was pretty sure it wouldn't make them like me.

Ares turned to glare at our spectators, which gave me a moment to breathe. There were five police cars now, and a line of officers crouching behind them, pistols trained on us.

"This is a private matter!" Ares bellowed. "Be gone!"

He swept his hand, and a wall of red flame rolled across the patrol cars. The police barely had time to dive for cover before their vehicles exploded. The crowd behind them scattered, screaming.

Ares roared with laughter. "Now, little hero. Let's add you to the barbecue."

He slashed. I deflected his blade. I got close enough to strike, tried to fake him out with a feint, but my blow was knocked aside. The waves were hitting me in the back now. Ares was up to his thighs, wading in after me.

I felt the rhythm of the sea, the waves growing larger as the tide rolled in, and suddenly I had an idea. *Little waves*, I thought. And the water behind me seemed to recede. I was holding back the tide by force of will, but tension was building, like carbonation behind a cork.

Ares came toward, grinning confidently. I lowered my blade, as if I were too exhausted to go on. *Wait for it*, I told the sea. The pressure now was almost lifting me off my feet. Ares raised his sword. I released the tide and jumped, rocketing straight over Ares on a wave.

A six-foot wall of water smashed him full in the face, leaving him cursing and sputtering with a mouth full of seaweed. I landed behind him with a splash and feinted toward his head, as I'd done before. He turned in time to raise his sword, but this time he was disoriented, he didn't anticipate the trick. I changed direction, lunged to the side, and stabbed Riptide straight down into the water, sending the point through the god's heel.

The roar that followed made Hades's earthquake look like a minor event. The very sea was blasted back from Ares, leaving a wet circle of sand fifty feet wide.

Ichor, the golden blood of the gods, flowed from a gash in the war god's boot. The expression on his face was beyond hatred. It was pain, shock, complete disbelief that he'd been wounded.

He limped toward me, muttering ancient Greek curses. Something stopped him.

It was as if a cloud covered the sun, but worse. Light faded. Sound and color drained away. A cold, heavy presence passed over the beach, slowing time, dropping the temperature to freezing, and making me feel like life was hopeless, fighting was useless.

The darkness lifted.

Ares looked stunned.

Police cars were burning behind us. The crowd of spectators had fled. Annabeth and Grover stood on the beach, in shock, watching the water flood back around Ares's feet, his glowing golden ichor dissipating in the tide.

Ares lowered his sword.

"You have made an enemy, godling," he told me. "You have sealed your fate. Every time you raise your blade in battle, every time you hope for success, you will feel my curse. Beware, Perseus Jackson. Beware."

His body began to glow.

"Percy!" Annabeth shouted. "Don't watch!"

I turned away as the god Ares revealed his true immortal form. I somehow knew that if I looked, I would disintegrate into ashes.

The light died.

I looked back. Ares was gone. The tide rolled out to reveal Hades's bronze helm of darkness. I picked it up and walked toward my friends.

But before I got there, I heard the flapping of leathery wings. Three evil-looking grandmothers with lace hats and fiery whips drifted down from the sky and landed in front of me.

The middle Fury, the one who had been Mrs. Dodds, stepped forward. Her fangs were bared, but for once she didn't look threatening. She looked more disappointed, as if she'd been planning to have me for supper, but had decided I might give her indigestion.

"We saw the whole thing," she hissed. "So . . . it truly was not you?"

I tossed her the helmet, which she caught in surprise.

"Return that to Lord Hades," I said. "Tell him the truth. Tell him to call off the war."

She hesitated, then ran a forked tongue over her green, leathery lips. "Live well, Percy Jackson. Become a true hero.

Because if you do not, if you ever come into my clutches again . . ."

She cackled, savoring the idea. Then she and her sisters rose on their bats' wings, fluttered into the smoke-filled sky, and disappeared.

I joined Grover and Annabeth, who were staring at me in amazement.

"Percy . . ." Grover said. "That was so incredibly . . ."

"Terrifying," said Annabeth.

"Cool!" Grover corrected.

I didn't feel terrified. I certainly didn't feel cool. I was tired and sore and completely drained of energy.

"Did you guys feel that . . . whatever it was?" I asked.

They both nodded uneasily.

"Must've been the Furies overhead," Grover said.

But I wasn't so sure. Something had stopped Ares from killing me, and whatever could do that was a lot stronger than the Furies.

I looked at Annabeth, and an understanding passed between us. I knew now what was in that pit, what had spoken from the entrance of Tartarus.

I reclaimed my backpack from Grover and looked inside. The master bolt was still there. Such a small thing to almost cause World War III.

"We have to get back to New York," I said. "By tonight."

"That's impossible," Annabeth said, "unless we—"

"Fly," I agreed.

She stared at me. "Fly, like, in an airplane, which you

were warned never to do lest Zeus strike you out of the sky, *and* carrying a weapon that has more destructive power than a nuclear bomb?"

"Yeah," I said. "Pretty much exactly like that. Come on."

TWENTY-ONE

I SETTLE MY TAB

It's funny how humans can wrap their mind around things and fit them into their version of reality. Chiron had told me that long ago. As usual, I didn't appreciate his wisdom until much later.

According to the L.A. news, the explosion at the Santa Monica beach had been caused when a crazy kidnapper fired a shotgun at a police car. He accidentally hit a gas main that had ruptured during the earthquake.

This crazy kidnapper (a.k.a. Ares) was the same man who had abducted me and two other adolescents in New York and brought us across country on a ten-day odyssey of terror.

Poor little Percy Jackson wasn't an international criminal after all. He'd caused a commotion on that Greyhound bus in New Jersey trying to get away from his captor (and afterward, witnesses would even swear they had seen the leather-clad man on the bus—"Why didn't I remember him before?"). The crazy man had caused the explosion in the St. Louis Arch. After all, no kid could've done that. A concerned waitress in Denver had seen the man threatening his abductees outside her diner, gotten a friend to take a photo, and notified the police. Finally, brave Percy Jackson (I was beginning to like this kid) had stolen a gun from his captor in Los Angeles and battled him shotgun-to-rifle on the beach. Police had arrived just in time. But in the spectacular explosion, five police cars had been destroyed and the captor had fled. No fatalities had occurred. Percy Jackson and his two friends were safely in police custody.

The reporters fed us this whole story. We just nodded and acted tearful and exhausted (which wasn't hard), and played victimized kids for the cameras.

"All I want," I said, choking back my tears, "is to see my loving stepfather again. Every time I saw him on TV, calling me a delinquent punk, I knew . . . somehow . . . we would be okay. And I know he'll want to reward each and every person in this beautiful city of Los Angeles with a free major appliance from his store. Here's the phone number." The police and reporters were so moved that they passed around the hat and raised money for three tickets on the next plane to New York.

I knew there was no choice but to fly. I hoped Zeus would cut me some slack, considering the circumstances. But it was still hard to force myself on board the flight.

Takeoff was a nightmare. Every spot of turbulence was scarier than a Greek monster. I didn't unclench my hands from the armrests until we touched down safely at La Guardia. The local press was waiting for us outside security, but we managed to evade them thanks to Annabeth, who lured them away in her invisible Yankees cap, shouting, "They're over by the frozen yogurt! Come on!," then rejoined us at baggage claim.

We split up at the taxi stand. I told Annabeth and Grover to get back to Half-Blood Hill and let Chiron know what had happened. They protested, and it was hard to let them go after all we'd been through, but I knew I had to do this last part of the quest by myself. If things went wrong, if the gods didn't believe me . . . I wanted Annabeth and Grover to survive to tell Chiron the truth.

I hopped in a taxi and headed into Manhattan.

Thirty minutes later, I walked into the lobby of the Empire State Building.

I must have looked like a homeless kid, with my tattered clothes and my scraped-up face. I hadn't slept in at least twenty-four hours.

I went up to the guard at the front desk and said, "Six hundredth floor."

He was reading a huge book with a picture of a wizard on the front. I wasn't much into fantasy, but the book must've been good, because the guard took a while to look up. "No such floor, kiddo."

"I need an audience with Zeus."

He gave me a vacant smile. "Sorry?"

"You heard me."

I was about to decide this guy was just a regular mortal, and I'd better run for it before he called the straitjacket patrol, when he said, "No appointment, no audience, kiddo. Lord Zeus doesn't see anyone unannounced."

"Oh, I think he'll make an exception." I slipped off my backpack and unzipped the top.

The guard looked inside at the metal cylinder, not getting what it was for a few seconds. Then his face went pale. "That isn't . . ."

"Yes, it is," I promised. "You want me take it out and—"

"No! No!" He scrambled out of his seat, fumbled around his desk for a key card, then handed it to me. "Insert this in the security slot. Make sure nobody else is in the elevator with you."

I did as he told me. As soon as the elevator doors closed, I slipped the key into the slot. The card disappeared and a new button appeared on the console, a red one that said 600.

I pressed it and waited, and waited.

Muzak played. "Raindrops keep falling on my head. . . ."

Finally, *ding*. The doors slid open. I stepped out and almost had a heart attack.

I was standing on a narrow stone walkway in the middle of the air. Below me was Manhattan, from the height of an airplane. In front of me, white marble steps wound up the spine of a cloud, into the sky. My eyes followed the stairway to its end, where my brain just could not accept what I saw.

Look again, my brain said.

We're looking, my eyes insisted. It's really there.

From the top of the clouds rose the decapitated peak of a mountain, its summit covered with snow. Clinging to the mountainside were dozens of multileveled palaces—a city of mansions—all with white-columned porticos, gilded terraces, and bronze braziers glowing with a thousand fires.

Roads wound crazily up to the peak, where the largest palace gleamed against the snow. Precariously perched gardens bloomed with olive trees and rosebushes. I could make out an open-air market filled with colorful tents, a stone amphitheater built on one side of the mountain, a hippodrome and a coliseum on the other. It was an Ancient Greek city, except it wasn't in ruins. It was new, and clean, and colorful, the way Athens must've looked twenty-five hundred years ago.

This place can't be here, I told myself. The tip of a mountain hanging over New York City like a billion-ton asteroid? How could something like that be anchored above the Empire State Building, in plain sight of millions of people, and not get noticed?

But here it was. And here I was.

My trip through Olympus was a daze. I passed some giggling wood nymphs who threw olives at me from their garden. Hawkers in the market offered to sell me ambrosia-on-a-stick, and a new shield, and a genuine glitter-weave replica of the Golden Fleece, as seen on Hephaestus-TV. The nine muses were tuning their instruments for a concert in the park while a small crowd gathered—satyrs and naiads and a bunch of good-looking teenagers who might've been minor gods and goddesses. Nobody seemed worried about an impending civil war. In fact, everybody seemed in a festive mood. Several of them turned to watch me pass, and whispered to themselves.

I climbed the main road, toward the big palace at the peak. It was a reverse copy of the palace in the Underworld.

There, everything had been black and bronze. Here, everything glittered white and silver.

I realized Hades must've built his palace to resemble this one. He wasn't welcomed in Olympus except on the winter solstice, so he'd built his own Olympus underground. Despite my bad experience with him, I felt a little sorry for the guy. To be banished from this place seemed really unfair. It would make anybody bitter.

Steps led up to a central courtyard. Past that, the throne room.

Room really isn't the right word. The place made Grand Central Station look like a broom closet. Massive columns rose to a domed ceiling, which was gilded with moving constellations.

Twelve thrones, built for beings the size of Hades, were arranged in an inverted U, just like the cabins at Camp Half-Blood. An enormous fire crackled in the central hearth pit. The thrones were empty except for two at the end: the head throne on the right, and the one to its immediate left. I didn't have to be told who the two gods were that were sitting there, waiting for me to approach. I came toward them, my legs trembling.

The gods were in giant human form, as Hades had been, but I could barely look at them without feeling a tingle, as if my body were starting to burn. Zeus, the Lord of the Gods, wore a dark blue pinstriped suit. He sat on a simple throne of solid platinum. He had a well-trimmed beard, marbled gray and black like a storm cloud. His face was proud and handsome and grim, his eyes rainy gray.

As I got nearer to him, the air crackled and smelled of ozone.

The god sitting next to him was his brother, without a doubt, but he was dressed very differently. He reminded me of a beachcomber from Key West. He wore leather sandals, khaki Bermuda shorts, and a Tommy Bahama shirt with coconuts and parrots all over it. His skin was deeply tanned, his hands scarred like an old-time fisherman's. His hair was black, like mine. His face had that same brooding look that had always gotten me branded a rebel. But his eyes, sea-green like mine, were surrounded by sun-crinkles that told me he smiled a lot, too.

His throne was a deep-sea fisherman's chair. It was the simple swiveling kind, with a black leather seat and a built-in holster for a fishing pole. Instead of a pole, the holster held a bronze trident, flickering with green light around the tips.

The gods weren't moving or speaking, but there was tension in the air, as if they'd just finished an argument.

I approached the fisherman's throne and knelt at his feet. "Father." I dared not look up. My heart was racing. I could feel the energy emanating from the two gods. If I said the wrong thing, I had no doubt they could blast me into dust.

To my left, Zeus spoke. "Should you not address the master of this house first, boy?"

I kept my head down, and waited.

"Peace, brother," Poseidon finally said. His voice stirred my oldest memories: that warm glow I remembered as a baby, the sensation of this god's hand on my forehead. "The boy defers to his father. This is only right."

"You still claim him then?" Zeus asked, menacingly. "You claim this child whom you sired against our sacred oath?"

"I have admitted my wrongdoing," Poseidon said. "Now I would hear him speak."

Wrongdoing.

A lump welled up in my throat. Was that all I was? A wrongdoing? The result of a god's mistake?

"I have spared him once already," Zeus grumbled. "Daring to fly through my domain . . . pah! I should have blasted him out of the sky for his impudence."

"And risk destroying your own master bolt?" Poseidon asked calmly. "Let us hear him out, brother."

Zeus grumbled some more. "I shall listen," he decided. "Then I shall make up my mind whether or not to cast this boy down from Olympus."

"Perseus," Poseidon said. "Look at me."

I did, and I wasn't sure what I saw in his face. There was no clear sign of love or approval. Nothing to encourage me. It was like looking at the ocean: some days, you could tell what mood it was in. Most days, though, it was unreadable, mysterious.

I got the feeling Poseidon really didn't know what to think of me. He didn't know whether he was happy to have me as a son or not. In a strange way, I was glad that Poseidon was so distant. If he'd tried to apologize, or told me he loved me, or even smiled, it would've felt fake. Like a human dad, making some lame excuse for not being around. I could live with that. After all, I wasn't sure about him yet, either.

"Address Lord Zeus, boy," Poseidon told me. "Tell him your story."

So I told Zeus everything, just as it had happened. I took out the metal cylinder, which began sparking in the Sky God's presence, and laid it at his feet.

There was a long silence, broken only by the crackle of the hearth fire.

Zeus opened his palm. The lightning bolt flew into it. As he closed his fist, the metallic points flared with electricity, until he was holding what looked more like the classic thunderbolt, a twenty-foot javelin of arcing, hissing energy that made the hairs on my scalp rise.

"I sense the boy tells the truth," Zeus muttered. "But that Ares would do such a thing . . . it is most unlike him."

"He is proud and impulsive," Poseidon said. "It runs in the family."

"Lord?" I asked.

They both said, "Yes?"

"Ares didn't act alone. Someone else—something else— came up with the idea."

I described my dreams, and the feeling I'd had on the beach, that momentary breath of evil that had seemed to stop the world, and made Ares back off from killing me.

"In the dreams," I said, "the voice told me to bring the bolt to the Underworld. Ares hinted that he'd been having dreams, too. I think he was being used, just as I was, to start a war."

"You are accusing Hades, after all?" Zeus asked.

"No," I said. "I mean, Lord Zeus, I've been in the presence of Hades. This feeling on the beach was different. It was the same thing I felt when I got close to that pit. That was the entrance to Tartarus, wasn't it? Something powerful and evil is stirring down there . . . something even older than the gods."

Poseidon and Zeus looked at each other. They had a quick, intense discussion in Ancient Greek. I only caught one word. *Father.*

Poseidon made some kind of suggestion, but Zeus cut him off. Poseidon tried to argue. Zeus held up his hand angrily. "We will speak of this no more," Zeus said. "I must go personally to purify this thunderbolt in the waters of Lemnos, to remove the human taint from its metal."

He rose and looked at me. His expression softened just a fraction of a degree. "You have done me a service, boy. Few heroes could have accomplished as much."

"I had help, sir," I said. "Grover Underwood and Annabeth Chase—"

"To show you my thanks, I shall spare your life. I do not trust you, Perseus Jackson. I do not like what your arrival means for the future of Olympus. But for the sake of peace in the family, I shall let you live."

"Um . . . thank you, sir."

"Do not presume to fly again. Do not let me find you

here when I return. Otherwise you shall taste this bolt. And it shall be your last sensation."

Thunder shook the palace. With a blinding flash of lightning, Zeus was gone.

I was alone in the throne room with my father.

"Your uncle," Poseidon sighed, "has always had a flair for dramatic exits. I think he would've done well as the god of theater."

An uncomfortable silence.

"Sir," I said, "what was in that pit?"

Poseidon regarded me. "Have you not guessed?"

"Kronos," I said. "The king of the Titans."

Even in the throne room of Olympus, far away from Tartarus, the name *Kronos* darkened the room, made the hearth fire seem not quite so warm on my back.

Poseidon gripped his trident. "In the First War, Percy, Zeus cut our father Kronos into a thousand pieces, just as Kronos had done to his own father, Ouranos. Zeus cast Kronos's remains into the darkest pit of Tartarus. The Titan army was scattered, their mountain fortress on Etna destroyed, their monstrous allies driven to the farthest corners of the earth. And yet Titans cannot die, any more than we gods can. Whatever is left of Kronos is still alive in some hideous way, still conscious in his eternal pain, still hungering for power."

"He's healing," I said. "He's coming back."

Poseidon shook his head. "From time to time, over the eons, Kronos has stirred. He enters men's nightmares and breathes evil thoughts. He wakens restless monsters from the depths. But to suggest he could rise from the pit is another thing."

"That's what he intends, Father. That's what he said."

Poseidon was silent for a long time.

"Lord Zeus has closed discussion on this matter. He will not allow talk of Kronos. You have completed your quest, child. That is all you need to do."

"But—" I stopped myself. Arguing would do no good. It would very possibly anger the only god who I had on my side. "As . . . as you wish, Father."

A faint smile played on his lips. "Obedience does not come naturally to you, does it?"

"No . . . sir."

"I must take some blame for that, I suppose. The sea does not like to be restrained." He rose to his full height and took up his trident. Then he shimmered and became the size of a regular man, standing directly in front of me. "You must go, child. But first, know that your mother has returned."

I stared at him, completely stunned. "My mother?"

"You will find her at home. Hades sent her when you recovered his helm. Even the Lord of Death pays his debts."

My heart was pounding. I couldn't believe it. "Do you . . . would you . . ."

I wanted to ask if Poseidon would come with me to see her, but then I realized that was ridiculous. I imagined loading the God of the Sea into a taxi and taking him to the Upper East Side. If he'd wanted to see my mom all these years, he would have. And there was Smelly Gabe to think about.

Poseidon's eyes took on a little sadness. "When you return home, Percy, you must make an important choice. You will find a package waiting in your room."

"A package?"

"You will understand when you see it. No one can choose your path, Percy. You must decide."

I nodded, though I didn't know what he meant.

"Your mother is a queen among women," Poseidon said wistfully. "I had not met such a mortal woman in a thousand years. Still . . . I am sorry you were born, child. I have brought you a hero's fate, and a hero's fate is never happy. It is never anything but tragic."

I tried not to feel hurt. Here was my own dad, telling me he was sorry I'd been born. "I don't mind, Father."

"Not yet, perhaps," he said. "Not yet. But it was an unforgivable mistake on my part."

"I'll leave you then." I bowed awkwardly. "I—I won't bother you again."

I was five steps away when he called, "Perseus."

I turned.

There was a different light in his eyes, a fiery kind of pride. "You did well, Perseus. Do not misunderstand me. Whatever else you do, know that you are mine. You are a true son of the Sea God."

As I walked back through the city of the gods, conversations stopped. The muses paused their concert. People and satyrs and naiads all turned toward me, their faces filled with respect and gratitude, and as I passed, they knelt, as if I were some kind of hero.

Fifteen minutes later, still in a trance, I was back on the streets of Manhattan.

I caught a taxi to my mom's apartment, rang the doorbell, and there she was—my beautiful mother, smelling of peppermint and licorice, the weariness and worry evaporating from her face as soon as she saw me.

"Percy! Oh, thank goodness. Oh, my baby."

She crushed the air right out of me. We stood in the hallway as she cried and ran her hands through my hair.

I'll admit it—my eyes were a little misty, too. I was shaking, I was so relieved to see her.

She told me she'd just appeared at the apartment that morning, scaring Gabe half out of his wits. She didn't remember anything since the Minotaur, and couldn't believe it when Gabe told her I was a wanted criminal, traveling across the country, blowing up national monuments. She'd been going out of her mind with worry all day because she hadn't heard the news. Gabe had forced her to go into work, saying she had a month's salary to make up and she'd better get started.

I swallowed back my anger and told her my own story. I tried to make it sound less scary than it had been, but that wasn't easy. I was just getting to the fight with Ares when Gabe's voice interrupted from the living room. "Hey, Sally! That meat loaf done yet or what?"

She closed her eyes. "He isn't going to be happy to see you, Percy. The store got half a million phone calls today from Los Angeles . . . something about free appliances."

"Oh, yeah. About that . . ."

She managed a weak smile. "Just don't make him angrier, all right? Come on."

In the month I'd been gone, the apartment had turned into Gabeland. Garbage was ankle deep on the carpet. The sofa had been reupholstered in beer cans. Dirty socks and underwear hung off the lampshades.

Gabe and three of his big goony friends were playing poker at the table.

When Gabe saw me, his cigar dropped out of his mouth. His face got redder than lava. "You got nerve coming here, you little punk. I thought the police—"

"He's not a fugitive after all," my mom interjected. "Isn't that wonderful, Gabe?"

Gabe looked back and forth between us. He didn't seem to think my homecoming was so wonderful.

"Bad enough I had to give back your life insurance money, Sally," he growled. "Get me the phone. I'll call the cops."

"Gabe, no!"

He raised his eyebrows. "Did you just say 'no'? You think I'm gonna put up with this punk again? I can still press charges against him for ruining my Camaro."

"But—"

He raised his hand, and my mother flinched.

For the first time, I realized something. Gabe had hit my mother. I didn't know when, or how much. But I was sure he'd done it. Maybe it had been going on for years, when I wasn't around.

A balloon of anger started expanding in my chest. I came toward Gabe, instinctively taking my pen out of my pocket.

He just laughed. "What, punk? You gonna write on me? You touch me, and you are going to jail forever, you understand?"

"Hey, Gabe," his friend Eddie interrupted. "He's just a kid."

Gabe looked at him resentfully and mimicked in a falsetto voice: "*Just a kid.*"

His other friends laughed like idiots.

"I'll be nice to you, punk." Gabe showed me his tobacco-stained teeth. "I'll give you five minutes to get your stuff and clear out. After that, I call the police."

"Gabe!" my mother pleaded.

"He ran away," Gabe told her. "Let him stay gone."

I was itching to uncap Riptide, but even if I did, the blade wouldn't hurt humans. And Gabe, by the loosest definition, was human.

My mother took my arm. "Please, Percy. Come on. We'll go to your room."

I let her pull me away, my hands still trembling with rage.

My room had been completely filled with Gabe's junk. There were stacks of used car batteries, a rotting bouquet of sympathy flowers with a card from somebody who'd seen his Barbara Walters interview.

"Gabe is just upset, honey," my mother told me. "I'll talk to him later. I'm sure it will work out."

"Mom, it'll never work out. Not as long as Gabe's here."

She wrung her hands nervously. "I can . . . I'll take you to work with me for the rest of the summer. In the fall, maybe there's another boarding school—"

"Mom."

She lowered her eyes. "I'm trying, Percy. I just . . . I need some time."

A package appeared on my bed. At least, I could've sworn it hadn't been there a moment before.

It was a battered cardboard box about the right size to fit a basketball. The address on the mailing slip was in my own handwriting:

> The Gods
> Mount Olympus
> 600th Floor,
> Empire State Building
> New York, NY
>
> With best wishes,
> PERCY JACKSON

Over the top in black marker, in a man's clear, bold print, was the address of our apartment, and the words: RETURN TO SENDER.

Suddenly I understood what Poseidon had told me on Olympus.

A package. A decision.

Whatever else you do, know that you are mine. You are a true son of the Sea God.

I looked at my mother. "Mom, do you want Gabe gone?"

"Percy, it isn't that simple. I—"

"Mom, just tell me. That jerk has been hitting you. Do you want him gone or not?"

She hesitated, then nodded almost imperceptibly. "Yes, Percy. I do. And I'm trying to get up my courage to tell him. But you can't do this for me. You can't solve my problems."

I looked at the box.

I *could* solve her problem. I wanted to slice that package open, plop it on the poker table, and take out what was inside. I could start my very own statue garden, right there in the living room.

That's what a Greek hero would do in the stories, I thought. That's what Gabe deserves.

But a hero's story always ended in tragedy. Poseidon had told me that.

I remembered the Underworld. I thought about Gabe's spirit drifting forever in the Fields of Asphodel, or condemned to some hideous torture behind the barbed wire of the Fields of Punishment—an eternal poker game, sitting up to his waist in boiling oil listening to opera music. Did I have the right to send someone there? Even Gabe?

A month ago, I wouldn't have hesitated. Now . . .

"I can do it," I told my mom. "One look inside this box, and he'll never bother you again."

She glanced at the package, and seemed to understand immediately. "No, Percy," she said, stepping away. "You can't."

"Poseidon called you a queen," I told her. "He said he hadn't met a woman like you in a thousand years."

Her cheeks flushed. "Percy—"

"You deserve better than this, Mom. You should go to college, get your degree. You can write your novel, meet a nice guy maybe, live in a nice house. You don't need to protect me anymore by staying with Gabe. Let me get rid of him."

She wiped a tear off her cheek. "You sound so much like your father," she said. "He offered to stop the tide for me once. He offered to build me a palace at the bottom of the sea. He thought he could solve all my problems with a wave of his hand."

"What's wrong with that?"

Her multicolored eyes seemed to search inside me. "I think you know, Percy. I think you're enough like me to understand. If my life is going to mean anything, I have to live it myself. I can't let a god take care of me . . . or my son. I have to . . . find the courage on my own. Your quest has reminded me of that."

We listened to the sound of poker chips and swearing, ESPN from the living room television.

"I'll leave the box," I said. "If he threatens you . . ."

She looked pale, but she nodded. "Where will you go, Percy?"

"Half-Blood Hill."

"For the summer . . . or forever?"

"I guess that depends."

We locked eyes, and I sensed that we had an agreement.

We would see how things stood at the end of the summer.

She kissed my forehead. "You'll be a hero, Percy. You'll be the greatest of all."

I took one last look around my bedroom. I had a feeling I'd never see it again. Then I walked with my mother to the front door.

"Leaving so soon, punk?" Gabe called after me. "Good riddance."

I had one last twinge of doubt. How could I turn down the perfect chance to take revenge on him? I was leaving here without saving my mother.

"Hey, Sally," he yelled. "What about that meat loaf, huh?"

A steely look of anger flared in my mother's eyes, and I thought, just maybe, I was leaving her in good hands after all. Her own.

"The meat loaf is coming right up, dear," she told Gabe. "Meat loaf surprise."

She looked at me, and winked.

The last thing I saw as the door swung closed was my mother staring at Gabe, as if she were contemplating how he would look as a garden statue.

TWENTY-TWO

THE PROPHECY COMES TRUE

We were the first heroes to return alive to Half-Blood Hill since Luke, so of course everybody treated us as if we'd won some reality-TV contest. According to camp tradition, we wore laurel wreaths to a big feast prepared in our honor, then led a procession down to the bonfire, where we got to burn the burial shrouds our cabins had made for us in our absence.

Annabeth's shroud was so beautiful—gray silk with embroidered owls—I told her it seemed a shame not to bury her in it. She punched me and told me to shut up.

Being the son of Poseidon, I didn't have any cabin mates, so the Ares cabin had volunteered to make my shroud. They'd taken an old bedsheet and painted smiley faces with X'ed-out eyes around the border, and the word LOSER painted really big in the middle.

It was fun to burn.

As Apollo's cabin led the sing-along and passed out s'mores, I was surrounded by my old Hermes cabinmates, Annabeth's friends from Athena, and Grover's satyr buddies, who were admiring the brand-new searcher's license he'd received from the Council of Cloven Elders. The council had called Grover's performance on the quest "Brave to the point of indigestion. Horns-and-whiskers above anything we have seen in the past."

The only ones not in a party mood were Clarisse and her cabinmates, whose poisonous looks told me they'd never forgive me for disgracing their dad.

That was okay with me.

Even Dionysus's welcome-home speech wasn't enough to dampen my spirits. "Yes, yes, so the little brat didn't get himself killed and now he'll have an even bigger head. Well, huzzah for that. In other announcements, there will be *no* canoe races this Saturday. . . ."

I moved back into cabin three, but it didn't feel so lonely anymore. I had my friends to train with during the day. At night, I lay awake and listened to the sea, knowing my father was out there. Maybe he wasn't quite sure about me yet, maybe he hadn't even wanted me born, but he was watching. And so far, he was proud of what I'd done.

As for my mother, she had a chance at a new life. Her letter arrived a week after I got back to camp. She told me Gabe had left mysteriously—disappeared off the face of the planet, in fact. She'd reported him missing to the police, but she had a funny feeling they would never find him.

On a completely unrelated subject, she'd sold her first life-size concrete sculpture, entitled *The Poker Player*, to a collector, through an art gallery in Soho. She'd gotten so much money for it, she'd put a deposit down on a new apartment and made a payment on her first semester's tuition at NYU. The Soho gallery was clamoring for more of her work, which they called "a huge step forward in super-ugly neorealism."

But don't worry, my mom wrote. *I'm done with sculpture. I've disposed of that box of tools you left me. It's time for me to turn to writing.*

At the bottom, she wrote a P.S.: *Percy, I've found a good private school here in the city. I've put a deposit down to hold you a spot, in case you want to enroll for seventh grade. You could live at home. But if you want to go year-round at Half-Blood Hill, I'll understand.*

I folded the note carefully and set it on my bedside table. Every night before I went to sleep, I read it again, and I tried to decide how to answer her.

On the Fourth of July, the whole camp gathered at the beach for a fireworks display by cabin nine. Being Hephaestus's kids, they weren't going to settle for a few lame red-white-and-blue explosions. They'd anchored a barge offshore and loaded it with rockets the size of Patriot missiles. According to Annabeth, who'd seen the show before, the blasts would be sequenced so tightly they'd look like frames of animation across the sky. The finale was supposed to be a couple of hundred-foot-tall Spartan warriors who would crackle to life above the ocean, fight a battle, then explode into a million colors.

As Annabeth and I were spreading a picnic blanket, Grover showed up to tell us good-bye. He was dressed in his usual jeans and T-shirt and sneakers, but in the last few weeks he'd started to look older, almost high-school age. His goatee had gotten thicker. He'd put on weight. His horns had grown at least an inch, so he now had to wear his rasta cap all the time to pass as human.

"I'm off," he said. "I just came to say . . . well, you know."

I tried to feel happy for him. After all, it wasn't every day a satyr got permission to go look for the great god Pan. But it was hard saying good-bye. I'd only known Grover a year, yet he was my oldest friend.

Annabeth gave him a hug. She told him to keep his fake feet on.

I asked him where he was going to search first.

"Kind of a secret," he said, looking embarrassed. "I wish you could come with me, guys, but humans and Pan . . ."

"We understand," Annabeth said. "You got enough tin cans for the trip?"

"Yeah."

"And you remembered your reed pipes?"

"Jeez, Annabeth," he grumbled. "You're like an old mama goat."

But he didn't really sound annoyed.

He gripped his walking stick and slung a backpack over his shoulder. He looked like any hitchhiker you might see on an American highway—nothing like the little runty boy I used to defend from bullies at Yancy Academy.

"Well," he said, "wish me luck."

He gave Annabeth another hug. He clapped me on the shoulder, then headed back through the dunes.

Fireworks exploded to life overhead: Hercules killing

the Nemean lion, Artemis chasing the boar, George Washington (who, by the way, was a son of Athena) crossing the Delaware.

"Hey, Grover," I called.

He turned at the edge of the woods.

"Wherever you're going—I hope they make good enchiladas."

Grover grinned, and then he was gone, the trees closing around him.

"We'll see him again," Annabeth said.

I tried to believe it. The fact that no searcher had ever come back in two thousand years . . . well, I decided not to think about that. Grover would be the first. He had to be.

July passed.

I spent my days devising new strategies for capture-the-flag and making alliances with the other cabins to keep the banner out of Ares's hands. I got to the top of the climbing wall for the first time without getting scorched by lava.

From time to time, I'd walk past the Big House, glance up at the attic windows, and think about the Oracle. I tried to convince myself that its prophecy had come to completion.

You shall go west, and face the god who has turned.

Been there, done that—even though the traitor god had turned out to be Ares rather than Hades.

You shall find what was stolen, and see it safe returned.

Check. One master bolt delivered. One helm of darkness back on Hades's oily head.

You shall be betrayed by one who calls you a friend.

This line still bothered me. Ares had pretended to be my friend, then betrayed me. That must be what the Oracle meant. . . .

And you shall fail to save what matters most, in the end.

I *had* failed to save my mom, but only because I'd let her save herself, and I knew that was the right thing.

So why was I still uneasy?

The last night of the summer session came all too quickly.

The campers had one last meal together. We burned part of our dinner for the gods. At the bonfire, the senior counselors awarded the end-of-summer beads.

I got my own leather necklace, and when I saw the bead for my first summer, I was glad the firelight covered my blushing. The design was pitch black, with a sea-green trident shimmering in the center.

"The choice was unanimous," Luke announced. "This bead commemorates the first Son of the Sea God at this camp, and the quest he undertook into the darkest part of the Underworld to stop a war!"

The entire camp got to their feet and cheered. Even Ares's cabin felt obliged to stand. Athena's cabin steered Annabeth to the front so she could share in the applause.

I'm not sure I'd ever felt as happy or sad as I did at that moment. I'd finally found a family, people who cared about me and thought I'd done something right. And in the morning, most of them would be leaving for the year.

* * *

The next morning, I found a form letter on my bedside table.

I knew Dionysus must've filled it out, because he stubbornly insisted on getting my name wrong:

> Dear _____ Peter Johnson _____ ,
> If you intend to stay at Camp Half-Blood year-round, you must inform the Big House by noon today. If you do not announce your intentions, we will assume you have vacated your cabin or died a horrible death. Cleaning harpies will begin work at sundown. They will be authorized to eat any unregistered campers. All personal articles left behind will be incinerated in the lava pit.
> Have a nice day!
> Mr. D (Dionysus)
> Camp Director, Olympian Council #12

That's another thing about ADHD. Deadlines just aren't real to me until I'm staring one in the face. Summer was over, and I still hadn't answered my mother, or the camp, about whether I'd be staying. Now I had only a few hours to decide.

The decision should have been easy. I mean, nine months of hero training or nine months of sitting in a classroom—duh.

But there was my mom to consider. For the first time, I had the chance to live with her for a whole year, without Gabe. I had a chance be at home and knock around the city in my free time. I remembered what Annabeth had said so long ago on our quest: *The real world is where the monsters are. That's where you learn whether you're any good or not.*

I thought about the fate of Thalia, daughter of Zeus. I wondered how many monsters would attack me if I left Half-Blood Hill. If I stayed in one place for a whole school year, without Chiron or my friends around to help me, would my mother and I even survive until the next summer? That was assuming the spelling tests and five-paragraph essays didn't kill me. I decided I'd go down to the arena and do some sword practice. Maybe that would clear my head.

The campgrounds were mostly deserted, shimmering in the August heat. All the campers were in their cabins packing up, or running around with brooms and mops, getting ready for final inspection. Argus was helping some of the Aphrodite kids haul their Gucci suitcases and makeup kits over the hill, where the camp's shuttle bus would be waiting to take them to the airport.

Don't think about leaving yet, I told myself. Just train.

I got to the sword-fighters arena and found that Luke had had the same idea. His gym bag was plopped at the edge of the stage. He was working solo, whaling on battle dummies with a sword I'd never seen before. It must've been a regular steel blade, because he was slashing the dummies' heads right off, stabbing through their straw-stuffed guts. His orange counselor's shirt was dripping with sweat. His expression was so intense, his life might've really been in danger. I watched, fascinated, as he disemboweled the whole row of dummies, hacking off limbs and basically reducing them to a pile of straw and armor.

They were only dummies, but I still couldn't help being awed by Luke's skill. The guy was an incredible fighter. It made me wonder, again, how he possibly could've failed at his quest.

Finally, he saw me, and stopped mid-swing. "Percy."

"Um, sorry," I said, embarrassed. "I just—"

"It's okay," he said, lowering his sword. "Just doing some last-minute practice."

"Those dummies won't be bothering anybody anymore."

Luke shrugged. "We build new ones every summer."

Now that his sword wasn't swirling around, I could see something odd about it. The blade was two different types of metal—one edge bronze, the other steel.

Luke noticed me looking at it. "Oh, this? New toy. This is Backbiter."

"Backbiter?"

Luke turned the blade in the light so it glinted wickedly. "One side is celestial bronze. The other is tempered steel. Works on mortals and immortals both."

I thought about what Chiron had told me when I started my quest—that a hero should never harm mortals unless absolutely necessary.

"I didn't know they could make weapons like that."

"*They* probably can't," Luke agreed. "It's one of a kind."

He gave me a tiny smile, then slid the sword into its scabbard. "Listen, I was going to come looking for you.

What do you say we go down to the woods one last time, look for something to fight?"

I don't know why I hesitated. I should've felt relieved that Luke was being so friendly. Ever since I'd gotten back from the quest, he'd been acting a little distant. I was afraid he might resent me for all the attention I'd gotten.

"You think it's a good idea?" I asked. "I mean——"

"Aw, come on." He rummaged in his gym bag and pulled out a six-pack of Cokes. "Drinks are on me."

I stared at the Cokes, wondering where the heck he'd gotten them. There were no regular mortal sodas at the camp store. No way to smuggle them in unless you talked to a satyr, maybe.

Of course, the magic dinner goblets would fill with anything you want, but it just didn't taste the same as a real Coke, straight out of the can.

Sugar and caffeine. My willpower crumbled.

"Sure," I decided. "Why not?"

We walked down to the woods and kicked around for some kind of monster to fight, but it was too hot. All the monsters with any sense must've been taking siestas in their nice cool caves.

We found a shady spot by the creek where I'd broken Clarisse's spear during my first capture the flag game. We sat on a big rock, drank our Cokes, and watched the sunlight in the woods.

After a while Luke said, "You miss being on a quest?"

"With monsters attacking me every three feet? Are you kidding?"

Luke raised an eyebrow.

"Yeah, I miss it," I admitted. "You?"

A shadow passed over his face.

I was used to hearing from the girls how good-looking Luke was, but at the moment, he looked weary, and angry, and not at all handsome. His blond hair was gray in the sunlight. The scar on his face looked deeper than usual. I could imagine him as an old man.

"I've lived at Half-Blood Hill year-round since I was fourteen," he told me. "Ever since Thalia . . . well, you know. I trained, and trained, and trained. I never got to be a normal teenager, out there in the real world. Then they threw me one quest, and when I came back, it was like, 'Okay, ride's over. Have a nice life.'"

He crumpled his Coke can and threw into the creek, which really shocked me. One of the first things you learn at Camp Half-Blood is: Don't litter. You'll hear from the nymphs and the naiads. They'll get even. You'll crawl into bed one night and find your sheets filled with centipedes and mud.

"The heck with laurel wreaths," Luke said. "I'm not going to end up like those dusty trophies in the Big House attic."

"You make it sound like you're leaving."

Luke gave me a twisted smile. "Oh, I'm leaving, all right, Percy. I brought you down here to say good-bye."

He snapped his fingers. A small fire burned a hole in the ground at my feet. Out crawled something glistening black, about the size of my hand. A scorpion.

I started to go for my pen.

"I wouldn't," Luke cautioned. "Pit scorpions can jump up to fifteen feet. Its stinger can pierce right through your clothes. You'll be dead in sixty seconds."

"Luke, what—"

Then it hit me.

You will be betrayed by one who calls you a friend.

"You," I said.

He stood calmly and brushed off his jeans.

The scorpion paid him no attention. It kept its beady black eyes on me, clamping its pincers as it crawled onto my shoe.

"I saw a lot out there in the world, Percy," Luke said. "Didn't you feel it—the darkness gathering, the monsters growing stronger? Didn't you realize how useless it all is? All the heroics—being pawns of the gods. They should've been overthrown thousands of years ago, but they've hung on, thanks to us half-bloods."

I couldn't believe this was happening.

"Luke . . . you're talking about our parents," I said.

He laughed. "That's supposed to make me love them? Their precious 'Western civilization' is a disease, Percy. It's killing the world. The only way to stop it is to burn it to the ground, start over with something more honest."

"You're as crazy as Ares."

His eyes flared. "Ares is a fool. He never realized the true master he was serving. If I had time, Percy, I could explain. But I'm afraid you won't live that long."

The scorpion crawled onto my pants leg.

There had to be a way out of this. I needed time to think.

"Kronos," I said. "That's who you serve."

The air got colder.

"You should be careful with names," Luke warned.

"Kronos got you to steal the master bolt and the helm. He spoke to you in your dreams."

Luke's eye twitched. "He spoke to you, too, Percy. You should've listened."

"He's brainwashing you, Luke."

"You're wrong. He showed me that my talents are being wasted. You know what my quest was two years ago, Percy? My father, Hermes, wanted me to steal a golden apple from the Garden of the Hesperides and return it to Olympus. After all the training I'd done, *that* was the best he could think up."

"That's not an easy quest," I said. "Hercules did it."

"Exactly," Luke said. "Where's the glory in repeating what others have done? All the gods know how to do is replay their past. My heart wasn't in it. The dragon in the garden gave me this"—he pointed angrily at his scar—"and when I came back, all I got was pity. I wanted to pull Olympus down stone by stone right then, but I bided my time. I began to dream of Kronos. He convinced me to steal something worthwhile, something no hero had ever had the courage to take. When we went on that winter-solstice field trip, while the other campers were asleep, I snuck into the throne room and took Zeus's master bolt right from his chair. Hades's helm of darkness, too. You wouldn't believe how easy it was. The Olympians are so arrogant; they never dreamed someone would dare steal from them. Their security is horrible. I was halfway across New Jersey before I heard the storms rumbling, and I knew they'd discovered my theft."

The scorpion was sitting on my knee now, staring at me with its glittering eyes. I tried to keep my voice level. "So why didn't you bring the items to Kronos?"

Luke's smile wavered. "I . . . I got overconfident. Zeus sent out his sons and daughters to find the stolen bolt— Artemis, Apollo, my father, Hermes. But it was Ares who caught me. I could have beaten him, but I wasn't careful enough. He disarmed me, took the items of power, threatened to return them to Olympus and burn me alive. Then Kronos's voice came to me and told me what to say. I put the idea in Ares's head about a great war between the gods. I said all he had to do was hide the items away for a while and watch the others fight. Ares got a wicked gleam in his eyes. I knew he was hooked. He let me go, and I returned to Olympus before anyone noticed my absence." Luke drew his new sword. He ran his thumb down the flat of the blade, as if he were hypnotized by its beauty. "Afterward, the Lord of the Titans . . . h-he punished me with nightmares. I swore not to fail again. Back at Camp Half-Blood, in my dreams, I was told that a second hero would arrive, one who could be tricked into taking the bolt and the helm the rest of the way—from Ares down to Tartarus."

"*You* summoned the hellhound, that night in the forest."

"We had to make Chiron think the camp wasn't safe for

you, so he would start you on your quest. We had to confirm his fears that Hades was after you. And it worked."

"The flying shoes were cursed," I said. "They were supposed to drag me and the backpack into Tartarus."

"And they would have, if you'd been wearing them. But you gave them to the satyr, which wasn't part of the plan. Grover messes up everything he touches. He even confused the curse."

Luke looked down at the scorpion, which was now sitting on my thigh. "You should have died in Tartarus, Percy. But don't worry, I'll leave you with my little friend to set things right."

"Thalia gave her life to save you," I said, gritting my teeth. "And this is how you repay her?"

"Don't speak of Thalia!" he shouted. "The gods *let* her die! That's one of the many things they will pay for."

"You're being used, Luke. You and Ares both. Don't listen to Kronos."

"*I've* been used?" Luke's voice turned shrill. "Look at yourself. What has your dad ever done for you? Kronos will rise. You've only delayed his plans. He will cast the Olympians into Tartarus and drive humanity back to their caves. All except the strongest—the ones who serve him."

"Call off the bug," I said. "If you're so strong, fight me yourself."

Luke smiled. "Nice try, Percy. But I'm not Ares. You can't bait me. My lord is waiting, and he's got plenty of quests for me to undertake."

"Luke—"

"Good-bye, Percy. There is a new Golden Age coming. You won't be part of it."

He slashed his sword in an arc and disappeared in a ripple of darkness.

The scorpion lunged.

I swatted it away with my hand and uncapped my sword. The thing jumped at me and I cut it in half in midair.

I was about to congratulate myself until I looked down at my hand. My palm had a huge red welt, oozing and smoking with yellow guck. The thing had gotten me after all.

My ears pounded. My vision went foggy. The water, I thought. It healed me before.

I stumbled to the creek and submerged my hand, but nothing seemed to happen. The poison was too strong. My vision was getting dark. I could barely stand up.

Sixty seconds, Luke had told me.

I had to get back to camp. If I collapsed out here, my body would be dinner for a monster. Nobody would ever know what had happened.

My legs felt like lead. My forehead was burning. I stumbled toward the camp, and the nymphs stirred from their trees.

"Help," I croaked. "Please . . ."

Two of them took my arms, pulling me along. I remember making it to the clearing, a counselor shouting for help, a centaur blowing a conch horn.

Then everything went black.

* * *

I woke with a drinking straw in my mouth. I was sipping something that tasted like liquid chocolate-chip cookies. Nectar.

I opened my eyes.

I was propped up in bed in the sickroom of the Big House, my right hand bandaged like a club. Argus stood guard in the corner. Annabeth sat next to me, holding my nectar glass and dabbing a washcloth on my forehead.

"Here we are again," I said.

"You idiot," Annabeth said, which is how I knew she was overjoyed to see me conscious. "You were green and turning gray when we found you. If it weren't for Chiron's healing . . ."

"Now, now," Chiron's voice said. "Percy's constitution deserves some of the credit."

He was sitting near the foot of my bed in human form, which was why I hadn't noticed him yet. His lower half was magically compacted into the wheelchair, his upper half dressed in a coat and tie. He smiled, but his face looked weary and pale, the way it did when he'd been up all night grading Latin papers.

"How are you feeling?" he asked.

"Like my insides have been frozen, then microwaved."

"Apt, considering that was pit scorpion venom. Now you must tell me, if you can, exactly what happened."

Between sips of nectar, I told them the story.

The room was quiet for a long time.

"I can't believe that Luke . . ." Annabeth's voice faltered. Her expression turned angry and sad. "Yes. Yes, I *can* believe it. May the gods curse him. . . . He was never the same after his quest."

"This must be reported to Olympus," Chiron murmured. "I will go at once."

"Luke is out there right now," I said. "I have to go after him."

Chiron shook his head. "No, Percy. The gods—"

"Won't even *talk* about Kronos," I snapped. "Zeus declared the matter closed!"

"Percy, I know this is hard. But you must not rush out for vengeance. You aren't ready."

I didn't like it, but part of me suspected Chiron was right. One look at my hand, and I knew I wasn't going to be sword fighting any time soon. "Chiron . . . your prophecy from the Oracle . . . it was about Kronos, wasn't it? Was I in it? And Annabeth?"

Chiron glanced nervously at the ceiling. "Percy, it isn't my place—"

"You've been ordered not to talk to me about it, haven't you?"

His eyes were sympathetic, but sad. "You will be a great hero, child. I will do my best to prepare you. But if I'm right about the path ahead of you . . ."

Thunder boomed overhead, rattling the windows.

"All right!" Chiron shouted. "Fine!"

He sighed in frustration. "The gods have their reasons, Percy. Knowing too much of your future is never a good thing."

"We can't just sit back and do nothing," I said.

"*We* will not sit back," Chiron promised. "But *you* must be careful. Kronos wants you to come unraveled. He wants your life disrupted, your thoughts clouded with fear and anger. Do not give him what he wants. Train patiently. Your time will come."

"Assuming I live that long."

Chiron put his hand on my ankle. "You'll have to trust me, Percy. You will live. But first you must decide your path for the coming year. I cannot tell you the right choice. . . ." I got the feeling that he had a very definite opinion, and it was taking all his willpower not to advise me. "But you must decide whether to stay at Camp Half-Blood year-round, or return to the mortal world for seventh grade and be a summer camper. Think on that. When I get back from Olympus, you must tell me your decision."

I wanted to protest. I wanted to ask him more questions. But his expression told me there could be no more discussion; he had said as much as he could.

"I'll be back as soon as I can," Chiron promised. "Argus will watch over you."

He glanced at Annabeth. "Oh, and, my dear . . . whenever you're ready, they're here."

"Who's here?" I asked.

Nobody answered.

Chiron rolled himself out of the room. I heard the wheels of his chair clunk carefully down the front steps, two at a time.

Annabeth studied the ice in my drink.

"What's wrong?" I asked her.

"Nothing." She set the glass on the table. "I . . . just took your advice about something. You . . . um . . . need anything?"

"Yeah. Help me up. I want to go outside."

"Percy, that isn't a good idea."

I slid my legs out of bed. Annabeth caught me before I could crumple to the floor. A wave of nausea rolled over me.

Annabeth said, "I told you . . ."

"I'm fine," I insisted. I didn't want to lie in bed like an invalid while Luke was out there planning to destroy the Western world.

I managed a step forward. Then another, still leaning heavily on Annabeth. Argus followed us outside, but he kept his distance.

By the time we reached the porch, my face was beaded with sweat. My stomach had twisted into knots. But I had managed to make it all the way to the railing.

It was dusk. The camp looked completely deserted. The cabins were dark and the volleyball pit silent. No canoes cut the surface of the lake. Beyond the woods and the strawberry fields, the Long Island Sound glittered in the last light of the sun.

"What are you going to do?" Annabeth asked me.

"I don't know."

I told her I got the feeling Chiron wanted me to stay year-round, to put in more individual training time, but I wasn't sure that's what I wanted. I admitted I'd feel bad about leaving her alone, though, with only Clarisse for company. . . .

Annabeth pursed her lips, then said quietly, "I'm going home for the year, Percy."

I stared at her. "You mean, to your dad's?"

She pointed toward the crest of Half-Blood Hill. Next to Thalia's pine tree, at the very edge of the camp's magical boundaries, a family stood silhouetted—two little children, a woman, and a tall man with blond hair. They seemed to be waiting. The man was holding a backpack that looked like the one Annabeth had gotten from Waterland in Denver.

"I wrote him a letter when we got back," Annabeth said. "Just like you suggested. I told him . . . I was sorry. I'd come home for the school year if he still wanted me. He wrote back immediately. We decided . . . we'd give it another try."

"That took guts."

She pursed her lips. "You won't try anything stupid during the school year, will you? At least . . . not without sending me an Iris-message?"

I managed a smile. "I won't go looking for trouble. I usually don't have to."

"When I get back next summer," she said, "we'll hunt down Luke. We'll ask for a quest, but if we don't get approval, we'll sneak off and do it anyway. Agreed?"

"Sounds like a plan worthy of Athena."

She held out her hand. I shook it.

"Take care, Seaweed Brain," Annabeth told me. "Keep your eyes open."

"You too, Wise Girl."

I watched her walk up the hill and join her family. She

gave her father an awkward hug and looked back at the valley one last time. She touched Thalia's pine tree, then allowed herself to be lead over the crest and into the mortal world.

For the first time at camp, I felt truly alone. I looked out at Long Island Sound and I remembered my father saying, *The sea does not like to be restrained.*

I made my decision.

I wondered, if Poseidon were watching, would he approve of my choice?

"I'll be back next summer," I promised him. "I'll survive until then. After all, I am your son." I asked Argus to take me down to cabin three, so I could pack my bags for home.

ACKNOWLEDGMENTS

Without the assistance of numerous valiant helpers, I would have been slain by monsters many times over as I endeavored to bring this story to print. Thanks to my elder son, Haley Michael, who heard the story first; my younger son, Patrick John, who at the age of six is the level-headed one in the family; and my wife, Becky, who puts up with my many long hours at Camp Half-Blood. Thanks also to my cadre of middle-school beta testers: Travis Stoll, clever and quick as Hermes; C. C. Kellogg, beloved as Athena; Allison Bauer, clear-eyed as Artemis the Huntress; and Mrs. Margaret Floyd, the wise and kindly seer of middle-school English. My appreciation also to Professor Egbert J. Bakker, classicist extraordinaire; Nancy Gallt, agent *summa cum laude*; Jonathan Burnham, Jennifer Besser, and Sarah Hughes for believing in Percy.

DON'T MISS THE NEXT EXCITING
ADVENTURE IN THE
PERCY JACKSON & THE OLYMPIANS
SERIES

THE SEA OF MONSTERS

THE
SEA OF
MONSTERS

My nightmare started like this.

I was standing on a deserted street in some little beach town. It was the middle of the night. A storm was blowing. Wind and rain ripped at the palm trees along the sidewalk. Pink and yellow stucco buildings lined the street, their windows boarded up. A block away, past a line of hibiscus bushes, the ocean churned.

Florida, I thought. Though I wasn't sure how I knew that. I'd never been to Florida.

Then I heard hooves clattering against the pavement. I turned and saw my friend Grover running for his life.

Yeah, I said *hooves*.

Grover is a satyr. From the waist up, he looks like a typical gangly teenager with a peach-fuzz goatee and a bad case of acne. He walks with a strange limp, but unless you happen to catch him without his pants on (which I don't recommend), you'd never know there was anything un-human about him. Baggy jeans and fake feet hide the fact that he's got furry hindquarters and hooves.

Grover had been my best friend in sixth grade. He'd gone on this adventure with me and a girl named Annabeth to save the world, but I hadn't seen him since last July, when he set off alone on a dangerous quest—a quest no satyr had ever returned from.

Anyway, in my dream, Grover was hauling goat tail, holding his human shoes in his hands the way he does when he needs to move fast. He clopped past the little tourist shops and surfboard rental places. The wind bent the palm trees almost to the ground.

Grover was terrified of something behind him. He must've just come from the beach. Wet sand was caked in his fur. He'd escaped from somewhere. He was trying to get away from . . . something.

A bone-rattling growl cut through the storm. Behind Grover, at the far end of the block, a shadowy figure loomed. It swatted aside a street lamp, which burst in a shower of sparks.

Grover stumbled, whimpering in fear. He muttered to himself, *Have to get away. Have to warn them!*

I couldn't see what was chasing him, but I could hear it muttering and cursing. The ground shook as it got closer. Grover dashed around a street corner and faltered. He'd run into a dead-end courtyard full of shops. No time to back up. The nearest door had been blown open by the storm. The sign above the darkened display window read: ST. AUGUSTINE BRIDAL BOUTIQUE.

Grover dashed inside. He dove behind a rack of wedding dresses.

The monster's shadow passed in front of the shop. I could smell the thing—a sickening combination of wet sheep wool and rotten meat and that weird sour body odor only monsters have, like a skunk that's been living off Mexican food.

Grover trembled behind the wedding dresses. The monster's shadow passed on.

Silence except for the rain. Grover took a deep breath. Maybe the thing was gone.

Then lightning flashed. The entire front of the store exploded, and a monstrous voice bellowed: "MIIIIINE!"

I sat bolt upright, shivering in my bed.

There was no storm. No monster.

Morning sunlight filtered through my bedroom window.

I thought I saw a shadow flicker across the glass—a humanlike shape. But then there was a knock on my bedroom door—my mom called: "Percy, you're going to be late"—and the shadow at the window disappeared.

It must've been my imagination. A fifth-story window with a rickety old fire escape . . . there couldn't have been anyone out there.

"Come on, dear," my mother called again. "Last day of school. You should be excited! You've almost made it!"

"Coming," I managed.

I felt under my pillow. My fingers closed reassuringly around the ballpoint pen I always slept with. I brought it out, studied the Ancient Greek writing engraved on the side: *Anaklusmos*. Riptide.

I thought about uncapping it, but something held me back. I hadn't used Riptide for so long. . . .

Besides, my mom had made me promise not to use deadly weapons in the apartment after I'd swung a javelin the wrong way and taken out her china cabinet. I put Anaklusmos on my nightstand and dragged myself out of bed.

I got dressed as quickly as I could. I tried not to think about my nightmare or monsters or the shadow at my window.

Have to get away. Have to warn them!

What had Grover meant?

I made a three-fingered claw over my heart and pushed outward—an ancient gesture Grover had once taught me for warding off evil.

The dream couldn't have been real.

Last day of school. My mom was right, I should have been excited. For the first time in my life, I'd almost made it an entire year without getting expelled. No weird accidents. No fights in the classroom. No teachers turning into monsters and trying to kill me with poisoned cafeteria food or exploding homework. Tomorrow, I'd be on my way to my favorite place in the world—Camp Half-Blood.

Only one more day to go. Surely even I couldn't mess that up.

As usual, I didn't have a clue how wrong I was.

My mom made blue waffles and blue eggs for breakfast. She's funny that way, celebrating special occasions with blue food. I think it's her way of saying anything is possible. Percy can pass seventh grade. Waffles can be blue. Little miracles like that.

I ate at the kitchen table while my mom washed dishes. She was dressed in her work uniform—a starry blue skirt and a red-and-white striped blouse she wore to sell candy at Sweet on America. Her long brown hair was pulled back in a ponytail.

The waffles tasted great, but I guess I wasn't digging in like I usually did. My mom looked over and frowned. "Percy, are you all right?"

"Yeah . . . fine."

But she could always tell when something was bothering me. She dried her hands and sat down across from me. "School, or . . ."

She didn't need to finish. I knew what she was asking.

"I think Grover's in trouble," I said, and I told her about my dream.

She pursed her lips. We didn't talk much about the *other*

part of my life. We tried to live as normally as possible, but my mom knew all about Grover.

"I wouldn't be too worried, dear," she said. "Grover is a big satyr now. If there were a problem, I'm sure we would've heard from . . . from camp. . . ." Her shoulders tensed as she said the word *camp*.

"What is it?" I asked.

"Nothing," she said. "I'll tell you what. This afternoon we'll celebrate the end of school. I'll take you and Tyson to Rockefeller Center—to that skateboard shop you like."

Oh, man, that was tempting. We were always struggling with money. Between my mom's night classes and my private school tuition, we could never afford to do special stuff like shop for a skateboard. But something in her voice bothered me.

"Wait a minute," I said. "I thought we were packing me up for camp tonight."

She twisted her dishrag. "Ah, dear, about that . . . I got a message from Chiron last night."

My heart sank. Chiron was the activities director at Camp Half-Blood. He wouldn't contact us unless something serious was going on. "What did he say?"

"He thinks . . . it might not be safe for you to come to camp just yet. We might have to postpone."

"*Postpone?* Mom, how could it not be *safe*? I'm a half-blood! It's like the only safe place on earth for me!"

"Usually, dear. But with the problems they're having—"

"*What* problems?"

"Percy . . . I'm very, very sorry. I was hoping to talk to you about it this afternoon. I can't explain it all now. I'm not even sure Chiron can. Everything happened so suddenly."

My mind was reeling. How could I *not* go to camp? I wanted to ask a million questions, but just then the kitchen clock chimed the half-hour.

My mom looked almost relieved. "Seven-thirty, dear. You should go. Tyson will be waiting."

"But—"

"Percy, we'll talk this afternoon. Go on to school."

That was the last thing I wanted to do, but my mom had this fragile look in her eyes—a kind of warning, like if I pushed her too hard she'd start to cry. Besides, she was right about my friend Tyson. I had to meet him at the subway station on time or he'd get upset. He was scared of traveling underground alone.

I gathered up my stuff, but I stopped in the doorway. "Mom, this problem at camp. Does it . . . could it have anything to do with my dream about Grover?"

She wouldn't meet my eyes. "We'll talk this afternoon, dear. I'll explain . . . as much as I can."

Reluctantly, I told her good-bye. I jogged downstairs to catch the Number Two train.

I didn't know it at the time, but my mom and I would never get to have our afternoon talk.

In fact, I wouldn't be seeing home for a long, long time.

As I stepped outside, I glanced at the brownstone

building across the street. Just for a second I saw a dark shape in the morning sunlight—a human silhouette against the brick wall, a shadow that belonged to no one.

Then it rippled and vanished.

RICK RIORDAN

THE HEROES OF OLYMPUS

THE LOST HERO

DISNEP · HYPERION

Los Angeles   New York

For Haley and Patrick, always the first to hear stories.
Without them, Camp Half-Blood would not exist.

JASON

EVEN BEFORE HE GOT ELECTROCUTED, Jason was having a rotten day.

He woke in the backseat of a school bus, not sure where he was, holding hands with a girl he didn't know. That wasn't necessarily the rotten part. The girl was cute, but he couldn't figure out who she was or what he was doing there. He sat up and rubbed his eyes, trying to think.

A few dozen kids sprawled in the seats in front of him, listening to iPods, talking, or sleeping. They all looked around his age...fifteen? Sixteen? Okay, that was scary. He didn't know his own age.

The bus rumbled along a bumpy road. Out the windows, desert rolled by under a bright blue sky. Jason was pretty sure he didn't live in the desert. He tried to think back...the last thing he remembered...

The girl squeezed his hand. "Jason, you okay?"

She wore faded jeans, hiking boots, and a fleece

snowboarding jacket. Her chocolate brown hair was cut choppy and uneven, with thin strands braided down the sides. She wore no makeup like she was trying not to draw attention to herself, but it didn't work. She was seriously pretty. Her eyes seemed to change color like a kaleidoscope—brown, blue, and green.

Jason let go of her hand. "Um, I don't—"

In the front of the bus, a teacher shouted, "All right, cupcakes, listen up!"

The guy was obviously a coach. His baseball cap was pulled low over his hair, so you could just see his beady eyes. He had a wispy goatee and a sour face, like he'd eaten something moldy. His buff arms and chest pushed against a bright orange polo shirt. His nylon workout pants and Nikes were spotless white. A whistle hung from his neck, and a megaphone was clipped to his belt. He would've looked pretty scary if he hadn't been five feet zero. When he stood up in the aisle, one of the students called, "Stand up, Coach Hedge!"

"I heard that!" The coach scanned the bus for the offender. Then his eyes fixed on Jason, and his scowl deepened.

A jolt went down Jason's spine. He was sure the coach knew he didn't belong there. He was going to call Jason out, demand to know what he was doing on the bus—and Jason wouldn't have a clue what to say.

But Coach Hedge looked away and cleared his throat. "We'll arrive in five minutes! Stay with your partner. Don't lose your worksheet. And if any of you precious little cupcakes causes any trouble on this trip, I will personally send you back to campus the hard way."

He picked up a baseball bat and made like he was hitting a homer.

Jason looked at the girl next to him. "Can he talk to us that way?"

She shrugged. "Always does. This is the Wilderness School. 'Where kids are the animals.'"

She said it like it was a joke they'd shared before.

"This is some kind of mistake," Jason said. "I'm not supposed to be here."

The boy in front of him turned and laughed. "Yeah, right, Jason. We've all been framed! I didn't run away six times. Piper didn't steal a BMW."

The girl blushed. "I didn't steal that car, Leo!"

"Oh, I forgot, Piper. What was your story? You 'talked' the dealer into lending it to you?" He raised his eyebrows at Jason like, *Can you believe her?*

Leo looked like a Latino Santa's elf, with curly black hair, pointy ears, a cheerful, babyish face, and a mischievous smile that told you right away this guy should not be trusted around matches or sharp objects. His long, nimble fingers wouldn't stop moving—drumming on the seat, sweeping his hair behind his ears, fiddling with the buttons of his army fatigue jacket. Either the kid was naturally hyper or he was hopped up on enough sugar and caffeine to give a heart attack to a water buffalo.

"Anyway," Leo said, "I hope you've got your worksheet, 'cause I used mine for spit wads days ago. Why are you looking at me like that? Somebody draw on my face again?"

"I don't know you," Jason said.

Leo gave him a crocodile grin. "Sure. I'm not your best friend. I'm his evil clone."

"Leo Valdez!" Coach Hedge yelled from the front. "Problem back there?"

Leo winked at Jason. "Watch this." He turned to the front. "Sorry, Coach! I was having trouble hearing you. Could you use your megaphone, please?"

Coach Hedge grunted like he was pleased to have an excuse. He unclipped the megaphone from his belt and continued giving directions, but his voice came out like Darth Vader's. The kids cracked up. The coach tried again, but this time the megaphone blared: "The cow says moo!"

The kids howled, and the coach slammed down the megaphone. "Valdez!"

Piper stifled a laugh. "My god, Leo. How did you do that?"

Leo slipped a tiny Phillips head screwdriver from his sleeve. "I'm a special boy."

"Guys, seriously," Jason pleaded. "What am I doing here? Where are we going?"

Piper knit her eyebrows. "Jason, are you joking?"

"No! I have no idea—"

"Aw, yeah, he's joking," Leo said. "He's trying to get me back for that shaving cream on the Jell-O thing, aren't you?"

Jason stared at him blankly.

"No, I think he's serious." Piper tried to take his hand again, but he pulled it away.

"I'm sorry," he said. "I don't—I can't—"

"That's it!" Coach Hedge yelled from the front. "The back row has just volunteered to clean up after lunch!"

The rest of the kids cheered.

"There's a shocker," Leo muttered.

But Piper kept her eyes on Jason, like she couldn't decide whether to be hurt or worried. "Did you hit your head or something? You really don't know who we are?"

Jason shrugged helplessly. "It's worse than that. I don't know who *I* am."

The bus dropped them in front of a big red stucco complex like a museum, just sitting in the middle of nowhere. Maybe that's what it was: the National Museum of Nowhere, Jason thought. A cold wind blew across the desert. Jason hadn't paid much attention to what he was wearing, but it wasn't nearly warm enough: jeans and sneakers, a purple T-shirt, and a thin black windbreaker.

"So, a crash course for the amnesiac," Leo said, in a helpful tone that made Jason think this was not going to be helpful. "We go to the 'Wilderness School'"—Leo made air quotes with his fingers. "Which means we're 'bad kids.' Your family, or the court, or whoever, decided you were too much trouble, so they shipped you off to this lovely prison—sorry, 'boarding school'—in Armpit, Nevada, where you learn valuable nature skills like running ten miles a day through the cacti and weaving daisies into hats! And for a special treat we go on 'educational' field trips with Coach Hedge, who keeps order with a baseball bat. Is it all coming back to you now?"

"No." Jason glanced apprehensively at the other kids: maybe twenty guys, half that many girls. None of them looked like hardened criminals, but he wondered what they'd all done to get sentenced to a school for delinquents, and he wondered why he belonged with them.

Leo rolled his eyes. "You're really gonna play this out, huh? Okay, so the three of us started here together this semester. We're totally tight. You do everything I say and give me your dessert and do my chores—"

"Leo!" Piper snapped.

"Fine. Ignore that last part. But we *are* friends. Well, Piper's a little more than your friend, the last few weeks—"

"Leo, stop it!" Piper's face turned red. Jason could feel his face burning too. He thought he'd remember if he'd been going out with a girl like Piper.

"He's got amnesia or something," Piper said. "We've got to tell somebody."

Leo scoffed. "Who, Coach Hedge? He'd try to fix Jason by whacking him upside the head."

The coach was at the front of the group, barking orders and blowing his whistle to keep the kids in line; but every so often he'd glance back at Jason and scowl.

"Leo, Jason needs help," Piper insisted. "He's got a concussion or—"

"Yo, Piper." One of the other guys dropped back to join them as the group was heading into the museum. The new guy wedged himself between Jason and Piper and knocked Leo down. "Don't talk to these bottom-feeders. You're my partner, remember?"

The new guy had dark hair cut Superman style, a deep tan, and teeth so white they should've come with a warning label: DO NOT STARE DIRECTLY AT TEETH. PERMANENT BLINDNESS

MAY OCCUR. He wore a Dallas Cowboys jersey, Western jeans and boots, and he smiled like he was God's gift to juvenile delinquent girls everywhere. Jason hated him instantly.

"Go away, Dylan," Piper grumbled. "I didn't ask to work with you."

"Ah, that's no way to be. This is your lucky day!" Dylan hooked his arm through hers and dragged her through the museum entrance. Piper shot one last look over her shoulder like, *911.*

Leo got up and brushed himself off. "I hate that guy." He offered Jason his arm, like they should go skipping inside together. "'I'm Dylan. I'm so cool, I want to date myself, but I can't figure out how! You want to date me instead? You're so lucky!'"

"Leo," Jason said, "you're weird."

"Yeah, you tell me that a lot." Leo grinned. "But if you don't remember me, that means I can reuse all my old jokes. Come on!"

Jason figured that if this was his best friend, his life must be pretty messed up; but he followed Leo into the museum.

They walked through the building, stopping here and there for Coach Hedge to lecture them with his megaphone, which alternately made him sound like a Sith Lord or blared out random comments like "The pig says oink."

Leo kept pulling out nuts, bolts, and pipe cleaners from the pockets of his army jacket and putting them together, like he had to keep his hands busy at all times.

Jason was too distracted to pay much attention to the

exhibits, but they were about the Grand Canyon and the Hualapai tribe, which owned the museum.

Some girls kept looking over at Piper and Dylan and snickering. Jason figured these girls were the popular clique. They wore matching jeans and pink tops and enough makeup for a Halloween party.

One of them said, "Hey, Piper, does your tribe run this place? Do you get in free if you do a rain dance?"

The other girls laughed. Even Piper's so-called partner Dylan suppressed a smile. Piper's snowboarding jacket sleeves hid her hands, but Jason got the feeling she was clenching her fists.

"My dad's Cherokee," she said. "Not Hualapai. 'Course, you'd need a few brain cells to know the difference, Isabel."

Isabel widened her eyes in mock surprise, so that she looked like an owl with a makeup addiction. "Oh, sorry! Was your *mom* in this tribe? Oh, that's right. You never knew your mom."

Piper charged her, but before a fight could start, Coach Hedge barked, "Enough back there! Set a good example or I'll break out my baseball bat!"

The group shuffled on to the next exhibit, but the girls kept calling out little comments to Piper.

"Good to be back on the rez?" one asked in a sweet voice.

"Dad's probably too drunk to work," another said with fake sympathy. "That's why she turned klepto."

Piper ignored them, but Jason was ready to punch them himself. He might not remember Piper, or even who he was, but he knew he hated mean kids.

Leo caught his arm. "Be cool. Piper doesn't like us fighting her battles. Besides, if those girls found out the truth about her dad, they'd be all bowing down to her and screaming, 'We're not worthy!'"

"Why? What about her dad?"

Leo laughed in disbelief. "You're not kidding? You really don't remember that your girlfriend's dad—"

"Look, I wish I did, but I don't even remember *her*, much less her dad."

Leo whistled. "Whatever. We *have* to talk when we get back to the dorm."

They reached the far end of the exhibit hall, where some big glass doors led out to a terrace.

"All right, cupcakes," Coach Hedge announced. "You are about to see the Grand Canyon. Try not to break it. The skywalk can hold the weight of seventy jumbo jets, so you featherweights should be safe out there. If possible, try to avoid pushing each other over the edge, as that would cause me extra paperwork."

The coach opened the doors, and they all stepped outside. The Grand Canyon spread before them, live and in person. Extending over the edge was a horseshoe-shaped walkway made of glass, so you could see right through it.

"Man," Leo said. "That's pretty wicked."

Jason had to agree. Despite his amnesia and his feeling that he didn't belong there, he couldn't help being impressed.

The canyon was bigger and wider than you could appreciate from a picture. They were up so high that birds circled below their feet. Five hundred feet down, a river snaked along the canyon floor. Banks of storm clouds had moved overhead while they'd been inside, casting shadows like angry faces across the cliffs. As far as Jason could see in any direction, red and gray ravines cut through the desert like some crazy god had taken a knife to it.

Jason got a piercing pain behind his eyes. *Crazy gods...* Where had he come up with that idea? He felt like he'd gotten close to something important—something he should know about. He also got the unmistakable feeling he was in danger.

"You all right?" Leo asked. "You're not going to throw up over the side, are you? 'Cause I should've brought my camera."

Jason grabbed the railing. He was shivering and sweaty, but it had nothing to do with heights. He blinked, and the pain behind his eyes subsided.

"I'm fine," he managed. "Just a headache."

Thunder rumbled overhead. A cold wind almost knocked him sideways.

"This can't be safe." Leo squinted at the clouds. "Storm's right over us, but it's clear all the way around. Weird, huh?"

Jason looked up and saw Leo was right. A dark circle of clouds had parked itself over the skywalk, but the rest of the sky in every direction was perfectly clear. Jason had a bad feeling about that.

"All right, cupcakes!" Coach Hedge yelled. He frowned at the storm like it bothered him too. "We may have to cut this short, so get to work! Remember, complete sentences!"

The storm rumbled, and Jason's head began to hurt again. Not knowing why he did it, he reached into his jeans pocket and brought out a coin—a circle of gold the size of a half-dollar, but thicker and more uneven. Stamped on one side was a picture of a battle-ax. On the other was some guy's face wreathed in laurels. The inscription said something like IVLIVS.

"Dang, is that gold?" Leo asked. "You been holding out on me!"

Jason put the coin away, wondering how he'd come to have it, and why he had the feeling he was going to need it soon.

"It's nothing," he said. "Just a coin."

Leo shrugged. Maybe his mind had to keep moving as much as his hands. "Come on," he said. "Dare you to spit over the edge."

They didn't try very hard on the worksheet. For one thing, Jason was too distracted by the storm and his own mixed-up feelings. For another thing, he didn't have any idea how to "name three sedimentary strata you observe" or "describe two examples of erosion."

Leo was no help. He was too busy building a helicopter out of pipe cleaners.

"Check it out." He launched the copter. Jason figured it would plummet, but the pipe-cleaner blades actually spun. The little copter made it halfway across the canyon before it lost momentum and spiraled into the void.

"How'd you do that?" Jason asked.

Leo shrugged. "Would've been cooler if I had some rubber bands."

"Seriously," Jason said, "are we friends?"

"Last I checked."

"You sure? What was the first day we met? What did we talk about?"

"It was..." Leo frowned. "I don't recall exactly. I'm ADHD, man. You can't expect me to remember details."

"But I don't remember you *at all*. I don't remember anyone here. What if—"

"You're right and everyone else is wrong?" Leo asked. "You think you just appeared here this morning, and we've all got fake memories of you?"

A little voice in Jason's head said, *That's exactly what I think.*

But it sounded crazy. Everybody here took him for granted. Everyone acted like he was a normal part of the class—except for Coach Hedge.

"Take the worksheet." Jason handed Leo the paper. "I'll be right back."

Before Leo could protest, Jason headed across the skywalk.

Their school group had the place to themselves. Maybe it was too early in the day for tourists, or maybe the weird weather had scared them off. The Wilderness School kids had spread out in pairs across the skywalk. Most were joking around or talking. Some of the guys were dropping pennies over the side. About fifty feet away, Piper was trying to fill out her worksheet, but her stupid partner Dylan was hitting on her, putting his hand on her shoulder and giving her that blinding white smile. She kept pushing him away, and when she saw Jason she gave him a look like, *Throttle this guy for me.*

Jason motioned for her to hang on. He walked up to Coach Hedge, who was leaning on his baseball bat, studying the storm clouds.

"Did you do this?" the coach asked him.

Jason took a step back. "Do what?" It sounded like the coach had just asked if he'd made the thunderstorm.

Coach Hedge glared at him, his beady little eyes glinting under the brim of his cap. "Don't play games with me, kid. What are you doing here, and why are you messing up my job?"

"You mean...you *don't* know me?" Jason said. "I'm not one of your students?"

Hedge snorted. "Never seen you before today."

Jason was so relieved he almost wanted to cry. At least he wasn't going insane. He *was* in the wrong place. "Look, sir, I don't know how I got here. I just woke up on the school bus. All I know is I'm not supposed to be here."

"Got that right." Hedge's gruff voice dropped to a murmur, like he was sharing a secret. "You got a powerful way with the Mist, kid, if you can make all these people think they know you; but you can't fool me. I've been smelling monster for days now. I knew we had an infiltrator, but you don't smell like a monster. You smell like a half-blood. So—who are you, and where'd you come from?"

Most of what the coach said didn't make sense, but Jason decided to answer honestly. "I don't know who I am. I don't have any memories. You've got to help me."

Coach Hedge studied his face like he was trying to read Jason's thoughts.

"Great," Hedge muttered. "You're being truthful."

"Of course I am! And what was all that about monsters and half-bloods? Are those code words or something?"

Hedge narrowed his eyes. Part of Jason wondered if the guy was just nuts. But the other part knew better.

"Look, kid," Hedge said, "I don't know who you are. I just know *what* you are, and it means trouble. Now I got to protect three of you rather than two. Are you the special package? Is that it?"

"What are you talking about?"

Hedge looked at the storm. The clouds were getting thicker and darker, hovering right over the skywalk.

"This morning," Hedge said, "I got a message from camp. They said an extraction team is on the way. They're coming to pick up a special package, but they wouldn't give me details. I thought to myself, Fine. The two I'm watching are pretty powerful, older than most. I know they're being stalked. I can smell a monster in the group. I figure that's why the camp is suddenly frantic to pick them up. But then *you* pop up out of nowhere. So, are you the special package?"

The pain behind Jason's eyes got worse than ever. *Half-bloods. Camp. Monsters.* He still didn't know what Hedge was talking about, but the words gave him a massive brain freeze—like his mind was trying to access information that should've been there but wasn't.

He stumbled, and Coach Hedge caught him. For a short guy, the coach had hands like steel. "Whoa, there, cupcake. You say you got no memories, huh? Fine. I'll just have to watch you, too, until the team gets here. We'll let the director figure things out."

"What director?" Jason said. "What camp?"

"Just sit tight. Reinforcements should be here soon. Hopefully nothing happens before—"

Lightning crackled overhead. The wind picked up with a vengeance. Worksheets flew into the Grand Canyon, and the entire bridge shuddered. Kids screamed, stumbling and grabbing the rails.

"I had to say something," Hedge grumbled. He bellowed into his megaphone: "Everyone inside! The cow says moo! Off the skywalk!"

"I thought you said this thing was stable!" Jason shouted over the wind.

"Under normal circumstances," Hedge agreed, "which these aren't. Come on!"

JASON

THE STORM CHURNED INTO A MINIATURE HURRICANE. Funnel clouds snaked toward the skywalk like the tendrils of a monster jellyfish.

Kids screamed and ran for the building. The wind snatched away their notebooks, jackets, hats, and backpacks. Jason skidded across the slick floor.

Leo lost his balance and almost toppled over the railing, but Jason grabbed his jacket and pulled him back.

"Thanks, man!" Leo yelled.

"Go, go, go!" said Coach Hedge.

Piper and Dylan were holding the doors open, herding the other kids inside. Piper's snowboarding jacket was flapping wildly, her dark hair all in her face. Jason thought she must've been freezing, but she looked calm and confident—telling the others it would be okay, encouraging them to keep moving.

Jason, Leo, and Coach Hedge ran toward them, but it was

like running through quicksand. The wind seemed to fight them, pushing them back.

Dylan and Piper pushed one more kid inside, then lost their grip on the doors. They slammed shut, closing off the skywalk.

Piper tugged at the handles. Inside, the kids pounded on the glass, but the doors seemed to be stuck.

"Dylan, help!" Piper shouted.

Dylan just stood there with an idiotic grin, his Cowboys jersey rippling in the wind, like he was suddenly enjoying the storm.

"Sorry, Piper," he said. "I'm done helping."

He flicked his wrist, and Piper flew backward, slamming into the doors and sliding to the skywalk deck.

"Piper!" Jason tried to charge forward, but the wind was against him, and Coach Hedge pushed him back.

"Coach," Jason said, "let me go!"

"Jason, Leo, stay behind me," the coach ordered. "This is my fight. I should've known that was our monster."

"What?" Leo demanded. A rogue worksheet slapped him in the face, but he swatted it away. "What monster?"

The coach's cap blew off, and sticking up above his curly hair were two bumps—like the knots cartoon characters get when they're bonked on the head. Coach Hedge lifted his baseball bat—but it wasn't a regular bat anymore. Somehow it had changed into a crudely shaped tree-branch club, with twigs and leaves still attached.

Dylan gave him that psycho happy smile. "Oh, come on,

Coach. Let the boy attack me! After all, you're getting too old for this. Isn't that why they *retired* you to this stupid school? I've been on your team the entire season, and you didn't even know. You're losing your nose, grandpa."

The coach made an angry sound like an animal bleating. "That's it, cupcake. You're going down."

"You think you can protect three half-bloods at once, old man?" Dylan laughed. "Good luck."

Dylan pointed at Leo, and a funnel cloud materialized around him. Leo flew off the skywalk like he'd been tossed. Somehow he managed to twist in midair, and slammed sideways into the canyon wall. He skidded, clawing furiously for any handhold. Finally he grabbed a thin ledge about fifty feet below the skywalk and hung there by his fingertips.

"Help!" he yelled up at them. "Rope, please? Bungee cord? Something?"

Coach Hedge cursed and tossed Jason his club. "I don't know who you are, kid, but I hope you're good. Keep that *thing* busy"—he stabbed a thumb at Dylan—"while I get Leo."

"Get him how?" Jason demanded. "You going to fly?"

"Not fly. Climb." Hedge kicked off his shoes, and Jason almost had a coronary. The coach didn't have any feet. He had hooves—goat's hooves. Which meant those things on his head, Jason realized, weren't bumps. They were horns.

"You're a faun," Jason said.

"*Satyr!*" Hedge snapped. "Fauns are Roman. But we'll talk about that later."

Hedge leaped over the railing. He sailed toward the canyon wall and hit hooves first. He bounded down the cliff with impossible agility, finding footholds no bigger than postage stamps, dodging whirlwinds that tried to attack him as he picked his way toward Leo.

"Isn't that cute!" Dylan turned toward Jason. "Now it's your turn, boy."

Jason threw the club. It seemed useless with the winds so strong, but the club flew right at Dylan, even curving when he tried to dodge, and smacked him on the head so hard he fell to his knees.

Piper wasn't as dazed as she appeared. Her fingers closed around the club when it rolled next to her, but before she could use it, Dylan rose. Blood—*golden* blood—trickled from his forehead.

"Nice try, boy." He glared at Jason. "But you'll have to do better."

The skywalk shuddered. Hairline fractures appeared in the glass. Inside the museum, kids stopped banging on the doors. They backed away, watching in terror.

Dylan's body dissolved into smoke, as if his molecules were coming unglued. He had the same face, the same brilliant white smile, but his whole form was suddenly composed of swirling black vapor, his eyes like electrical sparks in a living storm cloud. He sprouted black smoky wings and rose above the skywalk. If angels could be evil, Jason decided, they would look exactly like this.

"You're a *ventus*," Jason said, though he had no idea how he knew that word. "A storm spirit."

Dylan's laugh sounded like a tornado tearing off a roof. "I'm glad I waited, demigod. Leo and Piper I've known about for weeks. Could've killed them at any time. But my mistress said a third was coming—someone special. She'll reward me greatly for your death!"

Two more funnel clouds touched down on either side of Dylan and turned into *venti*—ghostly young men with smoky wings and eyes that flickered with lightning.

Piper stayed down, pretending to be dazed, her hand still gripping the club. Her face was pale, but she gave Jason a determined look, and he understood the message: *Keep their attention. I'll brain them from behind.*

Cute, smart, *and* violent. Jason wished he remembered having her as a girlfriend.

He clenched his fists and got ready to charge, but he never got a chance.

Dylan raised his hand, arcs of electricity running between his fingers, and blasted Jason in the chest.

Bang! Jason found himself flat on his back. His mouth tasted like burning aluminum foil. He lifted his head and saw that his clothes were smoking. The lightning bolt had gone straight though his body and blasted off his left shoe. His toes were black with soot.

The storm spirits were laughing. The winds raged. Piper was screaming defiantly, but it all sounded tinny and far away.

Out of the corner of his eye, Jason saw Coach Hedge climbing the cliff with Leo on his back. Piper was on her feet, desperately swinging the club to fend off the two extra storm spirits, but they were just toying with her. The club went right through their bodies like they weren't there. And Dylan, a dark and winged tornado with eyes, loomed over Jason.

"Stop," Jason croaked. He rose unsteadily to his feet, and he wasn't sure who was more surprised: him, or the storm spirits.

"How are you alive?" Dylan's form flickered. "That was enough lightning to kill twenty men!"

"My turn," Jason said.

He reached in his pocket and pulled out the gold coin. He let his instincts take over, flipping the coin in the air like he'd done it a thousand times. He caught it in his palm, and suddenly he was holding a sword—a wickedly sharp double-edged weapon. The ridged grip fit his fingers perfectly, and the whole thing was gold—hilt, handle, and blade.

Dylan snarled and backed up. He looked at his two comrades and yelled, "Well? Kill him!"

The other storm spirits didn't look happy with that order, but they flew at Jason, their fingers crackling with electricity.

Jason swung at the first spirit. His blade passed through it, and the creature's smoky form disintegrated. The second spirit let loose a bolt of lightning, but Jason's blade absorbed the charge. Jason stepped in—one quick thrust, and the second storm spirit dissolved into gold powder.

Dylan wailed in outrage. He looked down as if expecting his comrades to re-form, but their gold dust remains dispersed in the wind. "Impossible! Who *are* you, half-blood?"

Piper was so stunned she dropped her club. "Jason, how...?"

Then Coach Hedge leaped back onto the skywalk and dumped Leo like a sack of flour.

"Spirits, fear me!" Hedge bellowed, flexing his short arms. Then he looked around and realized there was only Dylan.

"Curse it, boy!" he snapped at Jason. "Didn't you leave some for me? I like a challenge!"

Leo got to his feet, breathing hard. He looked completely humiliated, his hands bleeding from clawing at the rocks. "Yo, Coach Supergoat, whatever you are—I just fell down the freaking Grand Canyon! Stop asking for challenges!"

Dylan hissed at them, but Jason could see fear in his eyes. "You have no idea how many enemies you've awakened, half-bloods. My mistress will destroy *all* demigods. This war you *cannot* win."

Above them, the storm exploded into a full-force gale. Cracks expanded in the skywalk. Sheets of rain poured down, and Jason had to crouch to keep his balance.

A hole opened in the clouds—a swirling vortex of black and silver.

"The mistress calls me back!" Dylan shouted with glee. "And you, demigod, will come with me!"

He lunged at Jason, but Piper tackled the monster from behind. Even though he was made of smoke, Piper somehow managed to connect. Both of them went sprawling. Leo, Jason, and the coach surged forward to help, but the spirit screamed with rage. He let loose a torrent that knocked them all backward. Jason and Coach Hedge landed on their butts. Jason's sword skidded across the glass. Leo hit the back of his head and curled on his side, dazed and groaning. Piper got the worst of it. She was thrown off Dylan's back and hit the railing, tumbling over the side until she was hanging by one hand over the abyss.

Jason started toward her, but Dylan screamed, "I'll settle for this one!"

He grabbed Leo's arm and began to rise, towing a half-conscious Leo below him. The storm spun faster, pulling them upward like a vacuum cleaner.

"Help!" Piper yelled. "Somebody!"

Then she slipped, screaming as she fell.

"Jason, go!" Hedge yelled. "Save her!"

The coach launched himself at the spirit with some serious goat fu—lashing out with his hooves, knocking Leo free from the spirit's grasp. Leo dropped safely to the floor, but Dylan grappled the coach's arms instead. Hedge tried to head-butt him, then kicked him and called him a cupcake. They rose into the air, gaining speed.

Coach Hedge shouted down once more, "Save her! I got this!" Then the satyr and the storm spirit spiraled into the clouds and disappeared.

Save her? Jason thought. *She's gone!*

But again his instincts won. He ran to the railing, thinking, *I'm a lunatic,* and jumped over the side.

Jason wasn't scared of heights. He was scared of being smashed against the canyon floor five hundred feet below. He figured he hadn't accomplished anything except for dying along with Piper, but he tucked in his arms and plummeted headfirst. The sides of the canyon raced past like a film on fast-forward. His face felt like it was peeling off.

In a heartbeat, he caught up with Piper, who was flailing wildly. He tackled her waist and closed his eyes, waiting for death. Piper screamed. The wind whistled in Jason's ears. He wondered what dying would feel like. He was thinking, probably not so good. He wished somehow they could never hit bottom.

Suddenly the wind died. Piper's scream turned into a strangled gasp. Jason thought they must be dead, but he hadn't felt any impact.

"J-J-Jason," Piper managed.

He opened his eyes. They weren't falling. They were floating in midair, a hundred feet above the river.

He hugged Piper tight, and she repositioned herself so she was hugging him too. They were nose to nose. Her heart beat so hard, Jason could feel it through her clothes.

Her breath smelled like cinnamon. She said, "How did you—"

"I didn't," he said. "I think I would know if I could fly...."

But then he thought: *I don't even know who I am.*

He imagined going up. Piper yelped as they shot a few feet higher. They weren't exactly floating, Jason decided. He could feel pressure under his feet like they were balancing at the top of a geyser.

"The air is supporting us," he said.

"Well, tell it to support us more! Get us out of here!"

Jason looked down. The easiest thing would be to sink gently to the canyon floor. Then he looked up. The rain had stopped. The storm clouds didn't seem as bad, but they were still rumbling and flashing. There was no guarantee the spirits were gone for good. He had no idea what had happened to Coach Hedge. And he'd left Leo up there, barely conscious.

"We have to help them," Piper said, as if reading his thoughts. "Can you—"

"Let's see." Jason thought *Up*, and instantly they shot skyward.

The fact he was riding the winds might've been cool under different circumstances, but he was too much in shock. As soon as they landed on the skywalk, they ran to Leo.

Piper turned Leo over, and he groaned. His army coat was soaked from the rain. His curly hair glittered gold from rolling around in monster dust. But at least he wasn't dead.

"Stupid...ugly...goat," he muttered.

"Where did he go?" Piper asked.

Leo pointed straight up. "Never came down. Please tell me he didn't actually save my life."

"Twice," Jason said.

Leo groaned even louder. "What happened? The tornado guy, the gold sword...I hit my head. That's it, right? I'm hallucinating?"

Jason had forgotten about the sword. He walked over to where it was lying and picked it up. The blade was well balanced. On a hunch he flipped it. Midspin, the sword shrank back into a coin and landed in his palm.

"Yep," Leo said. "Definitely hallucinating."

Piper shivered in her rain-soaked clothes. "Jason, those things—"

"*Venti,*" he said. "Storm spirits."

"Okay. You acted like...like you'd seen them before. Who *are* you?"

He shook his head. "That's what I've been trying to tell you. I don't know."

The storm dissipated. The other kids from the Wilderness

School were staring out the glass doors in horror. Security guards were working on the locks now, but they didn't seem to be having any luck.

"Coach Hedge said he had to protect three people," Jason remembered. "I think he meant us."

"And that thing Dylan turned into..." Piper shuddered. "God, I can't believe it was *hitting* on me. He called us... what, *demigods*?"

Leo lay on his back, staring at the sky. He didn't seem anxious to get up. "Don't know what *demi* means," he said. "But I'm not feeling too godly. You guys feeling godly?"

There was a brittle sound like dry twigs snapping, and the cracks in the skywalk began to widen.

"We need to get off this thing," Jason said. "Maybe if we—"

"Ohhh-kay," Leo interrupted. "Look up there and tell me if those are flying horses."

At first Jason thought Leo *had* hit his head too hard. Then he saw a dark shape descending from the east—too slow for a plane, too large for a bird. As it got closer he could see a pair of winged animals—gray, four-legged, exactly like horses— except each one had a twenty-foot wingspan. And they were pulling a brightly painted box with two wheels: a chariot.

"Reinforcements," he said. "Hedge told me an extraction squad was coming for us."

"Extraction squad?" Leo struggled to his feet. "That sounds painful."

"And where are they extracting us *to*?" Piper asked.

Jason watched as the chariot landed on the far end of the

skywalk. The flying horses tucked in their wings and cantered nervously across the glass, as if they sensed it was near
breaking. Two teenagers stood in the chariot—a tall blond
girl maybe a little older than Jason, and a bulky dude with a
shaved head and a face like a pile of bricks. They both wore
jeans and orange T-shirts, with shields tossed over their backs.
The girl leaped off before the chariot had even finished moving. She pulled a knife and ran toward Jason's group while
the bulky dude was reining in the horses.

"Where is he?" the girl demanded. Her gray eyes were
fierce and a little startling.

"Where's who?" Jason asked.

She frowned like his answer was unacceptable. Then she
turned to Leo and Piper. "What about Gleeson? Where is
your protector, Gleeson Hedge?"

The coach's first name was Gleeson? Jason might've
laughed if the morning hadn't been quite so weird and scary.
Gleeson Hedge: football coach, goat man, protector of demigods. Sure. Why not?

Leo cleared his throat. "He got taken by some . . . tornado
things."

"*Venti*," Jason said. "Storm spirits."

The blond girl arched an eyebrow. "You mean *anemoi thuellai*? That's the Greek term. Who are you, and what happened?"

Jason did his best to explain, though it was hard to meet
those intense gray eyes. About halfway through the story, the
other guy from the chariot came over. He stood there glaring
at them, his arms crossed. He had a tattoo of a rainbow on
his biceps, which seemed a little unusual.

When Jason had finished his story, the blond girl didn't look satisfied. "No, no, no! She *told* me he would be here. She told me if I came here, I'd find the answer."

"Annabeth," the bald guy grunted. "Check it out." He pointed at Jason's feet.

Jason hadn't thought much about it, but he was still missing his left shoe, which had been blown off by the lightning. His bare foot felt okay, but it looked like a lump of charcoal.

"The guy with one shoe," said the bald dude. "He's the answer."

"No, Butch," the girl insisted. "He can't be. I was tricked." She glared at the sky as though it had done something wrong. "What do you want from me?" she screamed. "What have you done with him?"

The skywalk shuddered, and the horses whinnied urgently.

"Annabeth," said the bald dude, Butch, "we gotta leave. Let's get these three to camp and figure it out there. Those storm spirits might come back."

She fumed for a moment. "Fine." She fixed Jason with a resentful look. "We'll settle this later."

She turned on her heel and marched toward the chariot.

Piper shook her head. "What's *her* problem? What's going on?"

"Seriously," Leo agreed.

"We have to get you out of here," Butch said. "I'll explain on the way."

"I'm not going anywhere with *her*." Jason gestured toward the blonde. "She looks like she wants to kill me."

Butch hesitated. "Annabeth's okay. You gotta cut her some

slack. She had a vision telling her to come here, to find a guy with one shoe. That was supposed to be the answer to her problem."

"What problem?" Piper asked.

"She's been looking for one of our campers, who's been missing three days," Butch said. "She's going out of her mind with worry. She hoped he'd be here."

"Who?" Jason asked.

"Her boyfriend," Butch said. "A guy named Percy Jackson."

III

PIPER

AFTER A MORNING OF STORM SPIRITS, goat men, and flying boyfriends, Piper should've been losing her mind. Instead, all she felt was dread.

It's starting, she thought. *Just like the dream said.*

She stood in back of the chariot with Leo and Jason, while the bald guy, Butch, handled the reins, and the blond girl, Annabeth, adjusted a bronze navigation device. They rose over the Grand Canyon and headed east, icy wind ripping straight through Piper's jacket. Behind them, more storm clouds were gathering.

The chariot lurched and bumped. It had no seat belts and the back was wide open, so Piper wondered if Jason would catch her again if she fell. That had been the most disturbing part of the morning—not that Jason could fly, but that he'd held her in his arms and yet didn't know who she was.

All semester she'd worked on a relationship, trying to get

Jason to notice her as more than a friend. Finally she'd gotten the big dope to kiss her. The last few weeks had been the best of her life. And then, three nights ago, the dream had ruined everything—that horrible voice, giving her horrible news. She hadn't told anyone about it, not even Jason.

Now she didn't even have *him*. It was like someone had wiped his memory, and she was stuck in the worst "do over" of all time. She wanted to scream. Jason stood right next to her: those sky blue eyes, close-cropped blond hair, that cute little scar on his upper lip. His face was kind and gentle, but always a little sad. And he just stared at the horizon, not even noticing her.

Meanwhile, Leo was being annoying, as usual. "This is so cool!" He spit a pegasus feather out of his mouth. "Where are we going?"

"A safe place," Annabeth said. "The *only* safe place for kids like us. Camp Half-Blood."

"Half-Blood?" Piper was immediately on guard. She hated that word. She'd been called a half-blood too many times— half Cherokee, half white—and it was never a compliment. "Is that some kind of bad joke?"

"She means we're demigods," Jason said. "Half god, half mortal."

Annabeth looked back. "You seem to know a lot, Jason. But, yes, demigods. My mom is Athena, goddess of wisdom. Butch here is the son of Iris, the rainbow goddess."

Leo choked. "Your mom is a rainbow goddess?"

"Got a problem with that?" Butch said.

"No, no," Leo said. "Rainbows. Very macho."

"Butch is our best equestrian," Annabeth said. "He gets along great with the pegasi."

"Rainbows, ponies," Leo muttered.

"I'm gonna toss you off this chariot," Butch warned.

"Demigods," Piper said. "You mean you think you're . . . you think we're—"

Lightning flashed. The chariot shuddered, and Jason yelled, "Left wheel's on fire!"

Piper stepped back. Sure enough, the wheel was burning, white flames lapping up the side of the chariot.

The wind roared. Piper glanced behind them and saw dark shapes forming in the clouds, more storm spirits spiraling toward the chariot—except these looked more like horses than angels.

She started to say, "Why are they—"

"*Anemoi* come in different shapes," Annabeth said. "Sometimes human, sometimes stallions, depending on how chaotic they are. Hold on. This is going to get rough."

Butch flicked the reins. The pegasi put on a burst of speed, and the chariot blurred. Piper's stomach crawled into her throat. Her vision went black, and when it came back to normal, they were in a totally different place.

A cold gray ocean stretched out to the left. Snow-covered fields, roads, and forests spread to the right. Directly below them was a green valley, like an island of springtime, rimmed with snowy hills on three sides and water to the north. Piper saw a cluster of buildings like ancient Greek temples, a big blue mansion, ball courts, a lake, and a climbing wall that seemed to be on fire. But before she could really process all she was seeing, their wheels came off and the chariot dropped out of the sky.

Annabeth and Butch tried to maintain control. The pegasi labored to hold the chariot in a flight pattern, but they seemed exhausted from their burst of speed, and bearing the chariot and the weight of five people was just too much.

"The lake!" Annabeth yelled. "Aim for the lake!"

Piper remembered something her dad had once told her, about hitting water from up high being as bad as hitting cement.

And then—*BOOM*.

The biggest shock was the cold. She was underwater, so disoriented that she didn't know which way was up.

She just had time to think: *This would be a stupid way to die.* Then faces appeared in the green murk—girls with long black hair and glowing yellow eyes. They smiled at her, grabbed her shoulders, and hauled her up.

They tossed her, gasping and shivering, onto the shore. Nearby, Butch stood in the lake, cutting the wrecked harnesses off the pegasi. Fortunately, the horses looked okay, but they were flapping their wings and splashing water everywhere. Jason, Leo, and Annabeth were already on shore, surrounded by kids giving them blankets and asking questions. Somebody took Piper by the arms and helped her stand. Apparently kids fell into the lake a lot, because a detail of campers ran up with big bronze leaf blower–looking things and blasted Piper with hot air; and in about two seconds her clothes were dry.

There were at least twenty campers milling around— the youngest maybe nine, the oldest college age, eighteen or nineteen—and all of them had orange T-shirts like Annabeth's. Piper looked back at the water and saw those strange girls just below the surface, their hair floating in the current. They waved like, *toodle-oo*, and disappeared into the depths. A second later the wreckage of the chariot was tossed from the lake and landed nearby with a wet crunch.

"Annabeth!" A guy with a bow and quiver on his back pushed through the crowd. "I said you could *borrow* the chariot, not destroy it!"

"Will, I'm sorry," Annabeth sighed. "I'll get it fixed, I promise."

Will scowled at his broken chariot. Then he sized up Piper, Leo, and Jason. "These are the ones? Way older than thirteen. Why haven't they been claimed already?"

"Claimed?" Leo asked.

Before Annabeth could explain, Will said, "Any sign of Percy?"

"No," Annabeth admitted.

The campers muttered. Piper had no idea who this guy Percy was, but his disappearance seemed to be a big deal.

Another girl stepped forward—tall, Asian, dark hair in ringlets, plenty of jewelry, and perfect makeup. Somehow she managed to make jeans and an orange T-shirt look glamorous. She glanced at Leo, fixed her eyes on Jason like he might be worthy of her attention, then curled her lip at Piper as if she were a week-old burrito that had just been pulled out of a Dumpster. Piper knew this girl's type. She'd dealt with a lot of girls like this at Wilderness School and every other stupid school her father had sent her to. Piper knew instantly they were going to be enemies.

"Well," the girl said, "I hope they're worth the trouble."

Leo snorted. "Gee, thanks. What are we, your new pets?"

"No kidding," Jason said. "How about some answers before you start judging us—like, what is this place, why are we here, how long do we have to stay?"

Piper had the same questions, but a wave of anxiety washed over her. *Worth the trouble.* If they only knew about her dream. They had no idea. . . .

"Jason," Annabeth said, "I promise we'll answer your questions. And Drew"—she frowned at the glamour girl—"all demigods are worth saving. But I'll admit, the trip didn't accomplish what I hoped."

"Hey," Piper said, "we didn't ask to be brought here."

Drew sniffed. "And nobody *wants* you, hon. Does your hair always look like a dead badger?"

Piper stepped forward, ready to smack her, but Annabeth said, "Piper, stop."

Piper did. She wasn't a bit scared of Drew, but Annabeth didn't seem like somebody she wanted for an enemy.

"We need to make our new arrivals feel welcome," Annabeth said, with another pointed look at Drew. "We'll assign them each a guide, give them a tour of camp. Hopefully by the campfire tonight, they'll be claimed."

"Would somebody tell me what *claimed* means?" Piper asked.

Suddenly there was a collective gasp. The campers backed

away. At first Piper thought she'd done something wrong. Then she realized their faces were bathed in a strange red light, as if someone had lit a torch behind her. She turned and almost forgot how to breathe.

Floating over Leo's head was a blazing holographic image —a fiery hammer.

"That," Annabeth said, "is claiming."

"What'd I do?" Leo backed toward the lake. Then he glanced up and yelped. "Is my hair on fire?" He ducked, but the symbol followed him, bobbing and weaving so it looked like he was trying to write something in flames with his head.

"This can't be good," Butch muttered. "The curse—"

"Butch, shut up," Annabeth said. "Leo, you've just been claimed—"

"By a god," Jason interrupted. "That's the symbol of Vulcan, isn't it?"

All eyes turned to him.

"Jason," Annabeth said carefully, "how did you know that?"

"I'm not sure."

"Vulcan?" Leo demanded. "I don't even LIKE *Star Trek*. What are you talking about?"

"Vulcan is the Roman name for Hephaestus," Annabeth said, "the god of blacksmiths and fire."

The fiery hammer faded, but Leo kept swatting the air like he was afraid it was following him. "The god of *what*? Who?"

Annabeth turned to the guy with the bow. "Will, would you take Leo, give him a tour? Introduce him to his bunkmates in Cabin Nine."

"Sure, Annabeth."

"What's Cabin Nine?" Leo asked. "And I'm not a Vulcan!"

"Come on, Mr. Spock, I'll explain everything." Will put a hand on his shoulder and steered him off toward the cabins.

Annabeth turned her attention back to Jason. Usually Piper didn't like it when other girls checked out her boyfriend, but Annabeth didn't seem to care that he was a good-looking guy. She studied him more like he was a complicated blueprint. Finally she said, "Hold out your arm."

Piper saw what she was looking at, and her eyes widened.

Jason had taken off his windbreaker after his dip in the lake, leaving his arms bare, and on the inside of his right forearm was a tattoo. How had Piper never noticed it before? She'd looked at Jason's arms a million times. The tattoo couldn't have just *appeared*, but it was darkly etched, impossible to miss: a dozen straight lines like a bar code, and over that an eagle with the letters SPQR.

"I've never seen marks like this," Annabeth said. "Where did you get them?"

Jason shook his head. "I'm getting really tired of saying this, but I don't know."

The other campers pushed forward, trying to get a look at Jason's tattoo. The marks seemed to bother them *a lot*—almost like a declaration of war.

"They look burned into your skin," Annabeth noticed.

"They were," Jason said. Then he winced as if his head was aching. "I mean . . . I think so. I don't remember."

No one said anything. It was clear the campers saw Annabeth as the leader. They were waiting for her verdict.

"He needs to go straight to Chiron," Annabeth decided. "Drew, would you—"

"Absolutely." Drew laced her arm through Jason's. "This way, sweetie. I'll introduce you to our director. He's . . . an *interesting* guy." She flashed Piper a smug look and led Jason toward the big blue house on the hill.

The crowd began to disperse, until only Annabeth and Piper were left.

"Who's Chiron?" Piper asked. "Is Jason in some kind of trouble?"

Annabeth hesitated. "Good question, Piper. Come on, I'll give you a tour. We need to talk."

IV

PIPER

PIPER SOON REALIZED ANNABETH'S HEART wasn't in the tour.

She talked about all this amazing stuff the camp offered—magic archery, pegasus riding, the lava wall, fighting monsters—but she showed no excitement, as if her mind were elsewhere. She pointed out the open-air dining pavilion that overlooked Long Island Sound. (Yes, Long Island, New York; they'd traveled *that* far on the chariot.) Annabeth explained how Camp Half-Blood was mostly a summer camp, but some kids stayed here year-round, and they'd added so many campers it was always crowded now, even in winter.

Piper wondered who ran the camp, and how they'd known Piper and her friends belonged here. She wondered if she'd have to stay full-time, or if she'd be any good at the activities. Could you flunk out of monster fighting? A million questions bubbled in her head, but given Annabeth's mood, she decided to keep quiet.

As they climbed a hill at the edge of camp, Piper turned and got an amazing view of the valley—a big stretch of woods to the northwest, a beautiful beach, the creek, the canoe lake, lush green fields, and the whole layout of the cabins—a bizarre assortment of buildings arranged like a Greek omega, Ω, with a loop of cabins around a central green, and two wings sticking out the bottom on either side. Piper counted twenty cabins in all. One glowed golden, another silver. One had grass on the roof. Another was bright red with barbed wire trenches. One cabin was black with fiery green torches out front.

All of it seemed like a different world from the snowy hills and fields outside.

"The valley is protected from mortal eyes," Annabeth said. "As you can see, the weather is controlled, too. Each cabin represents a Greek god—a place for that god's children to live."

She looked at Piper like she was trying to judge how Piper was handling the news.

"You're saying Mom was a goddess."

Annabeth nodded. "You're taking this awfully calmly."

Piper couldn't tell her why. She couldn't admit that this just confirmed some weird feelings she'd had for years, arguments she'd had with her father about why there were no photos of Mom in the house, and why Dad would never tell her exactly how or why her mom had left them. But mostly, the dream had warned her this was coming. *Soon they will find you, demigod,* that voice had rumbled. *When they do, follow our directions. Cooperate, and your father might live.*

Piper took a shaky breath. "I guess after this morning, it's a little easier to believe. So who's my mom?"

"We should know soon," Annabeth said. "You're what—fifteen? Gods are supposed to claim you when you're thirteen. That was the deal."

"The deal?"

"They made a promise last summer...well, long story ...but they promised not to ignore their demigod children anymore, to claim them by the time they turn thirteen. Sometimes it takes a little longer, but you saw how fast Leo was claimed once he got here. Should happen for you soon. Tonight at the campfire, I bet we'll get a sign."

Piper wondered if she'd have a big flaming hammer over her head, or with her luck, something even more embarrassing. A flaming wombat, maybe. Whoever her mother was, Piper had no reason to think she'd be proud to claim a kleptomaniac daughter with massive problems. "Why thirteen?"

"The older you get," Annabeth said, "the more monsters notice you, try to kill you. 'Round thirteen is usually when it starts. That's why we send protectors into the schools to find you guys, get you to camp before it's too late."

"Like Coach Hedge?"

Annabeth nodded. "He's—he was a satyr: half man, half goat. Satyrs work for the camp, finding demigods, protecting them, bringing them in when the time is right."

Piper had no trouble believing Coach Hedge was half goat. She'd seen the guy eat. She'd never liked the coach much, but she couldn't believe he'd sacrificed himself to save them.

"What happened to him?" she asked. "When we went up into the clouds, did he . . . is he gone for good?"

"Hard to say." Annabeth's expression was pained. "Storm spirits . . . difficult to battle. Even our best weapons, Celestial bronze, will pass right through them unless you can catch them by surprise."

"Jason's sword just turned them to dust," Piper remembered.

"He was lucky, then. If you hit a monster just right, you can dissolve them, send their essence back to Tartarus."

"Tartarus?"

"A huge abyss in the Underworld, where the worst monsters come from. Kind of like a bottomless pit of evil. Anyway, once monsters dissolve, it usually takes months, even years before they can re-form again. But since this storm spirit Dylan got away—well, I don't know why he'd keep Hedge alive. Hedge was a protector, though. He knew the risks. Satyrs don't have mortal souls. He'll be reincarnated as a tree or a flower or something."

Piper tried to imagine Coach Hedge as a clump of very angry pansies. That made her feel even worse.

She gazed at the cabins below, and an uneasy feeling settled over her. Hedge had died to get her here safely. Her mom's cabin was down there somewhere, which meant she had brothers and sisters, more people she'd have to betray. *Do what we tell you*, the voice had said. *Or the consequences will be painful.* She tucked her hands under her arms, trying to stop them from shaking.

"It'll be okay," Annabeth promised. "You have friends

here. We've all been through a lot of weird stuff. We know what you're going through."

I doubt that, Piper thought.

"I've been kicked out of five different schools the past five years," she said. "My dad's running out of places to put me."

"Only five?" Annabeth didn't sound like she was teasing. "Piper, we've all been labeled troublemakers. I ran away from home when I was seven."

"Seriously?"

"Oh, yeah. Most of us are diagnosed with attention deficit disorder or dyslexia, or both—"

"Leo's ADHD," Piper said.

"Right. It's because we're hardwired for battle. Restless, impulsive—we don't fit in with regular kids. You should hear how much trouble Percy—" Her face darkened. "Anyway, demigods get a bad rep. How'd you get in trouble?"

Usually when someone asked that question, Piper started a fight, or changed the subject, or caused some kind of distraction. But for some reason she found herself telling the truth.

"I steal stuff," she said. "Well, not really *steal*..."

"Is your family poor?"

Piper laughed bitterly. "Not even. I did it...I don't know why. For attention, I guess. My dad never had time for me unless I got in trouble."

Annabeth nodded. "I can relate. But you said you didn't really steal? What do you mean?"

"Well...nobody ever believes me. The police, teachers —even the people I took stuff from: they're so embarrassed, they'll deny what happened. But the truth is, I don't steal anything. I just ask people for things. And they give me stuff. Even a BMW convertible. I just asked. And the dealer said, 'Sure. Take it.' Later, he realized what he'd done, I guess. Then the police came after me."

Piper waited. She was used to people calling her a liar, but when she looked up, Annabeth just nodded.

"Interesting. If your *dad* were the god, I'd say you're a child of Hermes, god of thieves. He can be pretty convincing. But your dad is mortal...."

"Very," Piper agreed.

Annabeth shook her head, apparently mystified. "I don't know, then. With luck, your mom will claim you tonight."

Piper almost hoped it wouldn't happen. If her mom were a goddess, would she know about that dream? Would she know what Piper had been asked to do? Piper wondered if Olympian gods ever blasted their kids with lightning for being evil, or grounded them in the Underworld.

Annabeth was studying her. Piper decided she was going to have to be careful what she said from now on. Annabeth was obviously pretty smart. If anyone could figure out Piper's secret...

"Come on," Annabeth said at last. "There's something else I need to check."

They hiked a little farther until they reached a cave near the top of the hill. Bones and old swords littered the ground. Torches flanked the entrance, which was covered in a velvet curtain embroidered with snakes. It looked like the set for some kind of twisted puppet show.

"What's in there?" Piper asked.

Annabeth poked her head inside, then sighed and closed the curtains. "Nothing, right now. A friend's place. I've been expecting her for a few days, but so far, nothing."

"Your friend lives in a cave?"

Annabeth almost managed a smile. "Actually, her family has a luxury condo in Queens, and she goes to a finishing school in Connecticut. But when she's here at camp, yeah, she lives in the cave. She's our oracle, tells the future. I was hoping she could help me—"

"Find Percy," Piper guessed.

All the energy drained out of Annabeth, like she'd been holding it together for as long as she could. She sat down on a rock, and her expression was so full of pain, Piper felt like a voyeur.

She forced herself to look away. Her eyes drifted to the crest of the hill, where a single pine tree dominated the skyline. Something glittered in its lowest branch—like a fuzzy gold bath mat.

No... not a bath mat. It was a sheep's fleece.

Okay, Piper thought. Greek camp. They've got a replica of the Golden Fleece.

Then she noticed the base of the tree. At first she thought it was wrapped in a pile of massive purple cables. But the cables had reptilian scales, clawed feet, and a snakelike head with yellow eyes and smoking nostrils.

"That's—a dragon," she stammered. "That's the *actual* Golden Fleece?"

Annabeth nodded, but it was clear she wasn't really

listening. Her shoulders drooped. She rubbed her face and took a shaky breath. "Sorry. A little tired."

"You look ready to drop," Piper said. "How long have been searching for your boyfriend?"

"Three days, six hours, and about twelve minutes."

"And you've got no idea what happened to him?"

Annabeth shook her head miserably. "We were so excited because we both started winter break early. We met up at camp on Tuesday, figured we had three weeks together. It was going to be great. Then after the campfire, he—he kissed me good night, went back to his cabin, and in the morning, he was gone. We searched the whole camp. We contacted his mom. We've tried to reach him every way we know how. Nothing. He just disappeared."

Piper was thinking: *Three days ago.* The same night she'd had her dream. "How long were you guys together?"

"Since August," Annabeth said. "August eighteenth."

"Almost exactly when I met Jason," Piper said. "But we've only been together a few weeks."

Annabeth winced. "Piper . . . about that. Maybe you should sit down."

Piper knew where this was going. Panic started building inside her, like her lungs were filling with water. "Look, I know Jason thought—he thought he just *appeared* at our school today. But that's not true. I've known him for four months."

"Piper," Annabeth said sadly. "It's the Mist."

"Missed . . . what?"

"M-i-s-t. It's a kind of veil separating the mortal world from the mortal world from the magic world. Mortal minds—they can't process strange stuff like gods and monsters, so the Mist bends reality. It makes mortals see things in a way they *can* understand —like their eyes might just skip over this valley completely, or they might look at that dragon and see a pile of cables."

Piper swallowed. "No. You said yourself I'm not a regular mortal. I'm a demigod."

"Even demigods can be affected. I've seen it lots of times. Monsters infiltrate some place like a school, pass themselves off as human, and everyone *thinks* they remember that person. They believe he's always been around. The Mist can change memories, even create memories of things that never happened—"

"But Jason's not a monster!" Piper insisted. "He's a human guy, or demigod, or whatever you want to call him. My memories aren't fake. They're *so* real. The time we set Coach Hedge's pants on fire. The time Jason and I watched a meteor shower on the dorm roof and I finally got the stupid guy to kiss me...."

She found herself rambling, telling Annabeth about her whole semester at Wilderness School. She'd liked Jason from the first week they'd met. He was so nice to her, and so patient, he could even put up with hyperactive Leo and his stupid jokes. He'd accepted her for herself and didn't judge her because of the stupid things she'd done. They'd spent hours talking, looking at the stars, and eventually—*finally*—holding hands. All that *couldn't* be fake.

Annabeth pursed her lips. "Piper, your memories are a lot sharper than most. I'll admit that, and I don't know why that is. But if you know him so well—"

"I do!"

"Then where is he from?"

Piper felt like she'd been hit between the eyes. "He must have told me, but—"

"Did you ever notice his tattoo before today? Did he ever tell you anything about his parents, or his friends, or his last school?"

"I—I don't know, but—"

"Piper, what's his last name?"

Her mind went blank. She didn't know Jason's last name. How could that be?

She started to cry. She felt like a total fool, but she sat down on the rock next to Annabeth and just fell to pieces. It was too much. Did *everything* that was good in her stupid, miserable life have to be taken away?

Yes, the dream had told her. *Yes, unless you do exactly what we say.*

"Hey," Annabeth said. "We'll figure it out. Jason's here now. Who knows? Maybe it'll work out with you guys for real."

Not likely, Piper thought. Not if the dream had told her the truth. But she couldn't say that.

She brushed a tear from her cheek. "You brought me up here so no one would see me blubbering, huh?"

Annabeth shrugged. "I figured it would be hard for you. I know what it's like to lose your boyfriend."

"But I still can't believe... I *know* we had something. And now it's just gone, like he doesn't even recognize me. If he really did just show up today, then why? How'd he get there? Why can't he remember anything?"

"Good questions," Annabeth said. "Hopefully Chiron can figure that out. But for now, we need to get you settled. You ready to go back down?"

Piper gazed at the crazy assortment of cabins in the valley. Her new home, a family who supposedly understood her—but soon they'd be just another bunch of people she'd disappointed, just another place she'd been kicked out of. *You'll betray them for us,* the voice had warned. *Or you'll lose everything.*

She didn't have a choice.

"Yeah," she lied. "I'm ready."

On the central green, a group of campers was playing basketball. They were incredible shots. Nothing bounced off the rim. Three-pointers went in automatically.

"Apollo's cabin," Annabeth explained. "Bunch of show-offs with missile weapons—arrows, basketballs."

They walked past a central fire pit, where two guys were hacking at each other with swords.

"Real blades?" Piper noted. "Isn't that dangerous?"

"That's sort of the point," Annabeth said. "Uh, sorry. Bad pun. That's my cabin over there. Number Six." She nodded to a gray building with a carved owl over the door. Through the open doorway, Piper could see bookshelves, weapon displays, and one of those computerized SMART Boards they have in classrooms. Two girls were drawing a map that looked like a battle diagram.

"Speaking of blades," Annabeth said, "come here."

She led Piper around the side of the cabin, to a big metal shed that looked like it was meant for gardening tools. Annabeth unlocked it, and inside were *not* gardening tools, unless you wanted to make war on your tomato plants. The shed was lined with all sorts of weapons—from swords to spears to clubs like Coach Hedge's.

"Every demigod needs a weapon," Annabeth said. "Hephaestus makes the best, but we have a pretty good selection, too. Athena's all about strategy—matching the right weapon to the right person. Let's see..."

Piper didn't feel much like shopping for deadly objects, but she knew Annabeth was trying to do something nice for her.

Annabeth handed her a massive sword, which Piper could hardly lift.

"No," they both said at once.

Annabeth rummaged a little farther in the shed and brought out something else.

"A shotgun?" Piper asked.

"Mossberg 500." Annabeth checked the pump action like it was no big deal. "Don't worry. It doesn't hurt humans. It's modified to shoot Celestial bronze, so it only kills monsters."

"Um, I don't think that's my style," Piper said.

"Mmm, yeah," Annabeth agreed. "Too flashy."

She put the shotgun back and started poking through a rack of crossbows when something in the corner of the shed caught Piper's eye.

"What is that?" she said. "A knife?"

Annabeth dug it out and blew the dust off the scabbard. It looked like it hadn't seen the light of day in centuries.

"I don't know, Piper." Annabeth sounded uneasy. "I don't think you want this one. Swords are usually better."

"You use a knife." Piper pointed to the one strapped to Annabeth's belt.

"Yeah, but..." Annabeth shrugged. "Well, take a look if you want."

The sheath was worn black leather, bound in bronze. Nothing fancy, nothing flashy. The polished wood handle fit beautifully in Piper's hand. When she unsheathed it, she found a triangular blade eighteen inches long—bronze gleaming like it had been polished yesterday. The edges were deadly sharp. Her reflection in the blade caught her by surprise. She looked older, more serious, not as scared as she felt.

"It suits you," Annabeth admitted. "That kind of blade is called a parazonium. It was mostly ceremonial, carried by high-ranking officers in the Greek armies. It showed you were a person of power and wealth, but in a fight, it could protect you just fine."

"I like it," Piper said. "Why didn't you think it was right?"

Annabeth exhaled. "That blade has a long story. Most people would be afraid to claim it. Its first owner...well, things didn't turn out too well for her. Her name was Helen."

Piper let that sink in. "Wait, you mean *the* Helen? Helen of Troy?"

Annabeth nodded.

Suddenly Piper felt like she should be handling the dagger with surgical gloves. "And it's just sitting in your toolshed?"

"We're surrounded by Ancient Greek stuff," Annabeth said. "This isn't a museum. Weapons like that—they're meant to be used. They're our heritage as demigods. That was a wedding present from Menelaus, Helen's first husband. She named the dagger Katoptris."

"Meaning?"

"Mirror," Annabeth said. "Looking glass. Probably because that's the only thing Helen used it for. I don't think it's ever seen battle."

Piper looked at the blade again. For a moment, her own image stared up at her, but then the reflection changed. She saw flames, and a grotesque face like something carved from bedrock. She heard the same laughter as in her dream. She saw her dad in chains, tied to a post in front of a roaring bonfire.

She dropped the blade.

"Piper?" Annabeth shouted to the Apollo kids on the court, "Medic! I need some help over here!"

"No, it's—it's okay," Piper managed.

"You sure?"

"Yeah. I just..." She had to control herself. With trembling fingers, she picked up the dagger. "I just got overwhelmed. So much happening today. But...I want to keep the dagger, if that's okay."

Annabeth hesitated. Then she waved off the Apollo kids. "Okay, if you're sure. You turned really pale, there. I thought you were having a seizure or something."

"I'm fine," Piper promised, though her heart was still racing. "Is there...um, a phone at camp? Can I call my dad?"

Annabeth's gray eyes were almost as unnerving as the dagger blade. She seemed to be calculating a million possibilities, trying to read Piper's thoughts.

"We aren't allowed phones," she said. "Most demigods, if they use a cell phone, it's like sending up a signal, letting monsters know where you are. But...I've got one." She slipped it out of her pocket. "Kind of against the rules, but if it can be our secret..."

Piper took it gratefully, trying not to let her hands shake. She stepped away from Annabeth and turned to face the commons area.

She called her dad's private line, even though she knew what would happen. Voice mail. She'd been trying for three days, ever since the dream. Wilderness School only allowed phone privileges once a day, but she'd called every evening, and gotten nowhere.

Reluctantly she dialed the other number. Her dad's personal assistant answered immediately. "Mr. McLean's office."

"Jane," Piper said, gritting her teeth. "Where's my dad?"

Jane was silent for a moment, probably wondering if she could get away with hanging up. "Piper, I thought you weren't supposed to call from school."

"Maybe I'm not at school," Piper said. "Maybe I ran away to live among the woodland creatures."

"Mmm." Jane didn't sound concerned. "Well, I'll tell him you called."

"Where is he?"

"Out."

"You don't know, do you?" Piper lowered her voice, hoping Annabeth was too nice to eavesdrop. "When are you going to call the police, Jane? He could be in trouble."

"Piper, we are not going to turn this into a media circus. I'm sure he's fine. He does take off occasionally. He always comes back."

"So it's true. You *don't* know—"

"I have to go, Piper," Jane snapped. "Enjoy school."

The line went dead. Piper cursed. She walked back to Annabeth and handed her the phone.

"No luck?" Annabeth asked.

Piper didn't answer. She didn't trust herself not to start crying again.

Annabeth glanced at the phone display and hesitated. "Your last name is McLean? Sorry, it's not my business. But that sounds really familiar."

"Common name."

"Yeah, I guess. What does your dad do?"

"He's got a degree in the arts," Piper said automatically. "He's a Cherokee artist."

Her standard response. Not a lie, just not the whole truth. Most people, when they heard that, figured her dad sold Indian souvenirs at a roadside stand on a reservation. Sitting Bull bobble-heads, wampum necklaces, Big Chief tablets—that kind of thing.

"Oh." Annabeth didn't look convinced, but she put the phone away. "You feeling okay? Want to keep going?"

Piper fastened her new dagger to her belt and promised

herself that later, when she was alone, she'd figure out how it worked. "Sure," she said. "I want to see everything."

All the cabins were cool, but none of them struck Piper as *hers*. No burning signs—wombats or otherwise—appeared over her head.

Cabin Eight was entirely silver and glowed like moonlight.

"Artemis?" Piper guessed.

"You know Greek mythology," Annabeth said.

"I did some reading when my dad was working on a project last year."

"I thought he did Cherokee art."

Piper bit back a curse. "Oh, right. But—you know, he does other stuff too."

Piper thought she'd blown it: McLean, Greek mythology. Thankfully, Annabeth didn't seem to make the connection.

"Anyway," Annabeth continued, "Artemis is goddess of the moon, goddess of hunting. But no campers. Artemis was an eternal maiden, so she doesn't have any kids."

"Oh." That kind of bummed Piper out. She'd always liked the stories of Artemis, and figured she would make a cool mom.

"Well, there *are* the Hunters of Artemis," Annabeth amended. "They visit sometimes. They're not the children of Artemis, but they're her handmaidens—this band of immortal teenage girls who adventure together and hunt monsters and stuff."

Piper perked up. "That sounds cool. They get to be immortal?"

"Unless they die in combat, or break their vows. Did I mention they have to swear off boys? No dating—ever. For eternity."

"Oh," Piper said. "Never mind."

Annabeth laughed. For a moment she looked almost happy, and Piper thought she'd be a cool friend to hang out with in better times.

Forget it, Piper reminded herself. You're not going to make any friends here. Not once they find out.

They passed the next cabin, Number Ten, which was decorated like a Barbie house with lace curtains, a pink door, and potted carnations in the windows. They walked by the doorway, and the smell of perfume almost made Piper gag.

"Gah, is that where supermodels go to die?"

Annabeth smirked. "Aphrodite's cabin. Goddess of love. Drew is the head counselor."

"Figures," Piper grumbled.

"They're not all bad," Annabeth said. "The last head counselor we had was great."

"What happened to her?"

Annabeth's expression darkened. "We should keep moving."

They looked at the other cabins, but Piper just got more depressed. She wondered if she could be the daughter of Demeter, the farming goddess. Then again, Piper killed every plant she ever touched. Athena was cool. Or maybe Hecate, the magic goddess. But it didn't really matter. Even here, where everyone was supposed to find a lost parent, she knew she would still end up the unwanted kid. She was not looking forward to the campfire tonight.

"We started with the twelve Olympian gods," Annabeth explained. "Male gods on the left, female on the right. Then last year, we added a whole bunch of new cabins for the other gods who didn't have thrones on Olympus—Hecate, Hades, Iris—"

"What are the two big ones on the end?" Piper asked.

Annabeth frowned. "Zeus and Hera. King and queen of the gods."

Piper headed that way, and Annabeth followed, though she didn't act very excited. The Zeus cabin reminded Piper of a bank. It was white marble with big columns out front and polished bronze doors emblazoned with lightning bolts.

Hera's cabin was smaller but done in the same style, except the doors were carved with peacock feather designs, shimmering in different colors.

Unlike the other cabins, which were all noisy and open and full of activity, the Zeus and Hera cabins looked closed and silent.

"Are they empty?" Piper asked.

Annabeth nodded. "Zeus went a long time without having any children. Well, mostly. Zeus, Poseidon, and Hades, the eldest brothers among the gods—they're called the Big Three. Their kids are really powerful, really dangerous. For the last seventy years or so, they tried to avoid having demigod children."

"*Tried* to avoid it?"

"Sometimes they...um, cheated. I've got a friend, Thalia

Grace, who's the daughter of Zeus. But she gave up camp life and became a Hunter of Artemis. My boyfriend, Percy, he's a son of Poseidon. And there's a kid who shows up sometimes, Nico—son of Hades. Except for them, there are no demigod children of the Big Three gods. At least, not that we know of."

"And Hera?" Piper looked at the peacock-decorated doors. The cabin bothered her, though she wasn't sure why.

"Goddess of marriage." Annabeth's tone was carefully controlled, like she was trying to avoid cursing. "She doesn't have kids with anyone but Zeus. So, yeah, no demigods. The cabin's just honorary."

"You don't like her," Piper noticed.

"We have a long history," Annabeth admitted. "I thought we'd made peace, but when Percy disappeared . . . I got this weird dream vision from her."

"Telling you to come get us," Piper said. "But you thought Percy would be there."

"It's probably better I don't talk about it," Annabeth said. "I've got nothing good to say about Hera right now."

Piper looked down at the base of the doors. "So who goes in here?"

"No one. The cabin is just honorary, like I said. No one goes in."

"Someone does." Piper pointed at a footprint on the dusty threshold. On instinct, she pushed the doors and they swung open easily.

Annabeth stepped back. "Um, Piper, I don't think we should—"

"We're supposed to do dangerous stuff, right?" And Piper walked inside.

Hera's cabin was not someplace Piper would want to live. It was as cold as a freezer, with a circle of white columns around a central statue of the goddess, ten feet tall, seated on a throne in flowing golden robes. Piper had always thought of Greek statues as white with blank eyes, but this one was brightly painted so it looked almost human—except huge. Hera's piercing eyes seemed to follow Piper.

At the goddess's feet, a fire burned in a bronze brazier. Piper wondered who tended it if the cabin was always empty. A stone hawk sat on Hera's shoulder, and in her hand was a staff topped with a lotus flower. The goddess's hair was done in black plaits. Her face smiled, but the eyes were cold and calculating, as if she were saying: *Mother knows best. Now don't cross me or I will have to step on you.*

There was nothing else in the cabin—no beds, no furniture, no bathroom, no windows, nothing that anyone could actually use to live. For a goddess of home and marriage, Hera's place reminded Piper of a tomb.

No, this wasn't her mom. At least Piper was sure of *that*. She hadn't come in here because she felt a *good* connection, but because her sense of dread was stronger here. Her dream—that horrible ultimatum she'd been handed—had something to do with this cabin.

She froze. They weren't alone. Behind the statue, at a little altar in the back, stood a figure covered in a black shawl. Only her hands were visible, palms up. She seemed to be chanting something like a spell or a prayer.

Annabeth gasped. "Rachel?"

The other girl turned. She dropped her shawl, revealing a mane of curly red hair and a freckled face that didn't go with the seriousness of the cabin or the black shawl at all. She looked about seventeen, a totally normal teen in a green blouse and tattered jeans covered with marker doodles. Despite the cold floor, she was barefoot.

"Hey!" She ran to give Annabeth a hug. "I'm so sorry! I came as fast as I could."

They talked for a few minutes about Annabeth's boyfriend and how there was no news, et cetera, until finally Annabeth remembered Piper, who was standing there feeling uncomfortable.

"I'm being rude," Annabeth apologized. "Rachel, this is Piper, one of the half-bloods we rescued today. Piper, this is Rachel Elizabeth Dare, our oracle."

"The friend who lives in the cave," Piper guessed.

Rachel grinned. "That's me."

"So you're an oracle?" Piper asked. "You can tell the future?"

"More like the future mugs me from time to time," Rachel said. "I speak prophecies. The oracle's spirit kind of hijacks me every once in a while and speaks important stuff that doesn't make any sense to anybody. But yeah, the prophecies tell the future."

"Oh." Piper shifted from foot to foot. "That's cool."

Rachel laughed. "Don't worry. Everybody finds it a little creepy. Even me. But usually I'm harmless."

"You're a demigod?"

"Nope," Rachel said. "Just mortal."

"Then what are you..." Piper waved her hand around the room.

Rachel's smile faded. She glanced at Annabeth, then back at Piper. "Just a hunch. Something about this cabin and Percy's disappearance. They're connected somehow. I've learned to follow my hunches, especially the last month, since the gods went silent."

"Went silent?" Piper asked.

Rachel frowned at Annabeth. "You haven't told her yet?"

"I was getting to that," Annabeth said. "Piper, for the last month...well, it's normal for the gods not to talk to their children very much, but usually we can count on some messages now and then. Some of us can even visit Olympus. I spent practically all semester at the Empire State Building."

"Excuse me?"

"The entrance to Mount Olympus these days."

"Oh," Piper said. "Sure, why not?"

"Annabeth was redesigning Olympus after it was damaged in the Titan War," Rachel explained. "She's an amazing architect. You should see the salad bar—"

"Anyway," Annabeth said, "starting about a month ago, Olympus fell silent. The entrance closed, and no one could get in. Nobody knows why. It's like the gods have sealed themselves off. Even my mom won't answer my prayers, and our camp director, Dionysus, was recalled."

"Your camp director was the god of...wine?"

"Yeah, it's a—"

"Long story," Piper guessed. "Right. Go on."

"That's it, really," Annabeth said. "Demigods still get claimed, but nothing else. No messages. No visits. No sign the gods are even listening. It's like something has happened —something *really* bad. Then Percy disappeared."

"And Jason showed up on our field trip," Piper supplied. "With no memory."

"Who's Jason?" Rachel asked.

"My—" Piper stopped herself before she could say "boyfriend," but the effort made her chest hurt. "My friend. But Annabeth, you said Hera sent you a dream vision."

"Right," Annabeth said. "The first communication from a god in a month, and it's Hera, the least helpful goddess, and she contacts me, her least favorite demigod. She tells me I'll find out what happened to Percy if I go to the Grand Canyon skywalk and look for a guy with one shoe. Instead, I find you guys, and the guy with one shoe is Jason. It doesn't make sense."

"Something bad is happening," Rachel agreed. She looked at Piper, and Piper felt an overwhelming desire to tell them about her dream, to confess that *she* knew what was happening—at least part of the story. And the bad stuff was only beginning.

"Guys," she said. "I—I need to—"

Before she could continue, Rachel's body stiffened. Her eyes began to glow with a greenish light, and she grabbed Piper by the shoulders.

Piper tried to back away, but Rachel's hands were like steel clamps.

Free me, she said. But it wasn't Rachel's voice. It sounded like an older woman, speaking from somewhere far away, down a long, echoing pipe. *Free me, Piper McLean, or the earth shall swallow us. It must be by the solstice.*

The room started spinning. Annabeth tried to separate Piper from Rachel, but it was no use. Green smoke enveloped them, and Piper was no longer sure if she was awake or dreaming. The giant statue of the goddess seemed to rise from its throne. It leaned over Piper, its eyes boring into her. The statue's mouth opened, its breath like horribly thick perfume. It spoke in the same echoing voice: *Our enemies stir. The fiery one is only the first. Bow to his will, and their king shall rise, dooming us all. FREE ME!*

Piper's knees buckled, and everything went black.

V

LEO

LEO'S TOUR WAS GOING GREAT UNTIL he learned about the dragon.

The archer dude, Will Solace, seemed pretty cool. Everything he showed Leo was so amazing, it should've been illegal. Real Greek warships moored at the beach that sometimes had practice fights with flaming arrows and explosives? Sweet! Arts & crafts sessions where you could make sculptures with chain saws and blowtorches? Leo was like, *Sign me up!* The woods were stocked with dangerous monsters, and no one should ever go in there alone? Nice! And the camp was overflowing with fine-looking girls. Leo didn't quite understand the whole related-to-the-gods business, but he hoped that didn't mean he was cousins with all these ladies. That would suck. At the very least, he wanted to check out those underwater girls in the lake again. They were definitely worth drowning for.

Will showed him the cabins, the dining pavilion, and the sword arena.

"Do I get a sword?" Leo asked.

Will glanced at him like he found the idea disturbing. "You'll probably make your own, seeing as how you're in Cabin Nine."

"Yeah, what's up with that? Vulcan?"

"Usually we don't call the gods by their Roman names," Will said. "The original names are Greek. Your dad is Hephaestus."

"Festus?" Leo had heard somebody say that before, but he was still dismayed. "Sounds like the god of cowboys."

"*He*-phaestus," Will corrected. "God of blacksmiths and fire."

Leo had heard that too, but he was trying not to think about it. The god of fire ... seriously? Considering what had happened to his mom, that seemed like a sick joke.

"So the flaming hammer over my head," Leo said. "Good thing, or bad thing?"

Will took a while to answer. "You were claimed almost immediately. That's usually good."

"But that Rainbow Pony dude, Butch—he mentioned a curse."

"Ah ... look, it's nothing. Since Cabin Nine's last head counselor died—"

"Died? Like, painfully?"

"I ought to let your bunkmates tell you about it."

"Yeah, where *are* my home dawgs? Shouldn't their counselor be giving me the VIP tour?"

"He, um, can't. You'll see why." Will forged ahead before Leo could ask anything else.

"Curses and death," Leo said to himself. "This just gets better and better."

He was halfway across the green when he spotted his old babysitter. And she was *not* the kind of person he expected to see at a demigod camp.

Leo froze in his tracks.

"What's wrong?" Will asked.

Tía Callida—*Auntie* Callida. That's what she'd called herself, but Leo hadn't seen her since he was five years old. She was just standing there, in the shadow of a big white cabin at the end of the green, watching him. She wore her black linen widow's dress, with a black shawl pulled over her hair. Her face hadn't changed—leathery skin, piercing dark eyes. Her withered hands were like claws. She looked ancient, but no different than Leo remembered.

"That old lady..." Leo said. "What's she doing here?"

Will tried to follow his gaze. "What old lady?"

"Dude, *the* old lady. The one in black. How many old ladies do you see over there?"

Will frowned. "I think you've had a long day, Leo. The Mist could still be playing tricks on your mind. How about we head straight to your cabin now?"

Leo wanted to protest, but when he looked back toward the big white cabin, Tía Callida was gone. He was *sure* she'd been there, almost as if thinking about his mom had summoned Callida back from the past.

And that wasn't good, because Tía Callida had tried to kill him.

"Just messing with you, man." Leo pulled some gears and levers from his pockets and started fiddling with them to calm his nerves. He couldn't have everybody at camp thinking he was crazy. At least, not crazier than he really was.

"Let's go see Cabin Nine," he said. "I'm in the mood for a good curse."

From the outside, the Hephaestus cabin looked like an oversize RV with shiny metal walls and metal-slatted windows. The entrance was like a bank vault door, circular and several feet thick. It opened with lots of brass gears turning and hydraulic pistons blowing smoke.

Leo whistled. "They got a steampunk theme going on, huh?"

Inside, the cabin seemed deserted. Steel bunks were folded against the walls like high-tech Murphy beds. Each had a digital control panel, blinking LED lights, glowing gems, and interlocking gears. Leo figured each camper had his own combination lock to release his bed, and there was probably an alcove behind it with storage, maybe some traps to keep out unwanted visitors. At least, that's the way Leo would've designed it. A fire pole came down from the second floor, even though the cabin didn't appear to *have* a second floor from the outside. A circular staircase led down into some kind of basement. The walls were lined with every kind of power tool Leo could imagine, plus a huge assortment of knives, swords, and other implements of destruction. A large workbench overflowed with scrap metal—screws, bolts, washers, nails, rivets, and a million other machine parts. Leo had a strong urge to shovel them all into his coat pockets. He loved that kind of stuff. But he'd need a hundred more coats to fit it all.

Looking around, he could almost imagine he was back in his mom's machine shop. Not the weapons, maybe—but the tools, the piles of scrap, the smell of grease and metal and hot engines. She would've loved this place.

He pushed that thought away. He didn't like painful memories. *Keep moving*—that was his motto. Don't dwell on things. Don't stay in one place too long. It was the only way to stay ahead of the sadness.

He picked a long implement from the wall. "A weed whacker? What's the god of fire want with a weed whacker?"

A voice in the shadows said, "You'd be surprised."

At the back of the room, one of the bunk beds was occupied. A curtain of dark camouflage material retracted, and Leo could see the guy who'd been invisible a second before. It was hard to tell much about him because he was covered in a body cast. His head was wrapped in gauze except for his face, which was puffy and bruised. He looked like the Pillsbury Doughboy after a beat-down.

"I'm Jake Mason," the guy said. "I'd shake your hand, but..."

"Yeah," Leo said. "Don't get up."

The guy cracked a smile, then winced like it hurt to move his face. Leo wondered what had happened to him, but he was afraid to ask.

"Welcome to Cabin Nine," Jake said. "Been almost a year since we had any new kids. I'm head counselor for now."

"For now?" Leo asked.

Will Solace cleared his throat. "So where is everybody, Jake?"

"Down at the forges," Jake said wistfully. "They're working on . . . you know, that problem."

"Oh." Will changed the subject. "So, you got a spare bed for Leo?"

Jake studied Leo, sizing him up. "You believe in curses, Leo? Or ghosts?"

I just saw my evil babysitter Tía Callida, Leo thought. She's *got* to be dead after all these years. And I can't go a day without remembering my mom in that machine shop fire. Don't talk to me about ghosts, doughboy.

But aloud, he said, "Ghosts? Pfft. Nah. I'm cool. A storm spirit chucked me down the Grand Canyon this morning, but you know, all in a day's work, right?"

Jake nodded. "That's good. Because I'll give you the best bed in the cabin—Beckendorf's."

"Whoa, Jake," Will said. "You sure?"

Jake called out: "Bunk 1-A, please."

The whole cabin rumbled. A circular section of the floor spiraled open like a camera lens, and a full-size bed popped up. The bronze frame had a built-in game station at the foot-board, a stereo system in the headboard, a glass-door refrigerator mounted into the base, and a whole bunch of control panels running down the side.

Leo jumped right in and lay back with arms behind his head. "I can handle this."

"It retracts into a private room below," Jake said.

"Oh, heck, yes," Leo said. "See y'all. I'll be down in the Leo Cave. Which button do I press?"

"Hold on," Will Solace protested. "You guys have private underground rooms?"

Jake probably would've smiled if it didn't hurt so much. "We got lots of secrets, Will. You Apollo guys can't have all the fun. Our campers have been excavating the tunnel system under Cabin Nine for almost a century. We still haven't found the end. Anyway, Leo, if you don't mind sleeping in a dead man's bed, it's yours."

Suddenly Leo didn't feel like kicking back. He sat up, careful not to touch any of the buttons. "The counselor who died—this was his bed?"

"Yeah," Jake said. "Charles Beckendorf."

Leo imagined saw blades coming through the mattress, or maybe a grenade sewn inside the pillows. "He didn't, like, die *in* this bed, did he?"

"No," Jake said. "In the Titan War, last summer."

"The Titan War," Leo repeated, "which has *nothing* to do with this very fine bed?"

"The Titans," Will said, like Leo was an idiot. "The big powerful guys that ruled the world before the gods. They tried to make a comeback last summer. Their leader, Kronos, built a new palace on top of Mount Tam in California. Their armies came to New York and almost destroyed Mount Olympus. A lot of demigods died trying to stop them."

"I'm guessing this wasn't on the news?" Leo said.

It seemed like a fair question, but Will shook his head in

disbelief. "You didn't hear about Mount St. Helens erupting, or the freak storms across the country, or that building collapsing in St. Louis?"

Leo shrugged. Last summer, he'd been on the run from another foster home. Then a truancy officer caught him in New Mexico, and the court sentenced him to the nearest correctional facility—the Wilderness School. "Guess I was busy."

"Doesn't matter," Jake said. "You were lucky to miss it. T he thing is, Beckendorf was one of the first casualties, and ever since then—"

"Your cabin's been cursed," Leo guessed.

Jake didn't answer. Then again, the dude was in a body cast. That *was* an answer. Leo started noticing little things that he hadn't seen before—an explosion mark on the wall, a stain on the floor that might've been oil...or blood. Broken swords and smashed machines kicked into the corners of the room, maybe out of frustration. The place *did* feel unlucky.

Jake sighed halfheartedly. "Well, I should get some sleep. I hope you like it here, Leo. It used to be...really nice."

He closed his eyes, and the camouflage curtain drew itself across the bed.

"Come on, Leo," Will said. "I'll take you to the forges."

As they were leaving, Leo looked back at his new bed, and he could almost imagine a dead counselor sitting there —another ghost who wasn't going to leave Leo alone.

LEO

"How did he die?" Leo asked. "I mean Beckendorf."

Will Solace trudged ahead. "Explosion. Beckendorf and Percy Jackson blew up a cruise ship full of monsters. Beckendorf didn't make it out."

There was that name again—Percy Jackson, Annabeth's missing boyfriend. That guy must've been into everything around here, Leo thought.

"So Beckendorf was pretty popular?" Leo asked. "I mean —before he blew up?"

"He was awesome," Will agreed. "It was hard on the whole camp when he died. Jake—he became head counselor in the middle of the war. Same as I did, actually. Jake did his best, but he never wanted to be leader. He just likes building stuff. Then after the war, things started to go wrong. Cabin Nine's chariots blew up. Their automatons went haywire. Their inventions started to malfunction. It was like a curse, and eventually people started calling it that—the Curse of Cabin Nine. Then Jake had his accident—"

"Which had something to do with the problem he mentioned," Leo guessed.

"They're working on it," Will said without enthusiasm. "And here we are."

The forge looked like a steam-powered locomotive had smashed into the Greek Parthenon and they had fused together. White marble columns lined the soot-stained walls. Chimneys pumped smoke over an elaborate gable carved with a bunch of gods and monsters. The building sat at the edge of a stream, with several waterwheels turning a series of bronze gears. Leo heard machinery grinding inside, fires roaring, and hammers ringing on anvils.

They stepped through the doorway, and a dozen guys and girls who'd been working on various projects all froze. The noise died down to the roar of the forge and the *click-click-click* of gears and levers.

"'Sup, guys," Will said. "This is your new brother, Leo —um, what's your last name?"

"Valdez." Leo looked around at the other campers. Was he really related to all of them? His cousins came from some big families, but he'd always just had his mom—until she died.

Kids came up and started shaking hands and introducing themselves. Their names blurred together: Shane, Christopher, Nyssa, Harley (yeah, like the motorcycle). Leo knew he'd never keep everybody straight. Too many of them. Too overwhelming.

None of them looked like the others—all different face types, skin tone, hair color, height. You'd never think, *Hey, look, it's the Hephaestus Bunch!* But they all had powerful hands, rough with calluses and stained with engine grease. Even little Harley, who couldn't have been more than eight, looked like he could go six rounds with Chuck Norris without breaking a sweat.

And all the kids shared a sad kind of seriousness. Their shoulders slumped like life had beaten them down pretty hard. Several looked like they'd been physically beaten up, too. Leo counted two arm slings, one pair of crutches, an eye patch, six Ace bandages, and about seven thousand Band-Aids.

"Well, all right!" Leo said. "I hear this is the party cabin!"

Nobody laughed. They all just stared at him.

Will Solace patted Leo's shoulder. "I'll leave you guys to get acquainted. Somebody show Leo to dinner when it's time?"

"I got it," one of the girls said. Nyssa, Leo remembered. She wore camo pants, a tank top that showed off her buff arms, and a red bandanna over a mop of dark hair. Except for the smiley-face Band-Aid on her chin, she looked like one of those female action heroes, like any second she was going to grab a machine gun and start mowing down evil aliens.

"Cool," Leo said. "I always wanted a sister who could beat me up."

Nyssa didn't smile. "Come on, joker boy. I'll show you around."

• • •

Leo was no stranger to workshops. He'd grown up around grease monkeys and power tools. His mom used to joke that his first pacifier was a lug wrench. But he'd never seen any place like the camp forge.

One guy was working on a battle-ax. He kept testing the blade on a slab of concrete. Each time he swung, the ax cut into the slab like it was warm cheese, but the guy looked unsatisfied and went back to honing the edge.

"What's he planning to kill with that thing?" Leo asked Nyssa. "A battleship?"

"You never know. Even with Celestial bronze—"

"That's the metal?"

She nodded. "Mined from Mount Olympus itself. Extremely rare. Anyway, it usually disintegrates monsters on contact, but big powerful ones have notoriously tough hides. Drakons, for instances—"

"You mean dragons?"

"Similar species. You'll learn the difference in monster-fighting class."

"Monster-fighting class. Yeah, I already got my black belt in that."

She didn't crack a smile. Leo hoped she wasn't this serious all the time. His dad's side of the family had to have *some* sense of humor, right?

They passed a couple of guys making a bronze windup toy. At least that's what it looked like. It was a six-inch-tall centaur—half man, half horse—armed with a miniature bow. One of the campers cranked the centaur's tail, and it whirred to life. It galloped across the table, yelling, "Die, mosquito! Die, mosquito!" and shooting everything in sight.

Apparently this had happened before, because everybody knew to hit the floor except Leo. Six needle-sized arrows embedded themselves in his shirt before a camper grabbed a hammer and smashed the centaur to pieces.

"Stupid curse!" The camper waved his hammer at the sky. "I just want a magic bug killer! Is that too much to ask?"

"Ouch," Leo said.

Nyssa pulled the needles out of his shirt. "Ah, you're fine. Let's move on before they rebuild it."

Leo rubbed his chest as they walked. "That sort of thing happen a lot?"

"Lately," Nyssa said, "everything we build turns to junk."

"The curse?"

Nyssa frowned. "I don't believe in curses. But *something's* wrong. And if we don't figure out the dragon problem, it's gonna get even worse."

"The dragon problem?" Leo hoped she was talking about a miniature dragon, maybe one that killed cockroaches, but he got the feeling he wasn't going to be so lucky.

Nyssa took him over to a big wall map that a couple of girls were studying. The map showed the camp—a semicircle of land with Long Island Sound on the north shore, the woods to the west, the cabins to the east, and a ring of hills to the south.

"It's got to be in the hills," the first girl said.

"We *looked* in the hills," the second argued. "The woods are a better hiding place."

"But we already set traps—"

"Hold up," Leo said. "You guys lost a dragon? A *real* full-size dragon?"

"It's a bronze dragon," Nyssa said. "But yes, it's a life-size automaton. Hephaestus cabin built it years ago. Then it was lost in the woods until a few summers back, when Beckendorf found it in pieces and rebuilt it. It's been helping protect the camp, but, um, it's a little unpredictable."

"Unpredictable," Leo said.

"It goes haywire and smashes down cabins, sets people on fire, tries to eat the satyrs."

"That's pretty unpredictable."

Nyssa nodded. "Beckendorf was the only one who could control it. Then he died, and the dragon just got worse and worse. Finally it went berserk and ran off. Occasionally it shows up, demolishes something, and runs away again. Everyone expects us to find it and destroy it—"

"*Destroy* it?" Leo was appalled. "You've got a life-size bronze dragon, and you want to *destroy* it?"

"It breathes fire," Nyssa explained. "It's deadly and out of control."

"But it's a dragon! Dude, that's so awesome. Can't you try talking to it, controlling it?"

"We tried. Jake Mason tried. You saw how well that worked."

Leo thought about Jake, wrapped in a body cast, lying alone on his bunk. "Still—"

"There's no other option." Nyssa turned to the other girls. "Let's try more traps in the woods—here, here, and here. Bait them with thirty-weight motor oil."

"The dragon drinks that?" Leo asked.

"Yeah." Nyssa sighed regretfully. "He used to like it with a little Tabasco sauce, right before bed. If he springs a trap, we can come in with acid sprayers—should melt through his hide. Then we get metal cutters and...and finish the job."

They all looked sad. Leo realized they didn't want to kill the dragon any more than he did.

"Guys," he said. "There has to be another way."

Nyssa looked doubtful, but a few other campers stopped what they were working on and drifted over to hear the conversation.

"Like what?" one asked. "The thing breathes fire. We can't even get close."

Fire, Leo thought. Oh, man, the things he could tell them about fire.... But he had to be careful, even if these were his brothers and sisters. *Especially* if he had to live with them.

"Well..." He hesitated. "Hephaestus is the god of fire, right? So don't any of you have like fire resistance or something?"

Nobody acted as if it was a crazy question, which was a relief, but Nyssa shook her head gravely.

"That's a Cyclops ability, Leo. Demigod children of Hephaestus...we're just good with our hands. We're builders, craftsmen, weaponsmiths—stuff like that."

Leo's shoulders slumped. "Oh."

A guy in back said, "Well, a long *time* ago—"

"Yeah, okay," Nyssa conceded. "A long time ago some children of Hephaestus were born with power over fire. But that ability was very, very rare. And always dangerous. No demigod like that has been born in centuries. The last one . . ." She looked at one of the other kids for help.

"Sixteen sixty-six," the girl offered. "Guy named Thomas Faynor. He started the Great Fire of London, destroyed most of the city."

"Right," Nyssa said. "When a child of Hephaestus like that appears, it usually means something catastrophic is about to happen. And we don't need any more catastrophes."

Leo tried to keep his face clear of emotion, which wasn't his strong suit. "I guess I see your point. Too bad, though. If you could resist flames, you could get close to the dragon."

"Then it would kill you with its claws and fangs," Nyssa said. "Or simply step on you. No, we've got to destroy it. Trust me, if anyone *could* figure out another answer . . ."

She didn't finish, but Leo got the message. This was the cabin's big test. If they could do something only Beckendorf could do, if they could subdue the dragon without killing it, then maybe their curse would be lifted. But they were stumped for ideas. Any camper who figured out how would be a hero.

A conch horn blew in the distance. Campers started putting up their tools and projects. Leo hadn't realized it was getting so late, but he looked through the windows and saw the sun going down. His ADHD did that to him sometimes. If he was bored, a fifty-minute class seemed like six hours. If he was interested in something, like touring a demigod camp, hours slipped away and *bam*—the day was over.

"Dinner," Nyssa said. "Come on, Leo."

"Up at the pavilion, right?" he asked.

She nodded.

"You guys go ahead," Leo said. "Can you ... give me a second?"

Nyssa hesitated. Then her expression softened. "Sure. It's a lot to process. I remember my first day. Come up when you're ready. Just don't touch anything. Almost every project in here can kill you if you're not careful."

"No touching," Leo promised.

His cabinmates filed out of the forge. Soon Leo was alone with the sounds of the bellows, the waterwheels, and small machines clicking and whirring.

He stared at the map of camp—the locations where his newfound siblings were going to put traps to catch a dragon. It was wrong. Plain wrong.

Very rare, he thought. And always dangerous.

He held out his hand and studied his fingers. They were long and thin, not callused like the other Hephaestus campers'. Leo had never been the biggest or the strongest kid. He'd survived in tough neighborhoods, tough schools, tough foster homes by using his wits. He was the class clown, the court jester, because he'd learned early that if you cracked jokes and pretended you weren't scared, you usually didn't get beat up. Even the baddest gangster kids would tolerate you, keep you around for laughs. Plus, humor was a good way to hide the pain. And if that didn't work, there was always Plan B. Run away. Over and over.

There *was* a Plan C, but he'd promised himself never to use it again.

He felt an urge to try it now—something he hadn't done since the accident, since his mom's death.

He extended his fingers and felt them tingle, like they were waking up—pins and needles. Then flames flickered to life, curls of red-hot fire dancing across his palm.

VII

JASON

As soon as Jason saw the house, he knew he was a dead man.

"Here we are!" Drew said cheerfully. "The Big House, camp headquarters."

It didn't look threatening, just a four-story manor painted baby blue with white trim. The wraparound porch had lounge chairs, a card table, and an empty wheelchair. Wind chimes shaped like nymphs turned into trees as they spun. Jason could imagine old people coming here for summer vacation, sitting on the porch and sipping prune juice while they watched the sunset. Still, the windows seemed to glare down at him like angry eyes. The wide-open doorway looked ready to swallow him. On the highest gable, a bronze eagle weathervane spun in the wind and pointed straight in his direction, as if telling him to turn around.

Every molecule in Jason's body told him he was on enemy ground.

"I am *not* supposed to be here," he said.

Drew circled her arm through his. "Oh, please. You're *perfect* here, sweetie. Believe me, I've seen a lot of heroes."

Drew smelled like Christmas—a strange combination of pine and nutmeg. Jason wondered if she always smelled like that, or if it was some kind of special perfume for the holidays. Her pink eyeliner was really distracting. Every time she blinked, he felt compelled to look at her. Maybe that was the point, to show off her warm brown eyes. She was pretty. No doubt about that. But she made Jason feel uncomfortable.

He slipped his arm away as gently as he could. "Look, I appreciate—"

"Is it that girl?" Drew pouted. "Oh, please, tell me you are *not* dating the Dumpster Queen."

"You mean Piper? Um . . ."

Jason wasn't sure how to answer. He didn't think he'd ever seen Piper before today, but he felt strangely guilty about it. He knew he shouldn't be in this place. He shouldn't befriend these people, and certainly he shouldn't date one of them. Still . . . Piper had been holding his hand when he woke up on that bus. She believed she was his girlfriend. She'd been brave on the skywalk, fighting those *venti*, and when Jason had caught her in midair and they'd held each other face-to-face, he couldn't pretend he wasn't a little tempted to kiss her. But that wasn't right. He didn't even know his own story. He couldn't play with her emotions like that.

Drew rolled her eyes. "Let me help you decide, sweetie. You can do better. A guy with your looks and obvious talent?"

She wasn't looking at him, though. She was staring at a spot right above his head.

"You're waiting for a sign," he guessed. "Like what popped over Leo's head."

"What? No! Well... yes. I mean, from what I heard, you're pretty powerful, right? You're going to be important at camp, so I figure your parent will claim you right away. And I'd love to see that. I wanna be with you every step of the way! So is your dad or mom the god? Please tell me it's not your mom. I would hate it if you were an *Aphrodite* kid."

"Why?"

"Then you'd be my half brother, silly. You can't date somebody from your own cabin. Yuck!"

"But aren't all the gods related?" Jason asked. "So isn't everyone here your cousin or something?"

"Aren't you cute! Sweetie, the godly side of your family doesn't count except for your parent. So anybody from another cabin—they're fair game. So who's your godly parent—mom or dad?"

As usual, Jason didn't have an answer. He looked up, but no glowing sign popped above his head. At the top of the Big House, the weathervane was still pointing his direction, that bronze eagle glaring as if to say, *Turn around, kid, while you still can.*

Then he heard footsteps on the front porch. No—not footsteps—*hooves.*

"Chiron!" Drew called. "This is Jason. He's totally awesome!"

Jason backed up so fast he almost tripped. Rounding the corner of the porch was a man on horseback. Except he wasn't on horseback—he was part of the horse. From the waist up he was human, with curly brown hair and a well-trimmed beard. He wore a T-shirt that said *World's Best Centaur*, and had a quiver and bow strapped to his back. His head was so high up he had to duck to avoid the porch lights, because from the waist down, he was a white stallion.

Chiron started to smile at Jason. Then the color drained from his face.

"You..." The centaur's eyes flared like a cornered animal's. "You should be dead."

Chiron ordered Jason—well, *invited*, but it sounded like an order—to come inside the house. He told Drew to go back to her cabin, which Drew didn't look happy about.

The centaur trotted over to the empty wheelchair on the porch. He slipped off his quiver and bow and backed up to the chair, which opened like a magician's box. Chiron gingerly stepped into it with his back legs and began scrunching himself into a space that should've been much too small. Jason imagined a truck's reversing noises—*beep, beep, beep*—as the centaur's lower half disappeared and the chair folded up, popping out a set of fake human legs covered in a blanket, so Chiron appeared to be a regular mortal guy in a wheelchair.

"Follow me," he ordered. "We have lemonade."

The living room looked like it had been swallowed by a rain forest. Grapevines curved up the walls and across the ceiling, which Jason found a little strange. He didn't think plants grew like that inside, especially in the winter, but these were leafy green and bursting with bunches of red grapes.

Leather couches faced a stone fireplace with a crackling fire. Wedged in one corner, an old-style Pac-Man arcade game beeped and blinked. Mounted on the walls was an assortment of masks—smiley/frowny Greek theater types, feathered Mardi Gras masks, Venetian *Carnevale* masks with big beaklike noses, carved wooden masks from Africa. Grapevines grew through their mouths so they seemed to have leafy tongues. Some had red grapes bulging through their eyeholes.

But the weirdest thing was the stuffed leopard's head above the fireplace. It looked so real, its eyes seemed to follow Jason. Then it snarled, and Jason nearly leaped out of his skin.

"Now, Seymour," Chiron chided. "Jason is a friend. Behave yourself."

"That thing is alive!" Jason said.

Chiron rummaged through the side pocket of his wheelchair and brought out a package of Snausages. He threw one to the leopard, who snapped it up and licked his lips.

"You must excuse the décor," Chiron said. "All this was a parting gift from our old director before he was recalled to Mount Olympus. He thought it would help us to remember him. Mr. D has a strange sense of humor."

"Mr. D," Jason said. "Dionysus?"

"Mmm hmm." Chiron poured lemonade, though his hands were trembling a little. "As for Seymour, well, Mr. D liberated him from a Long Island garage sale. The leopard is Mr. D's sacred animal, you see, and Mr. D was appalled that someone would stuff such a noble creature. He decided to grant it life, on the assumption that life as a mounted head was better than no life at all. I must say it's a kinder fate than Seymour's previous owner got."

Seymour bared his fangs and sniffed the air, as if hunting for more Snausages.

"If he's only a head," Jason said, "where does the food go when he eats?"

"Better not to ask," Chiron said. "Please, sit."

Jason took some lemonade, though his stomach was fluttering. Chiron sat back in his wheelchair and tried for a smile, but Jason could tell it was forced. The old man's eyes were as deep and dark as wells.

"So, Jason," he said, "would you mind telling me—ah—where you're from?"

"I wish I knew." Jason told him the whole story, from waking up on the bus to crash-landing at Camp Half-Blood. He didn't see any point in hiding the details, and Chiron was a good listener. He didn't react to the story, other than to nod encouragingly for more.

When Jason was done, the old man sipped his lemonade.

"I see," Chiron said. "And you must have questions for me."

"Only one," Jason admitted. "What did you mean when you said that I should be dead?"

Chiron studied him with concern, as if he expected Jason to burst into flames. "My boy, do you know what those marks on your arm mean? The color of your shirt? Do you remember anything?"

Jason looked at the tattoo on his forearm: SPQR, the eagle, twelve straight lines.

"No," he said. "Nothing."

"Do you know where you are?" Chiron asked. "Do you understand what this place is, and who I am?"

"You're Chiron the centaur," Jason said. "I'm guessing you're the same one from the old stories, who used to train the Greek heroes like Heracles. This is a camp for demigods, children of the Olympian gods."

"So you believe those gods still exist?"

"Yes," Jason said immediately. "I mean, I don't think we should *worship* them or sacrifice chickens to them or anything, but they're still around because they're a powerful part of civilization. They move from country to country as the center of power shifts—like they moved from Ancient Greece to Rome."

"I couldn't have said it better." Something about Chiron's voice had changed. *"So you already know the gods are real. You have already been claimed, haven't you?"*

"Maybe," Jason answered. *"I'm not really sure."*

Seymour the leopard snarled.

Chiron waited, and Jason realized what had just happened. The centaur had switched to another language and Jason had understood, automatically answering in the same tongue.

"Quis erat—" Jason faltered, then made a conscious effort to speak English. "What was that?"

"You know Latin," Chiron observed. "Most demigods recognize a few phrases, of course. It's in their blood, but not as much as Ancient Greek. None can speak Latin fluently without practice."

Jason tried to wrap his mind around what that meant, but too many pieces were missing from his memory. He still had the feeling that he shouldn't be here. It was wrong—and dangerous. But at least Chiron wasn't threatening. In fact the centaur seemed concerned for him, afraid for his safety.

The fire reflected in Chiron's eyes, making them dance fretfully. "I taught your namesake, you know, the original Jason. He had a hard path. I've seen many heroes come and go. Occasionally, they have happy endings. Mostly, they don't. It breaks my heart, like losing a child each time one of my pupils dies. But you—you are not like any pupil I've ever taught. Your presence here could be a disaster."

"Thanks," Jason said. "You must be an inspiring teacher."

"I am sorry, my boy. But it's true. I had hoped that after Percy's success—"

"Percy Jackson, you mean. Annabeth's boyfriend, the one who's missing."

Chiron nodded. "I hoped that after he succeeded in the Titan War and saved Mount Olympus, we might have some peace. I might be able to enjoy one final triumph, a happy ending, and perhaps retire quietly. I should have known better. The last chapter approaches, just as it did before. The worst is yet to come."

In the corner, the arcade game made a sad *pew-pew-pew-pew* sound, like a Pac-Man had just died.

"Ohh-kay," Jason said. "So—last chapter, happened before,

worst yet to come. Sounds fun, but can we go back to the part where I'm supposed to be dead? I don't like that part."

"I'm afraid I can't explain, my boy. I swore on the River Styx and on all things sacred that I would never..." Chiron frowned. "But you're here, in violation of the same oath. That too, should not be possible. I don't understand. Who would've done such a thing? Who—"

Seymour the leopard howled. His mouth froze, half open. The arcade game stopped beeping. The fire stopped crackling, its flames hardening like red glass. The masks stared down silently at Jason with their grotesque grape eyes and leafy tongues.

"Chiron?" Jason asked. "What's going—"

The old centaur had frozen, too. Jason jumped off the couch, but Chiron kept staring at the same spot, his mouth open mid-sentence. His eyes didn't blink. His chest didn't move.

Jason, a voice said.

For a horrible moment, he thought the leopard had spoken. Then dark mist boiled out of Seymour's mouth, and an even worse thought occurred to Jason: *storm spirits*.

He grabbed the golden coin from his pocket. With a quick flip, it changed into a sword.

The mist took the form of a woman in black robes. Her face was hooded, but her eyes glowed in the darkness. Over her shoulders she wore a goatskin cloak. Jason wasn't sure how he knew it was goatskin, but he recognized it and knew it was important.

Would you attack your patron? the woman chided. Her voice echoed in Jason's head. *Lower your sword.*

"Who are you?" he demanded. "How did you—"

Our time is limited, Jason. My prison grows stronger by the hour. It took me a full month to gather enough energy to work even the smallest magic through its bonds. I've managed to bring you here, but now I have little time left, and even less power. This may be the last time I can speak to you.

"You're in prison?" Jason decided maybe he wouldn't lower his sword. "Look, I don't know you, and you're not my patron."

You know me, she insisted. *I have known you since your birth.*

"I don't remember. I don't remember anything."

No, you don't, she agreed. *That also was necessary. Long ago, your father gave me your life as a gift to placate my anger. He named you Jason, after my favorite mortal. You belong to me.*

"Whoa," Jason said. "I don't belong to anyone."

Now is the time to pay your debt, she said. *Find my prison. Free me, or their king will rise from the earth, and I will be destroyed. You will never retrieve your memory.*

"Is that a threat? You *took* my memories?"

You have until sunset on the solstice, Jason. Four short days. Do not fail me.

The dark woman dissolved, and the mist curled into the leopard's mouth.

Time unfroze. Seymour's howl turned into a cough like he'd sucked in a hair ball. The fire crackled to life, the arcade machine beeped, and Chiron said, "—would dare to bring you here?"

"Probably the lady in the mist," Jason offered.

Chiron looked up in surprise. "Weren't you just sitting... why do you have a sword drawn?"

"I hate to tell you this," Jason said, "but I think your leopard just ate a goddess."

He told Chiron about the frozen-in-time visit, the dark misty figure that disappeared into Seymour's mouth.

"Oh, dear," Chiron murmured. "That does explain a lot."

"Then why don't you explain a lot to me?" Jason said. "Please."

Before Chiron could say anything, footsteps reverberated on the porch outside. The front door blew open, and Annabeth and another girl, a redhead, burst in, dragging Piper between them. Piper's head lolled like she was unconscious.

"What happened?" Jason rushed over. "What's wrong with her?"

"Hera's cabin," Annabeth gasped, like they'd run all the way. "Vision. Bad."

The redheaded girl looked up, and Jason saw that she'd been crying.

"I think..." The redheaded girl gulped. "I think I may have killed her."

VIII

JASON

JASON AND THE REDHEAD, WHO INTRODUCED herself as
Rachel, put Piper on the couch while Annabeth rushed down
the hall to get a med kit. Piper was still breathing, but she
wouldn't wake up. She seemed to be in some kind of coma.

"We've got to heal her," Jason insisted. "There's a way,
right?"

Seeing her so pale, barely breathing, Jason felt a surge of
protectiveness. Maybe he didn't really know her. Maybe she
wasn't his girlfriend. But they'd survived the Grand Canyon
together. They'd come all this way. He'd left her side for a
little while, and *this* had happened.

Chiron put his hand on her forehead and grimaced. "Her
mind is in a fragile state. Rachel, what happened?"

"I wish I knew," she said. "As soon as I got to camp, I had
a premonition about Hera's cabin. I went inside. Annabeth
and Piper came in while I was there. We talked, and then—I
just blanked out. Annabeth said I spoke in a different voice."

"A prophecy?" Chiron asked.

"No. The spirit of Delphi comes from within. I know how that feels. This was like long distance, a power trying to speak through me."

Annabeth ran in with a leather pouch. She knelt next to Piper. "Chiron, what happened back there—I've never seen anything like it. I've heard Rachel's prophecy voice. This was different. She sounded like an older woman. She grabbed Piper's shoulders and told her—"

"To free her from a prison?" Jason guessed.

Annabeth stared at him. "How did you know that?"

Chiron made a three-fingered gesture over his heart, like a ward against evil.

"Jason, tell them. Annabeth, the medicine bag, please."

Chiron trickled drops from a medicine vial into Piper's mouth while Jason explained what had happened when the room froze—the dark misty woman who had claimed to be Jason's patron.

When he was done, no one spoke, which made him more anxious.

"So does this happen often?" he asked. "Supernatural phone calls from convicts demanding you bust them out of jail?"

"Your patron," Annabeth said. "Not your godly parent?"

"No, she said *patron*. She also said my dad had given her my life."

Annabeth frowned. "I've never of heard anything like that before. You said the storm spirit on the skywalk—he claimed to be working for some mistress who was giving him orders, right? Could it be this woman you saw, messing with your mind?"

"I don't think so," Jason said. "If she were my enemy, why would she be asking for my help? She's imprisoned. She's worried about some enemy getting more powerful. Something about a king rising from the earth on the solstice—"

Annabeth turned to Chiron. "Not Kronos. Please tell me it's not that."

The centaur looked miserable. He held Piper's wrist, checking her pulse.

At last he said, "It is not Kronos. That threat is ended. But..."

"But what?" Annabeth asked.

Chiron closed the medicine bag. "Piper needs rest. We should discuss this later."

"Or now," Jason said. "Sir, Mr. Chiron, you told me the greatest threat was coming. The last chapter. You can't possibly mean something worse than an army of Titans, right?"

"Oh," Rachel said in a small voice. "Oh, dear. The woman was Hera. Of course. Her cabin, her voice. She showed herself to Jason at the same moment."

"Hera?" Annabeth's snarl was even fiercer than Seymour's. "*She* took you over? She did this to Piper?"

"I think Rachel's right," Jason said. "The woman did seem like a goddess. And she wore this—this goatskin cloak. That's a symbol of Juno, isn't it?"

"It is?" Annabeth scowled. "I've never heard that."

Chiron nodded reluctantly. "Of Juno, Hera's Roman

aspect, in her most warlike state. The goatskin cloak was a symbol of the Roman soldier."

"So Hera is imprisoned?" Rachel asked. "Who could do that to the queen of the gods?"

Annabeth crossed her arms. "Well, whoever they are, maybe we should thank them. If they can shut up Hera—"

"Annabeth," Chiron warned, "she is still one of the Olympians. In many ways, she is the glue that holds the gods' family together. If she truly has been imprisoned and is in danger of destruction, this could shake the foundations of the world. It could unravel the stability of Olympus, which is never great even in the best of times. And if Hera has asked Jason for help—"

"Fine," Annabeth grumbled. "Well, we know Titans can capture a god, right? Atlas captured Artemis a few years ago. And in the old stories, the gods captured each other in traps all the time. But something worse than a Titan . . . ?"

Jason looked at the leopard's head. Seymour was smacking his lips like the goddess had tasted much better than a Snausage. "Hera said she'd been trying to break through her prison bonds for a month."

"Which is how long Olympus has been closed," Annabeth said. "So the gods must know something bad is going on."

"But why use her energy to send me here?" Jason asked. "She wiped my memory, plopped me into the Wilderness School field trip, and sent you a dream vision to come pick me up. Why am I so important? Why not just send up an emergency flare to the other gods—let them know where she is so they bust her out?"

"The gods need heroes to do their will down here on earth," Rachel said. "That's right, isn't it? Their fates are always intertwined with demigods."

"That's true," Annabeth said, "but Jason's got a point. Why him? Why take his memory?"

"And Piper's involved somehow," Rachel said. "Hera sent her the same message—*Free me*. And, Annabeth, this must have something to do with Percy's disappearing."

Annabeth fixed her eyes on Chiron. "Why are you so quiet, Chiron? What is it we're facing?"

The old centaur's face looked like it had aged ten years in a matter of minutes. The lines around his eyes were deeply etched. "My dear, in this, I cannot help you. I am so sorry."

Annabeth blinked. "You've never...you've *never* kept information from me. Even the last great prophecy—"

"I will be in my office." His voice was heavy. "I need some time to think before dinner. Rachel, will you watch the girl? Call Argus to bring her to the infirmary, if you'd like. And Annabeth, you should speak with Jason. Tell him about—about the Greek and Roman gods."

"But..."

The centaur turned his wheelchair and rolled off down the hallway. Annabeth's eyes turned stormy. She muttered something in Greek, and Jason got the feeling it wasn't complimentary toward centaurs.

"I'm sorry," Jason said. "I think my being here—I don't know. I've messed things up coming to the camp, somehow. Chiron said he'd sworn an oath and couldn't talk about it."

"What oath?" Annabeth demanded. "I've never seen him

act this way. And why would he tell me to talk to you about the gods..."

Her voice trailed off. Apparently she'd just noticed Jason's sword sitting on the coffee table. She touched the blade gingerly, like it might be hot.

"Is this gold?" she said. "Do you remember where you got it?"

"No," Jason said. "Like I said, I don't remember anything."

Annabeth nodded, like she'd just come up with a rather desperate plan. "If Chiron won't help, we'll need to figure things out ourselves. Which means... Cabin Fifteen. Rachel, you'll keep an eye on Piper?"

"Sure," Rachel promised. "Good luck, you two."

"Hold on," Jason said. "What's in Cabin Fifteen?"

Annabeth stood. "Maybe a way to get your memory back."

They headed toward a newer wing of cabins in the southwest corner of the green. Some were fancy, with glowing walls or blazing torches, but Cabin Fifteen was not so dramatic. It looked like an old-fashioned prairie house with mud walls and a rush roof. On the door hung a wreath of crimson flowers —red poppies, Jason thought, though he wasn't sure how he knew.

"You think this is my parent's cabin?" he asked.

"No," Annabeth said. "This is the cabin for Hypnos, the god of sleep."

"Then why—"

"You've forgotten everything," she said. "If there's any god who can help us figure out memory loss, it's Hypnos."

Inside, even though it was almost dinnertime, three kids

were sound asleep under piles of covers. A warm fire crackled in the hearth. Above the mantel hung a tree branch, each twig dripping white liquid into a collection of tin bowls. Jason was tempted to catch a drop on his finger just to see what it was, but he held himself back.

Soft violin music played from somewhere. The air smelled like fresh laundry. The cabin was so cozy and peaceful that Jason's eyelids started to feel heavy. A nap sounded like a great idea. He was exhausted. There were plenty of empty beds, all with feather pillows and fresh sheets and fluffy quilts and—

Annabeth nudged him. "Snap out of it."

Jason blinked. He realized his knees had been starting to buckle.

"Cabin Fifteen does that to everyone," Annabeth warned. "If you ask me, this place is even more dangerous than the Ares cabin. At least with Ares, you can learn where the land mines are."

"Land mines?"

She walked up to the nearest snoring kid and shook his shoulder. "Clovis! Wake up!"

The kid looked like a baby cow. He had a blond tuft of hair on a wedge-shaped head, with thick features and a thick neck. His body was stocky, but he had spindly little arms like he'd never lifted anything heavier than a pillow.

"Clovis!" Annabeth shook harder, then finally knocked on his forehead about six times.

"Wh-wh-what?" Clovis complained, sitting up and squinting. He yawned hugely, and both Annabeth and Jason yawned too.

"Stop that!" Annabeth said. "We need your help."

"I was sleeping."

"You're *always* sleeping."

"Good night."

Before he could pass out, Annabeth yanked his pillow off the bed.

"That's not fair," Clovis complained meekly. "Give it back."

"First help," Annabeth said. "Then sleep."

Clovis sighed. His breath smelled like warm milk. "Fine. What?"

Annabeth explained about Jason's problem. Every once in a while she'd snap her fingers under Clovis's nose to keep him awake.

Clovis must have been really excited, because when Annabeth was done, he didn't pass out. He actually stood and stretched, then blinked at Jason. "So you don't remember anything, huh?"

"Just impressions," Jason said. "Feelings, like..."

"Yes?" Clovis said.

"Like I know I shouldn't be here. At this camp. I'm in danger."

"Hmm. Close your eyes."

Jason glanced at Annabeth, but she nodded reassuringly.

Jason was afraid he'd end up snoring in one of the bunks forever, but he closed his eyes. His thoughts became murky, as if he were sinking into a dark lake.

The next thing he knew, his eyes snapped open. He was sitting in a chair by the fire. Clovis and Annabeth knelt next to him.

"—serious, all right," Clovis was saying.

"What happened?" Jason said. "How long—"

"Just a few minutes," Annabeth said. "But it was tense. You almost dissolved."

Jason hoped she didn't mean *literally*, but her expression was solemn.

"Usually," Clovis said, "memories are lost for a good reason. They sink under the surface like dreams, and with a good sleep, I can bring them back. But this . . ."

"Lethe?" Annabeth asked.

"No," Clovis said. "Not even Lethe."

"Lethe?" Jason asked.

Clovis pointed to the tree branch dripping milky drops above the fireplace. "The River Lethe in the Underworld. It dissolves your memories, wipes your mind clean permanently. That's the branch of a poplar tree from the Underworld, dipped into the Lethe. It's the symbol of my father, Hypnos. Lethe is not a place you want to go swimming."

Annabeth nodded. "Percy went there once. He told me it was powerful enough to wipe the mind of a Titan."

Jason was suddenly glad he hadn't touched the branch. "But . . . that's not my problem?"

"No," Clovis agreed. "Your mind wasn't wiped, and your memories weren't buried. They've been stolen."

The fire crackled. Drops of Lethe water plinked into the tin cups on the mantel. One of the other Hypnos campers muttered in his sleep—something about a duck.

"Stolen," Jason said. "How?"

"A god," Clovis said. "Only a god would have that kind of power."

"We know that," said Jason. "It was Juno. But how did she do it, and why?"

Clovis scratched his neck. "Juno?"

"He means Hera," Annabeth said. "For some reason, Jason likes the Roman names."

"Hmm," Clovis said.

"What?" Jason asked. "Does that mean something?"

"Hmm," Clovis said again, and this time Jason realized he was snoring.

"Clovis!" he yelled.

"What? What?" His eyes fluttered open. "We were talking about pillows, right? No, gods. I remember. Greek and Roman. Sure, could be important."

"But they're the same gods," Annabeth said. "Just different names."

"Not exactly," Clovis said.

Jason sat forward, now very much awake. "What do you mean, not exactly?"

"Well…" Clovis yawned. "Some gods are only Roman. Like Janus, or Pompona. But even the major Greek gods—it's not just their names that changed when they moved to Rome. Their appearances changed. Their attributes changed. They even had slightly different personalities."

"But…" Annabeth faltered. "Okay, so maybe people saw them differently through the centuries. That doesn't change who they are."

"Sure it does." Clovis began to nod off, and Jason snapped his fingers under his nose.

"Coming, Mother!" he yelped. "I mean… Yeah, I'm

awake. So, um, personalities. The gods change to reflect their host cultures. You know that, Annabeth. I mean, these days, Zeus likes tailored suits, reality television, and that Chinese food place on East Twenty-eighth Street, right? It was the same in Roman times, and the gods were Roman almost as long as they were Greek. It was a big empire, lasted for centuries. So of course their Roman aspects are still a big part of their character."

"Makes sense," Jason said.

Annabeth shook her head, mystified. "But how do you know all this, Clovis?"

"Oh, I spend a lot of time dreaming. I see the gods there all the time—always shifting forms. Dreams are fluid, you know. You can be in different places at once, always changing identities. It's a lot like being a god, actually. Like recently, I dreamed I was watching a Michael Jackson concert, and then I was onstage *with* Michael Jackson, and we were singing this duet, and I could *not* remember the words for 'The Girl Is Mine.' Oh, man, it was so embarrassing, I—"

"Clovis," Annabeth interrupted. "Back to Rome?"

"Right, Rome," Clovis said. "So we call the gods by their Greek names because that's their original form. But saying their Roman aspects are exactly the same—that's not true. In Rome, they became more warlike. They didn't mingle with mortals as much. They were harsher, more powerful—the gods of an empire."

"Like the dark side of the gods?" Annabeth asked.

"Not exactly," Clovis said. "They stood for discipline, honor, strength—"

"Good things, then," Jason said. For some reason, he felt the need to speak up for the Roman gods, though wasn't sure why it mattered to him. "I mean, discipline is important, right? That's what made Rome last so long."

Clovis gave him a curious look. "That's true. But the Roman gods weren't very friendly. For instance, my dad, Hypnos...he didn't do much except sleep in Greek times. In Roman times, they called him Somnus. He liked killing people who didn't stay alert at their jobs. If they nodded off at the wrong time, *boom*—they never woke up. He killed the helmsman of Aeneas when they were sailing from Troy."

"Nice guy," Annabeth said. "But I still don't understand what it has to do with Jason."

"Neither do I," Clovis said. "But if Hera took your memory, only she can give it back. And if I had to meet the queen of the gods, I'd hope she was more in a Hera mood than a Juno mood. Can I go back to sleep now?"

Annabeth stared at the branch above the fire, dripping Lethe water into the cups. She looked so worried, Jason wondered if she was considering a drink to forget her troubles. Then she stood and tossed Clovis his pillow. "Thanks, Clovis. We'll see you at dinner."

"Can I get room service?" Clovis yawned and stumbled to his bunk. "I feel like...*zzzz*..." He collapsed with his butt in the air and his face buried in pillow.

"Won't he suffocate?" Jason asked.

"He'll be fine," Annabeth said. "But I'm beginning to think that you are in serious trouble."

IX

PIPER

PIPER DREAMED ABOUT HER LAST DAY with her dad.

They were on the beach near Big Sur, taking a break from surfing. The morning had been so perfect, Piper knew something had to go wrong soon—a rabid horde of paparazzi, or maybe a great white shark attack. No way her luck could hold.

But so far, they'd had excellent waves, an overcast sky, and a mile of oceanfront completely to themselves. Dad had found this out-of-the-way spot, rented a beachfront villa *and* the properties on either side, and somehow managed to keep it secret. If he stayed there too long, Piper knew the photographers would find him. They always did.

"Nice job out there, Pipes." He gave her the smile he was famous for: perfect teeth, dimpled chin, a twinkle in his dark eyes that always made grown women scream and ask him to sign their bodies in permanent marker. (*Seriously*, Piper thought, *get a life*.) His close-cropped black hair gleamed with salt water. "You're getting better at hanging ten."

Piper flushed with pride, though she suspected Dad was just being nice. She still spent most of her time wiping out. It took special talent to run over yourself with a surfboard. Her *dad* was the natural surfer—which made no sense since he'd been raised a poor kid in Oklahoma, hundreds of miles from the ocean—but he was amazing on the curls. Piper would've given up surfing a long time ago except it let her spend time with him. There weren't many ways she could do that.

"Sandwich?" Dad dug into the picnic basket his chef, Arno, had made. "Let's see: turkey pesto, crabcake wasabi —ah, a Piper special. Peanut butter and jelly."

She took the sandwich, though her stomach was too upset to eat. She always asked for PB&J. Piper was vegetarian, for one thing. She had been ever since they'd driven past that slaughterhouse in Chino and the smell had made her insides want to come outside. But it was more than that. PB&J was simple food, like a regular kid would have for lunch. Sometimes she pretended her dad had actually made it for her, not a personal chef from France who liked to wrap the sandwich in gold leaf paper with a light-up sparkler instead of a toothpick.

Couldn't anything be simple? That's why she turned down the fancy clothes Dad always offered, the designer shoes, the trips to the salon. She cut her own hair with a pair of plastic Garfield safety scissors, deliberately making it uneven. She preferred to wear beat-up running shoes, jeans, a T-shirt, and her old Polartec jacket from the time they went snowboarding.

And she hated the snobby private schools Dad thought were good for her. She kept getting herself kicked out. He kept finding more schools.

Yesterday, she'd pulled her biggest heist yet—driving that "borrowed" BMW out of the dealership. She *had* to pull a bigger stunt each time, because it took more and more to get Dad's attention.

Now she regretted it. Dad didn't know yet.

She'd meant to tell him that morning. Then he'd surprised her with this trip, and she couldn't ruin it. It was the first time they'd had a day together in what—three months?

"What's wrong?" He passed her a soda.

"Dad, there's something—"

"Hold on, Pipes. That's a serious face. Ready for Any Three Questions?"

They'd been playing that game for years—her dad's way of staying connected in the shortest possible amount of time. They could ask each other any three questions. Nothing off-limits, and you had to answer honestly. The rest of the time, Dad promised to stay out of her business—which was easy, since he was never around.

Piper knew most kids would find a Q&A like this with their parents totally mortifying. But she looked forward to it. It was like surfing—not easy, but a way to feel like she actually had a father.

"First question," she said. "Mom."

No surprise. That was always one of her topics.

Her dad shrugged with resignation. "What do you want to know, Piper? I've already told you—she disappeared. I don't know why, or where she went. After you were born, she simply left. I never heard from her again."

"Do you think she's still alive?"

It wasn't a real question. Dad was allowed to say he didn't know. But she wanted to hear how he'd answer.

He stared at the waves.

"Your Grandpa Tom," he said at last, "he used to tell me that if you walked far enough toward the sunset, you'd come to Ghost Country, where you could talk to the dead. He said a long time ago, you could bring the dead back; but then mankind messed up. Well, it's a long story."

"Like the Land of the Dead for the Greeks," Piper remembered. "It was in the west, too. And Orpheus—he tried to bring his wife back."

Dad nodded. A year before, he'd had his biggest role as an Ancient Greek king. Piper had helped him research the myths—all those old stories about people getting turned to stone and boiled in lakes of lava. They'd had a fun time reading together, and it made Piper's life seem not so bad. For a while she'd felt closer to her dad, but like everything, it didn't last.

"Lot of similarities between Greek and Cherokee," Dad agreed. "Wonder what your grandpa would think if he saw us now, sitting at the end of the western land. He'd probably think we're ghosts."

"So you're saying you believe those stories? You think Mom is dead?"

His eyes watered, and Piper saw the sadness behind them. She figured that's why women were so attracted to him. On the surface, he seemed confident and rugged, but his eyes held so much sadness. Women wanted to find out why. They wanted to comfort him, and they never could. Dad told

Piper it was a Cherokee thing—they all had that darkness inside them from generations of pain and suffering. But Piper thought it was more than that.

"I don't believe the stories," he said. "They're fun to tell, but if I really believed in Ghost Country, or animal spirits, or Greek gods...I don't think I could sleep at night. I'd always be looking for somebody to blame."

Somebody to blame for Grandpa Tom dying of lung cancer, Piper thought, before Dad got famous and had the money to help. For Mom—the only woman he'd ever loved —abandoning him without even a good-bye note, leaving him with a newborn girl he wasn't ready to care for. For his being so successful, and yet still not happy.

"I don't know if she's alive," he said. "But I do think she might as well be in Ghost Country, Piper. There's no getting her back. If I believed otherwise...I don't think I could stand that, either."

Behind them, a car door opened. Piper turned, and her heart sank. Jane was marching toward them in her business suit, wobbling over the sand in her high heels, her PDA in hand. The look on her face was partly annoyed, partly triumphant, and Piper knew she'd been in touch with the police.

Please fall down, Piper prayed. *If there's any animal spirit or Greek god that can help, make Jane take a header. I'm not asking for permanent damage, just knock her out for the rest of the day, please?*

But Jane kept advancing.

"Dad," Piper said quickly. "Something happened yester-day...."

But he'd seen Jane, too. He was already reconstructing his business face. Jane wouldn't be here if it wasn't serious. A studio head called—a project fell through—or Piper had messed up again.

"We'll get back to that, Pipes," he promised. "I'd better see what Jane wants. You know how she is."

Yes—Piper knew. Dad trudged across the sand to meet her. Piper couldn't hear them talking, but she didn't need to. She was good at reading faces. Jane gave him the facts about the stolen car, occasionally pointing at Piper like she was a disgusting pet that had whizzed on the carpet.

Dad's energy and enthusiasm drained away. He gestured for Jane to wait. Then he walked back to Piper. She couldn't stand that look in his eyes—like she'd betrayed his trust.

"You told me you would try, Piper," he said.

"Dad, I hate that school. I can't do it. I wanted to tell you about the BMW, but—"

"They've expelled you," he said. "A car, Piper? You're sixteen next year. I would buy you any car you want. How could you—"

"You mean *Jane* would buy me a car?" Piper demanded. She couldn't help it. The anger just welled up and spilled out of her. "Dad, just listen for once. Don't make me wait for you to ask your stupid three questions. I want to go to regular school. I want *you* to take me to parents' night, not Jane. Or homeschool me! I learned so much when we read about Greece together. We could do that all the time! We could—"

"Don't make this about me," her dad said. "I do the best I can, Piper. We've had this conversation."

No, she thought. *You've cut off this conversation. For years.*

Her dad sighed. "Jane's talked to the police, brokered a deal. The dealership won't press charges, but you have to agree to go to a boarding school in Nevada. They specialize in problems . . . in kids with tough issues."

"That's what I am." Her voice trembled. "A problem."

"Piper . . . you said you'd try. You let me down. I don't know what else to do."

"Do anything," she said. "But do it yourself! Don't let Jane handle it for you. You can't just send me away."

Dad looked down at the picnic basket. His sandwich sat uneaten on a piece of gold leaf paper. They'd planned for a whole afternoon in the surf. Now that was ruined.

Piper couldn't believe he'd really give in to Jane's wishes. Not this time. Not on something as huge as boarding school.

"Go see her," Dad said. "She's got the details."

"Dad . . ."

He looked away, gazing at the ocean like he could see all the way to Ghost Country. Piper promised herself she wouldn't cry. She headed up the beach toward Jane, who smiled coldly and held up a plane ticket. As usual, she'd already arranged everything. Piper was just another problem of the day that Jane could now check off her list.

Piper's dream changed.

She stood on a mountaintop at night, city lights glimmering below. In front of her, a bonfire blazed. Purplish flames seemed to cast more shadows than light, but the heat was so intense, her clothes steamed.

"This is your second warning," a voice rumbled, so powerful it shook the earth. Piper had heard that voice before in her dreams. She'd tried to convince herself it wasn't as scary as she remembered, but it was worse.

Behind the bonfire, a huge face loomed out of the darkness. It seemed to float above the flames, but Piper knew it must be connected to an enormous body. The crude features might've been chiseled out of rock. The face hardly seemed alive except for its piercing white eyes, like raw diamonds, and its horrible frame of locs, braided with human bones. It smiled, and Piper shivered.

"You'll do what you're told," the giant said. "You'll go on the quest. Do our bidding, and you may walk away alive. Otherwise—"

He gestured to one side of the fire. Piper's father was hanging unconscious, tied to a stake.

She tried to cry out. She wanted to call to her dad, and demand the giant let him go, but her voice wouldn't work.

"I'll be watching," the giant said. "Serve me, and you both live. You have the word of Enceladus. Fail me . . . well, I've slept for millennia, young demigod. I am *very* hungry. Fail, and I'll eat well."

The giant roared with laughter. The earth trembled. A crevice opened at Piper's feet, and she tumbled into darkness.

She woke feeling like she'd been trampled by an Irish step-dancing troupe. Her chest hurt, and she could barely breathe. She reached down and closed her hand around the hilt of the dagger Annabeth had given her—Katoptris, Helen of Troy's weapon.

So Camp Half-Blood hadn't been a dream.

"How are you feeling?" someone asked.

Piper tried to focus. She was lying in a bed with a white curtain on one side, like in a nurse's office. That redheaded girl, Rachel Dare, sat next to her. On the wall was a poster of a cartoon satyr who looked disturbingly like Coach Hedge with a thermometer sticking out of his mouth. The caption read: *Don't let sickness get your goat!*

"Where—" Piper's voice died when she saw the guy at the door.

He looked like a typical California surfer dude—buff and tan, blond hair, dressed in shorts and a T-shirt. But he had hundreds of blue eyes all over his body—along his arms, down his legs, and all over his face. Even his feet had eyes, peering up at her from between the straps of his sandals.

"That's Argus," Rachel said, "our head of security. He's just keeping an eye on things . . . so to speak."

Argus nodded. The eye on his chin winked.

"Where—?" Piper tried again, but she felt like she was talking through a mouthful of cotton.

"You're in the Big House," Rachel said. "Camp offices. We brought you here when you collapsed."

"You grabbed me," Piper remembered. "Hera's voice—"

"I'm so sorry about that," Rachel said. "Believe me, it was *not* my idea to get possessed. Chiron healed you with some nectar—"

"Nectar?"

"The drink of the gods. In small amounts, it heals demigods, if it doesn't—ah—burn you to ashes."

"Oh. Fun."

Rachel sat forward. "Do you remember your vision?"

Piper had a moment of dread, thinking she meant the dream about the giant. Then she realized Rachel was talking about what happened in Hera's cabin.

"Something's wrong with the goddess," Piper said. "She told me to free her, like she's trapped. She mentioned the earth swallowing us, and a fiery one, and something about the solstice."

In the corner, Argus made a rumbling sound in his chest. His eyes all fluttered at once.

"Hera created Argus," Rachel explained. "He's actually very sensitive when it comes to her safety. We're trying to keep him from crying, because last time that happened... well, it caused quite a flood."

Argus sniffled. He grabbed a fistful of Kleenex from the bedside table and started dabbing eyes all over his body.

"So..." Piper tried not to stare as Argus wiped the tears from his elbows. "What's happened to Hera?"

"We're not sure," Rachel said. "Annabeth and Jason were here for you, by the way. Jason didn't want to leave you, but Annabeth had an idea—something that might restore his memories."

"That's... that's great."

Jason had been here for her? She wished she'd been conscious for that. But if he got his memories back, would that be a good thing? She was still holding out hope that they really did know each other. She didn't want their relationship to be just a trick of the Mist.

Get over yourself, she thought. If she was going to save her dad, it didn't matter whether Jason liked her or not. He would hate her eventually. Everyone here would.

She looked down at the ceremonial dagger strapped to her side. Annabeth had said it was a sign of power and status, but not normally used in battle. All show and no substance. A fake, just like Piper. And its name was Katoptris, looking glass. She didn't dare unsheathe it again, because she couldn't bear to see her own reflection.

"Don't worry." Rachel squeezed her arm. "Jason seems like a good guy. He had a vision too, a lot like yours. Whatever's happening with Hera—I think you two are meant to work together."

Rachel smiled like this was good news, but Piper's spirits plunged even further. She'd thought that this quest—whatever it was—would involve nameless people. Now Rachel was basically telling her: *Good news! Not only is your dad being held ransom by a cannibal giant, you also get to betray the guy you like! How awesome is that?*

"Hey," Rachel said. "No need to cry. You'll figure it out."

Piper wiped her eyes, trying to get control of herself. This wasn't like her. She was supposed to be tough—a hardened car thief, the scourge of L.A. private schools. Here she was, crying like a baby. "How can you know what I'm facing?"

Rachel shrugged. "I know it's a hard choice, and your options aren't great. Like I said, I get hunches sometimes.

But you're going to be claimed at the campfire. I'm almost sure. When you know who your godly parent is, things might be clearer."

Clearer, Piper thought. Not necessarily better.

She sat up in bed. Her forehead ached like someone had driven a spike between her eyes. *There's no getting your mother back,* her dad had told her. But apparently, tonight, her mom might claim her. For the first time, Piper wasn't sure she wanted that.

"I hope it's Athena." She looked up, afraid Rachel might make fun of her, but the oracle just smiled.

"Piper, I don't blame you. Truthfully? I think Annabeth is hoping that too. You guys are a lot alike."

The comparison made Piper feel even guiltier. "Another hunch? You don't know anything about me."

"You'd be surprised."

"You're just saying that because you're an oracle, aren't you? You're supposed to sound all mysterious."

Rachel laughed. "Don't be giving away my secrets, Piper. And don't worry. Things will work out—just maybe not the way you plan."

"That's not making me feel better."

Somewhere in the distance, a conch horn blew. Argus grumbled and opened the door.

"Dinner?" Piper guessed.

"You slept through it," Rachel said. "Time for the campfire. Let's go find out who you are."

X

PIPER

THE WHOLE CAMPFIRE IDEA FREAKED PIPER OUT. It made her think of that huge purple bonfire in the dreams, and her father tied to a stake.

What she got instead was almost as terrifying: a sing-along. The amphitheater steps were carved into the side of a hill, facing a stone-lined fire pit. Fifty or sixty kids filled the rows, clustered into groups under various banners.

Piper spotted Jason in the front next to Annabeth. Leo was nearby, sitting with a bunch of burly-looking campers under a steel gray banner emblazoned with a hammer. Standing in front of the fire, half a dozen campers with guitars and strange, old-fashioned harps—lyres?—were jumping around, leading a song about pieces of armor, something about how their grandma got dressed for war. Everybody was singing with them and making gestures for the pieces of armor and joking around. It was quite possibly the weirdest thing Piper had ever seen—one of those campfire songs that would've been completely embarrassing in daylight; but in the dark, with everybody participating, it was kind of corny and fun. As the energy level got higher, the flames did too, turning from red to orange to gold.

Finally the song ended with a lot of rowdy applause. A guy on a horse trotted up. At least in the flickering light, Piper *thought* it was a guy on a horse. Then she realized it was a centaur—his bottom half a white stallion, his top half a middle-aged guy with curly hair and a trimmed beard. He brandished a spear impaled with toasted marshmallows. "Very nice! And a special welcome to our new arrivals. I am Chiron, camp activities director, and I'm happy you have all arrived here alive and with most of your limbs attached. In a moment, I promise we'll get to the s'mores, but first—"

"What about capture the flag?" somebody yelled. Grumbling broke out among some kids in armor, sitting under a red banner with the emblem of a boar's head.

"Yes," the centaur said. "I know the Ares cabin is anxious to return to the woods for our regular games."

"And kill people!" one of them shouted.

"However," Chiron said, "until the dragon is brought under control, that won't be possible. Cabin Nine, anything to report on that?"

He turned to Leo's group. Leo winked at Piper and shot her with a finger gun. The girl next to him stood uncomfortably. She wore an army jacket a lot like Leo's, with her hair covered in a red bandanna. "We're working on it."

More grumbling.

"How, Nyssa?" an Ares kid demanded.

"Really hard," the girl said.

Nyssa sat down to a lot of yelling and complaining, which caused the fire to sputter chaotically. Chiron stamped his hoof against the fire pit stones—*bang, bang, bang*—and the campers fell silent.

"We will have to be patient," Chiron said. "In the meantime, we have more pressing matters to discuss."

"Percy?" someone asked. The fire dimmed even further, but Piper didn't need the mood flames to sense the crowd's anxiety.

Chiron gestured to Annabeth. She took a deep breath and stood.

"I didn't find Percy," she announced. Her voice caught a little when she said his name. "He wasn't at the Grand Canyon like I thought. But we're not giving up. We've got teams everywhere. Grover, Tyson, Nico, the Hunters of Artemis —everyone's out looking. We *will* find him. Chiron's talking about something different. A new quest."

"It's the Great Prophecy, isn't it?" a girl called out.

Everyone turned. The voice had come from a group in back, sitting under a rose-colored banner with a dove emblem. They'd been chatting among themselves and not paying much attention until their leader stood up: Drew.

Everyone else looked surprised. Apparently Drew didn't address the crowd very often.

"Drew?" Annabeth said. "What do you mean?"

"Well, *come on*." Drew spread her hands like the truth was obvious. "Olympus is closed. Percy's disappeared. Hera sends you a vision and you come back with three new demigods in one day. I mean, something weird is going on. The Great Prophecy has started, right?"

Piper whispered to Rachel, "What's she talking about—the Great Prophecy?"

Then she realized everyone else was looking at Rachel, too.

"Well?" Drew called down. "You're the oracle. Has it started or not?"

Rachel's eyes looked scary in the firelight. Piper was afraid she might clench up and start channeling a freaky peacock goddess again, but she stepped forward calmly and addressed the camp.

"Yes," she said. "The Great Prophecy has begun."

Pandemonium broke out.

Piper caught Jason's eye. He mouthed, *You all right?* She nodded and managed a smile, but then looked away. It was too painful seeing him and not being with him.

When the talking finally subsided, Rachel took another step toward the audience, and fifty-plus demigods leaned away from her, as if one skinny redheaded mortal was more intimidating than all of them put together.

"For those of you who have not heard it," Rachel said, "the Great Prophecy was my first prediction. It arrived in August. It goes like this:

> *"Seven half-bloods shall answer the call.*
> *To storm or fire the world must fall—"*

Jason shot to his feet. His eyes looked wild, like he'd just been tasered.

Even Rachel seemed caught off guard. "J-Jason?" she said. "What's—"

"*Ut cum spiritu postrema sacramentum dejuremus,*" he chanted. "*Et hostes ornamenta addent ad ianuam necem.*"

An uneasy silence settled on the group. Piper could see from their faces that several of them were trying to translate the lines. She could tell it was Latin, but she wasn't sure why her hopefully future boyfriend was suddenly chanting like a Catholic priest.

"You just…finished the prophecy," Rachel stammered. "—*An oath to keep with a final breath/And foes bear arms to the Doors of Death.* How did you—"

"I know those lines." Jason winced and put his hands to his temples. "I don't know how, but I *know* that prophecy."

"In Latin, no less," Drew called out. "Handsome *and* smart."

There was some giggling from the Aphrodite cabin. God, what a bunch of losers, Piper thought. But it didn't do much to break the tension. The campfire was burning a chaotic, nervous shade of green.

Jason sat down, looking embarrassed, but Annabeth put a hand on his shoulder and muttered something reassuring. Piper felt a pang of jealousy. It should have been *her* next to him, comforting him.

Rachel Dare still looked a little shaken. She glanced back at Chiron for guidance, but the centaur stood grim and silent, as if he were watching a play he couldn't interrupt—a tragedy that ended with a lot of people dead onstage.

"Well," Rachel said, trying to regain her composure. "So,

yeah, that's the Great Prophecy. We hoped it might not happen for years, but I fear it's starting now. I can't give you proof. It's just a feeling. And like Drew said, some weird stuff is happening. The seven demigods, whoever they are, have not been gathered yet. I get the feeling some are here tonight. Some are not here."

The campers began to stir and mutter, looking at each other nervously, until a drowsy voice in the crowd called out, "I'm here! Oh . . . were you calling roll?"

"Go back to sleep, Clovis," someone yelled, and a lot of people laughed.

"Anyway," Rachel continued, "we don't know what the Great Prophecy means. We don't know what challenge the demigods will face, but since the *first* Great Prophecy predicted the Titan War, we can guess the *second* Great Prophecy will predict something at least that bad."

"Or worse," Chiron murmured.

Maybe he didn't mean everyone to overhear, but they did. The campfire immediately turned dark purple, the same color as Piper's dream.

"What we *do* know," Rachel said, "is that the first phase has begun. A major problem has arisen, and we need a quest to solve it. Hera, the queen of the gods, has been taken."

Shocked silence. Then fifty demigods started talking at once.

Chiron pounded his hoof again, but Rachel still had to wait before she could get back their attention.

She told them about the incident on the Grand Canyon skywalk—how Gleeson Hedge had sacrificed himself when the storm spirits attacked, and the spirits had warned it was only the beginning. They apparently served some great mistress who would destroy all demigods.

Then Rachel told them about Piper passing out in Hera's cabin. Piper tried to keep a calm expression, even when she noticed Drew in the back row, pantomiming a faint, and her friends giggling. Finally Rachel told them about Jason's vision in the living room of the Big House. The message Hera had delivered there was so similar that Piper got a chill. The only difference: Hera had warned Piper not to betray her: *Bow to his will, and their king shall rise, dooming us all.* Hera *knew* about the giant's threat. But if that was true, why hadn't she warned Jason, and exposed Piper as an enemy agent?

"Jason," Rachel said. "Um... do you remember your last name?"

He looked self-conscious, but he shook his head.

"We'll just call you Jason, then," Rachel said. "It's clear Hera herself has issued you a quest."

Rachel paused, as if giving Jason a chance to protest his destiny. Everyone's eyes were on him; there was so much pressure, Piper thought she would've buckled in his position. Yet he looked brave and determined. He set his jaw and nodded. "I agree."

"You must save Hera to prevent a great evil," Rachel continued. "Some sort of king from rising. For reasons we don't yet understand, it must happen by the winter solstice, only four days from now."

"That's the council day of the gods," Annabeth said. "If the gods don't *already* know Hera's gone, they will definitely notice her absence by then. They'll probably break out fighting, accusing each other of taking her. That's what they usually do."

"The winter solstice," Chiron spoke up, "is also the time of greatest darkness. The gods gather that day, as mortals always have, because there is strength in numbers. The solstice is a day when evil magic is strong. *Ancient* magic, older than the gods. It is a day when things ... stir."

The way he said it, stirring sounded absolutely sinister—like it should be a first-degree felony, not something you did to cookie dough.

"Okay," Annabeth said, glaring at the centaur. "Thank you, Captain Sunshine. Whatever's going on, I agree with Rachel. Jason has been chosen to lead this quest, so—"

"Why hasn't he been claimed?" somebody yelled from the Ares cabin. "If he's so important—"

"He has been claimed," Chiron announced. "Long ago. Jason, give them a demonstration."

At first, Jason didn't seem to understand. He stepped forward nervously, but Piper couldn't help thinking how amazing he looked with his blond hair glowing in the firelight, his regal features like a Roman statue's. He glanced at Piper, and she nodded encouragingly. She mimicked flipping a coin.

Jason reached into his pocket. His coin flashed in the air, and when he caught it in his hand, he was holding a lance—a rod of gold about seven feet long, with a spear tip at one end.

The other demigods gasped. Rachel and Annabeth stepped back to avoid the point, which looked sharp as an ice pick.

"Wasn't that..." Annabeth hesitated. "I thought you had a sword."

"Um, it came up tails, I think," Jason said. "Same coin, long-range weapon form."

"Dude, I want one!" yelled somebody from Ares cabin.

"Better than Clarisse's electric spear, Lamer!" one of his brothers agreed.

"Electric," Jason murmured, like that was a good idea. "Back away."

Annabeth and Rachel got the message. Jason raised his javelin, and thunder broke open the sky. Every hair on Piper's arms stood straight up. Lightning arced down through the golden spear point and hit the campfire with the force of an artillery shell.

When the smoke cleared, and the ringing in Piper's ears subsided, the entire camp sat frozen in shock, half blind, covered in ashes, staring at the place where the fire had been. Cinders rained down everywhere. A burning log had impaled itself a few inches from the sleeping kid Clovis, who hadn't even stirred.

Jason lowered his lance. "Um...sorry."

Chiron brushed some burning coals out of his beard. He grimaced as if his worst fears had been confirmed. "A little overkill, perhaps, but you've made your point. And I believe we know who your father is."

"Jupiter," Jason said. "I mean Zeus. Lord of the Sky."

Piper couldn't help smiling. It made perfect sense. The most powerful god, the father of all the greatest heroes in the ancient myths—no one else could possibly be Jason's dad.

Apparently, the rest of the camp wasn't so sure. Everything broke into chaos, with dozens of people asking questions until Annabeth raised her arms.

"Hold it!" she said. "How can he be the son of Zeus? The Big Three . . . their pact not to have mortal kids . . . how could we not have known about him sooner?"

Chiron didn't answer, but Piper got the feeling he knew. And the truth was not good.

"The important thing," Rachel said, "is that Jason's here now. He has a quest to fulfill, which means he will need his own prophecy."

She closed her eyes and swooned. Two campers rushed forward and caught her. A third ran to the side of the amphitheater and grabbed a bronze three-legged stool, like they'd been trained for this duty. They eased Rachel onto the stool in front of the ruined hearth. Without the fire, the night was dark, but green mist started swirling around Rachel's feet. When she opened her eyes, they were glowing. Emerald smoke issued from her mouth. The voice that came out was raspy and ancient—the sound a snake would make if it could talk:

> *"Child of lightning, beware the earth,*
> *The giants' revenge the seven shall birth,*
> *The forge and dove shall break the cage,*
> *And death unleash through Hera's rage."*

On the last word, Rachel collapsed, but her helpers were waiting to catch her. They carried her away from the hearth and laid her in the corner to rest.

"Is that normal?" Piper asked. Then she realized she'd spoken into the silence, and everyone was looking at her. "I mean ... does she spew green smoke a lot?"

"Gods, you're dense!" Drew sneered. "She just issued a prophecy—Jason's prophecy to save Hera! Why don't you just—"

"Drew," Annabeth snapped. "Piper asked a fair question. Something about that prophecy *definitely* isn't normal. If breaking Hera's cage unleashes her rage and causes a bunch of death ... why would we free her? It might be a trap, or—or maybe Hera will turn on her rescuers. She's never been kind to heroes."

Jason rose. "I don't have much choice. Hera took my memory. I need it back. Besides, we can't just *not* help the queen of the heavens if she's in trouble."

A girl from Hephaestus cabin stood up—Nyssa, the one with the red bandanna. "Maybe. But you should listen to Annabeth. Hera can be vengeful. She threw her own son— our dad—down a mountain just because he was ugly."

"*Real* ugly," snickered someone from Aphrodite.

"Shut up!" Nyssa growled. "Anyway, we've also got to think —why beware the earth? And what's the giants' revenge? What are we dealing with here that's powerful enough to kidnap the queen of the heavens?"

No one answered, but Piper noticed Annabeth and Chiron having a silent exchange. Piper thought it went something like:

Annabeth: *The giants' revenge ... no, it can't be.*

Chiron: *Don't speak of it here. Don't scare them.*

Annabeth: *You're kidding me! We can't be* that *unlucky.*

Chiron: *Later, child. If you told them everything, they would be too terrified to proceed.*

Piper knew it was crazy to think she could read their expressions so well—two people she barely knew. But she was absolutely positive she understood them, and it scared the jujubes out of her.

Annabeth took a deep breath. "It's Jason's quest," she announced, "so it's Jason's choice. Obviously, he's the child of lightning. According to tradition, he may choose any two companions."

Someone from the Hermes cabin yelled, "Well, you, obviously, Annabeth. You've got the most experience."

"No, Travis," Annabeth said. "First off, I'm *not* helping Hera. Every time I've tried, she's deceived me, or it's come back to bite me later. Forget it. No way. Secondly, I'm leaving first thing in the morning to find Percy."

"It's connected," Piper blurted out, not sure how she got the courage. "You know that's true, don't you? This whole business, your boyfriend's disappearance—it's all connected."

"How?" demanded Drew. "If you're so smart, how?"

Piper tried to form an answer, but she couldn't.

Annabeth saved her. "You may be right, Piper. If this is connected, I'll find out from the other end—by searching for Percy. As I said, I'm not about to rush off to rescue Hera, even if her disappearance sets the rest of the Olympians fighting again. But there's another reason I can't go. The prophecy says otherwise."

"It says who *I* pick," Jason agreed. "*The forge and dove shall break the cage*. The forge is the symbol of Vul—Hephaestus."

Under the Cabin Nine banner, Nyssa's shoulders slumped, like she'd just been given a heavy anvil to carry. "If you have to beware the earth," she said, "you should avoid traveling overland. You'll need air transport."

Piper was about to call out that Jason could fly. But then she thought better of it. That was for Jason to tell them, and he wasn't volunteering the information. Maybe he figured he'd freaked them out enough for one night.

"The flying chariot's broken," Nyssa continued, "and the pegasi, we're using them to search for Percy. But maybe Hephaestus cabin can help figure out something else to help. With Jake incapacitated, I'm senior camper. I can volunteer for the quest."

She didn't sound enthusiastic.

Then Leo stood up. He'd been so quiet, Piper had almost forgotten he was there, which was totally *not* like Leo.

"It's me," he said.

His cabinmates stirred. Several tried to pull him back to his seat, but Leo resisted.

"No, it's me. I know it is. I've got an idea for the transportation problem. Let me try. I can fix this!"

Jason studied him for a moment. Piper was sure he was going to tell Leo no. Then he smiled. "We started this together, Leo. Seems only right you come along. You find us a ride, you're in."

"Yes!" Leo pumped his fist.

"It'll be dangerous," Nyssa warned him. "Hardship, monsters, terrible suffering. Possibly none of you will come back alive."

"Oh." Suddenly Leo didn't look so excited. Then he remembered everyone was watching. "I mean...Oh, cool! Suffering? I love suffering! Let's do this."

Annabeth nodded. "Then, Jason, you only need to choose the third quest member. The dove—"

"Oh, absolutely!" Drew was on her feet and flashing Jason a smile. "The dove is Aphrodite. Everybody knows that. I am *totally* yours."

Piper's hands clenched. She stepped forward. "No."

Drew rolled her eyes. "Oh, please, Dumpster girl. Back off."

"*I* had the vision of Hera; not you. I have to do this."

"Anyone can have a vision," Drew said. "You were just at the right place at the right time." She turned to Jason. "Look, fighting is all fine, I suppose. And people who build things..." She looked at Leo in disdain. "Well, I suppose someone has to get their hands dirty. But you need *charm* on your side. I can be very persuasive. I could help a lot."

The campers started murmuring about how Drew *was* pretty persuasive. Piper could see Drew winning them over. Even Chiron was scratching his beard, like Drew's participation suddenly made sense to him.

"Well..." Annabeth said. "Given the wording of the prophecy—"

"No!" Piper's own voice sounded strange in her ears—more insistent, richer in tone. "I'm supposed to go."

Then the weirdest thing happened. Everyone started nodding, muttering that hmm, Piper's point of view made sense too. Drew looked around, incredulous. Even some of her own campers were nodding.

"Get over it!" Drew snapped at the crowd. "What can Piper do?"

Piper tried to respond, but her confidence started to wane. What *could* she offer? She wasn't a fighter, or a planner, or a fixer. She had no skills except getting into trouble and occasionally convincing people to do stupid things.

Plus, she was a liar. She needed to go on this quest for reasons that went way beyond Jason—and if she did go, she'd end up betraying everyone there. She heard that voice from the dream: *Do our bidding, and you may walk away alive.* How could she make a choice like that—between helping her father and helping Jason?

"Well," Drew said smugly, "I guess that settles it."

Suddenly there was collective gasp. Everyone stared at Piper like she'd just exploded. She wondered what she'd done wrong. Then she realized there was a reddish glow around her.

"What?" she demanded.

She looked above her, but there was no burning symbol like the one that had appeared over Leo. Then she looked down and yelped.

Her clothes . . . what in the world was she *wearing*? She despised dresses. She didn't *own* a dress. But now she was adorned in a beautiful white sleeveless gown that went down to her ankles, with a V-neck so low it was totally embarrassing. Delicate gold armbands circled her biceps. An intricate necklace of amber, coral, and gold flowers glittered on her chest, and her hair...

"Oh, god," she said. "What's happened?"

A stunned Annabeth pointed at Piper's dagger, which was now oiled and gleaming, hanging at her side on a golden cord. Piper didn't want to draw it. She was afraid of what she would see. But her curiosity won out. She unsheathed Katoptris and stared at her reflection in the polished metal blade. Her hair was perfect: lush and long and chocolate brown, braided with gold ribbons down one side so it fell across her shoulder. She even wore makeup, better than Piper would ever know how to do herself—subtle touches that made her lips cherry red and brought out all the different colors in her eyes.

She was... she was...

"Beautiful," Jason exclaimed. "Piper, you... you're a knockout."

Under different circumstances, that would've been the happiest moment of her life. But now everyone was staring at her like she was a freak. Drew's face was full of horror and revulsion. "No!" she cried. "Not possible!"

"This isn't me," Piper protested. "I—don't understand."

Chiron the centaur folded his front legs and bowed to her, and all the campers followed his example.

"Hail, Piper McLean," Chiron announced gravely, as if he were speaking at her funeral. "Daughter of Aphrodite, lady of the doves, goddess of love."

XI

LEO

LEO DIDN'T STICK AROUND AFTER PIPER turned beautiful. Sure, it was amazing and all—*She's got makeup! It's a miracle!* —but Leo had problems to deal with. He ducked out of the amphitheater and ran into the darkness, wondering what he'd gotten himself into.

He'd stood up in front of a bunch of stronger, braver demigods and volunteered—*volunteered*—for a mission that would probably get him killed.

He hadn't mentioned seeing Tía Callida, his old babysitter, but as soon as he'd heard about Jason's vision—the lady in the black dress and shawl—Leo knew it was the same woman. Tía Callida was Hera. His evil babysitter was the queen of the gods. Stuff like that could really deep-fry your brain.

He trudged toward the woods and tried not to think about his childhood—all the messed-up things that had led to his mother's death. But he couldn't help it.

• • •

The first time Tía Callida tried to kill him, he must've been about two. Tía Callida was looking after him while his mother was at the machine shop. She wasn't really his aunt, of course —just one of the old women in the community, a generic *tía* who helped watch the kids. She smelled like a honey-baked ham, and always wore a widow's dress with a black shawl.

"Let's set you down for a nap," she said. "Let's see if you are my brave little hero, eh?"

Leo was sleepy. She nestled him into his blankets in a warm mound of red and yellow—pillows? The bed was like a cubby-hole in the wall, made of blackened bricks, with a metal slot over his head and a square hole far above, where he could see the stars. He remembered resting comfortably, grabbing at sparks like fireflies. He dozed, and dreamed of a boat made of fire, sailing through the cinders. He imagined himself on board, navigating the sky. Somewhere nearby, Tía Callida sat in her rocking chair—*creak, creak, creak*—and sang a lullaby. Even at two, Leo knew the difference between English and Spanish, and he remembered being puzzled because Tía Callida was singing in a language that was neither.

Everything was fine until his mother came home. She screamed and raced over to snatch him up, yelling at Tía Callida, "How could you?" But the old lady had disappeared.

Leo remembered looking over his mother's shoulder at the flames curling around his blankets. Only years later had he realized he'd been sleeping in a blazing fireplace.

The weirdest thing? Tía Callida hadn't been arrested or even banished from their house. She appeared again several times over the next few years. Once when Leo was three, she let him play with knives. "You must learn your blades early," she insisted, "if you are to be my hero someday." Leo managed not to kill himself, but he got the feeling Tía Callida wouldn't have cared one way or the other.

When Leo was four, Tía found a rattlesnake for him in a nearby cow pasture. She gave him a stick and encouraged him to poke the animal. "Where is your bravery, little hero? Show me the Fates were right to choose you." Leo stared down at those amber eyes, hearing the dry *shh-shh-ssh* of the snake's rattle. He couldn't bring himself to poke the snake. It didn't seem fair. Apparently the snake felt the same way about biting a little kid. Leo could've sworn it looked at Tía Callida like, *Are you nuts, lady?* Then it disappeared into the tall grass.

The last time she babysat him, Leo was five. She brought him a pack of crayons and a pad of paper. They sat together at the picnic table in back of the apartment complex, under an old pecan tree. While Tía Callida sang her strange songs, Leo drew a picture of the boat he'd seen in the flames, with colorful sails and rows of oars, a curved stern, and an awesome figurehead. When he was almost done, about to sign his name the way he'd learned in kindergarten, a wind snatched the picture away. It flew into the sky and disappeared.

Leo wanted to cry. He'd spent so much time on that picture—but Tía Callida just clucked with disappointment.

"It isn't time yet, little hero. Someday, you'll have your quest. You'll find your destiny, and your hard journey will finally make sense. But first you must face many sorrows. I regret that, but heroes cannot be shaped any other way. Now, make me a fire, eh? Warm these old bones."

A few minutes later, Leo's mom came out and shrieked with horror. Tía Callida was gone, but Leo sat in the middle of a smoking fire. The pad of paper was reduced to ashes. Crayons had melted into a bubbling puddle of multicolored goo, and Leo's hands were ablaze, slowly burning through the picnic table. For years afterward, people in the apartment complex would wonder how someone had seared the impressions of a five-year-old's hands an inch deep into solid wood.

Now Leo was sure that Tía Callida, his psychotic babysitter, had been Hera all along. That made her, what—his godly grandmother? His family was even more messed up than he realized.

He wondered if his mother had known the truth. Leo remembered after that last visit, his mom took him inside and had a long talk with him, but he only understood some of it.

"She can't come back again." His mom had a beautiful face with kind eyes, and curly dark hair, but she looked older than she was because of hard work. The lines around her eyes were deeply etched. Her hands were callused. She was the first person from their family to graduate from college. She had a degree in mechanical engineering and could design anything, fix anything, build anything.

No one would hire her. No company would take her seriously, so she ended up in the machine shop, trying to make enough money to support the two of them. She always smelled of machine oil, and when she talked with Leo, she switched from Spanish to English constantly—using them like complementary tools. It took Leo years to realize that not everyone spoke that way. She'd even taught him Morse code as a kind of game, so they could tap messages to each other when they were in different rooms: *I love you. You okay?* Simple things like that.

"I don't care what Callida says," his mom told him. "I don't care about destiny and the Fates. You're too young for that. You're still my baby."

She took his hands, looking for burn marks, but of course there weren't any. "Leo, listen to me. Fire is a tool, like anything else, but it's more dangerous than most. You don't know your limits. Please, promise me—no more fire until you meet your father. Someday, *mijo*, you *will* meet him. He'll explain everything."

Leo had heard that since he could remember. Someday he would meet his dad. His mom wouldn't answer any questions about him. Leo had never met him, never even seen pictures, but she talked like he'd just gone to the store for some milk and he'd be back any minute. Leo tried to believe her. Someday, everything would make sense.

For the next couple of years, they were happy. Leo almost forgot about Tía Callida. He still dreamed of the flying boat, but the other strange events seemed like a dream too.

It all came apart when he was eight. By then, he was spending every free hour at the shop with his mom. He knew how to use the machines. He could measure and do math better than most adults. He'd learned to think three-dimensionally, solving mechanical problems in his head the way his mom did.

One night, they stayed late because his mom was finishing

a drill bit design she hoped to patent. If she could sell the prototype, it might change their lives. She'd finally get a break.

As she worked, Leo passed her supplies and told her corny jokes, trying to keep her spirits up. He loved it when he could make her laugh. She'd smile and say, "Your father would be proud of you, *mijo*. You'll meet him soon, I'm sure."

Mom's workspace was at the very back of the shop. It was kind of creepy at night, because they were the only ones there. Every sound echoed through the dark warehouse, but Leo didn't mind as long as he was with his mom. If he did wander the shop, they could always keep in touch with Morse code taps. Whenever they were ready to leave, they had to walk through the entire shop, through the break room, and out to the parking lot, locking the doors behind them.

That night after finishing up, they'd just gotten to the break room when his mom realized she didn't have her keys.

"That's funny." She frowned. "I know I had them. Wait here, *mijo*. I'll only be a minute."

She gave him one more smile—the last one he'd ever get —and she went back into the warehouse.

She'd only been gone a few heartbeats when the interior door slammed shut. Then the exterior door locked itself.

"Mom?" Leo's heart pounded. Something heavy crashed inside the warehouse. He ran to the door, but no matter how hard he pulled or kicked, it wouldn't open. "Mom!" Frantically, he tapped a message on the wall: *You okay?*

"She can't hear you," a voice said.

Leo turned and found himself facing a strange woman. At

first he thought it was Tía Callida. She was wrapped in black robes, with a veil covering her face.

"Tía?" he said.

The woman chuckled, a slow gentle sound, as if she were half asleep. "I am not your guardian. Merely a family resemblance."

"What—what do you want? Where's my mom?"

"Ah...loyal to your mother. How nice. But you see, I have children too...and I understand you will fight them someday. When they try to wake me, you will prevent them. I cannot allow that."

"I don't know you. I don't want to fight anybody."

She muttered like a sleepwalker in a trance, "A wise choice."

With a chill, Leo realized the woman was, in fact, asleep. Behind the veil, her eyes were closed. But even stranger: her clothes were not made of cloth. They were made of *earth*—dry black dirt, churning and shifting around her. Her pale, sleeping face was barely visible behind a curtain of dust, and he had the horrible sense that she had just risen from the grave. If the woman was asleep, Leo wanted her to stay that way. He knew that fully awake, she would be even more terrible.

"I cannot destroy you yet," the woman murmured. "The Fates will not allow it. But they do not protect your mother, and they cannot stop me from breaking your spirit. Remember this night, little hero, when they ask you to oppose me."

"Leave my mother alone!" Fear rose in his throat as the woman shuffled forward. She moved more like an avalanche than a person, a dark wall of earth shifting toward him.

"How will you stop me?" she whispered.

She walked straight through a table, the particles of her body reassembling on the other side.

She loomed over Leo, and he knew she would pass right through him, too. He was the only thing between her and his mother.

His hands caught fire.

A sleepy smile spread across the woman's face, as if she'd already won. Leo screamed with desperation. His vision turned red. Flames washed over the earthen woman, the walls, the locked doors. And Leo lost consciousness.

When he woke, he was in an ambulance.

The paramedic tried to be kind. She told him the warehouse had burned down. His mother hadn't made it out. The paramedic said she was sorry, but Leo felt hollow. He'd lost control, just like his mother had warned. Her death was his fault.

Soon the police came to get him, and they weren't as nice. The fire had started in the break room, they said, right where Leo was standing. He'd survived by some miracle, but what kind of child locked the doors of his mother's workplace, knowing she was inside, and started a fire?

Later, his neighbors at the apartment complex told the police what a strange boy he was. They talked about the burned handprints on the picnic table. They'd always known something was wrong with Esperanza Valdez's son.

His relatives wouldn't take him in. His Aunt Rosa called him a *diablo* and shouted at the social workers to take him away. So Leo went to his first foster home. A few days later, he ran away. Some foster homes lasted longer than others. He would joke around, make a few friends, pretend that nothing bothered him, but he always ended up running sooner or later. It was the only thing that made the pain better—feeling like he was moving, getting farther and farther away from the ashes of that machine shop.

He'd promised himself he would never play with fire again. He hadn't thought about Tía Callida, or the sleeping woman wrapped in earthen robes, for a long time.

He was almost to the woods when he imagined Tía Callida's voice: *It wasn't your fault, little hero. Our enemy wakes. It's time to stop running.*

"Hera," Leo muttered, "you're not even here, are you? You're in a cage somewhere."

There was no answer.

But now, at least, Leo understood something. Hera had been watching him his entire life. Somehow, she'd known that one day she would need him. Maybe those Fates she mentioned could tell the future. Leo wasn't sure. But he knew he was *meant* to go on this quest. Jason's prophecy warned them to beware the earth, and Leo knew it had something to do with that sleeping woman in the shop, wrapped in robes of shifting dirt.

You'll find your destiny, Tía Callida had promised, *and your hard journey will finally make sense.*

Leo might find out what that flying boat in his dreams meant. He might meet his father, or even get to avenge his mother's death.

But first things first. He'd promised Jason a flying ride.

Not the boat from his dreams—not yet. There wasn't time to build something that complicated. He needed a quicker solution. He needed a dragon.

He hesitated at the edge of the woods, peering into absolute blackness. Owls hooted, and something far away hissed like a chorus of snakes.

Leo remembered what Will Solace had told him: No one should go in the woods alone, definitely not unarmed. Leo had nothing—no sword, no flashlight, no help.

He glanced back at the lights of the cabins. He could turn around now and tell everyone he'd been joking. *Psych!* Nyssa could go on the quest instead. He could stay at camp and learn to be part of the Hephaestus cabin, but he wondered how long it would be before he looked like his bunkmates—sad, dejected, convinced of his own bad luck.

They cannot stop me from breaking your spirit, the sleeping woman had said. *Remember this night, little hero, when they ask you to oppose me.*

"Believe me, lady," Leo muttered, "I remember. And whoever you are, I'm gonna face-plant you hard, Leo-style."

He took a deep breath and plunged into the forest.

XII

LEO

THE WOODS WEREN'T LIKE ANYPLACE he'd been before. Leo had been raised in a north Houston apartment complex. The wildest things he'd ever seen were that rattlesnake in the cow pasture and his Aunt Rosa in her nightgown, until he was sent to Wilderness School.

Even there, the school had been in the desert. No trees with gnarled roots to trip over. No streams to fall into. No branches casting dark, creepy shadows and owls looking down at him with their big reflective eyes. This was the Twilight Zone.

He stumbled along until he was sure no one back at the cabins could possibly see him. Then he summoned fire. Flames danced along his fingertips, casting enough light to see. He hadn't tried to keep a sustained burn going since he was five, at that picnic table. Since his mom's death, he'd been too afraid to try anything. Even this tiny fire made him feel guilty.

He kept walking, looking for dragon-type clues—giant

footprints, trampled trees, swaths of burning forest. Something that big couldn't exactly sneak around, right? But he saw *nada*. Once he glimpsed a large, furry shape like a wolf or a bear, but it stayed away from his fire, which was fine by Leo.

Then, at the bottom of a clearing, he saw the first trap—a hundred-foot-wide crater ringed with boulders.

Leo had to admit it was pretty ingenious. In the center of the depression, a metal vat the size of a hot tub had been filled with bubbly dark liquid—Tabasco sauce and motor oil. On a pedestal suspended over the vat, an electric fan rotated in a circle, spreading the fumes across the forest. Could metal dragons smell?

The vat seemed to be unguarded. But Leo looked closely, and in the dim light of the stars and his handheld fire, he could see the glint of metal beneath the dirt and leaves—a bronze net lining the entire crater. Or maybe *see* wasn't the right word—he could sense it there, as if the mechanism was emitting heat, revealing itself to him. Six large strips of bronze stretched out from the vat like the spokes of a wheel. They would be pressure sensitive, Leo guessed. As soon as the dragon stepped on one, the net would spring closed, and *voilà*—one gift-wrapped monster.

Leo edged closer. He put his foot on the nearest trigger strip. As he expected, nothing happened. They had to have set the net for something really heavy. Otherwise they could catch an animal, human, smaller monster, whatever. He doubted there was anything else as heavy as a metal dragon in these woods. At least, he hoped there wasn't.

He picked his way down the crater and approached the

vat. The fumes were almost overpowering, and his eyes started watering. He remembered a time when Tía Callida (Hera, whatever) had made him chop jalapeños in the kitchen and he'd gotten the juice in his eyes. Serious pain. But of course she'd been like, "Endure it, little hero. The Aztecs of your mother's homeland used to punish bad children by holding them over a fire filled with chili peppers. They raised many heroes that way."

A total psycho, that lady. Leo was so glad he was on a quest to rescue her.

Tía Callida would've loved this vat, because it was *way* worse than jalapeño juice. Leo looked for a trigger—something that would disable the net. He didn't see anything.

He had a moment of panic. Nyssa had said there were several traps like this in the woods, and they were planning more. What if the dragon had already stepped into another one? How could Leo possibly find them all?

He continued to search, but he didn't see any release mechanism. No large button labeled OFF. It occurred to him that there might not *be* one. He started to despair—and then he heard the sound.

It was more of a tremor—the deep sort of rumbling you hear in your gut rather than your ears. It gave him the jitters, but he didn't look around for the source. He just kept examining the trap, thinking, *Must be a long way off. It's pounding its way through the woods. I gotta hurry.*

Then he heard a grinding snort, like steam forced out of a metal barrel.

His neck tingled. He turned slowly. At the edge of the pit,

fifty feet away, two glowing red eyes were staring at him. The creature gleamed in the moonlight, and Leo couldn't believe something that huge had sneaked up on him so fast. Too late, he realized its gaze was fixed on the fire in his hand, and he extinguished the flames.

He could still see the dragon just fine. It was about sixty feet long, snout to tail, its body made of interlocking bronze plates. Its claws were the size of butcher knives, and its mouth was lined with hundreds of dagger-sharp metal teeth. Steam came out of its nostrils. It snarled like a chain saw cutting through a tree. It could've bitten Leo in half, easy, or stomped him flat. It was the most beautiful thing he'd ever seen, except for one problem that completely ruined Leo's plan.

"You don't have wings," Leo said.

The dragon's snarl died. It tilted its head as if to say, *Why aren't you running away in terror?*

"Hey, no offense," Leo said. "You're amazing! Good god, who *made* you? Are you hydraulic or nuclear-powered or what? But if it was me, I would've put wings on you. What kind of dragon doesn't have wings? I guess maybe you're too heavy to fly? I should've thought of that."

The dragon snorted, more confused now. It was supposed to trample Leo. This conversation thing wasn't part of the plan. It took a step forward, and Leo shouted, "No!"

The dragon snarled again.

"It's a trap, bronze brain," Leo said. "They're trying to catch you."

The dragon opened its mouth and blew fire. A column of white-hot flames billowed over Leo, more than he'd ever tried to endure before. He felt as if he were being hosed down with a powerful, very hot fire hose. It stung a little, but he stood his ground. When the flames died, he was perfectly fine. Even his clothes were okay, which Leo didn't understand, but for which he was grateful. He liked his army jacket, and having his pants seared off would've been pretty embarrassing.

The dragon stared at Leo. Its face didn't actually change, being made of metal and all, but Leo thought he could read its expression: *Why no crispy critter?* A spark flew out of its neck like it was about to short-circuit.

"You can't burn me," Leo said, trying to sound stern and calm. He'd never had a dog before, but he talked to the dragon the way he thought you'd talk to a dog. "Stay, boy. Don't come any closer. I don't want you to get caught. See, they think you're broken and have to be scrapped. But I don't believe that. I can fix you if you'll let me—"

The dragon creaked, roared, and charged. The trap sprang. The floor of the crater erupted with a sound like a thousand trash can lids banging together. Dirt and leaves flew, metal net flashing. Leo was knocked off his feet, turned upside down, and doused in Tabasco sauce and oil. He found himself sandwiched between the vat and the dragon as it thrashed, trying to free itself from the net that had wrapped around them both.

The dragon blew flames in every direction, lighting up the sky and setting trees on fire. Oil and sauce burned all over them. It didn't hurt Leo, but it left a nasty taste in his mouth.

"Will you stop that!" he yelled.

The dragon kept squirming. Leo realized he would get

crushed if he didn't move. It wasn't easy, but he managed to wriggle out from between the dragon and the vat. He squirmed his way through the net. Fortunately the holes were plenty big enough for a skinny kid.

He ran to the dragon's head. It tried to snap at him, but its teeth were tangled in the mesh. It blew fire again, but seemed to be running out of energy. This time the flames were only orange. They sputtered before they even reached Leo's face.

"Listen, man," Leo said, "you're just going to show them where you are. Then they'll come and break out the acid and the metal cutters. Is that what you want?"

The dragon's jaw made a creaking sound, like it was trying to talk.

"Okay, then," Leo said. "You'll have to trust me."

And Leo set to work.

It took him almost an hour to find the control panel. It was right behind the dragon's head, which made sense. He'd elected to keep the dragon in the net, because it was easier to work with the dragon constrained, but the dragon didn't like it.

"Hold still!" Leo scolded.

The dragon made another creaking sound that might've been a whimper.

Leo examined the wires inside the dragon's head. He was distracted by a sound in the woods, but when he looked up it was just a tree spirit—a dryad, Leo thought they were called—putting out the flames in her branches. Fortunately, the dragon hadn't started an all-out forest fire, but still the dryad wasn't too pleased. The girl's dress was smoking. She smothered the flames with a silky blanket, and when she saw Leo looking at her, she made a gesture that was probably very rude in Dryad. Then she disappeared in a green poof of mist.

Leo returned his attention to the wiring. It was ingenious, definitely, and it made sense to him. This was the motor control relay. This processed sensory input from the eyes. This disk...

"Ha," he said. "Well, no wonder."

Creak? the dragon asked with its jaw.

"You've got a corroded control disk. Probably regulates your higher reasoning circuits, right? Rusty brain, man. No wonder you're a little...confused." He almost said *crazy*, but he caught himself. "I wish I had a replacement disk, but... this is a complicated piece of circuitry. I'm gonna have to take it out and clean it. Only be a minute." He pulled out the disk, and the dragon went absolutely still. The glow died in its eyes. Leo slid off its back and began polishing the disk. He mopped up some oil and Tabasco sauce with his sleeve, which helped cut through the grime, but the more he cleaned, the more concerned he got. Some of the circuits were beyond repair. He could make it better, but not perfect. For that, he'd need a completely new disk, and he had no idea how to build one.

He tried to work quickly. He wasn't sure how long the dragon's control disk could be off without damaging it— maybe forever—but he didn't want to take chances. Once he'd done the best he could, he climbed back up to the dragon's head and started cleaning the wiring and gearboxes, getting himself filthy in the process.

"Clean hands, dirty equipment," he muttered, something

his mother used to say. By the time he was through, his hands were black with grease and his clothes looked like he'd just lost a mud-wrestling contest, but the mechanisms looked a lot better. He slipped in the disk, connected the last wire, and sparks flew. The dragon shuddered. Its eyes began to glow.

"Better?" Leo asked.

The dragon made a sound like a high-speed drill. It opened its mouth and all its teeth rotated.

"I guess that's a *yes*. Hold on, I'll free you."

Another thirty minutes to find the release clamps for the net and untangle the dragon, but finally it stood and shook the last bit of netting off its back. It roared triumphantly and shot fire at the sky.

"Seriously," Leo said. "Could you not show off?"

Creak? the dragon asked.

"You need a name," Leo decided. "I'm calling you Festus."

The dragon whirred its teeth and grinned. At least Leo hoped it was a grin.

"Cool," Leo said. "But we still have a problem, because you don't have wings."

Festus tilted his head and snorted steam. Then he lowered his back in an unmistakable gesture. He wanted Leo to climb on.

"Where we going?" Leo asked.

But he was too excited to wait for an answer. He climbed onto the dragon's back, and Festus bounded off into the woods.

• • •

Leo lost track of time and all sense of direction. It seemed impossible the woods could be so deep and wild, but the dragon traveled until the trees were like skyscrapers and the canopy of leaves completely blotted out the stars. Even the fire in Leo's hand couldn't have lit the way, but the dragon's glowing red eyes acted like headlights.

Finally they crossed a stream and came to a dead end, a limestone cliff a hundred feet tall—a solid, sheer mass the dragon couldn't possibly climb.

Festus stopped at the base and lifted one leg like a dog pointing.

"What is it?" Leo slid to the ground. He walked up to the cliff—nothing but solid rock. The dragon kept pointing.

"It's not going to move out of your way," Leo told him.

The loose wire in the dragon's neck sparked, but otherwise he stayed still. Leo put his hand on the cliff. Suddenly his fingers smoldered. Lines of fire spread from his fingertips like ignited gunpowder, sizzling across the limestone. The burning lines raced across the cliff face until they had outlined a glowing red door five times as tall as Leo. He backed up and the door swung open, disturbingly silently for such a big slab of rock.

"Perfectly balanced," he muttered. "That's some first-rate engineering."

The dragon unfroze and marched inside, as if he were coming home.

Leo stepped through, and the door began to close. He had a moment of panic, remembering that night in the machine shop long ago, when he'd been locked in. What if he got stuck in here? But then lights flickered on—a combination of electric fluorescents and wall-mounted torches. When Leo saw the cavern, he forgot about leaving.

"Festus," he muttered. "What *is* this place?"

The dragon stomped to the center of the room, leaving tracks in the thick dust, and curled up on a large circular platform.

The cave was the size of an airplane hangar, with endless worktables and storage cages, rows of garage-sized doors along either wall, and staircases that led up to a network of catwalks high above. Equipment was everywhere—hydraulic lifts, welding torches, hazard suits, air-spades, forklifts, plus something that looked suspiciously like a nuclear reaction chamber. Bulletin boards were covered with tattered, faded blueprints. And weapons, armor, shields—war supplies all over the place, a lot of them only partially finished.

Hanging from chains far above the dragon's platform was an old tattered banner almost too faded to read. The letters were Greek, but Leo somehow knew what they said: BUNKER 9.

Did that mean nine as in the Hephaestus cabin, or nine as in there were eight others? Leo looked at Festus, still curled up on the platform, and it occurred to him that the dragon looked so content because it *was* home. It had probably been built on that pad.

"Do the other kids know...?" Leo's question died as he asked it. Clearly, this place had been abandoned for decades. Cobwebs and dust covered everything. The floor revealed no footprints except for his, and the huge paw prints of the dragon. He was the first one in this bunker since...since a long time ago. Bunker 9 had been abandoned with a lot of projects half finished on the tables. Locked up and forgotten, but why?

Leo looked at a map on the wall—a battle map of camp, but the paper was as cracked and yellow as onionskin. A date at the bottom read, 1864.

"No way," he muttered.

Then he spotted a blueprint on a nearby bulletin board, and his heart almost leaped out of his throat. He ran to the worktable and stared up at a white-line drawing almost faded beyond recognition: a Greek ship from several different angles. Faintly scrawled words underneath it read: PROPHECY? UNCLEAR. FLIGHT?

It was the ship he'd seen in his dreams—the flying ship. Someone had tried to build it here, or at least sketched out the idea. Then it was left, forgotten...a prophecy yet to come. And weirdest of all, the ship's figurehead was exactly like the one Leo had drawn when he was five—the head of a dragon.

"Looks like you, Festus," he murmured. "That's creepy."

The figurehead gave him an uneasy feeling, but Leo's mind spun with too many other questions to think about it for long. He touched the blueprint, hoping he could take it down to study, but the paper crackled at his touch, so he left it alone. He looked around for other clues. No boats. No pieces that looked like parts of this project, but there were so many doors and storerooms to explore.

Festus snorted like he was trying to get Leo's attention, reminding him they didn't have all night. It was true. Leo figured it would be morning in a few hours, and he'd gotten completely sidetracked. He'd saved the dragon, but it wasn't going to help him on the quest. He needed something that would fly.

Festus nudged something toward him—a leather tool belt that had been left next to his construction pad. Then the dragon switched on his glowing red eye beams and turned them toward the ceiling. Leo looked up to where the spotlights were pointing, and yelped when he recognized the shapes hanging above them in the darkness.

"Festus," he said in a small voice. "We've got work to do."

XIII

JASON

JASON DREAMED OF WOLVES.

He stood in a clearing in the middle of a redwood forest. In front of him rose the ruins of a stone mansion. Low gray clouds blended with the ground fog, and cold rain hung in the air. A pack of large gray beasts milled around him, brushing against his legs, snarling and baring their teeth. They gently nudged him toward the ruins.

Jason had no desire to become the world's largest dog biscuit, so he decided to do what they wanted.

The ground squelched under his boots as he walked. Stone spires of chimneys, no longer attached to anything, rose up like totem poles. The house must've been enormous once, multi-storied with massive log walls and a soaring gabled roof, but now nothing remained but its stone skeleton. Jason passed under a crumbling doorway and found himself in a kind of courtyard.

Before him was a drained reflecting pool, long and

rectangular. Jason couldn't tell how deep it was, because the bottom was filled with mist. A dirt path led all the way around, and the house's uneven walls rose on either side. Wolves paced under the archways of rough red volcanic stone.

At the far end of the pool sat a giant she-wolf, several feet taller than Jason. Her eyes glowed silver in the fog, and her coat was the same color as the rocks—warm chocolaty red.

"I know this place," Jason said.

The wolf regarded him. She didn't exactly speak, but Jason could understand her. The movements of her ears and whiskers, the flash of her eyes, the way she curled her lips—all of these were part of her language.

Of course, the she-wolf said. *You began your journey here as a pup. Now you must find your way back. A new quest, a new start.*

"That isn't fair," Jason said. But as soon as he spoke, he knew there was no point complaining to the she-wolf.

Wolves didn't feel sympathy. They never expected fairness. The wolf said: *Conquer or die. This is always our way.*

Jason wanted to protest that he couldn't conquer if he didn't know who he was, or where he was supposed to go. But he knew this wolf. Her name was simply Lupa, the Mother Wolf, the greatest of her kind. Long ago she'd found him in this place, protected him, nurtured him, *chosen* him, but if Jason showed weakness, she would tear him to shreds. Rather than being her pup, he would become her dinner. In the wolf pack, weakness was not an option.

"Can you guide me?" Jason asked.

Lupa made a rumbling noise deep in her throat, and the mist in the pool dissolved.

At first Jason wasn't sure what he was seeing. At opposite ends of the pool, two dark spires had erupted from the cement floor like the drill bits of some massive tunneling machines boring through the surface. Jason couldn't tell if the spires were made of rock or petrified vines, but they were formed of thick tendrils that came together in a point at the top. Each spire was about five feet tall, but they weren't identical. The one closest to Jason was darker and seemed like a solid mass, its tendrils fused together. As he watched, it pushed a little farther out of the earth and expanded a little wider.

On Lupa's end of the pool, the second spire's tendrils were more open, like the bars of a cage. Inside, Jason could vaguely see a misty figure struggling, shifting within its confines.

"Hera," Jason said.

The she-wolf growled in agreement. The other wolves circled the pool, their fur standing up on their backs as they snarled at the spires.

The enemy has chosen this place to awaken her most powerful son, the giant king, Lupa said. *Our sacred place, where demigods are claimed—the place of death or life. The burned house. The house of the wolf. It is an abomination. You must stop her.*

"Her?" Jason was confused. "You mean, Hera?"

The she-wolf gnashed her teeth impatiently. *Use your senses, pup. I care nothing for Juno, but if she falls, our enemy wakes. And that will be the end for all of us. You know this place. You can find it again. Cleanse our house. Stop this before it is too late.*

The dark spire grew slowly larger, like the bulb of some horrible flower. Jason sensed that if it ever opened, it would release something he did *not* want to meet.

"Who am I?" Jason asked the she-wolf. "At least tell me that."

Wolves don't have much of a sense of humor, but Jason could tell the question amused Lupa, as if Jason were a cub just trying out his claws, practicing to be the alpha male.

You are our saving grace, as always. The she-wolf curled her lip, as if she had just made a clever joke. *Do not fail, son of Jupiter.*

XIV

JASON

JASON WOKE TO THE SOUND OF THUNDER. Then he remembered where he was. It was always thundering in Cabin One.

Above his cot, the domed ceiling was decorated with a blue-and-white mosaic like a cloudy sky. The cloud tiles shifted across the ceiling, changing from white to black. Thunder rumbled through the room, and gold tiles flashed like veins of lightning.

Except for the cot that the other campers had brought him, the cabin had no regular furniture—no chairs, tables, or dressers. As far as Jason could tell, it didn't even have a bathroom. The walls were carved with alcoves, each holding a bronze brazier or a golden eagle statue on a marble pedestal. In the center of the room, a twenty-foot-tall, full-color statue of Zeus in classic Greek robes stood with a shield at his side and a lightning bolt raised, ready to smite somebody.

Jason studied the statue, looking for anything he had in common with the Lord of the Sky. Black hair? Nope. Grumbly expression? Well, maybe. Beard? No thanks. In his robes and sandals, Zeus looked like a really buff, really angry hippie.

Yeah, Cabin One. A big honor, the other campers had told him. Sure, if you liked sleeping in a cold temple by yourself with Hippie Zeus frowning down at you all night.

Jason got up and rubbed his neck. His whole body was stiff from bad sleep and summoning lightning. That little trick last night hadn't been as easy as he had let on. It had almost made him pass out.

Next to the cot, new clothes were laid out for him: jeans, sneakers, and an orange Camp Half-Blood shirt. He definitely needed a change of clothes, but looking down at his tattered purple shirt, he was reluctant to change. It felt wrong somehow, putting on the camp shirt. He still couldn't believe he belonged here, despite everything they'd told him.

He thought about his dream, hoping more memories would come back to him about Lupa, or that ruined house in the redwoods. He knew he'd been there before. The wolf was real. But his head ached when he tried to remember. The marks on his forearm seemed to burn.

If he could find those ruins, he could find his past. Whatever was growing inside that rock spire, Jason had to stop it.

He looked at Hippie Zeus. "You're welcome to help."

The statue said nothing.

"Thanks, Pops," Jason muttered.

He changed clothes and checked his reflection in Zeus's shield. His face looked watery and strange in the metal, like he was dissolving in a pool of gold. Definitely he didn't look as good as Piper had last night after she'd suddenly been transformed.

Jason still wasn't sure how he felt about that. He'd acted like an idiot, announcing in front of everyone that she was a knockout. Not like there'd been anything wrong with her *before*. Sure, she looked great after Aphrodite zapped her, but she also didn't look like herself, not comfortable with the attention.

Jason had felt bad for her. Maybe that was crazy, considering she'd just been claimed by a goddess and turned into the most gorgeous girl at camp. Everybody had started fawning over her, telling her how amazing she was and how obviously *she* should be the one who went on the quest—but that attention had nothing to do with who she was. New dress, new makeup, glowing pink aura, and *boom*: suddenly people liked her. Jason felt like he understood that.

Last night when he'd called down lightning, the other campers' reactions had seemed familiar to him. He was pretty sure he'd been dealing with that for a long time—people looking at him in awe just because he was the son of Zeus, treating him special, but it didn't have anything to do with *him*. Nobody cared about *him*, just his big scary daddy standing behind him with the doomsday bolt, as if to say, *Respect this kid or eat voltage!*

After the campfire, when people started heading back to their cabins, Jason had gone up to Piper and formally asked her to come with him on the quest.

She'd still been in a state of shock, but she nodded, rubbing her arms, which must've been cold in that sleeveless dress.

"Aphrodite took my snowboarding jacket," she muttered. "Mugged by my own mom."

In the first row of the amphitheater, Jason found a blanket and wrapped it around her shoulders. "We'll get you a new jacket," he promised.

She managed a smile. He wanted to wrap his arms around her, but he restrained himself. He didn't want her to think he was as shallow as everyone else—trying to make a move on her because she'd turned all beautiful.

He was glad Piper was going with him on the quest. Jason had tried to act brave at the campfire, but it was just that— an act. The idea of going up against an evil force powerful enough to kidnap Hera scared him witless, especially since he didn't even know his own past. He'd need help, and it felt right: Piper should be with him. But things were already complicated without figuring out how much he liked her, and why. He'd already messed with her head enough.

He slipped on his new shoes, ready to get out of that cold, empty cabin. Then he spotted something he hadn't noticed the night before. A brazier had been moved out of one of the alcoves to create a sleeping niche, with a bedroll, a backpack, even some pictures taped to the wall.

Jason walked over. Whoever had slept there, it had been a long time ago. The bedroll smelled musty. The backpack was covered with a thin film of dust. Some of the photos once taped to the wall had lost their stickiness and fallen to the floor.

One picture showed Annabeth—much younger, maybe eight, but Jason could tell it was she: same blond hair and gray eyes, same distracted look like she was thinking a million things at once. She stood next to a sandy-haired guy about fourteen or fifteen, with a mischievous smile and ragged leather armor over a T-shirt. He was pointing to an alley behind them, like he was telling the photographer, *Let's go meet things in a dark alley and kill them!* A second photo showed Annabeth and the same guy sitting at a campfire, laughing hysterically.

Finally Jason picked up one of the photos that had fallen. It was a strip of pictures like you'd take in a do-it-yourself photo booth: Annabeth and the sandy-haired guy, but with another girl between them. She was maybe fifteen, with black hair—choppy like Piper's—a black leather jacket, and silver jewelry, so she looked kind of goth; but she was caught mid-laugh, and it was clear she was with her two best friends.

"That's Thalia," someone said.

Jason turned.

Annabeth was peering over his shoulder. Her expression was sad, like the picture brought back hard memories. "She's the other child of Zeus who lived here—but not for long. Sorry, I should've knocked."

"It's fine," Jason said. "Not like I think of this place as home."

Annabeth was dressed for travel, with a winter coat over her camp clothes, her knife at her belt, and a backpack across her shoulder.

Jason said, "Don't suppose you've changed your mind about coming with us?"

She shook her head. "You got a good team already. I'm off to look for Percy."

Jason was a little disappointed. He would've appreciated having somebody on the trip who knew what they were doing, so he wouldn't feel like he was leading Piper and Leo off a cliff.

"Hey, you'll do fine," Annabeth promised. "Something tells me this isn't your first quest."

Jason had a vague suspicion she was right, but that didn't make him feel any better. Everyone seemed to think he was so brave and confident, but they didn't see how lost he really felt. How could they trust him when he didn't even know who he was?

He looked at the pictures of Annabeth smiling. He wondered how long it had been since she'd smiled. She must really like this Percy guy to search for him so hard, and that made Jason a little envious. Was anyone searching for *him* right now? What if somebody cared for *him* that much and was going out of her mind with worry, and he couldn't even remember his old life?

"You know who I am," he guessed. "Don't you?"

Annabeth gripped the hilt of her dagger. She looked for a chair to sit on, but of course there weren't any. "Honestly, Jason . . . I'm not sure. My best guess, you're a loner. It happens sometimes. For one reason or another, the camp never found you, but you survived anyway by constantly moving around. Trained yourself to fight. Handled the monsters on your own. You beat the odds."

"The first thing Chiron said to me," Jason remembered, "was *you should be dead.*"

"That could be why," Annabeth said. "Most demigods

would never make it on their own. And a child of Zeus—
I mean, it doesn't get any more dangerous than that. The
chances of your reaching age fifteen without finding Camp
Half-Blood or dying—microscopic. But like I said, it does
happen. Thalia ran away when she was young. She survived
on her own for years. Even took care of me for a while. So
maybe you were a loner too."

Jason held out his arm. "And these marks?"

Annabeth glanced at the tattoos. Clearly, they bothered
her. "Well, the eagle is the symbol of Zeus, so that makes
sense. The twelve lines—maybe they stand for years, if you'd
been making them since you were three years old. SPQR—
that's the motto of the old Roman Empire: *Senatus Populusque
Romanus*, the Senate and the People of Rome. Though why
you would burn that on your own arm, I don't know. Unless
you had a *really* harsh Latin teacher . . ."

Jason was pretty sure that wasn't the reason. It also didn't
seem possible he'd been on his own his whole life. But what
else made sense? Annabeth had been pretty clear—Camp
Half-Blood was the only safe place in the world for demigods.

"I, um . . . had a weird dream last night," he said. It seemed
like a stupid thing to confide, but Annabeth didn't look
surprised.

"Happens all the time to demigods," she said. "What did
you see?"

He told her about the wolves and the ruined house and
the two rock spires. As he talked, Annabeth started pacing,
looking more and more agitated.

"You don't remember where this house is?" she asked.

Jason shook his head. "But I'm sure I've been there before."

"Redwoods," she mused. "Could be northern California. And the she-wolf... I've studied goddesses, spirits, and monsters my whole life. I've never heard of Lupa."

"She said the enemy was a 'her.' I thought maybe it was Hera, but—"

"I wouldn't trust Hera, but I don't think she's the enemy. And that thing rising out of the earth—" Annabeth's expression darkened. "You've got to stop it."

"You know what it is, don't you?" he asked. "Or at least, you've got a guess. I saw your face last night at the campfire. You looked at Chiron like it was suddenly dawning on you, but you didn't want to scare us."

Annabeth hesitated. "Jason, the thing about prophecies... the more you know, the more you try to change them, and that can be disastrous. Chiron believes it's better that you find your own path, find out things in your own time. If he'd told me everything he knew before my first quest with Percy ...I've got to admit, I'm not sure I would've been able to go through with it. For your quest, it's even more important."

"That bad, huh?"

"Not if you succeed. At least...I hope not."

"But I don't even know where to start. Where am I supposed to go?"

"Follow the monsters," Annabeth suggested.

Jason thought about that. The storm spirit who'd attacked him at the Grand Canyon had said he was being recalled to his boss. If Jason could track the storm spirits, he might be able to find the person controlling them. And maybe that would lead him to Hera's prison.

"Okay," he said. "How do I find storm winds?"

"Personally, I'd ask a wind god," Annabeth said. "Aeolus is the master of all the winds, but he's a little...unpredictable. No one finds him unless he wants to be found. I'd try one of the four seasonal wind gods that work for Aeolus. The nearest one, the one who has the most dealings with heroes, is Boreas, the North Wind."

"So if I looked him up on Google maps—"

"Oh, he's not hard to find," Annabeth promised. "He settled in North America like all the other gods. So of course he picked the oldest northern settlement, about as far north as you can go."

"Maine?" Jason guessed.

"Farther."

Jason tried to envision a map. What was farther north than Maine? The oldest northern settlement...

"Canada," he decided. "Quebec."

Annabeth smiled. "I hope you speak French."

Jason actually felt a spark of excitement. Quebec—at least now he had a goal. Find the North Wind, track down the storm spirits, find out who they worked for and where that ruined house was. Free Hera. All in four days. Cake.

"Thanks, Annabeth." He looked at the photo booth pictures still in his hand. "So, um...you said it was dangerous being a child of Zeus. What happened to Thalia?"

"Oh, she's fine," Annabeth said. "She became a Hunter of

Artemis—one of the handmaidens of the goddess. They roam around the country killing monsters. We don't see them at camp very often."

Jason glanced over at the huge statue of Zeus. He understood why Thalia had slept in this alcove. It was the only place in the cabin not in Hippie Zeus's line of sight. And even that hadn't been enough. She'd chosen to follow Artemis and be part of a group rather than stay in this cold drafty temple alone with her twenty-foot-tall dad—*Jason's dad*—glowering down at her. *Eat voltage!* Jason didn't have any trouble understanding Thalia's feelings. He wondered if there was a Hunters group for guys.

"Who's the other kid in the photo?" he asked. "The sandy-haired guy."

Annabeth's expression tightened. Touchy subject.

"That's Luke," she said. "He's dead now."

Jason decided it was best not to ask more, but the way Annabeth said Luke's name, he wondered if maybe Percy Jackson wasn't the only boy Annabeth had ever liked.

He focused again on Thalia's face. He kept thinking this photo of her was important. He was missing something.

Jason felt a strange sense of connection to this other child of Zeus—someone who might understand his confusion, maybe even answer some questions. But another voice inside him, an insistent whisper, said: *Dangerous. Stay away*.

"How old is she now?" he asked.

"Hard to say. She was a tree for a while. Now she's immortal."

"What?"

His expression must've been pretty good, because Annabeth laughed. "Don't worry. It's not something all children of Zeus go through. It's a long story, but...well, she was out of commission for a long time. If she'd aged regularly, she'd be in her twenties now, but she still looks the same as in that picture, like she's about...well, about your age. Fifteen or sixteen?"

Something the she-wolf had said in his dream nagged at Jason. He found himself asking, "What's her last name?"

Annabeth looked uneasy. "She didn't use a last name, really. If she had to, she'd use her mom's, but they didn't get along. Thalia ran away when she was pretty young."

Jason waited.

"Grace," Annabeth said. "Thalia Grace."

Jason's fingers went numb. The picture fluttered to the floor.

"You okay?" Annabeth asked.

A shred of memory had ignited—maybe a tiny piece that Hera had forgotten to steal. Or maybe she'd left it there on purpose—just enough for him to remember that name, and know that digging up his past was terribly, terribly dangerous.

You should be dead, Chiron had said. It wasn't a comment about Jason beating the odds as a loner. Chiron knew something specific—something about Jason's family.

The she-wolf's words in his dream finally made sense to him, her clever joke at his expense. He could imagine Lupa growling a wolfish laugh.

"What is it?" Annabeth pressed.

Jason couldn't keep this to himself. It would kill him, and

he had to get Annabeth's help. If she knew Thalia, maybe she could advise him.

"You have to swear not to tell anyone else," he said.

"Jason—"

"Swear it," he urged. "Until I figure out what's going on, what this all means—" He rubbed the burned tattoos on his forearm. "You have to keep a secret."

Annabeth hesitated, but her curiosity won out. "All right. Until you tell me it's okay, I won't share what you say with anyone else. I swear on the River Styx."

Thunder rumbled, even louder than usual for the cabin.

You are our saving Grace, the wolf had snarled.

Jason picked up the photo from the floor.

"My last name is Grace," he said. "This is my sister."

Annabeth turned pale. Jason could see her wrestling with dismay, disbelief, anger. She thought he was lying. His claim was impossible. And part of him felt the same way, but as soon as he spoke the words, he knew they were true.

Then the doors of the cabin burst open. Half a dozen campers spilled in, led by the bald guy from Iris, Butch.

"Hurry!" he said, and Jason couldn't tell if his expression was excitement or fear. "The dragon is back."

PIPER

PIPER WOKE UP AND IMMEDIATELY GRABBED a mirror. There were plenty of those in the Aphrodite cabin. She sat on her bunk, looked at her reflection and groaned.

She was *still* gorgeous.

Last night after the campfire, she'd tried everything. She messed up her hair, washed the makeup off her face, cried to make her eyes red. Nothing worked. Her hair popped back to perfection. The magic makeup reapplied itself. Her eyes refused to get puffy or bloodshot.

She would've changed clothes, but she had nothing to change into. The other Aphrodite campers offered her some (laughing behind her back, she was sure), but each outfit was even more fashionable and ridiculous than what she had on.

Now, after a horrible night's sleep, still no change. Piper normally looked like a zombie in the morning, but her hair was styled like a supermodel's and her skin was perfect. Even that horrible zit at the base of her nose, which she'd had for so many days she'd started to call it Bob, had disappeared.

She growled in frustration and raked her fingers through her hair. No use. The do just popped back into place. She looked like Cherokee Barbie.

From across the cabin, Drew called, "Oh, honey, it won't go away." Her voice dripped with false sympathy. "Mom's blessing will last *at least* another day. Maybe a week if you're lucky."

Piper gritted her teeth. "A *week*?"

The other Aphrodite kids—about a dozen girls and five guys—smirked and snickered at her discomfort. Piper knew she should play cool, not let them get under her skin. She'd dealt with shallow, popular kids plenty of times. But this was different. These were her brothers and sisters, even if she had *nothing* in common with them, and how Aphrodite had managed to have so many kids so close in age . . . Never mind. She didn't want to know.

"Don't worry, hon." Drew blotted her fluorescent lipstick. "You're thinking you don't belong here? We couldn't agree more. Isn't that right, *Mitchell*?"

One of the guys flinched. "Um, yeah. Sure."

"Mmm-hmm." Drew took out her mascara and checked her lashes. Everyone else watched, not daring to speak. "So anyways, people, fifteen minutes until breakfast. The cabin's not going to clean itself! And Mitchell, I think you've learned your lesson. Right, sweetie? So you're on garbage patrol just for today, mm-kay? Show Piper how it's done, 'cause I have a feeling she'll have that job soon—*if* she survives her *quest*. Now, get to work, everybody! It's my bathroom time!"

Everybody started rushing around, making beds and folding clothes, while Drew scooped up her makeup kit, hair dryer, and brush and marched into the bathroom.

Someone inside yelped, and a girl about eleven was kicked out, hastily wrapped in towels with shampoo still in her hair.

The door slammed shut, and the girl started to cry. A couple of older campers comforted her and wiped the bubbles out of her hair.

"Seriously?" Piper said to no one in particular. "You let Drew treat you like this?"

A few kids shot Piper nervous looks, like they might actually agree, but they said nothing.

The campers kept working, though Piper couldn't see why the cabin needed much cleaning. It was a life-size dollhouse, with pink walls and white window trim. The lace curtains were pastel blue and green, which of course matched the sheets and feather comforters on all the beds.

The guys had one row of bunks separated by a curtain, but their section of the cabin was just as neat and orderly as the girls'. Something was *definitely* unnatural about that. Every camper had a wooden camp chest at the foot of their bunk with their name painted on it, and Piper guessed that the clothes in each chest were neatly folded and color coordinated. The only bit of individualism was how the campers decorated their private bunk spaces. Each had slightly different pictures tacked up of whatever celebrities they thought were hot. A few had personal photos, too, but most were actors or singers or whatever.

Piper hoped she might not see *The Poster*. It had been almost a year since the movie, and she thought by now surely everyone had torn down those old tattered advertisements and tacked up something newer. But no such luck. She spotted one on the wall by the storage closet, in the middle of a collage of famous heartthrobs.

The title was lurid red: KING OF SPARTA. Under that, the poster showed the leading man—a three-quarters shot of bare-chested bronze flesh, with ripped pectorals and six-pack abs. He was clad in only a Greek war kilt and a purple cape, sword in hand. He looked like he'd just been rubbed in oil, his short black hair gleaming and rivulets of sweat pouring off his rugged face, those dark sad eyes facing the camera as if to say, *I will kill your men and steal your women! Ha-ha!*

It was the most ridiculous poster of all time. Piper and her dad had had a good laugh over it the first time they saw it. Then the movie made a bajillion dollars. The poster graphic popped up everywhere. Piper couldn't get away from it at school, walking down the street, even online. It became *The Poster*, the most embarrassing thing in her life. And yeah, it was a picture of her dad.

She turned away so no one would think she was staring at it. Maybe when everyone went to breakfast she could tear it down and they wouldn't notice.

She tried to look busy, but she didn't have any extra clothes to fold. She straightened her bed, then realized the top blanket was the one Jason had wrapped around her shoulders last night. She picked it up and pressed it to her face. It smelled of wood smoke, but unfortunately not of Jason. He was the *only* person who'd been genuinely nice to her after the claiming, like he cared about how she felt, not just about her stupid new clothes. God, she'd wanted to kiss him, but he'd seemed so uncomfortable, almost scared of her. She couldn't really blame him. She'd been glowing pink.

"'Scuse me," said a voice by her feet. The garbage patrol guy, Mitchell, was crawling around on all fours, picking up chocolate wrappers and crumpled notes from under the bunk beds. Apparently the Aphrodite kids weren't one hundred percent neat freaks after all.

She moved out of his way. "What'd you do to make Drew mad?"

He glanced over at the bathroom door to make sure it was still closed. "Last night, after you were claimed, I said you might not be so bad."

It wasn't much of a compliment, but Piper was stunned. An Aphrodite kid had actually stood up for her?

"Thanks," she said.

Mitchell shrugged. "Yeah, well. See where it got me. But for what it's worth, welcome to Cabin Ten."

A girl with blond pigtails and braces raced up with a pile of clothes in her arms. She looked around furtively like she was delivering nuclear materials.

"I brought you these," she whispered.

"Piper, meet Lacy," Mitchell said, still crawling around on the floor.

"Hi," Lacy said breathlessly. "You *can* change clothes. The blessing won't stop you. This is just, you know, a backpack, some rations, ambrosia and nectar for emergencies, some jeans, a few extra shirts, and a warm jacket. The boots might be a little snug. But—well—we took up a collection. Good luck on your quest!"

Lacy dumped the things on the bed and started to hurry away, but Piper caught her arm. "Hold on. At least let me thank you! Why are you rushing off?"

Lacy looked like she might shake apart from nervousness. "Oh, well—"

"Drew might find out," Mitchell explained.

"I might have to wear the shoes of shame!" Lacy gulped.

"The what?" Piper asked.

Lacy and Mitchell both pointed to a black shelf mounted in the corner of the room, like an altar. Displayed on it were a hideous pair of orthopedic nurse's shoes, bright white with thick soles.

"I had to wear them for a week once," Lacy whimpered. "They don't go with *anything*!"

"And there're worse punishments," Mitchell warned. "Drew can charmspeak, see? Not many Aphrodite kids have that power; but if she tries hard enough, she can get you to do some pretty embarrassing things. Piper, you're the first person I've seen in a long time who is able to resist her."

"Charmspeak…" Piper remembered last night, the way the crowd at the campfire had swayed back and forth between Drew's opinion and hers. "You mean, like, you could talk someone into doing things. Or…giving you things. Like a car?"

"Oh, don't give Drew any ideas!" Lacy gasped.

"But yeah," Mitchell said. "She could do that."

"So that's why she's head counselor," Piper said. "She convinced you all?"

Mitchell picked a nasty wad of gum from under Piper's bed. "Nah, she inherited the post when Silena Beauregard died in the war. Drew was second oldest. Oldest camper automatically gets the post, unless somebody with more years or more completed quests wants to challenge, in which case there's a duel, but that hardly ever happens. Anyway, we've been stuck with Drew in charge since August. She decided to make some, ah, *changes* in the way the cabin is run."

"Yes, I did!" Suddenly Drew was there, leaning against the bunk. Lacy squeaked like a guinea pig and tried to run, but Drew put an arm out to stop her. She looked down at Mitchell. "I think you missed some trash, sweetie. You'd better make another pass."

Piper glanced toward the bathroom and saw that Drew had dumped everything from the bathroom waste bin—some pretty *nasty* things—all over the floor.

Mitchell sat up on his haunches. He glared at Drew like he was about to attack (which Piper would've paid money to see), but finally he snapped, "Fine."

Drew smiled. "See, Piper, hon, we're a good cabin here. A good family! Silena Beauregard, though...you could take a warning from her. She was secretly passing information to Kronos in the Titan War, helping the *enemy*."

Drew smiled all sweet and innocent, with her glittery pink makeup and her blow-dried hair lush and smelling like nutmeg. She looked like any popular teenage girl from any high school. But her eyes were as cold as steel. Piper got the feeling Drew was looking straight into her soul, pulling out her secrets.

Helping the enemy.

"Oh, none of the other cabins talk about it," Drew confided. "They act like Silena Beauregard was a hero."

"She sacrificed her life to make things right," Mitchell grumbled. "She *was* a hero."

"Mmm-hmm," Drew said. "Another day on garbage patrol, Mitchell. But *anyways*, Silena lost track of what this cabin is about. We match up cute couples at camp! Then we break them apart and start over! It's the best fun ever. We don't have any business getting involved in other stuff like wars and quests. *I* certainly haven't been on any quests. They're a waste of time!"

Lacy raised her hand nervously. "But last night you said you wanted to go on a—"

Drew glared at her, and Lacy's voice died.

"Most of all," Drew continued, "we certainly don't need our image tarnished by spies, do we, *Piper*?"

Piper tried to answer, but she couldn't. There was no way Drew could know about her dreams or her dad's kidnapping, was there?

"It's too bad you won't be around," Drew sighed. "But if you survive your little quest, don't worry, I'll find *somebody* to match up with you. Maybe one of those gross Hephaestus guys. Or Clovis? He's pretty repulsive." Drew looked her over with a mix of pity and disgust. "Honestly, I didn't think it was *possible* for Aphrodite to have an ugly child, but...who *was* your father? Was he some sort of mutant, or—"

"Tristan McLean," Piper snapped.

As soon as she said it, she hated herself. She never, *ever* played the "famous dad" card. But Drew had driven her over the edge. "My dad's Tristan McLean."

The stunned silence was gratifying for a few seconds, but Piper felt ashamed of herself. Everybody turned and looked at *The Poster*, her dad flexing his muscles for the whole world to see.

"Oh my god!" half the girls screamed at once.

"Sweet!" a guy said. "The dude with the sword who killed that other dude in that movie?"

"He is *so* hot for an old guy," a girl said, and then she blushed. "I mean I'm sorry. I know he's your *dad*. That's *so* weird!"

"It's weird, all right," Piper agreed.

"Do you think you could get me his autograph?" another girl asked.

Piper forced a smile. She couldn't say, *If my dad survives....*

"Yeah, no problem," she managed.

The girl squealed in excitement, and more kids surged forward, asking a dozen questions at once.

"Have you ever been on the set?"

"Do you live in a mansion?"

"Do you have lunch with movie stars?"

"Have you had your rite of passage?"

That one caught Piper off guard. "Rite of what?" she asked.

The girls and guys giggled and shoved each other around like this was an embarrassing topic.

"The rite of passage for an Aphrodite child," one explained. "You get someone to fall in love with you. Then you break their heart. Dump them. Once you do that, you've proven yourself worthy of Aphrodite."

Piper stared at the crowd to see if they were joking. "Break someone's heart on purpose? That's terrible!"

The others looked confused.

"Why?" a guy asked.

"Oh my god!" a girl said. "I bet Aphrodite broke your *dad's* heart! I bet he never loved anyone again, did he? That's so romantic! When you have your rite of passage, you can be just like Mom!"

"Forget it!" Piper yelled, a little louder than she'd intended. The other kids backed away. "I'm *not* breaking somebody's heart just for a stupid rite of passage!"

Which of course gave Drew a chance to take back control. "Well, there you go!" she cut in. "Silena said the same thing. She broke the tradition, fell in love with that Beckendorf boy, and *stayed* in love. If you ask me, that's why things ended tragically for her."

"That's not true!" Lacy squeaked, but Drew glared at her, and she immediately melted back into the crowd.

"Hardly matters," Drew continued, "because, Piper, hon, you couldn't break anyone's heart anyway. And this nonsense about your dad being Tristan McLean—that's *so* begging for attention."

Several of the kids blinked uncertainly.

"You mean he's *not* her dad?" one asked.

Drew rolled her eyes. "Please. Now, it's time for breakfast, people, and Piper here has to start that little quest. So let's get her packed and get her out of here!"

Drew broke up the crowd and got everyone moving. She called them "hon" and "dear," but her tone made it clear she expected to be obeyed. Mitchell and Lacy helped Piper pack. They even guarded the bathroom while Piper went in and changed into a better traveling outfit. The hand-me-downs weren't fancy—thank god—just well-worn jeans, a T-shirt, a comfortable winter coat, and hiking boots that fit perfectly. She strapped her dagger, Katoptris, to her belt.

When Piper came out, she felt almost normal again. The other campers were standing at their bunks while Drew came around and inspected. Piper turned to Mitchell and Lacy and mouthed, *Thank you.* Mitchell nodded grimly. Lacy flashed a full-braces smile. Piper doubted Drew had ever thanked them for anything. She also noticed that the *King of Sparta* poster had been wadded up and thrown in the trash. Drew's orders, no doubt. Even though Piper had wanted to take the poster down herself, now she was totally steamed.

When Drew spotted her, she clapped in mock applause. "Very nice! Our little quest girl all dressed in Dumpster clothes again. Now, off you go! No need to eat breakfast with us. Good luck with . . . whatever. Bye!"

Piper shouldered her bag. She could feel everyone else's eyes on her as she walked to the door. She could just leave and forget about it. That would've been the easy thing. What did she care about this cabin, these shallow kids?

Except that some of them had tried to help her. Some of them had even stood up to Drew for her.

She turned at the door. "You know, you all don't have to follow Drew's orders."

The other kids shifted. Several glanced at Drew, but she looked too stunned to respond.

"Umm," one managed, "she's our head counselor."

"She's a tyrant," Piper corrected. "You can think for yourselves. There's got to be more to Aphrodite than *this*."

"More than this," one kid echoed.

"Think for ourselves," a second muttered.

"People!" Drew screeched. "Don't be stupid! She's charmspeaking you."

"No," Piper said. "I'm just telling the truth."

At least, Piper thought that was the case. She didn't understand exactly how this charmspeaking business worked, but she didn't feel like she was putting any special power into her words. She didn't want to win an argument by tricking people. That would make her no better than Drew. Piper simply meant what she said. Besides, even if she tried charmspeaking, she had a feeling it wouldn't work very well on another charmspeaker like Drew.

Drew sneered at her. "You may have a little power, Miss Movie Star. But you don't know the first thing about Aphrodite. You have such great ideas? What do you think this cabin is about, then? Tell them. Then maybe I'll tell them a few things about *you*, huh?"

Piper wanted to make a withering retort, but her anger turned to panic. She was a spy for the enemy, just like Silena

Beauregard. An Aphrodite traitor. Did Drew know about that, or was she bluffing? Under Drew's glare, her confidence began to crumble.

"Not this," Piper managed. "Aphrodite is not about this."

Then she turned and stormed out before the others could see her blushing.

Behind her, Drew started laughing. "*Not this*? Hear that, people? She doesn't have a clue!"

Piper promised herself she would never *ever* go back to that cabin. She blinked away her tears and stormed across the green, not sure where she was going—until she saw the dragon swooping down from the sky.

XVI

PIPER

"Leo?" she yelled.

Sure enough, there he was, sitting atop a giant bronze death machine and grinning like a lunatic. Even before he landed, the camp alarm went up. A conch horn blew. All the satyrs started screaming, "Don't kill me!" Half the camp ran outside in a mixture of pajamas and armor. The dragon set down right in the middle of the green, and Leo yelled, "It's cool! Don't shoot!"

Hesitantly, the archers lowered their bows. The warriors backed away, keeping their spears and swords ready. They made a loose wide ring around the metal monster. Other demigods hid behind their cabin doors or peeped out the windows. Nobody seemed anxious to get close.

Piper couldn't blame them. The dragon was huge. It glistened in the morning sun like a living penny sculpture —different shades of copper and bronze—a sixty-foot-long serpent with steel talons and drill-bit teeth and glowing ruby eyes. It had bat-shaped wings twice its length that unfurled like metallic sails, making a sound like coins cascading out of a slot machine every time they flapped.

"It's beautiful," Piper muttered. The other demigods stared at her like she was insane.

The dragon reared its head and shot a column of fire into the sky. Campers scrambled away and hefted their weapons, but Leo slid calmly off the dragon's back. He held up his hands like he was surrendering, except he still had that crazy grin on his face.

"People of Earth, I come in peace!" he shouted. He looked like he'd been rolling around in the campfire. His army coat and his face were smeared with soot. His hands were grease-stained, and he wore a new tool belt around his waist. His eyes were bloodshot. His curly hair was so oily it stuck up in porcupine quills, and he smelled strangely of Tabasco sauce. But he looked absolutely delighted. "Festus is just saying hello!"

"That thing is dangerous!" an Ares girl shouted, brandishing her spear. "Kill it now!"

"Stand down!" someone ordered.

To Piper's surprise, it was Jason. He pushed through the crowd, flanked by Annabeth and that girl from the Hephaestus cabin, Nyssa.

Jason gazed up at the dragon and shook his head in amazement. "Leo, what have you done?"

"Found a ride!" Leo beamed. "You said I could go on the quest if I got you a ride. Well, I got you a class-A metallic flying bad boy! Festus can take us anywhere!"

"It—has wings," Nyssa stammered. Her jaw looked like it might drop off her face.

"Yeah!" Leo said. "I found them and reattached them."

"But it never had wings. Where did you find them?"

Leo hesitated, and Piper could tell he was hiding something.

"In...the woods," he said. "Repaired his circuits, too, mostly, so no more problems with him going haywire."

"Mostly?" Nyssa asked.

The dragon's head twitched. It tilted to one side and a stream of black liquid—maybe oil, *hopefully* just oil—poured out of its ear, all over Leo.

"Just a few kinks to work out," Leo said.

"But how did you survive...?" Nyssa was still staring at the creature in awe. "I mean, the fire breath..."

"I'm quick," Leo said. "And lucky. Now, am I on this quest, or what?"

Jason scratched his head. "You named him Festus? You know that in Latin, 'festus' means 'happy'? You want us to ride off to save the world on Happy the Dragon?"

The dragon twitched and shuddered and flapped his wings.

"That's a yes, bro!" Leo said. "Now, um, I'd really suggest we get going, guys. I already picked up some supplies in the —um, in the woods. And all these people with weapons are making Festus nervous."

Jason frowned. "But we haven't planned anything yet. We can't just—"

"Go," Annabeth said. She was the only one who didn't look nervous at all. Her expression was sad and wistful, like this reminded her of better times. "Jason, you've only got three days until the solstice now, and you should never keep a nervous dragon waiting. This is certainly a good omen. Go!"

Jason nodded. Then he smiled at Piper. "You ready, partner?"

Piper looked at the bronze dragon wings shining against the sky, and those talons that could've shredded her to pieces.

"You bet," she said.

Flying on the dragon was the most amazing experience ever, Piper thought.

Up high, the air was freezing cold; but the dragon's metal hide generated so much heat, it was like they were flying in a protective bubble. Talk about seat warmers! And the grooves in the dragon's back were designed like high-tech saddles, so they weren't uncomfortable at all. Leo showed them how to hook their feet in the chinks of the armor, like in stirrups, and use the leather safety harnesses cleverly concealed under the exterior plating. They sat single file: Leo in front, then Piper, then Jason, and Piper was very aware of Jason right behind her. She wished he would hold on to her, maybe wrap his arms around her waist; but sadly, he didn't.

Leo used the reins to steer the dragon into the sky like he'd been doing it all his life. The metal wings worked perfectly, and soon the coast of Long Island was just a hazy line behind them. They shot over Connecticut and climbed into the gray winter clouds.

Leo grinned back at them. "Cool, right?"

"What if we get spotted?" Piper asked.

"The Mist," Jason said. "It keeps mortals from seeing magic things. If they spot us, they'll probably mistake us for a small plane or something."

Piper glanced over her shoulder. "You sure about that?"

"No," he admitted. Then Piper saw he was clutching a photo in his hand—a picture of a girl with dark hair.

She gave Jason a quizzical look, but he blushed and put the photo in his pocket. "We're making good time. Probably get there by tonight."

Piper wondered who the girl in the picture was, but she didn't want to ask; and if Jason didn't volunteer the information, that wasn't a good sign. Had he remembered something about his life before? Was that a photo of his real girlfriend?

Stop it, she thought. You'll just torture yourself.

She asked a safer question. "Where are we heading?"

"To find the god of the North Wind," Jason said. "And chase some storm spirits."

XVII

LEO

LEO WAS TOTALLY BUZZING.

The expression on everyone's faces when he flew the dragon into camp? Priceless! He thought his cabinmates were going to bust a lug nut.

Festus had been awesome too. He hadn't blowtorched a single cabin or eaten any satyrs, even if he did dribble a little oil from his ear. Okay, a *lot* of oil. Leo could work on that later.

So maybe Leo didn't seize the chance to tell everybody about Bunker 9 or the flying boat design. He needed some time to think about all that. He could tell them when he came back.

If I come back, part of him thought.

Nah, he'd come back. He'd scored a sweet magic tool belt from the bunker, plus a lot of cool supplies now safely stowed in his backpack. Besides, he had a fire-breathing, only slightly leaky dragon on his side. What could go wrong?

Well, the control disk could bust, the bad part of him suggested. *Festus could eat you.*

Okay, so the dragon wasn't *quite* as fixed as Leo might've let on. He'd worked all night attaching those wings, but he hadn't found an extra dragon brain anywhere in the bunker. Hey, they were under a time limit! Three days until the solstice. They had to get going. Besides, Leo had cleaned the disk pretty well. Most of the circuits were still good. It would just have to hold together.

His bad side started to think, *Yeah, but what if—*

"Shut up, me," Leo said aloud.

"What?" Piper asked.

"Nothing," he said. "Long night. I think I'm hallucinating. It's cool."

Sitting in front, Leo couldn't see their faces, but he assumed from their silence that his friends were not pleased to have a sleepless, hallucinating dragon driver.

"Just joking." Leo decided it might be good to change the subject. "So what's the plan, bro? You said something about catching wind, or breaking wind, or something?"

As they flew over New England, Jason laid out the game plan: First, find some guy named Boreas and grill him for information—

"His name is *Boreas*?" Leo had to ask. "What is he, the God of Boring?"

Second, Jason continued, they had to find those *venti* that had attacked them at the Grand Canyon—

"Can we just call them storm spirits?" Leo asked. "*Venti* makes them sound like evil espresso drinks."

And third, Jason finished, they had to find out who the storm spirits worked for, so they could find Hera and free her.

"So you want to look for Dylan, the nasty storm dude, *on purpose*," Leo said. "The guy who threw me off the skywalk and sucked Coach Hedge into the clouds."

"That's about it," Jason said. "Well...there may be a wolf involved, too. But I think she's friendly. She probably won't eat us, unless we show weakness."

Jason told them about his dream—the big nasty mother wolf and a burned-out house with stone spires growing out of the swimming pool.

"Uh-huh," Leo said. "But you don't know where this place is."

"Nope," Jason admitted.

"There's also giants," Piper added. "The prophecy said *the giants' revenge.*"

"Hold on," Leo said. "Giants—like more than one? Why can't it be just one giant who wants revenge?"

"I don't think so," Piper said. "I remember in some of the old Greek stories, there was something about an army of giants."

"Great," Leo muttered. "Of course, with our luck, it's an army. So you know anything else about these giants? Didn't you do a bunch of myth research for that movie with your dad?"

"Your dad's an actor?" Jason asked.

Leo laughed. "I keep forgetting about your amnesia. Heh. Forgetting about amnesia. That's funny. But yeah, her dad's Tristan McLean."

"Uh— Sorry, what was he in?"

"It doesn't matter," Piper said quickly. "The giants—well, there were lots of giants in Greek mythology. But if I'm thinking of the right ones, they were bad news. Huge, almost impossible to kill. They could throw mountains and stuff. I think they were related to the Titans. They rose from the earth after Kronos lost the war—I mean the *first* Titan war, thousands of years ago—and they tried to destroy Olympus. If we're talking about the same giants—"

"Chiron said it was happening again," Jason remembered. "The last chapter. That's what he meant. No wonder he didn't want us to know all the details."

Leo whistled. "So... giants who can throw mountains. Friendly wolves that will eat us if we show weakness. Evil espresso drinks. Gotcha. Maybe this isn't the time to bring up my psycho babysitter."

"Is that another joke?" Piper asked.

Leo told them about Tía Callida, who was really Hera, and how she'd appeared to him at camp. He didn't tell them about his fire abilities. That was still a touchy subject, especially after Nyssa had told him fire demigods tended to destroy cities and stuff. Besides, then Leo would have to get into how he'd caused his mom's death, and... No. He wasn't ready to go there. He did manage to tell about the night she died, not mentioning the fire, just saying the machine shop collapsed. It was easier without having to look at his friends, just keeping his eyes straight ahead as they flew.

And he told them about the strange woman in earthen

robes who seemed to be asleep, and seemed to know the future.

Leo estimated the whole state of Massachusetts passed below them before his friends spoke.

"That's . . . disturbing," Piper said.

"'Bout sums it up," Leo agreed. "Thing is, everybody says don't trust Hera. She hates demigods. And the prophecy said we'd cause death if we unleash her rage. So I'm wondering . . . why are we doing this?"

"She chose us," Jason said. "All three of us. We're the first of the seven who have to gather for the Great Prophecy. This quest is the beginning of something much bigger."

That didn't make Leo feel any better, but he couldn't argue with Jason's point. It *did* feel like this was the start of something huge. He just wished that if there were four more demigods destined to help them, they'd show up quick. Leo didn't want to hog all the terrifying life-threatening adventures.

"Besides," Jason continued, "helping Hera is the only way I can get back my memory. And that dark spire in my dream seemed to be feeding on Hera's energy. If that thing unleashes a king of the giants by destroying Hera—"

"Not a good trade-off," Piper agreed. "At least Hera is on our side—mostly. Losing her would throw the gods into chaos. She's the main one who keeps peace in the family. And a war with the giants could be even more destructive than the Titan War."

Jason nodded. "Chiron also talked about worse forces stirring on the solstice, with it being a good time for dark magic, and all—something that could awaken if Hera were sacrificed on that day. And this mistress who's controlling the storm spirits, the one who wants to kill all the demigods—"

"Might be that weird sleeping lady," Leo finished. "Dirt Woman fully awake? Not something I want to see."

"But who is she?" Jason asked. "And what does she have to do with giants?"

Good questions, but none of them had answers. They flew in silence while Leo wondered if he'd done the right thing, sharing so much. He'd never told anyone about that night at the warehouse. Even if he hadn't given them the whole story, it still felt strange, like he'd opened up his chest and taken out all the gears that made him tick. His body was shaking, and not from the cold. He hoped Piper, sitting behind him, couldn't tell.

The forge and dove shall break the cage. Wasn't that the prophecy line? That meant Piper and he would have to figure out how to break into that magic rock prison, assuming they could find it. Then they'd unleash Hera's rage, causing a lot of death. Well, that sounded fun! Leo had seen Tía Callida in action; she liked knives, snakes, and putting babies in roaring fires. Yeah, definitely let's unleash her rage. Great idea.

Festus kept flying. The wind got colder, and below them snowy forests seemed to go on forever. Leo didn't know exactly where Quebec was. He'd told Festus to take them to the palace of Boreas, and Festus kept going north. Hopefully, the dragon knew the way, and they wouldn't end up at the North Pole.

"Why don't you get some sleep?" Piper said in his ear. "You were up all night."

Leo wanted to protest, but the word *sleep* sounded really good. "You won't let me fall off?"

Piper patted his shoulder. "Trust me, Valdez. Beautiful people never lie."

"Right," he muttered. He leaned forward against the warm bronze of the dragon's neck, and closed his eyes.

XVIII

LEO

IT SEEMED HE SLEPT ONLY FOR SECONDS, but when Piper shook him awake, the daylight was fading.

"We're here," she said.

Leo rubbed the sleep out of his eyes. Below them, a city sat on a cliff overlooking a river. The plains around it were dusted with snow, but the city itself glowed warmly in the winter sunset. Buildings crowded together inside high walls like a medieval town, way older than any place Leo had seen before. In the center was an actual castle—at least Leo assumed it was a castle—with massive red brick walls and a square tower with a peaked, green gabled roof.

"Tell me that's Quebec and not Santa's workshop," Leo said.

"Yeah, Quebec City," Piper confirmed. "One of the oldest cities in North America. Founded around sixteen hundred or so?"

Leo raised an eyebrow. "Your dad do a movie about that too?"

She made a face at him, which Leo was used to, but it didn't quite work with her new glamorous makeup. "I *read* sometimes, okay? Just because Aphrodite claimed me, doesn't mean I have to be an airhead."

"Feisty!" Leo said. "So you know so much, what's that castle?"

"A hotel, I think."

Leo laughed. "No way."

But as they got closer, Leo saw she was right. The grand entrance was bustling with doormen, valets, and porters taking bags. Sleek black luxury cars idled in the drive. People in elegant suits and winter cloaks hurried to get out of the cold.

"The North Wind is staying in a hotel?" Leo said. "That can't be—"

"Heads up, guys," Jason interrupted. "We got company!"

Leo looked below and saw what Jason meant. Rising from the top of the tower were two winged figures—angry angels, with nasty-looking swords.

Festus didn't like the angel guys. He swooped to a halt in midair, wings beating and talons bared, and made a rumbling sound in his throat that Leo recognized. He was getting ready to blow fire.

"Steady, boy," Leo muttered. Something told him the angels would not take kindly to getting torched.

"I don't like this," Jason said. "They look like storm spirits."

At first Leo thought he was right, but as the angels got closer, he could see they were much more solid than *venti*. They looked like regular teenagers except for their icy white hair and feathery purple wings. Their bronze swords were jagged, like icicles. Their faces looked similar enough that they might've been brothers, but they definitely weren't twins.

One was the size of an ox, with a bright red hockey jersey, baggy sweatpants, and black leather cleats. The guy clearly had been in too many fights, because both his eyes were black, and when he bared his teeth, several of them were missing.

The other guy looked like he'd just stepped off one of Leo's mom's 1980s rock album covers—Journey, maybe, or Hall & Oates, or something even lamer. His ice-white hair was long and feathered into a mullet. He wore pointy-toed leather shoes, designer pants that were way too tight, and a god-awful silk shirt with the top three buttons open. Maybe he thought he looked like a groovy love god, but the guy couldn't have weighed more than ninety pounds, and he had a bad case of acne.

The angels pulled up in front of the dragon and hovered there, swords at the ready.

The hockey ox grunted. "No clearance."

"'Scuse me?" Leo said.

"You have no flight plan on file," explained the groovy love god. On top of his other problems, he had a French accent so bad Leo was sure it was fake. "This is restricted airspace."

"Destroy them?" The ox showed off his gap-toothed grin.

The dragon began to hiss steam, ready to defend them. Jason summoned his golden sword, but Leo cried, "Hold on!

Let's have some manners here, boys. Can I at least find out who has the honor of destroying me?"

"I am Cal!" the ox grunted. He looked very proud of himself, like he'd taken a long time to memorize that sentence.

"That's short for Calais," the love god said. "Sadly, my brother cannot say words with more than two syllables—"

"Pizza! Hockey! Destroy!" Cal offered.

"—which includes his own name," the love god finished.

"I am Cal," Cal repeated. "And this is Zethes! My brother!"

"Wow," Leo said. "That was almost three sentences, man! Way to go."

Cal grunted, obviously pleased with himself.

"Stupid buffoon," his brother grumbled. "They make fun of you. But no matter. I am Zethes, which is short for Zethes. And the lady there—" He winked at Piper, but the wink was more like a facial seizure. "She can call me anything she likes. Perhaps she would like to have dinner with a famous demigod before we must destroy you?"

Piper made a sound like gagging on a cough drop. "That's . . . a truly horrifying offer."

"It is no problem." Zethes wiggled his eyebrows. "We are a very romantic people, we Boreads."

"Boreads?" Jason cut in. "Do you mean, like, the sons of Boreas?"

"Ah, so you've heard of us!" Zethes looked pleased. "We are our father's gatekeepers. So you understand, we cannot have unauthorized people flying in his airspace on creaky dragons, scaring the silly mortal peoples."

He pointed below, and Leo saw that the mortals were

starting to take notice. Several were pointing up—not with alarm, yet—more with confusion and annoyance, like the dragon was a traffic helicopter flying too low.

"Which is sadly why, unless this is an emergency landing," Zethes said, brushing his hair out of his acne-covered face, "we will have to destroy you painfully."

"Destroy!" Cal agreed, with a little more enthusiasm than Leo thought necessary.

"Wait!" Piper said. "This *is* an emergency landing."

"Awww!" Cal looked so disappointed, Leo almost felt sorry for him.

Zethes studied Piper, which of course he'd already been doing. "How does the pretty girl decide this is an emergency, then?"

"We have to see Boreas. It's totally urgent! Please?" She forced a smile, which Leo figured must've been killing her; but she still had that blessing of Aphrodite thing going on, and she looked great. Something about her voice, too—Leo found himself believing every word. Jason was nodding, looking absolutely convinced.

Zethes picked at his silk shirt, probably making sure it was still open wide enough. "Well…I hate to disappoint a lovely lady, but you see, my sister, she would have an avalanche if we allowed you—"

"And our dragon is malfunctioning!" Piper added. "It could crash any minute!"

Festus shuddered helpfully, then turned his head and spilled gunk out of his ear, splattering a black Mercedes in the parking lot below.

"No destroy?" Cal whimpered.

Zethes pondered the problem. Then he gave Piper another spasmodic wink. "Well, you are pretty. I mean, you're *right*. A malfunctioning dragon—this could be an emergency."

"Destroy them later?" Cal offered, which was probably as close to friendly as he ever got.

"It will take some explaining," Zethes decided. "Father has not been kind to visitors lately. But, yes. Come, faulty dragon people. Follow us."

The Boreads sheathed their swords and pulled smaller weapons from their belts—or at least Leo thought they were weapons. Then the Boreads switched them on, and Leo realized they were flashlights with orange cones, like the ones traffic controller guys use on a runway. Cal and Zethes turned and swooped toward the hotel's tower.

Leo turned to his friends. "I love these guys. Follow them?"

Jason and Piper didn't look eager.

"I guess," Jason decided. "We're here now. But I wonder why Boreas hasn't been kind to visitors."

"Pfft, he just hasn't met us." Leo whistled. "Festus, after those flashlights!"

As they got closer, Leo worried they'd crash into the tower. The Boreads made right for the green gabled peak and didn't slow down. Then a section of the slanted roof slid open, revealing an entrance easily wide enough for Festus. The top and bottom were lined with icicles like jagged teeth.

"This cannot be good," Jason muttered, but Leo spurred the dragon downward, and they swooped in after the Boreads.

They landed in what must have been the penthouse suite; but the place had been hit by a flash freeze. The entry hall had vaulted ceilings forty feet high, huge draped windows, and lush oriental carpets. A staircase at the back of the room led up to another equally massive hall, and more corridors branched off to the left and right. But the ice made the room's beauty a little frightening. When Leo slid off the dragon, the carpet crunched under his feet. A fine layer of frost covered the furniture. The curtains didn't budge because they were frozen solid, and the ice-coated windows let in weird watery light from the sunset. Even the ceiling was furry with icicles. As for the stairs, Leo was sure he'd slip and break his neck if he tried to climb them.

"Guys," Leo said, "fix the thermostat in here, and I would totally move in."

"Not me." Jason looked uneasily at the staircase. "Something feels wrong. Something up there..."

Festus shuddered and snorted flames. Frost started to form on his scales.

"No, no, no." Zethes marched over, though how he could walk in those pointy leather shoes, Leo had no idea. "The dragon must be deactivated. We can't have fire in here. The heat ruins my hair."

Festus growled and spun his drill-bit teeth.

"'S'okay, boy." Leo turned to Zethes. "The dragon's a little touchy about the whole *deactivation* concept. But I've got a better solution."

"Destroy?" Cal suggested.

"No, man. You gotta stop with the *destroy* talk. Just wait."

"Leo," Piper said nervously, "what are you—"

"Watch and learn, beauty queen. When I was repairing Festus last night, I found all kinds of buttons. Some, you do *not* want to know what they do. But others...Ah, here we go."

Leo hooked his fingers behind the dragon's left foreleg. He pulled a switch, and the dragon shuddered from head to toe. Everyone backed away as Festus folded like origami. His bronze plating stacked together. His neck and tail contracted into his body. His wings collapsed and his trunk compacted until he was a rectangular metal wedge the size of a suitcase.

Leo tried to lift it, but the thing weighed about six billion pounds. "Um...yeah. Hold on. I think—aha."

He pushed another button. A handle flipped up on the top, and wheels clicked out on the bottom.

"Ta-da!" he announced. "The world's heaviest carry-on bag!"

"That's impossible," Jason said. "Something that big couldn't—"

"Stop!" Zethes ordered. He and Cal both drew their swords and glared at Leo.

Leo raised his hands. "Okay...what'd I do? Stay calm, guys. If it bothers you that much, I don't *have* to take the dragon as carry-on—"

"Who are you?" Zethes shoved the point of his sword against Leo's chest. "A child of the South Wind, spying on us?"

"What? No!" Leo said. "Son of Hephaestus. Friendly blacksmith, no harm to anyone!"

Cal growled. He put his face up to Leo's, and he definitely

wasn't any prettier at point-blank, with his bruised eyes and bashed-in mouth. "Smell fire," he said. "Fire is bad."

"Oh." Leo's heart raced. "Yeah, well . . . my clothes are kind of singed, and I've been working with oil, and—"

"No!" Zethes pushed Leo back at sword point. "We can *smell* fire, demigod. We assumed it was from the creaky dragon, but now the dragon is a suitcase. And I still smell fire . . . on *you*."

If it hadn't been like three degrees in the penthouse, Leo would've started sweating. "Hey . . . look . . . I don't know—" He glanced at his friends desperately. "Guys, a little help?"

Jason already had his gold coin in his hand. He stepped forward, his eyes on Zethes. "Look, there's been a mistake. Leo isn't a fire guy. Tell them, Leo. Tell them you're not a fire guy."

"Um . . ."

"Zethes?" Piper tried her dazzling smile again, though she looked a little too nervous and cold to pull it off. "We're all friends here. Put down your swords and let's talk."

"The girl is pretty," Zethes admitted, "and of course she cannot help being attracted to my amazingness; but sadly, I cannot romance her at this time." He poked his sword point farther into Leo's chest, and Leo could feel the frost spreading across his shirt, turning his skin numb.

He wished he could reactivate Festus. He needed some backup. But it would've taken several minutes, even if he could reach the button, with two purple-winged crazy guys in his path.

"Destroy him now?" Cal asked his brother.

Zethes nodded. "Sadly, I think—"

"No," Jason insisted. He sounded calm enough, but Leo figured he was about two seconds away from flipping that coin and going into full gladiator mode. "Leo's just a son of Hephaestus. He's no threat. Piper here is a daughter of Aphrodite. I'm the son of Zeus. We're on a peaceful..."

Jason's voice faltered, because both Boreads had suddenly turned on him.

"What did you say?" Zethes demanded. "You are the son of Zeus?"

"Um...yeah," Jason said. "That's a good thing, right? My name is Jason."

Cal looked so surprised, he almost dropped his sword. "Can't be Jason," he said. "Doesn't look the same."

Zethes stepped forward and squinted at Jason's face. "No, he is not *our* Jason. Our Jason was more stylish. Not as much as me—but stylish. Besides, our Jason died millennia ago."

"Wait," Jason said. "*Your* Jason...you mean the original Jason? The Golden Fleece guy?"

"Of course," Zethes said. "We were his crewmates aboard his ship, the *Argo*, in the old times, when we were mortal demigods. Then we accepted immortality to serve our father, so I could look this good for all time, and my silly brother could enjoy pizza and hockey."

"Hockey!" Cal agreed.

"But Jason—*our* Jason—he died a mortal death," Zethes said. "You can't be him."

"I'm not," Jason agreed.

"So, destroy?" Cal asked. Clearly the conversation was giving his two brain cells a serious workout.

"No," Zethes said regretfully. "If he is a son of Zeus, he could be the one we've been watching for."

"Watching for?" Leo asked. "You mean like in a good way: you'll shower him with fabulous prizes? Or watching for like in a *bad* way: he's in trouble?"

A girl's voice said, "That depends on my father's will."

Leo looked up the staircase. His heart nearly stopped. At the top stood a girl in a white silk dress. Her skin was unnaturally pale, the color of snow, but her hair was a lush mane of black, and her eyes were coffee brown. She focused on Leo with no expression, no smile, no friendliness. But it didn't matter. Leo was in love. She was the most dazzling girl he'd ever seen.

Then she looked at Jason and Piper, and seemed to understand the situation immediately.

"Father will want to see the one called Jason," the girl said.

"Then it *is* him?" Zethes asked excitedly.

"We'll see," the girl said. "Zethes, bring our guests."

Leo grabbed the handle of his bronze dragon suitcase. He wasn't sure how he'd lug it up the stairs, but he *had* to get next to that girl and ask her some important questions—like her e-mail address and phone number.

Before he could take a step, she froze him with a look. Not *literally* froze, but she might as well have.

"Not you, Leo Valdez," she said.

In the back of his mind, Leo wondered how she knew his

name; but mostly he was just concentrating on how crushed he felt.

"Why not?" He probably sounded like a whiny kindergartner, but he couldn't help it.

"You cannot be in the presence of my father," the girl said. "Fire and ice—it would not be wise."

"We're going together," Jason insisted, putting his hand on Leo's shoulder, "or not at all."

The girl tilted her head, like she wasn't used to people refusing her orders. "He will not be harmed, Jason Grace, unless you make trouble. Calais, keep Leo Valdez here. Guard him, but do not kill him."

Cal pouted. "Just a little?"

"No," the girl insisted. "And take care of his interesting suitcase, until Father passes judgment."

Jason and Piper looked at Leo, their expressions asking him a silent question: *How do you want to play this?*

Leo felt a surge of gratitude. They were ready to fight for him. They wouldn't leave him alone with the hockey ox. Part of him wanted to go for it, bust out his new tool belt and see what he could do, maybe even summon a fireball or two and warm this place up. But the Boread guys scared him. And that gorgeous girl scared him more, even if he still wanted her number.

"It's fine, guys," he said. "No sense causing trouble if we don't have to. You go ahead."

"Listen to your friend," the pale girl said. "Leo Valdez will be perfectly safe. I wish I could say the same for you, son of Zeus. Now come, King Boreas is waiting."

XIX

JASON

JASON DIDN'T WANT TO LEAVE LEO, but he was starting to think that hanging out with Cal the hockey jock might be the *least* dangerous option in this place.

As they climbed the icy staircase, Zethes stayed behind them, his blade drawn. The guy might've looked like a disco-era reject, but there was nothing funny about his sword. Jason figured one hit from that thing would probably turn him into a Popsicle.

Then there was the ice princess. Every once in a while she'd turn and give Jason a smile, but there was no warmth in her expression. She regarded Jason like he was an especially interesting science specimen—one she couldn't wait to dissect.

If these were Boreas's kids, Jason wasn't sure he wanted to meet Daddy. Annabeth had told him Boreas was the friendliest of the wind gods. Apparently that meant he didn't kill heroes quite as fast as the others did.

Jason worried that he'd led his friends into a trap. If things went bad, he wasn't sure he could get them out alive. Without thinking about it, he took Piper's hand for reassurance.

She raised her eyebrows, but she didn't let go.

"It'll be fine," she promised. "Just a talk, right?"

At the top of the stairs, the ice princess looked back and noticed them holding hands. Her smile faded. Suddenly Jason's hand in Piper's turned ice cold—*burning* cold. He let go, and his fingers were smoking with frost. So were Piper's.

"Warmth is not a good idea here," the princess advised, "especially when *I* am your best chance of staying alive. Please, this way."

Piper gave him a nervous frown like, *What was that about?*

Jason didn't have an answer. Zethes poked him in the back with his icicle sword, and they followed the princess down a massive hallway decked in frosty tapestries.

Freezing winds blew back and forth, and Jason's thoughts moved almost as fast. He'd had a lot of time to think while they rode the dragon north, but he felt as confused as ever.

Thalia's picture was still in his pocket, though he didn't need to look at it anymore. Her image had burned itself into his mind. It was bad enough not remembering his past, but to know he had a sister out there somewhere who might have answers and to have no way of finding her—that just drove him up the wall.

In the picture, Thalia looked nothing like him. They both had blue eyes, but that was it. Her hair was black. Her complexion was more Mediterranean. Her facial features were sharper—like a hawk's.

Still, Thalia looked *so* familiar. Hera had left him just

enough memory that he could be certain Thalia was his sister. But Annabeth had acted completely surprised when he'd told her, like she'd never heard of Thalia's having a brother. Did Thalia even know about him? How had they been separated?

Hera had taken those memories. She'd stolen everything from Jason's past, plopped him into a new life, and now she expected him to save her from some prison just so he could get back what she'd taken. It made Jason so angry, he wanted to walk away, let Hera rot in that cage: but he couldn't. He was hooked. He had to know more, and that made him even more resentful.

"Hey." Piper touched his arm. "You still with me?"

"Yeah...yeah, sorry."

He was grateful for Piper. He needed a friend, and he was glad she'd started losing the Aphrodite blessing. The makeup was fading. Her hair was slowly going back to its old choppy style with the little braids down the sides. It made her look more real, and as far as Jason was concerned, more beautiful.

He was sure now that they'd never known each other before the Grand Canyon. Their relationship was just a trick of the Mist in Piper's mind. But the longer he spent with her, the more he wished it had been real.

Stop that, he told himself. It wasn't fair to Piper, thinking that way. Jason had no idea what was waiting for him back in his old life—or *who* might be waiting. But he was pretty sure his past wouldn't mix with Camp Half-Blood. After this quest, who knew what would happen? Assuming they even survived.

At the end of the hallway they found themselves in front

of a set of oaken doors carved with a map of the world. In each corner was a man's bearded face, blowing wind. Jason was pretty sure he'd seen maps like this before. But in this version, all the wind guys were Winter, blowing ice and snow from every corner of the world.

The princess turned. Her brown eyes glittered, and Jason felt like he was a Christmas present she was hoping to open.

"This is the throne room," she said. "Be on your best behavior, Jason Grace. My father can be...chilly. I will translate for you, and try to encourage him to hear you out. I do hope he spares you. We could have such fun."

Jason guessed this girl's definition of fun was not the same as his.

"Um, okay," he managed. "But really, we're just here for a little talk. We'll be leaving right afterward."

The girl smiled. "I love heroes. So blissfully ignorant."

Piper rested her hand on her dagger. "Well, how about you enlighten us? You say you're going to translate for us, and we don't even know who you are. What's your name?"

The girl sniffed with distaste. "I suppose I shouldn't be surprised you don't recognize me. Even in the ancient times the Greeks did not know me well. Their island homes were too warm, too far from my domain. I am Khione, daughter of Boreas, goddess of snow."

She stirred the air with her finger, and a miniature blizzard swirled around her—big, fluffy flakes as soft as cotton.

"Now, come," Khione said. The oaken doors blew open, and cold blue light spilled out of the room. "Hopefully you will survive your little talk."

JASON

IF THE ENTRY HALL HAD BEEN COLD, the throne room was like a meat locker.

Mist hung in the air. Jason shivered, and his breath steamed. Along the walls, purple tapestries showed scenes of snowy forests, barren mountains, and glaciers. High above, ribbons of colored light—the aurora borealis—pulsed along the ceiling. A layer of snow covered the floor, so Jason had to step carefully. All around the room stood life-size ice sculpture warriors—some in Greek armor, some medieval, some in modern camouflage—all frozen in various attack positions, swords raised, guns locked and loaded.

At least Jason *thought* they were sculptures. Then he tried to step between two Greek spearmen, and they moved with surprising speed, their joints cracking and spraying ice crystals as they crossed their javelins to block Jason's path.

From the far end of the hall, a man's voice rang out in a language that sounded like French. The room was so long and misty, Jason couldn't see the other end; but whatever the man said, the ice guards uncrossed their javelins.

"It's fine," Khione said. "My father has ordered them not to kill you just yet."

"Super," Jason said.

Zethes prodded him in the back with his sword. "Keep moving, Jason Junior."

"Please don't call me that."

"My father is not a patient man," Zethes warned, "and the beautiful Piper, sadly, is losing her magic hairdo very fast. Later, perhaps, I can lend her something from my wide assortment of hair products."

"Thanks," Piper grumbled.

They kept walking, and the mist parted to reveal a man on an ice throne. He was sturdily built, dressed in a stylish white suit that seemed woven from snow, with dark purple wings that spread out to either side. His long hair and shaggy beard were encrusted with icicles, so Jason couldn't tell if his hair was gray or just white with frost. His arched eyebrows made him look angry, but his eyes twinkled more warmly than his daughter's—as if he might have a sense of humor buried somewhere under that permafrost. Jason hoped so.

"*Bienvenu,*" the king said. "*Je suis Boreas le Roi. Et vous?*"

Khione the snow goddess was about to speak, but Piper stepped forward and curtsied.

"*Votre Majesté,*" she said, "*je suis Piper McLean. Et c'est Jason, fils de Zeus.*"

The king smiled with pleasant surprise. "*Vous parlez français? Très bien!*"

"Piper, you speak French?" Jason asked.

Piper frowned. "No. Why?"

"You just spoke French."

Piper blinked. "I did?"

The king said something else, and Piper nodded. *"Oui, Votre Majesté."*

The king laughed and clapped his hands, obviously delighted. He said a few more sentences, then swept his hand toward his daughter as if shooing her away.

Khione looked miffed. "The king says—"

"He says I'm a daughter of Aphrodite," Piper interrupted, "so naturally I can speak French, which is the language of love. I had no idea. His Majesty says Khione won't have to translate now."

Behind them, Zethes snorted, and Khione shot him a murderous look. She bowed stiffly to her father and took a step back.

The king sized up Jason, and Jason decided it would be a good idea to bow. "Your Majesty, I'm Jason Grace. Thank you for, um, not killing us. May I ask...why does a Greek god speak French?"

Piper had another exchange with the king.

"He speaks the language of his host country," Piper translated. "He says all gods do this. Most Greek gods speak English, as they now reside in the United States, but Boreas was never welcomed in their realm. His domain was always far to the north. These days he likes Quebec, so he speaks French."

The king said something else, and Piper turned pale.

"The king says..." She faltered. "He says—"

"Oh, allow me," Khione said. "My father says he has orders to kill you. Did I not mention that earlier?"

Jason tensed. The king was still smiling amiably, like he'd just delivered great news.

"Kill us?" Jason said. "Why?"

"Because," the king said, in heavily accented English, "my lord Aeolus has commanded it."

Boreas rose. He stepped down from his throne and furled his wings against his back. As he approached, Khione and Zethes bowed. Jason and Piper followed their example.

"I shall deign to speak your language," Boreas said, "as Piper McLean has honored me in mine. *Toujours*, I have had a fondness for the children of Aphrodite. As for you, Jason Grace, my master Aeolus would not expect me to kill a son of Lord Zeus...without first hearing you out."

Jason's gold coin seemed to grow heavy in his pocket. If he were forced to fight, he didn't like his chances. Two seconds at least to summon his blade. Then he'd be facing a god, two of his children, and an army of freeze-dried warriors.

"Aeolus is the master of the winds, right?" Jason asked. "Why would he want us dead?"

"You are demigods," Boreas said, as if this explained everything. "Aeolus's job is to contain the winds, and demigods have always caused him many headaches. They ask him for favors. They unleash winds and cause chaos. But the final insult was the battle with Typhon last summer...."

Boreas waved his hand, and a sheet of ice like a flat-screen TV appeared in the air. Images of a battle flickered across the surface—a giant wrapped in storm clouds, wading across a river toward the Manhattan skyline. Tiny, glowing figures —the gods, Jason guessed—swarmed around him like angry wasps, pounding the monster with lightning and fire. Finally the river erupted in a massive whirlpool, and the smoky form sank beneath the waves and disappeared.

"The storm giant, Typhon," Boreas explained. "The first time the gods defeated him, eons ago, he did not die quietly. His death released a host of storm spirits—wild winds that answered to no one. It was Aeolus's job to track them all down and imprison them in his fortress. The other gods—they did not help. They did not even apologize for the inconvenience. It took Aeolus centuries to track down all the storm spirits, and naturally this irritated him. Then, last summer, Typhon was defeated again—"

"And his death released another wave of *venti*," Jason guessed. "Which made Aeolus even angrier."

"*C'est vrai*," Boreas agreed.

"But, Your Majesty," Piper said, "the gods had no choice but to battle Typhon. He was going to destroy Olympus! Besides, why punish demigods for that?"

The king shrugged. "Aeolus cannot take out his anger on the gods. They are his bosses, and very powerful. So he gets even with the demigods who helped them in the war. He issued orders to us: demigods who come to us for aid are no longer to be tolerated. We are to crush your little mortal faces."

There was an uncomfortable silence.

"That sounds . . . extreme," Jason ventured. "But you're not going to crush our faces yet, right? You're going to listen to us first, 'cause once you hear about our quest—"

"Yes, yes," the king agreed. "You see, Aeolus also said that a son of Zeus might seek my aid, and if this happened, I should listen to you before destroying you, as you might— how did he put it?—make all our lives very interesting. I am only obligated to *listen,* however. After that, I am free to pass judgment as I see fit. But I *will* listen first. Khione wishes this also. It may be that we will not kill you."

Jason felt like he could almost breathe again. "Great. Thanks."

"Do not thank me." Boreas smiled. "There are many ways you could make our lives interesting. Sometimes we keep demigods for our amusement, as you can see."

He gestured around the room to the various ice statues.

Piper made a strangled noise. "You mean—they're all demigods? Frozen demigods? They're alive?"

"An interesting question," Boreas conceded, as if it had never occurred to him before. "They do not move unless they are obeying my orders. The rest of the time, they are merely frozen. Unless they were to melt, I suppose, which would be very messy."

Khione stepped behind Jason and put her cold fingers on his neck. "My father gives me such lovely presents," she murmured in his ear. "Join our court. Perhaps I'll let your friends go."

"What?" Zethes broke in. "If Khione gets this one, then I deserve the girl. Khione always gets more presents!"

"Now, children," Boreas said sternly. "Our guests will think you are spoiled! Besides, you moved too fast. We have not even heard the demigod's story yet. Then we will decide what to do with them. Please, Jason Grace, entertain us."

Jason felt his brain shutting down. He didn't look at Piper for fear he'd completely lose it. He'd gotten them into this, and now they were going to die—or worse, they'd be amusements for Boreas's children and end up frozen forever in this throne room, slowly corroding from freezer burn.

Khione purred and stroked his neck. Jason didn't plan it, but electricity sparked along his skin. There was a loud *pop*, and Khione flew backward, skidding across the floor.

Zethes laughed. "That is good! I'm glad you did that, even though I have to kill you now."

For a moment, Khione was too stunned to react. Then the air around her began to swirl with a micro-blizzard. "You dare—"

"Stop," Jason ordered, with as much force as he could muster. "You're not going to kill us. And you're not going to keep us. We're on a quest for the queen of the gods herself, so unless you want Hera busting down your doors, you're going to let us go."

He sounded a lot more confident than he felt, but it got their attention. Khione's blizzard swirled to a stop. Zethes lowered his sword. They both looked uncertainly at their father.

"Hmm," Boreas said. His eyes twinkled, but Jason couldn't tell if it was with anger or amusement. "A son of Zeus, favored by Hera? This is definitely a first. Tell us your story."

Jason would've botched it right there. He hadn't been expecting to get the chance to talk, and now that he could, his voice abandoned him.

Piper saved him. "Your Majesty." She curtsied again with incredible poise, considering her life was on the line. She told Boreas the whole story, from the Grand Canyon to the prophecy, much better and faster than Jason could have.

"All we ask for is guidance," Piper concluded. "These storm spirits attacked us, and they're working for some evil mistress. If we find them, maybe we can find Hera."

The king stroked the icicles in his beard. Out the windows, night had fallen, and the only light came from the aurora borealis overhead, washing everything in red and blue.

"I know of these storm spirits," Boreas said. "I know where they are kept, and of the prisoner they took."

"You mean Coach Hedge?" Jason asked. "He's alive?"

Boreas waved aside the question. "For now. But the one who controls these storm winds... It would be madness to oppose her. You would be better staying here as frozen statues."

"Hera's in trouble," Jason said. "In three days she's going to be—I don't know—consumed, destroyed, something. And a giant is going to rise."

"Yes," Boreas agreed. Was it Jason's imagination, or did he shoot Khione an angry look? "Many horrible things are waking. Even my children do not tell me all the news they should. The Great Stirring of monsters that began with Kronos—your father Zeus foolishly believed it would end when the Titans were defeated. But just as it was before, so it is now. The final battle is yet to come, and the one who will wake is more terrible than any Titan. Storm spirits—these are only beginning. The earth has many more horrors to yield up. When monsters no longer stay in Tartarus, and souls are no longer confined to Hades . . . Olympus has good reason to fear."

Jason wasn't sure what all this meant, but he didn't like the way Khione was smiling—like *this* was her definition of fun.

"So you'll help us?" Jason asked the king.

Boreas scowled. "I did not say that."

"Please, Your Majesty," Piper said.

Everyone's eyes turned toward her. She had to be scared out of her mind, but she looked beautiful and confident—and it had nothing to do with the blessing of Aphrodite. She looked herself again, in day-old traveling clothes with choppy hair and no makeup. But she almost glowed with warmth in that cold throne room. "If you tell us where the storm spirits are, we can capture them and bring them to Aeolus. You'd look good in front of your boss. Aeolus might pardon us and the other demigods. We could even rescue Gleeson Hedge. Everyone wins."

"She's pretty," Zethes mumbled. "I mean, she's right."

"Father, don't listen to her," Khione said. "She's a child of Aphrodite. She dares to charmspeak a god? Freeze her now!"

Boreas considered this. Jason slipped his hand in his pocket and got ready to bring out the gold coin. If things went wrong, he'd have to move fast.

The movement caught Boreas's eye. "What is that on your forearm, demigod?"

Jason hadn't realized his coat sleeve had gotten pushed

up, revealing the edge of his tattoo. Reluctantly, he showed Boreas his marks.

The god's eyes widened. Khione actually hissed and stepped away.

Then Boreas did something unexpected. He laughed so loudly, an icicle cracked from the ceiling and crashed next to his throne. The god's form began to flicker. His beard disappeared. He grew taller and thinner, and his clothes changed into a Roman toga, lined with purple. His head was crowned with a frosty laurel wreath, and a gladius—a Roman sword like Jason's—hung at his side.

"Aquilon," Jason said, though where he got the god's Roman name from, he had no idea.

The god inclined his head. "You recognize me better in this form, yes? And yet you said you came from Camp Half-Blood?"

Jason shifted his feet. "Uh . . . yes, Your Majesty."

"And Hera sent you there. . . ." The winter god's eyes were full of mirth. "I understand now. Oh, she plays a dangerous game. Bold, but dangerous! No wonder Olympus is closed. They must be trembling at the gamble she has taken."

"Jason," Piper said nervously, "why did Boreas change shape? The toga, the wreath. What's going on?"

"It's his Roman form," Jason said. "But what's going on—I don't know."

The god laughed. "No, I'm sure you don't. This should be very interesting to watch."

"Does that mean you'll let us go?" Piper asked.

"My dear," Boreas said, "there is no reason for me to kill

you. If Hera's plan fails, which I think it will, you will tear each other apart. Aeolus will never have to worry about demigods again."

Jason felt as if Khione's cold fingers were on his neck again, but it wasn't her—it was just the feeling that Boreas was right. That sense of wrongness which had bothered Jason since he got to Camp Half-Blood, and Chiron's comment about his arrival being disastrous—Boreas knew what they meant.

"I don't suppose you could explain?" Jason asked.

"Oh, perish the thought! It is not for me to interfere in Hera's plan. No wonder she took your memory." Boreas chuckled, apparently still having a great time imagining demigods tearing each other apart. "You know, I have a reputation as a helpful wind god. Unlike my brethren, I've been known to fall in love with mortals. Why, my sons Zethes and Calais started as demigods—"

"Which explains why they are idiots," Khione growled.

"Stop it!" Zethes snapped back. "Just because you were born a full goddess—"

"Both of you, freeze," Boreas ordered. Apparently, that word carried a lot of weight in the household, because the two siblings went absolutely still. "Now, as I was saying, I have a good reputation, but it is rare that Boreas plays an important role in the affairs of gods. I sit here in my palace, at the edge of civilization, and so rarely have amusements. Why, even that fool Notus, the South Wind, gets spring break in Cancún. What do I get? A winter festival with naked Québécois rolling around in the snow!"

"I like the winter festival," Zethes muttered.

"My point," Boreas snapped, "is that I now have a chance to be the center. Oh, yes, I will let you go on this quest. You will find your storm spirits in the windy city, of course. Chicago—"

"Father!" Khione protested.

Boreas ignored his daughter. "If you can capture the winds, you may be able to gain safe entrance to the court of Aeolus. If by some miracle you succeed, be sure to tell him you captured the winds on my orders."

"Okay, sure," Jason said. "So Chicago is where we'll find this lady who's controlling the winds? She's the one who's trapped Hera?"

"Ah." Boreas grinned. "Those are two different questions, son of Jupiter."

Jupiter, Jason noticed. *Before, he called me son of Zeus.*

"The one who controls the winds," Boreas continued, "yes, you will find her in Chicago. But *she* is only a servant—a servant who is very likely to destroy you. If you succeed against her and take the winds, then you may go to Aeolus. Only he has knowledge of all the winds on the earth. All secrets come to his fortress eventually. If anyone can tell you where Hera is imprisoned, it is Aeolus. As for who you will meet when you finally find Hera's cage—truly, if I told you that, you would beg me to freeze you."

"Father," Khione protested, "you can't simply let them—"

"I can do what I like," he said, his voice hardening. "I am still master here, am I not?"

The way Boreas glared at his daughter, it was obvious they had some ongoing argument. Khione's eyes flashed with anger, but she clenched her teeth. "As you wish, Father."

"Now go, demigods," Boreas said, "before I change my mind. Zethes, escort them out safely."

They all bowed, and the god of the North Wind dissolved into mist.

Back in the entry hall, Cal and Leo were waiting for them. Leo looked cold but unharmed. He'd even gotten cleaned up, and his clothes looked newly washed, like he'd used the hotel's valet service. Festus the dragon was back in normal form, snorting fire over his scales to keep himself defrosted.

As Khione led them down the stairs, Jason noticed that Leo's eyes followed her. Leo started combing his hair back with his hands. Uh-oh, Jason thought. He made a mental note to warn Leo about the snow goddess later. She was not someone to get a crush on.

At the bottom step, Khione turned to Piper. "You have fooled my father, girl. But you have not fooled me. We are not done. And you, Jason Grace, I will see you as a statue in the throne room soon enough."

"Boreas is right," Jason said. "You're a spoiled kid. See you around, ice princess."

Khione's eyes flared pure white. For once, she seemed at a loss for words. She stormed back up the stairs—literally. Halfway up, she turned into a blizzard and disappeared.

"Be careful," Zethes warned. "She never forgets an insult."

Cal grunted in agreement. "Bad sister."

"She's the goddess of snow," Jason said. "What's she going to do, throw snowballs at us?" But as he said it, Jason had a feeling Khione could do a whole lot worse.

Leo looked devastated. "What happened up there? You made her mad? Is she mad at me too? Guys, that was my prom date!"

"We'll explain later," Piper promised, but when she glanced at Jason, he realized she expected *him* to explain.

What *had* happened up there? Jason wasn't sure. Boreas had turned into Aquilon, his Roman form, as if Jason's presence caused him to go schizophrenic.

The idea that Jason had been sent to Camp Half-Blood seemed to amuse the god, but Boreas/Aquilon hadn't let them go out of kindness. Cruel excitement had danced in his eyes, as if he'd just placed a bet on a dogfight.

You will tear each other apart, he'd said with delight. *Aeolus will never have to worry about demigods again.*

Jason looked away from Piper, trying not to show how unnerved he was. "Yeah," he agreed, "we'll explain later."

"Be careful, pretty girl," Zethes said. "The winds between here and Chicago are bad-tempered. Many other evil things are stirring. I am sorry you will not be staying. You would make a lovely ice statue, in which I could check my reflection."

"Thanks," Piper said. "But I'd sooner play hockey with Cal."

"Hockey?" Cal's eyes lit up.

"Joking," Piper said. "And the storm winds aren't our worst problem, are they?"

"Oh, no," Zethes agreed. "Something else. Something worse."

"Worse," Cal echoed.

"Can you tell me?" Piper gave them a smile.

This time, the charm didn't work. The purple-winged Boreads shook their heads in unison. The hangar doors opened onto a freezing starry night, and Festus the dragon stomped his feet, anxious to fly.

"Ask Aeolus what is worse," Zethes said darkly. "He knows. Good luck."

He almost sounded like he cared what happened to them, even though a few minutes ago he'd wanted to make Piper into an ice sculpture.

Cal patted Leo on the shoulder. "Don't get destroyed," he said, which was probably the longest sentence he'd ever attempted. "Next time—hockey. Pizza."

"Come on, guys." Jason stared out at the dark. He was anxious to get out of that cold penthouse, but he had a feeling it was the most hospitable place they'd see for a while. "Let's go to Chicago and try not to get destroyed."

XXI

PIPER

PIPER DIDN'T RELAX UNTIL THE GLOW OF Quebec City faded behind them.

"You were amazing," Jason told her.

The compliment should've made her day. But all she could think about was the trouble ahead. *Evil things are stirring,* Zethes had warned them. She knew that firsthand. The closer they got to the solstice, the less time Piper had to make her decision.

She told Jason in French: "If you knew the truth about me, you wouldn't think I was so amazing."

"What'd you say?" he asked.

"I said I only talked to Boreas. It wasn't so amazing."

She didn't turn to look, but she imagined him smiling.

"Hey," he said, "you saved me from joining Khione's sub-zero hero collection. I owe you one."

That was definitely the easy part, she thought. There was no way Piper would've let that ice witch keep Jason. What bothered Piper more was the way Boreas had changed form, and why he'd let them go. It had something to do with Jason's past, those tattoos on his arm. Boreas assumed Jason was some sort of Roman, and Romans didn't mix with Greeks. She kept waiting for Jason to offer an explanation, but he clearly didn't want to talk about it.

Until now, Piper had been able to dismiss Jason's feeling that he didn't belong at Camp Half-Blood. Obviously he was a demigod. Of course he belonged. But now . . . what if he was something else? What if he really was an enemy? She couldn't stand that idea any more than she could stand Khione.

Leo passed them some sandwiches from his pack. He'd been quiet ever since they'd told him what happened in the throne room. "I still can't believe Khione," he said. "She looked so nice."

"Trust me, man," Jason said. "Snow may be pretty, but up close it's cold and nasty. We'll find you a better prom date."

Piper smiled, but Leo didn't look pleased. He hadn't said much about his time in the palace, or why the Boreads had singled him out for smelling like fire. Piper got the feeling he was hiding something. Whatever it was, his mood seemed to be affecting Festus, who grumbled and steamed as he tried to keep himself warm in the cold Canadian air. Happy the Dragon was not so happy.

They ate their sandwiches as they flew. Piper had no idea how Leo had stocked up on supplies, but he'd even remembered to bring veggie rations for her. The cheese and avocado sandwich was awesome.

Nobody talked. Whatever they might find in Chicago,

they all knew Boreas had only let them go because he figured they were already on a suicide mission.

The moon rose and stars turned overhead. Piper's eyes started to feel heavy. The encounter with Boreas and his children had scared her more than she wanted to admit. Now that she had a full stomach, her adrenaline was fading.

Suck it up, cupcake! Coach Hedge would've yelled at her. *Don't be a wimp!*

Piper had been thinking about the coach ever since Boreas mentioned he was still alive. She'd never liked Hedge, but he'd leaped off a cliff to save Leo, and he'd sacrificed himself to protect them on the skywalk. She now realized that all the times at school the coach had pushed her, yelled at her to run faster or do more push-ups, or even when he'd turned his back and let her fight her own battles with the mean girls, the old goat man had been trying to help her in his own irritating way—trying to prepare her for life as a demigod.

On the skywalk, Dylan the storm spirit had said something about the coach, too: how he'd been retired to Wilderness School because he was getting too old, like it was some sort of punishment. Piper wondered what that was about, and if it explained why the coach was always so grumpy. Whatever the truth, now that Piper knew Hedge was alive, she had a strong compulsion to save him.

Don't get ahead of yourself, she chided. *You've got bigger problems. This trip won't have a happy ending.*

She was a traitor, just like Silena Beauregard. It was only a matter of time before her friends found out.

She looked up at the stars and thought about a night

long ago when she and her dad had camped out in front of Grandpa Tom's house. Grandpa Tom had died years before, but Dad had kept his house in Oklahoma because it was where he grew up.

They'd gone back for a few days, with the idea of getting the place fixed up to sell, although Piper wasn't sure who'd want to buy a run-down cabin with shutters instead of windows and two tiny rooms that smelled like cigars. The first night had been so stifling hot—no air conditioning in the middle of August—that Dad suggested they sleep outside.

They'd spread their sleeping bags and listened to the cicadas buzzing in the trees. Piper pointed out the constellations she'd been reading about—Hercules, Apollo's lyre, Sagittarius the centaur.

Her dad crossed his arms behind his head. In his old T-shirt and jeans he looked like just another guy from Tahlequah, Oklahoma, a Cherokee who might've never left tribal lands. "Your grandpa would say those Greek patterns are a bunch of bull. He told me the stars were creatures with glowing fur, like magic hedgehogs. Once, long ago, some hunters even captured a few in the forest. They didn't know what they'd done until nighttime, when the star creatures began to glow. Golden sparks flew from their fur, so the Cherokee released them back into the sky."

"You believe in magic hedgehogs?" Piper asked.

Her dad laughed. "I think Grandpa Tom was full of bull, too, just like the Greeks. But it's a big sky. I suppose there's room for Hercules and hedgehogs."

They sat for a while, until Piper got the nerve to ask a

question that had been bugging her. "Dad, why don't you ever play Native American parts?"

The week before, he'd turned down several million dollars to play Tonto in a remake of *The Lone Ranger*. Piper was still trying to figure out why. He'd played all kinds of roles —a Latino teacher in a tough L.A. school, a dashing Israeli spy in an action-adventure blockbuster, even a Syrian terrorist in a James Bond movie. And, of course, he would always be known as the King of Sparta. But if the part was Native American—it didn't matter what *kind* of role it was—Dad turned it down.

He winked at her. "Too close to home, Pipes. Easier to pretend I'm something I'm not."

"Doesn't that get old? Aren't you ever tempted, like, if you found the perfect part that could change people's opinions?"

"If there's a part like that, Pipes," he said sadly, "I haven't found it."

She looked at the stars, trying to imagine them as glowing hedgehogs. All she saw were the stick figures she knew—Hercules running across the sky, on his way to kill monsters. Dad was probably right. The Greeks and the Cherokee were equally crazy. The stars were just balls of fire.

"Dad," she said, "if you don't like being close to home, why are we sleeping in Grandpa Tom's yard?"

His laughter echoed in the quiet Oklahoma night. "I think you know me too well, Pipes."

"You're not really going to sell this place, are you?"

"Nope," he sighed. "I'm probably not."

Piper blinked, shaking herself out of the memory. She

realized she'd been falling asleep on the dragon's back. How could her dad pretend to be so many things he wasn't? She was trying to do that now, and it was tearing her apart.

Maybe she could pretend for a little while longer. She could dream of finding a way to save her father without betraying her friends—even if right now a happy ending seemed about as likely as magic hedgehogs.

She leaned back against Jason's warm chest. He didn't complain. As soon as she closed her eyes, she drifted off to sleep.

In her dream, she was back on the mountaintop. The ghostly purple bonfire cast shadows across the trees. Piper's eyes stung from smoke, and the ground was so warm, the soles of her boots felt sticky.

A voice from the dark rumbled, "You forget your duty."

Piper couldn't see him, but it was definitely her least favorite giant—the one who called himself Enceladus. She looked around for any sign of her father, but the pole where he'd been chained was no longer there.

"Where is he?" she demanded. "What've you done with him?"

The giant's laugh was like lava hissing down a volcano. "His body is safe enough, though I fear the poor man's mind can't take much more of my company. For some reason he finds me—disturbing. You must hurry, girl, or I fear there will be little left of him to save."

"Let him go!" she screamed. "Take me instead. He's just a mortal!"

"But, my dear," the giant rumbled, "we must prove our love

for our parents. That's what *I'm* doing. Show me you value your father's life by doing what I ask. Who's more important —your father, or a deceitful goddess who used you, toyed with your emotions, manipulated your memories, eh? What is Hera to you?"

Piper began to tremble. So much anger and fear boiled inside her, she could hardly talk. "You're asking me to betray my friends."

"Sadly, my dear, your friends are destined to die. Their quest is impossible. Even if you succeeded, you heard the prophecy: unleashing Hera's rage would mean your destruction. The only question now—will you die with your friends, or live with your father?"

The bonfire roared. Piper tried to step back, but her feet were heavy. She realized the ground was pulling her down, clinging to her boots like wet sand. When she looked up, a shower of purple sparks had spread across the sky, and the sun was rising in the east. A patchwork of cities glowed in the valley below, and far to the west, over a line of rolling hills, she saw a familiar landmark rising from a sea of fog.

"Why are you showing me this?" Piper asked. "You're revealing where you are."

"Yes, you know this place," the giant said. "Lead your friends here instead of their true destination, and I will deal with them. Or even better, arrange their deaths before you arrive. I don't care which. Just be at the summit by noon on the solstice, and you may collect your father and go in peace."

"I can't," Piper said. "You can't ask me—"

"To betray that foolish boy Valdez, who always irritated

you and is now hiding secrets from you? To give up a boyfriend you never really had? Is that more important than your own father?"

"I'll find a way to defeat you," Piper said. "I'll save my father *and* my friends."

The giant growled in the shadows. "I was once proud too. I thought the gods could never defeat me. Then they hurled a mountain on top of me, crushed me into the ground, where I struggled for eons, half-conscious in pain. That taught me patience, girl. It taught me not to act rashly. Now I've clawed my way back with the help of the waking earth. I am only the first. My brethren will follow. We will not be denied our vengeance—not this time. And you, Piper McLean, need a lesson in humility. I'll show you how easily your rebellious spirit can be brought to earth."

The dream dissolved. And Piper woke up screaming, free-falling through the air.

XXII

PIPER

PIPER TUMBLED THROUGH THE SKY. Far below she saw city lights glimmering in the early dawn, and several hundred yards away the body of the bronze dragon spinning out of control, its wings limp, fire flickering in its mouth like a badly wired lightbulb.

A body shot past her—Leo, screaming and frantically grabbing at the clouds. "Not coooooool!"

She tried to call to him, but he was already too far below.

Somewhere above her, Jason yelled, "Piper, level out! Extend your arms and legs!"

It was hard to control her fear, but she did what he said and regained some balance. She fell spread-eagle like a skydiver, the wind underneath her like a solid block of ice. Then Jason was there, wrapping his arms around her waist.

Thank god, Piper thought. But part of her also thought: Great. Second time this week he's hugged me, and both times it's because I'm plummeting to my death.

"We have to get Leo!" she shouted.

Their fall slowed as Jason controlled the winds, but they still lurched up and down like the winds didn't want to cooperate.

"Gonna get rough," Jason warned. "Hold on!"

Piper locked her arms around him, and Jason shot toward the ground. Piper probably screamed, but the sound was ripped from her mouth. Her vision blurred.

And then, *thump!* They slammed into another warm body—Leo, still wriggling and cursing.

"Stop fighting!" Jason said. "It's me!"

"My dragon!" Leo yelled. "You gotta save Festus!"

Jason was already struggling to keep the three of them aloft, and Piper knew there was no way he could help a fifty-ton metal dragon. But before she could try to reason with Leo, she heard an explosion below them. A fireball rolled into the sky from behind a warehouse complex, and Leo sobbed, "Festus!"

Jason's face reddened with strain as he tried to maintain an air cushion beneath them, but intermittent slow-downs were the best he could manage. Rather than free-falling, it felt like they were bouncing down a giant staircase, a hundred feet at a time, which wasn't doing Piper's stomach any favors.

As they wobbled and zigzagged, Piper could make out details of the factory complex below—warehouses, smoke-stacks, barbed-wire fences, and parking lots lined with snow-covered vehicles. They were still high enough so that hitting the ground would flatten them into roadkill—or skykill—when Jason groaned, "I can't—"

And they dropped like stones.

They hit the roof of the largest warehouse and crashed through into darkness.

Unfortunately, Piper tried to land on her feet. Her feet didn't like that. Pain flared in her left ankle as she crumpled against a cold metal surface.

For a few seconds she wasn't conscious of anything but pain—pain so bad that her ears rang and her vision went red.

Then she heard Jason's voice somewhere below, echoing through the building. "Piper! Where's Piper?"

"Ow, bro!" Leo groaned. "That's my back! I'm not a sofa! Piper, where'd you go?"

"Here," she managed, her voice a whimper.

She heard shuffling and grunting, then feet pounding on metal steps.

Her vision began to clear. She was on a metal catwalk that ringed the warehouse interior. Leo and Jason had landed on ground level, and were now coming up the stairs toward her. She looked at her foot, and a wave of nausea swept over her. Her toes weren't supposed to point that way, were they?

Oh, god. She forced herself to look away before she threw up. Focus on something else. Anything else.

The hole they'd made in the roof was a ragged starburst twenty feet above. How they'd even survived that drop, she had no idea. Hanging from the ceiling, a few electric bulbs flickered dimly, but they didn't do much to light the enormous space. Next to Piper, the corrugated metal wall was emblazoned with a company logo, but it was almost completely spray-painted over with graffiti. Down in the shadowy warehouse, she could make out huge machines, robotic arms, half-finished trucks on an assembly line. The place looked like it had been abandoned for years.

Jason and Leo reached her side.

Leo started to ask, "You okay...?" Then he saw her foot. "Oh no, you're not."

"Thanks for the reassurance," Piper groaned.

"You'll be fine," Jason said, though Piper could hear the worry in his voice. "Leo, you got any first aid supplies?"

"Yeah—yeah, sure." He dug around in his tool belt and pulled out a wad of gauze and a roll of duct tape—both of which seemed too big for the belt's pockets. Piper had noticed the tool belt yesterday morning, but she hadn't thought to ask Leo about it. It didn't look like anything special—just one of those wraparound leather aprons with a bunch of pockets, like a blacksmith or a carpenter might wear. And it seemed to be empty.

"How did you—" Piper tried to sit up, and winced. "How did you pull that stuff from an empty belt?"

"Magic," Leo said. "Haven't figured it out completely, but I can summon just about any regular tool out of the pockets, plus some other helpful stuff." He reached into another pocket and pulled out a little tin box. "Breath mint?"

Jason snatched away the mints. "That's great, Leo. Now, can you fix her foot?"

"I'm a mechanic, man. Maybe if she was a car..." He snapped his fingers. "Wait, what was that godly healing stuff they fed you at camp—Rambo food?"

"Ambrosia, dummy," Piper said through gritted teeth. "There should be some in my bag, if it's not crushed."

Jason carefully pulled her backpack off her shoulders. He rummaged through the supplies the Aphrodite kids had packed for her, and found a Ziploc full of smashed pastry squares like lemon bars. He broke off a piece and fed it to her.

The taste was nothing like she expected. It reminded her of Dad's black bean soup from when she was a little girl. He used to feed it to her whenever she got sick. The memory relaxed her, though it made her sad. The pain in her ankle subsided.

"More," she said.

Jason frowned. "Piper, we shouldn't risk it. They said too much could burn you up. I think I should try to set your foot."

Piper's stomach fluttered. "Have you ever done that before?"

"Yeah . . . I think so."

Leo found an old piece of wood and broke it in half for a splint. Then he got the gauze and duct tape ready.

"I hold her leg still," Jason told him. "Piper, this is going to hurt."

When Jason set the foot, Piper flinched so hard she punched Leo in the arm, and he yelled almost as much as she did. When her vision cleared and she could breathe normally again, she found that her foot was pointing the right way, her ankle splinted with plywood, gauze, and duct tape.

"Ow," she said.

"Jeez, beauty queen!" Leo rubbed his arm. "Glad my face wasn't there."

"Sorry," she said. "And don't call me 'beauty queen,' or I'll punch you again."

"You both did great." Jason found a canteen in Piper's pack and gave her some water. After a few minutes, her stomach began to calm down.

Once she wasn't screaming in pain, she could hear the wind howling outside. Snowflakes fluttered through the hole in the roof, and after their meeting with Khione, snow was the last thing Piper wanted to see.

"What happened to the dragon?" she asked. "Where are we?"

Leo's expression turned sullen. "I don't know with Festus. He just jerked sideways like he hit an invisible wall and started to fall."

Piper remembered Enceladus's warning: *I'll show you how easily your rebellious spirit can be brought to earth.* Had he managed to strike them down from so far away? It seemed impossible. If he were that powerful, why would he need her to betray her friends when he could just kill them himself? And how could the giant be keeping an eye on her in a snowstorm thousands of miles away?

Leo pointed to the logo on the wall. "As far as where we are..." It was hard to see through the graffiti, but Piper could make out a large red eye with the stenciled words: MONOCLE MOTORS, ASSEMBLY PLANT 1.

"Closed car plant," Leo said. "I'm guessing we crash-landed in Detroit."

Piper had heard about closed car plants in Detroit, so that

made sense. But it seemed like a pretty depressing place to land. "How far is that from Chicago?"

Jason handed her the canteen. "Maybe three-fourths of the way from Quebec? The thing is, without the dragon, we're stuck traveling overland."

"No way," Leo said. "It isn't safe."

Piper thought about the way the ground had pulled at her feet in the dream, and what King Boreas had said about the earth yielding up more horrors. "He's right. Besides, I don't know if I can walk. And three people—Jason, you can't fly that many across country by yourself."

"No way," Jason said. "Leo, are you sure the dragon didn't malfunction? I mean, Festus is old, and—"

"And I might not have repaired him right?"

"I didn't say that," Jason protested. "It's just—maybe you could fix it."

"I don't know." Leo sounded crestfallen. He pulled a few screws out of his pockets and started fiddling with them. "I'd have to find where he landed, if he's even in one piece."

"It was my fault," Piper said without thinking. She just couldn't stand it anymore. The secret about her father was heating up inside her like too much ambrosia. If she kept lying to her friends, she felt like she'd burn to ashes.

"Piper," Jason said gently, "you were asleep when Festus conked out. It couldn't be your fault."

"Yeah, you're just shaken up," Leo agreed. He didn't even try to make a joke at her expense. "You're in pain. Just rest."

She wanted to tell them everything, but the words stuck

in her throat. They were both being so kind to her. Yet if Enceladus was watching her somehow, saying the wrong thing could get her father killed.

Leo stood. "Look, um, Jason, why don't you stay with her, bro? I'll scout around for Festus. I think he fell outside the warehouse somewhere. If I can find him, maybe I can figure out what happened and fix him."

"It's too dangerous," Jason said. "You shouldn't go by yourself."

"Ah, I got duct tape and breath mints. I'll be fine," Leo said, a little too quickly, and Piper realized he was a lot more shaken up than he was letting on. "You guys just don't run off without me."

Leo reached into his magic tool belt, pulled out a flashlight, and headed down the stairs, leaving Piper and Jason alone.

Jason gave her a smile, though he looked kind of nervous. It was the exact expression he'd had on his face after he'd kissed her the first time, up on the Wilderness School dorm roof—that cute little scar on his lip curving into a crescent. The memory gave her a warm feeling. Then she remembered that the kiss had never really happened.

"You look better," Jason offered.

Piper wasn't sure if he meant her foot, or the fact that she wasn't magically beautified anymore. Her jeans were tattered from the fall through the roof. Her boots were splattered with melted dirty snow. She didn't know what her face looked like, but probably horrible.

Why did it matter? She'd never cared about things like that before. She wondered if it was her stupid mother, the goddess of love, messing with her thoughts. If Piper started getting urges to read fashion magazines, she was going to have to find Aphrodite and smack her.

She decided to focus on her ankle instead. As long as she didn't move it, the pain wasn't bad. "You did a good job," she told Jason. "Where'd you learn first aid?"

He shrugged. "Same answer as always. I don't know."

"But you're starting to have some memories, aren't you? Like that prophecy in Latin back at camp, or that dream about the wolf."

"It's fuzzy," he said. "Like déjà vu. Ever forgotten a word or a name, and you know it should be on the tip of your tongue, but it isn't? It's like that—only with my whole life."

Piper sort of knew what he meant. The last three months —a life she thought she'd had, a relationship with Jason—had turned out to be Mist.

A boyfriend you never really had, Enceladus had said. *Is that more important than your own father?*

She should've kept her mouth shut, but she voiced the question that had been on her mind since yesterday.

"That photo in your pocket," she said. "Is that someone from your past?"

Jason pulled back.

"I'm sorry," she said. "None of my business. Forget it."

"No—it's okay." His features relaxed. "Just, I'm trying to figure things out. Her name's Thalia. She's my sister. I don't remember any details. I'm not even sure how I know, but— um, why are you smiling?"

"Nothing." Piper tried to kill the smile. *Not* an old

girlfriend. She felt ridiculously happy. "Um, it's just—that's great you remembered. Annabeth told me she became a Hunter of Artemis, right?"

Jason nodded. "I get the feeling I'm supposed to find her. Hera left me that memory for a reason. It's got something to do with this quest. But...I also have the feeling it could be dangerous. I'm not sure I *want* to find out the truth. Is that crazy?"

"No," Piper said. "Not at all."

She stared at the logo on the wall: MONOCLE MOTORS, the single red eye. Something about that logo bothered her.

Maybe it was the idea Enceladus was watching her, holding her father for leverage. She had to save him, but how could she betray her friends?

"Jason," she said. "Speaking of the truth, I need to tell you something—something about my dad—"

She didn't get the chance. Somewhere below, metal clanged against metal, like a door slamming shut. The sound echoed through the warehouse.

Jason stood. He took out his coin and flipped it, snatching his golden sword out of the air. He peered over the railing. "Leo?" he called.

No answer.

He crouched next to Piper. "I don't like this."

"He could be in trouble," Piper said. "Go check."

"I can't leave you alone."

"I'll be fine." She felt terrified, but she wasn't about to admit it. She drew her dagger Katoptris and tried to look confident. "Anyone gets close, I'll skewer them."

Jason hesitated. "I'll leave you the pack. If I'm not back in five minutes—"

"Panic?" she suggested.

He managed a smile. "Glad you're back to normal. The makeup and the dress were a lot more intimidating than the dagger."

"Get going, Sparky, before I skewer *you*."

"Sparky?"

Even offended, Jason looked hot. It wasn't fair. Then he made his way to the stairs and disappeared into the dark.

Piper counted her breaths, trying to gauge how much time had passed. She lost track at around forty-three. Then something in the warehouse went *bang!*

The echo died. Piper's heart pounded, but she didn't call out. Her instincts told her it might not be a good idea.

She stared at her splinted ankle. *It's not like I can run.* Then she looked up again at the Monocle Motors sign. A little voice in her head pestered her, warning of danger. Something from Greek mythology...

Her hand went to her backpack. She took out the ambrosia squares. Too much would burn her up, but would a little more fix her ankle?

Boom. The sound was closer this time, directly below her. She dug out a whole square of ambrosia and stuffed it in her mouth. Her heart raced faster. Her skin felt feverish.

Hesitantly, she flexed her ankle against the splint. No pain, no stiffness at all. She cut through the duct tape with her dagger and heard heavy steps on the stairs—like metal boots.

Had it been five minutes? Longer? The steps didn't sound

like Jason, but maybe he was carrying Leo. Finally she couldn't stand it. Gripping her dagger, she called out, "Jason?"

"Yeah," he said from the darkness. "On my way up."

Definitely Jason's voice. So why did all her instincts say *Run?*

With effort, she got to her feet.

The steps came closer.

"It's okay," Jason's voice promised.

At the top of the stairs, a face appeared out of the darkness —a hideous black grin, a smashed nose, and a single bloodshot eye in the middle of his forehead.

"It's fine," the Cyclops said, in a perfect imitation of Jason's voice. "You're just in time for dinner."

XXIII

LEO

LEO WISHED THE DRAGON HADN'T LANDED on the toilets.

Of all the places to crash, a line of Porta-Potties would not have been his first choice. A dozen of the blue plastic boxes had been set up in the factory yard, and Festus had flattened them all. Fortunately, they hadn't been used in a long time, and the fireball from the crash incinerated most of the contents; but still, there were some pretty gross chemicals leaking out of the wreckage. Leo had to pick his way through and try not to breathe through his nose. Heavy snow was coming down, but the dragon's hide was still steaming hot. Of course, that didn't bother Leo.

After a few minutes climbing over Festus's inanimate body, Leo started to get irritated. The dragon looked perfectly fine. Yes, it had fallen out of the sky and landed with a big *ka-boom*, but its body wasn't even dented. The fireball had apparently come from built up gasses inside the toilet units, not from the dragon itself. Festus's wings were intact. Nothing seemed broken. There was no reason it should have stopped.

"Not my fault," he muttered. "Festus, you're making me look bad."

Then he opened the control panel on the dragon's head, and Leo's heart sank. "Oh, Festus, what the heck?"

The wiring had frozen over. Leo knew it had been okay yesterday. He'd worked so hard to repair the corroded lines, but something had caused a flash freeze inside the dragon's skull, where it should've been too hot for ice to form. The ice had caused the wiring to overload and char the control disk. Leo couldn't see any reason that would've happened. Sure, the dragon was old, but still, it didn't make sense.

He could replace the wires. That wasn't the problem. But the charred control disk was not good. The Greek letters and pictures carved around the edges, which probably held all kinds of magic, were blurred and blackened.

The one piece of hardware Leo couldn't replace—and it was damaged. *Again.*

He imagined his mom's voice: *Most problems look worse than they are,* mijo. *Nothing is unfixable.*

His mom could repair just about anything, but Leo was pretty sure she'd never worked on a fifty-year-old magic metal dragon.

He clenched his teeth and decided he had to try. He wasn't walking from Detroit to Chicago in a snowstorm, and he wasn't going to be responsible for stranding his friends.

"Right," he muttered, brushing the snow off his shoulders.

"Gimme a nylon bristle detail brush, some nitrile gloves, and maybe a can of that aerosol cleaning solvent."

The tool belt obliged. Leo couldn't help smiling as he pulled out the supplies. The belt's pockets did have limits. They wouldn't give him anything magic, like Jason's sword, or anything huge, like a chain saw. He'd tried asking for both. And if he asked for too many things at once, the belt needed a cooldown time before it could work again. The more complicated the request, the longer the cooldown. But anything small and simple like you might find around a workshop—all Leo had to do was ask.

He began cleaning off the control disk. While he worked, snow collected on the cooling dragon. Leo had to stop from time to time to summon fire and melt it away, but mostly he went into autopilot mode, his hands working by themselves as his thoughts wandered.

Leo couldn't believe how stupid he'd acted back at Boreas's palace. He should've figured a family of winter gods would hate him on sight. Son of the fire god flying a fire-breathing dragon into an ice penthouse—yeah, maybe not the best move. Still, he hated feeling like a reject. Jason and Piper got to visit the throne room. Leo got to wait in the lobby with Cal, the demigod of hockey and major head injuries.

Fire is bad, Cal had told him.

That pretty much summed it up. Leo knew he couldn't keep the truth from his friends much longer. Ever since Camp Half-Blood, one line of that Great Prophecy kept coming back to him: *To storm or fire the world must fall.*

And Leo was the fire guy, the first one since 1666 when London had burned down. If he told his friends what he could really do—*Hey, guess what, guys? I might destroy the world!*—why would anyone welcome him back at camp? Leo would have to go on the run again. Even though he knew that drill, the idea depressed him.

Then there was Khione. Dang, that girl was fine. Leo knew he'd acted like a total fool, but he couldn't help himself. He'd had his clothes cleaned with the one-hour valet service—which had been totally sweet, by the way. He'd combed his hair—never an easy job—and even discovered the tool bag could make breath mints, all in hopes that he could get close to her. Naturally, no such luck.

Getting frozen out—story of his life—by his relatives, foster homes, you name it. Even at Wilderness School, Leo had spent the last few weeks feeling like a third wheel as Jason and Piper, his only friends, became a couple. He was happy for them and all, but still it made him feel like they didn't need him anymore.

When he'd found out that Jason's whole time at school had been an illusion—a kind of a memory burp—Leo had been secretly excited. It was a chance for a reset. Now Jason and Piper were heading toward being a couple again—that was obvious from the way they'd acted in the warehouse just now, like they wanted to talk in private without Leo around. What had he expected? He'd wind up the odd man out again. Khione had just given him the cold shoulder a little quicker than most.

"Enough, Valdez," he scolded himself. "Nobody's going

to play any violins for you just because you're not important. Fix the stupid dragon."

He got so involved with his work, he wasn't sure how much time had passed before he heard the voice.

You're wrong, Leo, it said.

He fumbled his brush and dropped it into the dragon's head. He stood, but he couldn't see who'd spoken. Then he looked at the ground. Snow and chemical sludge from the toilets, even the asphalt itself was shifting like it was turning to liquid. A ten-foot-wide area formed eyes, a nose, and a mouth—the giant face of a sleeping woman.

She didn't exactly speak. Her lips didn't move. But Leo could hear her voice in his head, as if the vibrations were coming through the ground, straight into his feet and resonating up his skeleton.

They need you desperately, she said. *In some ways, you are the most important of the seven—like the control disk in the dragon's brain. Without you, the power of the others means nothing. They will never reach me, never stop me. And I will fully wake.*

"You." Leo was shaking so badly he wasn't sure he'd spoken aloud. He hadn't heard that voice since he was eight, but it was her: the earthen woman from the machine shop. "You killed my mom."

The face shifted. The mouth formed a sleepy smile like it was having a pleasant dream. *Ah, but Leo. I am your mother too—the First Mother. Do not oppose me. Walk away now. Let my son Porphyrion rise and become king, and I will ease your burdens. You will tread lightly on the earth.*

Leo grabbed the nearest thing he could find—a Porta-Potty seat—and threw it at the face. "Leave me alone!"

The toilet seat sank into the liquid earth. Snow and sludge rippled, and the face dissolved.

Leo stared at the ground, waiting for the face to reappear. But it didn't. Leo wanted to think he'd imagined it.

Then from the direction of the factory, he heard a crash —like two dump trucks slamming together. Metal crumpled and groaned, and the noise echoed across the yard. Instantly Leo knew that Jason and Piper were in trouble.

Walk away now, the voice had urged.

"Not likely," Leo growled. "Gimme the biggest hammer you got."

He reached into his tool belt and pulled out a three-pound club hammer with a double-faced head the size of a baked potato. Then he jumped off the dragon's back and ran toward the warehouse.

XXIV

LEO

LEO STOPPED AT THE DOORS AND TRIED to control his breathing. The voice of the earth woman still rang in his ears, reminding him of his mother's death. The last thing he wanted to do was plunge into another dark warehouse. Suddenly he felt eight years old again, alone and helpless as someone he cared about was trapped and in trouble.

Stop it, he told himself. That's how she wants you to feel.

But that didn't make him any less scared. He took a deep breath and peered inside. Nothing looked different. Gray morning light filtered through the hole in the roof. A few lightbulbs flickered, but most of the factory floor was still lost in shadows. He could make out the catwalk above, the dim shapes of heavy machinery along the assembly line, but no movement. No sign of his friends.

He almost called out, but something stopped him—a sense he couldn't identify. Then he realized it was *smell*. Something smelled wrong—like burning motor oil and sour breath.

Something not human was inside the factory. Leo was certain. His body shifted into high gear, all his nerves tingling.

Somewhere on the factory floor, Piper's voice cried out: "Leo, help!"

But Leo held his tongue. How could Piper have gotten off the catwalk with her broken ankle?

He slipped inside and ducked behind a cargo container. Slowly, gripping his hammer, he worked his way toward the center of the room, hiding behind boxes and hollow truck chassis. Finally he reached the assembly line. He crouched behind the nearest piece of machinery—a crane with a robotic arm.

Piper's voice called out again: "Leo?" Less certain this time, but very close.

Leo peeked around the machinery. Hanging directly above the assembly line, suspended by a chain from a crane on the opposite side, was a massive truck engine—just dangling thirty feet up, as if it had been left there when the factory was abandoned. Below it on the conveyor belt sat a truck chassis, and clustered around it were three dark shapes the size of forklifts. Nearby, dangling from chains on two other robotic arms, were two smaller shapes—maybe more engines, but one of them was twisting around as if it were alive.

Then one of the forklift shapes rose, and Leo realized it was a humanoid of massive size. "Told you it was nothing," the thing rumbled. Its voice was too deep and feral to be human.

One of the other forklift-sized lumps shifted, and called out in Piper's voice: "Leo, help me! Help—" Then the voice changed, becoming a masculine snarl. "Bah, there's nobody out there. No demigod could be that quiet, eh?"

The first monster chuckled. "Probably ran away, if he knows what's good for him. Or the girl was lying about a third demigod. Let's get cooking."

Snap. A bright orange light sizzled to life—an emergency flare—and Leo was temporarily blinded. He ducked behind the crane until the spots cleared from his eyes. Then he took another peep and saw a nightmare scene even Tía Callida couldn't have dreamed up.

The two smaller things dangling from crane arms weren't engines. They were Jason and Piper. Both hung upside down, tied by their ankles and cocooned with chains up to their necks. Piper was flailing around, trying to free herself. Her mouth was gagged, but at least she was alive. Jason didn't look so good. He hung limply, his eyes rolled up in his head. A red welt the size of an apple had swollen over his left eyebrow.

On the conveyor belt, the bed of the unfinished pickup truck was being used as a fire pit. The emergency flare had ignited a mixture of tires and wood, which, from the smell of it, had been doused in kerosene. A big metal pole was suspended over the flames—a spit, Leo realized, which meant this was a cooking fire.

But most terrifying of all were the cooks.

Monocle Motors: that single red eye logo. Why hadn't Leo realized?

Three massive humanoids gathered around the fire. Two

were standing, stoking the flames. The largest one crouched with his back to Leo. The two facing him were each ten feet tall, with hairy muscular bodies and skin that glowed red in the firelight. One of the monsters wore a chain mail loincloth that looked really uncomfortable. The other wore a ragged fuzzy toga made of fiberglass insulation, which also would not have made Leo's top ten wardrobe ideas. Other than that, the two monsters could've been twins. Each had a brutish face with a single eye in the center of his forehead. The cooks were Cyclopes.

Leo's legs started quaking. He'd seen some weird things so far—storm spirits and winged gods and a metal dragon that liked Tabasco sauce. But this was different. These were actual, flesh-and-blood, ten-foot-tall living monsters who wanted to eat his friends for dinner.

He was so terrified he could hardly think. If only he had Festus. He could use a fire-breathing sixty-foot-long tank about now. But all he had was a tool belt and a backpack. His three-pound club hammer looked awfully small compared to those Cyclopes.

This is what the sleeping earth lady had been talking about. She wanted Leo to walk away and leave his friends to die.

That decided it. No way was Leo going to let that earth lady make him feel powerless—never again. Leo slipped off his backpack and quietly started to unzip it.

The Cyclops in the chain mail loincloth walked over to Piper, who squirmed and tried to head-butt him in the eye. "Can I take her gag off now? I like it when they scream."

The question was directed at the third Cyclops, apparently

the leader. The crouching figure grunted, and Loincloth ripped the gag off Piper's mouth.

She didn't scream. She took a shaky breath like she was trying to keep herself calm.

Meanwhile, Leo found what he wanted in the pack: a stack of tiny remote control units he'd picked up in Bunker 9. At least he *hoped* that's what they were. The robotic crane's maintenance panel was easy to find. He slipped a screwdriver from his tool belt and went to work, but he had to go slowly. The leader Cyclops was only twenty feet in front of him. The monsters obviously had excellent senses. Pulling off his plan without making noise seemed impossible, but he didn't have much choice.

The Cyclops in the toga poked at the fire, which was now blazing away and billowing noxious black smoke toward the ceiling. His buddy Loincloth glowered at Piper, waiting for her to do something entertaining. "Scream, girl! I like funny screaming!"

When Piper finally spoke, her tone was calm and reasonable, like she was correcting a naughty puppy. "Oh, Mr. Cyclops, you don't want to kill us. It would be much better if you let us go."

Loincloth scratched his ugly head. He turned to his friend in the fiberglass toga. "She's kind of pretty, Torque. Maybe I should let her go."

Torque, the dude in the toga, growled. "I saw her first, Sump. *I'll* let her go!"

Sump and Torque started to argue, but the third Cyclops rose and shouted, "Fools!"

Leo almost dropped his screwdriver. The third Cyclops was a *female*. She was several feet taller than Torque or Sump, and even beefier. She wore a tent of chain mail cut like one of those sack dresses Leo's mean Aunt Rosa used to wear. What'd they call that—a muumuu? Yeah, the Cyclops lady had a chain mail muumuu. Her greasy black hair was matted in pigtails, woven with copper wires and metal washers. Her nose and mouth were thick and smashed together, like she spent her free time ramming her face into walls; but her single red eye glittered with evil intelligence.

The woman Cyclops stalked over to Sump and pushed him aside, knocking him over the conveyor belt. Torque backed up quickly.

"The girl is Venus spawn," the lady Cyclops snarled. "She's using charmspeak on you."

Piper started to say, "Please, ma'am—"

"Rarr!" The lady Cyclops grabbed Piper around the waist. "Don't try your pretty talk on me, girl! I'm Ma Gasket! I've eaten heroes tougher than you for lunch!"

Leo feared Piper would get crushed, but Ma Gasket just dropped her and let her dangle from her chain. Then she started yelling at Sump about how stupid he was.

Leo's hands worked furiously. He twisted wires and turned switches, hardly thinking about what he was doing. He finished attaching the remote. Then he crept over to the next robotic arm while the Cyclopes were talking.

"—eat her last, Ma?" Sump was saying.

"Idiot!" Ma Gasket yelled, and Leo realized Sump and Torque must be her sons. If so, ugly definitely ran in the family. "I should've thrown you out on the streets when you were babies, like *proper* Cyclops children. You might have learned some useful skills. Curse my soft heart that I kept you!"

"Soft heart?" Torque muttered.

"What was that, you ingrate?"

"Nothing, Ma. I said you got a soft heart. We get to work for you, feed you, file your toenails—"

"And you should be grateful!" Ma Gasket bellowed. "Now, stoke the fire, Torque! And Sump, you idiot, my case of salsa is in the other warehouse. Don't tell me you expect me to eat these demigods without salsa!"

"Yes, Ma," Sump said. "I mean no, Ma. I mean—"

"Go get it!" Ma Gasket picked up a nearby truck chassis and slammed it over Sump's head. Sump crumpled to his knees. Leo was sure a hit like that would kill him, but Sump apparently got hit by trucks a lot. He managed to push the chassis off his head. Then he staggered to his feet and ran off to fetch the salsa.

Now's the time, Leo thought. While they're separated.

He finished wiring the second machine and moved toward a third. As he dashed between robotic arms, the Cyclopes didn't see him, but Piper did. Her expression turned from terror to disbelief, and she gasped.

Ma Gasket turned to her. "What's the matter, girl? So fragile I broke you?"

Thankfully, Piper was a quick thinker. She looked away from Leo and said, "I think it's my ribs, ma'am. If I'm busted up inside, I'll taste terrible."

Ma Gasket bellowed with laughter. "Good one. The last hero we ate—remember him, Torque? Son of Mercury, wasn't he?"

"Yes, Ma," Torque said. "Tasty. Little bit stringy."

"He tried a trick like that. Said he was on medication. But he tasted fine!"

"Tasted like mutton," Torque recalled. "Purple shirt. Talked in Latin. Yes, a bit stringy, but good."

Leo's fingers froze on the maintenance panel. Apparently, Piper was having the same thought he was, because she asked, "Purple shirt? Latin?"

"Good eating," Ma Gasket said fondly. "Point is, girl, we're not as dumb as people think! We're not falling for those stupid tricks and riddles, not us northern Cyclopes."

Leo forced himself back to work, but his mind was racing. A kid who spoke Latin had been caught here—in a purple shirt like Jason's? He didn't know what that meant, but he had to leave the interrogation to Piper. If he was going to have any chance of defeating these monsters, he had to move fast before Sump came back with the salsa.

He looked up at the engine block suspended right above the Cyclopes' campsite. He wished he could use that—it would make a great weapon. But the crane holding it was on the opposite side of the conveyor belt. There was no way Leo could get over there without being seen, and besides, he was running short on time.

The last part of his plan was the trickiest. From his tool belt he summoned some wires, a radio adapter, and a smaller screwdriver and started to build a universal remote. For the first time, he said a silent thank-you to his dad—Hephaestus —for the magic tool belt. *Get me out of here,* he prayed, *and maybe you're not such a jerk.*

Piper kept talking, laying on the praise. "Oh, I've heard about the northern Cyclopes!" Which Leo figured was bull, but she sounded convincing. "I never knew you were so big and clever!"

"Flattery won't work either," Ma Gasket said, though she sounded pleased. "It's true, you'll be breakfast for the best Cyclopes around."

"But aren't Cyclopes good?" Piper asked. "I thought you made weapons for the gods."

"Bah! I'm very good. Good at eating people. Good at smashing. And good at building things, yes, but not for the gods. Our cousins, the elder Cyclopes, they do this, yes. Thinking they're so high and mighty 'cause they're a few thousand years older. Then there's our southern cousins, living on islands and tending sheep. Morons! But we Hyperborean Cyclopes, the northern clan, we're the best! Founded Monocle Motors in this old factory—the best weapons, armor, chariots, fuel-efficient SUVs! And yet—bah! Forced to shut down. Laid off most of our tribe. The war was too quick. Titans lost. No good! No more need for Cyclops weapons."

"Oh, no," Piper sympathized. "I'm sure you made some amazing weapons."

Torque grinned. "Squeaky war hammer!" He picked up a large pole with an accordion-looking metal box on the end.

He slammed it against the floor and the cement cracked, but there was also a sound like the world's largest rubber ducky getting stomped.

"Terrifying," Piper said.

Torque looked pleased. "Not as good as the exploding ax, but this one can be used more than once."

"Can I see it?" Piper asked. "If you could just free my hands—"

Torque stepped forward eagerly, but Ma Gasket said, "Stupid! She's tricking you again. Enough talk! Slay the boy first before he dies on his own. I like my meat fresh."

No! Leo's fingers flew, connecting the wires for the remote. *Just a few more minutes!*

"Hey, wait," Piper said, trying to get the Cyclopes' attention. "Hey, can I just ask—"

The wires sparked in Leo's hand. The Cyclopes froze and turned in his direction. Then Torque picked up a truck and threw it at him.

Leo rolled as the truck steamrolled over the machinery. If he'd been a half-second slower, he would've been smashed.

He got to his feet, and Ma Gasket spotted him. She yelled, "Torque, you pathetic excuse for a Cyclops, get him!"

Torque barreled toward him. Leo frantically gunned the toggle on his makeshift remote.

Torque was fifty feet away. Twenty feet.

Then the first robotic arm whirred to life. A three-ton yellow metal claw slammed the Cyclops in the back so hard, he landed flat on his face. Before Torque could recover, the robotic hand grabbed him by one leg and hurled him straight up.

"AHHHHH!" Torque rocketed into the gloom. The ceiling was too dark and too high up to see exactly what happened, but judging from the harsh metal *clang*, Leo guessed the Cyclops had hit one of the support girders.

Torque never came down. Instead, yellow dust rained to the floor. Torque had disintegrated.

Ma Gasket stared at Leo in shock. "My son... You... You..."

As if on cue, Sump lumbered into the firelight with a case of salsa. "Ma, I got the extra-spicy—"

He never finished his sentence. Leo spun the remote's toggle, and the second robotic arm whacked Sump in the chest. The salsa case exploded like a piñata and Sump flew backward, right into the base of Leo's third machine. Sump may have been immune to getting hit with truck chassis, but he wasn't immune to robotic arms that could deliver ten thousand pounds of force. The third crane arm slammed him against the floor so hard, he exploded into dust like a broken flour sack.

Two Cyclopes down. Leo was beginning to feel like Commander Tool Belt when Ma Gasket locked her eye on him. She grabbed the nearest crane arm and ripped it off its pedestal with a savage roar. "You busted my boys! Only *I* get to bust my boys!"

Leo punched a button, and the two remaining arms swung into action. Ma Gasket caught the first one and tore it in half. The second arm smacked her in the head, but that only seemed to make her mad. She grabbed it by the clamps, ripped it free, and swung it like a baseball bat. It missed Piper and Jason by an inch. Then Ma Gasket let it go—spinning it toward Leo. He yelped and rolled to one side as it demolished the machine next to him.

Leo started to realize that an angry Cyclops mother was not something you wanted to fight with a universal remote and a screwdriver. The future for Commander Tool Belt was not looking so hot.

She stood about twenty feet from him now, next to the cooking fire. Her fists were clenched, her teeth bared. She looked ridiculous in her chain mail muumuu and her greasy pigtails—but given the murderous glare in her huge red eye and the fact that she was twelve feet tall, Leo wasn't laughing.

"Any more tricks, demigod?" Ma Gasket demanded.

Leo glanced up. The engine block suspended on the chain —if only he'd had time to rig it. If only he could get Ma Gasket to take one step forward. The chain itself...that one link...Leo shouldn't have been able to see it, especially from so far down, but his senses told him there was metal fatigue.

"Heck, yeah, I got tricks!" Leo raised his remote control. "Take one more step, and I'll destroy you with fire!"

Ma Gasket laughed. "Would you? Cyclopes are immune to fire, you idiot. But if you wish to play with flames, let me help!"

She scooped red-hot coals into her bare hands and flung them at Leo. They landed all around his feet.

"You missed," he said incredulously. Then Ma Gasket

grinned and picked up a barrel next to the truck. Leo just had time to read the stenciled word on the side—KEROSENE —before Ma Gasket threw it. The barrel split on the floor in front of him, spilling lighter fluid everywhere.

Coals sparked. Leo closed his eyes, and Piper screamed, "No!"

A firestorm erupted around him. When Leo opened his eyes he was bathed in flames swirling twenty feet into the air.

Ma Gasket shrieked with delight, but Leo didn't offer the fire any good fuel. The kerosene burned off, dying down to small fiery patches on the floor.

Piper gasped. "Leo?"

Ma Gasket looked astonished. "You live?" Then she took that extra step forward, which put her right where Leo wanted. "What are you?"

"The son of Hephaestus," Leo said. "And I warned you I'd destroy you with fire."

He pointed one finger in the air and summoned all his will. He'd never tried to do anything so focused and intense —but he shot a bolt of white-hot flames at the chain suspending the engine block above the Cyclops's head—aiming for the link that looked weaker than the rest.

The flames died. Nothing happened. Ma Gasket laughed. "An impressive try, son of Hephaestus. It's been many centuries since I saw a fire user. You'll make a spicy appetizer!"

The chain snapped—that single link heated beyond its tolerance point—and the engine block fell, deadly and silent.

"I don't think so," Leo said.

Ma Gasket didn't even have time to look up.

Smash! No more Cyclops—just a pile of dust under a five-ton engine block.

"Not immune to engines, huh?" Leo said. "Boo-yah!"

Then he fell to his knees, his head buzzing. After a few minutes he realized Piper was calling his name.

"Leo! Are you all right? Can you move?"

He stumbled to his feet. He'd never tried to summon such an intense fire before, and it had left him completely drained.

It took him a long time to get Piper down from her chains. Then together they lowered Jason, who was still unconscious. Piper managed to trickle a little nectar into his mouth, and he groaned. The welt on his head started to shrink. His color came back a little.

"Yeah, he's got a nice thick skull," Leo said. "I think he's gonna be fine."

"Thank god," Piper sighed. Then she looked at Leo with something like fear. "How did you—the fire—have you always...?"

Leo looked down. "Always," he said. "I'm a freaking menace. Sorry, I should've told you guys sooner but—"

"Sorry?" Piper punched his arm. When he looked up, she was grinning. "That was amazing, Valdez! You saved our lives. What are you sorry about?"

Leo blinked. He started to smile, but his sense of relief was ruined when he noticed something next to Piper's foot.

Yellow dust—the powdered remains of one of the Cyclopes, maybe Torque—was shifting across the floor like an invisible wind was pushing it back together.

"They're forming again," Leo said. "Look."

Piper stepped away from the dust. "That's not possible. Annabeth told me monsters dissipate when they're killed. They go back to Tartarus and can't return for a long time."

"Well, nobody told the dust that." Leo watched as it collected into a pile, then very slowly spread out, forming a shape with arms and legs.

"Oh, god." Piper turned pale. "Boreas said something about this—the earth yielding up horrors. 'When monsters no longer stay in Tartarus, and souls are no longer confined to Hades.' How long do you think we have?"

Leo thought about the face that had formed in the ground outside—the sleeping woman who was *definitely* a horror from the earth.

"I don't know," he said. "But we need to get out of here."

XXV

JASON

JASON DREAMED HE WAS WRAPPED in chains, hanging upside down like a hunk of meat. Everything hurt—his arms, his legs, his chest, his head. Especially his head. It felt like an overinflated water balloon.

"If I'm dead," he murmured, "why does it hurt so much?"

"You're not dead, my hero," said a woman's voice. "It is not your time. Come, speak with me."

Jason's thoughts floated away from his body. He heard monsters yelling, his friends screaming, fiery explosions, but it all seemed to be happening on another plane of existence —getting farther and farther away.

He found himself standing in an earthen cage. Tendrils of tree roots and stone whirled together, confining him. Outside the bars, he could see the floor of a dry reflecting pool, another earthen spire growing at the far end, and above them, the ruined red stones of a burned-out house.

Next to him in the cage, a woman sat cross-legged in black

robes, her head covered by a shroud. She pushed aside her veil, revealing a face that was proud and beautiful—but also hardened with suffering.

"Hera," Jason said.

"Welcome to my prison," said the goddess. "You will not die today, Jason. Your friends will see you through—for now."

"For now?" he asked.

Hera gestured at the tendrils of her cage. "There are worse trials to come. The very earth stirs against us."

"You're a goddess," Jason said. "Why can't you just escape?"

Hera smiled sadly. Her form began to glow, until her brilliance filled the cage with painful light. The air hummed with power, molecules splitting apart like a nuclear explosion. Jason suspected if he were actually there in the flesh, he would've been vaporized.

The cage should've been blasted to rubble. The ground should've split and the ruined house should've been leveled. But when the glow died, the cage hadn't budged. Nothing outside the bars had changed. Only Hera looked different—a little more stooped and tired.

"Some powers are even greater than the gods," she said. "I am not easily contained. I can be in many places at once. But when the greater part of my essence is caught, it is like a foot in a bear trap, you might say. I can't escape, and I am concealed from the eyes of the other gods. Only you can find me, and I grow weaker by the day."

"Then why did you come here?" Jason asked. "How were you caught?"

The goddess sighed. "I could not stay idle. Your father

Jupiter believes he can withdraw from the world, and thus lull our enemies back to sleep. He believes we Olympians have become too involved in the affairs of mortals, in the fates of our demigod children, especially since we agreed to claim them all after the war. He believes this is what has caused our enemies to stir. That is why he closed Olympus."

"But you don't agree."

"No," she said. "Often I do not understand my husband's moods or his decisions, but even for Zeus, this seemed paranoid. I cannot fathom why he was so insistent and so convinced. It was...unlike him. As Hera, I might have been content to follow my lord's wishes. But I am also Juno." Her image flickered, and Jason saw armor under her simple black robes, a goatskin cloak—the symbol of a Roman warrior—across her bronze mantle. "Juno Moneta they once called me—Juno, the One Who Warns. I was guardian of the state, patron of Eternal Rome. I could not sit by while the descendants of my people were attacked. I sensed danger at this sacred spot. A voice—" She hesitated. "A voice told me I should come here. Gods do not have what you might call a conscience, nor do we have dreams; but the voice was like that—soft and persistent, warning me to come here. And so the same day Zeus closed Olympus, I slipped away without telling him my plans, so he could not stop me. And I came here to investigate."

"It was a trap," Jason guessed.

The goddess nodded. "Only too late did I realize how quickly the earth was stirring. I was even more foolish than Jupiter—a slave to my own impulses. This is exactly how it happened the first time. I was taken captive by the giants, and my imprisonment started a war. Now our enemies rise again. The gods can only defeat them with the help of the greatest living heroes. And the one whom the giants serve... *she* cannot be defeated at all—only kept asleep."

"I don't understand."

"You will soon," Hera said.

The cage began to constrict, the tendrils spiraling tighter. Hera's form shivered like a candle flame in the breeze. Outside the cage, Jason could see shapes gathering at the edge of the pool—lumbering humanoids with hunched backs and bald heads. Unless Jason's eyes were tricking him—they had more than one set of arms. He heard wolves too, but not the wolves he'd seen with Lupa. He could tell from their howls this was a different pack—hungrier, more aggressive, out for blood.

"Hurry, Jason," Hera said. "My keepers approach, and you begin to wake. I will not be strong enough to appear to you again, even in dreams."

"Wait," he said. "Boreas told us you'd made a dangerous gamble. What did he mean?"

Hera's eyes looked wild, and Jason wondered if she really *had* done something crazy.

"An exchange," she said. "The only way to bring peace. The enemy counts on our divisions, and if we are divided, we *will* be destroyed. You are my peace offering, Jason—a bridge to overcome millennia of hatred."

"What? I don't—"

"I cannot tell you more," Hera said. "You have only lived

this long because I have taken your memory. Find this place. Return to your starting point. Your sister will help."

"Thalia?"

The scene began to dissolve. "Good-bye, Jason. Beware Chicago. Your most dangerous mortal enemy waits there. If you are to die, it will be by her hand."

"Who?" he demanded.

But Hera's image faded, and Jason awoke.

His eyes snapped open. "Cyclops!"

"Whoa, sleepyhead." Piper sat behind him on the bronze dragon, holding his waist to keep him balanced. Leo sat in front, driving. They flew peacefully through the winter sky as if nothing had happened.

"D-Detroit," Jason stammered. "Didn't we crash-land? I thought—"

"It's okay," Leo said. "We got away, but you got a nasty concussion. How you feeling?"

Jason's head throbbed. He remembered the factory, then walking down the catwalk, then a creature looming over him —a face with one eye, a massive fist—and everything went black.

"How did you—the Cyclops—"

"Leo ripped them apart," Piper said. "He was amazing. He can summon fire—"

"It was nothing," Leo said quickly.

Piper laughed. "Shut up, Valdez. I'm going to tell him. Get over it."

And she did—how Leo single-handedly defeated the Cyclopes family; how they freed Jason, then noticed the Cyclopes starting to re-form; how Leo had replaced the dragon's wiring and gotten them back in the air just as they'd started to hear the Cyclopes roaring for vengeance inside the factory.

Jason was impressed. Taking out three Cyclopes with nothing but a tool kit? Not bad. It didn't exactly scare him to hear how close he'd come to death, but it did make him feel horrible. He'd stepped right into an ambush and spent the whole fight knocked out while his friends fended for themselves. What kind of quest leader was he?

When Piper told him about the other kid the Cyclopes claimed to have eaten, the one in the purple shirt who spoke Latin, Jason felt like his head was going to explode. A son of Mercury... Jason felt like he should know that kid, but the name was missing from his mind.

"I'm not alone, then," he said. "There are others like me."

"Jason," Piper said, "you were never alone. You've got us."

"I—I know...but something Hera said. I was having a dream...."

He told them what he'd seen, and what the goddess had said inside her cage.

"An exchange?" Piper asked. "What does that mean?"

Jason shook his head. "But Hera's gamble is *me*. Just by sending me to Camp Half-Blood, I have a feeling she broke some kind of rule, something that could blow up in a big way—"

"Or save us," Piper said hopefully. "That bit about the sleeping enemy—that sounds like the lady Leo told us about."

Leo cleared his throat. "About that . . . she kind of appeared to me back in Detroit, in a pool of Porta-Potty sludge."

Jason wasn't sure he'd heard that right. "Did you say . . . Porta-Potty?"

Leo told them about the big face in the factory yard. "I don't know if she's completely unkillable," he said, "but she cannot be defeated by toilet seats. I can vouch for that. She wanted me to betray you guys, and I was like, 'Pfft, right, I'm gonna listen to a face in the potty sludge.'"

"She's trying to divide us." Piper slipped her arms from around Jason's waist. He could sense her tension without even looking at her.

"What's wrong?" he asked.

"I just . . . Why are they toying with us? Who is this lady, and how is she connected to Enceladus?"

"Enceladus?" Jason didn't think he'd heard that name before.

"I mean . . ." Piper's voice quavered. "That's one of the giants. Just one of the names I could remember."

Jason got the feeling there was a lot more bothering her, but he decided not to press her. She'd had a rough morning.

Leo scratched his head. "Well, I dunno about Enchiladas—"

"Enceladus," Piper corrected.

"Whatever. But Old Potty Face mentioned another name. Porpoise Fear, or something?"

"Porphyrion?" Piper asked. "He was the giant king, I think."

Jason envisioned that dark spire in the old reflecting pool —growing larger as Hera got weaker. "I'm going to take a wild guess," he said. "In the old stories, Porphyrion kidnapped Hera. That was the first shot in the war between the giants and the gods."

"I think so," Piper agreed. "But those myths are really garbled and conflicted. It's almost like nobody wanted that story to survive. I just remember there was a war, and the giants were almost impossible to kill."

"Heroes and gods had to work together," Jason said. "That's what Hera told me."

"Kind of hard to do," Leo grumbled, "if the gods won't even talk to us."

They flew west, and Jason became lost in his thoughts—all of them bad. He wasn't sure how much time passed before the dragon dove through a break in the clouds, and below them, glittering in the winter sun, was a city at the edge of a massive lake. A crescent of skyscrapers lined the shore. Behind them, stretching out to the western horizon, was a vast grid of snow-covered neighborhoods and roads.

"Chicago," Jason said.

He thought about what Hera had said in his dream. His worst mortal enemy would be waiting here. If he was going to die, it would be by her hand.

"One problem down," Leo said. "We got here alive. Now, how do we find the storm spirits?"

Jason saw a flash of movement below them. At first he thought it was a small plane, but it was too small, too dark and fast. The thing spiraled toward the skyscrapers, weaving and changing shape—and, just for a moment it became the smoky figure of a horse.

"How about we follow that one," Jason suggested, "and see where it goes?"

XXVI

JASON

JASON WAS AFRAID THEY'D LOSE THEIR TARGET. The *ventus* moved like . . . well, like the wind.

"Speed up!" he urged.

"Bro," Leo said, "if I get any closer, he'll spot us. Bronze dragon ain't exactly a stealth plane."

"Slow down!" Piper yelped.

The storm spirit dove into the grid of downtown streets. Festus tried to follow, but his wingspan was way too wide. His left wing clipped the edge of a building, slicing off a stone gargoyle before Leo pulled up.

"Get above the buildings," Jason suggested. "We'll track him from there."

"You want to drive this thing?" Leo grumbled, but he did what Jason asked.

After a few minutes, Jason spotted the storm spirit again, zipping through the streets with no apparent purpose—blowing over pedestrians, ruffling flags, making cars swerve.

"Oh great," Piper said. "There're two."

She was right. A second *ventus* blasted around the corner of the Renaissance Hotel and linked up with the first. They wove together in a chaotic dance, shooting to the top of a skyscraper, bending a radio tower, and diving back down toward the street.

"Those guys do *not* need any more caffeine," Leo said.

"I guess Chicago's a good place to hang out," Piper said. "Nobody's going to question a couple more evil winds."

"More than a couple," Jason said. "Look."

The dragon circled over a wide avenue next to a lakeside park. Storm spirits were converging—at least a dozen of them, whirling around a big public art installation.

"Which one do you think is Dylan?" Leo asked. "I wanna throw something at him."

But Jason focused on the art installation. The closer they got to it, the faster his heart beat. It was just a public fountain, but it was unpleasantly familiar. Two five-story monoliths rose from either end of a long granite reflecting pool. The monoliths seemed to be built of video screens, flashing the combined image of a giant face that spewed water into the pool.

Maybe it was just a coincidence, but it looked like a high-tech, super-size version of that ruined reflecting pool he'd seen in his dreams, with those two dark masses jutting from either end. As Jason watched, the image on the screens changed to a woman's face with her eyes closed.

"Leo..." he said nervously.

"I see her," Leo said. "I don't like her, but I see her."

Then the screens went dark. The *venti* swirled together into a single funnel cloud and skittered across the fountain, kicking up a waterspout almost as high as the monoliths. They got to its center, popped off a drain cover, and disappeared underground.

"Did they just go down a drain?" Piper asked. "How are we supposed to follow them?"

"Maybe we shouldn't," Leo said. "That fountain thing is giving me seriously bad vibes. And aren't we supposed to, like, beware the earth?"

Jason felt the same way, but they had to follow. It was their only way forward. They had to find Hera, and they now had only two days until the solstice.

"Put us down in that park," he suggested. "We'll check it out on foot."

Festus landed in an open area between the lake and the skyline. The signs said Grant Park, and Jason imagined it would've been a nice place in the summer; but now it was a field of ice, snow, and salted walkways. The dragon's hot metal feet hissed as they touched down. Festus flapped his wings unhappily and shot fire into the sky, but there was no one around to notice. The wind coming off the lake was bitter cold. Anyone with sense would be inside. Jason's eyes stung so badly, he could barely see.

They dismounted, and Festus the dragon stomped his feet. One of his ruby eyes flickered, so it looked like he was blinking.

"Is that normal?" Jason asked.

Leo pulled a rubber mallet from his tool bag. He whacked the dragon's bad eye, and the light went back to normal. "Yes," Leo said. "Festus can't hang around here, though, in the middle of the park. They'll arrest him for loitering. Maybe if I had a dog whistle..."

He rummaged in his tool belt, but came up with nothing.

"Too specialized?" he guessed. "Okay, give me a safety whistle. They got that in lots of machine shops."

This time, Leo pulled out a big plastic orange whistle. "Coach Hedge would be jealous! Okay, Festus, listen." Leo blew the whistle. The shrill sound probably rolled all the way across Lake Michigan. "You hear that, come find me, okay? Until then, you fly wherever you want. Just try not to barbecue any pedestrians."

The dragon snorted—hopefully in agreement. Then he spread his wings and launched into the air.

Piper took one step and winced. "Ah!"

"Your ankle?" Jason felt bad he'd forgotten about her injury back in the Cyclops factory. "That nectar we gave you might be wearing off."

"It's fine." She shivered, and Jason remembered his promise to get her a new snowboarding coat. He hoped he lived long enough to find her one. She took a few more steps with only a slight limp, but Jason could tell she was trying not to grimace.

"Let's get out of the wind," he suggested.

"Down a drain?" Piper shuddered. "Sounds cozy."

They wrapped themselves up as best they could and headed toward the fountain.

• • •

According to the plaque, it was called Crown Fountain. All the water had emptied out except for a few patches that were starting to freeze. It didn't seem right to Jason that the fountain would have water in it in the winter anyway. Then again, those big monitors had flashed the face of their mysterious enemy Dirt Woman. Nothing about this place was right.

They stepped to the center of the pool. No spirits tried to stop them. The giant monitor walls stayed dark. The drain hole was easily big enough for a person, and a maintenance ladder led down into the gloom.

Jason went first. As he climbed, he braced himself for horrible sewer smells, but it wasn't that bad. The ladder dropped into a brickwork tunnel running north to south. The air was warm and dry, with only a trickle of water on the floor.

Piper and Leo climbed down after him.

"Are all sewers this nice?" Piper wondered.

"No," Leo said. "Trust me."

Jason frowned. "How do you know—"

"Hey, man, I ran away six times. I've slept in some weird places, okay? Now, which way do we go?"

Jason tilted his head, listening, then pointed south. "That way."

"How can you be sure?" Piper asked.

"There's a draft blowing south," Jason said. "Maybe the *venti* went with the flow."

It wasn't much of a lead, but nobody offered anything better.

Unfortunately, as soon as they started walking, Piper stumbled. Jason had to catch her.

"Stupid ankle," she cursed.

"Let's rest," Jason decided. "We could all use it. We've been going nonstop for over a day. Leo, can you pull any food from that tool belt besides breath mints?"

"Thought you'd never ask. Chef Leo is on it!"

Piper and Jason sat on a brick ledge while Leo shuffled through his pack.

Jason was glad to rest. He was still tired and dizzy, and hungry, too. But mostly, he wasn't eager to face whatever lay ahead. He turned his gold coin in his fingers.

If you are to die, Hera had warned, *it will be by her hand.*

Whoever "her" was. After Khione, the Cyclops mother, and the weird sleeping lady, the last thing Jason needed was another psycho villainess in his life.

"It wasn't your fault," Piper said.

He looked at her blankly. "What?"

"Getting jumped by the Cyclopes," she said. "It wasn't your fault."

He looked down at the coin in his palm. "I was stupid. I left you alone and walked into a trap. I should've known. . . ."

He didn't finish. There were too many things he should have known—who he was, how to fight monsters, how Cyclopes lured their victims by mimicking voices and hiding in shadows and a hundred other tricks. All that information was supposed to be in his head. He could feel the places it should be—like empty pockets. If Hera wanted him to succeed, why had she stolen the memories that could help him? She claimed his amnesia had kept him alive, but that made no sense. He was starting to understand why Annabeth had wanted to leave the goddess in her cage.

"Hey." Piper nudged his arm. "Cut yourself some slack. Just because you're the son of Zeus doesn't mean you're a one-man army."

A few feet away, Leo lit a small cooking fire. He hummed as he pulled supplies out of his pack and his tool belt.

In the firelight, Piper's eyes seemed to dance. Jason had been studying them for days now, and he still couldn't decide what color they were.

"I know this must suck for you," he said. "Not just the quest, I mean. 'The way I appeared on the bus, the Mist messing with your mind, and making you think I was . . . you know."

She dropped her gaze. "Yeah, well. None of us asked for this. It's not your fault."

She tugged at the little braids on each side of her head. Again, Jason thought how glad he was that she'd lost the Aphrodite blessing. With the makeup and the dress and the perfect hair, she'd looked about twenty-five, glamorous, and completely out of his league. He'd never thought of beauty as a form of power, but that's the way Piper had seemed—*powerful*.

He liked regular Piper better—someone he could hang out with. But the weird thing was, he couldn't quite get that other image out of his head. It hadn't been an illusion. That side of Piper was there too. She just did her best to hide it.

"Back in the factory," Jason said, "you were going to say something about your dad."

She traced her finger over the bricks, almost like she was writing out a scream she didn't want to vocalize. "Was I?"

"Piper," he said, "he's in some kind of trouble, isn't he?"

Over at the fire, Leo stirred some sizzling bell peppers and meat in a pan. "Yeah, baby! Almost there."

Piper looked on the verge of tears. "Jason . . . I can't talk about it."

"We're your friends. Let us help."

That seemed to make her feel worse. She took a shaky breath. "I wish I could, but—"

"And bingo!" Leo announced.

He came over with three plates stacked on his arms like a waiter. Jason had no idea where he'd gotten all the food, or how he'd put it together so fast, but it looked amazing: pepper and beef tacos with chips and salsa.

"Leo," Piper said in amazement. "How did you—?"

"Chef Leo's Taco Garage is fixing you up!" he said proudly. "And by the way, it's tofu, not beef, beauty queen, so don't freak. Just dig in!"

Jason wasn't sure about tofu, but the tacos tasted as good as they smelled. While they ate, Leo tried to lighten the mood and joke around. Jason was grateful Leo was with them. It made being with Piper a little less intense and uncomfortable. At the same time, he kind of wished he *was* alone with her; but he chided himself for feeling that way.

After Piper ate, Jason encouraged her to get some sleep. Without another word, she curled up and put her head in his lap. In two seconds she was snoring.

Jason looked up at Leo, who was obviously trying not to laugh.

They sat in silence for a few minutes, drinking lemonade Leo had made from canteen water and powdered mix.

"Good, huh?" Leo grinned.

"You should start a stand," Jason said. "Make some serious coin."

But as he stared at the embers of the fire, something began to bother him. "Leo...about this fire stuff you can do...is it true?"

Leo's smile faltered. "Yeah, well..." He opened his hand. A small ball of flame burst to life, dancing across his palm.

"That is so cool," Jason said. "Why didn't you say anything?"

Leo closed his hand and the fire went out. "Didn't want to look like a freak."

"I have lightning and wind powers," Jason reminded him. "Piper can turn beautiful and charm people into giving her BMWs. You're no more a freak than we are. And, hey, maybe you can fly, too. Like jump off a building and yell, 'Flame on!'"

Leo snorted. "If I did that, you would see a flaming kid falling to his death, and I would be yelling something a little stronger than 'Flame on!' Trust me, Hephaestus cabin doesn't see fire powers as cool. Nyssa told me they're super rare. When a demigod like me comes around, bad things happen. *Really* bad."

"Maybe it's the other way around," Jason suggested. "Maybe people with special gifts show up when bad things are happening because that's when they're needed most."

Leo cleared away the plates. "Maybe. But I'm telling you . . . it's not always a gift."

Jason fell silent. "You're talking about your mom, aren't you? The night she died."

Leo didn't answer. He didn't have to. The fact that he was quiet, not joking around—that told Jason enough.

"Leo, her death wasn't your fault. Whatever happened that night—it wasn't because you could summon fire. This Dirt Woman, whoever she is, has been trying to ruin you for years, mess up your confidence, take away everything you care about. She's trying to make you feel like a failure. You're not. You're important."

"That's what she said." Leo looked up, his eyes full of pain. "She said I was meant to do something important—something that would make or break that big prophecy about the seven demigods. That's what scares me. I don't know if I'm up to it."

Jason wanted to tell him everything would be all right, but it would've sounded fake. Jason didn't know *what* would happen. They were demigods, which meant sometimes things didn't end okay. Sometimes you got eaten by the Cyclops.

If you asked most kids, "Hey, you want to summon fire or lightning or magical makeup?" they'd think it sounded pretty cool. But those powers went along with hard stuff, like sitting in a sewer in the middle of winter, running from monsters, losing your memory, watching your friends almost get cooked, and having dreams that warned you of your own death.

Leo poked at the remnants of his fire, turning over red-hot

coals with his bare hand. "You ever wonder about the other four demigods? I mean...if we're three of the ones from the Great Prophecy, who are the others? Where are they?"

Jason had thought about it, all right, but he tried to push it out of his mind. He had a horrible suspicion that *he* would be expected to lead those other demigods, and he was afraid he would fail.

You'll tear each other apart, Boreas had promised.

Jason had been trained never to show fear. He was sure of that from his dream with the wolves. He was supposed to act confident, even if he didn't feel it. But Leo and Piper were depending on him, and he was terrified of failing them. If he had to lead a group of six—six who might not get along—that would be even worse.

"I don't know," he said at last. "I guess the other four will show up when the time is right. Who knows? Maybe they're on some other quest right now."

Leo grunted. "I bet their sewer is nicer than ours."

The draft picked up, blowing toward the south end of the tunnel.

"Get some rest, Leo," Jason said. "I'll take first watch."

It was hard to measure time, but Jason figured his friends slept about four hours. Jason didn't mind. Now that he was resting, he didn't really feel the need for more sleep. He'd been conked out long enough on the dragon. Plus, he needed time to think about the quest, his sister Thalia, and Hera's warnings. He also didn't mind Piper's using him for a pillow. She had a cute way of breathing when she slept—inhaling through the nose, exhaling with a little puff through the mouth. He was almost disappointed when she woke up.

Finally they broke camp and started down the tunnel.

It twisted and turned and seemed to go on forever. Jason wasn't sure what to expect at the end—a dungeon, a mad scientist's lab, or maybe a sewer reservoir where all Porta-Potty sludge ends up, forming an evil toilet face large enough to swallow the world.

Instead, they found polished steel elevator doors, each one engraved with a cursive letter *M*. Next to the elevator was a directory, like for a department store.

"M for Macy's?" Piper guessed. "I think they have one in downtown Chicago."

"Or Monocle Motors still?" Leo said. "Guys, read the directory. It's messed up."

Parking, Kennels, Main Entrance	Sewer Level
Furnishings and Café M	1
Women's Fashion and Magical Appliances	2
Men's Wear and Weaponry	3
Cosmetics, Potions, Poisons & Sundries	4

"Kennels for what?" Piper said. "And what kind of department store has its entrance in a sewer?"

"Or sells poisons," Leo said. "Man, what does 'sundries' even mean? Is that like underwear?"

Jason took a deep breath. "When in doubt, start at the top."

• • •

The doors slid open on the fourth floor, and the scent of perfume wafted into the elevator. Jason stepped out first, sword ready.

"Guys," he said. "You've got to see this."

Piper joined him and caught her breath. "This is *not* Macy's."

The department store looked like the inside of a kaleidoscope. The entire ceiling was a stained glass mosaic with astrological signs around a giant sun. The daylight streaming through it washed everything in a thousand different colors. The upper floors made a ring of balconies around a huge central atrium, so they could see all the way down to the ground floor. Gold railings glittered so brightly, they were hard to look at.

Aside from the stained glass ceiling and the elevator, Jason couldn't see any other windows or doors, but two sets of glass escalators ran between the levels. The carpeting was a riot of oriental patterns and colors, and the racks of merchandise were just as bizarre. There was too much to take in at once, but Jason saw normal stuff like shirt racks and shoe trees mixed in with armored manikins, beds of nails, and fur coats that seemed to be moving.

Leo stepped to the railing and looked down. "Check it out."

In the middle of the atrium a fountain sprayed water twenty feet into the air, changing color from red to yellow to blue. The pool glittered with gold coins, and on either side of the fountain stood a gilded cage—like an oversize canary cage.

Inside one, a miniature hurricane swirled, and lightning flashed. Somebody had imprisoned the storm spirits, and the cage shuddered as they tried to get out. In the other, frozen like a statue, was a short, buff satyr, holding a tree-branch club.

"Coach Hedge!" Piper said. "We've got to get down there."

A voice said, "May I help you find something?"

All three of them jumped back.

A woman had just *appeared* in front of them. She wore an elegant black dress with diamond jewelry, and she looked like a retired fashion model—maybe fifty years old, though it was hard for Jason to judge. Her long dark hair swept over one shoulder, and her face was gorgeous in that surreal supermodel way—thin and haughty and cold, not quite human. With their long red-painted nails, her fingers looked more like talons.

She smiled. "I'm so happy to see new customers. How may I help you?"

Leo glanced at Jason like, *All yours.*

"Um," Jason started, "is this your store?"

The woman nodded. "I found it abandoned, you know. I understand so many stores are, these days. I decided it would make the perfect place. I love collecting tasteful objects, helping people, and offering quality goods at a reasonable price. So this seemed a good...how do you say...first acquisition in this country."

She spoke with a pleasing accent, but Jason couldn't guess where from. Clearly she wasn't hostile, though. Jason started to relax. Her voice was rich and exotic. Jason wanted to hear more.

"So you're new to America?" he asked.

"I am ... new," the woman agreed. "I am the Princess of Colchis. My friends call me Your Highness. Now, what are you looking for?"

Jason had heard of rich foreigners buying American department stores. Of course most of the time they didn't sell poisons, living fur coats, storm spirits, or satyrs, but still —with a nice voice like that, the Princess of Colchis couldn't be all bad.

Piper poked him in the ribs. "Jason ..."

"Um, right. Actually, Your Highness ..." He pointed to the gilded cage on the first floor. "That's our friend down t here, Gleeson Hedge. The satyr. Could we ... have him back, please?"

"Of course!" the princess agreed immediately. "I would love to show you my inventory. First, may I know your names?"

Jason hesitated. It seemed like a bad idea to give out their names. A memory tugged at the back of his mind—something Hera had warned him about, but it seemed fuzzy.

On the other hand, Her Highness was on the verge of cooperating. If they could get what they wanted without a fight, that would be better. Besides, this lady didn't seem like an enemy.

Piper started to say, "Jason, I wouldn't—"

"This is Piper," he said. "This is Leo. I'm Jason."

The princess fixed her eyes on him and, just for a moment,

her face literally glowed, blazing with so much anger, Jason could see her skull beneath her skin. Jason's mind was getting blurrier, but he knew something didn't seem right. Then the moment passed, and Her Highness looked like a normal elegant woman again, with a cordial smile and a soothing voice.

"Jason. What an interesting name," she said, her eyes as cold as the Chicago wind. "I think we'll have to make a special deal for you. Come, children. Let's go shopping."

XXVII

PIPER

PIPER WANTED TO RUN FOR THE ELEVATOR.

Her second choice: attack the weird princess now, because she was sure a fight was coming. The way the lady's face glowed when she'd heard Jason's name had been bad enough. Now Her Highness was smiling like nothing had happened, and Jason and Leo didn't seem to think anything was wrong.

The princess gestured toward the cosmetics counter. "Shall we start with the potions?"

"Cool," Jason said.

"Guys," Piper interrupted, "we're here to get the storm spirits and Coach Hedge. If this—*princess*—is really our friend—"

"Oh, I'm better than a friend, my dear," Her Highness said. "I'm a saleswoman." Her diamonds sparkled, and her eyes glittered like a snake's—cold and dark. "Don't worry. We'll work our way down to the first floor, eh?"

Leo nodded eagerly. "Sure, yeah! That sounds okay. Right, Piper?"

Piper did her best to stare daggers at him: *No, it is not okay!*

"Of course it's okay." Her Highness put her hands on Leo's and Jason's shoulders and steered them toward the cosmetics. "Come along, boys."

Piper didn't have much choice except to follow.

She hated department stores—mostly because she'd gotten caught stealing from several of them. Well, not exactly *caught*, and not exactly *stealing*. She'd talked salesmen into giving her computers, new boots, a gold ring, once even a lawn mower, though she had no idea why she wanted one. She never kept the stuff. She just did it to get her dad's attention. Usually she talked her neighborhood UPS guy into taking the stuff back. But of course the salesmen she duped always came to their senses and called the police, who eventually tracked her down.

Anyway, she wasn't thrilled to be back in a department store—especially one run by a crazy princess who glowed in the dark.

"And here," the princess said, "is the finest assortment of magical mixtures anywhere."

The counter was crammed with bubbling beakers and smoking vials on tripods. Lining the display shelves were crystal flasks—some shaped like swans or honey bear dispensers. The liquids inside were every color, from glowing white to polka-dotted. And the smells—ugh! Some were pleasant, like fresh-baked cookies or roses, but they were mixed with the scents of burning tires, skunk spray, and gym lockers.

The princess pointed to a bloodred vial—a simple test tube with a cork stopper. "This one will heal any disease."

"Even cancer?" Leo asked. "Leprosy? Hangnails?"

"Any disease, sweet boy. And this vial"—she pointed to a swan-shaped container with blue liquid inside—"will kill you very painfully."

"Awesome," Jason said. His voice sounded dazed and sleepy.

"Jason," Piper said. "We've got a job to do. Remember?" She tried to put power into her words, to snap him out of his trance with charmspeak, but her voice sounded shaky even to her. This princess woman scared her too much, made her confidence crumble, just the way she'd felt back in the Aphrodite cabin with Drew.

"Job to do," Jason muttered. "Sure. But shopping first, okay?"

The princess beamed at him. "Then we have potions for resisting fire—"

"Got that covered," Leo said.

"Indeed?" The princess studied Leo's face more closely. "You don't appear to be wearing my trademark sunscreen... but no matter. We also have potions that cause blindness, insanity, sleep, or—"

"Wait." Piper was still staring at the red vial. "Could that potion cure lost memory?"

The princess narrowed her eyes. "Possibly. Yes. Quite

possibly. Why, my dear? Have you forgotten something important?"

Piper tried to keep her expression neutral, but if that vial could cure Jason's memory...

Do I really want that? she wondered.

If Jason found out who he was, he might not even be her friend. Hera had taken away his memories for a reason. She'd told him it was the only way he'd survive at Camp Half-Blood. What if Jason found out that he was their enemy, or something? He might come out of his amnesia and decide he hated Piper. He might have a girlfriend wherever he came from.

It doesn't matter, she decided, which kind of surprised her.

Jason always looked so anguished when he tried to remember things. Piper hated seeing him that way. She wanted to help him because she cared about him, even if that meant losing him. And maybe it would make this trip through Her Craziness's department store worthwhile.

"How much?" Piper asked.

The princess got a faraway look in her eyes. "Well, now... The price is always tricky. I love helping people. Honestly, I do. And I always keep my bargains, but sometimes people try to cheat me." Her gaze drifted to Jason. "Once, for instance, I met a handsome young man who wanted a treasure from my father's kingdom. We made a bargain, and I promised to help him steal it."

"From your own dad?" Jason still looked half in a trance, but the idea seemed to bother him.

"Oh, don't worry," the princess said. "I demanded a high

price. The young man had to take me away with him. He was quite good-looking, dashing, strong..." She looked at Piper. "I'm sure, my dear, you understand how one might be attracted to such a hero, and want to help him."

Piper tried to control her emotions, but she probably blushed. She got the creepiest feeling the princess could read her thoughts.

She also found the princess's story disturbingly familiar. Pieces of old myths she'd read with her dad started coming together, but this woman couldn't be the one she was thinking of.

"At any rate," Her Highness continued, "my hero had to do many impossible tasks, and I'm not bragging when I say he couldn't have done them without me. I betrayed my own family to win the hero his prize. And still he cheated me of my payment."

"Cheated?" Jason frowned, as if trying to remember something important.

"That's messed up," Leo said.

Her Highness patted his cheek affectionately. "I'm sure you don't need to worry, Leo. You seem honest. You would always pay a fair price, wouldn't you?"

Leo nodded. "What were we buying again? I'll take two."

Piper broke in: "So, the vial, Your Highness—how much?"

The princess assessed Piper's clothes, her face, her posture, as if putting a price tag on one slightly used demigod.

"Would you give anything for it, my dear?" the princess asked. "I sense that you would."

The words washed over Piper as powerfully as a good

surfing wave. The force of the suggestion nearly lifted her off her feet. She wanted to pay any price. She wanted to say yes.

Then her stomach twisted. Piper realized she was being charmspoken. She'd sensed something like it before, when Drew spoke at the campfire, but this was a thousand times more potent. No wonder her friends were dazed. Was *this* what people felt when Piper used charmspeak? A feeling of guilt settled over her.

She summoned all her willpower. "No, I won't pay *any* price. But a fair price, maybe. After that, we need to leave. Right, guys?"

Just for a moment, her words seemed to have some effect. The boys looked confused.

"Leave?" Jason said.

"You mean … after shopping?" Leo asked.

Piper wanted to scream, but the princess tilted her head, examining Piper with newfound respect.

"Impressive," the princess said. "Not many people could resist my suggestions. Are you a child of Aphrodite, my dear? Ah, yes—I should have seen it. No matter. Perhaps we should shop a while longer before you decide what to buy, eh?"

"But the vial—"

"Now, boys." She turned to Jason and Leo. Her voice was so much more powerful than Piper's, so full of confidence, Piper didn't stand a chance. "Would you like to see more?"

"Sure," Jason said.

"Okay," Leo said.

"Excellent," the princess said. "You'll need all the help you can get if you're to make it to the Bay Area."

Piper's hand moved to her dagger. She thought about her dream of the mountaintop—the scene Enceladus had shown her, a place she knew, where she was supposed to betray her friends in two days.

"The Bay Area?" Piper said. "Why the Bay Area?"

The princess smiled. "Well, that's where they'll die, isn't it?"

Then she led them toward the escalators, Jason and Leo still looking excited to shop.

XXVIII

PIPER

PIPER CORNERED THE PRINCESS as Jason and Leo went off to check out the living fur coats.

"You want them shopping for their deaths?" Piper demanded.

"Mmm." The princess blew dust off a display case of swords. "I'm a seer, my dear. I know your little secret. But we don't want to dwell on that, do we? The boys are having such fun."

Leo laughed as he tried on a hat that seemed to be made from enchanted raccoon fur. Its ringed tail twitched, and its little legs wiggled frantically as Leo walked. Jason was ogling the men's sportswear. Boys interested in shopping for clothes? A definite sign they were under an evil spell.

Piper glared at the princess. "Who are you?"

"I told you, my dear. I'm the Princess of Colchis."

"Where's Colchis?"

The princess's expression turned a little sad. "Where *was*

Colchis, you mean. My father ruled the far shores of the Black Sea, as far to the east as a Greek ship could sail in those days. But Colchis is no more—lost eons ago."

"Eons?" Piper asked. The princess looked no more than fifty, but a bad feeling started settling over Piper—something King Boreas had mentioned back in Quebec. "How old are you?"

The princess laughed. "A lady should avoid asking or answering that question. Let's just say the, ah, immigration process to enter your country took quite a while. My patron finally brought me through. She made all this possible." The princess swept her hand around the department store.

Piper's mouth tasted like metal. "Your patron..."

"Oh, yes. She doesn't bring just anyone through, mind you—only those who have special talents, such as me. And really, she insists on so little—a store entrance that must be underground so she can, ah, monitor my clientele; and a favor now and then. In exchange for a new life? Really, it was the best bargain I'd made in centuries."

Run, Piper thought. *We have to get out of here.*

But before she could even turn her thoughts into words, Jason called, "Hey, check it out!"

From a rack labeled DISTRESSED CLOTHING, he held up a purple T-shirt like the one he'd worn on the school field trip —except this shirt looked as if it had been clawed by tigers.

Jason frowned. "Why does this look so familiar?"

"Jason, it's like *yours,*" Piper said. "Now we really have to leave." But she wasn't sure he could even hear her anymore through the princess's enchantment.

"Nonsense," the princess said. "The boys aren't done, are they? And yes, my dear. Those shirts are very popular—trade-ins from previous customers. It suits you."

Leo picked up an orange Camp Half-Blood tee with a hole through the middle, as if it had been hit by a javelin. Next to that was a dented bronze breastplate pitted with corrosion —acid, maybe?—and a Roman toga slashed to pieces and stained with something that looked disturbingly like dried blood.

"Your Highness," Piper said, trying to control her nerves. "Why don't you tell the boys how you betrayed your family? I'm sure they'd like to hear that story."

Her words didn't have any effect on the princess, but the boys turned, suddenly interested.

"More story?" Leo asked.

"I like more story!" Jason agreed.

The princess flashed Piper an irritated look. "Oh, one will do strange things for love, Piper. You should know that. I fell for that young hero, in fact, because your mother Aphrodite had me under a spell. If it wasn't for her—but I can't hold a grudge against a goddess, can I?"

The princess's tone made her meaning clear: *I can take it out on you.*

"But that hero took you with him when he fled Colchis," Piper remembered. "Didn't he, Your Highness? He married you just as he promised."

The look in the princess's eyes made Piper want to apologize, but she didn't back down.

"At first," Her Highness admitted, "it seemed he would

keep his word. But even after I helped him steal my father's treasure, he *still* needed my help. As we fled, my brother's fleet came after us. His warships overtook us. He would have destroyed us, but I convinced my brother to come aboard our ship first and talk under a flag of truce. He trusted me."

"And you killed your own brother," Piper said, the horrible story all coming back to her, along with a name—an infamous name that began with the letter *M*.

"What?" Jason stirred. For a moment he looked almost like himself. "Killed your own—"

"No," the princess snapped. "Those stories are lies. It was my new husband and his men who killed my brother, though they couldn't have done it without my deception. They threw his body into the sea, and the pursuing fleet had to stop and search for it so they could give my brother a proper burial. This gave us time to get away. All this, I did for my husband. And he forgot our bargain. He betrayed me in the end."

Jason still looked uncomfortable. "What did he do?"

The princess held the sliced-up toga against Jason's chest, as if measuring him for an assassination. "Don't you know the story, my boy? You of all people should. You were named for him."

"Jason," Piper said. "The *original* Jason. But then you're—you should be dead!"

The princess smiled. "As I said, a new life in a new country. Certainly I made mistakes. I turned my back on my own people. I was called a traitor, a thief, a liar, a murderess. But I acted out of love." She turned to the boys and gave them a pitiful look, batting her eyelashes. Piper could feel the sorcery washing over them, taking control more firmly than ever. "Wouldn't you do the same for someone you loved, my dears?"

"Oh, sure," Jason said.

"Okay," Leo said.

"Guys!" Piper ground her teeth in frustration. "Don't you see who she is? Don't you—"

"Let's continue, shall we?" the princess said breezily. "I believe you wanted to talk about a price for the storm spirits —and your satyr."

Leo got distracted on the second floor with the appliances.

"No way," he said. "Is that an armored forge?"

Before Piper could stop him, he hopped off the escalator and ran over to a big oval oven that looked like a barbecue on steroids.

When they caught up with him, the princess said, "You have good taste. This is the H-2000, designed by Hephaestus himself. Hot enough to melt Celestial bronze or Imperial gold."

Jason flinched as if he recognized that term. "Imperial gold?"

The princess nodded. "Yes, my dear. Like that weapon so cleverly concealed in your pocket. To be properly forged, Imperial gold had to be consecrated in the Temple of Jupiter on Capitoline Hill in Rome. Quite a powerful and rare metal, but like the Roman emperors, quite volatile. Be sure never to break that blade...." She smiled pleasantly. "Rome was *after* my time, of course, but I do hear stories. And now over here—this golden throne is one of my finest luxury items.

Hephaestus made it as a punishment for his mother, Hera. Sit in it and you'll be immediately trapped."

Leo apparently took this as an order. He began walking toward it in a trance.

"Leo, don't!" Piper warned.

He blinked. "How much for both?"

"Oh, the seat I could let you have for five great deeds. The forge, seven years of servitude. And for only a bit of your strength—" She led Leo into the appliance section, giving him prices on various items.

Piper didn't want to leave him alone with her, but she had to try reasoning with Jason. She pulled him aside and slapped him across the face.

"Ow," he muttered sleepily. "What was that for?"

"Snap out of it!" Piper hissed.

"What do you mean?"

"She's charmspeaking you. Can't you feel it?"

He knit his eyebrows. "She seems okay."

"She's not okay! She shouldn't even be alive! She was married to Jason—the *other* Jason—three thousand years ago. Remember what Boreas said—something about the souls no longer being confined to Hades? It's not just monsters who can't stay dead. She's come back from the Underworld!"

Jason shook his head uneasily. "She's not a ghost."

"No, she's worse! She's—"

"Children." The princess was back with Leo in tow. "If you please, we will now see what you came for. That is what you want, yes?"

Piper had to choke back a scream. She was tempted to

pull out her dagger and take on this witch herself, but she didn't like her chances—not in the middle of Her Highness's department store while her friends were under a spell. Piper couldn't even be sure they'd take her side in a fight. She had to figure out a better plan.

They took the escalator down to the base of the fountain. For the first time, Piper noticed two large bronze sundials —each about the size of a trampoline—inlaid on the marble tile floor to the north and south of the fountain. The gilded oversize canary cages stood to the east and west, and the farthest one held the storm spirits. They were so densely packed, spinning around like a super-concentrated tornado, that Piper couldn't tell how many there were—dozens, at least.

"Hey," Leo said, "Coach Hedge looks okay!"

They ran to the nearest canary cage. The old satyr seemed to have been petrified at the moment he was sucked into the sky above the Grand Canyon. He was frozen mid-shout, his club raised over his head like he was ordering the gym class to drop and give him fifty. His curly hair stuck up at odd angles. If Piper just concentrated on certain details—the bright orange polo shirt, the wispy goatee, the whistle around his neck—she could imagine Coach Hedge as his good old annoying self. But it was hard to ignore the stubby horns on his head, and the fact that he had furry goat legs and hooves instead of workout pants and Nikes.

"Yes," the princess said. "I always keep my wares in good condition. We can certainly barter for the storm spirits and the satyr. A package deal. If we come to terms, I'll even throw in the vial of healing potion, and you can go in peace." She gave Piper a shrewd look. "That's better than starting unpleasantness, isn't it, dear?"

Don't trust her, warned a voice in her head. If Piper was right about this lady's identity, nobody would be leaving in peace. A fair deal wasn't possible. It was all a trick. But her friends were looking at her, nodding urgently and mouthing, *Say yes!* Piper needed more to time to think.

"We can negotiate," she said.

"Totally!" Leo agreed. "Name your price."

"Leo!" Piper snapped.

The princess chuckled. "Name my price? Perhaps not the best haggling strategy, my boy, but at least you know a thing's value. Freedom is very valuable indeed. You would ask me to release this satyr, who attacked my storm winds—"

"Who attacked us," Piper interjected.

Her Highness shrugged. "As I said, my patron asks me for small favors from time to time. Sending the storm spirits to abduct you—that was one. I assure you it was nothing personal. And no harm done, as you came here, in the end, of your own free will! At any rate, you want the satyr freed, and you want my storm spirits—who are very valuable servants, by the way—so you can hand them over to that tyrant Aeolus. Doesn't seem quite fair, does it? The price will be high."

Piper could see that her friends were ready to offer anything, promise anything. Before they could speak, she played her last card.

"You're Medea," she said. "You helped the original Jason steal the Golden Fleece. You're one of the most evil villains in Greek mythology. Jason, Leo—don't trust her."

Piper put all the intensity she could gather into those words. She was utterly sincere, and it seemed to have some effect. Jason stepped away from the sorceress.

Leo scratched his head and looked around like he was coming out of a dream.

"What are we doing, again?"

"Boys!" The princess spread her hands in a welcoming gesture. Her diamond jewelry glittered, and her painted fingers curled like blood-tipped claws. "It's true, I'm Medea. But I'm so misunderstood. Oh, Piper, my dear, you don't know what it was like for women in the old days. We had no power, no leverage. Often we couldn't even choose our own husbands. But *I* was different. I chose my own destiny by becoming a sorceress. Is that so wrong? I made a pact with Jason: my help to win the fleece, in exchange for his love. A fair deal. He became a famous hero! Without me, he would've died unknown on the shores of Colchis."

Jason—Piper's Jason—scowled. "Then...you really did die three thousand years ago? You came back from the Underworld?"

"Death no longer holds me, young hero," Medea said. "Thanks to my patron, I am flesh and blood again."

"You...re-formed?" Leo blinked. "Like a monster?"

Medea spread her fingers, and steam hissed from her nails, like water splashed on hot iron. "You have no idea what's happening, do you, my dears? It is so much worse than a stirring of monsters from Tartarus. My patron knows that giants and monsters are not her greatest servants. *I* am mortal. I learn from my mistakes. And now that I have returned to the living, I will not be cheated again. Now, here is my price for what you ask."

"Guys," Piper said. "The original Jason left Medea because she was crazy and bloodthirsty."

"Lies!" Medea said.

"On the way back from Colchis, Jason's ship landed at another kingdom, and Jason agreed to dump Medea and marry the king's daughter."

"After I bore him two children!" Medea said. "Still he broke his promise! I ask you, was that right?"

Jason and Leo dutifully shook their heads, but Piper wasn't through.

"It may not have been right," she said, "but neither was Medea's revenge. She murdered her own children to get back at Jason. She poisoned his new wife and fled the kingdom."

Medea snarled. "An invention to ruin my reputation! The people of the Corinth—that unruly mob—killed my children and drove me out. Jason did nothing to protect me. He robbed me of everything. So yes, I sneaked back into the palace and poisoned his lovely new bride. It was only fair—a suitable price."

"You're insane," Piper said.

"I am the victim!" Medea wailed. "I died with my dreams shattered, but no longer. I know now not to trust heroes. When they come asking for treasures, they will pay a heavy price. Especially when the one asking has the name of Jason!"

The fountain turned bright red. Piper drew her dagger, but her hand was shaking almost too badly to hold it. "Jason, Leo—it's time to go. *Now.*"

"Before you've closed the deal?" Medea asked. "What of your quest, boys? And my price is so easy. Did you know this fountain is magic? If a dead man were to be thrown into it, even if he was chopped to pieces, he would pop back out fully formed—stronger and more powerful than ever."

"Seriously?" Leo asked.

"Leo, she's lying," Piper said. "She did that trick with somebody before—a king, I think. She convinced his daughters to cut him to pieces so he could come out of the water young and healthy again, but it just killed him!"

"Ridiculous," Medea said, and Piper could hear the power charged in every syllable. "Leo, Jason—my price is so simple. Why don't you two fight? If you get injured, or even killed, no problem. We'll just throw you into the fountain and you'll be better than ever. You *do* want to fight, don't you? You resent each other!"

"Guys, no!" Piper said. But they were already glaring at each other, as if it was just dawning on them how they really felt.

Piper had never felt more helpless. Now she understood what real sorcery looked like. She'd always thought magic meant wands and fireballs, but this was worse. Medea didn't just rely on poisons and potions. Her most potent weapon was her voice.

Leo scowled. "Jason's always the star. He always gets the attention and takes me for granted."

"You're annoying, Leo," Jason said. "You never take anything seriously. You can't even fix a dragon."

"Stop!" Piper pleaded, but both drew weapons—Jason his gold sword, and Leo a hammer from his tool belt.

"Let them go, Piper," Medea urged. "I'm doing you a favor. Let it happen now, and it will make your choice so much easier. Enceladus will be pleased. You could have your father back today!"

Medea's charmspeak didn't work on her, but the sorceress still had a persuasive voice. *Her father back today?* Despite her best intentions, Piper wanted that. She wanted her father back so much, it hurt.

"You work for Enceladus," she said.

Medea laughed. "Serve a giant? No. But we all serve the same greater cause—a patron you cannot begin to challenge. Walk away, child of Aphrodite. This does not have to be your death, too. Save yourself, and your father can go free."

Leo and Jason were still facing off, ready to fight, but they looked unsteady and confused—waiting for another order. Part of them had to be resisting, Piper hoped. This went completely against their nature.

"Listen to me, girl." Medea plucked a diamond off her bracelet and threw it into a spray of water from the fountain. As it passed through the multicolored light, Medea said, "O Iris, goddess of the rainbow, show me the office of Tristan McLean."

The mist shimmered, and Piper saw her father's study. Sitting behind his desk, talking on the phone, was her dad's assistant, Jane, in her dark business suit, her hair swirled in a tight bun.

"Hello, Jane," Medea said.

Jane hung up the phone calmly. "How can I help you, ma'am? Hello, Piper."

"You—" Piper was so angry she could hardly talk.

"Yes, child," Medea said. "Your father's assistant. Quite easy to manipulate. An organized mind for a mortal, but incredibly weak."

"Thank you, ma'am," Jane said.

"Don't mention it," Medea said. "I just wanted to congratulate you, Jane. Getting Mr. McLean to leave town so suddenly, take his jet to Oakland without alerting the press or the police—well done! No one seems to know where he's gone. And telling him his daughter's life was on the line— that was a nice touch to get his cooperation."

"Yes," Jane agreed in a bland tone, as if she were sleepwalking. "He was quite cooperative when he believed Piper was in danger."

Piper looked down at her dagger. The blade trembled in her hand. She couldn't use it for a weapon any better than Helen of Troy could, but it was still a looking glass, and what she saw in it was a scared girl with no chance of winning.

"I may have new orders for you, Jane," Medea said. "If the girl cooperates, it may be time for Mr. McLean to come home. Would you arrange a suitable cover story for his absence, just in case? And I imagine the poor man will need some time in a psychiatric hospital."

"Yes, ma'am. I will stand by."

The image faded, and Medea turned to Piper. "There, you see?"

"You lured my dad into a trap," Piper said. "You helped the giant—"

"Oh, please, dear. You'll work yourself into a fit! I've been preparing for this war for years, even before I was brought back to life. I'm a seer, as I said. I can tell the future as well as your little oracle. Years ago, still suffering in the Fields of Punishment, I had a vision of the seven in your so-called Great Prophecy. I saw your friend Leo here, and saw that he would be an important enemy someday. I stirred the consciousness of my patron, gave her this information, and she managed to wake just a little—just enough to visit him."

"Leo's mother," Piper said. "Leo, listen to this! She helped get your mother killed!"

"Uh-huh," Leo mumbled, in a daze. He frowned at his hammer. "So . . . I just attack Jason? That's okay?"

"Perfectly safe," Medea promised. "And Jason, strike him hard. Show me you are worthy of your namesake."

"No!" Piper ordered. She knew it was her last chance. "Jason, Leo—she's tricking you. Put down your weapons."

The sorceress rolled her eyes. "Please, girl. You're no match for me. I trained with my aunt, the immortal Circe. I can drive men mad or heal them with my voice. What hope do these puny young heroes have against me? Now, boys, kill each other!"

"Jason, Leo, listen to me." Piper put all of her emotion into her voice. For years she'd been trying to control herself and not show weakness, but now she poured everything into her words—her fear, her desperation, her anger. She knew she might be signing her dad's death warrant, but she cared too much about her friends to let them hurt each other. "Medea is charming you. It's part of her magic. You are best friends. Don't fight each other. Fight *her*!"

They hesitated, and Piper could feel the spell shatter.

Jason blinked. "Leo, was I just about to stab you?"

"Something about my mother...?" Leo frowned, then turned toward Medea. "You...you're working for Dirt Woman. You sent her to the machine shop." He lifted his arm. "Lady, I got a three-pound hammer with your name on it."

"Bah!" Medea sneered. "I'll simply collect payment another way."

She pressed one of the mosaic tiles on the floor, and the building rumbled. Jason swung his sword at Medea, but she dissolved into smoke and reappeared at the base of the escalator.

"You're slow, hero!" She laughed. "Take your frustration out on my pets!"

Before Jason could go after her, the giant bronze sundials at either end of the fountain swung open. Two snarling gold beasts—flesh-and-blood winged dragons—crawled out from the pits below. Each was the size of a camper van, maybe not large compared to Festus, but large enough.

"So that's what's in the kennels," Leo said meekly.

The dragons spread their wings and hissed. Piper could feel the heat coming off their glittering skin. One turned his angry orange eyes on her.

"Don't look them in the eye!" Jason warned. "They'll paralyze you."

"Indeed!" Medea was leisurely riding the escalator up, leaning against the handrail as she watched the fun. "These two dears have been with me a long time—sun dragons, you know, gifts from my grandfather Helios. They pulled my chariot when I left Corinth, and now they will be your destruction. Ta-ta!"

The dragons lunged. Leo and Jason charged to intercept. Piper was amazed how fearlessly the boys attacked—working like a team who had trained together for years.

Medea was almost to the second floor, where she'd be able to choose from a wide assortment of deadly appliances.

"Oh, no, you don't," Piper growled, and took off after her.

When Medea spotted Piper, she started climbing in earnest. She was quick for a three-thousand-year-old lady. Piper climbed at top speed, taking the steps three at a time, and still she couldn't catch her. Medea didn't stop at floor two. She hopped the next escalator and continued to ascend.

The potions, Piper thought. Of course that's what she would go for. She was famous for potions.

Down below, Piper heard the battle raging. Leo was blowing his safety whistle, and Jason was yelling to keep the dragons' attention. Piper didn't dare look—not while she was running with a dagger in her hand. She could just see herself tripping and stabbing herself in the nose. That would be super heroic.

She grabbed a shield from an armored manikin on floor three and continued to climb. She imagined Coach Hedge yelling in her mind, just like back in gym class at Wilderness School: *Move it, McLean! You call that escalator-climbing?*

She reached the top floor, breathing hard, but she was too late. Medea had reached the potions counter.

The sorceress grabbed a swan-shaped vial—the blue one that caused painful death—and Piper did the only thing that came to mind. She threw her shield.

Medea turned triumphantly just in time to get hit in the chest by a fifty-pound metal Frisbee. She stumbled backward, crashing over the counter, breaking vials and knocking down shelves. When the sorceress stood from the wreckage, her dress was stained a dozen different colors. Many of the stains were smoldering and glowing.

"Fool!" Medea wailed. "Do you have any idea what so many potions will do when mixed?"

"Kill you?" Piper said hopefully.

The carpet began to steam around Medea's feet. She coughed, and her face contorted in pain—or was she faking?

Below, Leo called, "Jason, help!"

Piper risked a quick look, and almost sobbed in despair. One of the dragons had Leo pinned to the floor. It was baring its fangs, ready to snap. Jason was all the way across the room battling the other dragon, much too far away to assist.

"You've doomed us all!" Medea screamed. Smoke was rolling across the carpet as the stain spread, throwing sparks and setting fires in the clothing racks. "You have only seconds before this concoction consumes everything and destroys the building. There's no time—"

CRASH! The stained glass ceiling splintered in a rain of multicolored shards, and Festus the bronze dragon dropped into the department store.

He hurtled into the fray, snatching up a sun dragon in each claw. Only now did Piper appreciate just how big and strong their metal friend was.

"That's my boy!" Leo yelled.

Festus flew halfway up the atrium, then hurled the sun dragons into the pits they'd come from. Leo raced to the fountain and pressed the marble tile, closing the sundials. They shuddered as the dragons banged against them, trying to get out, but for the moment they were contained.

Medea cursed in some ancient language. The whole fourth floor was on fire now. The air filled with noxious gas. Even with the roof open, Piper could feel the heat intensifying. She backed up to the edge of the railing, keeping her dagger pointed toward Medea.

"I will not be abandoned again!" The sorceress knelt and snatched up the red healing potion, which had somehow survived the crash. "You want your boyfriend's memory restored? Take me with you!"

Piper glanced behind her. Leo and Jason were on board Festus's back. The bronze dragon flapped his mighty wings, snatched the two cages with the satyr and the storm spirits in his claws, and began to ascend.

The building rumbled. Fire and the smoke curled up the walls, melting the railings, turning the air to acid.

"You'll never survive your quest without me!" Medea growled. "Your boy hero will stay ignorant forever, and your father will die. Take me with you!"

For one heartbeat, Piper was tempted. Then she saw Medea's grim smile. The sorceress was confident in her powers of persuasion, confident that she could always make a deal, always escape and win in the end.

"Not today, witch." Piper jumped over the side. She plummeted for only a second before Leo and Jason caught her, hauling her aboard the dragon.

She heard Medea screaming in rage as they soared through the broken roof and over downtown Chicago. Then the department store exploded behind them.

XXIX

LEO

LEO KEPT LOOKING BACK. HE HALF EXPECTED to see those nasty sun dragons toting a flying chariot with a screaming magical saleswoman throwing potions, but nothing followed them.

He steered the dragon toward the southwest. Eventually, the smoke from the burning department store faded in the distance, but Leo didn't relax until the suburbs of Chicago gave way to snowy fields, and the sun began to set.

"Good job, Festus." He patted the dragon's metal hide. "You did awesome."

The dragon shuddered. Gears popped and clicked in his neck.

Leo frowned. He didn't like those noises. If the control disk was failing again—No, hopefully it was something minor. Something he could fix.

"I'll give you a tune-up next time we land," Leo promised. "You've earned some motor oil and Tabasco sauce."

Festus whirled his teeth, but even that sounded weak. He flew at a steady pace, his great wings angling to catch the wind, but he was carrying a heavy load. Two cages in his claws plus three people on his back—the more Leo thought about it, the more worried he got. Even metal dragons had limits.

"Leo." Piper patted his shoulder. "You feeling okay?"

"Yeah . . . not bad for a brainwashed zombie." He hoped he didn't look as embarrassed as he felt. "Thanks for saving us back there, beauty queen. If you hadn't talked me out of that spell—"

"Don't worry about it," Piper said.

But Leo worried a lot. He felt terrible about how easily Medea had set him against his best friend. And those feelings hadn't come from nowhere—his resentment of the way Jason always got the spotlight and didn't really seem to need him. Leo did feel that way sometimes, even if he wasn't proud of it.

What bothered him more was the news about his mom. Medea had seen the future down in the Underworld. That was how her patron, the woman in the black earthen robes, had come to the machine shop seven years ago to scare him, ruin his life. That's how his mother had died—because of something Leo might do someday. So in a weird way, even if his fire powers weren't to blame, Mom's death was *still* his fault.

When they had left Medea in that exploding store, Leo had felt a little too good. He hoped she wouldn't make it out, and would go right back to the Fields of Punishment, where she belonged. Those feelings didn't make him proud, either.

And if souls were coming back from the Underworld . . . was it possible Leo's mom could be brought back?

He tried to put the idea aside. That was Frankenstein thinking. It wasn't natural. It wasn't right. Medea might've been brought back to life, but she hadn't seemed quite human, with the hissing nails and the glowing head and whatnot.

No, Leo's mom had passed on. Thinking any other way would just drive Leo nuts. Still, the thought kept poking at him, like an echo of Medea's voice.

"We're going to have to put down soon," he warned his friends. "Couple more hours, maybe, to make sure Medea's not following us. I don't think Festus can fly much longer than that."

"Yeah," Piper agreed. "Coach Hedge probably wants to get out of his canary cage, too. Question is—where are we going?"

"The Bay Area," Leo guessed. His memories of the department store were fuzzy, but he seemed to remember hearing that. "Didn't Medea say something about Oakland?"

Piper didn't respond for so long, Leo wondered if he'd said something wrong.

"Piper's dad," Jason put in. "Something's happened to your dad, right? He got lured into some kind of trap."

Piper let out a shaky breath. "Look, Medea said you would both *die* in the Bay Area. And besides... even if we went there, the Bay Area is huge! First we need to find Aeolus and drop off the storm spirits. Boreas said Aeolus was the only one who could tell us exactly where to go."

Leo grunted. "So how do we find Aeolus?"

Jason leaned forward. "You mean you don't see it?" He pointed ahead of them, but Leo didn't see anything except clouds and the lights of a few towns glowing in the dusk.

"What?" Leo asked.

"That...whatever it is," Jason said. "In the air."

Leo glanced back. Piper looked just as confused as he was.

"Right," Leo said. "Could you be more specific on the 'whatever-it-is' part?"

"Like a vapor trail," Jason said. "Except it's glowing. Really faint, but it's definitely there. We've been following it since Chicago, so I figured you saw it."

Leo shook his head. "Maybe Festus can sense it. You think Aeolus made it?"

"Well, it's a magic trail in the wind," Jason said. "Aeolus is the wind god. I think he knows we've got prisoners for him. He's telling us where to fly."

"Or it's another trap," Piper said.

Her tone worried Leo. She didn't just sound nervous. She sounded broken with despair, like they'd already sealed their fate, and like it was her fault.

"Pipes, you all right?" he asked.

"Don't call me that."

"Okay, fine. You don't like any of the names I make up for you. But if your dad's in trouble and we can help—"

"You can't," she said, her voice getting shakier. "Look, I'm tired. If you don't mind..."

She leaned back against Jason and closed her eyes.

All right, Leo thought—pretty clear signal she didn't want to talk.

They flew in silence for a while. Festus seemed to know where he was going. He kept his course, gently curving toward the southwest and hopefully Aeolus's fortress. Another wind god to visit, a whole new flavor of crazy— Oh, boy, Leo couldn't wait.

He had way too much on his mind to sleep, but now that he was out of danger, his body had different ideas. His energy level was crashing. The monotonous beat of the dragon's wings made his eyes feel heavy. His head started to nod.

"Catch a few Z's," Jason said. "It's cool. Hand me the reins."

"Nah, I'm okay—"

"Leo," Jason said, "you're not a machine. Besides, I'm the only one who can see the vapor trail. I'll make sure we stay on course."

Leo's eyes started to close on their own. "All right. Maybe just..."

He didn't finish the sentence before slumping forward against the dragon's warm neck.

In his dream, he heard a voice full of static, like a bad AM radio: "Hello? Is this thing working?"

Leo's vision came into focus—sort of. Everything was hazy and gray, with bands of interference running across his sight. He'd never dreamed with a bad connection before.

He seemed to be in a workshop. Out of the corners of his eyes he saw bench saws, metal lathes, and tool cages. A forge glowed cheerfully against one wall.

It wasn't the camp forge—too big. Not Bunker 9—much warmer and more comfortable, obviously not abandoned.

Then Leo realized something was blocking the middle of his view—something large and fuzzy, and so close, Leo had to cross his eyes to see it properly. It was a large ugly face.

"Holy mother!" he yelped.

The face backed away and came into focus. Staring down at him was a bearded man in grimy blue coveralls. His face was lumpy and covered with welts, as if he'd been bitten by a million bees, or dragged across gravel. Possibly both.

"Humph," the man said. "Holy *father*, boy. I should think you'd know the difference."

Leo blinked. "Hephaestus?"

Being in the presence of his father for the first time, Leo probably should've been speechless or awestruck or something. But after what he'd been through the last couple of days, with Cyclopes and a sorceress and a face in the potty sludge, all Leo felt was a surge of complete annoyance.

"Now you show up?" he demanded. "After fifteen years? Great parenting, Fur Face. Where do you get off sticking your ugly nose into my dreams?"

The god raised an eyebrow. A little spark caught fire in his beard. Then he threw back his head and laughed so loudly, the tools rattled on the workbenches.

"You sound just like your mother," Hephaestus said. "I miss Esperanza."

"She's been dead seven years." Leo's voice trembled. "Not that you'd care."

"But I do care, boy. About both of you."

"Uh-huh. Which is why I never saw you before today."

The god made a rumbling sound in his throat, but he looked more uncomfortable than angry. He pulled a miniature motor from his pocket and began fiddling absently with the pistons—just the way Leo did when he was nervous.

"I'm not good with children," the god confessed. "Or people. Well, any organic life forms, really. I thought about speaking to you at your mom's funeral. Then again when you were in fifth grade...that science project you made, steam-powered chicken chucker. Very impressive."

"You saw that?"

Hephaestus pointed to the nearest worktable, where a shiny bronze mirror showed a hazy image of Leo asleep on the dragon's back.

"Is that me?" Leo asked. "Like—me right now, having this dream—looking at me having a dream?"

Hephaestus scratched his beard. "Now you've confused me. But yes—it's you. I'm always keeping an eye on you, Leo. But talking to you is, um...different."

"You're scared," Leo said.

"Grommets and gears!" the god yelled. "Of course not!"

"Yeah, you're scared." But Leo's anger seeped away. He'd spent years thinking about what he'd say to his dad if they ever met—how Leo would chew him out for being a dead beat. Now, looking at that bronze mirror, Leo thought about his dad watching his progress over the years, even his stupid science experiments.

Maybe Hephaestus was still a jerk, but Leo kind of understood where he was coming from. Leo knew about running away from people, not fitting in. He knew about hiding out in a workshop rather than trying to deal with organic life forms.

"So," Leo grumbled, "you keep track of all your kids? You got like twelve back at camp. How'd you even— Never mind. I don't want to know."

Hephaestus might've blushed, but his face was so beat up and red, it was hard to tell. "Gods are different from mortals, boy. We can exist in many places at once—wherever people call on us, wherever our sphere of influence is strong. In fact, it's rare our entire essence is ever together in one place—our true form. It's dangerous, powerful enough to destroy any mortal who looks upon us. So, yes...lots of children. Add to that our different aspects, Greek and Roman—" The god's fingers froze on his engine project. "Er, that is to say, being a god is complicated. And yes, I try to keep an eye on all my children, but you especially."

Leo was pretty sure Hephaestus had almost slipped and said something important, but he wasn't sure what.

"Why contact me now?" Leo asked. "I thought the gods had gone silent."

"We have," Hephaestus grumped. "Zeus's orders—very strange, even for him. He's blocked all visions, dreams, and Iris-messages to and from Olympus. Hermes is sitting around bored out of his mind because he can't deliver the mail. Fortunately, I kept my old pirate broadcasting equipment."

Hephaestus patted a machine on the table. It looked like a combination satellite dish, V-6 engine, and espresso maker. Each time Hephaestus jostled the machine, Leo's dream flickered and changed color.

"Used this in the Cold War," the god said fondly. "Radio Free Hephaestus. Those were the days. I keep it around for pay-for-view, mostly, or making viral brain videos—"

"Viral brain videos?"

"But now it's come in handy again. If Zeus knew I was contacting you, he'd have my hide."

"Why is Zeus being such a jerk?"

"Hrumph. He excels at that, boy." Hephaestus called him *boy* as if Leo were an annoying machine part—an extra washer, maybe, that had no clear purpose, but that Hephaestus didn't want to throw away for fear he might need it someday.

Not exactly heartwarming. Then again, Leo wasn't sure he wanted to be called "son." Leo wasn't about to start calling this big awkward ugly guy "Dad."

Hephaestus got tired of his engine and tossed it over his shoulder. Before it could hit the floor, it sprouted helicopter wings and flew itself into a recycling bin.

"It was the second Titan War, I suppose," Hephaestus said. "That's what got Zeus upset. We gods were...well, embarrassed. Don't think there's any other way to say it."

"But you won," Leo said.

The god grunted. "We won because the demigods of"—again he hesitated, as if he'd almost made a slip—"of Camp Half-Blood took the lead. We won because our children fought our battles for us, smarter than we did. If we'd relied on Zeus's plan, we would've all gone down to Tartarus fighting the storm giant Typhon, and Kronos would've won. Bad enough mortals won our war for us, but then that young upstart, Percy Jackson—"

"The guy who's missing."

"Hmph. Yes. Him. He had the nerve to turn down our

offer of immortality and tell us to pay better attention to our children. Er, no offense."

"Oh, how could I take offense? Please, go on ignoring me."

"Mighty understanding of you..." Hephaestus frowned, then sighed wearily. "That was sarcasm, wasn't it? Machines don't have sarcasm, usually. But as I was saying, the gods felt ashamed, shown up by mortals. At first, of course, we were grateful. But after a few months, those feelings turned bitter. We're gods, after all. We need to be admired, looked up to, held in awe and admiration."

"Even if you're wrong?"

"Especially then! And to have Jackson refuse our gift, as if being mortal were somehow *better* than being a god... well, that stuck in Zeus's craw. He decided it was high time we got back to traditional values. Gods were to be respected. Our children were to be seen and not visited. Olympus was closed. At least that was *part* of his reasoning. And, of course, we started hearing of bad things stirring under the earth."

"The giants, you mean. Monsters re-forming instantly. The dead rising again. Little stuff like that?"

"Aye, boy." Hephaestus turned a knob on his pirate broadcasting machine. Leo's dream sharpened to full color, but the god's face was such a riot of red welts and yellow and black bruises, Leo wished it would go back to black and white.

"Zeus thinks he can reverse the tide," the god said, "lull the earth back to sleep as long as we stay quiet. None of us really believes that. And I don't mind saying, we're in no shape to fight another war. We barely survived the Titans. If we're repeating the old pattern, what comes next is even worse."

"The giants," Leo said. "Hera said demigods and gods had to join forces to defeat them. Is that true?"

"Mmm. I hate to agree with my mother about anything, but yes. Those giants are tough to kill, boy. They're a different breed."

"Breed? You make them sound like racehorses."

"Ha!" the god said. "More like war dogs. Back in the beginning, y'see, everything in creation came from the same parents—Gaea and Ouranos, Earth and Sky. They had their different batches of children—your Titans, your Elder Cyclopes, and so forth. Then Kronos, the head Titan—well, you've probably heard how he chopped up his father Ouranos with a scythe and took over the world. Then we gods came along, children of the Titans, and defeated *them*. But that wasn't the end of it. The earth bore a new batch of children, except they were sired by Tartarus, the spirit of the eternal abyss—the darkest, most evil place in the Underworld. Those children, the giants, were bred for one purpose—revenge on *us* for the fall of the Titans. They rose up to destroy Olympus, and they came awfully close."

Hephaestus's beard began to smolder. He absently swatted out the flames. "What my blasted mother Hera is doing now—she's a meddling fool playing a dangerous game, but she's right about one thing: you demigods have to unite. That's the only way to open Zeus's eyes, convince the Olympians they must accept your help. And that's the only way to defeat what's coming. You're a big part of that, Leo. "

The god's gaze seemed far away. Leo wondered if he really could split himself into different parts—where else was he right now? Maybe his Greek side was fixing a car or going on a date, while his Roman side was watching a ball game and ordering pizza. Leo tried to imagine what it would feel like to have multiple personalities. He hoped it wasn't hereditary.

"Why me?" he asked, and as soon as he said it, more questions flooded out. "Why claim me now? Why not when I was thirteen, like you're supposed to? Or you could've claimed me at seven, before my mom died! Why didn't you find me earlier? Why didn't you warn me about *this*?"

Leo's hand burst into flames.

Hephaestus regarded him sadly. "Hardest part, boy. Letting my children walk their own paths. Interfering doesn't work. The Fates make sure of that. As for the claiming, you were a special case, boy. The timing had to be right. I can't explain it much more, but—"

Leo's dream went fuzzy. Just for a moment, it turned into a rerun of *Wheel of Fortune*. Then Hephaestus came back into focus.

"Blast," he said. "I can't talk much longer. Zeus is sensing an illegal dream. He is lord of the air, after all, including the airwaves. Just listen, boy: you have a role to play. Your friend Jason is right—fire is a gift, not a curse. I don't give that blessing to just anyone. They'll never defeat the giants without you, much less the mistress they serve. She's worse than any god or Titan."

"Who?" Leo demanded.

Hephaestus frowned, his image becoming fuzzier. "I told you. Yes, I'm pretty sure I told you. Just be warned: along the way, you're going to lose some friends and some valuable tools.

But that isn't your fault, Leo. Nothing lasts forever, not even the best machines. And everything can be reused."

"What do you mean? I don't like the sound of that."

"No, you shouldn't." Hephaestus's image was barely visible now, just a blob in the static. "Just watch out for—"

Leo's dream switched to *Wheel of Fortune* just as the wheel hit Bankrupt and the audience said, "Awwww!"

Then Leo snapped awake to Jason and Piper screaming.

X X X

LEO

THEY SPIRALED THROUGH THE DARK in a free fall, still on the dragon's back, but Festus's hide was cold. His ruby eyes were dim.

"Not again!" Leo yelled. "You can't fall again!"

He could barely hold on. The wind stung his eyes, but he managed to pull open the panel on the dragon's neck. He toggled the switches. He tugged the wires. The dragon's wings flapped once, but Leo caught a whiff of burning bronze. The drive system was overloaded. Festus didn't have the strength to keep flying, and Leo couldn't get to the main control panel on the dragon's head—not in midair. He saw the lights of a city below them—just flashes in the dark as they plummeted in circles. They had only seconds before they crashed.

"Jason!" he screamed. "Take Piper and fly out of here!"

"What?"

"We need to lighten the load! I might be able to reboot Festus, but he's carrying too much weight!"

"What about you?" Piper cried. "If you can't reboot him—"

"I'll be fine," Leo yelled. "Just follow me to the ground. Go!"

Jason grabbed Piper around the waist. They both unbuckled their harnesses, and in a flash they were gone—shooting into the air.

"Now," Leo said. "Just you and me, Festus—and two heavy cages. You can do it, boy!"

Leo talked to the dragon while he worked, falling at terminal velocity. He could see the city lights below him, getting closer and closer. He summoned fire in his hand so he could see what he was doing, but the wind kept extinguishing it.

He pulled a wire that he thought connected the dragon's nerve center to its head, hoping for a little wake-up jolt.

Festus groaned—metal creaking inside his neck. His eyes flickered weakly to life, and he spread his wings. Their fall turned into a steep glide.

"Good!" Leo said. "Come on, big boy. Come on!"

They were still flying in way too hot, and the ground was too close. Leo needed a place to land—fast.

There was a big river—no. Not good for a fire-breathing dragon. He'd never get Festus out from the bottom if he sank, especially in freezing temperatures. Then, on the riverbanks, Leo spotted a white mansion with a huge snowy lawn inside a tall brick perimeter fence—like some rich person's private compound, all of it blazing with light. A perfect landing field. He did his best to steer the dragon toward it, and Festus seemed to come back to life. They could make this!

Then everything went wrong. As they approached the

lawn, spotlights along the fence fixed on them, blinding Leo. He heard bursts like tracer fire, the sound of metal being cut to shreds—and *BOOM*.

Leo blacked out.

When Leo came to his senses, Jason and Piper were leaning over him. He was lying in the snow, covered in mud and grease. He spit a clump of frozen grass out of his mouth.

"Where—"

"Lie still." Piper had tears in her eyes. "You rolled pretty hard when—when Festus—"

"Where is he?" Leo sat up, but his head felt like it was floating. They'd landed inside the compound. Something had happened on the way in—gunfire?

"Seriously, Leo," Jason said. "You could be hurt. You shouldn't—"

Leo pushed himself to his feet. Then he saw the wreckage. Festus must have dropped the big canary cages as he came over the fence, because they'd rolled in different directions and landed on their sides, perfectly undamaged.

Festus hadn't been so lucky.

The dragon had disintegrated. His limbs were scattered across the lawn. His tail hung on the fence. The main section of his body had plowed a trench twenty feet wide and fifty feet long across the mansion's yard before breaking apart. What remained of his hide was a charred, smoking pile of scraps. Only his neck and head were somewhat intact, resting across a row of frozen rosebushes like a pillow.

"No," Leo sobbed. He ran to the dragon's head and stroked

its snout. The dragon's eyes flickered weakly. Oil leaked out of his ear.

"You can't go," Leo pleaded. "You're the best thing I ever fixed."

The dragon's head whirred its gears, as if it were purring. Jason and Piper stood next to him, but Leo kept his eyes fixed on the dragon.

He remembered what Hephaestus had said: *That isn't your fault, Leo. Nothing lasts forever, not even the best machines.*

His dad had been trying to warn him.

"It's not fair," he said.

The dragon clicked. Long *creak*. Two short *clicks. Creak. Creak.* Almost like a pattern ... triggering an old memory in Leo's mind. Leo realized Festus was trying to say something. He was using Morse code—just like Leo's mom had taught him years ago. Leo listened more intently, translating the clicks into letters: a simple message repeating over and over.

"Yeah," Leo said. "I understand. I will. I promise."

The dragon's eyes went dark. Festus was gone.

Leo cried. He wasn't even embarrassed. His friends stood on either side, patting his shoulders, saying comforting things; but the buzzing in Leo's ears drowned out their words.

Finally Jason said, "I'm so sorry, man. What did you promise Festus?"

Leo sniffled. He opened the dragon's head panel, just to be sure, but the control disk was cracked and burned beyond repair.

"Something my dad told me," Leo said. "Everything can be reused."

"Your dad talked to you?" Jason asked. "When was this?"

Leo didn't answer. He worked at the dragon's neck hinges until the head was detached. It weighed about a hundred pounds, but Leo managed to hold it in his arms. He looked up at the starry sky and said, "Take him back to the bunker, Dad. Please, until I can reuse him. I've never asked you for anything."

The wind picked up, and the dragon's head floated out of Leo's arms like it weighed nothing. It flew into the sky and disappeared.

Piper looked at him in amazement. "He *answered* you?"

"I had a dream," Leo managed. "Tell you later."

He knew he owed his friends a better explanation, but Leo could barely speak. He felt like a broken machine himself —like someone had removed one little part of him, and now he'd never be complete. He might move, he might talk, he might keep going and do his job. But he'd always be off balance, never calibrated exactly right.

Still, he couldn't afford to break down completely. Otherwise, Festus had died for nothing. He had to finish this quest —for his friends, for his mom, for his dragon.

He looked around. The large white mansion glowed in the center of the grounds. Tall brick walls with lights and security cameras surrounded the perimeter, but now Leo could see —or rather *sense*—just how well those walls were defended.

"Where are we?" he asked. "I mean, what city?"

"Omaha, Nebraska," Piper said. "I saw a billboard as we flew in. But I don't know what this mansion is. We came in right behind you, but as you were landing, Leo, I swear it looked like—I don't know—"

"Lasers," Leo said. He picked up a piece of dragon wreckage and threw it toward the top of the fence. Immediately a turret popped up from the brick wall and a beam of pure heat incinerated the bronze plating to ashes.

Jason whistled. "Some defense system. How are we even alive?"

"Festus," Leo said miserably. "He took the fire. The lasers sliced him to bits as he came in so they didn't focus on you. I led him into a death trap."

"You couldn't have known," Piper said. "He saved our lives again."

"But what now?" Jason said. "The main gates are locked, and I'm guessing I can't fly us out of here without getting shot down."

Leo looked up the walkway at the big white mansion. "Since we can't go out, we'll have to go in."

XXXI

JASON

JASON WOULD'VE DIED FIVE TIMES on the way to the front door if not for Leo.

First it was the motion-activated trapdoor on the sidewalk, then the lasers on the steps, then the nerve gas dispenser on the porch railing, the pressure-sensitive poison spikes in the welcome mat, and of course the exploding doorbell.

Leo deactivated all of them. It was like he could smell the traps, and he picked just the right tool out of his belt to disable them.

"You're amazing, man," Jason said.

Leo scowled as he examined the front door lock. "Yeah, amazing," he said. "Can't fix a dragon right, but I'm amazing."

"Hey, that wasn't your—"

"Front door's already unlocked," Leo announced.

Piper stared at the door in disbelief. "It is? All those traps, and the *door's* unlocked?"

Leo turned the knob. The door swung open easily. He stepped inside without hesitation.

Before Jason could follow, Piper caught his arm. "He's going to need some time to get over Festus. Don't take it personally."

"Yeah," Jason said. "Yeah, okay."

But still he felt terrible. Back in Medea's store, he'd said some pretty harsh stuff to Leo—stuff a friend shouldn't say, not to mention the fact he'd almost skewered Leo with a sword. If it hadn't been for Piper, they'd both be dead. And Piper hadn't gotten out of that encounter easily, either.

"Piper," he said, "I know I was in a daze back in Chicago, but that stuff about your dad—if he's in trouble, I want to help. I don't care if it's a trap or not."

Her eyes were always different colors, but now they looked shattered, as if she'd seen something she just couldn't cope with. "Jason, you don't know what you're saying. Please—don't make me feel worse. Come on. We should stick together."

She ducked inside.

"Together," Jason said to himself. "Yeah, we're doing great with that."

Jason's first impression of the house: Dark.

From the echo of his footsteps he could tell the entry hall was enormous, even bigger than Boreas's penthouse; but the only illumination came from the yard lights outside. A faint glow peeked through the breaks in the thick velvet curtains. The windows rose about ten feet tall. Spaced between them along the walls were life-size metal statues. As Jason's eyes adjusted, he saw sofas arranged in a U in the middle of the room, with a central coffee table and one large chair at the far end. A massive chandelier glinted overhead. Along the back wall stood a row of closed doors.

"Where's the light switch?" His voice echoed alarmingly through the room.

"Don't see one," Leo said.

"Fire?" Piper suggested.

Leo held out his hand, but nothing happened. "It's not working."

"Your fire is out? Why?" Piper asked.

"Well, if I knew that—"

"Okay, okay," she said. "What do we do—explore?"

Leo shook his head. "After all those traps outside? Bad idea."

Jason's skin tingled. He hated being a demigod. Looking around, he didn't see a comfortable room to hang out in. He imagined vicious storm spirits lurking in the curtains, dragons under the carpet, a chandelier made of lethal ice shards, ready to impale them.

"Leo's right," he said. "We're not separating again—not like in Detroit."

"Oh, thank you for reminding me of the Cyclopes." Piper's voice quavered. "I needed that."

"It's a few hours until dawn," Jason guessed. "Too cold to wait outside. Let's bring the cages in and make camp in this room. Wait for daylight; then we can decide what to do."

Nobody offered a better idea, so they rolled in the cages

with Coach Hedge and the storm spirits, then settled in. Thankfully, Leo didn't find any poison throw pillows or electric whoopee cushions on the sofas.

Leo didn't seem in the mood to make more tacos. Besides, they had no fire, so they settled for cold rations.

As Jason ate, he studied the metal statues along the walls. They looked like Greek gods or heroes. Maybe that was a good sign. Or maybe they were used for target practice. On the coffee table sat a tea service and a stack of glossy brochures, but Jason couldn't make out the words. The big chair at the other end of the table looked like a throne. None of them tried to sit in it.

The canary cages didn't make the place any less creepy. The *venti* kept churning in their prison, hissing and spinning, and Jason got the uncomfortable feeling they were watching him. He could sense their hatred for the children of Zeus—the lord of the sky who'd ordered Aeolus to imprison their kind. The *venti* would like nothing better than to tear Jason apart.

As for Coach Hedge, he was still frozen mid-shout, his cudgel raised. Leo was working on the cage, trying to open it with various tools, but the lock seemed to be giving him a hard time. Jason decided not to sit next to him in case Hedge suddenly unfroze and went into ninja goat mode.

Despite how wired he felt, once his stomach was full, Jason started to nod off. The couches were a little too comfortable —a lot better than a dragon's back—and he'd taken the last two watches while his friends slept. He was exhausted.

Piper had already curled up on the other sofa. Jason wondered if she was really asleep or dodging a conversation about her dad. Whatever Medea had meant in Chicago, about Piper getting her dad back if she cooperated—it didn't sound good. If Piper had risked her own dad to save them, that made Jason feel even guiltier.

And they were running out of time. If Jason had his days straight, this was early morning of December 20. Which meant tomorrow was the winter solstice.

"Get some sleep," Leo said, still working on the locked cage. "It's your turn."

Jason took a deep breath. "Leo, I'm sorry about that stuff I said in Chicago. That wasn't me. You're not annoying and you *do* take stuff seriously—especially your work. I wish I could do half the things you can do."

Leo lowered his screwdriver. He looked at the ceiling and shook his head like, *What am I gonna do with this guy?*

"I try very hard to be annoying," Leo said. "Don't insult my ability to *annoy*. And how am I supposed to resent you if you go apologizing? I'm a lowly mechanic. You're like the prince of the sky, son of the Lord of the Universe. I'm *supposed* to resent you."

"Lord of the Universe?"

"Sure, you're all—*bam!* Lightning man. And 'Watch me fly. I am the eagle that soars—'"

"Shut up, Valdez."

Leo managed a little smile. "Yeah, see. I *do* annoy you."

"I apologize for apologizing."

"Thank you." He went back to work, but the tension had eased between them. Leo still looked sad and exhausted—just not quite so angry.

"Go to sleep, Jason," he ordered. "It's gonna take a few hours to get this goat man free. Then I still got to figure out how to make the winds a smaller holding cell, 'cause I am *not* lugging that canary cage to California."

"You did fix Festus, you know," Jason said. "You gave him a purpose again. I think this quest was the high point of his life."

Jason was afraid he'd blown it and made Leo mad again, but Leo just sighed.

"I hope," he said. "Now, sleep, man. I want some time without you organic life forms."

Jason wasn't quite sure what that meant, but he didn't argue. He closed his eyes and had a long, blissfully dreamless sleep.

He only woke when the yelling started.

"Ahhhgggggggh!"

Jason leaped to his feet. He wasn't sure what was more jarring—the full sunlight that now bathed the room, or the screaming satyr.

"Coach is awake," Leo said, which was kind of unnecessary. Gleeson Hedge was capering around on his furry hindquarters, swinging his club and yelling, "Die!" as he smashed the tea set, whacked the sofas, and charged at the throne.

"Coach!" Jason yelled.

Hedge turned, breathing hard. His eyes were so wild, Jason was afraid he might attack. The satyr was still wearing his orange polo shirt and his coach's whistle, but his horns were clearly visible above his curly hair, and his beefy hindquarters were definitely all goat. Could you call a goat *beefy*? Jason put the thought aside.

"You're the new kid," Hedge said, lowering his club. "Jason." He looked at Leo, then Piper, who'd apparently also just woken up. Her hair looked like it had become a nest for a friendly hamster.

"Valdez, McLean," the coach said. "What's going on? We were at the Grand Canyon. The *anemoi thuellai* were attacking and—" He zeroed in on the storm spirit cage, and his eyes went back to DEFCON 1. "Die!"

"Whoa, Coach!" Leo stepped in his path, which was pretty brave, even though Hedge was six inches shorter. "It's okay. They're locked up. We just sprang you from the other cage."

"Cage? Cage? What's going on? Just because I'm a satyr doesn't mean I can't have you doing plank push-ups, Valdez!"

Jason cleared his throat. "Coach—Gleeson—um, whatever you want us to call you. You saved us at the Grand Canyon. You were totally brave."

"Of course I was!"

"The extraction team came and took us to Camp Half-Blood. We thought we'd lost you. Then we got word the storm spirits had taken you back to their—um, operator, Medea."

"That witch! Wait—that's impossible. She's mortal. She's dead."

"Yeah, well," Leo said, "somehow she got not dead anymore."

Hedge nodded, his eyes narrowing. "So! You were sent on a dangerous quest to rescue me. Excellent!"

"Um." Piper got to her feet, holding out her hands so Coach Hedge wouldn't attack her. "Actually, Glee—can I still call you Coach Hedge? Gleeson seems *wrong*. We're on a quest for something else. We kind of found you by accident."

"Oh." The coach's spirits seemed to deflate, but only for a second. Then his eyes lit up again. "But there are no accidents! Not on quests. This was *meant* to happen! So, this is the witch's lair, eh? Why is everything gold?"

"Gold?" Jason looked around. From the way Leo and Piper caught their breath, he guessed they hadn't noticed yet either.

The room was full of gold—the statues, the tea set Hedge had smashed, the chair that was definitely a throne. Even the curtains—which seemed to have opened by themselves at daybreak—appeared to be woven of gold fiber.

"Nice," Leo said. "No wonder they got so much security."

"This isn't—" Piper stammered. "This isn't Medea's place, Coach. It's some rich person's mansion in Omaha. We got away from Medea and crash-landed here."

"It's destiny, cupcakes!" Hedge insisted. "I'm meant to protect you. What's the quest?"

Before Jason could decide if he wanted to explain or just shove Coach Hedge back into his cage, a door opened at the far end of the room.

A pudgy man in a white bathrobe stepped out with a golden toothbrush in his mouth. He had a white beard and one of those long, old-fashioned sleeping caps pressed down over his white hair. He froze when he saw them, and the toothbrush fell out of his mouth.

He glanced into the room behind him and called, "Son? Lit, come out here, please. There are strange people in the throne room."

Coach Hedge did the obvious thing. He raised his club and shouted, "Die!"

XXXII

JASON

IT TOOK ALL THREE OF THEM to hold back the satyr.

"Whoa, Coach!" Jason said. "Bring it down a few notches."

A younger man charged into the room. Jason guessed he must be Lit, the old guy's son. He was dressed in pajama pants with a sleeveless T-shirt that said CORNHUSKERS, and he held a sword that looked like it could husk a lot of things besides corn. His ripped arms were covered in scars, and his face, framed by curly dark hair, would've been handsome if it wasn't also sliced up.

Lit immediately zeroed in on Jason like he was the biggest threat, and stalked toward him, swinging his sword overhead.

"Hold on!" Piper stepped forward, trying for her best calming voice. "This is just a misunderstanding! Everything's fine."

Lit stopped in his tracks, but he still looked wary.

It didn't help that Hedge was screaming, "I'll get them! Don't worry!"

"Coach," Jason pleaded, "they may be friendly. Besides, we're trespassing in their house."

"Thank you!" said the old man in the bathrobe. "Now, who are you, and why are you here?"

"Let's all put our weapons down," Piper said. "Coach, you first."

Hedge clenched his jaw. "Just one thwack?"

"No," Piper said.

"What about a compromise? I'll kill them first, and if it turns out they were friendly, I'll apologize."

"No!" Piper insisted.

"Meh." Coach Hedge lowered his club.

Piper gave Lit a friendly *sorry-about-that* smile. Even with her hair messed up and wearing two-day-old clothes, she looked extremely cute, and Jason felt a little jealous she was giving Lit that smile.

Lit huffed and sheathed his sword. "You speak well, girl—fortunately for your friends, or I would've run them through."

"Appreciate it," Leo said. "I try not to get run through before lunchtime."

The old man in the bathrobe sighed, kicking the teapot that Coach Hedge had smashed. "Well, since you're here. Please, sit down."

Lit frowned. "Your Majesty—"

"No, no, it's fine, Lit," the old man said. "New land, new customs. They may sit in my presence. After all, they've seen me in my nightclothes. No sense observing formalities." He did his best to smile, though it looked a little forced. "Welcome to my humble home. I am King Midas."

* * *

"Midas? Impossible," said Coach Hedge. "He died."

They were sitting on the sofas now, while the king reclined on his throne. Tricky to do that in a bathrobe, and Jason kept worrying the old guy would forget and uncross his legs. Hopefully he was wearing golden boxers under there.

Lit stood behind the throne, both hands on his sword, glancing at Piper and flexing his muscular arms just to be annoying. Jason wondered if *he* looked that ripped holding a sword. Sadly, he doubted it.

Piper sat forward. "What our satyr friend means, Your Majesty, is that you're the second mortal we've met who should be—sorry—dead. King Midas lived thousands of years ago."

"Interesting." The king gazed out the windows at the brilliant blue skies and the winter sunlight. In the distance, downtown Omaha looked like a cluster of children's blocks —way too clean and small for a regular city.

"You know," the king said, "I think I *was* a bit dead for a while. It's strange. Seems like a dream, doesn't it, Lit?"

"A very long dream, Your Majesty."

"And yet, now we're here. I'm enjoying myself very much. I like being alive better."

"But how?" Piper asked. "You didn't happen to have a... patron?"

Midas hesitated, but there was a sly twinkle in his eyes. "Does it matter, my dear?"

"We could kill them again," Hedge suggested.

"Coach, not helping," Jason said. "Why don't you go outside and stand guard?"

Leo coughed. "Is that safe? They've got some serious security."

"Oh, yes," the king said. "Sorry about that. But it's lovely stuff, isn't it? Amazing what gold can still buy. Such excellent toys you have in this country!"

He fished a remote control out of his bathrobe pocket and pressed a few buttons—a pass code, Jason guessed.

"There," Midas said. "Safe to go out now."

Coach Hedge grunted. "Fine. But if you need me..." He winked at Jason meaningfully. Then he pointed at himself, pointed two fingers at their hosts, and sliced a finger across his throat. Very subtle sign language.

"Yeah, thanks," Jason said.

After the satyr left, Piper tried another diplomatic smile. "So...you don't know how you got here?"

"Oh, well, yes. Sort of," the king said. He frowned at Lit. "Why did we pick Omaha, again? I know it wasn't the weather."

"The oracle," Lit said.

"Yes! I was told there was an oracle in Omaha." The king shrugged. "Apparently I was mistaken. But this is a rather nice house, isn't it? Lit—it's short for Lityerses, by the way—horrible name, but his mother insisted—Lit has plenty of wide-open space to practice his swordplay. He has quite a reputation for that. They called him the Reaper of Men back in the old days."

"Oh." Piper tried to sound enthusiastic. "How nice."

Lit's smile was more of a cruel sneer. Jason was now one hundred percent sure he didn't like this guy, and he was starting to regret sending Hedge outside.

"So," Jason said. "All this gold—"

The king's eyes lit up. "Are you here for gold, my boy? Please, take a brochure!"

Jason looked at the brochures on the coffee table. The title said GOLD: *Invest for Eternity.* "Um, you sell gold?"

"No, no," the king said. "I *make* it. In uncertain times like these, gold is the wisest investment, don't you think? Governments fall. The dead rise. Giants attack Olympus. But gold retains its value!"

Leo frowned. "I've seen that commercial."

"Oh, don't be fooled by cheap imitators!" the king said. "I assure you, I can beat any price for a serious investor. I can make a wide assortment of gold items at a moment's notice."

"But..." Piper shook her head in confusion. "Your Majesty, you gave up the golden touch, didn't you?"

The king looked astonished. "Gave it up?"

"Yes," Piper said. "You got it from some god—"

"Dionysus," the king agreed. "I'd rescued one of his satyrs, and in return, the god granted me one wish. I chose the golden touch."

"But you accidentally turned your own daughter to gold," Piper remembered. "And you realized how greedy you'd been. So you repented."

"Repented!" King Midas looked at Lit incredulously. "You see, son? You're away for a few thousand years, and the story gets twisted all around. My dear girl, did those stories ever *say* I'd lost my magic touch?"

"Well, I guess not. They just said you learned how to reverse it with running water, and you brought your daughter back to life."

"That's all true. Sometimes I still have to reverse my touch. There's no running water in the house because I don't want accidents"—he gestured to his statues—"but we chose to live next to a river just in case. Occasionally, I'll forget and pat Lit on the back—"

Lit retreated a few steps. "I hate that."

"I *told* you I was sorry, son. At any rate, gold is wonderful. Why would I give it up?"

"Well..." Piper looked truly lost now. "Isn't that the point of the story? That you learned your lesson?"

Midas laughed. "My dear, may I see your backpack for a moment? Toss it here."

Piper hesitated, but she wasn't eager to offend the king. She dumped everything out of the pack and tossed it to Midas. As soon as he caught it, the pack turned to gold, like frost spreading across the fabric. It still looked flexible and soft, but definitely gold. The king tossed it back.

"As you see, I can still turn anything to gold," Midas said. "That pack is magic now, as well. Go ahead—put your little storm spirit enemies in there."

"Seriously?" Leo was suddenly interested. He took the bag from Piper and held it up to the cage. As soon as he unzipped the backpack, the winds stirred and howled in protest. The cage bars shuddered. The door of the prison flew open and the winds got vacuumed straight into the pack. Leo zipped it shut and grinned. "Gotta admit. That's cool."

"You see?" Midas said. "My golden touch a *curse*? Please. I didn't learn any lesson, and life isn't a story, girl. Honestly, my daughter Zoe was much more pleasant as a gold statue."

"She talked a lot," Lit offered.

"Exactly! And so I turned her back to gold." Midas pointed. There in the corner was a golden statue of a girl with a shocked expression, as if she were thinking, *Dad!*

"That's horrible!" Piper said.

"Nonsense. She doesn't mind. Besides, if I'd learned my lesson, would I have gotten these?"

Midas pulled off his oversize sleeping cap, and Jason didn't know whether to laugh or get sick. Midas had long fuzzy gray ears sticking up from his white hair—like Bugs Bunny's, but they weren't rabbit ears. They were donkey ears.

"Oh, wow," Leo said. "I didn't need to see that."

"Terrible, isn't it?" Midas sighed. "A few years after the golden touch incident, I judged a music contest between Apollo and Pan, and I declared Pan the winner. Apollo, sore loser, said I must have the ears of an ass, and *voilà*. This was my reward for being truthful. I tried to keep them a secret. Only my barber knew, but he couldn't help blabbing." Midas pointed out another golden statue—a bald man in a toga, holding a pair of shears. "That's him. He won't be telling anyone's secrets again."

The king smiled. Suddenly he didn't strike Jason as a harmless old man in a bathrobe. His eyes had a merry glow to them—the look of a madman who knew he was mad, accepted his madness, and enjoyed it. "Yes, gold has many uses. I think that *must* be why I was brought back, eh Lit? To bankroll our patron."

Lit nodded. "That and my good sword arm."

Jason glanced at his friends. Suddenly the air in the room seemed much colder.

"So you do have a patron," Jason said. "You work for the giants."

King Midas waved his hand dismissively. "Well, I don't care for giants myself, of course. But even supernatural armies need to get paid. I do owe my patron a great debt. I tried to explain that to the last group that came through, but they were very unfriendly. Wouldn't cooperate at all."

Jason slipped his hand into his pocket and grabbed his gold coin. "The last group?"

"Hunters," Lit snarled. "Blasted girls from Artemis."

Jason felt a spark of electricity—a *literal* spark—travel down his spine. He caught a whiff of electrical fire like he'd just melted some of the springs in the sofa.

His *sister* had been here.

"When?" he demanded. "What happened?"

Lit shrugged. "Few days ago? I didn't get to kill them, unfortunately. They were looking for some evil wolves, or something. Said they were following a trail, heading west. Missing demigod—I don't recall."

Percy Jackson, Jason thought. Annabeth had mentioned the Hunters were looking for him. And in Jason's dream of the burned-out house in the redwoods, he'd heard enemy wolves baying. Hera had called them her keepers. It had to be connected somehow.

Midas scratched his donkey ears. "Very unpleasant young ladies, those Hunters," he recalled. "They absolutely refused to be turned into gold. Much of the security system outside I installed to keep that sort of thing from happening again, you know. I don't have time for those who aren't serious investors."

Jason stood warily and glanced at his friends. They got the message.

"Well," Piper said, managing a smile. "It's been a great visit. Welcome back to life. Thanks for the gold bag."

"Oh, but you can't leave!" Midas said. "I know you're not serious investors, but that's all right! I have to rebuild my collection."

Lit was smiling cruelly. The king rose, and Leo and Piper moved away from him.

"Don't worry," the king assured them. "You don't *have* to be turned to gold. I give all my guests a choice—join my collection, or die at the hands of Lityerses. Really, it's good either way."

Piper tried to use her charmspeak. "Your Majesty, you can't—"

Quicker than any old man should've been able to move, Midas lashed out and grabbed her wrist.

"No!" Jason yelled.

But a frost of gold spread over Piper, and in a heartbeat she was a glittering statue. Leo tried to summon fire, but he'd forgotten his power wasn't working. Midas touched his hand, and Leo transformed into solid metal.

Jason was so horrified he couldn't move. His friends—just *gone*. And he hadn't been able to stop it.

Midas smiled apologetically. "Gold trumps fire, I'm afraid." He waved around him at all the gold curtains and furniture. "In this room, my power dampens all others: fire ... even charmspeak. Which leaves me only one more trophy to collect."

"Hedge!" Jason yelled. "Need help in here!"

For once, the satyr didn't charge in. Jason wondered if the

lasers had gotten him, or if he was sitting at the bottom of a trap pit.

Midas chuckled. "No goat to the rescue? Sad. But don't worry, my boy. It's really not painful. Lit can tell you."

Jason fixed on an idea. "I choose combat. You said I could choose to fight Lit instead."

Midas looked mildly disappointed, but he shrugged. "I said you could *die* fighting Lit. But of course, if you wish."

The king backed away, and Lit raised his sword.

"I'm going to enjoy this," Lit said. "I am the Reaper of Men!"

"Come on, Cornhusker." Jason summoned his own weapon. This time it came up as a javelin, and Jason was glad for the extra length.

"Oh, gold weapon!" Midas said. "Very nice."

Lit charged.

The guy was fast. He slashed and sliced, and Jason could barely dodge the strikes, but his mind went into a different mode—analyzing patterns, learning Lit's style, which was all offense, no defense.

Jason countered, sidestepped, and blocked. Lit seemed surprised to find him still alive.

"What is that style?" Lit growled. "You don't fight like a Greek."

"Legion training," Jason said, though he wasn't sure how he knew that. "It's Roman."

"Roman?" Lit struck again, and Jason deflected his blade. "What is *Roman*?"

"News flash," Jason said. "While you were dead, Rome defeated Greece. Created the greatest empire of all time."

"Impossible," Lit said. "Never even heard of them."

Jason spun on one heel, smacked Lit in the chest with the butt of his javelin, and sent him toppling into Midas's throne.

"Oh, dear," Midas said. "Lit?"

"I'm fine," Lit growled.

"You'd better help him up," Jason said.

Lit cried, "Dad, no!"

Too late. Midas put his hand on his son's shoulder, and suddenly a very angry-looking gold statue was sitting on Midas's throne.

"Curses!" Midas wailed. "That was a naughty trick, demigod. I'll get you for that." He patted Lit's golden shoulder. "Don't worry, son. I'll get you down to the river right after I collect this prize."

Midas raced forward. Jason dodged, but the old man was fast, too. Jason kicked the coffee table into the old man's legs and knocked him over, but Midas wouldn't stay down for long.

Then Jason glanced at Piper's golden statue. Anger washed over him. He was the son of Zeus. He could *not* fail his friends.

He felt a tugging sensation in his gut, and the air pressure dropped so rapidly that his ears popped. Midas must've felt it too, because he stumbled to his feet and grabbed his donkey ears.

"Ow! What are you doing?" he demanded. "My power is supreme here!"

Thunder rumbled. Outside, the sky turned black.

"You know another good use for gold?" Jason said.

Midas raised his eyebrows, suddenly excited. "Yes?"

"It's an excellent conductor of electricity."

Jason raised his javelin, and the ceiling exploded. A lightning bolt ripped through the roof like it was an eggshell, connected with the tip of Jason's spear, and sent out arcs of energy that blasted the sofas to shreds. Chunks of ceiling plaster crashed down. The chandelier groaned and snapped off its chain, and Midas screamed as it pinned him to the floor. The glass immediately turned into gold.

When the rumbling stopped, freezing rain poured into the building. Midas cursed in Ancient Greek, thoroughly pinned under his chandelier. The rain soaked everything, turning the gold chandelier back to glass. Piper and Leo were slowly changing too, along with the other statues in the room.

Then the front door burst open, and Coach Hedge charged in, club ready. His mouth was covered with dirt, snow, and grass.

"What'd I miss?" he asked.

"Where were you?" Jason demanded. His head was spinning from summoning the lightning bolt, and it was all he could do to keep from passing out. "I was screaming for help."

Hedge belched. "Getting a snack. Sorry. Who needs killing?"

"No one, now!" Jason said. "Just grab Leo. I'll get Piper."

"Don't leave me like this!" Midas wailed.

All around him the statues of his victims were turning to flesh—his daughter, his barber, and a whole lot of angry-looking guys with swords.

Jason grabbed Piper's golden bag and his own supplies.

Then he threw a rug over the golden statue of Lit on the throne. Hopefully that would keep the Reaper of Men from turning back to flesh—at least until after Midas's victims did.

"Let's get out of here," Jason told Hedge. "I think these guys will want some quality time with Midas."

XXXIII

PIPER

PIPER WOKE UP COLD AND SHIVERING.

She'd had the worst dream about an old guy with donkey ears chasing her around and shouting, *You're it!*

"Oh, god." Her teeth chattered. "He turned me to gold!"

"You're okay now." Jason leaned over and tucked a warm blanket around her, but she still felt as cold as a Boread.

She blinked, trying to figure out where they were. Next to her, a campfire blazed, turning the air sharp with smoke. Firelight flickered against rock walls. They were in a shallow cave, but it didn't offer much protection. Outside, the wind howled. Snow blew sideways. It might've been day or night. The storm made it too dark to tell.

"L-L-Leo?" Piper managed.

"Present and un-gold-ified." Leo was also wrapped in blankets. He didn't look great, but better than Piper felt. "I got the precious metal treatment too," he said. "But I came out of it faster. Dunno why. We had to dunk you in the river to get you back completely. Tried to dry you off, but... it's really, really cold."

"You've got hypothermia," Jason said. "We risked as much nectar as we could. Coach Hedge did a little nature magic—"

"Sports medicine." The coach's ugly face loomed over her. "Kind of a hobby of mine. Your breath might smell like wild mushrooms and Gatorade for a few days, but it'll pass. You probably won't die. Probably."

"Thanks," Piper said weakly. "How did you beat Midas?"

Jason told her the story, putting most of it down to luck.

The coach snorted. "Kid's being modest. You should've seen him. Hi-yah! Slice! Boom with the lightning!"

"Coach, you didn't even see it," Jason said. "You were outside eating the lawn."

But the satyr was just warming up. "Then I came in with my club, and we dominated that room. Afterward, I told him, 'Kid, I'm proud of you! If you could just work on your upper body strength—'"

"Coach," said Jason.

"Yeah?"

"Shut up, please."

"Sure." The coach sat down at the fire and started chewing his cudgel.

Jason put his hand on Piper's forehead and checked her temperature. "Leo, can you stoke the fire?"

"On it." Leo summoned a baseball-sized clump of flames and lobbed it into the campfire.

"Do I look that bad?" Piper shivered.

"Nah," Jason said.

"You're a terrible liar," she said. "Where are we?"

"Pikes Peak," Jason said. "Colorado."

"But that's, what—five hundred miles from Omaha?"

"Something like that," Jason agreed. "I harnessed the storm spirits to bring us this far. They didn't like it—went a little faster than I wanted, almost crashed us into the mountainside before I could get them back in the bag. I'm not going to be trying that again."

"Why are we here?"

Leo sniffed. "That's what *I* asked him."

Jason gazed into the storm as if watching for something. "That glittery wind trail we saw yesterday? It was still in the sky, though it had faded a lot. I followed it until I couldn't see it anymore. Then—honestly I'm not sure. I just felt like this was the right place to stop."

"'Course it is." Coach Hedge spit out some cudgel splinters. "Aeolus's floating palace should be anchored above us, right at the peak. This is one of his favorite spots to dock."

"Maybe that was it." Jason knit his eyebrows. "I don't know. Something else, too..."

"The Hunters were heading west," Piper remembered. "Do you think they're around here?"

Jason rubbed his forearm as if the tattoos were bothering him. "I don't see how anyone could survive on the mountain right now. The storm's pretty bad. It's already the evening before the solstice, but we didn't have much choice except to wait out the storm here. We had to give you some time to rest before we tried moving."

He didn't need to convince her. The wind howling outside the cave scared her, and she couldn't stop shivering.

"We have to get you warm." Jason sat next to her and held out his arms a little awkwardly. "Uh, you mind if I . . ."

"I suppose." She tried to sound nonchalant.

He put his arms around her and held her. They scooted closer to the fire. Coach Hedge chewed on his club and spit splinters into the fire.

Leo broke out some cooking supplies and started frying burger patties on an iron skillet. "So, guys, long as you're cuddled up for story time . . . something I've been meaning to tell you. On the way to Omaha, I had this dream. Kinda hard to understand with the static and the *Wheel of Fortune* breaking in—"

"*Wheel of Fortune?*" Piper assumed Leo was kidding, but when he looked up from his burgers, his expression was deadly serious.

"The thing is," he said, "my dad Hephaestus talked to me."

Leo told them about his dream. In the firelight, with the wind howling, the story was even creepier. Piper could imagine the static-filled voice of the god warning about giants who were the sons of Tartarus, and about Leo losing some friends along the way.

She tried to concentrate on something good: Jason's arms around her, the warmth slowly spreading into her body, but she was terrified. "I don't understand. If demigods and gods have to work together to kill the giants, why would the gods stay silent? If they need us—"

"Ha," said Coach Hedge. "The gods *hate* needing humans. They like to be needed *by* humans, but not the other way around. Things will have to get a whole lot worse before Zeus admits he made a mistake closing Olympus."

"Coach," Piper said, "that was almost an intelligent comment."

Hedge huffed. "What? I'm intelligent! I'm not surprised you cupcakes haven't heard of the Giant War. The gods don't like to talk about it. Bad PR to admit you needed mortals to help beat an enemy. That's just embarrassing."

"There's more, though," Jason said. "When I dreamed about Hera in her cage, she said Zeus was acting unusually paranoid. And Hera—she said she went to those ruins because a voice had been speaking in her head. What if someone's influencing the gods, like Medea influenced us?"

Piper shuddered. She'd had a similar thought—that some force they couldn't see was manipulating things behind the scenes, helping the giants. Maybe the same force was keeping Enceladus informed about their movements, and had even knocked their dragon out of the sky over Detroit. Perhaps Leo's sleeping Dirt Woman, or another servant of hers...

Leo set hamburger buns on the skillet to toast. "Yeah, Hephaestus said something similar, like Zeus was acting weirder than usual. But what bothered me was the stuff my dad *didn't* say. Like a couple of times he was talking about the demigods, and how he had so many kids and all. I don't know. He acted like getting the greatest demigods together was going to be almost impossible—like Hera was trying, but it was a really stupid thing to do, and there was some secret Hephaestus wasn't supposed to tell me."

Jason shifted. Piper could feel the tension in his arms.

"Chiron was the same way back at camp," he said. "He mentioned a sacred oath not to discuss—something. Coach, you know anything about that?"

"Nah. I'm just a satyr. They don't tell us the juicy stuff. Especially an old—" He stopped himself.

"An old guy like you?" Piper asked. "But you're not that old, are you?"

"Hundred and six," the coach muttered.

Leo coughed. "Say what?"

"Don't catch your panties on fire, Valdez. That's just fifty-three in human years. Still, yeah, I made some enemies on the Council of Cloven Elders. I've been a protector a *long* time. But they started saying I was getting unpredictable. Too violent. Can you imagine?"

"Wow." Piper tried not to look at her friends. "That's hard to believe."

Coach scowled. "Yeah, then finally we get a good war going with the Titans, and do they put me on the front lines? No! They send me as far away as possible—the Canadian frontier, can you believe it? Then after the war, they put me out to pasture. The Wilderness School. Bah! Like I'm too old to be helpful just because I like playing offense. All those flower-pickers on the Council—talking about nature."

"I thought satyrs liked nature," Piper ventured.

"Shoot, I love nature," Hedge said. "Nature means big

things killing and eating little things! And when you're a —you know—vertically challenged satyr like me, you get in good shape, you carry a big stick, and you don't take nothing from no one! That's nature." Hedge snorted indignantly. "Flower-pickers. Anyway, I hope you got something vegetarian cooking, Valdez. I don't do flesh."

"Yeah, Coach. Don't eat your cudgel. I got some tofu patties here. Piper's a vegetarian too. I'll throw them on in a second."

The smell of frying burgers filled the air. Piper usually hated the smell of cooking meat, but her stomach rumbled like it wanted to mutiny.

I'm losing it, she thought. Think broccoli. Carrots. Lentils.

Her stomach wasn't the only thing rebelling. Lying by the fire, with Jason holding her, Piper's conscience felt like a hot bullet slowly working its way toward her heart. All the guilt she'd been holding in for the last week, since the giant Enceladus had first sent her a dream, was about to kill her.

Her friends wanted to help her. Jason even said he'd walk into a trap to save her dad. And Piper had shut them out.

For all she knew, she'd already doomed her father when she attacked Medea.

She choked back a sob. Maybe she'd done the right thing in Chicago by saving her friends, but she'd only delayed her problem. She could never betray her friends, but the tiniest part of her was desperate enough to think, *What if I did?*

She tried to imagine what her dad would say. *Hey, Dad, if you were ever chained up by a cannibal giant and I had to betray a couple of friends to save you, what should I do?*

Funny, that had never come up when they did Any Three Questions. Her dad would never take the question seriously, of course. He'd probably tell her one of Grandpa Tom's old stories—something with glowing hedgehogs and talking birds—and then laugh about it as if the advice was silly.

Piper wished she remembered her grandpa better. Sometimes she dreamed about that little two-room house in Oklahoma. She wondered what it would've been like to grow up there.

Her dad would think that was nuts. He had spent his whole life running away from that place, distancing himself from the rez, playing any role except Native American. He'd always told Piper how lucky she was to grow up rich and well cared-for, in a nice house in California.

She'd learned to be vaguely uncomfortable about her ancestry—like Dad's old pictures from the eighties, when he had feathered hair and crazy clothes. *Can you believe I ever looked like that?* he'd say. Being Cherokee was the same way for him—something funny and mildly embarrassing.

But what else were they? Dad didn't seem to know. Maybe that's why he was always so unhappy, changing roles. Maybe that's why Piper started stealing things, looking for something her dad couldn't give her.

Leo put tofu patties on the skillet. The wind kept raging. Piper thought of an old story her dad had told her...one that maybe *did* answer some of her questions.

One day in second grade she'd come home in tears and demanded why her father had named her Piper. The kids were making fun of her because Piper Cherokee was a kind of airplane.

Her dad laughed, as if that had never occurred to him. "No, Pipes. Fine airplane. That's not how I named you. Grandpa Tom picked out your name. First time he heard you cry, he said you had a powerful voice—better than any reed flute piper. He said you'd learn to sing the hardest Cherokee songs, even the snake song."

"The snake song?"

Dad told her the legend—how one day a Cherokee woman had seen a snake playing too near her children and killed it with a rock, not realizing it was the king of rattlesnakes. The snakes prepared for war on the humans, but the woman's husband tried to make peace. He promised he'd do anything to repay the rattlesnakes. The snakes held him to his word. They told him to send his wife to the well so the snakes could bite her and take her life in exchange. The man was heartbroken, but he did what they asked. Afterward, the snakes were impressed that the man had given up so much and kept his promise. They taught him the snake song for all the Cherokee to use. From that point on, if any Cherokee met a snake and sang that song, the snake would recognize the Cherokee as a friend, and would not bite.

"That's awful!" Piper had said. "He let his wife die?"

Her dad spread his hands. "It was a hard sacrifice. But one life brought generations of peace between snakes and Cherokee. Grandpa Tom believed that Cherokee music could solve almost any problem. He thought you'd know lots of songs, and be the greatest musician of the family. That's why we named you Piper."

A hard sacrifice. Had her grandfather foreseen something about her, even when she was a baby? Had he sensed she was a child of Aphrodite? Her dad would probably tell her that was crazy. Grandpa Tom was no oracle.

But still... she'd made a promise to help on this quest. Her friends were counting on her. They'd saved her when Midas had turned her to gold. They'd brought her back to life. She couldn't repay them with lies.

Gradually, she started to feel warmer. She stopped shivering and settled against Jason's chest. Leo handed out the food. Piper didn't want to move, talk, or do anything to disrupt the moment. But she had to.

"We need to talk." She sat up so she could face Jason. "I don't want to hide anything from you guys anymore."

They looked at her with their mouths full of burger. Too late to change her mind now.

"Three nights before the Grand Canyon trip," she said, "I had a dream vision—a giant, telling me my father had been taken hostage. He told me I had to cooperate, or my dad would be killed."

The flames crackled.

Finally Jason said, "Enceladus? You mentioned that name before."

Coach Hedge whistled. "Big giant. Breathes fire. Not somebody I'd want barbecuing my daddy goat."

Jason gave him a *shut up* look. "Piper, go on. What happened next?"

"I—I tried to reach my dad, but all I got was his personal assistant, and she told me not to worry."

"Jane?" Leo remembered. "Didn't Medea say something about controlling her?"

Piper nodded. "To get my dad back, I had to sabotage this quest. I didn't realize it would be the three of us. Then after we started the quest, Enceladus sent me another warning: He told me he wanted you two dead. He wants me to lead you to a mountain. I don't know exactly which one, but it's in the Bay Area—I could see the Golden Gate Bridge from the summit. I have to be there by noon on the solstice, tomorrow. An exchange."

She couldn't meet her friends' eyes. She waited for them to yell at her, or turn their backs, or kick her out into the snowstorm.

Instead, Jason scooted next to her and put his arm around her again. "God, Piper. I'm so sorry."

Leo nodded. "No kidding. You've been carrying this around for a week? Piper, we could *help* you."

She glared at them. "Why don't you yell at me or something? I was ordered to kill you!"

"Aw, come on," Jason said. "You've saved us both on this quest. I'd put my life in your hands any day."

"Same," Leo said. "Can I have a hug too?"

"You don't get it!" Piper said. "I've probably just killed my dad, telling you this."

"I doubt it." Coach Hedge belched. He was eating his

tofu burger folded inside the paper plate, chewing it all like a taco. "Giant hasn't gotten what he wants yet, so he still needs your dad for leverage. He'll wait until the deadline passes, see if you show up. He wants you to divert the quest to this mountain, right?"

Piper nodded uncertainly.

"So that means Hera is being kept somewhere else," Hedge reasoned. "And she has to be saved by the same day. So you have to choose—rescue your dad, or rescue Hera. If you go after Hera, *then* Enceladus takes care of your dad. Besides, Enceladus would never let you go even if you cooperated. You're obviously one of the seven in the Great Prophecy."

One of the seven. She'd talked about this before with Jason and Leo, and she supposed it must be true, but she still had trouble believing it. She didn't feel that important. She was just a stupid child of Aphrodite. How could she be worth deceiving and killing?

"So we have no choice," she said miserably. "We have to save Hera, or the giant king gets unleashed. That's our quest. The world depends on it. And Enceladus seems to have ways of watching me. He isn't stupid. He'll know if we change course and go the wrong way. He'll kill my dad."

"He's not going to kill your dad," Leo said. "We'll save him."

"We don't have time!" Piper cried. "Besides, it's a trap."

"We're your friends, beauty queen," Leo said. "We're not going to let your dad die. We just gotta figure out a plan."

Coach Hedge grumbled. "Would help if we knew where this mountain was. Maybe Aeolus can tell you that. The Bay

Area has a bad reputation for demigods. Old home of the Titans, Mount Othrys, sits over Mount Tam, where Atlas holds up the sky. I hope that's not the mountain you saw."

Piper tried to remember the vista in her dreams. "I don't think so. This was inland."

Jason frowned at the fire, like he was trying to remember something.

"Bad reputation...that doesn't seem right. The Bay Area..."

"You think you've been there?" Piper asked.

"I..." He looked like he was almost on the edge of a breakthrough. Then the anguish came back into his eyes. "I don't know. Hedge, what happened to Mount Othrys?"

Hedge took another bite of paper and burger. "Well, Kronos built a new palace there last summer. Big nasty place, was going to be the headquarters for his new kingdom and all. Weren't any battles there, though. Kronos marched on Manhattan, tried to take Olympus. If I remember right, he left some other Titans in charge of his palace, but after Kronos got defeated in Manhattan, the whole palace just crumbled on its own."

"No," Jason said.

Everyone looked at him.

"What do you mean, 'No'?" Leo asked.

"That's not what happened. I—" He tensed, looking toward the cave entrance. "Did you hear that?"

For a second, nothing. Then Piper heard it: howls piercing the night.

XXXIV

PIPER

"Wolves," Piper said. "They sound close."

Jason rose and summoned his sword. Leo and Coach Hedge got to their feet too. Piper tried, but black spots danced before her eyes.

"Stay there," Jason told her. "We'll protect you."

She gritted her teeth. She hated feeling helpless. She didn't *want* anyone to protect her. First the stupid ankle. Now stupid hypothermia. She wanted to be on her feet, with her dagger in her hand.

Then, just outside the firelight at the entrance of the cave, she saw a pair of red eyes glowing in the dark.

Okay, she thought. Maybe a little protection is fine.

More wolves edged into the firelight—black beasts bigger than Great Danes, with ice and snow caked on their fur. Their fangs gleamed, and their glowing red eyes looked disturbingly intelligent. The wolf in front was almost as tall as a horse, his mouth stained as if he'd just made a fresh kill.

Piper pulled her dagger out of its sheath.

Then Jason stepped forward and said something in Latin.

Piper didn't think a dead language would have much effect on wild animals, but the alpha wolf curled his lip. The fur stood up along his spine. One of his lieutenants tried to advance, but the alpha wolf snapped at his ear. Then all of the wolves backed into the dark.

"Dude, I gotta study Latin." Leo's hammer shook in his hand. "What'd you say, Jason?"

Hedge cursed. "Whatever it was, it wasn't enough. Look."

The wolves were coming back, but the alpha wolf wasn't with them. They didn't attack. They waited—at least a dozen now, in a rough semicircle just outside the firelight, blocking the cave exit.

The coach hefted his club. "Here's the plan. I'll kill them all, and you guys escape."

"Coach, they'll rip you apart," Piper said.

"Nah, I'm good."

Then Piper saw the silhouette of a man coming through the storm, wading through the wolf pack.

"Stick together," Jason said. "They respect a pack. And Hedge, no crazy stuff. We're not leaving you or anyone else behind."

Piper got a lump in her throat. She was the weak link in their "pack" right now. No doubt the wolves could smell her fear. She might as well be wearing a sign that said FREE LUNCH.

The wolves parted, and the man stepped into the firelight. His hair was greasy and ragged, the color of fireplace soot, topped with a crown of what looked like finger bones. His robes were tattered fur—wolf, rabbit, raccoon, deer, and several others Piper couldn't identify. The furs didn't look cured, and from the smell, they weren't very fresh. His frame was lithe and muscular, like a distance runner's. But the most horrible thing was his face. His thin pale skin was pulled tight over his skull. His teeth were sharpened like fangs. His eyes glowed bright red like his wolves'—and they fixed on Jason with absolute hatred.

"*Ecce*," he said, "*filli Romani.*"

"Speak English, wolf man!" Hedge bellowed.

The wolf man snarled. "Tell your faun to mind his tongue, son of Rome. Or he'll be my first snack."

Piper remembered that *faun* was the Roman name for *satyr*. Not exactly helpful information. Now, if she could remember who this wolf guy was in Greek mythology, and how to defeat him, *that* she could use.

The wolf man studied their little group. His nostrils twitched. "So it's true," he mused. "A child of Aphrodite. A son of Hephaestus. A faun. And a child of Rome, of Lord Jupiter, no less. All together, without killing each other. How interesting."

"You were told about us?" Jason asked. "By whom?"

The man snarled—perhaps a laugh, perhaps a challenge. "Oh, we've been patrolling for you all across the west, demigod, hoping we'd be the first to find you. The giant king will reward me well when he rises. I am Lycaon, king of the wolves. And my pack is hungry."

The wolves snarled in the darkness.

Out of the corner of her eye, Piper saw Leo put up his hammer and slip something else from his tool belt—a glass bottle full of clear liquid.

Piper racked her brain trying to place the wolf guy's name. She knew she'd heard it before, but she couldn't remember details.

Lycaon glared at Jason's sword. He moved to each side as if looking for an opening, but Jason's blade moved with him.

"Leave," Jason ordered. "There's no food for you here."

"Unless you want tofu burgers," Leo offered.

Lycaon bared his fangs. Apparently he wasn't a tofu fan.

"If I had my way," Lycaon said with regret, "I'd kill you first, son of Jupiter. Your father made me what I am. I was the powerful mortal king of Arcadia, with fifty fine sons, and Zeus slew them all with his lightning bolts."

"Ha," Coach Hedge said. "For good reason!"

Jason glanced over his shoulder. "Coach, you know this clown?"

"*I* do," Piper answered. The details of the myth came back to her—a short, horrible story she and her father had laughed at over breakfast. She wasn't laughing now.

"Lycaon invited Zeus to dinner," she said. "But the king wasn't sure it was really Zeus. So to test his powers, Lycaon tried to feed him human flesh. Zeus got outraged—"

"And killed my sons!" Lycaon howled. The wolves behind him howled too.

"So Zeus turned him into a wolf," Piper said. "They call . . . they call werewolves *lycanthropes*, named after him, the first werewolf."

"The king of wolves," Coach Hedge finished. "An immortal, smelly, vicious mutt."

Lycaon growled. "I will tear you apart, faun!"

"Oh, you want some goat, buddy? 'Cause I'll give you goat."

"Stop it," Jason said. "Lycaon, you said you *wanted* to kill me first, but...?"

"Sadly, Child of Rome, you are spoken for. Since this one" —he waggled his claws at Piper—"has failed to kill you, you are to be delivered alive to the Wolf House. One of my compatriots has asked for the honor of killing you herself."

"Who?" Jason said.

The wolf king snickered. "Oh, a great admirer of yours. Apparently, you made quite an impression on her. She will take care of you soon enough, and really I cannot complain. Spilling your blood at the Wolf House should mark my new territory quite well. Lupa will think twice about challenging my pack."

Piper's heart tried to jump out of her chest. She didn't understand everything Lycaon had said, but a woman who wanted to kill Jason? Medea, she thought. Somehow, she must've survived the explosion.

Piper struggled to her feet. Spots danced before her eyes again. The cave seemed to spin.

"You're going to leave now," Piper said, "before we destroy you."

She tried to put power into the words, but she was too weak. Shivering in her blankets, pale and sweaty and barely able to hold a knife, she couldn't have looked very threatening.

Lycaon's red eyes crinkled with humor. "A brave try, girl.

I admire that. Perhaps I'll make your end quick. Only the son of Jupiter is needed alive. The rest of you, I'm afraid, are dinner."

At that moment, Piper knew she was going to die. But at least she'd die on her feet, fighting next to Jason.

Jason took a step forward. "You're not killing anyone, wolf man. Not without going through me."

Lycaon howled and extended his claws. Jason slashed at him, but his golden sword passed straight through as if the wolf king wasn't there.

Lycaon laughed. "Gold, bronze, steel—none of these are any good against my wolves, son of Jupiter."

"Silver!" Piper cried. "Aren't werewolves hurt by silver?"

"We don't have any silver!" Jason said.

Wolves leaped into the firelight. Hedge charged forward with an elated "Woot!"

But Leo struck first. He threw his glass bottle and it shattered on the ground, splattering liquid all over the wolves —the unmistakable smell of gasoline. He shot a burst of fire at the puddle, and a wall of flames erupted.

Wolves yelped and retreated. Several caught fire and had to run back into the snow. Even Lycaon looked uneasily at the barrier of flames now separating his wolves from the demigods.

"Aw, c'mon," Coach Hedge complained. "I can't hit them if they're way over there."

Every time a wolf came closer, Leo shot a new wave of fire from his hands, but each effort seemed to make him a little more tired, and the gasoline was already dying down. "I can't summon any more gas!" Leo warned. Then his face turned red. "Wow, that came out wrong. I mean the *burning* kind. Gonna take the tool belt a while to recharge. What you got, man?"

"Nothing," Jason said. "Not even a weapon that works."

"Lightning?" Piper asked.

Jason concentrated, but nothing happened. "I think the snowstorm is interfering, or something."

"Unleash the *venti*!" Piper said.

"Then we'll have nothing to give Aeolus," Jason said. "We'll have come all this way for nothing."

Lycaon laughed. "I can smell your fear. A few more minutes of life, heroes. Pray to whatever gods you wish. Zeus did not grant me mercy, and you will have none from me."

The flames began to sputter out. Jason cursed and dropped his sword. He crouched like he was ready to go hand-to-hand. Leo pulled his hammer out of his pack. Piper raised her dagger—not much, but it was all she had. Coach Hedge hefted his club, and he was the only one who looked excited about dying.

Then a ripping sound cut through the wind—like a piece of tearing cardboard. A long stick sprouted from the neck of the nearest wolf—the shaft of a silver arrow. The wolf writhed and fell, melting into a puddle of shadow.

More arrows. More wolves fell. The pack broke in confusion. An arrow flashed toward Lycaon, but the wolf king caught it in midair. Then he yelled in pain. When he dropped the arrow, it left a charred, smoking gash across his palm. Another arrow caught him in the shoulder, and the wolf king staggered.

"Curse them!" Lycaon yelled. He growled at his pack, and the wolves turned and ran. Lycaon fixed Jason with those glowing red eyes. "This isn't over, boy."

The wolf king disappeared into the night.

Seconds later, Piper heard more wolves baying, but the sound was different—less threatening, more like hunting dogs on the scent. A smaller white wolf burst into the cave, followed by two more.

Hedge said, "Kill it?"

"No!" Piper said. "Wait."

The wolves tilted their heads and studied the campers with huge golden eyes.

A heartbeat later, their masters appeared: a troop of hunters in white-and-gray winter camouflage, at least half a dozen. All of them carried bows, with quivers of glowing silver arrows on their backs.

Their faces were covered with parka hoods, but clearly they were all girls. One, a little taller than the rest, crouched in the firelight and snatched up the arrow that had wounded Lycaon's hand.

"So close." She turned to her companions. "Phoebe, stay with me. Watch the entrance. The rest of you, follow Lycaon. We can't lose him now. I'll catch up with you."

The other hunters mumbled agreement and disappeared, heading after Lycaon's pack.

The girl in white turned toward them, her face still hidden

in her parka hood. "We've been following that demon's trail for over a week. Is everyone all right? No one got bit?"

Jason stood frozen, staring at the girl. Piper realized something about her voice sounded familiar. It was hard to pin down, but the way she spoke, the way she formed her words, reminded her of Jason.

"You're her," Piper guessed. "You're Thalia."

The girl tensed. Piper was afraid she might draw her bow, but instead she pulled down her parka hood. Her hair was spiky black, with a silver tiara across her brow. Her face had a super-healthy glow to it, as if she were a little more than human, and her eyes were brilliant blue. She was the girl from Jason's photograph.

"Do I know you?" Thalia asked.

Piper took a breath. "This might be a shock, but—"

"Thalia." Jason stepped forward, his voice trembling. "I'm Jason, your brother."

XXXV

LEO

LEO FIGURED HE HAD THE WORST LUCK in the group, and that was saying a lot. Why didn't *he* get to have the long-lost sister or the movie star dad who needed rescuing? All he got was a tool belt and a dragon that broke down halfway through the quest. Maybe it was the stupid curse of the Hephaestus cabin, but Leo didn't think so. His life had been unlucky way before he got to camp.

A thousand years from now, when this quest was being told around a campfire, he figured people would talk about brave Jason, beautiful Piper, and their sidekick Flaming Valdez, who accompanied them with a bag of magic screwdrivers and occasionally fixed tofu burgers.

If that wasn't bad enough, Leo fell in love with every girl he saw—as long as she was totally out of his league.

When he first saw Thalia, Leo immediately thought she was *way* too pretty to be Jason's sister. Then he thought he'd better not say that or he'd get in trouble. He liked her dark hair, her blue eyes, and her confident attitude. She looked like the kind of girl who could stomp anybody on the ball court or the battlefield, and wouldn't give Leo the time of day—just Leo's type!

For a minute, Jason and Thalia faced each other, stunned. Then Thalia rushed forward and hugged him.

"My gods! She told me you were dead!" She gripped Jason's face and seemed to be examining everything about it. "Thank Artemis, it *is* you. That little scar on your lip—you tried to eat a stapler when you were two!"

Leo laughed. "Seriously?"

Hedge nodded like he approved of Jason's taste. "Staplers —excellent source of iron."

"W-wait," Jason stammered. "Who told you I was dead? What happened?"

At the cave entrance, one of the white wolves barked. Thalia looked back at the wolf and nodded, but she kept her hands on Jason's face, like she was afraid he might vanish. "My wolf is telling me I don't have much time, and she's right. But we *have* to talk. Let's sit."

Piper did better than that. She collapsed. She would've cracked her head on the cave floor if Hedge hadn't caught her.

Thalia rushed over. "What's wrong with her? Ah—never mind. I see. Hypothermia. Ankle." She frowned at the satyr. "Don't you know nature healing?"

Hedge scoffed. "Why do you think she looks *this* good? Can't you smell the Gatorade?"

Thalia looked at Leo for the first time, and of course it was an accusatory glare, like *Why did you let the goat be a doctor?* As if that was Leo's fault.

"You and the satyr," Thalia ordered, "take this girl to my friend at the entrance. Phoebe's an excellent healer."

"It's cold out there!" Hedge said. "I'll freeze my horns off."

But Leo knew when they weren't wanted. "Come on, Hedge. These two need time to talk."

"Humph. Fine," the satyr muttered. "Didn't even get to brain anybody."

Hedge carried Piper toward the entrance. Leo was about to follow when Jason called, "Actually, man, could you, um, stick around?"

Leo saw something in Jason's eyes he didn't expect: Jason was asking for support. He wanted somebody else there. He was scared.

Leo grinned. "Sticking around is my specialty."

Thalia didn't look too happy about it, but the three of them sat at the fire. For a few minutes, nobody spoke. Jason studied his sister like she was a scary device—one that might explode if handled incorrectly. Thalia seemed more at ease, as if she was used to stumbling across stranger things than long-lost relatives. But still she regarded Jason in a kind of amazed trance, maybe remembering a little two-year-old who tried to eat a stapler. Leo took a few pieces of copper wire out of his pockets and twisted them together.

Finally he couldn't stand the silence. "So...the Hunters of Artemis. This whole 'not dating' thing—is that like *always*, or more of a seasonal thing, or what?"

Thalia stared at him as if he'd just evolved from pond scum. Yeah, he was *definitely* liking this girl.

Jason kicked him in the shin. "Don't mind Leo. He's just trying to break the ice. But, Thalia...what happened to our family? Who told you I was dead?"

Thalia tugged at a silver bracelet on her wrist. In the firelight, in her winter camouflage, she almost looked like Khione the snow princess—just as cold and beautiful.

"Do you remember anything?" she asked.

Jason shook his head. "I woke up three days ago on a bus with Leo and Piper."

"Which wasn't our fault," Leo added hastily. "Hera stole his memories."

Thalia tensed. "Hera? How do you know that?"

Jason explained about their quest—the prophecy at camp, Hera getting imprisoned, the giant taking Piper's dad, and the winter solstice deadline. Leo chimed in to add the important stuff: how he'd fixed the bronze dragon, could throw fireballs, and made excellent tacos.

Thalia was a good listener. Nothing seemed to surprise her—the monsters, the prophecies, the dead rising. But when Jason mentioned King Midas, she cursed in Ancient Greek.

"I knew we should've burned down his mansion," she said. "That man's a menace. But we were so intent on following Lycaon— Well, I'm glad you got away. So Hera's been... what, hiding you all these years?"

"I don't know." Jason brought out the photo from his pocket. "She left me just enough memory to recognize your face."

Thalia looked at the picture, and her expression softened. "I'd forgotten about that. I left it in Cabin One, didn't I?"

Jason nodded. "I think Hera wanted for us to meet. When we landed here, at this cave...I had a feeling it was important. Like I knew you were close by. Is that crazy?"

"Nah," Leo assured him. "We were absolutely destined to meet your hot sister."

Thalia ignored him. Probably she just didn't want to let on how much Leo impressed her.

"Jason," she said, "when you're dealing with the gods, *nothing* is too crazy. But you can't trust Hera, especially since we're children of Zeus. She *hates* all children of Zeus."

"But she said something about Zeus giving her my life as a peace offering. Does that make any sense?"

The color drained from Thalia's face. "Oh, gods. Mother wouldn't have...You don't remember— No, of course you don't."

"What?" Jason asked.

Thalia's features seemed to grow older in the firelight, like her immortality wasn't working so well. "Jason...I'm not sure how to say this. Our mom wasn't exactly stable. She caught Zeus's eye because she was a television actress, and she *was* beautiful, but she didn't handle the fame well. She drank, pulled stupid stunts. She was always in the tabloids. She could never get enough attention. Even before you were born, she and I argued all the time. She...she knew Dad was Zeus, and I think that was too much for her to take. It was like the ultimate achievement for her to attract the lord of the sky, and

she couldn't accept it when he left. The thing about the gods
... well, they don't hang around."

Leo remembered his own mom, the way she'd assured him
over and over that his dad would be back someday. But she'd
never acted mad about it. She didn't seem to want Hephaestus
for herself—only so Leo could know his father. She'd dealt
with working a dead-end job, living in a tiny apartment, never
having enough money—and she'd seemed fine with it. As
long as she had Leo, she always said, life would be okay.

He watched Jason's face—looking more and more devastated as Thalia described their mom—and for once, Leo didn't
feel jealous of his friend. Leo might have lost his mom. He
might have had some hard times. But at least he remembered
her. He found himself tapping out a Morse code message on
his knee: *Love you.* He felt bad for Jason, not having memories
like that—not having anything to fall back on.

"So..." Jason didn't seem able to finish the question.

"Jason, you got friends," Leo told him. "Now you got a
sister. You're not alone."

Thalia offered her hand, and Jason took it.

"When I was about seven," she said, "Zeus started visiting
Mom again. I think he felt bad about wrecking her life, and
he seemed—different somehow. A little older and sterner,
more fatherly toward me. For a while, Mom improved. She
loved having Zeus around, bringing her presents, causing the
sky to rumble. She always wanted more attention. That's the
year you were born. Mom... well, I never got along with her,
but you gave me a reason to hang around. You were so cute.

And I didn't trust Mom to look after you. Of course, Zeus eventually stopped coming by again. He probably couldn't stand Mom's demands anymore, always pestering him to let her visit Olympus, or to make her immortal or eternally beautiful. When he left for good, Mom got more and more unstable. That was about the time the monsters started attacking me. Mom blamed Hera. She claimed the goddess was coming after you too—that Hera had barely tolerated my birth, but *two* demigod children from the same family was too big an insult. Mom even said she hadn't wanted to name you Jason, but Zeus insisted, as a way to appease Hera because the goddess liked that name. I didn't know what to believe."

Leo fiddled with his copper wires. He felt like an intruder. He shouldn't be listening to this, but it also made him feel like he was getting to know Jason for the first time—like maybe being here now made up for those four months at Wilderness School, when Leo had just imagined they'd had a friendship.

"How did you guys get separated?" he asked.

Thalia squeezed her brother's hand. "If I'd known you were alive...gods, things would've been so different. But when you were two, Mom packed us in the car for a family vacation. We drove up north, toward the wine country, to this park she wanted to show us. I remember thinking it was strange because Mom never took us anywhere, and she was acting super nervous. I was holding your hand, walking you toward this big building in the middle of the park, and..." She took a shaky breath. "Mom told me to go back to the car and get the picnic basket. I didn't want to leave you alone with her, but it was only for a few minutes. When I came back...Mom was kneeling on the stone steps, hugging herself and crying. She said—she said you were gone. She said Hera claimed you and you were as good as dead. I didn't know what she'd done. I was afraid she'd completely lost her mind. I ran all over the place looking for you, but you'd just vanished. She had to drag me away, kicking and screaming. For the next few days I was hysterical. I don't remember everything, but I called the police on Mom and they questioned her for a long time. Afterward, we fought. She told me I'd betrayed her, that I should support her, like *she* was the only one who mattered. Finally I couldn't stand it. Your disappearance was the last straw. I ran away from home, and I never went back, not even when Mom died a few years ago. I thought you were gone forever. I never told anyone about you—not even Annabeth or Luke, my two best friends. It was just too painful."

"Chiron knew." Jason's voice sounded far away. "When I got to camp, he took one look at me and said, 'You should be dead.'"

"That doesn't make sense," Thalia insisted. "I never told him."

"Hey," Leo said. "Important thing is you've got each other now, right? You two are lucky."

Thalia nodded. "Leo's right. Look at you. You're *my* age. You've grown up."

"But where have I been?" Jason said. "How could I be missing all that time? And the Roman stuff..."

Thalia frowned. "The Roman stuff?"

"Your brother speaks Latin," Leo said. "He calls gods by their Roman names, and he's got tattoos." Leo pointed out the marks on Jason's arm. Then he gave Thalia the rundown about the other weird stuff that had happened: Boreas turning into Aquilon, Lycaon calling Jason a "child of Rome," and the wolves backing off when Jason spoke Latin to them.

Thalia plucked her bowstring. "Latin. Zeus sometimes spoke Latin, the second time he stayed with Mom. Like I said, he seemed different, more formal."

"You think he was in his Roman aspect?" Jason asked. "And that's why I think of myself as a child of Jupiter?"

"Possibly," Thalia said. "I've never heard of something like that happening, but it might explain why you think in Roman terms, why you can speak Latin rather than Ancient Greek. That would make you unique. Still, it doesn't explain how you've survived without Camp Half-Blood. A child of Zeus, or Jupiter, or whatever you want to call him—you would've been hounded by monsters. If you were on your own, you should've died years ago. I know *I* wouldn't have been able to survive without friends. You would've needed training, a safe haven—"

"He wasn't alone," Leo blurted out. "We've heard about others like him."

Thalia looked at him strangely. "What do you mean?"

Leo told her about the slashed-up purple shirt in Medea's department store, and the story the Cyclopes told about the child of Mercury who spoke Latin.

"Isn't there anywhere else for demigods?" Leo asked. "I mean besides Camp Half-Blood? Maybe some crazy Latin teacher has been abducting children of the gods or something, making them think like Romans."

As soon as he said it, Leo realized how stupid the idea sounded. Thalia's dazzling blue eyes studied him intently, making him feel like a suspect in a lineup.

"I've been all over the country," Thalia mused. "I've never seen evidence of a crazy Latin teacher, or demigods in purple shirts. Still..." Her voice trailed off, like she'd just had a troubling thought.

"What?" Jason asked.

Thalia shook her head. "I'll have to talk to the goddess. Maybe Artemis will guide us."

"She's still talking to you?" Jason asked. "Most of the gods have gone silent."

"Artemis follows her own rules," Thalia said. "She has to be careful not to let Zeus know, but she thinks Zeus is being ridiculous closing Olympus. She's the one who set us on the trail of Lycaon. She said we'd find a lead to a missing friend of ours."

"Percy Jackson," Leo guessed. "The guy Annabeth is looking for."

Thalia nodded, her face full of concern.

Leo wondered if anyone had ever looked that worried all the times *he'd* disappeared. He kind of doubted it.

"So what would Lycaon have to do with it?" Leo asked. "And how does it connect to us?"

"We need to find out soon," Thalia admitted. "If your deadline is tomorrow, we're wasting time. Aeolus could tell you—"

The white wolf appeared again at the doorway and yipped insistently.

"I have to get moving." Thalia stood. "Otherwise I'll lose the other Hunters' trail. First, though, I'll take you to Aeolus's palace."

"If you can't, it's okay," Jason said, though he sounded kind of distressed.

"Oh, please." Thalia smiled and helped him up. "I haven't had a brother in years. I think I can stand a few minutes with you before you get annoying. Now, let's go!"

XXXVI

LEO

WHEN LEO SAW HOW WELL PIPER AND HEDGE were being treated, he was thoroughly offended.

He'd imagined them freezing their hindquarters off in the snow, but the Hunter Phoebe had set up this silver tent pavilion thing right outside the cave. How she'd done it so fast, Leo had no idea, but inside was a kerosene heater keeping them toasty warm and a bunch of comfy throw pillows. Piper looked back to normal, decked out in a new parka, gloves, and camo pants like a Hunter. She and Hedge and Phoebe were kicking back, drinking hot chocolate.

"Oh, no way," Leo said. "We've been sitting in a *cave* and you get the luxury tent? Somebody give me hypothermia. I want hot chocolate and a parka!"

Phoebe sniffed. "Boys," she said, like it was the worst insult she could think of.

"It's all right, Phoebe," Thalia said. "They'll need extra coats. And I think we can spare some chocolate."

Phoebe grumbled, but soon Leo and Jason were also dressed in silvery winter clothes that were incredibly lightweight and warm. The hot chocolate was first-rate.

"Cheers!" said Coach Hedge. He crunched down his plastic thermos cup.

"That cannot be good for your intestines," Leo said.

Thalia patted Piper on the back. "You up for moving?"

Piper nodded. "Thanks to Phoebe, yeah. You guys are really good at this wilderness survival thing. I feel like I could run ten miles."

Thalia winked at Jason. "She's tough for a child of Aphrodite. I like this one."

"Hey, I could run ten miles too," Leo volunteered. "Tough Hephaestus kid here. Let's hit it."

Naturally, Thalia ignored him.

It took Phoebe exactly six seconds to break camp, which Leo could not believe. The tent self-collapsed into a square the size of a pack of chewing gum. Leo wanted to ask her for the blueprints, but they didn't have time.

Thalia ran uphill through the snow, hugging a tiny little path on the side of the mountain, and soon Leo was regretting trying to look macho, because the Hunters left him in the dust.

Coach Hedge leaped around like a happy mountain goat, coaxing them on like he used to do on track days at school. "Come on, Valdez! Pick up the pace! Let's chant. *I've got a girl in Kalamazoo—*"

"Let's not," Thalia snapped.

So they ran in silence.

Leo fell in next to Jason at the back of the group. "How you doing, man?"

Jason's expression was enough of an answer: *Not good.*

"Thalia takes it so calmly," Jason said. "Like it's no big deal that I appeared. I didn't know what I was expecting, but... she's not like me. She seems so much more *together.*"

"Hey, she's not fighting amnesia," Leo said. "Plus, she's had more time to get used to this whole demigod thing. You fight monsters and talk to gods for a while, you probably get used to surprises."

"Maybe," Jason said. "I just wish I understood what happened when I was two, why my mom got rid of me. Thalia ran away because of *me.*"

"Hey, whatever's happened, it wasn't your fault. And your sister is pretty cool. She's a *lot* like you."

Jason took that in silence. Leo wondered if he'd said the right things. He wanted to make Jason feel better, but this was way outside his comfort zone.

Leo wished he could reach inside his tool belt and pick just the right wrench to fix Jason's memory—maybe a little hammer —bonk the sticking spot and make everything run right. That would be a lot easier than trying to talk it through. *Not good with organic life forms.* Thanks for those inherited traits, Dad.

He was so lost in thought, he didn't realize the Hunters had stopped. He slammed into Thalia and nearly sent them both down the side of the mountain the hard way. Fortunately, the Hunter was light on her feet. She steadied them both, then pointed up.

"That," Leo choked, "is a really large rock."

They stood near the summit of Pikes Peak. Below them the world was blanketed in clouds. The air was so thin, Leo could hardly breathe. Night had set in, but a full moon shone and the stars were incredible. Stretching out to the north and south, peaks of other mountains rose from the clouds like islands—or teeth.

But the real show was above them. Hovering in the sky, about a quarter mile away, was a massive free-floating island of glowing purple stone. It was hard to judge its size, but Leo figured it was at least as wide as a football stadium and just as tall. The sides were rugged cliffs, riddled with caves, and every once in a while a gust of wind burst out with a sound like a pipe organ blast. At the top of the rock, brass walls ringed some kind of a fortress.

The only thing connecting Pikes Peak to the floating island was a narrow bridge of ice that glistened in the moonlight.

Then Leo realized the bridge wasn't exactly ice, because it wasn't solid. As the winds changed direction, the bridge snaked around—blurring and thinning, in some places even breaking into a dotted line like the vapor trail of a plane.

"We're not seriously crossing that," Leo said.

Thalia shrugged. "I'm not a big fan of heights, I'll admit. But if you want to get to Aeolus's fortress, this is the only way."

"Is the fortress always hanging there?" Piper asked. "How can people not notice it sitting on top of Pikes Peak?"

"The Mist," Thalia said. "Still, mortals do notice it indirectly. Some days, Pikes Peak looks purple. People say it's a trick of the light, but actually it's the color of Aeolus's palace, reflecting off the mountain face."

"It's enormous," Jason said.

Thalia laughed. "You should see Olympus, little brother."

"You're serious? You've been there?"

Thalia grimaced as if it wasn't a good memory. "We should go across in two different groups. The bridge is fragile."

"That's reassuring," Leo said. "Jason, can't you just fly us up there?"

Thalia laughed. Then she seemed to realize Leo's question wasn't a joke. "Wait...Jason, you can *fly?*"

Jason gazed up at the floating fortress. "Well, sort of. More like I can control the winds. But the winds up here are so strong, I'm not sure I'd want to try. Thalia, you mean...you can't fly?"

For a second, Thalia looked genuinely afraid. Then she got her expression under control. Leo realized she was a lot more scared of heights than she was letting on.

"Truthfully," she said, "I've never tried. Might be better if we stuck to the bridge."

Coach Hedge tapped the ice vapor trail with his hoof, then jumped onto the bridge. Amazingly, it held his weight. "Easy! I'll go first. Piper, come on, girl. I'll give you a hand."

"No, that's okay," Piper started to say, but the coach grabbed her hand and dragged her up the bridge.

When they were about halfway, the bridge still seemed to be holding them just fine.

Thalia turned to her Hunter friend. "Phoebe, I'll be back soon. Go find the others. Tell them I'm on my way."

"You sure?" Phoebe narrowed her eyes at Leo and Jason, like they might kidnap Thalia or something.

"It's fine," Thalia promised.

Phoebe nodded reluctantly, then raced down the mountain path, the white wolves at her heels.

"Jason, Leo, just be careful where you step," Thalia said. "It hardly ever breaks."

"It hasn't met me yet," Leo muttered, but he and Jason led the way up the bridge.

Halfway up, things went wrong, and of course it was Leo's fault. Piper and Hedge had already made it safely to the top and were waving at them, encouraging them to keep climbing, but Leo got distracted. He was thinking about bridges —how he would design something way more stable than this shifting ice vapor business if this were his palace. He was pondering braces and support columns. Then a sudden revelation stopped him in his tracks.

"Why do they have a bridge?" he asked.

Thalia frowned. "Leo, this isn't a good place to stop. What do you mean?"

"They're wind spirits," Leo said. "Can't they fly?"

"Yes, but sometimes they need a way to connect to the world below."

"So the bridge isn't always here?" Leo asked.

Thalia shook her head. "The wind spirits don't like to anchor to the earth, but sometimes it's necessary. Like now. They know you're coming."

Leo's mind was racing. He was so excited he could almost feel his body's temperature rising. He couldn't quite put his thoughts into words, but he knew he was on to something important.

"Leo?" Jason said. "What are you thinking?"

"Oh, gods," Thalia said. "Keep moving. Look at your feet."

Leo shuffled backward. With horror, he realized his body temperature really *was* rising, just as it had years ago at that picnic table under the pecan tree, when his anger had gotten away from him. Now, excitement was causing the reaction. His pants steamed in the cold air. His shoes were literally smoking, and the bridge didn't like it. The ice was thinning.

"Leo, stop it," Jason warned. "You're going to melt it."

"I'll try," Leo said. But his body was overheating on its own, running as fast as his thoughts. "Listen, Jason, what did Hera call you in that dream? She called you a *bridge*."

"Leo, seriously, cool down," Thalia said. "I don't know what you're talking about, but the bridge is—"

"Just listen," Leo insisted. "If Jason is a bridge, what's he connecting? Maybe two different places that normally don't get along—like the air palace and the ground. You had to be somewhere before this, right? And Hera said you were an exchange."

"An exchange." Thalia's eyes widened. "Oh, gods."

Jason frowned. "What are you two talking about?"

Thalia murmured something like a prayer. "I understand now why Artemis sent me here. Jason—she told me to hunt for Lycaon and I would find a clue about Percy. *You* are the clue. Artemis wanted us to meet so I could hear your story."

"I don't understand," he protested. "I don't have a story. I don't remember anything."

"But Leo's right," Thalia said. "It's all connected. If we just knew where—"

Leo snapped his fingers. "Jason, what did you call that place in your dream? That ruined house. The Wolf House?"

Thalia nearly choked. "The Wolf House? Jason, why didn't you tell me that! *That's* where they're keeping Hera?"

"You know where it is?" Jason asked.

Then the bridge dissolved. Leo would've fallen to his death, but Jason grabbed his coat and pulled him to safety. The two of them scrambled up the bridge, and when they turned, Thalia was on the other side of a thirty-foot chasm. The bridge was continuing to melt.

"Go!" Thalia shouted, backing down the bridge as it crumbled. "Find out where the giant is keeping Piper's dad. Save him! I'll take the Hunters to the Wolf House and hold it until you can get there. We can do both!"

"But where *is* the Wolf House?" Jason shouted.

"You know where it is, little brother!" She was so far away now that they could barely hear her voice over the wind. Leo was pretty sure she said: "I'll see you there. I promise."

Then she turned and raced down the dissolving bridge.

Leo and Jason had no time to stand around. They climbed for their lives, the ice vapor thinning under their feet. Several times, Jason grabbed Leo and used the winds to keep them aloft, but it was more like bungee jumping than flying.

When they reached the floating island, Piper and Coach Hedge pulled them aboard just as the last of the vapor bridge vanished. They stood gasping for breath at the base of a stone stairway chiseled into the side of the cliff, leading up to the fortress.

Leo looked back down. The top of Pikes Peak floated below them in a sea of clouds, but there was no sign of Thalia. And Leo had just burned their only exit.

"What happened?" Piper demanded. "Leo, why are your clothes smoking?"

"I got a little heated," he gasped. "Sorry, Jason. Honest. I didn't—"

"It's all right," Jason said, but his expression was grim. "We've got less than twenty-four hours to rescue a goddess and Piper's dad. Let's go see the king of the winds."

XXXVII

JASON

JASON HAD FOUND HIS SISTER AND lost her in less than an hour. As they climbed the cliffs of the floating island, he kept looking back, but Thalia was gone.

Despite what she'd said about meeting him again, Jason wondered. She'd found a new family with the Hunters, and a new mother in Artemis. She seemed so confident and comfortable with her life, Jason wasn't sure if he'd ever be part of it. And she seemed so set on finding her friend Percy. Had she ever searched for Jason that way?

Not fair, he told himself. *She thought you were dead.*

He could barely tolerate what she'd said about their mom. It was almost like Thalia had handed him a baby—a really loud, ugly baby—and said, *Here, this is yours. Carry it.* He didn't want to carry it. He didn't want to look at it or claim it. He didn't want to know that he had an unstable mother who'd gotten rid of him to appease a goddess. No wonder Thalia had run away.

Then he remembered the Zeus cabin at Camp Half-Blood —that tiny little alcove Thalia had used as a bunk, out of sight from the glowering statue of the sky god. Their dad wasn't much of a bargain, either. Jason understood why Thalia had renounced that part of her life too, but he was still resentful. He couldn't be so lucky. He was left holding the bag —literally.

The golden backpack of winds was strapped over his shoulders. The closer they got to Aeolus's palace, the heavier the bag got. The winds struggled, rumbling and bumping around.

The only one who seemed in a good mood was Coach Hedge. He kept bounding up the slippery staircase and trotting back down. "Come on, cupcakes! Only a few thousand more steps!"

As they climbed, Leo and Piper left Jason in his silence. Maybe they could sense his bad mood. Piper kept glancing back, worried, as if he were the one who'd almost died of hypothermia rather than she. Or maybe she was thinking about Thalia's idea. They'd told her what Thalia had said on the bridge—how they could save both her dad and Hera—but Jason didn't really understand how they were going to do that, and he wasn't sure if the possibility had made Piper more hopeful or just more anxious.

Leo kept swatting his own legs, checking for signs that his pants were on fire. He wasn't steaming anymore, but the incident on the ice bridge had really freaked Jason out. Leo hadn't seemed to realize that he had smoke coming out his ears and flames dancing through his hair. If Leo started spontaneously combusting every time he got excited, they were going to have a tough time taking him anywhere. Jason imagined trying to get food at a restaurant. *I'll have a cheeseburger and—Ahhh! My friend's on fire! Get me a bucket!*

Mostly, though, Jason worried about what Leo had said. Jason didn't want to be a bridge, or an exchange, or anything else. He just wanted to know where he'd come from. And Thalia had looked so unnerved when Leo mentioned the burned-out house in his dreams—the place the wolf Lupa had told him was his starting point. How did Thalia know that place, and why did she assume Jason could find it?

The answer seemed close. But the nearer Jason got to it, the less it cooperated, like the winds on his back.

Finally they arrived at the top of the island. Bronze walls marched all the way around the fortress grounds, though Jason couldn't imagine who would possibly attack this place. Twenty-foot-high gates opened for them, and a road of polished purple stone led up to the main citadel—a white-columned rotunda, Greek style, like one of the monuments in Washington, D.C.—except for the cluster of satellite dishes and radio towers on the roof.

"That's bizarre," Piper said.

"Guess you can't get cable on a floating island," Leo said. "Dang, check this guy's front yard."

The rotunda sat in the center of a quarter-mile circle. The grounds were amazing in a scary way. They were divided into four sections like big pizza slices, each one representing a season.

The section on their right was an icy waste, with bare trees and a frozen lake. Snowmen rolled across the landscape as the wind blew, so Jason wasn't sure if they were decorations or alive.

To their left was an autumn park with gold and red trees. Mounds of leaves blew into patterns—gods, people, animals that ran after each other before scattering back into leaves.

In the distance, Jason could see two more areas behind the rotunda. One looked like a green pasture with sheep made out of clouds. The last section was a desert where tumble-weeds scratched strange patterns in the sand like Greek let-ters, smiley faces, and a huge advertisement that read: WATCH AEOLUS NIGHTLY!

"One section for each of the four wind gods," Jason guessed. "Four cardinal directions."

"I'm loving that pasture." Coach Hedge licked his lips. "You guys mind—"

"Go ahead," Jason said. He was actually relieved to send the satyr off. It would be hard enough getting on Aeolus's good side without Coach Hedge waving his club and scream-ing, "Die!"

While the satyr ran off to attack springtime, Jason, Leo, and Piper walked down the road to the steps of the palace. They passed through the front doors into a white marble foyer decorated with purple banners that read OLYMPIAN WEATHER CHANNEL, and some that just read OW!

"Hello!" A woman floated up to them. *Literally* floated. She was pretty in that elfish way Jason associated with nature spirits at Camp Half-Blood—petite, slightly pointy ears, and an ageless face that could've been sixteen or thirty. Her brown eyes twinkled cheerfully. Even though there was no wind, her dark hair blew in slow motion, shampoo-commercial style. Her white gown billowed around her like parachute material. Jason couldn't tell if she had feet, but if so, they didn't touch the floor. She had a white tablet computer in her hand. "Are you from Lord Zeus?" she asked. "We've been expecting you."

Jason tried to respond, but it was a little hard to think straight, because he'd realized the woman was see-through. Her shape faded in and out like she was made of fog.

"Are you a ghost?" he asked.

Right away he knew he'd insulted her. The smile turned into a pout. "I'm an *aura*, sir. A wind nymph, as you might expect, working for the lord of the winds. My name is Mellie. We don't have *ghosts*."

Piper came to the rescue. "No, of course you don't! My friend simply mistook you for Helen of Troy, the most beautiful mortal of all time. It's an easy mistake."

Wow, she was good. The compliment seemed a little over the top, but Mellie the aura blushed. "Oh...well, then. So you *are* from Zeus?"

"Er," Jason said, "I'm the son of Zeus, yeah."

"Excellent! Please, right this way." She led them through some security doors into another lobby, consulting her tablet as she floated. She didn't look where she was going, but apparently it didn't matter as she drifted straight through a marble column with no problem. "We're out of prime time now, so that's good," she mused. "I can fit you in right before his 11:12 spot."

"Um, okay," Jason said.

The lobby was a pretty distracting place. Winds blasted

around them, so Jason felt like he was pushing through an invisible crowd. Doors blew open and slammed by themselves.

The things Jason *could* see were just as bizarre. Paper airplanes of all different sizes and shapes sped around, and other wind nymphs, *aurai*, would occasionally pluck them out of the air, unfold and read them, then toss them back into the air, where the planes would refold themselves and keep flying.

An ugly creature fluttered past. She looked like a mix between an old lady and a chicken on steroids. She had a wrinkled face with black hair tied in a hairnet, arms like a human plus wings like a chicken, and a fat, feathered body with talons for feet. It was amazing she could fly at all. She kept drifting around and bumping into things like a parade balloon.

"Not an *aura*?" Jason asked Mellie as the creature wobbled by.

Mellie laughed. "That's a harpy, of course. Our, ah, ugly stepsisters, I suppose you would say. Don't you have harpies on Olympus? They're spirits of violent gusts, unlike us *aurai*. We're all gentle breezes."

She batted her eyes at Jason.

"'Course you are," he said.

"So," Piper prompted, "you were taking us to see Aeolus?"

Mellie led them through a set of doors like an airlock. Above the interior door, a green light blinked.

"We have a few minutes before he starts," Mellie said cheerfully. "He probably won't kill you if we go in now. Come along!"

XXXVIII

JASON

Jason's jaw dropped. The central section of Aeolus's fortress was as big as a cathedral, with a soaring domed roof covered in silver. Television equipment floated randomly through the air—cameras, spotlights, set pieces, potted plants. And there was no floor. Leo almost fell into the chasm before Jason pulled him back.

"Holy—!" Leo gulped. "Hey, Mellie. A little warning next time!"

An enormous circular pit plunged into the heart of the mountain. It was probably half a mile deep, honeycombed with caves. Some of the tunnels probably led straight outside. Jason remembered seeing winds blast out of them when they'd been on Pikes Peak. Other caves were sealed with some glistening material like glass or wax. The whole cavern bustled with harpies, *aurai*, and paper airplanes, but for someone who couldn't fly, it would be a very long, very fatal fall.

"Oh, my," Mellie gasped. "I'm so sorry." She unclipped a walkie-talkie from somewhere inside her robes and spoke into it: "Hello, sets? Is that Nuggets? Hi, Nuggets. Could we get a floor in the main studio, please? Yes, a solid one. Thanks."

A few seconds later, an army of harpies rose from the pit—three dozen or so demon chicken ladies, all carrying squares of various building material. They went to work hammering and gluing—and using large quantities of duct tape, which didn't reassure Jason. In no time there was a makeshift floor snaking out over the chasm. It was made of plywood, marble blocks, carpet squares, wedges of grass sod—just about anything.

"That can't be safe," Jason said.

"Oh, it is!" Mellie assured him. "The harpies are very good."

Easy for her to say. She just drifted across without touching the floor, but Jason decided he had the best chance at surviving, since he could fly, so he stepped out first. Amazingly, the floor held.

Piper gripped his hand and followed him. "If I fall, you're catching me."

"Uh, sure." Jason hoped he wasn't blushing.

Leo stepped out next. "You're catching me, too, Superman. But I ain't holding your hand."

Mellie led them toward the middle of the chamber, where a loose sphere of flat-panel video screens floated around a kind of control center. A man hovered inside, checking monitors and reading paper airplane messages.

The man paid them no attention as Mellie brought them forward. She pushed a forty-two-inch Sony out of their way and led them into the control area.

Leo whistled. "I *got* to get a room like this."

The floating screens showed all sorts of television programs. Some Jason recognized—news broadcasts, mostly—but some programs looked a little strange: gladiators fighting, demigods battling monsters. Maybe they were movies, but they looked more like reality shows.

At the far end of the sphere was a silky blue backdrop like a cinema screen, with cameras and studio lights floating around it.

The man in the center was talking into an earpiece phone. He had a remote control in each hand and was pointing them at various screens, seemingly at random.

He wore a business suit that looked like the sky—blue mostly, but dappled with clouds that changed and darkened and moved across the fabric. He looked like he was in his sixties, with a shock of white hair, but he had a ton of stage makeup on, and that smooth plastic-surgery look to his face, so he appeared not really young, not really old, just *wrong*—like a Ken doll someone had halfway melted in a microwave. His eyes darted back and forth from screen to screen, like he was trying to absorb everything at once. He muttered things into his phone, and his mouth kept twitching. He was either amused, or crazy, or both.

Mellie floated toward him. "Ah, sir, Mr. Aeolus, these demigods—"

"Hold it!" He held up a hand to silence her, then pointed at one of the screens. "Watch!"

It was one of those storm-chaser programs, where insane thrill-seekers drive after tornados. As Jason watched, a Jeep plowed straight into a funnel cloud and got tossed into the sky.

Aeolus shrieked with delight. "The Disaster Channel. People do that *on purpose!*" He turned toward Jason with a mad grin. "Isn't that amazing? Let's watch it again."

"Um, sir," Mellie said, "this is Jason, son of—"

"Yes, yes, I remember," Aeolus said. "You're back. How did it go?"

Jason hesitated. "Sorry? I think you've mistaken me—"

"No, no, Jason Grace, aren't you? It was—what—last year? You were on your way to fight a sea monster, I believe."

"I—I don't remember."

Aeolus laughed. "Must not have been a very good sea monster! No, I remember every hero who's ever come to me for aid. Odysseus—gods, he docked at my island for a month! At least you only stayed a few days. Now, watch this video. These ducks get sucked straight into—"

"Sir," Mellie interrupted. "Two minutes to air."

"Air!" Aeolus exclaimed. "I love air. How do I look? Makeup!"

Immediately a small tornado of brushes, blotters, and cotton balls descended on Aeolus. They blurred across his face in a cloud of flesh-tone smoke until his coloration was even more gruesome than before. Wind swirled through his hair and left it sticking up like a frosted Christmas tree.

"Mr. Aeolus." Jason slipped off the golden backpack. "We brought you these rogue storm spirits."

"Did you!" Aeolus looked at the bag like it was a gift from a fan—something he really didn't want. "Well, how nice."

Leo nudged him, and Jason offered the bag. "Boreas sent us to capture them for you. We hope you'll accept them and stop—you know—ordering demigods to be killed."

Aeolus laughed, and looked incredulously at Mellie. "Demigods be killed—did I order that?"

Mellie checked her computer tablet. "Yes, sir, fifteenth of September. 'Storm spirits released by the death of Typhon, demigods to be held responsible,' etc.... yes, a general order for them all to be killed."

"Oh, pish," Aeolus said. "I was just grumpy. Rescind that order, Mellie, and um, who's on guard duty—Teriyaki?—Teri, take these storm spirits down to cell block Fourteen E, will you?"

A harpy swooped out of nowhere, snatched the golden bag, and spiraled into the abyss.

Aeolus grinned at Jason. "Now, sorry about that kill-on-sight business. But gods, I really was mad, wasn't I?" His face suddenly darkened, and his suit did the same, the lapels flashing with lightning. "You know... I remember now. Almost seemed like a voice was telling me to give that order. A little cold tingle on the back of my neck."

Jason tensed. A cold tingle on the back of his neck... Why did that sound so familiar? "A... um, voice in your head, sir?"

"Yes. How odd. Mellie, *should* we kill them?"

"No, sir," she said patiently. "They just brought us the storm spirits, which makes everything all right."

"Of course." Aeolus laughed. "Sorry. Mellie, let's send the demigods something nice. A box of chocolates, perhaps."

"A box of chocolates to *every* demigod in the world, sir?"

"No, too expensive. Never mind. Wait, it's time! I'm on!"

Aeolus flew off toward the blue screen as newscast music started to play.

Jason looked at Piper and Leo, who seemed just as confused as he was.

"Mellie," he said, "is he . . . always like that?"

She smiled sheepishly. "Well, you know what they say. If you don't like his mood, wait five minutes. That expression 'whichever way the wind blows'—that was based on him."

"And that thing about the sea monster," Jason said. "*Was* I here before?"

Mellie blushed. "I'm sorry, I don't remember. I'm Mr. Aeolus's new assistant. I've been with him longer than most, but still—not that long."

"How long do his assistants usually last?" Piper asked.

"Oh . . ." Mellie thought for a moment. "I've been doing this for . . . twelve hours?"

A voice blared from floating speakers: "And now, weather every twelve minutes! Here's your forecaster for Olympian Weather—the OW! channel—Aeolus!"

Lights blazed on Aeolus, who was now standing in front of the blue screen. His smile was unnaturally white, and he looked like he'd had so much caffeine his face was about to explode.

"Hello, Olympus! Aeolus, master of the winds here, with weather every twelve! We'll have a low-pressure system moving over Florida today, so expect milder temperatures since Demeter wishes to spare the citrus farmers!" He gestured at the blue screen, but when Jason checked the monitors, he saw that a digital image was being projected behind Aeolus, so it looked like he was standing in front of a U.S. map with animated smiley suns and frowny storm clouds. "Along the eastern seaboard—oh, hold on." He tapped his earpiece. "Sorry, folks! Poseidon is angry with Miami today, so it looks like that Florida freeze is back on! Sorry, Demeter. Over in the Midwest, I'm not sure what St. Louis did to offend Zeus, but you can expect winter storms! Boreas himself is being called down to punish the area with ice. Bad news, Missouri! No, wait. Hephaestus feels sorry for central Missouri, so you all will have much more moderate temperatures and sunny skies."

Aeolus kept going like that—forecasting each area of the country and changing his prediction two or three times as he got messages over his earpiece—the gods apparently putting in orders for various winds and weather.

"This can't be right," Jason whispered. "Weather isn't this random."

Mellie smirked. "And how often are the mortal weathermen right? They talk about fronts and air pressure and moisture, but the weather surprises them all the time. At least Aeolus tells us *why* it's so unpredictable. Very hard job, trying to appease all the gods at once. It's enough to drive anyone..."

She trailed off, but Jason knew what she meant. *Mad.* Aeolus was completely mad.

"And that's the weather," Aeolus concluded. "See you in twelve minutes, because I'm sure it'll change!"

The lights shut off, the video monitors went back to random coverage, and just for a moment, Aeolus's face sagged with weariness. Then he seemed to remember he had guests, and he put a smile back on.

"So, you brought me some rogue storm spirits," Aeolus said. "I suppose . . . thanks! And did you want something else? I assume so. Demigods always do."

Mellie said, "Um, sir, this is Zeus's son."

"Yes, yes. I know that. I said I remembered him from before."

"But, sir, they're here from *Olympus*."

Aeolus looked stunned. Then he laughed so abruptly, Jason almost jumped into the chasm. "You mean you're here on behalf of your father this time? Finally! I *knew* they would send someone to renegotiate my contract!"

"Um, what?" Jason asked.

"Oh, thank goodness!" Aeolus sighed with relief. "It's been what, three thousand years since Zeus made me master of the winds. Not that I'm ungrateful, of course! But really, my contract is so vague. Obviously I'm immortal, but 'master of the winds.' What does that mean? Am I a nature spirit? A demigod? A god? I *want* to be god of the winds, because the benefits are *so* much better. Can we start with that?"

Jason looked at his friends, mystified.

"Dude," Leo said, "you think we're here to promote you?"

"You are, then?" Aeolus grinned. His business suit turned completely blue—not a cloud in the fabric. "Marvelous! I mean, I think I've shown quite a bit of initiative with the weather channel, eh? And of course I'm in the press all the time. So many books have been written about me: *Into Thin Air, Up in the Air, Gone with the Wind*—"

"Er, I don't think those are about you," Jason said, before he noticed Mellie shaking her head.

"Nonsense," Aeolus said. "Mellie, they're biographies of me, aren't they?"

"Absolutely, sir," she squeaked.

"There, you see? I don't read. Who has time? But obviously the mortals love me. So, we'll change my official title to *god* of the winds. Then, about salary and staff—"

"Sir," Jason said, "we're not from Olympus."

Aeolus blinked. "But—"

"I'm the son of Zeus, yes," Jason said, "but we're not here to negotiate your contract. We're on a quest and we need your help."

Aeolus's expression hardened. "Like last time? Like *every* hero who comes here? Demigods! It's always about *you*, isn't it?"

"Sir, please, I don't remember last time, but if you helped me once before—"

"I'm always helping! Well, sometimes I'm destroying, but mostly I'm helping, and sometimes I'm asked to do both at the same time! Why, Aeneas, the first of your kind—"

"My kind?" Jason asked. "You mean, demigods?"

"Oh, please!" Aeolus said. "I mean your *line* of demigods. You know, Aeneas, son of Venus—the only surviving hero of Troy. When the Greeks burned down his city, he escaped to

Italy, where he founded the kingdom that would eventually become Rome, blah, blah, blah. *That's* what I meant."

"I don't get it," Jason admitted.

Aeolus rolled his eyes. "The point being, I was thrown in the middle of that conflict, too! Juno calls up: 'Oh, Aeolus, destroy Aeneas's ships for me. I don't like him.' Then Neptune says, 'No, you don't! That's my territory. Calm the winds.' Then Juno is like, 'No, wreck his ships, or I'll tell Jupiter you're uncooperative!' Do you think it's easy juggling requests like that?"

"No," Jason said. "I guess not."

"And don't get me started on Amelia Earhart! I'm *still* getting angry calls from Olympus about knocking *her* out of the sky!"

"We just want information," Piper said in her most calming voice. "We hear you know everything."

Aeolus straightened his lapels and looked slightly mollified. "Well...*that's* true, of course. For instance, I know that *this* business here"—he waggled his fingers at the three of them—"this harebrained scheme of Juno's to bring you all together is likely to end in bloodshed. As for you, Piper McLean, I know your father is in serious trouble." He held out his hand, and a scrap of paper fluttered into his grasp. It was a photo of Piper with a guy who must've been her dad. His face *did* look familiar. Jason was pretty sure he'd seen him in some movies.

Piper took the photo. Her hands were shaking. "This—this is from his wallet."

"Yes," Aeolus said. "All things lost in the wind eventually

come to me. The photo blew away when the Earthborn captured him."

"The what?" Piper asked.

Aeolus waved aside the question and narrowed his eyes at Leo. "Now, *you,* son of Hephaestus...yes, I see your future." Another paper fell into the wind god's hands—an old tattered drawing done in crayons.

Leo took it as if it might be coated in poison. He staggered backward.

"Leo?" Jason said. "What is it?"

"Something I—I drew when I was a kid." He folded it quickly and put it in his coat. "It's...yeah, it's nothing."

Aeolus laughed. "Really? Just the key to your success! Now, where were we? Ah, yes, you wanted information. Are you sure about that? Sometimes information can be dangerous."

He smiled at Jason like he was issuing a challenge. Behind him, Mellie shook her head in warning.

"Yeah," Jason said. "We need to find the lair of Enceladus."

Aeolus's smile melted. "The giant? Why would you want to go there? He's horrible! He doesn't even watch my program!"

Piper held up the photo. "Aeolus, he's got my father. We need to rescue him and find out where Hera is being held captive."

"Now, *that's* impossible," Aeolus said. "Even *I* can't see that, and believe me, I've tried. There's a veil of magic over Hera's location—very strong, impossible to locate."

"She's at a place called the Wolf House," Jason said.

"Hold on!" Aelous put a hand to his forehead and closed

his eyes. "I'm getting something! Yes, she's at a place called the Wolf House! Sadly, I don't know where that is."

"Enceladus does," Piper persisted. "If you help us find him, we could get the location of the goddess—"

"Yeah," Leo said, catching on. "And if we save her, she'd be really grateful to you—"

"And Zeus might promote you," Jason finished.

Aeolus's eyebrows crept up. "A promotion—and all you want from me is the giant's location?"

"Well, if you could get us there, too," Jason amended, "that would be great."

Mellie clapped her hands in excitement. "Oh, he could do that! He often sends helpful winds—"

"Mellie, quiet!" Aeolus snapped. "I have half a mind to fire you for letting these people in under false pretenses."

Her face paled. "Yes, sir. Sorry, sir."

"It wasn't her fault," Jason said. "But about that help . . ."

Aeolus tilted his head as if thinking. Then Jason realized the wind lord was listening to voices in his earpiece.

"Well . . . Zeus approves," Aeolus muttered. "He says . . . he says it would be better if you could avoid saving her until after the weekend, because he has a big party planned—Ow! That's Aphrodite yelling at him, reminding him that the solstice starts at dawn. She says I should help you. And Hephaestus . . . yes. Hmm. Very rare they agree on anything. Hold on . . ."

Jason smiled at his friends. Finally, they were having some good luck. Their godly parents were standing up for them.

Back toward the entrance, Jason heard a loud belch. Coach

Hedge waddled in from the lobby, grass all over his face. Mellie saw him coming across the makeshift floor and caught her breath. "Who is *that*?"

Jason stifled a cough. "That? That's just Coach Hedge. Uh, Gleeson Hedge. He's our..." Jason wasn't sure what to call him: *teacher, friend, problem*?

"Our guide."

"He's *so* goatly," Mellie murmured.

Behind her, Piper poofed out her cheeks, pretending to vomit.

"What's up, guys?" Hedge trotted over. "Wow, nice place. Oh! Sod squares."

"Coach, you just ate," Jason said. "And we're using the sod as a floor. This is, ah, Mellie—"

"An *aura*." Hedge smiled winningly. "Beautiful as a summer breeze."

Mellie blushed.

"And Aeolus here was just about to help us," Jason said.

"Yes," the wind lord muttered. "It seems so. You'll find Enceladus on Mount Diablo."

"Devil Mountain?" Leo asked. "That doesn't sound good."

"I remember that place!" Piper said. "I went there once with my dad. It's just east of San Francisco Bay."

"The Bay Area again?" The coach shook his head. "Not good. Not good at all."

"Now..." Aeolus began to smile. "As to getting you there—"

Suddenly his face went slack. He bent over and tapped his earpiece as if it were malfunctioning. When he straightened again, his eyes were wild. Despite the makeup, he looked like an old man—an old, very frightened man. "She hasn't spoke to me for centuries. I can't—yes, yes I understand."

He swallowed, regarding Jason as if he had suddenly turned into a giant cockroach. "I'm sorry, son of Jupiter. New orders. You all have to die."

Mellie squeaked. "But—but, sir! Zeus said to help them. Aphrodite, Hephaestus—"

"Mellie!" Aeolus snapped. "Your job is already on the line. Besides, there are some orders that transcend even the wishes of the gods, especially when it comes to the forces of nature."

"*Whose* orders?" Jason said. "Zeus will fire you if you don't help us!"

"I doubt it." Aeolus flicked his wrist, and far below them, a cell door opened in the pit. Jason could hear storm spirits screaming out of it, spiraling up toward them, howling for blood.

"Even Zeus understands the order of things," Aeolus said. "And if *she* is waking—by all the gods—she cannot be denied. Good-bye, heroes. I'm terribly sorry, but I'll have to make this quick. I'm back on the air in four minutes."

Jason summoned his sword. Coach Hedge pulled out his club. Mellie the aura yelled, "No!"

She dived at their feet just as the storm spirits hit with hurricane force, blasting the floor to pieces, shredding the carpet samples and marble and linoleum into what should've been lethal projectiles, had Mellie's robes not spread out like a shield and absorbed the brunt of the impact. The five of them fell into the pit, and Aeolus screamed above them, "Mellie, you are *so* fired!"

"Quick," Mellie yelled. "Son of Zeus, do you have any power over the air?"

"A little!"

"Then help me, or you're all dead!" Mellie grabbed his hand, and an electric charge went through Jason's arm. He understood what she needed. They had to control their fall and head for one of the open tunnels. The storm spirits were following them down, closing rapidly, bringing with them a cloud of deadly shrapnel.

Jason grabbed Piper's hand. "Group hug!"

Hedge, Leo, and Piper tried to huddle together, hanging on to Jason and Mellie as they fell.

"This is NOT GOOD!" Leo yelled.

"Bring it on, gas bags!" Hedge yelled up at the storm spirits. "I'll pulverize you!"

"He's magnificent," Mellie sighed.

"Concentrate?" Jason prompted.

"Right!" she said.

They channeled the wind so their fall became more of a tumble into the nearest open chute. Still, they slammed into the tunnel at painful speed and went rolling over each other down a steep vent that was not designed for people. There was no way they could stop.

Mellie's robes billowed around her. Jason and the others clung to her desperately, and they began to slow down, but the storm spirits were screaming into the tunnel behind them.

"Can't—hold—long," Mellie warned. "Stay together! When the winds hit—"

"You're doing great, Mellie," Hedge said. "My own mama was an *aura*, you know. She couldn't have done better herself."

"Iris-message me?" Mellie pleaded.

Hedge winked.

"Could you guys plan your date later?" Piper screamed. "Look!"

Behind them, the tunnel was turning dark. Jason could feel his ears pop as the pressure built.

"Can't hold them," Mellie warned. "But I'll try to shield you, do you one more favor."

"Thanks, Mellie," Jason said. "I hope you get a new job."

She smiled, and then dissolved, wrapping them in a warm gentle breeze. Then the real winds hit, shooting them into the sky so fast, Jason blacked out.

XXXIX

PIPER

PIPER DREAMED SHE WAS ON THE Wilderness School dorm roof.

The desert night was cold, but she'd brought blankets, and with Jason next to her, she didn't need any more warmth.

The air smelled of sage and burning mesquite. On the horizon, the Spring Mountains loomed like jagged black teeth, the dim glow of Las Vegas behind them.

The stars were so bright, Piper had been afraid they wouldn't be able to see the meteor shower. She didn't want Jason to think she'd dragged him up here on false pretenses. (Even though her pretenses had been *totally* false.) But the meteors did not disappoint. One streaked across the sky almost every minute—a line of white, yellow, or blue fire. Piper was sure her Grandpa Tom would have some Cherokee myth to explain them, but at the moment she was busy creating her own story.

Jason took her hand—*finally*—and pointed as two meteors skipped across the atmosphere and formed a cross.

"Wow," he said. "I can't believe Leo didn't want to see this."

"Actually, I didn't invite him," Piper said casually.

Jason smiled. "Oh, yeah?"

"Mm-hmm. You ever feel like three would be a crowd?"

"Yeah," Jason admitted. "Like right now. You know how much trouble we'd get in if we got caught up here?"

"Oh, I'd make up something," Piper said. "I can be very persuasive. So you want to dance, or what?"

He laughed. His eyes were amazing, and his smile was even better in the starlight. "With no music. At night. On a rooftop. Sounds dangerous."

"I'm a dangerous girl."

"That, I can believe."

He stood and offered her his hand. They slow danced a few steps, but it quickly turned into a kiss. Piper almost couldn't kiss him again, because she was too busy smiling.

Then her dream changed—or maybe she was dead in the Underworld—because she found herself back in Medea's department store.

"Please let this be a dream," she murmured, "and not my eternal punishment."

"No, dear," said a woman's honey-sweet voice. "No punishment."

Piper turned, afraid she'd see Medea, but a different

woman stood next to her, browsing through the fifty-percent-off rack.

The woman was gorgeous—shoulder-length hair, a graceful neck, perfect features, and an amazing figure tucked into jeans and a snowy white top.

Piper had seen her share of actresses—most of her dad's dates were knockout beautiful—but this lady was different. She was elegant without trying, fashionable without effort, stunning without makeup. After seeing Aeolus with his silly face-lifts and cosmetics, Piper thought this woman looked even more astonishing. There was nothing artificial about her.

Yet as Piper watched, the woman's appearance changed. Piper couldn't decide the color of her eyes, or the exact color of her hair. The woman became more and more beautiful, as if her image were aligning itself to Piper's thoughts—getting as close as possible to Piper's ideal of beauty.

"Aphrodite," Piper said. "Mom?"

The goddess smiled. "You're only dreaming, my sweet. If anyone wonders, I wasn't here. Okay?"

"I—" Piper wanted to ask a thousand questions, but they all crowded together in her head.

Aphrodite held up a turquoise dress. Piper thought it looked awesome, but the goddess made a face. "This isn't my color, is it? Pity, it's cute. Medea really does have some lovely things here."

"This—this building exploded," Piper stammered. "I saw it."

"Yes," Aphrodite agreed. "I suppose that's why everything's on sale. Just a memory, now. And I'm sorry to pull you out of your other dream. Much more pleasant, I know."

Piper's face burned. She didn't know whether she was more angry or embarrassed, but mostly she felt hollow with disappointment. "It wasn't real. It never even happened. So why do I remember it so vividly?"

Aphrodite smiled. "Because you are my daughter, Piper. You see possibilities much more vividly than others. You see what *could* be. And it still might be—don't give up. Unfortunately—" The goddess gestured around the department store. "You have other trials to face, first. Medea will be back, along with many other enemies. The Doors of Death have opened."

"What do you mean?"

Aphrodite winked at her. "You're a smart one, Piper. You know."

A cold feeling settled over her. "The sleeping woman, the one Medea and Midas called their patron. She's managed to open a new entrance from the Underworld. She's letting the dead escape back into the world."

"Mmm. And not just *any* dead. The worst, the most powerful, the ones most likely to hate the gods."

"The monsters are coming back from Tartarus the same way," Piper guessed. "That's why they don't stay disintegrated."

"Yes. Their *patron*, as you call her, has a special relationship with Tartarus, the spirit of the pit." Aphrodite held up a gold sequined top. "No... this would make me look ridiculous."

Piper laughed uneasily. "You? You can't look anything but perfect."

"You're sweet," Aphrodite said. "But beauty is about finding the right fit, the most natural fit. To be perfect, you have to feel perfect about yourself—avoid trying to be something you're not. For a goddess, that's especially hard. We can change so easily."

"My dad thought you were perfect." Piper's voice quavered. "He never got over you."

Aphrodite's gaze became distant. "Yes... Tristan. Oh, he was amazing. So gentle and kind, funny and handsome. Yet he had so much sadness inside."

"Could we please not talk about him in the past tense?"

"I'm sorry, dear. I didn't want to leave your father, of course. It's always so hard, but it was for the best. If he had realized who I actually was—"

"Wait—he didn't *know* you were a goddess?"

"Of course not." Aphrodite sounded offended. "I wouldn't do that to him. For most mortals, that's simply too hard to accept. It can ruin their lives! Ask your friend Jason—*lovely* boy, by the way. His poor mother was destroyed when she found out she'd fallen in love with Zeus. No, it was much better Tristan believed that I was a mortal woman who left him without explanation. Better a bittersweet memory than an immortal, unattainable goddess. Which brings me to an important matter..."

She opened her hand and showed Piper a glowing glass vial of pink liquid. "This is one of Medea's kinder mixtures. It erases only recent memories. When you save your father, *if* you can save him, you should give him this."

Piper couldn't believe what she was hearing. "You want me to dope my dad? You want me to make him forget what he's been through?"

Aphrodite held up the vial. The liquid cast a pink glow over her face. "Your father acts confident, Piper, but he walks a fine line between two worlds. He's worked his whole life to deny the old stories about gods and spirits, yet he fears those stories might be real. He fears that he's shut off an important part of himself, and someday it will destroy him. Now he's been captured by a giant. He's living a nightmare. Even if he survives . . . if he has to spend the rest of his life with those memories, knowing that gods and spirits walk the earth, it will shatter him. That's what our enemy hopes for. She will break him, and thus break your spirit."

Piper wanted to shout that Aphrodite was wrong. Her dad was the strongest person she knew. Piper would never take his memories the way Hera had taken Jason's.

But somehow she couldn't stay angry with Aphrodite. She remembered what her dad had said months ago, at the beach at Big Sur: *If I really believed in Ghost Country, or animal spirits, or Greek gods . . . I don't think I could sleep at night. I'd always be looking for somebody to blame.*

Now Piper wanted someone to blame, too.

"Who is she?" Piper demanded. "The one controlling the giants?"

Aphrodite pursed her lips. She moved to the next rack, which held battered armor and ripped togas, but Aphrodite looked through them as if they were designer outfits.

"You have a strong will," she mused. "I'm never given much credit among the gods. My children are laughed at. They're dismissed as conceited and shallow."

"Some of them are."

Aphrodite laughed. "Granted. Perhaps I'm conceited and shallow, too, sometimes. A girl has to indulge. Oh, this is nice." She picked up a burned and stained bronze breastplate and held it up for Piper to see. "No?"

"No," Piper said. "Are you going to answer my question?"

"Patience, my sweet," the goddess said. "My point is that love is the most powerful motivator in the world. It spurs mortals to greatness. Their noblest, bravest acts are done for love."

Piper pulled out her dagger and studied its reflective blade. "Like Helen starting the Trojan War?"

"Ah, Katoptris." Aphrodite smiled. "I'm glad you found it. I get so much flack for that war, but honestly, Paris and Helen were a cute couple. And the heroes of that war are immortal now—at least in the memories of men. Love is powerful, Piper. It can bring even the gods to their knees. I told this to my son Aeneas when he escaped from Troy. He thought he had failed. He thought he was a loser! But he traveled to Italy—"

"And became the forebear of Rome."

"Exactly. You see, Piper, my children can be quite powerful. *You* can be quite powerful, because my lineage is unique. I am closer to the beginning of creation than any other Olympian."

Piper struggled to remember about Aphrodite's birth. "Didn't you . . . rise from the sea? Standing on a seashell?"

The goddess laughed. "That painter Botticelli had quite an imagination. I never stood on a seashell, thank you very much. But yes, I rose from the sea. The first beings to rise from Chaos were the Earth and Sky—Gaea and Ouranos. When their son the Titan Kronos killed Ouranos—"

"By chopping him to pieces with a scythe," Piper remembered.

Aphrodite wrinkled her nose. "Yes. The pieces of Ouranos fell into the sea. His immortal essence created sea foam. And from that foam—"

"You were born. I remember now. So you're—"

"The last child of Ouranos, who was greater than the gods or the Titans. So, in a strange way, I'm the eldest Olympian god. As I said, love is a powerful force. And you, my daughter, are much more than a pretty face. Which is why you already know who is waking the giants, and who has the power to open doors into the deepest parts of the earth."

Aphrodite waited, as if she could sense Piper slowly putting together the pieces of a puzzle, which made a dreadful picture.

"Gaea," Piper said. "The earth itself. That's our enemy."

She hoped Aphrodite would say no, but the goddess kept her eyes on the rack of tattered armor. "She has slumbered for eons, but she is slowly waking. Even asleep, she is powerful, but once she wakes . . . we will be doomed. You must defeat the giants before that happens, and lull Gaea back into her slumber. Otherwise the rebellion has only begun. The dead will continue to rise. Monsters will regenerate with even greater speed. The giants will lay waste to the birthplace of the gods. And if they do that, all civilization will burn."

"But *Gaea*? Mother Earth?"

"Do not underestimate her," Aphrodite warned. "She is a cruel deity. She orchestrated Ouranos's death. *She* gave Kronos the sickle and urged him to kill his own father. While the Titans ruled the world, she slumbered in peace. But when the gods overthrew them, Gaea woke again in all her anger and gave birth to a new race—the giants—to destroy Olympus once and for all."

"And it's happening again," Piper said. "The rise of the giants."

Aphrodite nodded. "Now you know. What will you do?"

"Me?" Piper clenched her fists. "What am I supposed to do? Put on a pretty dress and sweet-talk Gaea into going back to sleep?"

"I wish that would work," Aphrodite said. "But no, you will have to find your own strengths, and fight for what you love. Like my favored ones, Helen and Paris. Like my son Aeneas."

"Helen and Paris died," Piper said.

"And Aeneas became a hero," the goddess countered. "The first great hero of Rome. The result will depend on you, Piper, but I will tell you this: The seven greatest demigods must be gathered to defeat the giants, and that effort will not succeed without you. When the two sides meet . . . you will be the mediator. You will determine whether there is friendship or bloodshed."

"What two sides?"

Piper's vision began to dim.

"You must wake soon, my child," said the goddess. "I do not always agree with Hera, but she's taken a bold risk, and

I agree it must be done. Zeus has kept the two sides apart for too long. Only together will you have the power to save Olympus. Now, wake, and I hope you like the clothes I picked out."

"What clothes?" Piper demanded, but the dream faded to black.

X L

PIPER

PIPER WOKE AT A TABLE AT A SIDEWALK CAFÉ.

For a second, she thought she was still dreaming. It was a sunny morning. The air was brisk but not unpleasant for sitting outside. At the other tables, a mix of bicyclists, business people, and college kids sat chatting and drinking coffee.

She could smell eucalyptus trees. Lots of foot traffic passed in front of quaint little shops. The street was lined with bottlebrush trees and blooming azaleas as if winter was a foreign concept.

In other words: she was in California.

Her friends sat in chairs around her—all of them with their hands calmly folded across their chests, dozing pleasantly. And they all had new clothes on. Piper looked down at her own outfit and gasped. "Mother!"

She yelled louder than she meant. Jason flinched, bumping the table with his knees, and then all of them were awake.

"What?" Hedge demanded. "Fight who? Where?"

"Falling!" Leo grabbed the table. "No—not falling. Where are we?"

Jason blinked, trying to get his bearings. He focused on Piper and made a little choking sound. "What are you wearing?"

Piper probably blushed. She was wearing the turquoise dress she'd seen in her dream, with black leggings and black leather boots. She had on her favorite silver charm bracelet, even though she'd left that back home in L.A., and her old snowboarding jacket from her dad, which amazingly went with the outfit pretty well. She pulled out Katoptris, and judging from the reflection in the blade, she'd gotten her hair done, too.

"It's nothing," she said. "It's my—" She remembered Aphrodite's warning not to mention that they'd talked. "It's nothing."

Leo grinned. "Aphrodite strikes again, huh? You're gonna be the best-dressed warrior in town, beauty queen."

"Hey, Leo." Jason nudged his arm. "You look at yourself recently?"

"What...oh."

All of them had been give a makeover. Leo was wearing pinstriped pants, black leather shoes, a white collarless shirt with suspenders, and his tool belt, Ray-Ban sunglasses, and a porkpie hat.

"God, Leo." Piper tried not to laugh. "I think my dad wore that to his last premiere, minus the tool belt."

"Hey, shut up!"

"I think he looks good," said Coach Hedge. "'Course, I look better."

The satyr was a pastel nightmare. Aphrodite had given him a baggy canary yellow zoot suit with two-tone shoes that fit over his hooves. He had a matching yellow broad-brimmed hat, a rose-colored shirt, a baby blue tie, and a blue carnation in his lapel, which Hedge sniffed and then ate.

"Well," Jason said, "at least your mom overlooked me."

Piper knew that wasn't exactly true. Looking at him, her heart did a little tap dance. Jason was dressed simply in jeans and a clean purple T-shirt, like he'd worn at the Grand Canyon. He had new track shoes on, and his hair was newly trimmed. His eyes were the same color as the sky. Aphrodite's message was clear: *This one needs no improvement.*

And Piper agreed.

"Anyway," she said uncomfortably, "how did we get here?"

"Oh, that would be Mellie," Hedge said, chewing happily on his carnation. "Those winds shot us halfway across the country, I'd guess. We would've been smashed flat on impact, but Mellie's last gift—a nice soft breeze—cushioned our fall."

"And she got fired for us," Leo said. "Man, we suck."

"Ah, she'll be fine," Hedge said. "Besides, she couldn't help herself. I've got that effect on nymphs. I'll send her a message when we're through with this quest and help her figure something out. That is one *aura* I could settle down with and raise a herd of baby goats."

"I'm going to be sick," Piper said. "Anyone else want coffee?"

"Coffee!" Hedge's grin was stained blue from the flower. "I love coffee!"

"Um," Jason said, "but—money? Our packs?"

Piper looked down. Their packs were at their feet, and everything seemed to still be there. She reached into her coat pocket and felt two things she hadn't expected. One was a wad of cash. The other was a glass vial—the amnesia potion. She left the vial in her pocket and brought out the money.

Leo whistled. "Allowance? Piper, your mom rocks!"

"Waitress!" Hedge called. "Six double espressos, and whatever these guys want. Put it on the girl's tab."

It didn't take them long to figure out where they were. The menus said "Café Verve, Walnut Creek, CA." And according to the waitress, it was 9 A.M. on December 21, the winter solstice, which gave them three hours until Enceladus's deadline.

They didn't have to wonder where Mount Diablo was, either. They could see it on the horizon, right at the end of the street. After the Rockies, Mount Diablo didn't look very large, nor was it covered in snow. It seemed downright peaceful, its golden creases marbled with gray-green trees. But size was deceptive with mountains, Piper knew. It was probably much bigger up close. And appearances were deceptive too. Here they were—back in California—supposedly her home —with sunny skies, mild weather, laid-back people, and a plate of chocolate chip scones with coffee. And only a few miles away, somewhere on that peaceful mountain, a superpowerful, super-evil giant was about to have her father for lunch.

Leo pulled something out of his pocket—the old crayon drawing Aeolus had given him. Aphrodite must've thought it was important if she'd magically transferred it to his new outfit.

"What is that?" Piper asked.

Leo folded it up gingerly again and put it away. "Nothing. You don't want to see my kindergarten artwork."

"It's more than that," Jason guessed. "Aeolus said it was the key to our success."

Leo shook his head. "Not today. He was talking about . . . later."

"How can you be sure?" Piper asked.

"Trust me," Leo said. "Now—what's our game plan?"

Coach Hedge belched. He'd already had three espressos and a plate of doughnuts, along with two napkins and another flower from the vase on the table. He would've eaten the silverware, except Piper had slapped his hand.

"Climb the mountain," Hedge said. "Kill everything except Piper's dad. Leave."

"Thank you, General Eisenhower," Jason grumbled.

"Hey, I'm just saying!"

"Guys," Piper said. "There's more you need to know."

It was tricky, because she couldn't mention her mom; but she told them she'd figured some things out in her dreams. She told them about their real enemy: Gaea.

"Gaea?" Leo shook his head. "Isn't that Mother Nature? She's supposed to have, like, flowers in her hair and birds singing around her and deer and rabbits doing her laundry."

"Leo, that's Snow White," Piper said.

"Okay, but—"

"Listen, cupcake." Coach Hedge dabbed the espresso out of his goatee. "Piper's telling us some serious stuff, here. Gaea's no softie. I'm not even sure *I* could take her."

Leo whistled. "Really?"

Hedge nodded. "This earth lady—she and her old man the sky were nasty customers."

"Ouranos," Piper said. She couldn't help looking up at the blue sky, wondering if it had eyes.

"Right," Hedge said. "So Ouranos, he's not the best dad. He throws their first kids, the Cyclopes, into Tartarus. That makes Gaea mad, but she bides her time. Then they have another set of kids—the twelve Titans—and Gaea is afraid they'll get thrown into prison too. So she goes up to her son Kronos—"

"The big bad dude," Leo said. "The one they defeated last summer."

"Right. And Gaea's the one who gives him the scythe, and tells him, 'Hey, why don't I call your dad down here? And while he's talking to me, distracted, you can cut him to pieces. Then you can take over the world. Wouldn't that be great?'"

Nobody said anything. Piper's chocolate chip scone didn't look so appetizing anymore. Even though she'd heard the story before, she still couldn't quite get her mind around it. She tried to imagine a kid so messed up, he would kill his own dad just for power. Then she imagined a mom so messed up, she would convince her son to do it.

"Definitely not Snow White," she decided.

"Nah, Kronos was a bad guy," Hedge said. "But Gaea is

literally the *mother* of all bad guys. She's so old and powerful, so *huge*, that it's hard for her to be fully conscious. Most of the time, she sleeps, and that's the way we like her—snoring."

"But she talked to me," Leo said. "How can she be asleep?"

Gleeson brushed crumbs off his canary yellow lapel. He was on his sixth espresso now, and his pupils were as big as quarters. "Even in her sleep, part of her consciousness is active—dreaming, keeping watch, doing little things like causing volcanoes to explode and monsters to rise. Even now, she's not fully awake. Believe me, you don't want to see her fully awake."

"But she's getting more powerful," Piper said. "She's causing the giants to rise. And if their king comes back—this guy Porphyrion—"

"He'll raise an army to destroy the gods," Jason put in. "Starting with Hera. It'll be another war. And Gaea will wake up fully."

Gleeson nodded. "Which is why it's a good idea for us to stay off the ground as much as possible."

Leo looked warily at Mount Diablo. "So...climbing a mountain. That would be bad."

Piper's heart sank. First, she'd been asked to betray her friends. Now they were trying to help her rescue her dad even though they knew they were walking into a trap. The idea of fighting a giant had been scary enough. But the idea that Gaea was behind it—a force more powerful than a god or Titan...

"Guys, I can't ask you to do this," Piper said. "This is too dangerous."

"You kidding?" Gleeson belched and showed them his blue carnation smile. "Who's ready to beat stuff up?"

LEO

LEO HOPED THE TAXI COULD TAKE THEM all the way to the top.

No such luck. The cab made lurching, grinding sounds as it climbed the mountain road, and halfway up they found the ranger's station closed, a chain blocking the way.

"Far as I can go," the cabbie said. "You sure about this? Gonna be a long walk back, and my car's acting funny. I can't wait for you."

"We're sure." Leo was the first one out. He had a bad feeling about what was wrong with the cab, and when he looked down he saw he was right. The wheels were sinking into the road like it was made of quicksand. Not fast—just enough to make the driver think he had a transmission problem or a bad axle—but Leo knew different.

The road was hard-packed dirt. No reason at all it should have been soft, but already Leo's shoes were starting to sink. Gaea was messing with them.

While his friends got out, Leo paid the cabbie. He was generous—heck, why not? It was Aphrodite's money. Plus, he had a feeling he might never be coming off this mountain.

"Keep the change," he said. "And get out of here. Quick."

The driver didn't argue. Soon all they could see was his dust trail.

The view from the mountain was pretty amazing. The whole inland valley around Mount Diablo was a patchwork of towns—grids of tree-lined streets and nice middle-class suburbs, shops, and schools. All these normal people living normal lives—the kind Leo had never known.

"That's Concord," Jason said, pointing to the north. "Walnut Creek below us. To the south, Danville, past those hills. And that way..."

He pointed west, where a ridge of golden hills held back a layer of fog, like the rim of a bowl. "That's the Berkeley Hills. The East Bay. Past that, San Francisco."

"Jason?" Piper touched his arm. "You remember something? You've been here?"

"Yes...no." He gave her an anguished look. "It just seems important."

"That's Titan land." Coach Hedge nodded toward the west. "Bad place, Jason. Trust me, this is as close to 'Frisco as we want to get."

But Jason looked toward the foggy basin with such longing that Leo felt uneasy. Why did Jason seem so connected with that place—a place Hedge said was evil, full of bad magic and old enemies? What if Jason came from here? Everybody kept hinting Jason was an enemy, that his arrival at Camp Half-Blood was a dangerous mistake.

No, Leo thought. Ridiculous. Jason was their friend.

Leo tried to move his foot, but his heels were now completely embedded in the dirt.

"Hey, guys," he said. "Let's keep moving."

The others noticed the problem.

"Gaea is stronger here," Hedge grumbled. He popped his hooves free from his shoes, then handed the shoes to Leo. "Keep those for me, Valdez. They're nice."

Leo snorted. "Yes, sir, Coach. Would you like them polished?"

"That's varsity thinking, Valdez." Hedge nodded approvingly. "But first, we'd better hike up this mountain while we still can."

"How do we know where the giant is?" Piper asked.

Jason pointed toward the peak. Drifting across the summit was a plume of smoke. From a distance, Leo had thought it was a cloud, but it wasn't. Something was burning.

"Smoke equals fire," Jason said. "We'd better hurry."

The Wilderness School had taken Leo on several forced marches. He thought he was in good shape. But climbing a mountain when the earth was trying to swallow his feet was like jogging on a flypaper treadmill.

In no time, Leo had rolled up the sleeves on his collarless shirt, even though the wind was cold and sharp. He wished Aphrodite had given him walking shorts and some more comfortable shoes, but he was grateful for the Ray-Bans that kept the sun out of his eyes. He slipped his hands into his tool belt and started summoning supplies—gears, a tiny wrench, some strips of bronze. As he walked, he built—not really thinking about it, just fiddling with pieces.

By the time they neared the crest of the mountain, Leo was the most fashionably dressed sweaty, dirty hero ever. His hands were covered in machine grease.

The little object he'd made was like a windup toy—the kind that rattles and walks across a coffee table. He wasn't sure what it could do, but he slipped it into his tool belt.

He missed his army coat with all its pockets. Even more than that, he missed Festus. He could use a fire-breathing bronze dragon right now. But Leo knew Festus would not be coming back—at least, not in his old form.

He patted the picture in his pocket—the crayon drawing he'd made at the picnic table under the pecan tree when he was five years old. He remembered Tía Callida singing as he worked, and how upset he'd been when the winds had snatched the picture away. *It isn't time yet, little hero,* Tía Callida had told him. *Someday, yes. You'll have your quest. You will find your destiny, and your hard journey will finally make sense.*

Now Aeolus had returned the picture. Leo knew that meant his destiny was getting close; but the journey was as frustrating as this stupid mountain. Every time Leo thought they'd reached the summit, it turned out to be just another ridge with an even higher one behind it.

First things first, Leo told himself. Survive today. Figure out crayon drawing of destiny later.

Finally Jason crouched behind a wall of rock. He gestured for the others to do the same. Leo crawled up next to him. Piper had to pull Coach Hedge down.

"I don't want to get my outfit dirty!" Hedge complained.

"Shhh!" Piper said.

Reluctantly, the satyr knelt.

Just over the ridge where they were hiding, in the shadow of the mountain's final crest, was a forested depression about the size of a football field, where the giant Enceladus had set up camp.

Trees had been cut down to make a towering purple bonfire. The outer rim of the clearing was littered with extra logs and construction equipment—an earthmover; a big crane thing with rotating blades at the end like an electric shaver—must be a tree harvester, Leo thought—and a long metal column with an ax blade, like a sideways guillotine—a hydraulic ax.

Why a giant needed construction equipment, Leo wasn't sure. He didn't see how the creature in front of him could even fit in the driver's seat. The giant Enceladus was so large, so horrible, Leo didn't want to look at him.

But he forced himself to focus on the monster.

To start with, he was thirty feet tall—easily as tall as the treetops. Leo was sure the giant could've seen them behind their ridge, but he seemed intent on the weird purple bonfire, circling it and chanting under his breath. From the waist up, the giant appeared humanoid, his muscular chest clad in bronze armor, decorated with flame designs. His arms were completely ripped. Each of his biceps was bigger than Leo. His skin was bronze but sooty with ash. His face was crudely shaped, like a half-finished clay figure, but his eyes glowed white, and his hair was matted in shaggy locs down to his shoulders, braided with bones.

From the waist down, he was even more terrifying. His legs were scaly green, with claws instead of feet—like the forelegs of a dragon. In his hand, Enceladus held a spear the size of a flagpole. Every so often he dipped its tip in the fire, turning the metal molten red.

"Okay," Coach Hedge whispered. "Here's the plan—"

Leo elbowed him. "You're not charging him alone!"

"Aw, c'mon."

Piper choked back a sob. "Look."

Just visible on the other side of the bonfire was a man tied to a post. His head slumped like he was unconscious, so Leo couldn't make out his face, but Piper didn't seem to have any doubts.

"Dad," she said.

Leo swallowed. He wished this were a Tristan McLean movie. Then Piper's dad would be faking unconsciousness. He'd untie his bonds and knock out the giant with some cleverly hidden anti-giant gas. Heroic music would start to play, and Tristan McLean would make his amazing escape, running away in slow motion while the mountainside exploded behind him.

But this wasn't a movie. Tristan McLean was half dead and about to be eaten. The only people who could stop it —three fashionably dressed teenaged demigods and a megalomaniac goat.

"There's four of us," Hedge whispered urgently. "And only one of him."

"Did you miss the fact that he's thirty feet tall?" Leo asked.

"Okay," Hedge said. "So you, me, and Jason distract him. Piper sneaks around and frees her dad."

They all looked at Jason.

"What?" Jason asked. "I'm not the leader."

"Yes," Piper said. "You are."

They'd never really talked about it, but no one disagreed, not even Hedge. Coming this far had been a team effort, but when it came to a life-and-death decision, Leo knew Jason was the one to ask. Even if he had no memory, Jason had a kind of balance to him. You could just tell he'd been in battles before, and he knew how to keep his cool. Leo wasn't exactly the trusting type, but he trusted Jason with his life.

"I hate to say it," Jason sighed, "but Coach Hedge is right. A distraction is Piper's best chance."

Not a good chance, Leo thought. Not even a survivable chance. Just their *best* chance.

They couldn't sit there all day and talk about it, though. It had to be close to noon—the giant's deadline—and the ground was still trying to pull them down. Leo's knees had already sunk two inches into the dirt.

Leo looked at the construction equipment and got a crazy

idea. He brought out the little toy he'd made on the climb, and he realized what it could do—*if* he was lucky, which he almost never was.

"Let's boogie," he said. "Before I come to my senses."

XLII

LEO

THE PLAN WENT WRONG ALMOST IMMEDIATELY. Piper scrambled along the ridge, trying to keep her head down, while Leo, Jason, and Coach Hedge walked straight into the clearing.

Jason summoned his golden lance. He brandished it over his head and yelled, "Giant!" Which sounded pretty good, and a lot more confident than Leo could've managed. He was thinking more along the lines of, "We are pathetic ants! Don't kill us!"

Enceladus stopped chanting at the flames. He turned toward them and grinned, revealing fangs like a saber-toothed tiger's.

"Well," the giant rumbled. "What a nice surprise."

Leo didn't like the sound of that. His hand closed on his windup gadget. He stepped sideways, edging his way toward the bulldozer.

Coach Hedge shouted, "Let the movie star go, you big ugly cupcake! Or I'm gonna plant my hoof right up your—"

"Coach," Jason said. "Shut up."

Enceladus roared with laughter. "I've forgotten how funny satyrs are. When we rule the world, I think I'll keep your kind around. You can entertain me while I eat all the other mortals."

"Is that a compliment?" Hedge frowned at Leo. "I don't think that was a compliment."

Enceladus opened his mouth wide, and his teeth began to glow.

"Scatter!" Leo yelled.

Jason and Hedge dove to the left as the giant blew fire —a furnace blast so hot even Festus would've been jealous. Leo dodged behind the bulldozer, wound up his homemade device, and dropped it into the driver's seat. Then he ran to the right, heading for the tree harvester.

Out of the corner of his eye, he saw Jason rise and charge the giant. Coach Hedge ripped off his canary yellow jacket, which was now on fire, and bleated angrily. "I *liked* that outfit!" Then he raised his club and charged, too.

Before they could get very far, Enceladus slammed his spear against the ground. The entire mountain shook.

The shockwave sent Leo sprawling. He blinked, momentarily stunned. Through a haze of grassfire and bitter smoke, he saw Jason staggering to his feet on the other side of the clearing. Coach Hedge was knocked out cold. He'd fallen forward and hit his head on a log. His furry hindquarters were sticking straight up, with his canary yellow pants around his knees—a view Leo really didn't need.

The giant bellowed, "I see you, Piper McLean!" He turned and blew fire at a line of bushes to Leo's right. Piper ran into the clearing like a flushed quail, the underbrush burning behind her.

Enceladus laughed. "I'm happy you've arrived. And you brought me my prizes!"

Leo's gut twisted. This was the moment Piper had warned them about. They'd played right into Enceladus's hands.

The giant must've read Leo's expression, because he laughed even louder. "That's right, son of Hephaestus. I didn't expect you all to stay alive this long, but it doesn't matter. By bringing you here, Piper McLean has sealed the deal. If she betrays you, I'm as good as my word. She can take her father and go. What do I care about a movie star?"

Leo could see Piper's dad more clearly now. He wore a ragged dress shirt and torn slacks. His bare feet were caked with mud. He wasn't completely unconscious, because he lifted his head and groaned—yep, Tristan McLean all right. Leo had seen that face in enough movies. But he had a nasty cut down the side of his face, and he looked thin and sickly —not heroic at all.

"Dad!" Piper yelled.

Mr. McLean blinked, trying to focus. "Pipes . . . ? Where . . ."

Piper drew her dagger and faced Enceladus. "Let him go!"

"Of course, dear," the giant rumbled. "Swear your loyalty to me, and we have no problem. Only these others must die."

Piper looked back and forth between Leo and her dad.

"He'll kill you," Leo warned. "Don't trust him!"

"Oh, come now," Enceladus bellowed. "You know I was born to fight Athena herself? Mother Gaea made each of us giants with a specific purpose, designed to fight and destroy a particular god. I was Athena's nemesis, the *anti*-Athena, you might say. Compared to some of my brethren—I am small! But I am clever. And I keep my bargain with you, Piper McLean. It's part of my plan!"

Jason was on his feet now, lance ready; but before he could act, Enceladus roared—a call so loud it echoed down the valley and was probably heard all the way to San Francisco.

At the edge of the woods, half a dozen ogre-like creatures rose up. Leo realized with nauseating certainty that they hadn't simply been hiding there. They'd risen straight out of the earth.

The ogres shuffled forward. They were small compared to Enceladus, about seven feet tall. Each one of them had six arms—one pair in the regular spot, then an extra pair sprouting out the top of their shoulders, and another set shooting from the sides of their rib cages. They wore only ragged leather loincloths, and even across the clearing, Leo could smell them. Six guys who never bathed, with six armpits each. Leo decided if he survived this day, he'd have to take a three-hour shower just to forget the stench.

Leo stepped toward Piper. "What—what are those?"

Her blade reflected the purple light of the bonfire. "Gegenees."

"In English?" Leo asked.

"The Earthborn," she said. "Six-armed giants who fought Jason—the *first* Jason."

"Very good, my dear!" Enceladus sounded delighted. "They used to live on a miserable place in Greece called Bear Mountain. Mount Diablo is much nicer! They are lesser children of Mother Earth, but they serve their purpose. They're good with construction equipment—"

"Vroom, vroom!" one of the Earthborn bellowed, and the others took up the chant, each moving his six hands as though driving a car, as if it were some kind of weird religious ritual. "Vroom, vroom!"

"Yes, thank you, boys," Enceladus said. "They also have a score to settle with heroes. Especially anyone named Jason."

"Yay-son!" the Earthborn screamed. They all picked up clumps of earth, which solidified in their hands, turning to nasty pointed stones. "Where Yay-son? Kill Yay-son!"

Enceladus smiled. "You see, Piper, you have a choice. Save your father, or ah, *try* to save your friends and face certain death."

Piper stepped forward. Her eyes blazed with such rage, even the Earthborn backed away. She radiated power and beauty, but it had nothing to do with her clothes or her makeup.

"You will not take the people I love," she said. "None of them."

Her words rippled across the clearing with such force, the Earthborn muttered, "Okay. Okay, sorry," and began to retreat.

"Stand your ground, fools!" Enceladus bellowed. He

snarled at Piper. "This is why we wanted you alive, my dear. You could have been so useful to us. But as you wish. Earthborn! I will show you Jason."

Leo's heart sank. But the giant didn't point to Jason. He pointed to the other side of the bonfire, where Tristan McLean hung helpless and half conscious.

"There is Jason," Enceladus said with pleasure. "Tear him apart!"

Leo's biggest surprise: One look from Jason, and all three of them knew the game plan. When had that happened, that they could read each other so well?

Jason charged Enceladus, while Piper rushed to her father, and Leo dashed for the tree harvester, which stood between Mr. McLean and the Earthborn.

The Earthborn were fast, but Leo ran like a storm spirit. He leaped toward the harvester from five feet away and slammed into the driver's seat. His hands flew across the controls, and the machine responded with unnatural speed—coming to life as if it knew how important this was.

"Ha!" Leo screamed, and swung the crane arm through the bonfire, toppling burning logs onto the Earthborn and spraying sparks everywhere. Two giants went down under a fiery avalanche and melted back into the earth—hopefully to stay for a while.

The other four ogres stumbled across burning logs and hot coals while Leo brought the harvester around. He smashed a button, and on the end of the crane arm the wicked rotating blades began to whir.

Out of the corner of his eye, he could see Piper at the stake, cutting her father free. On the other side of the clearing, Jason fought the giant, somehow managing to dodge his massive spear and blasts of fire breath. Coach Hedge was still heroically passed out with his goat tail sticking up in the air.

The whole side of the mountain would soon be ablaze. The fire wouldn't bother Leo, but if his friends got trapped up here— No. He had to act quickly.

One of the Earthborn—apparently not the most intelligent one—charged the tree harvester, and Leo swung the crane arm in his direction. As soon as the blades touched the ogre, he dissolved like wet clay and splattered all over the clearing. Most of him flew into Leo's face.

He spit clay out of his mouth and turned the harvester toward the three remaining Earthborn, who backed up quickly.

"Bad vroom-vroom!" one yelled.

"Yeah, that's right!" Leo yelled at them. "You want some bad vroom-vroom? Come on!"

Unfortunately, they did. Three ogres with six arms, each throwing large, hard rocks at super speed—and Leo knew it was over. Somehow, he launched himself in a backward somersault off the harvester half a second before a boulder demolished the driver's seat. Rocks slammed into metal. By the time Leo stumbled to his feet, the harvester looked like a crushed soda can, sinking in the mud.

"Dozer!" Leo yelled.

The ogres were picking up more clumps of earth, but this time they were glaring in Piper's direction.

Thirty feet away, the bulldozer roared to life. Leo's make-shift gadget had done its job, burrowing into the earthmover's controls and giving it a temporary life of its own. It roared toward the enemy.

Just as Piper cut her father free and caught him in her arms, the giants launched their second volley of stones. The dozer swiveled in the mud, skidding to intercept, and most of the rocks slammed into its shovel. The force was so great it pushed the dozer back. Two rocks ricocheted and struck their throwers. Two more Earthborn melted into clay. Unfortunately, one rock hit the dozer's engine, sending up a cloud of oily smoke, and the dozer groaned to a stop. Another great toy broken.

Piper dragged her father below the ridge. The last Earthborn charged after her.

Leo was out of tricks, but he couldn't let that monster get to Piper. He ran forward, straight through the flames, and grabbed something—*anything*—from his tool belt.

"Hey, stupid!" he yelled, and threw a screwdriver at the Earthborn.

It didn't kill the ogre, but it sure got his attention. The screwdriver sank hilt-deep into the Earthborn's forehead like he was made of Play-Doh.

The Earthborn yelped in pain and skittered to a halt. He pulled out the screwdriver, turned and glared at Leo. Sadly, this last ogre looked like the biggest and nastiest of the bunch. Gaea had really gone all out creating him—with extra muscle upgrades, deluxe ugly face, the whole package.

Oh, great, Leo thought. I've made a friend.

"You die!" the Earthborn roared. "Friend of Yay-son dies!"

The ogre scooped up handfuls of dirt, which immediately hardened into rock cannonballs.

Leo's mind went blank. He reached into his tool belt, but he couldn't think of anything that would help. He was supposed to be clever—but he couldn't craft or build or tinker his way out of this one.

Fine, he thought. I'll go out blaze-of-glory style.

He burst into flames, yelled, "Hephacstus!" and charged at the ogre barehanded.

He never got there.

A blur of turquoise and black flashed behind the ogre. A gleaming bronze blade sliced up one side of the Earthborn and down the other.

Six large arms dropped to the ground, boulders rolling out of their useless hands. The Earthborn looked down, very surprised. He mumbled, "Arms go bye-bye."

Then he melted into the ground.

Piper stood there, breathing hard, her dagger covered with clay. Her dad sat at the ridge, dazed and wounded, but still alive.

Piper's expression was ferocious—almost crazy, like a cornered animal. Leo was glad she was on his side.

"Nobody hurts my friends," she said, and with a sudden warm feeling, Leo realized she was talking about him. Then she yelled, "Come on!"

Leo saw that the battle wasn't over. Jason was still fighting the giant Enceladus—and it wasn't going well.

XLIII

JASON

WHEN JASON'S LANCE BROKE, he knew he was dead.

The battle had started well enough. Jason's instincts kicked in, and his gut told him he'd dueled opponents almost this big before. Size and strength equaled slowness, so Jason just had to be quicker—pace himself, wear out his opponent, and avoid getting smashed or flame-broiled.

He rolled away from the giant's first spear thrust and jabbed Enceladus in the ankle. Jason's javelin managed to pierce the thick dragon hide, and golden *ichor*—the blood of immortals—trickled down the giant's clawed foot.

Enceladus bellowed in pain and blasted him with fire. Jason scrambled away, rolling behind the giant, and struck again behind his knee.

It went on like that for seconds, minutes—it was hard to judge. Jason heard combat across the clearing—construction equipment grinding, fire roaring, monsters shouting, and rocks smashing into metal. He heard Leo and Piper yelling defiantly, which meant they were still alive. Jason tried not to think about it. He couldn't afford to get distracted.

Enceladus's spear missed him by a millimeter. Jason kept dodging, but the ground stuck to his feet. Gaea was getting stronger, and the giant was getting faster. Enceladus might be slow, but he wasn't dumb. He began anticipating Jason's moves, and Jason's attacks were only annoying him, making him more enraged.

"I'm not some minor monster," Enceladus bellowed. "I am a giant, born to destroy gods! Your little gold toothpick can't kill me, boy."

Jason didn't waste energy replying. He was already tired. The ground clung to his feet, making him feel like he weighed an extra hundred pounds. The air was full of smoke that burned his lungs. Fires roared around him, stoked by the winds, and the temperature was approaching the heat of an oven.

Jason raised his javelin to block the giant's next strike—a big mistake. *Don't fight force with force,* a voice chided him— the wolf Lupa, who'd told him that long ago. He managed to deflect the spear, but it grazed his shoulder, and his arm went numb.

He backed up, almost tripping over a burning log.

He had to delay—to keep the giant's attention fixed on him while his friends dealt with the Earthborn and rescued Piper's dad. He couldn't fail.

He retreated, trying to lure the giant to the edge of the clearing. Enceladus could sense his weariness. The giant smiled, baring his fangs.

"The mighty Jason Grace," he taunted. "Yes, we know about you, son of Jupiter. The one who led the assault on Mount Othrys. The one who single-handedly slew the Titan Krios and toppled the black throne."

Jason's mind reeled. He didn't know these names, yet they made his skin tingle, as if his body remembered the pain his mind didn't.

"What are you talking about?" he asked. He realized his mistake when Enceladus breathed fire.

Distracted, Jason moved too slowly. The blast missed him, but heat blistered his back. He slammed into the ground, his clothes smoldering. He was blinded from ash and smoke, choking as he tried to breathe.

He scrambled back as the giant's spear cleaved the ground between his feet.

Jason managed to stand.

If he could only summon one good blast of lightning—but he was already drained, and in this condition, the effort might kill him. He didn't even know if electricity would harm the giant.

Death in battle is honorable, said Lupa's voice.

That's real comforting, Jason thought.

One last try: Jason took a deep breath and charged.

Enceladus let him approach, grinning with anticipation. At the last second, Jason faked a strike and rolled between the giant's legs. He came up quickly, thrusting with all his might, ready to stab the giant in the small of his back, but Enceladus anticipated the trick. He stepped aside with too much speed and agility for a giant, as if the earth were helping him move.

He swept his spear sideways, met Jason's javelin—and with a snap like a shotgun blast, the golden weapon shattered.

The explosion was hotter than the giant's breath, blinding Jason with golden light. The force knocked him off his feet and squeezed the breath out of him.

When he regained his focus, he was sitting at the rim of a crater. Enceladus stood at the other side, staggering and confused. The javelin's destruction had released so much energy, it had blasted a perfect cone-shaped pit thirty feet deep, fusing the dirt and rock into a slick glassy substance. Jason wasn't sure how he'd survived, but his clothes were steaming. He was out of energy. He had no weapon. And Enceladus was still very much alive.

Jason tried to get up, but his legs were like lead. Enceladus blinked at the destruction, then laughed. "Impressive! Unfortunately, that was your last trick, demigod."

Enceladus leaped the crater in a single bound, planting his feet on either side of Jason. The giant raised his spear, its tip hovering six feet over Jason's chest.

"And now," Enceladus said, "my first sacrifice to Gaea!"

XLIV

JASON

TIME SEEMED TO SLOW DOWN, WHICH WAS really frustrating, since Jason still couldn't move. He felt himself sinking into the earth like the ground was a waterbed—comfortable, urging him to relax and give up. He wondered if the stories of the Underworld were true. Would he end up in the Fields of Punishment or Elysium? If he couldn't remember any of his deeds, would they still count? He wondered if the judges would take that into consideration, or if his dad, Zeus, would write him a note: "Please excuse Jason from eternal damnation. He has had amnesia."

Jason couldn't feel his arms. He could see the tip of the spear coming toward his chest in slow motion. He knew he should move, but he couldn't seem to do it. Funny, he thought. All that effort to stay alive, and then, *boom*. You just lie there helplessly while a fire-breathing giant impales you.

Leo's voice yelled, "Heads up!"

A large black metal wedge slammed into Enceladus with a massive *thunk!* The giant toppled over and slid into the pit.

"Jason, get up!" Piper called. Her voice energized him, shook him out of his stupor. He sat up, his head groggy, while Piper grabbed him under his arms and hauled him to his feet.

"Don't die on me," she ordered. "You are *not* dying on me."

"Yes, ma'am." He felt light-headed, but she was about the most beautiful thing he'd ever seen. Her hair was smoldering. Her face was smudged with soot. She had a cut on her arm, her dress was torn, and she was missing a boot. Beautiful.

About a hundred feet behind her, Leo was standing over a piece of construction equipment—a long cannonlike thing with a single massive piston, the edge broken clean off.

Then Jason looked down in the crater and saw where the other end of the hydraulic ax had gone. Enceladus was struggling to rise, an ax blade the size of a washing machine stuck in his breastplate.

Amazingly, the giant managed to pull the ax blade free. He yelled in pain and the mountain trembled. Golden ichor soaked the front of his armor, but Enceladus stood.

Shakily, he bent down and retrieved his spear.

"Good try." The giant winced. "But I cannot be beaten."

As they watched, the giant's armor mended itself, and the ichor stopped flowing. Even the cuts on his dragon-scale legs, which Jason had worked so hard to make, were now just pale scars.

Leo ran up to them, saw the giant, and cursed. "What *is* it with this guy? Die, already!"

"My fate is preordained," Enceladus said. "Giants cannot be killed by gods or heroes."

"Only by both," Jason said. The giant's smile faltered, and Jason saw in his eyes something like fear. "It's true, isn't it? Gods and demigods have to work together to kill you."

"You will not live long enough to try!" The giant started stumbling up the crater's slope, slipping on the glassy sides.

"Anyone have a god handy?" Leo asked.

Jason's heart filled with dread. He looked at the giant below them, struggling to get out of the pit, and he knew what had to happen.

"Leo," he said, "if you've got a rope in that tool belt, get it ready."

He leaped at the giant with no weapon but his bare hands.

"Enceladus!" Piper yelled. "Look behind you!"

It was an obvious trick, but her voice was so compelling, even Jason bought it. The giant said, "What?" and turned like there was an enormous spider on his back.

Jason tackled his legs at just the right moment. The giant lost his balance. Enceladus slammed into the crater and slid to the bottom. While he tried to rise, Jason put his arms around the giant's neck. When Enceladus struggled to his feet, Jason was riding his shoulders.

"Get off!" Enceladus screamed. He tried to grab Jason's legs, but Jason scrabbled around, squirming and climbing over the giant's hair.

Father, Jason thought. *If I've ever done anything good, anything you approved of, help me now. I offer my own life—just save my friends.*

Suddenly he could smell the metallic scent of a storm. Darkness swallowed the sun. The giant froze, sensing it too.

Jason yelled to his friends, "Hit the deck!"

And every hair on his head stood straight up.

Crack!

Lightning surged through Jason's body, straight through Enceladus, and into the ground. The giant's back stiffened, and Jason was thrown clear. When he regained his bearings, he was slipping down the side of the crater, and the crater was cracking open. The lightning bolt had split the mountain itself. The earth rumbled and tore apart, and Enceladus's legs slid into the chasm. He clawed helplessly at the glassy sides of the pit, and just for a moment managed to hold on to the edge, his hands trembling.

He fixed Jason with a look of hatred. "You've won nothing, boy. My brothers are rising, and they are ten times as strong as I. We will destroy the gods at their roots! You will die, and Olympus will die with   "

The giant lost his grip and fell into the crevice.

The earth shook. Jason fell toward the rift.

"Grab hold!" Leo yelled.

Jason's feet were at the edge of the chasm when he grabbed the rope, and Leo and Piper pulled him up.

They stood together, exhausted and terrified, as the chasm closed like an angry mouth. The ground stopped pulling at their feet.

For now, Gaea was gone.

The mountainside was on fire. Smoke billowed hundreds

of feet into the air. Jason spotted a helicopter—maybe fire-fighters or reporters—coming toward them.

All around them was carnage. The Earthborn had melted into piles of clay, leaving behind only their rock missiles and some nasty bits of loincloth, but Jason figured they would re-form soon enough. Construction equipment lay in ruins. The ground was scarred and blackened.

Coach Hedge started to move. He sat up with a groan and rubbed his head. His canary yellow pants were now the color of Dijon mustard mixed with mud.

He blinked and looked around him at the battle scene. "Did I do this?"

Before Jason could reply, Hedge picked up his club and got shakily to his feet. "Yeah, you wanted some hoof? I gave you some hoof, cupcakes! Who's the goat, huh?"

He did a little dance, kicking rocks and making what were probably rude satyr gestures at the piles of clay.

Leo cracked a smile, and Jason couldn't help it—he started to laugh. It probably sounded a little hysterical, but it was such a relief to be alive, he didn't care.

Then a man stood up across the clearing. Tristan McLean staggered forward. His eyes were hollow, shell-shocked, like someone who'd just walked through a nuclear wasteland.

"Piper?" he called. His voice cracked. "Pipes, what—what is—"

He couldn't complete the thought. Piper ran over to him and hugged him tightly, but he almost didn't seem to know her.

Jason had felt a similar way—that morning at the Grand

Canyon, when he woke with no memory. But Mr. McLean had the opposite problem. He had too *many* memories, too much trauma his mind just couldn't handle. He was coming apart.

"We need to get him out of here," Jason said.

"Yeah, but how?" Leo said. "He's in no shape to walk."

Jason glanced up at the helicopter, which was now circling directly overhead. "Can you make us a bullhorn or something?" he asked Leo. "Piper has some talking to do."

XLV

PIPER

BORROWING THE HELICOPTER WAS EASY. Getting her dad on board was not.

Piper needed only a few words through Leo's improvised bullhorn to convince the pilot to land on the mountain. The Park Service copter was big enough for medical evacuations or search and rescue, and when Piper told the very nice ranger pilot lady that it would be a great idea to fly them to the Oakland Airport, she readily agreed.

"No," her dad muttered, as they picked him up off the ground. "Piper, what—there were monsters—there were monsters—"

She needed both Leo's and Jason's help to hold him, while Coach Hedge gathered their supplies. Fortunately Hedge had put his pants and shoes back on, so Piper didn't have to explain the goat legs.

It broke Piper's heart to see her dad like this—pushed beyond the breaking point, crying like a little boy. She didn't know what the giant had done to him exactly, how the monsters had shattered his spirit, but she didn't think she could stand to find out.

"It'll be okay, Dad," she said, making her voice as soothing as possible. She didn't want to charmspeak her own father, but it seemed the only way. "These people are my friends. We're going to help you. You're safe now."

He blinked, and looked up at helicopter rotors. "Blades. They had a machine with so many blades. They had six arms . . ."

When they got him to the bay doors, the pilot came over to help. "What's wrong with him?" she asked.

"Smoke inhalation," Jason suggested. "Or heat exhaustion."

"We should get him to a hospital," the pilot said.

"It's okay," Piper said. "The airport is good."

"Yeah, the airport is good," the pilot agreed immediately. Then she frowned, as if uncertain why she'd changed her mind. "Isn't he Tristan McLean, the movie star?"

"No," Piper said. "He only looks like him. Forget it."

"Yeah," the pilot said. "Only looks like him. I—" She blinked, confused. "I forgot what I was saying. Let's get going."

Jason raised his eyebrows at Piper, obviously impressed, but Piper felt miserable. She didn't want to twist people's minds, convince them of things they didn't believe. It felt so bossy, so *wrong*—like something Drew would do back at camp, or Medea in her evil department store. And how would it help her father? She couldn't convince him he would be okay, or that nothing had happened. His trauma was just too deep.

Finally they got him on board, and the helicopter took off. The pilot kept getting questions over her radio, asking her where she was going, but she ignored them. They veered away from the burning mountain and headed toward the Berkeley Hills.

"Piper." Her dad grasped her hand and held on like he was afraid he'd fall. "It's you? They told me—they told me you would die. They said . . . horrible things would happen."

"It's me, Dad." It took all her willpower not to cry. She had to be strong for him. "Everything's going to be okay."

"They were monsters," he said. "Real monsters. Earth spirits, right out of Grandpa Tom's stories—and the Earth Mother was angry with me. And the giant, Tsul'kälû, breathing fire—" He focused on Piper again, his eyes like broken glass, reflecting a crazy kind of light. "They said you were a demigod. Your mother was . . ."

"Aphrodite," Piper said. "Goddess of love."

"I—I—" He took a shaky breath, then seemed to forget how to exhale.

Piper's friends were careful not to watch. Leo fiddled with a lug nut from his tool belt. Jason gazed at the valley below —the roads backing up as mortals stopped their cars and gawked at the burning mountain. Gleeson chewed on the stub of his carnation, and for once the satyr didn't look in the mood to yell or boast.

Tristan McLean wasn't supposed to be seen like this. He was a star. He was confident, stylish, suave—always in control. That was the public image he projected. Piper had seen the image falter before. But this was different. Now it was broken, gone.

"I didn't know about Mom," Piper told him. "Not until you were taken. When we found out where you were, we came right away. My friends helped me. No one will hurt you again."

Her dad couldn't stop shivering. "You're heroes—you and your friends. I can't believe it. You're a *real* hero, not like me. Not playing a part. I'm so proud of you, Pipes." But the words were muttered listlessly, in a semi-trance.

He gazed down on the valley, and his grip on Piper's hand went slack. "Your mother never told me."

"She thought it was for the best." It sounded lame, even to Piper, and no amount of charmspeak could change that. But she didn't tell her dad what Aphrodite had really worried about: *If he has to spend the rest of his life with those memories, knowing that gods and spirits walk the earth, it will shatter him.*

Piper felt inside the pocket of her jacket. The vial was still there, warm to her touch.

But how could she erase his memories? Her dad finally knew who she was. He was proud of her, and for once she was his hero, not the other way around. He would never send her away now. They shared a secret.

How could she go back to the way things were?

She held his hand, speaking to him about small things— her time at the Wilderness School, her cabin at Camp Half-Blood. She told him how Coach Hedge ate carnations and got knocked on his butt on Mount Diablo, how Leo had tamed a dragon, and how Jason had made wolves back down by talking in Latin. Her friends smiled reluctantly as she recounted their adventures. Her dad seemed to relax as she talked, but he didn't smile. Piper wasn't even sure he heard her.

As they passed over the hills into the East Bay, Jason tensed. He leaned so far out the doorway Piper was afraid he'd fall.

He pointed. "What is that?"

Piper looked down, but she didn't see anything interesting —just hills, woods, houses, little roads snaking through the canyons. A highway cut through a tunnel in the hills, connecting the East Bay with the inland towns.

"Where?" Piper asked.

"That road," he said. "The one that goes through the hills."

Piper picked up the com helmet the pilot had given her and relayed the question over the radio. The answer wasn't very exciting.

"She says it's Highway 24," Piper reported. "That's the Caldecott Tunnel. Why?"

Jason stared intently at the tunnel entrance, but he said nothing. It disappeared from view as they flew over downtown Oakland, but Jason still stared into the distance, his expression almost as unsettled as Piper's dad's.

"Monsters," her dad said, a tear tracing his cheek. "I live in a world of monsters."

XLVI

PIPER

AIR TRAFFIC CONTROL DIDN'T WANT TO let an unscheduled helicopter land at the Oakland Airport—until Piper got on the radio. Then it turned out to be no problem.

They unloaded on the tarmac, and everyone looked at Piper.

"What now?" Jason asked her.

She felt uncomfortable. She didn't want to be in charge, but for her dad's sake, she had to appear confident. She had no plan. She'd just remembered that he'd flown into Oakland, which meant his private plane would still be here. But today was the solstice. They had to save Hera. They had no idea where to go or if they were even too late. And how could she leave her dad in this condition?

"First thing," she said. "I—I have to get my dad home. I'm sorry, guys."

Their faces fell.

"Oh," Leo said. "I mean, absolutely. He needs you right now. We can take it from here."

"Pipes, no." Her dad had been sitting in the helicopter doorway, a blanket around his shoulders. But he stumbled to his feet. "You have a mission. A quest. I can't—"

"I'll take care of him," said Coach Hedge.

Piper stared at him. The satyr was the last person she'd expected to offer. "You?" she asked.

"I'm a protector," Gleeson said. "That's my job, not fighting."

He sounded a little crestfallen, and Piper realized maybe she shouldn't have recounted how he got knocked unconscious in the last battle. In his own way, maybe the satyr was as sensitive as her dad.

Then Hedge straightened, and set his jaw. "Of course, I'm good at fighting, too." He glared at them all, daring them to argue.

"Yes," Jason said.

"Terrifying," Leo agreed.

The coach grunted. "But I'm a protector, and I can do this. Your dad's right, Piper. You need to carry on with the quest."

"But..." Piper's eyes stung, as if she were back in the forest fire. "Dad..."

He held out his arms, and she hugged him. He felt frail. He was trembling so much, it scared her.

"Let's give them a minute," Jason said, and they took the pilot a few yards down the tarmac.

"I can't believe it," her dad said. "I failed you."

"No, Dad!"

"The things they did, Piper, the visions they showed me..."

"Dad, listen." She took out the vial from her pocket. "Aphrodite gave me this, for you. It takes away your recent memories. It'll make it like none of this ever happened."

He gazed at her, as if translating her words from a foreign language. "But you're a hero. I would forget that?"

"Yes," Piper whispered. She forced an assuring tone into her voice. "Yes, you would. It'll be like—like before."

He closed his eyes and took a shaky breath. "I love you, Piper. I always have. I—I sent you away because I didn't want you exposed to my life. Not the way I grew up—the poverty, the hopelessness. Not the Hollywood insanity either. I thought—I thought I was protecting you." He managed a brittle laugh. "As if your life without me was better, or safer."

Piper took his hand. She'd heard him talk about protecting her before, but she'd never believed it. She'd always thought he was just rationalizing. Her dad seemed so confident and easygoing, like his life was a joyride. How could he claim she needed protecting from that?

Finally Piper understood he'd been acting for her benefit, trying not to show how scared and insecure he was. He really *had* been trying to protect her. And now his ability to cope had been destroyed.

She offered him the vial. "Take it. Maybe someday we'll be ready to talk about this again. When you're ready."

"When I'm ready," he murmured. "You make it sound like—like I'm the one growing up. I'm supposed to be the parent." He took the vial. His eyes glimmered with a small desperate hope. "I love you, Pipes."

"Love you, too, Dad."

He drank the pink liquid. His eyes rolled up into his head, and he slumped forward. Piper caught him, and her friends ran up to help.

"Got him," Hedge said. The satyr stumbled, but he was strong enough to hold Tristan McLean upright. "I already asked our ranger friend to call up his plane. It's on the way now. Home address?"

Piper was about to tell him. Then a thought occurred to her. She checked her dad's pocket, and his BlackBerry was still there. It seemed bizarre that he'd still have something so normal after all he'd been through, but she guessed Enceladus hadn't seen any reason to take it.

"Everything's on here," Piper said. "Address, his chauffeur's number. Just watch out for Jane."

Hedge's eyes lit up, like he sensed a possible fight. "Who's Jane?"

By the time Piper explained, her dad's sleek white Gulfstream had taxied next to the helicopter.

Hedge and the flight attendant got Piper's dad on board. Then Hedge came down one last time to say his good-byes. He gave Piper a hug and glared at Jason and Leo. "You cupcakes take care of this girl, you hear? Or I'm gonna make you do push-ups."

"You got it, Coach," Leo said, a smile tugging at his mouth.

"No push-ups," Jason promised.

Piper gave the old satyr one more hug. "Thank you, Gleeson. Take care of him, please."

"I got this, McLean," he assured her. "They got root beer and veggie enchiladas on this flight, and one hundred percent linen napkins—yum! I could get used to this."

Trotting up the stairs, he lost one shoe, and his hoof was visible for just a second. The flight attendant's eyes widened, but she looked away and pretended nothing was wrong. Piper figured she'd probably seen stranger things, working for Tristan McLean.

When the plane was heading down the runaway, Piper started to cry. She'd been holding it in too long and she just couldn't anymore. Before she knew it, Jason was hugging her, and Leo stood uncomfortably nearby, pulling Kleenex out of his tool belt.

"Your dad's in good hands," Jason said. "You did amazing."

She sobbed into his shirt. She allowed herself to be held for six deep breaths. Seven. Then she couldn't indulge herself anymore. They needed her. The helicopter pilot was already looking uncomfortable, like she was starting to wonder why she'd flown them here.

"Thank you, guys," Piper said. "I—"

She wanted to tell them how much they meant to her. They'd sacrificed everything, maybe even their quest, to help her. She couldn't repay them, couldn't even put her gratitude into words. But her friends' expressions told her they understood.

Then, right next to Jason, the air began to shimmer. At first Piper thought it was heat off the tarmac, or maybe gas fumes from the helicopter, but she'd seen something like this before in Medea's fountain. It was an Iris message. An image appeared in the air—a dark-haired girl in silver winter camouflage, holding a bow.

Jason stumbled back in surprise. "Thalia!"

"Thank the gods," said the Hunter. The scene behind her was hard to make out, but Piper heard yelling, metal clashing on metal, and explosions.

"We've found her," Thalia said. "Where are you?"

"Oakland," he said. "Where are you?"

"The Wolf House! Oakland is good; you're not too far. We're holding off the giant's minions, but we can't hold them forever. Get here before sunset, or it's all over."

"Then it's not too late?" Piper cried. Hope surged through her, but Thalia's expression quickly dampened it.

"Not yet," Thalia said. "But Jason—it's worse than I realized. Porphyrion is rising. Hurry."

"But where is the Wolf House?" he pleaded.

"Our last trip," Thalia said, her image starting to flicker. "The park. Jack London. Remember?"

This made no sense to Piper, but Jason looked like he'd been shot. He tottered, his face pale, and the Iris message disappeared.

"Bro, you all right?" Leo asked. "You know where she is?"

"Yes," Jason said. "Sonoma Valley. Not far. Not by air."

Piper turned to the ranger pilot, who'd been watching all this with an increasingly puzzled expression.

"Ma'am," Piper said with her best smile. "You don't mind helping us one more time, do you?"

"I don't mind," the pilot agreed.

"We can't take a mortal into battle," Jason said. "It's too dangerous." He turned to Leo. "Do you think you could fly this thing?"

"Um..." Leo's expression didn't exactly reassure Piper. But then he put his hand on the side of the helicopter, concentrating hard, as if listening to the machine.

"Bell 412HP utility helicopter," Leo said. "Composite four-blade main rotor, cruising speed twenty-two knots, service ceiling twenty-thousand feet. The tank is near full. Sure, I can fly it."

Piper smiled at the ranger again. "You don't have a problem with an under-aged unlicensed kid borrowing your copter, do you? We'll return it."

"I—" The pilot nearly choked on the words, but she got them out: "I don't have a problem with that."

Leo grinned. "Hop in, kids. Uncle Leo's gonna take you for a ride."

XLVII

LEO

FLY A HELICOPTER? SURE, WHY NOT. Leo had done plenty of crazier things that week.

The sun was going down as they flew north over the Richmond Bridge, and Leo couldn't believe the day had gone so quickly. Once again, nothing like ADHD and a good fight to the death to make time fly.

Piloting the chopper, he went back and forth between confidence and panic. If he didn't think about it, he found himself automatically flipping the right switches, checking the altimeter, easing back on the stick, and flying straight. If he allowed himself to consider what he was doing, he started freaking out. He imagined his Aunt Rosa yelling at him in Spanish, telling him he was a delinquent lunatic who was going to crash and burn. Part of him suspected she was right.

"Going okay?" Piper asked from the copilot's seat. She sounded more nervous than he was, so Leo put on a brave face.

"Aces," he said. "So what's the Wolf House?"

Jason knelt between their seats. "An abandoned mansion in the Sonoma Valley. A demigod built it—Jack London."

Leo couldn't place the name. "He an actor?"

"Writer," Piper said. "Adventure stuff, right? *Call of the Wild*? *White Fang*?"

"Yeah," Jason said. "He was a son of Mercury—I mean, Hermes. He was an adventurer, traveled the world. He was even a hobo for a while. Then he made a fortune writing. He bought a big ranch in the country and decided to build this huge mansion—the Wolf House."

"Named that 'cause he wrote about wolves?" Leo guessed.

"Partially," Jason said. "But the site, and the reason he wrote about wolves—he was dropping hints about his personal experience. There're a lot of holes in his life story—how he was born, who his dad was, why he wandered around so much—stuff you can only explain if you know he was a demigod."

The bay slipped behind them, and the helicopter continued north. Ahead of them, yellow hills rolled out as far as Leo could see.

"So Jack London went to Camp Half-Blood," Leo guessed.

"No," Jason said. "No, he didn't."

"Bro, you're freaking me out with the mysterious talk. Are you remembering your past or not?"

"Pieces," Jason said. "Only pieces. None of it good. The Wolf House is on sacred ground. It's where London started his journey as a child—where he found out he was a demigod. That's why he returned there. He thought he could live there, claim that land, but it wasn't meant for him. The Wolf House was cursed. It burned in a fire a week before he and his wife were supposed to move in. A few years later, London died, and his ashes were buried on the site."

"So," Piper said, "how do you know all this?"

A shadow crossed Jason's face. Probably just a cloud, but Leo could swear the shape looked like an eagle.

"I started my journey there too," Jason said. "It's a powerful place for demigods, a dangerous place. If Gaea can claim it, use its power to entomb Hera on the solstice and raise Porphyrion—that might be enough to awaken the earth goddess fully."

Leo kept his hand on the joystick, guiding the chopper at full speed—racing toward the north. He could see some weather ahead—a spot of darkness like a cloudbank or a storm, right where they were going.

Piper's dad had called him a hero earlier. And Leo couldn't believe some of the things he'd done—smacking around Cyclopes, disarming exploding doorbells, battling six-armed ogres with construction equipment. They seemed like they had happened to another person. He was just Leo Valdez, an orphaned kid from Houston. He'd spent his life running away, and part of him still wanted to run. What was he thinking, flying toward a cursed mansion to fight more evil monsters?

His mom's voice echoed in his head: *Nothing is unfixable.*

Except the fact that you're gone forever, Leo thought.

Seeing Piper and her dad back together had really driven that home. Even if Leo survived this quest and saved Hera,

Leo wouldn't have any happy reunions. He wouldn't be going back to a loving family. He wouldn't see his mom.

The helicopter shuddered. Metal creaked, and Leo could almost imagine the tapping was Morse code: *Not the end. Not the end.*

He leveled out the chopper, and the creaking stopped. He was just hearing things. He couldn't dwell on his mom, or the idea that kept bugging him—that Gaea was bringing souls back from the Underworld—so why couldn't he make some good come out of it? Thinking like that would drive him crazy. He had a job to do.

He let his instincts take over—just like flying the helicopter. If he thought about the quest too much, or what might happen afterward, he'd panic. The trick was not to think—just get through it.

"Thirty minutes out," he told his friends, though he wasn't sure how he knew. "If you want to get some rest, now's a good time."

Jason strapped himself into the back of the helicopter and passed out almost immediately. Piper and Leo stayed wide-awake.

After a few minutes of awkward silence, Leo said, "Your dad'll be fine, you know. Nobody's gonna mess with him with that crazy goat around."

Piper glanced over, and Leo was struck by how much she'd changed. Not just physically. Her presence was stronger. She seemed more... *here*. At Wilderness School she'd spent the semester trying not to be seen, hiding out in the back row of the classroom, the back of the bus, the corner of the lunchroom as far as possible from the loud kids. Now she would be impossible to miss. It didn't matter what she was wearing —you'd *have* to look at her.

"My dad," she said thoughtfully. "Yeah, I know. I was thinking about Jason. I'm worried about him."

Leo nodded. The closer they got to that bank of dark clouds, the more Leo worried, too. "He's starting to remember. That's got to make him a little edgy."

"But what if... what if he's a different person?"

Leo had had the same thought. If the Mist could affect their memories, could Jason's whole personality be an illusion, too? If their friend wasn't their friend, and they were heading into a cursed mansion—a dangerous place for demigods —what would happen if Jason's full memory came back in the middle of a battle?

"Nah," Leo decided. "After all we've been through? I can't see it. We're a team. Jason can handle it."

Piper smoothed her blue dress, which was tattered and burned from their fight on Mount Diablo. "I hope you're right. I need him..." She cleared her throat. "I mean I need to trust him...."

"I know," Leo said. After seeing her dad break down, Leo understood Piper couldn't afford to lose Jason as well. She'd just watched Tristan McLean, her cool suave movie star dad, reduced to near insanity. Leo could barely stand to watch that, but for *Piper*— Wow, Leo couldn't even imagine. He figured that would make her insecure about herself, too. If weakness was inherited, she'd be wondering, could *she* break down the same way her dad did?

"Hey, don't worry," Leo said. "Piper, you're the strongest, most powerful beauty queen I've ever met. You can trust yourself. For what it's worth, you can trust me too."

The helicopter dipped in a wind shear, and Leo almost jumped out of his skin. He cursed and righted the chopper.

Piper laughed nervously. "Trust you, huh?"

"Ah, shut up, already." But he grinned at her, and for a second, it felt like he was just relaxing comfortably with a friend.

Then they hit the storm clouds.

XLVIII

LEO

At first, Leo thought rocks were pelting the windshield. Then he realized it was sleet. Frost built up around the edges of the glass, and slushy waves of ice blotted out his view.

"An ice storm?" Piper shouted over the engine and the wind. "Is it supposed to be this cold in Sonoma?"

Leo wasn't sure, but something about this storm seemed conscious, malevolent—like it was intentionally slamming them.

Jason woke up quickly. He crawled forward, grabbing their seats for balance. "We've got to be getting close."

Leo was too busy wrestling with the stick to reply. Suddenly it wasn't so easy to drive the chopper. Its movements turned sluggish and jerky. The whole machine shuddered in the icy wind. The helicopter probably hadn't been prepped for cold-weather flying. The controls refused to respond, and they started to lose altitude.

Below them, the ground was a dark quilt of trees and fog. The ridge of a hill loomed in front of them and Leo yanked the stick, just clearing the treetops.

"There!" Jason shouted.

A small valley opened up before them, with the murky shape of a building in the middle. Leo aimed the helicopter straight for it. All around them were flashes of light that reminded Leo of the tracer fire at Midas's compound. Trees cracked and exploded at the edges of the clearing. Shapes moved through the mist. Combat seemed to be everywhere.

He set down the helicopter in an icy field about fifty yards from the house and killed the engine. He was about to relax when he heard a whistling sound and saw a dark shape hurtling toward them out of the mist.

"Out!" Leo screamed.

They leaped from the helicopter and barely cleared the rotors before a massive *BOOM* shook the ground, knocking Leo off his feet and splattering ice all over him.

He got up shakily and saw that the world's largest snowball —a chunk of snow, ice, and dirt the size of a garage—had completely flattened the Bell 412.

"You all right?" Jason ran up to him, Piper at his side. They both looked fine except for being speckled with snow and mud.

"Yeah." Leo shivered. "Guess we owe that ranger lady a new helicopter."

Piper pointed south. "Fighting's over there." Then she frowned. "No . . . it's all around us."

She was right. The sounds of combat rang across the valley. The snow and mist made it hard to tell for sure, but there seemed to be a circle of fighting all around the Wolf House.

Behind them loomed Jack London's dream home—a massive ruin of red and gray stones and rough-hewn timber beams. Leo could imagine how it had looked before it burned down—a combination log cabin and castle, like a billionaire lumberjack might build. But in the mist and sleet, the place had a lonely, haunted feel. Leo could totally believe the ruins were cursed.

"Jason!" a girl's voice called.

Thalia appeared from the fog, her parka caked with snow. Her bow was in her hand, and her quiver was almost empty. She ran toward them, but made it only a few steps before a six-armed ogre—one of the Earthborn—burst out of the storm behind her, a raised club in each hand.

"Look out!" Leo yelled. They rushed to help, but Thalia had it under control. She launched herself into a flip, notching an arrow as she pivoted like a gymnast and landed in a kneeling position. The ogre got a silver arrow right between the eyes and melted into a pile of clay.

Thalia stood and retrieved her arrow, but the point had snapped off. "That was my last one." She kicked the pile of clay resentfully. "Stupid ogre."

"Nice shot, though," Leo said.

Thalia ignored him as usual (which no doubt meant she thought he was as cool as ever). She hugged Jason and nodded to Piper. "Just in time. My Hunters are holding a perimeter around the mansion, but we'll be overrun any minute."

"By Earthborn?" Jason asked.

"*And* wolves—Lycaon's minions." Thalia blew a fleck of ice off her nose. "Also storm spirits—"

"But we gave them to Aeolus!" Piper protested.

"Who tried to kill us," Leo reminded her. "Maybe he's helping Gaea again."

"I don't know," Thalia said. "But the monsters keep re-forming almost as fast as we can kill them. We took the Wolf House with no problem: surprised the guards and sent them straight to Tartarus. But then this freak snowstorm blew in. Wave after wave of monsters started attacking. Now we're surrounded. I don't know who or what is leading the assault, but I think they planned this. It was a trap to kill anyone who tried to rescue Hera."

"Where is she?" Jason asked.

"Inside," Thalia said. "We tried to free her, but we can't figure out how to break the cage. It's only a few minutes until the sun goes down. Hera thinks that's the moment when Porphyrion will be reborn. Plus, most monsters are stronger at night. If we don't free Hera soon—"

She didn't need to finish the thought.

Leo, Jason, and Piper followed her into the ruined mansion.

Jason stepped over the threshold and immediately collapsed.

"Hey!" Leo caught him. "None of that, man. What's wrong?"

"This place..." Jason shook his head. "Sorry... It came rushing back to me."

"So you *have* been here," Piper said.

"We both have," Thalia said. Her expression was grim, like she was reliving someone's death. "This is where my mom took us when Jason was a child. She left him here, told me he was dead. He just disappeared."

"She gave me to the wolves," Jason murmured. "At Hera's insistence. She gave me to Lupa."

"That part I didn't know." Thalia frowned. "Who is Lupa?"

An explosion shook the building. Just outside, a blue mushroom cloud billowed up, raining snowflakes and ice like a nuclear blast made of cold instead of heat.

"Maybe this isn't the time for questions," Leo suggested. "Show us the goddess."

Once inside, Jason seemed to get his bearings. The house was built in a giant U, and Jason led them between the two wings to an outside courtyard with an empty reflecting pool. At the bottom of the pool, just as Jason had described from his dream, two spires of rock and root tendrils had cracked through the foundation.

One of the spires was much bigger—a solid dark mass about twenty feet high, and to Leo it looked like a stone body bag. Underneath the mass of fused tendrils he could make out the shape of a head, wide shoulders, a massive chest and arms, like the creature was stuck waist deep in the earth. No, not stuck—*rising*.

On the opposite end of the pool, the other spire was smaller and more loosely woven. Each tendril was as thick as a telephone pole, with so little space between them that Leo doubted he could've gotten his arm through. Still, he could see inside. And in the center of the cage stood Tía Callida.

She looked exactly like Leo remembered: dark hair covered with a shawl, the black dress of a widow, a wrinkled face with glinting, scary eyes.

She didn't glow or radiate any sort of power. She looked like a regular mortal woman, his good old psychotic babysitter.

Leo dropped into the pool and approached the cage. "*Hola, Tía*. Little bit of trouble?"

She crossed her arms and sighed in exasperation. "Don't inspect me like I'm one of your machines, Leo Valdez. Get me out of here!"

Thalia stepped next to him and looked at the cage with distaste—or maybe she was looking at the goddess. "We tried everything we could think of, Leo, but maybe my heart wasn't in it. If it was up to me, I'd just leave her in there."

"Ohh, Thalia Grace," the goddess said. "When I get out of here, you'll be sorry you were ever born."

"Save it!" Thalia snapped. "You've been nothing but a curse to every child of Zeus for ages. You sent a bunch of intestinally challenged cows after my friend Annabeth—"

"She was disrespectful!"

"You dropped a statue on my legs."

"It was an accident!"

"*And* you took my brother!" Thalia's voice cracked with emotion. "Here—on this spot. You ruined our lives. We should leave you to Gaea!"

"Hey," Jason intervened. "Thalia—Sis—I know. But this isn't the time. You should help your Hunters."

Thalia clenched her jaw. "Fine. For you, Jason. But if you ask me, she isn't worth it."

Thalia turned, leaped out of the pool, and stormed from the building.

Leo turned to Hera with grudging respect. "Intestinally challenged cows?"

"Focus on the cage, Leo," she grumbled. "And Jason—you are wiser than your sister. I chose my champion well."

"I'm not your champion, lady," Jason said. "I'm only helping you because you stole my memories and you're better than the alternative. Speaking of which, what's going on with that?"

He nodded to the other spire that looked like the king-size granite body bag. Was Leo imagining it, or had it grown taller since they'd gotten here?

"That, Jason," Hera said, "is the king of the giants being reborn."

"Gross," Piper said.

"Indeed," Hera said. "Porphyrion, the strongest of his kind. Gaea needed a great deal of power to raise him again —*my* power. For weeks I've grown weaker as my essence was used to grow him a new form."

"So you're like a heat lamp," Leo guessed. "Or fertilizer."

The goddess glared at him, but Leo didn't care. This old lady had been making his life miserable since he was a baby. He totally had rights to rag on her.

"Joke all you wish," Hera said in a clipped tone. "But at sundown, it will be too late. The giant will awake. He will offer me a choice: marry him, or be consumed by the earth. And I cannot marry him. We will all be destroyed. And as we die, Gaea will awaken."

Leo frowned at the giant's spire. "Can't we blow it up or something?"

"Without me, you do not have the power," Hera said. "You might as well try to destroy a mountain."

"Done that once today," Jason said.

"Just hurry up and let me out!" Hera demanded.

Jason scratched his head. "Leo, can you do it?"

"I don't know." Leo tried not to panic. "Besides, if she's a goddess, why hasn't she busted herself out?"

Hera paced furiously around her cage, cursing in Ancient Greek. "Use your brain, Leo Valdez. I *picked* you because you're intelligent. Once trapped, a god's power is useless. Your own father trapped me once in a golden chair. It was humiliating! I had to beg—*beg* him for my freedom and apologize for throwing him off Olympus."

"Sounds fair," Leo said.

Hera gave him the godly stink-eye. "I've watched you since you were a child, son of Hephaestus, because I knew you could aid me at this moment. If anyone can find a way to destroy this *abomination*, it is you."

"But it's not a machine. It's like Gaea thrust her hand out of the ground and..." Leo felt dizzy. The line of their prophecy came back to him: *The forge and dove shall break the cage.* "Hold on. I do have an idea. Piper, I'm going to need your help. And we're going to need time."

The air turned brittle with cold. The temperature dropped so fast, Leo's lips cracked and his breath changed to mist. Frost coated the walls of the Wolf House. *Venti* rushed in

—but instead of winged men, these were shaped like horses, with dark storm-cloud bodies and manes that crackled with lightning. Some had silver arrows sticking out of their flanks. Behind them came red-eyed wolves and the six-armed Earthborn.

Piper drew her dagger. Jason grabbed an ice-covered plank off the pool floor. Leo reached into his tool belt, but he was so shaken up, all he produced was a tin of breath mints. He shoved them back in, hoping nobody had noticed, and drew a hammer instead.

One of the wolves padded forward. It was dragging a human-size statue by the leg. At the edge of the pool, the wolf opened its maw and dropped the statue for them to see —an ice sculpture of a girl, an archer with short spiky hair and a surprised look on her face.

"Thalia!" Jason rushed forward, but Piper and Leo pulled him back. The ground around Thalia's statue was already webbed with ice. Leo feared if Jason touched her, he might freeze too.

"Who did this?" Jason yelled. His body crackled with electricity. "I'll kill you myself!"

From somewhere behind the monsters, Leo heard a girl's laughter, clear and cold. She stepped out of the mist in her snowy white dress, a silver crown atop her long black hair. She regarded them with those deep brown eyes Leo had thought were so beautiful in Quebec.

"Bon soir, mes amis," said Khione, the goddess of snow. She gave Leo a frosty smile. "Alas, son of Hephaestus, you say you need time? I'm afraid time is one tool you do not have."

XLIX

JASON

AFTER THE FIGHT ON MOUNT DIABLO, Jason didn't think he could ever feel more afraid or devastated.

Now his sister was frozen at his feet. He was surrounded by monsters. He'd broken his golden sword and replaced it with a piece of wood. He had approximately five minutes until the king of the giants busted out and destroyed them. Jason had already pulled his biggest ace, calling down Zeus's lightning when he'd fought Enceladus, and he doubted he'd have the strength or the cooperation from above to do it again. Which meant his only assets were one whiny imprisoned goddess, one sort-of girlfriend with a dagger, and Leo, who apparently thought he could defeat the armies of darkness with breath mints.

On top of all this, Jason's worst memories were flooding back. He knew for certain he'd done many dangerous things in his life, but he'd never been closer to death than he was right now.

The enemy was beautiful. Khione smiled, her dark eyes glittering, as a dagger of ice grew in her hand.

"What've you done?" Jason demanded.

"Oh, so many things," the snow goddess purred. "Your sister's not dead, if that's what you mean. She and her Hunters will make fine toys for our wolves. I thought we'd defrost them one at a time and hunt them down for amusement. Let *them* be the prey for once."

The wolves snarled appreciatively.

"Yes, my dears." Khione kept her eyes on Jason. "Your sister almost killed their king, you know. Lycaon's off in a cave somewhere, no doubt licking his wounds, but his minions have joined us to take revenge for their master. And soon Porphyrion will arise, and we shall rule the world."

"Traitor!" Hera shouted. "You meddlesome, D-list goddess! You aren't worthy to pour my wine, much less rule the world."

Khione sighed. "Tiresome as ever, Queen Hera. I've been wanting to shut you up for millennia."

Khione waved her hand, and ice encased the prison, sealing in the spaces between the earthen tendrils.

"That's better," the snow goddess said. "Now, demigods, about your death—"

"You're the one who tricked Hera into coming here," Jason said. "You gave Zeus the idea of closing Olympus."

The wolves snarled, and the storm spirits whinnied, ready to attack, but Khione held up her hand. "Patience, my loves. If he wants to talk, what matter? The sun is setting, and time is on our side. Of course, Jason Grace. Like snow, my voice is quiet and gentle, and very cold. It's easy for me to whisper to the other gods, especially when I am only confirming their own deepest fears. I also whispered in Aeolus's ear that he should issue an order to kill demigods. It is a small service for Gaea, but I'm sure I will be well rewarded when her sons the giants come to power."

"You could've killed us in Quebec," Jason said. "Why let us live?"

Khione wrinkled her nose. "Messy business, killing you in my father's house, especially when he insists on meeting all visitors. I did *try*, you remember. It would've been lovely if he'd agreed to turn you to ice. But once he'd given you guarantee of safe passage, I couldn't openly disobey him. My father is an old fool. He lives in fear of Zeus and Aeolus, but he's still powerful. Soon enough, when my new masters have awakened, I will depose Boreas and take the throne of the North Wind, but not just yet. Besides, my father did have a point. Your quest was suicidal. I fully expected you to fail."

"And to help us with that," Leo said, "you knocked our dragon out of the sky over Detroit. Those frozen wires in his head—that was *your* fault. You're gonna pay for that."

"You're also the one who kept Enceladus informed about us," Piper added. "We've been plagued by snowstorms the whole trip."

"Yes, I feel so close to all of you now!" Khione said. "Once you made it past Omaha, I decided to ask Lycaon to track you down so Jason could die here, at the Wolf House." Khione smiled at him. "You see, Jason, your blood spilled on this sacred ground will taint it for generations. Your demigod brethren will be outraged, especially when they find the bodies of these two from Camp Half-Blood. They'll believe the Greeks have conspired with giants. It will be...delicious."

Piper and Leo didn't seem to understand what she was saying. But Jason knew. His memories were returning enough for him to realize how dangerously effective Khione's plan could be.

"You'll set demigods against demigods," he said.

"It's so easy!" said Khione. "As I told you, I only encourage what you would do anyway."

"But why?" Piper spread her hands. "Khione, you'll tear the world apart. The giants will destroy everything. You don't want that. Call off your monsters."

Khione hesitated, then laughed. "Your persuasive powers are improving, girl. But I am a goddess. You can't charm-speak me. We wind gods are creatures of chaos! I'll overthrow Aeolus and let the storms run free. If we destroy the mortal world, all the better! They never honored me, even in Greek times. Humans and their talk of global warming. Pah! I'll cool them down quickly enough. When we retake the ancient places, I will cover the Acropolis in snow."

"The ancient places." Leo's eyes widened. "That's what Enceladus meant about destroying the roots of the gods. He meant Greece."

"You could join me, son of Hephaestus," Khione said. "I know you find me beautiful. It would be enough for my plan if these other two were to die. Reject that ridiculous destiny the Fates have given you. Live and be my champion, instead. Your skills would be quite useful."

Leo looked stunned. He glanced behind him, like Khione might be talking to somebody else. For a second Jason was worried. He figured Leo didn't have beautiful goddesses make him offers like this every day.

Then Leo laughed so hard, he doubled over. "Yeah, join you. Right. Until you get bored of me and turn me into a Leosicle? Lady, nobody messes with my dragon and gets away with it. I can't believe I thought you were hot."

Khione's face turned red. "Hot? You dare insult me? I am cold, Leo Valdez. Very, very cold."

She shot a blast of wintry sleet at the demigods, but Leo held up his hand. A wall of fire roared to life in front of them, and the snow dissolved in a steamy cloud.

Leo grinned. "See, lady, that's what happens to snow in Texas. It—freaking—melts."

Khione hissed. "Enough of this. Hera is failing. Porphyrion is rising. Kill the demigods. Let them be our king's first meal!"

Jason hefted his icy wooden plank—a stupid weapon to die fighting with—and the monsters charged.

L

JASON

A WOLF LAUNCHED ITSELF AT JASON. He stepped back and swung his scrap wood into the beast's snout with a satisfying crack. Maybe only silver could kill it, but a good old-fashioned board could still give it a Tylenol headache.

He turned toward the sound of hooves and saw a storm spirit horse bearing down on him. Jason concentrated and summoned the wind. Just before the spirit could trample him, Jason launched himself into the air, grabbed the horse's smoky neck, and pirouetted onto its back.

The storm spirit reared. It tried to shake Jason, then tried to dissolve into mist to lose him; but somehow Jason stayed on. He willed the horse to remain in solid form, and the horse seemed unable to refuse. Jason could feel it fighting against him. He could sense its raging thoughts—complete chaos straining to break free. It took all Jason's willpower to impose his own wishes and bring the horse under control. He thought about Aeolus, overseeing thousands and thousands of spirits like this, some much worse. No wonder the Master of the Winds had gone a little mad after centuries of that pressure. But Jason had only one spirit to master, and he *had* to win.

"You're mine now," Jason said.

The horse bucked, but Jason held fast. Its mane flickered as it circled around the empty pool, its hooves causing miniature thunderstorms—tempests—whenever they touched.

"Tempest?" Jason said. "Is that your name?"

The horse spirit shook its mane, evidently pleased to be recognized.

"Fine," Jason said. "Now, let's fight."

He charged into battle, swinging his icy piece of wood, knocking aside wolves and plunging straight through other *venti*. Tempest was a strong spirit, and every time he plowed through one of his brethren, he discharged so much electricity, the other spirit vaporized into a harmless cloud of mist.

Through the chaos, Jason caught glimpses of his friends. Piper was surrounded by Earthborn, but she seemed to be holding her own. She was so impressive-looking as she fought, almost glowing with beauty, that the Earthborn stared at her in awe, forgetting that they were supposed to kill her. They'd lower their clubs and watch dumbfounded as she smiled and charged them. They'd smile back—until she sliced them apart with her dagger, and they melted into mounds of mud.

Leo had taken on Khione herself. While fighting a goddess should've been suicide, Leo was the right man for the job. She kept summoning ice daggers to throw at him, blasts of winter air, tornadoes of snow. Leo burned through all of it. His whole body flickered with red tongues of flame like he'd been doused with gasoline. He advanced on the goddess, using two silver-tipped ball-peen hammers to smash any monsters that got in his way.

Jason realized that Leo was the only reason they were still alive. His fiery aura was heating up the whole courtyard, countering Khione's winter magic. Without him, they would've been frozen like the Hunters long ago. Wherever Leo went, ice melted off the stones. Even Thalia started to defrost a little when Leo stepped near her.

Khione slowly backed away. Her expression went from enraged to shocked to slightly panicked as Leo got closer.

Jason was running out of enemies. Wolves lay in dazed heaps. Some slunk away into the ruins, yelping from their wounds. Piper stabbed the last Earthborn, who toppled to the ground in a pile of sludge. Jason rode Tempest through the last *ventus*, breaking it into vapor. Then he wheeled around and saw Leo bearing down on the goddess of snow.

"You're too late," Khione snarled. "He's awake! And don't think you've won anything here, demigods. Hera's plan will never work. You'll be at each other's throats before you can ever stop us."

Leo set his hammers ablaze and threw them at the goddess, but she turned into snow—a white powdery image of herself. Leo's hammers slammed into the snow woman, breaking it into a steaming mound of mush.

Piper was breathing hard, but she smiled up at Jason. "Nice horse."

Tempest reared on his hind legs, arcing electricity across his hooves. A complete show-off.

Then Jason heard a cracking sound behind him. The melting ice on Hera's cage sloughed off in a curtain of slush, and the goddess called, "Oh, don't mind me! Just the queen of the heavens, dying over here!"

Jason dismounted and told Tempest to stay put. The three demigods jumped into the pool and ran to the spire.

Leo frowned. "Uh, Tía Callida, are you getting shorter?"

"No, you dolt! The earth is claiming me. Hurry!"

As much as Jason disliked Hera, what he saw inside the cage alarmed him. Not only was Hera sinking, the ground was rising around her like water in a tank. Liquid rock had already covered her shins. "The giant wakes!" Hera warned. "You only have seconds!"

"On it," Leo said. "Piper, I need your help. Talk to the cage."

"What?" she said.

"Talk to it. Use everything you've got. Convince Gaea to sleep. Lull her into a daze. Just slow her down, try to get the tendrils to loosen while I—"

"Right!" Piper cleared her throat and said, "Hey, Gaea. Nice night, huh? Boy, I'm tired. How about you? Ready for some sleep?"

The more she talked, the more confident she sounded. Jason felt his own eyes getting heavy, and he had to force himself not to focus on her words. It seemed to have some effect on the cage. The mud was rising more slowly. The tendrils seemed to soften just a little—becoming more like tree root than rock. Leo pulled a circular saw out of his tool belt. How it fit in there, Jason had no idea. Then Leo looked at the cord and grunted in frustration. "I don't have anywhere to plug it in!"

The spirit horse Tempest jumped into the pit and whinnied.

"Really?" Jason asked.

Tempest dipped his head and trotted over to Leo. Leo looked dubious, but he held up the plug, and a breeze whisked it into the horse's flank. Lightning sparked, connecting with the prongs of the plug, and the circular saw whirred to life.

"Sweet!" Leo grinned. "Your horse comes with AC outlets!"

Their good mood didn't last long. On the other side of the pool, the giant's spire crumbled with a sound like a tree snapping in half. Its outer sheath of tendrils exploded from the top down, raining stone and wood shards as the giant shook himself free and climbed out of the earth.

Jason hadn't thought anything could be scarier than Enceladus.

He was wrong.

Porphyrion was even taller, and even more ripped. He didn't radiate heat, or show any signs of breathing fire, but there was something more terrible about him—a kind of strength, even magnetism, as if the giant were so huge and dense he had his own gravitational field.

Like Enceladus, the giant king was humanoid from the waist up, clad in bronze armor, and from the waist down he had scaly dragon's legs; but his skin was the color of lima beans. His hair was green as summer leaves, braided in long locks and decorated with weapons—daggers, axes, and full-size swords, some of them bent and bloody—maybe trophies taken from demigods eons before. When the giant opened his eyes, they were blank white, like polished marble. He took a deep breath.

"Alive!" he bellowed. "Praise to Gaea!"

Jason made a heroic little whimpering sound he hoped his friends couldn't hear. He was very sure no demigod could solo this guy. Porphyrion could lift mountains. He could crush Jason with one finger.

"Leo," Jason said.

"Huh?" Leo's mouth was wide open. Even Piper seemed dazed.

"You guys keep working," Jason said. "Get Hera free!"

"What are you going to do?" Piper asked. "You can't seriously—"

"Entertain a giant?" Jason said. "I've got no choice."

"Excellent!" the giant roared as Jason approached. "An appetizer! Who are you—Hermes? Ares?"

Jason thought about going with that idea, but something told him not to.

"I'm Jason Grace," he said. "Son of Jupiter."

Those white eyes bored into him. Behind him, Leo's circular saw whirred, and Piper talked to the cage in soothing tones, trying to keep the fear out of her voice.

Porphyrion threw back his head and laughed. "Outstanding!" He looked up at the cloudy night sky. "So, Zeus, you sacrifice a son to me? The gesture is appreciated, but it will not save you."

The sky didn't even rumble. No help from above. Jason was on his own.

He dropped his makeshift club. His hands were covered in splinters, but that didn't matter now. He had to buy Leo and Piper some time, and he couldn't do that without a proper weapon.

It was time to act a whole lot more confident than he felt.

"If you knew who I was," Jason yelled up at the giant, "you'd be worried about me, not my father. I hope you enjoyed your two and a half minutes of rebirth, giant, because I'm going to send you right back to Tartarus."

The giant's eyes narrowed. He planted one foot outside the pool and crouched to get a better look at his opponent. "So . . . we'll start by boasting, will we? Just like old times! Very well, demigod. I am Porphyrion, king of the giants, son of Gaea. In olden times, I rose from Tartarus, the abyss of my father, to challenge the gods. To start the war, I stole Zeus's queen." He grinned at the goddess's cage. "Hello, Hera."

"My husband destroyed you once, monster!" Hera said. "He'll do it again!"

"But he didn't, my dear! Zeus wasn't powerful enough to kill me. He had to rely on a puny demigod to help, and even then, we almost won. This time, we will complete what we started. Gaea is waking. She has provisioned us with many fine servants. Our armies will shake the earth—and we will destroy you at the roots."

"You wouldn't dare," Hera said, but she was weakening. Jason could hear it in her voice. Piper kept whispering to the cage, and Leo kept sawing, but the earth was still rising inside Hera's prison, covering her up to her waist.

"Oh, yes," the giant said. "The Titans sought to attack

your new home in New York. Bold, but ineffective. Gaea is wiser and more patient. And we, her greatest children, are much, much stronger than Kronos. We know how to kill you Olympians once and for all. You must be dug up completely like rotten trees—your eldest roots torn out and burned."

The giant frowned at Piper and Leo, as if he'd just noticed them working at the cage. Jason stepped forward and yelled to get back Porphyrion's attention.

"You said a demigod killed you," he shouted. "How, if we're so puny?"

"Ha! You think I would explain it to you? I was created to be Zeus's replacement, born to destroy the lord of the sky. I shall take his throne. I shall take his wife—or, if she will not have me, I will let the earth consume her life force. What you see before you, child, is only my weakened form. I will grow stronger by the hour, until I am invincible. But I am already quite capable of smashing you to a grease spot!"

He rose to his full height and held out his hand. A twenty-foot spear shot from the earth. He grasped it, then stomped the ground with his dragon's feet. The ruins shook. All around the courtyard, monsters started to regather—storm spirits, wolves, and Earthborn, all answering the giant king's call.

"Great," Leo muttered. "We needed more enemies."

"Hurry," Hera said.

"I know!" Leo snapped.

"Go to sleep, cage," Piper said. "Nice, sleepy cage. Yes, I'm talking to a bunch of earthen tendrils. This isn't weird at all."

Porphyrion raked his spear across the top of the ruins, destroying a chimney and spraying wood and stone across the courtyard. "So, child of Zeus! I have finished my boasting. Now it's your turn. What were you saying about destroying me?"

Jason looked at the ring of monsters, waiting impatiently for their master's order to tear them to shreds. Leo's circular saw kept whirring, and Piper kept talking, but it seemed hopeless. Hera's cage was almost completely filled with earth.

"I'm the son of Jupiter!" he shouted, and just for effect, he summoned the winds, rising a few feet off the ground. "I'm a child of Rome, consul to demigods, praetor of the First Legion." Jason didn't know quite what he was saying, but he rattled off the words like he'd said them many times before. He held out his arms, showing the tattoo of the eagle and SPQR, and to his surprise the giant seemed to recognize it.

For a moment, Porphyrion actually looked uneasy.

"I slew the Trojan sea monster," Jason continued. "I toppled the black throne of Kronos, and destroyed the Titan Krios with my own hands. And now I'm going to destroy you, Porphyrion, and feed you to your own wolves."

"Wow, dude," Leo muttered. "You been eating red meat?"

Jason launched himself at the giant, determined to tear him apart.

The idea of fighting a forty-foot-tall immortal bare handed was so ridiculous, even the giant seemed surprised. Half flying, half leaping, Jason landed on the giant's scaly reptilian knee and climbed up the giant's arm before Porphyrion even realized what had happened.

"You dare?" the giant bellowed.

Jason reached his shoulders and ripped a sword out of the giant's weapon-filled braids. He yelled, "For Rome!" and drove the sword into the nearest convenient target—the giant's massive ear.

Lightning streaked out of the sky and blasted the sword, throwing Jason free. He rolled when he hit the ground. When he looked up, the giant was staggering. His hair was on fire, and the side of his face was blackened from lightning. The sword had splintered in his ear. Golden ichor ran down his jaw. The other weapons were sparking and smoldering in his braids.

Porphyrion almost fell. The circle of monsters let out a collective growl and moved forward—wolves and ogres fixing their eyes on Jason.

"No!" Porphyrion yelled. He regained his balance and glared at the demigod. "I will kill him myself."

The giant raised his spear and it began to glow. "You want to play with lightning, boy? You forget. I am the bane of Zeus. I was created to destroy your father, which means I know exactly what will kill *you*."

Something in Porphyrion's voice told Jason he wasn't bluffing.

Jason and his friends had had a good run. The three of them had done amazing things. Yeah, even *heroic* things. But as the giant raised his spear, Jason knew there was no way he could deflect this strike.

This was the end.

"Got it!" Leo yelled.

"Sleep!" Piper said, so forcefully, the nearest wolves fell to the ground and began snoring.

The stone and wood cage crumbled. Leo had sawed through the base of the thickest tendril and apparently cut off the cage's connection to Gaea. The tendrils turned to dust. The mud around Hera disintegrated. The goddess grew in size, glowing with power.

"Yes!" the goddess said. She threw off her black robes to reveal a white gown, her arms bedecked with golden jewelry. Her face was both terrible and beautiful, and a golden crown glowed in her long black hair. "Now I shall have my revenge!"

The giant Porphyrion backed away. He said nothing, but he gave Jason one last look of hatred. His message was clear: *Another time.* Then he slammed his spear against the earth, and the giant disappeared into the ground like he'd dropped down a chute.

Around the courtyard, monsters began to panic and retreat, but there was no escape for them.

Hera glowed brighter. She shouted, "Cover your eyes, my heroes!"

But Jason was too much in shock. He understood too late.

He watched as Hera turned into a supernova, exploding in a ring of force that vaporized every monster instantly. Jason fell, light searing into his mind, and his last thought was that his body was burning.

PIPER

"Jason!"

Piper kept calling his name as she held him, though she'd almost lost hope. He'd been unconscious for two minutes now. His body was steaming, his eyes rolled back in his head. She couldn't tell if he was even breathing.

"It's no use, child." Hera stood over them in her simple black robes and shawl.

Piper hadn't seen the goddess go nuclear. Thankfully she'd closed her eyes, but she could see the aftereffects. Every vestige of winter was gone from the valley. No signs of battle, either. The monsters had been vaporized. The ruins had been restored to what they were before—still ruins, but with no evidence that they'd been overrun by a horde of wolves, storm spirits, and six-armed ogres.

Even the Hunters had been revived. Most waited at a respectful distance in the meadow, but Thalia knelt by Piper's side, her hand on Jason's forehead.

Thalia glared up at the goddess. "This is your fault. Do something!"

"Do not address me that way, girl. I am the queen—"

"Fix him!"

Hera's eyes flickered with power. "I *did* warn him. I would never intentionally hurt the boy. He was to be my champion. I told them to close their eyes before I revealed my true form."

"Um..." Leo frowned. "True form is bad, right? So why did you do it?"

"I unleashed my power to help you, fool!" Hera cried. "I became pure energy so I could disintegrate the monsters, restore this place, and even save these miserable Hunters from the ice."

"But mortals can't look upon you in that form!" Thalia shouted. "You've killed him!"

Leo shook his head in dismay. "That's what our prophecy meant. *Death unleash, through Hera's rage.* Come on, lady. You're a goddess. Do some voodoo magic on him! Bring him back."

Piper half heard their conversation, but mostly she was focused on Jason's face. "He's breathing!" she announced.

"Impossible," Hera said. "I wish it were true, child, but no mortal has ever—"

"Jason," Piper called, putting every bit of her willpower into his name. She could *not* lose him. "Listen to me. You can do this. Come back. You're going to be fine."

Nothing happened. Had she imagined his breath stirring?

"Healing is not a power of Aphrodite," Hera said regretfully. "Even I cannot fix this, girl. His mortal spirit—"

"Jason," Piper said again, and she imagined her voice resonating through the earth, all the way down to the Underworld. "Wake up."

He gasped, and his eyes flew open. For a moment they were full of light—glowing pure gold. Then the light faded and his eyes were normal again. "What—what happened?"

"Impossible!" Hera said.

Piper wrapped him in a hug until he groaned, "Crushing me."

"Sorry," she said, so relieved, she laughed while wiping a tear from her eye.

Thalia gripped her brother's hand. "How do you feel?"

"Hot," he muttered. "Mouth is dry. And I saw something . . . really terrible."

"That was Hera," Thalia grumbled. "Her Majesty, the Loose Cannon."

"That's it, Thalia Grace," said the goddess. "I will turn you into an aardvark, so help me—"

"Stop it, you two," Piper said. Amazingly, they both shut up.

Piper helped Jason to his feet and gave him the last nectar from their supplies.

"Now . . ." Piper faced Thalia and Hera. "Hera—Your Majesty—we couldn't have rescued you without the Hunters. And Thalia, you never would've seen Jason again—*I* wouldn't have met him—if it weren't for Hera. You two make nice, because we've got bigger problems."

They both glared at her, and for three long seconds, Piper wasn't sure which one of them was going to kill her first.

Finally Thalia grunted. "You've got spirit, Piper." She pulled a silver card from her parka and tucked it into the pocket of Piper's snowboarding jacket. "You ever want to be a Hunter, call me. We could use you."

Hera crossed her arms. "Fortunately for *this* Hunter, you have a point, daughter of Aphrodite." She assessed Piper, as if seeing her clearly for the first time. "You wondered, Piper, why I chose you for this quest, why I didn't reveal your secret in the beginning, even when I knew Enceladus was using you. I must admit, until this moment I was not sure. Something told me you would be vital to the quest. Now I see I was right. You're even stronger than I realized. And you are correct about the dangers to come. We must work together."

Piper's face felt warm. She wasn't sure how to respond to Hera's compliment, but Leo stepped in.

"Yeah," he said, "I don't suppose that Porphyrion guy just melted and died, huh?"

"No," Hera agreed. "By saving me, and saving this place, you prevented Gaea from waking. You have bought us some time. But Porphyrion has risen. He simply knew better than to stay here, especially since he has not yet regained his full power. Giants can only be killed by a combination of god and demigod, working together. Once you freed me—"

"He ran away," Jason said. "But to where?"

Hera didn't answer, but a sense of dread washed over Piper. She remembered what Porphyrion had said about killing the Olympians by pulling up their roots. *Greece.* She looked at Thalia's grim expression, and guessed the Hunter had come to the same conclusion.

"I need to find Annabeth," Thalia said. "She has to know what's happened here."

"Thalia . . ." Jason gripped her hand. "We never got to talk about this place, or—"

"I know." Her expression softened. "I lost you here once. I don't want to leave you again. But we'll meet soon. I'll rendezvous with you back at Camp Half-Blood." She glanced at Hera. "You'll see them there safely? It's the least you can do."

"It's not your place to tell me—"

"Queen Hera," Piper interceded.

The goddess sighed. "Fine. Yes. Just off with you, Hunter!"

Thalia gave Jason a hug and said her good-byes. When the Hunters were gone, the courtyard seemed strangely quiet. The dry reflecting pool showed no sign of the earthen tendrils that had brought back the giant king or imprisoned Hera. The night sky was clear and starry. The wind rustled in the redwoods. Piper thought about that night in Oklahoma when she and her dad had slept in Grandpa Tom's front yard. She thought about the night on the Wilderness School dorm roof, when Jason had kissed her—in her Mist-altered memories, anyway.

"Jason, what happened to you here?" she asked. "I mean— I know your mom abandoned you here. But you said it was sacred ground for demigods. Why? What happened after you were on your own?"

Jason shook his head uneasily. "It's still murky. The wolves . . ."

"You were given a destiny," Hera said. "You were given into my service."

Jason scowled. "Because you forced my mom to do that. You couldn't stand knowing Zeus had two children with my mom. Knowing that he'd fallen for her *twice*. I was the price you demanded for leaving the rest of my family alone. "

"It was the right choice for you as well, Jason," Hera insisted. "The second time your mother managed to snare Zeus's affections, it was because she imagined him in a different aspect—the aspect of Jupiter. Never before had this happened—two children, Greek and Roman, born into the same family. You *had* to be separated from Thalia. This is where all demigods of your kind start their journey."

"Of his kind?" Piper asked.

"She means Roman," Jason said. "Demigods are left here. We meet the she-wolf goddess, Lupa, the same immortal wolf that raised Romulus and Remus."

Hera nodded. "And if you are strong enough, you live."

"But..." Leo looked mystified. "What happened after that? I mean, Jason never made it to camp."

"Not to Camp Half-Blood, no," Hera agreed.

Piper felt as if the sky were spiraling above her, making her dizzy. "You went somewhere else. That's where you've been all these years. Somewhere else for demigods—but where?"

Jason turned to the goddess. "The memories are coming back, but not the location. You're not going to tell me, are you?"

"No," Hera said. "That is part of your destiny, Jason. You must find your own way back. But when you do...you will unite two great powers. You will give us hope against the giants, and more importantly—against Gaea herself."

"You want us to help you," Jason said, "but you're holding back information."

"Giving you answers would make those answers invalid," Hera said. "That is the way of the Fates. You must forge your own path for it to mean anything. Already, you three have surprised me. I would not have thought it possible..."

The goddess shook her head. "Suffice it to say, you have performed well, demigods. But this is only the beginning. Now you must return to Camp Half-Blood, where you will begin planning for the next phase."

"Which you won't tell us about," Jason grumped. "And I suppose you destroyed my nice storm spirit horse, so we'll have to walk home?"

Hera waved aside the question. "Storm spirits are creatures of chaos. I did not destroy that one, though I have no idea where he went, or whether you'll see him again. But there is an easier way home for you. As you have done me a great service, so I can help you—at least this once. Farewell, demigods, for now."

The world turned upside down, and Piper almost blacked out.

When she could see straight again, she was back at camp, in the dining pavilion, in the middle of dinner. They were standing on the Aphrodite cabin's table, and Piper had one foot in Drew's pizza. Sixty campers rose at once, gawking at them in astonishment.

Whatever Hera had done to shoot them across the country, it wasn't good for Piper's stomach. She could barely control her nausea. Leo wasn't so lucky. He jumped off the table, ran to the nearest bronze brazier, and threw up in it—which was probably not a great burnt offering for the gods.

"Jason?" Chiron trotted forward. No doubt the old centaur had seen thousands of years' worth of weird stuff, but even he looked totally flabbergasted. "What— How—?"

The Aphrodite campers stared up at Piper with their mouths open. Piper figured she must look awful.

"Hi," she said, as casually as she could. "We're back."

PIPER

PIPER DIDN'T REMEMBER MUCH ABOUT the rest of the night. They told their story and answered a million questions from the other campers, but finally Chiron saw how tired they were and ordered them to bed.

It felt so good to sleep on a real mattress, and Piper was so exhausted, she crashed immediately, which spared her any worry about what it would be like returning to the Aphrodite cabin.

The next morning she woke in her bunk, feeling reinvigorated. The sun came through the windows along with a pleasant breeze. It might've been spring instead of winter. Birds sang. Monsters howled in the woods. Breakfast smells wafted from the dining pavilion—bacon, pancakes, and all sorts of wonderful things.

Drew and her gang were frowning down at her, their arms crossed.

"Morning." Piper sat up and smiled. "Beautiful day."

"You're going to make us late for breakfast," Drew said, "which means *you* get to clean the cabin for inspection."

A week ago, Piper would've either punched Drew in the face, or hidden back under her covers. Now she thought about the Cyclopes in Detroit, Medea in Chicago, Midas turning her to gold in Omaha. Looking at Drew, who used to bother her, Piper laughed.

Drew's smug expression crumbled. She backed up, then remembered she was supposed to be angry. "What are you—"

"Challenging you," Piper said. "How about noon in the arena? You can choose the weapons."

She got out of bed, stretched leisurely, and beamed at her cabinmates. She spotted Mitchell and Lacy, who'd helped her pack for the quest. They were smiling tentatively, their eyes flitting from Piper to Drew like this might be a very interesting tennis game.

"I missed you guys!" Piper announced. "We're going to have a great time when I'm senior counselor."

Drew turned bug juice red. Even her closest lieutenants looked a little nervous. This wasn't in their script.

"You—" Drew spluttered. "You ugly little witch! I've been here the longest. You can't just—"

"Challenge you?" Piper said. "Sure, I can. Camp rules: I've been claimed by Aphrodite. I've completed a quest, which is one more than *you've* completed. If I feel I can do a better job, I can challenge you. Unless you just want to step down. Did I get all that right, Mitchell?"

"Just right, Piper." Mitchell was grinning. Lacy was bouncing up and down like she was trying to achieve liftoff.

A few of the other kids started to grin, as if they were enjoying the different colors Drew's face was turning.

"Step down?" Drew shrieked. "You're crazy!"

Piper shrugged. Then fast as a viper she pulled Katoptris from under her pillow, unsheathed the dagger, and thrust the point under Drew's chin. Everybody else backed up fast. One guy crashed into a makeup table and sent up a plume of pink powder.

"A duel, then," Piper said cheerfully. "If you don't want to wait until noon, now is fine. You've turned this cabin into a dictatorship, Drew. Silena Beauregard knew better than that. Aphrodite is about love and beauty. *Being* loving. *Spreading* beauty. Good friends. Good times. Good deeds. Not just looking good. Silena made mistakes, but in the end she stood by her friends. That's why she was a hero. I'm going to set things right, and I've got a feeling Mom will be on my side. Want to find out?"

Drew went cross-eyed looking down the blade of Piper's dagger.

A second passed. Then two. Piper didn't care. She was absolutely happy and confident. It must've shown in her smile.

"I . . . step down," Drew grumbled. "But if you think I'm ever going to forget this, McLean—"

"Oh, I hope you won't," Piper said. "Now, run along to the dining pavilion, and explain to Chiron why we're late. There's been a change of leadership."

Drew backed to the door. Even her closest lieutenants didn't follow her. She was about to leave when Piper said, "Oh, and Drew, honey?"

The former counselor looked back reluctantly.

"In case you think I'm not a true daughter of Aphrodite," Piper said, "don't even *look* at Jason Grace. He may not know it yet, but he's *mine*. If you even try to make a move, I will load you into a catapult and shoot you across Long Island Sound."

Drew turned around so fast, she ran into the doorframe. Then she was gone.

The cabin was silent. The other campers stared at Piper. This was the part she was unsure of. She didn't want to rule by fear. She wasn't like Drew, but she didn't know if they'd accept her.

Then, spontaneously, the Aphrodite campers cheered so loudly, they must've been heard all across camp. They herded Piper out of the cabin, raised her on their shoulders, and carried her all the way to the dining pavilion—still in her pajamas, her hair still a mess, but she didn't care. She'd never felt better.

By afternoon, Piper had changed into comfortable camp clothes and led the Aphrodite cabin through their morning activities. She was ready for free time.

Some of the buzz of her victory had faded because she had an appointment at the Big House.

Chiron met her on the front porch in human form, compacted into his wheelchair. "Come inside, my dear. The video conference is ready."

The only computer at camp was in Chiron's office, and the whole room was shielded in bronze plating.

"Demigods and technology don't mix," Chiron explained. "Phone calls, texting, even browsing the Internet—all these things can attract monsters. Why, just this fall at a school in Cincinnati, we had to rescue a young hero who Googled the gorgons and got a little more than he bargained for, but never mind that. Here at camp, you're protected. Still...we try to be cautious. You'll only be able to talk for a few minutes."

"Got it," Piper said. "Thank you, Chiron."

He smiled and wheeled himself out of the office. Piper hesitated before clicking the call button. Chiron's office had a cluttered, cozy feel. One wall was covered with T-shirts from different conventions—PARTY PONIES '09 VEGAS, PARTY PONIES '10 HONOLULU, et cetera. Piper didn't know who the Party Ponies were, but judging from the stains, scorch marks, and weapon holes in the T-shirts, they must've had some pretty wild meetings. On the shelf over Chiron's desk sat an old-fashioned boom box with cassette tapes labeled "Dean Martin" and "Frank Sinatra" and "Greatest Hits of the 40s." Chiron was so old, Piper wondered if that meant 1940s, 1840s, or maybe just A.D. 40.

But most of the office's wall space was plastered with photos of demigods, like a hall of fame. One of the newer shots showed a teenage guy with dark hair and green eyes. Since he stood arm in arm with Annabeth, Piper assumed the guy must be Percy Jackson. In some of the older photos, she recognized famous people: businessmen, athletes, even some actors that her dad knew.

"Unbelievable," she muttered.

Piper wondered if her photo would go on that wall some-day. For the first time, she felt like she was part of something bigger than herself. Demigods had been around for centuries. Whatever she did, she did for all of them.

She took a deep breath and made the call. The video screen popped up.

Gleeson Hedge grinned at her from her dad's office. "Seen the news?"

"Kind of hard to miss," Piper said. "I hope you know what you're doing."

Chiron had shown her a newspaper at lunch. Her dad's mysterious return from nowhere had made the front page. His personal assistant Jane had been fired for covering up his disappearance and failing to notify the police. A new staff had been hired and personally vetted by Tristan McLean's "life coach," Gleeson Hedge. According to the paper, Mr. McLean claimed to have no memory of the last week, and the media was totally eating up the story. Some thought it was a clever marketing ploy for a movie—maybe McLean was going to play an amnesiac? Some thought he'd been kidnapped by terrorists, or rabid fans, or had heroically escaped from ransom seekers using his incredible King of Sparta fighting skills. Whatever the truth, Tristan McLean was more famous than ever.

"It's going great," Hedge promised. "But don't worry. We're going to keep him out of the public eye for the next month or so until things cool down. Your dad's got more important things to do—like resting, and talking to his daughter."

"Don't get too comfortable out there in Hollywood, Gleeson," Piper said.

Hedge snorted. "You kidding? These people make Aeolus look sane. I'll be back as soon as I can, but your dad's gotta get back on his feet first. He's a good guy. Oh, and by the way, I took care of that other little matter. The Park Service in the Bay Area just got an anonymous gift of a new helicopter. And that ranger pilot who helped us? She's got a very lucrative offer to fly for Mr. McLean."

"Thanks, Gleeson," Piper said. "For everything."

"Yeah, well. I don't try to be awesome. It just comes natural. Speaking of Aeolus's place, meet your dad's new assistant."

Hedge was nudged out of the way, and a pretty young lady grinned into the camera.

"Mellie?" Piper stared, but it was definitely her: the *aura* who'd helped them escape from Aeolus's fortress. "You're working for my dad now?"

"Isn't it great?"

"Does he know you're a—you know—wind spirit?"

"Oh, no. But I love this job. It's—um—a breeze."

Piper couldn't help but laugh. "I'm glad. That's awesome. But where—"

"Just a sec." Mellie kissed Gleeson on the cheek. "Come on, you old goat. Stop hogging the screen."

"What?" Hedge demanded. But Mellie steered him away and called, "Mr. McLean? She's on!"

A second later, Piper's dad appeared.

He broke into a huge grin. "Pipes!"

He looked great—back to normal, with his sparkling brown eyes, his half-day beard, his confident smile, and his newly trimmed hair like he was ready to shoot a scene. Piper was relieved, but she also felt a little sad. Back to normal wasn't necessarily what she'd wanted.

In her mind, she started the clock. On a normal call like this, on a workday, she hardly ever got her dad's attention for longer than thirty seconds.

"Hey," she said weakly. "You feeling okay?"

"Honey, I'm so sorry to worry you with this disappearance business. I don't know..." His smile wavered, and she could tell he was trying to remember—grasping for a memory that should have been there, but wasn't. "I'm not sure what happened, honestly. But I'm fine. Coach Hedge has been a godsend."

"A godsend," she repeated. Funny choice of words.

"He told me about your new school," Dad said. "I'm sorry the Wilderness School didn't work out, but you were right. Jane was wrong. I was a fool to listen to her."

Ten seconds left, maybe. But at least her dad sounded sincere, like he really did feel remorseful.

"You don't remember anything?" she said, a bit wistfully.

"Of course I do," he said.

A chill went down her neck. "You do?"

"I remember that I love you," he said. "And I'm proud of you. Are you happy at your new school?"

Piper blinked. She wasn't going to cry now. After all she'd been through, that would be ridiculous. "Yeah, Dad. It's more like a camp, not a school, but... Yeah, I think I'll be happy here."

"Call me as often as you can," he said. "And come home for Christmas. And Pipes..."

"Yes?"

He touched the screen as if trying to reach through with his hand. "You're a wonderful young lady. I don't tell you that often enough. You remind me so much of your mother. She'd be proud. And Grandpa Tom"—he chuckled—"he always said you'd be the most powerful voice in our family. You're going to outshine me some day, you know. They're going to remember me as Piper McLean's father, and that's the best legacy I can imagine."

Piper tried to answer, but she was afraid she'd break down. She just touched his fingers on the screen and nodded.

Mellie said something in the background, and her dad sighed. "Studio calling. I'm sorry, honey." And he did sound genuinely annoyed to go.

"It's okay, Dad," she managed. "Love you."

He winked. Then the video call went black.

Forty-five seconds? Maybe a full minute.

Piper smiled. A small improvement, but it was progress.

At the commons area, she found Jason relaxing on a bench, a basketball between his feet. He was sweaty from working out, but he looked great in his orange tank top and shorts. His various scars and bruises from the quest were healing, thanks to some medical attention from the Apollo cabin. His arms and legs were well muscled and tan—distracting as always. His close-cropped blond hair caught the afternoon light so it looked like it was turning to gold, Midas style.

"Hey," he said. "How did it go?"

It took her a second to focus on his question. "Hmm? Oh, yeah. Fine."

She sat next to him and they watched the campers going

back and forth. A couple of Demeter girls were playing tricks on two of the Apollo guys—making grass grow around their ankles as they shot baskets. Over at the camp store, the Hermes kids were putting up a sign that read: FLYING SHOES, SLIGHTLY USED, 50% OFF TODAY! Ares kids were lining their cabin with fresh barbed wire. The Hypnos cabin was snoring away. A normal day at camp.

Meanwhile, the Aphrodite kids were watching Piper and Jason, and trying to pretend they weren't. Piper was pretty sure she saw money change hands, like they were placing bets on a kiss.

"Get any sleep?" she asked him.

He looked at her as if she'd been reading his thoughts. "Not much. Dreams."

"About your past?"

He nodded.

She didn't push him. If he wanted to talk, that was fine, but she knew him better than to press the subject. She didn't even worry that her knowledge of him was mostly based on three months of false memories. *You can sense possibilities,* her mother had said. And Piper was determined to make those possibilities a reality.

Jason spun his basketball. "It's not good news," he warned. "My memories aren't good for—for any of us."

Piper was pretty sure he'd been about to say *for us*—as in the two of them, and she wondered if he'd remembered a girl from his past. But she didn't let it bother her. Not on a sunny winter day like this, with Jason next to her.

"We'll figure it out," she promised.

He looked at her hesitantly, like he wanted very much to believe her. "Annabeth and Rachel are coming in for the meeting tonight. I should probably wait until then to explain..."

"Okay." She plucked a blade of grass by her foot. She knew there were dangerous things in store for both of them. She would have to compete with Jason's past, and they might not even survive their war against the giants. But right now, they were both alive, and she was determined to enjoy this moment.

Jason studied her warily. His forearm tattoo was faint blue in the sunlight. "You're in a good mood. How can you be so sure things will work out?"

"Because you're going to lead us," she said simply. "I'd follow you anywhere."

Jason blinked. Then slowly, he smiled. "Dangerous thing to say."

"I'm a dangerous girl."

"That, I believe."

He got up and brushed off his shorts. He offered her a hand. "Leo says he's got something to show us out in the woods. You coming?"

"Wouldn't miss it." She took his hand and stood up.

For a moment, they kept holding hands. Jason tilted his head. "We should get going."

"Yep," she said. "Just a sec."

She let go of his hand, and took a card from her pocket —the silver calling card that Thalia had given her for the Hunters of Artemis. She dropped it into a nearby eternal fire and watched it burn. There would be no breaking hearts in

Aphrodite cabin from now on. That was one rite of passage they didn't need.

Across the green, her cabinmates looked disappointed that they hadn't witnessed a kiss. They started cashing in their bets.

But that was all right. Piper was patient, and she could see lots of good possibilities.

"Let's go," she told Jason. "We've got adventures to plan."

L I I I

LEO

LEO HADN'T FELT THIS JUMPY SINCE HE offered tofu burgers to the werewolves. When he got to the limestone cliff in the forest, he turned to the group and smiled nervously. "Here we go."

He willed his hand to catch fire, and set it against the door.

His cabinmates gasped.

"Leo!" Nyssa cried. "You're a fire user!"

"Yeah, thanks," he said. "I know."

Jake Mason, who was out of his body cast but still on crutches, said, "Holy Hephaestus. That means—it's so rare that—"

The massive stone door swung open, and everyone's mouth dropped. Leo's flaming hand seemed insignificant now. Even Piper and Jason looked stunned, and they'd seen enough amazing things lately.

Only Chiron didn't look surprised. The centaur knit his

bushy eyebrows and stroked his beard, as if the group was about to walk through a minefield.

That made Leo even more nervous, but he couldn't change his mind now. His instincts told him he was meant to share this place—at least with the Hephaestus cabin—and he couldn't hide it from Chiron or his two best friends.

"Welcome to Bunker Nine," he said, as confidently as he could. "C'mon in."

The group was silent as they toured the facility. Everything was just as Leo had left it—giant machines, worktables, old maps and schematics. Only one thing had changed. Festus's head was sitting on the central table, still battered and scorched from his final crash in Omaha.

Leo went over to it, a bitter taste in his mouth, and stroked the dragon's forehead. "I'm sorry, Festus. But I won't forget you."

Jason put a hand on Leo's shoulder. "Hephaestus brought it here for you?"

Leo nodded.

"But you can't repair him," Jason guessed.

"No way," Leo said. "But the head is going to be reused. Festus will be going with us."

Piper came over and frowned. "What do you mean?"

Before Leo could answer, Nyssa cried out, "Guys, look at this!"

She was standing at one of the worktables, flipping through a sketchbook—diagrams for hundreds of different machines and weapons.

"I've never seen anything like these," Nyssa said. "There are more amazing ideas here than in Daedalus's workshop. It would take a century just to prototype them all."

"Who built this place?" Jake Mason said. "And why?"

Chiron stayed silent, but Leo focused on the wall map he'd seen during his first visit. It showed Camp Half-Blood with a line of triremes in the Sound, catapults mounted in the hills around the valley, and spots marked for traps, trenches, and ambush sites.

"It's a wartime command center," he said. "The camp was attacked once, wasn't it?"

"In the Titan War?" Piper asked.

Nyssa shook her head. "No. Besides, that map looks *really* old. The date . . . does that say 1864?"

They all turned to Chiron.

The centaur's tail swished fretfully. "This camp has been attacked many times," he admitted. "That map is from the last Civil War."

Apparently, Leo wasn't the only one confused. The other Hephaestus campers looked at each other and frowned.

"Civil War . . ." Piper said. "You mean the American Civil War, like a hundred and fifty years ago?"

"Yes and no," Chiron said. "The two conflicts—mortal and demigod—mirrored each other, as they usually do in Western history. Look at any civil war or revolution from the fall of Rome onward, and it marks a time when demigods also fought one another. But *that* Civil War was particularly horrible. For American mortals, it is still their bloodiest conflict of all time—worse than their casualties in the two World

Wars. For demigods, it was equally devastating. Even back then, this valley was Camp Half-Blood. There was a horrible battle in these woods lasting for days, with terrible losses on both sides."

"Both sides," Leo said. "You mean the camp split apart?"

"No," Jason spoke up. "He means two different groups. Camp Half-Blood was one side in the war."

Leo wasn't sure he wanted an answer, but he asked, "Who was the other?"

Chiron glanced up at the tattered BUNKER 9 banner, as if remembering the day it was raised.

"The answer is dangerous," he warned. "It is something I swore upon the River Styx never to speak of. After the American Civil War, the gods were so horrified by the toll it took on their children, that they swore it would never happen again. The two groups were separated. The gods bent all their will, wove the Mist as tightly as they could, to make sure the enemies never remembered each other, never met on their quests, so that bloodshed could be avoided. This map is from the final dark days of 1864, the last time the two groups fought. We've had several close calls since then. The nineteen sixties were particularly dicey. But we've managed to avoid another civil war—at least so far. Just as Leo guessed, this bunker was a command center for the Hephaestus cabin. In the last century, it has been reopened a few times, usually as a hiding place in times of great unrest. But coming here is dangerous. It stirs old memories, awakens the old feuds. Even when the Titans threatened last year, I did not think it worth the risk to use this place."

Suddenly Leo's sense of triumph turned to guilt. "Hey, look, this place found *me*. It was meant to happen. It's a good thing."

"I hope you're right," Chiron said.

"I am!" Leo pulled the old drawing out of his pocket and spread it on the table for everyone to see.

"There," he said proudly. "Aeolus returned that to me. I drew it when I was five. That's my destiny."

Nyssa frowned. "Leo, it's a crayon drawing of a boat."

"Look." He pointed at the largest schematic on the bulletin board—the blueprint showing a Greek trireme. Slowly, his cabinmates' eyes widened as they compared the two designs. The number of masts and oars, even the decorations on the shields and sails were exactly the same as on Leo's drawing.

"That's impossible," Nyssa said. "That blueprint has to be a century old at least."

"'*Prophecy—Unclear—Flight,*'" Jake Mason read from the notes on the blueprint. "It's a diagram for a flying ship. Look, that's the landing gear. And weaponry—Holy Hephaestus: rotating ballista, mounted crossbows, Celestial bronze plating. That thing would be one spankin' hot war machine. Was it ever made?"

"Not yet," Leo said. "Look at the masthead."

There was no doubt—the figure at the front of the ship was the head of a dragon. A very particular dragon.

"Festus," Piper said. Everyone turned and looked at the dragon's head sitting on the table.

"He's meant to be our masthead," Leo said. "Our good

luck charm, our eyes at sea. I'm supposed to build this ship. I'm gonna call it the *Argo II*. And guys, I'll need your help."

"The *Argo II*." Piper smiled. "After Jason's ship."

Jason looked a little uncomfortable, but he nodded. "Leo's right. That ship is just what we need for our journey."

"What journey?" Nyssa said. "You just got back!"

Piper ran her fingers over the old crayon drawing. "We've got to confront Porphyrion, the giant king. He said he would destroy the gods at their roots."

"Indeed," Chiron said. "Much of Rachel's Great Prophecy is still a mystery to me, but one thing is clear. You three—Jason, Piper, and Leo—are among the seven demigods who must take on that quest. You must confront the giants in their homeland, where they are strongest. You must stop them before they can wake Gaea fully, before they destroy Mount Olympus."

"Um..." Nyssa shifted. "You don't mean Manhattan, do you?"

"No," Leo said. "The original Mount Olympus. We have to sail to Greece."

LIV

LEO

IT TOOK A FEW MINUTES FOR THAT TO settle in. Then the other Hephaestus campers started asking questions all at once. Who were the other four demigods? How long would it take to build the boat? Why didn't everyone get to go to Greece?

"Heroes!" Chiron struck his hoof on the floor. "All the details are not clear yet, but Leo is correct. He will need your help to build the *Argo II*. It is perhaps the greatest project Cabin Nine has even undertaken, even greater than the bronze dragon."

"It'll take a year at least," Nyssa guessed. "Do we have that much time?"

"You have six months at most," Chiron said. "You should sail by summer solstice, when the gods' power is strongest. Besides, we evidently cannot trust the wind gods, and the summer winds are the least powerful and easiest to navigate. You dare not sail any later, or you may be too late to stop the giants. You must avoid ground travel, using only air and sea, so this vehicle is perfect. Jason being the son of the sky god..."

His voice trailed off, but Leo figured Chiron was thinking about his missing student, Percy Jackson, the son of Poseidon. He would've been good on this voyage, too.

Jake Mason turned to Leo. "Well, one thing's for sure. *You* are now senior counselor. This is the biggest honor the cabin has ever had. Anyone object?"

Nobody did. All his cabinmates smiled at him, and Leo could almost feel their cabin's curse breaking, their sense of hopelessness melting away.

"It's official, then," Jake said. "You're the man."

For once, Leo was speechless. Ever since his mom died, he'd spent his life on the run. Now he'd found a home and a family. He'd found a job to do. And as scary as it was, Leo wasn't tempted to run—not even a little.

"Well," he said at last, "if you guys elect me leader, you must be even crazier than I am. So let's build a spankin' hot war machine!"

LV

JASON

JASON WAITED ALONE IN CABIN ONE.

Annabeth and Rachel were due any minute for the head counselors' meeting, and Jason needed time to think.

His dreams the night before had been worse than he'd wanted to share—even with Piper. His memory was still foggy, but bits and pieces were coming back. The night Lupa had tested him at the Wolf House, to decide if he would be a pup or food. Then the long trip south to...he couldn't remember, but he had flashes of his old life. The day he'd gotten his tattoo. The day he'd been raised on a shield and proclaimed a praetor. His friends' faces: Dakota, Gwendolyn, Hazel, Bobby. And Reyna. Definitely there'd been a girl named Reyna. He wasn't sure what she'd meant to him, but the memory made him question what he felt about Piper—and wonder if he was doing something wrong. The problem was, he liked Piper a lot.

Jason moved his stuff to the corner alcove where his sister

had once slept. He put Thalia's photograph back on the wall so he didn't feel alone. He stared up at the frowning statue of Zeus, mighty and proud, but the statue didn't scare him anymore. It just made him feel sad.

"I know you can hear me," Jason said to the statue.

The statue said nothing. Its painted eyes seemed to stare at him.

"I wish I could talk with you in person," Jason continued, "but I understand you can't do that. The Roman gods don't like to interact with mortals so much, and—well, you're the king. You've got to set an example."

More silence. Jason had hoped for something—a bigger than usual rumble of thunder, a bright light, a smile. No, never mind. A smile would've been creepy.

"I remember some things," he said. The more he talked, the less self-conscious he felt. "I remember that it's hard being a son of Jupiter. Everyone is always looking at me to be a leader, but I always feel alone. I guess you feel the same way up on Olympus. The other gods challenge your decisions. Sometimes you've got to make hard choices, and the others criticize you. And you can't come to my aid like other gods might. You've got to keep me at a distance so it doesn't look like you're playing favorites. I guess I just wanted to say..."

Jason took a deep breath. "I understand all that. It's okay. I'm going to try to do my best. I'll try to make you proud. But I could really use some guidance, Dad. If there's anything you can do—help me so I can help my friends. I'm afraid I'll get them killed. I don't know how to protect them."

The back of his neck tingled. He realized someone was

standing behind him. He turned and found a woman in a black hooded robe, with a goatskin cloak over her shoulders and a sheathed Roman sword—a *gladius*—in her hands.

"Hera," he said.

She pushed back her hood. "To you, I have always been Juno. And your father has already sent you guidance, Jason. He sent you Piper and Leo. They're not just your responsibility. They are also your friends. Listen to them, and you will do well."

"Did Jupiter send you here to tell me that?"

"No one sends me anywhere, hero," she said. "I am not a messenger."

"But you got me into this. Why did you send me to this camp?"

"I think you know," Juno said. "An exchange of leaders was necessary. It was the only way to bridge the gap."

"I didn't agree to it."

"No. But Zeus gave your life to me, and I am helping you fulfill your destiny."

Jason tried to control his anger. He looked down at his orange camp shirt and the tattoos on his arm, and he knew these things should not go together. He had become a contradiction—a mixture as dangerous as anything Medea could cook up.

"You're not giving me all my memories," he said. "Even though you promised."

"Most will return in time," Juno said. "But you must find your own way back. You need these next months with your new friends, your new home. You're gaining their trust. By the time you sail in your ship, you will be a leader at this camp. And you will be ready to be a peacemaker between two great powers."

"What if you're not telling the truth?" he asked. "What if you're doing this to cause another civil war?"

Juno's expression was impossible to read—amusement? Disdain? Affection? Possibly all three. As much as she appeared human, Jason knew she was not. He could still see that blinding light—the true form of the goddess that had seared itself into his brain. She was Juno and Hera. She existed in many places at once. Her reasons for doing something were never simple.

"I am the goddess of family," she said. "My family has been divided for too long."

"They divided us so we don't kill each other," Jason said. "That seems like a pretty good reason."

"The prophecy demands that we change. The giants will rise. Each can only be killed by a god and demigod working together. Those demigods must be the seven greatest of the age. As it stands, they are divided between two places. If we remain divided, we cannot win. Gaea is counting on this. You must unite the heroes of Olympus and sail together to meet the giants on the ancient battlegrounds of Greece. Only then will the gods be convinced to join you. It will be the most dangerous quest, the most important voyage, ever attempted by the children of the gods."

Jason looked up again at the glowering statue of his father.

"It's not fair," Jason said. "I could ruin everything."

"You could," Juno agreed. "But gods need heroes. We always have."

"Even you? I thought you hated heroes."

The goddess gave him a dry smile. "I have that reputation. But if you want the truth, Jason, I often envy other gods their mortal children. You demigods can span both worlds. I think this helps your godly parents—even Jupiter, curse him—to understand the mortal world better than I."

Juno sighed so unhappily that despite his anger, Jason almost felt sorry for her.

"I am the goddess of marriage," she said. "It is not in my nature to be faithless. I have only two godly children—Ares and Hephaestus—both of whom are disappointments. I have no mortal heroes to do my bidding, which is why I am so often bitter toward demigods—Heracles, Aeneas, all of them. But it is also why I favored the first Jason, a pure mortal, who had no godly parent to guide him. And why I am glad Zeus gave you to me. You will be my champion, Jason. You will be the greatest of heroes, and bring unity to the demigods, and thus to Olympus."

Her words settled over him, as heavy as sandbags. Two days ago, he'd been terrified by the idea of leading demigods into a Great Prophecy, sailing off to battle the giants and save the world.

He was still terrified, but something had changed. He no longer felt alone. He had friends now, and a home to fight for. He even had a patron goddess looking out for him, which had to count for something, even if she seemed a little untrustworthy.

Jason had to stand up and accept his destiny, just as he had done when he faced Porphyrion with his bare hands. Sure, it seemed impossible. He might die. But his friends were counting on him.

"And if I fail?" he asked.

"Great victory requires great risk," she admitted. "Fail, and there will be bloodshed like we have never seen. Demigods will destroy one another. The giants will overrun Olympus. Gaea will wake, and the earth will shake off everything we have built over five millennia. It will be the end of us all."

"Great. Just great."

Someone pounded on the cabin doors.

Juno pulled her hood back over her face. Then she handed Jason the sheathed *gladius*. "Take this for the weapon you lost. We will speak again. Like it or not, Jason, I am your sponsor, and your link to Olympus. We need each other."

The goddess vanished as the doors creaked open, and Piper walked in.

"Annabeth and Rachel are here," she said. "Chiron has summoned the council."

LVI

JASON

THE COUNCIL WAS NOTHING LIKE Jason imagined. For one thing, it was in the Big House rec room, around a Ping-Pong table, and one of the satyrs was serving nachos and sodas. Somebody had brought Seymour the leopard head in from the living room and hung him on the wall. Every once in a while, a counselor would toss him a Snausage.

Jason looked around the room and tried to remember everyone's name. Thankfully, Leo and Piper were sitting next to him—it was their first meeting as senior counselors. Clarisse, leader of the Ares cabin, had her boots on the table, but nobody seemed to care. Clovis from Hypnos cabin was snoring in the corner while Butch from Iris cabin was seeing how many pencils he could fit in Clovis's nostrils. Travis Stoll from Hermes was holding a lighter under a Ping-Pong ball to see if it would burn, and Will Solace from Apollo was absently wrapping and unwrapping an Ace bandage around his wrist. The counselor from Hecate cabin,

Lou Ellen something-or-other, was playing "got-your-nose" with Miranda Gardiner from Demeter, except that Lou Ellen really *had* magically disconnected Miranda's nose, and Miranda was trying to get it back.

Jason had hoped Thalia would show. She'd promised, after all—but she was nowhere to be seen. Chiron had told him not to worry about it. Thalia often got sidetracked fighting monsters or running quests for Artemis, and she would probably arrive soon. But still, Jason worried.

Rachel Dare, the oracle, sat next to Chiron at the head of the table. She was wearing her Clarion Academy school uniform dress, which seemed a bit odd, but she smiled at Jason.

Annabeth didn't look so relaxed. She wore armor over her camp clothes, with her knife at her side and her blond hair pulled back in a ponytail. As soon as Jason walked in, she fixed him with an expectant look, as if she were trying to extract information out of him by sheer willpower.

"Let's come to order," Chiron said. "Lou Ellen, please give Miranda her nose back. Travis, if you'd kindly extinguish the flaming Ping-Pong ball, and Butch, I think twenty pencils is really too many for any human nostril. Thank you. Now, as you can see, Jason, Piper, and Leo have returned successfully ... more or less. Some of you have heard parts of their story, but I will let them fill you in."

Everyone looked at Jason. He cleared his throat and began the story. Piper and Leo chimed in from time to time, filling in the details he forgot.

It only took a few minutes, but it seemed like longer with everyone watching him. The silence was heavy, and for so many ADHD demigods to sit still listening for that long, Jason knew the story must have sounded pretty wild. He ended with Hera's visit right before the meeting.

"So Hera was *here*," Annabeth said. "Talking to you."

Jason nodded. "Look, I'm not saying I trust her—"

"That's smart," Annabeth said.

"—but she isn't making this up about another group of demigods. That's where I came from."

"Romans." Clarisse tossed Seymour a Snausage. "You expect us to believe there's another camp with demigods, but they follow the Roman forms of the gods. And we've never even heard of them."

Piper sat forward. "The gods have kept the two groups apart, because every time they see each other, they try to kill each other."

"I can respect that," Clarisse said. "Still, why haven't we ever run across each other on quests?"

"Oh, yes," Chiron said sadly. "You have, many times. It's always a tragedy, and always the gods do their best to wipe clean the memories of those involved. The rivalry goes all the way back to the Trojan War, Clarisse. The Greeks invaded Troy and burned it to the ground. The Trojan hero Aeneas escaped, and eventually made his way to Italy, where he founded the race that would someday become Rome. The Romans grew more and more powerful, worshipping the same gods but under different names, and with slightly different personalities."

"More warlike," Jason said. "More united. More about expansion, conquest, and discipline."

"Yuck," Travis put in.

Several of the others looked equally uncomfortable, though Clarisse shrugged like it sounded okay to her.

Annabeth twirled her knife on the table. "And the Romans hated the Greeks. They took revenge when they conquered the Greek isles, and made them part of the Roman Empire."

"Not exactly *hated* them," Jason said. "The Romans admired Greek culture, and were a little jealous. In return, the Greeks thought the Romans were barbarians, but they respected their military power. So during Roman times, demigods started to divide—either Greek or Roman."

"And it's been that way ever since," Annabeth guessed. "But this is crazy. Chiron, where were the Romans during the Titan War? Didn't they want to help?"

Chiron tugged at his beard. "They *did* help, Annabeth. While you and Percy were leading the battle to save Manhattan, who do think conquered Mount Othrys, the Titans' base in California?"

"Hold on," Travis said. "You said Mount Othrys just crumbled when we beat Kronos."

"No," Jason said. He remembered flashes of the battle—a giant in starry armor and a helm mounted with ram's horns. He remembered his army of demigods scaling Mount Tam, fighting through hordes of snake monsters. "It didn't just fall. We destroyed their palace. I defeated the Titan Krios myself."

Annabeth's eyes were as stormy as a *ventus*. Jason could almost see her thoughts moving, putting the pieces together. "The Bay Area. We demigods were always told to stay away from it because Mount Othrys was there. But that wasn't the only reason, was it? The Roman camp—it's got to be somewhere near San Francisco. I bet it was put there to keep watch on the Titans' territory. Where is it?"

Chiron shifted in his wheelchair. "I cannot say. Honestly, even *I* have never been trusted with that information. My counterpart, Lupa, is not exactly the sharing type. Jason's memory, too, has been burned away."

"The camp's heavily veiled with magic," Jason said. "And heavily guarded. We could search for years and never find it."

Rachel Dare laced her fingers. Of all the people in the room, only she didn't seem nervous about the conversation. "But you'll try, won't you? You'll build Leo's boat, the *Argo II*. And before you make for Greece, you'll sail for the Roman camp. You'll need their help to confront the giants."

"Bad plan," Clarisse warned. "If those Romans see a warship coming, they'll assume we're attacking."

"You're probably right," Jason agreed. "But we have to try. I was sent here to learn about Camp Half-Blood, to try to convince you the two camps don't have to be enemies. A peace offering."

"Hmm," Rachel said. "Because Hera is convinced we need both camps to win the war with the giants. Seven heroes of Olympus—some Greek, some Roman."

Annabeth nodded. "Your Great Prophecy—what's the last line?"

"And foes bear arms to the Doors of Death."

"Gaea has opened the Doors of Death," Annabeth said. "She's letting out the worst villains of the Underworld to fight us. Medea, Midas—there'll be more, I'm sure. Maybe the line means that the Roman and Greek demigods will unite, and find the doors, and close them."

"Or it could mean they fight each other at the doors of death," Clarisse pointed out. "It doesn't say we'll cooperate."

There was silence as the campers let that happy thought sink in.

"I'm going," Annabeth said. "Jason, when you get this ship built, let me go with you."

"I was hoping you'd offer," Jason said. "You of all people —we'll need you."

"Wait." Leo frowned. "I mean that's cool with me and all. But why Annabeth of all people?"

Annabeth and Jason studied one another, and Jason knew she had put it together. She saw the dangerous truth.

"Hera said my coming here was an exchange of leaders," Jason said. "A way for the two camps to learn of each other's existence."

"Yeah?" Leo said. "So?"

"An exchange goes two ways," Jason said. "When I got here, my memory was wiped. I didn't know who I was or where I belonged. Fortunately, you guys took me in and I found a new home. I know you're not my enemy. The Roman camp—they're not so friendly. You prove your worth quickly, or you don't survive. They may not be so nice to him, and if they learn where he comes from, he's going to be in serious trouble."

"Him?" Leo said. "Who are you talking about?"

"My boyfriend," Annabeth said grimly. "He disappeared

around the same time Jason appeared. If Jason came to Camp Half-Blood—"

"Exactly," Jason agreed. "Percy Jackson is at the other camp, and he probably doesn't even remember who he is."

Gods in *The Lost Hero*

Aeolus   The Greek god of the winds. Roman form: Aeolus

Aphrodite   The Greek goddess of love and beauty. She was married to Hephaestus, but she loved Ares, the god of war. Roman form: Venus

Apollo   The Greek god of the sun, prophecy, music, and healing; the son of Zeus, and the twin of Artemis. Roman form: Apollo

Ares   The Greek god of war; the son of Zeus and Hera, and half brother to Athena. Roman form: Mars

Artemis   The Greek goddess of the hunt and the moon; the daughter of Zeus and the twin of Apollo. Roman form: Diana

Boreas   The Greek god of the north wind, one of the four directional *anemoi* (wind gods); the god of winter; father of Khione. Roman form: Aquilon

Demeter   The Greek goddess of agriculture, a daughter of the Titans Rhea and Kronos. Roman form: Ceres

Dionysus   The Greek god of wine; the son of Zeus. Roman form: Bacchus

Gaea   The Greek personification of Earth. Roman form: Terra

Hades   According to Greek mythology, ruler of the Underworld and god of the dead. Roman form: Pluto

Hecate   The Greek goddess of magic; the only child of the Titans Perses and Asteria. Roman form: Trivia

Hephaestus   The Greek god of fire and crafts and of blacksmiths; the son of Zeus and Hera, and married to Aphrodite. Roman form: Vulcan

Hera   The Greek goddess of marriage; Zeus's wife and sister. Roman form: Juno

Hermes   The Greek god of travelers, communication, and thieves; son of Zeus. Roman form: Mercury

Hypnos   The Greek god of sleep; the (fatherless) son of Nyx (Night) and brother of Thanatos (Death). Roman form: Somnus

Iris   The Greek goddess of the rainbow, and a messenger of the gods; the daughter of Thaumas and Electra. Roman form: Iris

Janus   The Roman god of gates, doors, and doorways, as well as beginnings and endings.

Khione   The Greek goddess of snow; daughter of Boreas

Notus   The Greek god of the south wind, one of the four directional *anemoi* (wind gods). Roman form: Favonius

Ouranos   The Greek personification of the sky. Roman form: Uranus

Pan The Greek god of the wild; the son of Hermes. Roman form: Faunus

Pompona The Roman goddess of plenty

Poseidon The Greek god of the sea; son of the Titans Kronos and Rhea, and brother of Zeus and Hades. Roman form: Neptune

Zeus The Greek god of the sky and king of the gods. Roman form: Jupiter

Turn the page to start the next adventure in
the HEROES OF OLYMPUS series,

THE SON OF NEPTUNE

PERCY

THE SNAKE-HAIRED LADIES WERE starting to annoy Percy.

They should have died three days ago when he dropped a crate of bowling balls on them at the Napa Bargain Mart. They should have died two days ago when he ran over them with a police car in Martinez. They *definitely* should have died this morning when he cut off their heads in Tilden Park.

No matter how many times Percy killed them and watched them crumble to powder, they just kept re-forming like large evil dust bunnies. He couldn't even seem to outrun them.

He reached the top of the hill and caught his breath. How long since he'd last killed them? Maybe two hours. They never seemed to stay dead longer than that.

The past few days, he'd hardly slept. He'd eaten whatever he could scrounge—vending machine gummi bears, stale bagels, even a Jack in the Crack burrito, which was a new personal low. His clothes were torn, burned, and splattered with monster slime.

He'd only survived this long because the two snake-haired ladies—*gorgons*, they called themselves—couldn't seem to kill him either. Their claws didn't cut his skin. Their teeth broke whenever they tried to bite him. But Percy couldn't keep going much longer. Soon he'd collapse from exhaustion, and then —as hard as he was to kill, he was pretty sure the gorgons would find a way.

Where to run?

He scanned his surroundings. Under different circumstances, he might've enjoyed the view. To his left, golden hills rolled inland, dotted with lakes, woods, and a few herds of cows. To his right, the flatlands of Berkeley and Oakland marched west—a vast checkerboard of neighborhoods, with several million people who probably did not want their morning interrupted by two monsters and a filthy demigod.

Farther west, San Francisco Bay glittered under a silvery haze. Past that, a wall of fog had swallowed most of San Francisco, leaving just the tops of skyscrapers and the towers of the Golden Gate Bridge.

A vague sadness weighed on Percy's chest. Something told him he'd been to San Francisco before. The city had some connection to Annabeth—the only person he could remember from his past. His memory of her was frustratingly dim. The wolf had promised he would see her again and regain his memory—*if* he succeeded in his journey.

Should he try to cross the bay?

It was tempting. He could feel the power of the ocean just over the horizon. Water always revived him. Salt water was the best. He'd discovered that two days ago when he had strangled a sea monster in the Carquinez Strait. If he could reach the bay, he might be able to make a last stand. Maybe he could even drown the gorgons. But the shore was at least two miles away. He'd have to cross an entire city.

He hesitated for another reason. The she-wolf Lupa had taught him to sharpen his senses—to trust the instincts that had been guiding him south. His homing radar was tingling like crazy now. The end of his journey was close—almost right under his feet. But how could that be? There was nothing on the hilltop.

The wind changed. Percy caught the sour scent of reptile. A hundred yards down the slope, something rustled through the woods—snapping branches, crunching leaves, hissing.

Gorgons.

For the millionth time, Percy wished their noses weren't so good. They had always said they could *smell* him because he was a demigod—the half-blood son of some old Roman god. Percy had tried rolling in mud, splashing through creeks, even keeping air-freshener sticks in his pockets so he'd have that new car smell; but apparently demigod stink was hard to mask.

He scrambled to the west side of the summit. It was too steep to descend. The slope plummeted eighty feet, straight to the roof of an apartment complex built into the hillside. Fifty feet below that, a highway emerged from the hill's base and wound its way toward Berkeley.

Great. No other way off the hill. He'd managed to get himself cornered.

He stared at the stream of cars flowing west toward San Francisco and wished he were in one of them. Then he realized the highway must cut through the hill. There must be a tunnel . . . right under his feet.

His internal radar went nuts. He *was* in the right place, just too high up. He had to check out that tunnel. He needed a way down to the highway—fast.

He slung off his backpack. He'd managed to grab a lot of supplies at the Napa Bargain Mart: a portable GPS, duct tape, lighter, superglue, water bottle, camping roll, a Comfy Panda Pillow Pet (as seen on TV), and a Swiss army knife—pretty much every tool a modern demigod could want. But he had nothing that would serve as a parachute or a sled.

That left him two options: jump eighty feet to his death, or stand and fight. Both options sounded pretty bad.

He cursed and pulled his pen from his pocket.

The pen didn't look like much, just a regular cheap ballpoint, but when Percy uncapped it, it grew into a glowing bronze sword. The blade balanced perfectly. The leather grip fit his hand like it had been custom designed for him. Etched along the guard was an Ancient Greek word Percy somehow understood: *Anaklusmos*—Riptide.

He'd woken up with this sword his first night at the Wolf House—two months ago? More? He'd lost track. He'd found himself in the courtyard of a burned-out mansion in the middle of the woods, wearing shorts, an orange T-shirt, and a leather necklace with a bunch of strange clay beads. Riptide had been in his hand, but Percy had had no idea how he'd gotten there, and only the vaguest idea who he was. He'd been barefoot, freezing, and confused. And then the wolves came. . . .

Right next to him, a familiar voice jolted him back to the present: "There you are!"

Percy stumbled away from the gorgon, almost falling off the edge of the hill.

It was the smiley one—Beano.

Okay, her name wasn't really Beano. As near as Percy could figure, he was dyslexic, because words got twisted around when he tried to read. The first time he'd seen the gorgon, posing as a Bargain Mart greeter with a big green button that read: *Welcome! My name is STHENO,* he'd thought it said BEANO.

She was still wearing her green Bargain Mart employee vest over a flower-print dress. If you looked just at her body, you might think she was somebody's dumpy old grandmother —until you looked down and realized she had rooster feet. Or you looked up and saw bronze boar tusks sticking out of the corners of her mouth. Her eyes glowed red, and her hair was a writhing nest of bright green snakes.

The most horrible thing about her? She was still holding her big silver platter of free samples: Crispy Cheese 'n' Wieners. Her platter was dented from all the times Percy had killed her, but those little samples looked perfectly fine. Stheno just kept toting them across California so she could offer Percy a snack before she killed him. Percy didn't know why she kept doing that, but if he ever needed a suit of armor, he was going to make it out of Crispy Cheese 'n' Wieners. They were indestructible.

"Try one?" Stheno offered.

Percy fended her off with his sword. "Where's your sister?"

"Oh, put the sword away," Stheno chided. "You know by now that even Celestial bronze can't kill us for long. Have a Cheese 'n' Wiener! They're on sale this week, and I'd hate to kill you on an empty stomach."

"Stheno!" The second gorgon appeared on Percy's right so fast, he didn't have time to react. Fortunately she was too busy glaring at her sister to pay him much attention. "I told you to sneak up on him and kill him!"

Stheno's smile wavered. "But, Euryale . . ." She said the name so it rhymed with *Muriel.* "Can't I give him a sample first?"

"No, you imbecile!" Euryale turned toward Percy and bared her fangs.

Except for her hair, which was a nest of coral snakes instead of green vipers, she looked exactly like her sister. Her Bargain Mart vest, her flowery dress, even her tusks were decorated with 50% OFF stickers. Her name badge read: *Hello! My name is* DIE, DEMIGOD SCUM!

"You've led us on quite a chase, Percy Jackson," Euryale said. "But now you're trapped, and we'll have our revenge!"

"The Cheese 'n' Wieners are only $2.99," Stheno added helpfully. "Grocery department, aisle three."

Euryale snarled. "Stheno, the Bargain Mart was a *front*! You're going native! Now, put down that ridiculous tray and help me kill this demigod. Or have you forgotten that he's the one who vaporized Medusa?"

Percy stepped back. Six more inches, and he'd be tumbling through thin air. "Look, ladies, we've been over this. I don't even *remember* killing Medusa. I don't remember anything! Can't we just call a truce and talk about your weekly specials?"

Stheno gave her sister a pouty look, which was hard to do with giant bronze tusks. "Can we?"

"No!" Euryale's red eyes bored into Percy. "I don't care what you remember, son of the sea god. I can smell Medusa's blood on you. It's faint, yes, several years old, but *you* were the last one to defeat her. She *still* has not returned from Tartarus. It's your fault!"

Percy didn't really get that. The whole "dying then returning from Tartarus" concept gave him a headache. Of course, so did the idea that a ballpoint pen could turn into a sword, or that monsters could disguise themselves with something called the Mist, or that Percy was the son of a barnacle-encrusted god from five thousand years ago. But he *did* believe it. Even though his memory was erased, he knew he was a demigod the same way he knew his name was Percy Jackson. From his very first conversation with Lupa the wolf, he'd accepted that this crazy messed-up world of gods and monsters was his reality. Which pretty much sucked.

"How about we call it a draw?" he said. "I can't kill you. You can't kill me. If you're Medusa's sisters—like *the* Medusa who turned people to stone—shouldn't I be petrified by now?"

"Heroes!" Euryale said with disgust. "They always bring that up, just like our mother! 'Why can't you turn people to stone? Your *sister* can turn people to stone.' Well, I'm sorry to disappoint you, boy! That was Medusa's curse alone. *She* was the most hideous one in the family. She got all the luck!"

Stheno looked hurt. "Mother said *I* was the most hideous."

"Quiet!" Euryale snapped. "As for you, Percy Jackson, it's

true you bear the mark of Achilles. That makes you a little tougher to kill. But don't worry. We'll find a way."

"The mark of what?"

"Achilles," Stheno said cheerfully. "Oh, he was *gorgeous*! Dipped in the River Styx as a child, you know, so he was invulnerable except for a tiny spot on his ankle. That's what happened to you, dear. Someone must've dumped you in the Styx and made your skin like iron. But not to worry. Heroes like you always have a weak spot. We just have to find it, and then we can kill you. Won't that be lovely? Have a Cheese 'n' Wiener!"

Percy tried to think. He didn't remember any dip in the Styx. Then again, he didn't remember much of anything. His skin didn't feel like iron, but it would explain how he'd held out so long against the gorgons.

Maybe if he just fell down the mountain...would he survive? He didn't want to risk it—not without something to slow the fall, or a sled, or...

He looked at Stheno's large silver platter of free samples. Hmm...

"Reconsidering?" Stheno asked. "Very wise, dear. I added some gorgon's blood to these, so your death will be quick and painless."

Percy's throat constricted. "You added your blood to the Cheese 'n' Wieners?"

"Just a little." Stheno smiled. "A tiny nick on my arm, but you're sweet to be concerned. Blood from our right side can cure anything, you know, but blood from our left side is deadly—"

"You dimwit!" Euryale screeched. "You're not supposed to tell him that! He won't eat the wieners if you tell him they're poisoned!"

Stheno looked stunned. "He won't? But I said it would be quick and painless."

"Never mind!" Euryale's fingernails grew into claws. "We'll kill him the hard way—just keep slashing until we find the weak spot. Once we defeat Percy Jackson, we'll be more famous than Medusa! Our patron will reward us greatly!"

Percy gripped his sword. He'd have to time his move perfectly—a few seconds of confusion, grab the platter with his left hand...

Keep them talking, he thought.

"Before you slash me to bits," he said, "who's this patron you mentioned?"

Euryale sneered. "The goddess Gaea, of course! The one who brought us back from oblivion! You won't live long enough to meet her, but your friends below will soon face her wrath. Even now, her armies are marching south. At the Feast of Fortune, she'll awaken, and the demigods will be cut down like—like—"

"Like our low prices at Bargain Mart!" Stheno suggested.

"Gah!" Euryale stormed toward her sister. Percy took the opening. He grabbed Stheno's platter, scattering poisoned Cheese 'n' Wieners, and slashed Riptide across Euryale's waist, cutting her in half.

He raised the platter, and Stheno found herself facing her own greasy reflection.

"Medusa!" she screamed.

Her sister Euryale had crumbled to dust, but she was already starting to re-form, like a snowman un-melting.

"Stheno, you fool!" she gurgled as her half-made face rose from the mound of dust. "That's just your own reflection! Get him!"

Percy slammed the metal tray on top of Stheno's head, and she passed out cold.

He put the platter behind his butt, said a silent prayer to whatever Roman god oversaw stupid sledding tricks, and jumped off the side of the hill.

RICK RIORDAN

◄ 1 ►

THE HIDDEN ORACLE

DISNEP • HYPERION

Los Angeles   New York

To the Muse Calliope
This is long overdue. Please don't hurt me.

CAMP HALF-BLOOD

Western Hills

The Northern Woods

Satyrs

Grove of Dodona

Zeus's Fist

Council of Cloven Elders Meeting Grove

Wolves

Bunker 9

Myrmekes' Lair

Zephyros Creek

Maenad Party Area

Geysers

Wreckage of Old Automatons

Longer Drakons

Pegasus Stables

The Southern Woods

To Peach Orchard

Archery Range

Combat Arena

N W E S

Strawberry Fields

K. LEFAIVER

1

Hoodlums punch my face
I would smite them if I could
Mortality blows

MY NAME IS APOLLO. I used to be a god.

In my four thousand six hundred and twelve years, I have done many things. I inflicted a plague on the Greeks who besieged Troy. I blessed Babe Ruth with three home runs in game four of the 1926 World Series. I visited my wrath upon Britney Spears at the 2007 MTV Video Music Awards.

But in all my immortal life, I never before crash-landed in a Dumpster.

I'm not even sure how it happened.

I simply woke up falling. Skyscrapers spiraled in and out of view. Flames streamed off my body. I tried to fly. I tried to change into a cloud or teleport across the world or do a hundred other things that should have been easy for me, but I just kept falling. I plunged into a narrow canyon between two buildings and BAM!

Is anything sadder than the sound of a god hitting a pile of garbage bags?

I lay groaning and aching in the open Dumpster. My nostrils burned with the stench of rancid bologna and used diapers. My ribs felt broken, though that shouldn't have been possible.

My mind stewed in confusion, but one memory floated to the surface—the voice of my father, Zeus: *YOUR FAULT. YOUR PUNISHMENT.*

I realized what had happened to me. And I sobbed in despair.

Even for a god of poetry such as myself, it is difficult to describe how I felt. How could you—a mere mortal—possibly understand? Imagine being stripped of your clothes, then blasted with a fire hose in front of a laughing crowd. Imagine the ice-cold water filling your mouth and lungs, the pressure bruising your skin, turning your joints to putty. Imagine feeling helpless, ashamed, completely vulnerable—publicly and brutally stripped of everything that makes you *you*. My humiliation was worse than that.

YOUR FAULT, Zeus's voice rang in my head.

"No!" I cried miserably. "No, it wasn't! Please!"

Nobody answered. On either side of me, rusty fire escapes zigzagged up brick walls. Above, the winter sky was gray and unforgiving.

I tried to remember the details of my sentencing. Had my father told me how long this punishment would last? What was I supposed to do to regain his favor?

My memory was too fuzzy. I could barely recall what Zeus looked like, much less why he'd decided to toss me to earth. There'd been a war with the giants, I thought. The gods had been caught off guard, embarrassed, almost defeated.

The only thing I knew for certain: my punishment was

unfair. Zeus needed someone to blame, so of course he'd picked the handsomest, most talented, most popular god in the pantheon: me.

I lay in the garbage, staring at the label inside the Dumpster lid: FOR PICK-UP, CALL 1-555-STENCHY.

Zeus will reconsider, I told myself. *He's just trying to scare me. Any moment, he will yank me back to Olympus and let me off with a warning.*

"Yes . . ." My voice sounded hollow and desperate. "Yes, that's it."

I tried to move. I wanted to be on my feet when Zeus came to apologize. My ribs throbbed. My stomach clenched. I clawed the rim of the Dumpster and managed to drag myself over the side. I toppled out and landed on my shoulder, which made a cracking sound against the asphalt.

"*Araggeeddeee,*" I whimpered through the pain. "Stand up. Stand up."

Getting to my feet was not easy. My head spun. I almost passed out from the effort. I stood in a dead-end alley. About fifty feet away, the only exit opened onto a street with grimy storefronts for a bail bondsman's office and a pawnshop. I was somewhere on the west side of Manhattan, I guessed, or perhaps Crown Heights, in Brooklyn. Zeus must have been really angry with me.

I inspected my new body. I appeared to be a teenaged Caucasian male, clad in sneakers, blue jeans, and a green polo shirt. How utterly *drab.* I felt sick, weak, and so, so human.

I will never understand how you mortals tolerate it. You live your entire life trapped in a sack of meat, unable to enjoy simple pleasures like changing into a hummingbird or dissolving into pure light.

And now, heavens help me, I was one of you—just another meat sack.

I fumbled through my pants pockets, hoping I still had the keys to my sun chariot. No such luck. I found a cheap nylon wallet containing a hundred dollars in American currency— lunch money for my first day as a mortal, perhaps—along with a New York State junior driver's license featuring a photo of a dorky, curly-haired teen who could not possibly be me, with the name *Lester Papadopoulos*. The cruelty of Zeus knew no bounds!

I peered into the Dumpster, hoping my bow, quiver, and lyre might have fallen to earth with me. I would have set- tled for my harmonica. There was nothing.

I took a deep breath. *Cheer up*, I told myself. *I must have retained some of my godly abilities. Matters could be worse.*

A raspy voice called, "Hey, Cade, take a look at this loser."

Blocking the alley's exit were two young men: one squat and platinum blond, the other tall and redheaded. Both wore oversize hoodies and baggy pants. Serpentine tattoo designs covered their necks. All they were missing were the words I'M A THUG printed in large letters across their foreheads.

The redhead zeroed in on the wallet in my hand. "Now, be nice, Mikey. This guy looks friendly enough." He grinned and pulled a hunting knife from his belt. "In fact, I bet he wants to give us all his money."

———

I blame my disorientation for what happened next.

I knew my immortality had been stripped away, but I still considered myself the mighty Apollo! One cannot change one's way of thinking as easily as one might, say, turn into a snow leopard.

Also, on previous occasions when Zeus had punished me by making me mortal (yes, it had happened twice before), I had retained massive strength and at least some of my godly powers. I assumed the same would be true now.

I was *not* going to allow two young mortal ruffians to take Lester Papadopoulos's wallet.

I stood up straight, hoping Cade and Mikey would be intimidated by my regal bearing and divine beauty. (Surely those qualities could not be taken from me, no matter what my driver's license photo looked like.) I ignored the warm Dumpster juice trickling down my neck.

"I am Apollo," I announced. "You mortals have three choices: offer me tribute, flee, or be destroyed."

I wanted my words to echo through the alley, shake the towers of New York, and cause the skies to rain smoking ruin. None of that happened. On the word *destroyed*, my voice squeaked.

The redhead Cade grinned even wider. I thought how amusing it would be if I could make the snake tattoos around his neck come alive and strangle him to death.

"What do you think, Mikey?" he asked his friend. "Should we give this guy tribute?"

Mikey scowled. With his bristly blond hair, his cruel small eyes, and his thick frame, he reminded me of the monstrous sow that terrorized the village of Crommyon back in the good old days.

"Not feeling the tribute, Cade." His voice sounded like he'd been eating lit cigarettes. "What were the other options?"

"Fleeing?" said Cade.

"Nah," said Mikey.

"Being destroyed?"

Mikey snorted. "How about we destroy *him* instead?"

Cade flipped his knife and caught it by the handle. "I can live with that. After you."

I slipped the wallet into my back pocket. I raised my fists. I did not like the idea of flattening mortals into flesh waffles, but I was sure I could do it. Even in my weakened state, I would be far stronger than any human.

"I warned you," I said. "My powers are far beyond your comprehension."

Mikey cracked his knuckles. "Uh-huh."

He lumbered forward.

As soon as he was in range, I struck. I put all my wrath into that punch. It should have been enough to vaporize Mikey and leave a thug-shaped impression on the asphalt.

Instead he ducked, which I found quite annoying.

I stumbled forward. I have to say that when Prometheus fashioned you humans out of clay he did a shoddy job. Mortal legs are clumsy. I tried to compensate, drawing upon my boundless reserves of agility, but Mikey kicked me in the back. I fell on my divine face.

My nostrils inflated like air bags. My ears popped. The

taste of copper filled my mouth. I rolled over, groaning, and found the two blurry thugs staring down at me.

"Mikey," said Cade, "are you comprehending this guy's power?"

"Nah," said Mikey. "I'm not comprehending it."

"Fools!" I croaked. "I will destroy you!"

"Yeah, sure." Cade tossed away his knife. "But first I think we'll stomp you."

Cade raised his boot over my face, and the world went black.

2

A girl from nowhere
Completes my embarrassment
Stupid bananas

I HAD NOT BEEN STOMPED so badly since my guitar contest against Chuck Berry in 1957.

As Cade and Mikey kicked me, I curled into a ball, trying to protect my ribs and head. The pain was intolerable. I retched and shuddered. I blacked out and came to, my vision swimming with red splotches. When my attackers got tired of kicking me, they hit me over the head with a bag of garbage, which burst and covered me in coffee grounds and moldy fruit peels.

At last they stepped away, breathing heavily. Rough hands patted me down and took my wallet.

"Lookee here," said Cade. "Some cash and an ID for . . . Lester Papadopoulos."

Mikey laughed. "*Lester?* That's even worse than Apollo."

I touched my nose, which felt roughly the size and texture of a water-bed mattress. My fingers came away glistening red.

"Blood," I muttered. "That's not possible."

"It's very possible, Lester." Cade crouched next to me. "And there might be more blood in your near future. You want to explain why you don't have a credit card? Or a phone? I'd hate to think I did all that stomping for just a hundred bucks."

I stared at the blood on my fingertips. I was a god. I did not *have* blood. Even when I'd been turned mortal before, golden ichor still ran through my veins. I had never before been so . . . *converted*. It must be a mistake. A trick. Something.

I tried to sit up.

My hand hit a banana peel and I fell again. My attackers howled in delight.

"I love this guy!" Mikey said.

"Yeah, but the boss told us he'd be loaded," Cade complained.

"Boss . . ." I muttered. "Boss?"

"That's right, Lester." Cade flicked a finger against the side of my head. "'Go to that alley,' the boss told us. 'Easy score.' He said we should rough you up, take whatever you had. But this"—he waved the cash under my nose—"this isn't much of a payday."

Despite my predicament, I felt a surge of hopefulness. If these thugs had been sent here to find me, their "boss" must be a god. No mortal could have known I would fall to earth at this spot. Perhaps Cade and Mikey were not human either. Perhaps they were cleverly disguised monsters or spirits. At least that would explain why they had beaten me so easily.

"Who—who is your boss?" I struggled to my feet, coffee grounds dribbling from my shoulders. My dizziness made me feel as if I were flying too close to the fumes of primordial

Chaos, but I refused to be humbled. "Did Zeus send you? Or perhaps Ares? I demand an audience!"

Mikey and Cade looked at each other as if to say, *Can you believe this guy?*

Cade picked up his knife. "You don't take a hint, do you, Lester?"

Mikey pulled off his belt—a length of bike chain—and wrapped it around his fist.

I decided to sing them into submission. They may have resisted my fists, but no mortal could resist my golden voice. I was trying to decide between "You Send Me" and an original composition, "I'm Your Poetry God, Baby," when a voice yelled, "HEY!"

The hooligans turned. Above us, on the second-story fire escape landing, stood a girl of about twelve. "Leave him alone," she ordered.

My first thought was that Artemis had come to my aid. My sister often appeared as a twelve-year-old girl for reasons I'd never fully understood. But something told me this was not she.

The girl on the fire escape did not exactly inspire fear. She was small and pudgy, with dark hair chopped in a messy pageboy style and black cat-eye glasses with rhinestones glittering in the corners. Despite the cold, she wore no coat. Her outfit looked like it had been picked by a kindergartener—red sneakers, yellow tights, and a green tank dress. Perhaps she was on her way to a costume party dressed as a traffic light.

Still . . . there was something fierce in her expression.

She had the same obstinate scowl my old girlfriend Cyrene used to get whenever she wrestled lions.

Mikey and Cade did not seem impressed.

"Get lost, kid," Mikey told her.

The girl stamped her foot, causing the fire escape to shudder. "My alley. My rules!" Her bossy nasal voice made her sound like she was chiding a playmate in a game of make-believe. "Whatever that loser has is mine, including his money!"

"Why is everyone calling me a loser?" I asked weakly. The comment seemed unfair, even if I was beat-up and covered in garbage; but no one paid me any attention.

Cade glared at the girl. The red from his hair seemed to be seeping into his face. "You've got to be kidding me. Beat it, you brat!" He picked up a rotten apple and threw it.

The girl didn't flinch. The fruit landed at her feet and rolled harmlessly to a stop.

"You want to play with food?" The girl wiped her nose. "Okay."

I didn't see her kick the apple, but it came flying back with deadly accuracy and hit Cade in the nose. He collapsed on his rump.

Mikey snarled. He marched toward the fire escape ladder, but a banana peel seemed to slither directly into his path. He slipped and fell hard. "OWWW!"

I backed away from the fallen thugs. I wondered if I should make a run for it, but I could barely hobble. I also did not want to be assaulted with old fruit.

The girl climbed over the railing. She dropped to the

ground with surprising nimbleness and grabbed a sack of garbage from the Dumpster.

"Stop!" Cade did a sort of scuttling crab walk to get away from the girl. "Let's talk about this!"

Mikey groaned and rolled onto his back.

The girl pouted. Her lips were chapped. She had wispy black fuzz at the corners of her mouth.

"I don't like you guys," she said. "You should go."

"Yeah!" Cade said. "Sure! Just . . ."

He reached for the money scattered among the coffee grounds.

The girl swung her garbage bag. In mid arc the plastic exploded, disgorging an impossible number of rotten bananas. They knocked Cade flat. Mikey was plastered with so many peels he looked like he was being attacked by carnivorous starfish.

"Leave my alley," the girl said. "Now."

In the Dumpster, more trash bags burst like popcorn kernels, showering Cade and Mikey with radishes, potato peelings, and other compost material. Miraculously, none of it got on me. Despite their injuries, the two thugs scrambled to their feet and ran away, screaming.

I turned toward my pint-size savior. I was no stranger to dangerous women. My sister could rain down arrows of death. My stepmother, Hera, regularly drove mortals mad so that they would hack each other to pieces. But this garbage-wielding twelve-year-old made me nervous.

"Thank you," I ventured.

The girl crossed her arms. On her middle fingers she wore matching gold rings with crescent signets. Her eyes glinted darkly like a crow's. (I can make that comparison because I invented crows.)

"Don't thank me," she said. "You're still in my alley."

She walked a full circle around me, scrutinizing my appearance as if I were a prize cow. (I can also make that comparison, because I used to collect prize cows.)

"You're the god Apollo?" She sounded less than awe-struck. She also didn't seem fazed by the idea of gods walking among mortals.

"You were listening, then?"

She nodded. "You don't look like a god."

"I'm not at my best," I admitted. "My father, Zeus, has exiled me from Olympus. And who are you?"

She smelled faintly of apple pie, which was surprising, since she looked so grubby. Part of me wanted to find a fresh towel, clean her face, and give her money for a hot meal. Part of me wanted to fend her off with a chair in case she decided to bite me. She reminded me of the strays my sister was always adopting: dogs, panthers, homeless maidens, small dragons.

"Name is Meg," she said.

"Short for Megara? Or Margaret?"

"Margaret. But don't ever call me Margaret."

"And are you a demigod, Meg?"

She pushed up her glasses. "Why would you think that?"

Again she didn't seem surprised by the question. I sensed she had heard the term *demigod* before.

"Well," I said, "you obviously have some power. You chased off those hooligans with rotten fruit. Perhaps you have banana-kinesis? Or you can control garbage? I once knew a Roman goddess, Cloacina, who presided over the city's sewer system. Perhaps you're related . . . ?"

Meg pouted. I got the impression I might have said something wrong, though I couldn't imagine what.

"I think I'll just take your money," Meg said. "Go on. Get out of here."

"No, wait!" Desperation crept into my voice. "Please, I—I may need a bit of assistance."

I felt ridiculous, of course. Me—the god of prophecy, plague, archery, healing, music, and several other things I couldn't remember at the moment—asking a colorfully dressed street urchin for help. But I had no one else. If this child chose to take my money and kick me into the cruel winter streets, I didn't think I could stop her.

"Say I believe you . . ." Meg's voice took on a singsong tone, as if she were about to announce the rules of the game: *I'll be the princess, and you'll be the scullery maid.* "Say I decide to help. What then?"

Good question, I thought. "We . . . we are in Manhattan?"

"Mm-hmm." She twirled and did a playful skip-kick. "Hell's Kitchen."

It seemed wrong for a child to say *Hell's Kitchen.* Then again, it seemed wrong for a child to live in an alley and have garbage fights with thugs.

I considered walking to the Empire State Building. That was the modern gateway to Mount Olympus, but I doubted the guards would let me up to the secret six hundredth floor. Zeus would not make it so easy.

Perhaps I could find my old friend Chiron the centaur. He had a training camp on Long Island. He could offer me shelter and guidance. But that would be a dangerous journey. A defenseless god makes for a juicy target. Any monster along the way would cheerfully disembowel me. Jealous spirits and minor gods might also welcome the opportunity. Then there was Cade and Mikey's mysterious "boss." I had no idea who he was, or whether he had other, worse minions to send against me.

Even if I made it to Long Island, my new mortal eyes might not be able to *find* Chiron's camp in its magically camouflaged valley. I needed a guide to get me there— someone experienced and close by. . . .

"I have an idea." I stood as straight as my injuries allowed. It wasn't easy to look confident with a bloody nose and coffee grounds dripping off my clothes. "I know someone who might help. He lives on the Upper East Side. Take me to him, and I shall reward you."

Meg made a sound between a sneeze and a laugh. "Reward me with what?" She danced around, plucking twenty-dollar bills from the trash. "I'm already taking all your money."

"Hey!"

She tossed me my wallet, now empty except for Lester Papadopoulos's junior driver's license.

Meg sang, "I've got your money, I've got your money."

I stifled a growl. "Listen, child, I won't be mortal forever. Someday I will become a god again. Then I will reward those who helped me—and punish those who didn't."

She put her hands on her hips. "How do *you* know what will happen? Have you ever been mortal before?"

"Yes, actually. Twice! Both times, my punishment only lasted a few years at most!"

"Oh, yeah? And how did you get back to being all goddy or whatever?"

"*Goddy* is not a word," I pointed out, though my poetic sensibilities were already thinking of ways I might use it. "Usually Zeus requires me to work as a slave for some important demigod. This fellow uptown I mentioned, for instance. He'd be perfect! I do whatever tasks my new master requires for a few years. As long as I behave, I am allowed back to Olympus. Right now I just have to recover my strength and figure out—"

"How do you know for sure which demigod?"

I blinked. "What?"

"Which demigod you're supposed to serve, dummy."

"I . . . uh. Well, it's usually obvious. I just sort of run into them. That's why I want to get to the Upper East Side. My new master will claim my service and—"

"I'm Meg McCaffrey!" Meg blew me a raspberry. "And I claim your service!"

Overhead, thunder rumbled in the gray sky. The sound echoed through the city canyons like divine laughter.

Whatever was left of my pride turned to ice water and trickled into my socks. "I walked right into that, didn't I?"

"Yep!" Meg bounced up and down in her red sneakers. "We're going to have fun!"

With great difficulty, I resisted the urge to weep. "Are you sure you're not Artemis in disguise?"

"I'm that other thing," Meg said, counting my money. "The thing you said before. A demigod."

"How do you know?"

"Just do." She gave me a smug smile. "And now I have a sidekick god named Lester!"

I raised my face to the heavens. "Please, Father, I get the point. Please, I can't do this!"

Zeus did not answer. He was probably too busy recording my humiliation to share on Snapchat.

"Cheer up," Meg told me. "Who's that guy you wanted to see—the guy on the Upper East Side?"

"Another demigod," I said. "He knows the way to a camp where I might find shelter, guidance, food—"

"Food?" Meg's ears perked up almost as much as the points on her glasses. "*Good* food?"

"Well, normally I just eat ambrosia, but, yes, I suppose."

"Then that's my first order! We're going to find this guy to take us to the camp place!"

I sighed miserably. It was going to be a very long servitude.

"As you wish," I said. "Let's find Percy Jackson."

3

Used to be goddy
Now uptown feeling shoddy
Bah, haiku don't rhyme

AS WE TRUDGED up Madison Avenue, my mind swirled with questions: Why hadn't Zeus given me a winter coat? Why did Percy Jackson live so far uptown? Why did pedestrians keep staring at me?

I wondered if my divine radiance was starting to return. Perhaps the New Yorkers were awed by my obvious power and unearthly good looks.

Meg McCaffrey set me straight.

"You smell," she said. "You look like you've just been mugged."

"I *have* just been mugged. Also enslaved by a small child."

"It's not slavery." She chewed off a piece of her thumb cuticle and spit it out. "It's more like mutual cooperation."

"Mutual in the sense that you give orders and I am forced to cooperate?"

"Yep." She stopped in front of a storefront window. "See? You look gross."

My reflection stared back at me, except it was *not* my

reflection. It couldn't be. The face was the same as on Lester Papadopoulos's ID.

I looked about sixteen. My medium-length hair was dark and curly—a style I had rocked in Athenian times, and again in the 1970s. My eyes were blue. My face was pleasing enough in a dorkish way, but it was marred by a swollen eggplant-colored nose, which had dripped a gruesome mustache of blood down my upper lip. Even worse, my cheeks were covered with some sort of rash that looked suspiciously like . . . My heart climbed into my throat.

"Horrors!" I cried. "Is that— Is that *acne?*"

Immortal gods do not *get* acne. It is one of our inalienable rights. Yet I leaned closer to the glass and saw that my skin was indeed a scarred landscape of whiteheads and pustules.

I balled my fists and wailed to the cruel sky, "Zeus, what have I done to deserve this?"

Meg tugged at my sleeve. "You're going to get yourself arrested."

"What does it matter? I have been made a teenager, and not even one with perfect skin! I bet I don't even have . . ." With a cold sense of dread, I lifted my shirt. My midriff was covered with a floral pattern of bruises from my fall into the Dumpster and my subsequent kicking. But even worse, I had *flab*.

"Oh, no, no, no." I staggered around the sidewalk, hoping the flab would not follow me. "Where are my eight-pack abs? I *always* have eight-pack abs. I *never* have love handles. Never in four thousand years!"

Meg made another snorting laugh. "Sheesh, crybaby, you're fine."

"I'm fat!"

"You're average. Average people don't have eight-pack abs. C'mon."

I wanted to protest that I was not average *nor* a person, but with growing despair, I realized the term now fit me perfectly.

On the other side of the storefront window, a security guard's face loomed, scowling at me. I allowed Meg to pull me farther down the street.

She skipped along, occasionally stopping to pick up a coin or swing herself around a streetlamp. The child seemed unfazed by the cold weather, the dangerous journey ahead, and the fact that I was suffering from acne.

"How are you so calm?" I demanded. "You are a demigod, walking with a god, on your way to a camp to meet others of your kind. Doesn't any of that surprise you?"

"Eh." She folded one of my twenty-dollar bills into a paper airplane. "I've seen a bunch of weird stuff."

I was tempted to ask what could be weirder than the morning we had just had. I decided I might not be able to stand the stress of knowing. "Where are you from?"

"I told you. The alley."

"No, but . . . your parents? Family? Friends?"

A ripple of discomfort passed over her face. She returned her attention to her twenty-dollar airplane. "Not important."

My highly advanced people-reading skills told me she was hiding something, but that was not unusual for demigods. For children blessed with an immortal parent, they were strangely sensitive about their backgrounds. "And you've never heard of Camp Half-Blood? Or Camp Jupiter?"

"Nuh-uh." She tested the airplane's point on her fingertip. "How much farther to Perry's house?"

"Percy's. I'm not sure. A few more blocks . . . I think."

That seemed to satisfy Meg. She hopscotched ahead, throwing the cash airplane and retrieving it. She cartwheeled through the intersection at East Seventy-Second Street—her clothes a flurry of traffic-light colors so bright I worried the drivers might get confused and run her down. Fortunately, New York drivers were used to swerving around oblivious pedestrians.

I decided Meg must be a feral demigod. They were rare but not unheard of. Without any support network, without being discovered by other demigods or taken in for proper training, she had still managed to survive. But her luck would not last. Monsters usually began hunting down and killing young heroes around the time they turned thirteen, when their true powers began to manifest. Meg did not have long. She needed to be brought to Camp Half-Blood as much as I did. She was fortunate to have met me.

(I know that last statement seems obvious. *Everyone* who meets me is fortunate, but you take my meaning.)

Had I been my usual omniscient self, I could have gleaned Meg's destiny. I could have looked into her soul and seen all I needed to know about her godly parentage, her powers, her motives and secrets.

Now I was blind to such things. I could only be sure she was a demigod because she had successfully claimed my service. Zeus had affirmed her right with a clap of thunder. I felt the binding upon me like a shroud of tightly wrapped banana peels. Whoever Meg McCaffrey was, however she had happened to find me, our fates were now intertwined.

It was almost as embarrassing as the acne.

We turned east on Eighty-Second Street.

By the time we reached Second Avenue, the neighborhood started to look familiar—rows of apartment buildings, hardware shops, convenience stores, and Indian restaurants. I knew that Percy Jackson lived around here somewhere, but my trips across the sky in the sun chariot had given me something of a Google Earth orientation. I wasn't used to traveling at street level.

Also, in this mortal form, my flawless memory had become . . . flawed. Mortal fears and needs clouded my thoughts. I wanted to eat. I wanted to use the restroom. My body hurt. My clothes stank. I felt as if my brain had been stuffed with wet cotton. Honestly, how do you humans stand it?

After a few more blocks, a mixture of sleet and rain began to fall. Meg tried to catch the precipitation on her tongue, which I thought a very ineffective way to get a drink—and of dirty water, no less. I shivered and concentrated on happy thoughts: the Bahamas, the Nine Muses in perfect harmony, the many horrible punishments I would visit on Cade and Mikey when I became a god again.

I still wondered about their boss, and how he had known where I would fall to earth. No mortal could've had that knowledge. In fact, the more I thought about it, I didn't see how even a god (other than myself) could have foreseen the future so accurately. After all, I had been the god of prophecy, master of the Oracle of Delphi, distributor of the highest quality sneak previews of destiny for millennia.

Of course, I had no shortage of enemies. One of the natural consequences of being so awesome is that I attracted envy from all quarters. But I could only think of one adversary who might be able to tell the future. And if *he* came looking for me in my weakened state . . .

I tamped down that thought. I had enough to worry about. No point scaring myself to death with what-ifs.

We began searching side streets, checking names on apartment mailboxes and intercom panels. The Upper East Side had a surprising number of Jacksons. I found that annoying.

After several failed attempts, we turned a corner and there—parked under a crape myrtle—sat an older model blue Prius. Its hood bore the unmistakable dents of pegasus hooves. (How was I sure? I know my hoof marks. Also, normal horses do not gallop over Toyotas. Pegasi often do.)

"Aha," I told Meg. "We're getting close."

Half a block down, I recognized the building: a five-story brick row house with rusty air conditioner units sagging from the windows. *"Voilà!"* I cried.

At the front steps, Meg stopped as if she'd run into an invisible barrier. She stared back toward Second Avenue, her dark eyes turbulent.

"What's wrong?" I asked.

"Thought I saw them again."

"Them?" I followed her gaze but saw nothing unusual. "The thugs from the alley?"

"No. Couple of . . ." She waggled her fingers. "Shiny blobs. Saw them back on Park Avenue."

My pulse increased from an andante tempo to a lively allegretto. "Shiny blobs? Why didn't you say anything?"

She tapped the temples of her glasses. "I've seen a lot of weird stuff. Told you that. Mostly, things don't bother me, but . . ."

"But if they are following us," I said, "that would be bad."

I scanned the street again. I saw nothing amiss, but I didn't doubt Meg had seen shiny blobs. Many spirits could appear that way. My own father, Zeus, once took the form of a shiny blob to woo a mortal woman. (Why the mortal woman found that attractive, I have no idea.)

"We should get inside," I said. "Percy Jackson will help us."

Still, Meg held back. She had shown no fear while pelting muggers with garbage in a blind alley, but now she seemed to be having second thoughts about ringing a doorbell. It occurred to me she might have met demigods before. Perhaps those meetings had not gone well.

"Meg," I said, "I realize some demigods are not good. I could tell you stories of all the ones I've had to kill or transform into herbs—"

"Herbs?"

"But Percy Jackson has always been reliable. You have nothing to fear. Besides, he likes me. I taught him everything he knows."

She frowned. "You did?"

I found her innocence somewhat charming. So many obvious things she did not know. "Of course. Now let's go up."

I rang the buzzer. A few moments later, the garbled voice of a woman answered, "Yes?"

"Hello," I said. "This is Apollo."

Static.

"The *god* Apollo," I said, thinking perhaps I should be more specific. "Is Percy home?"

More static, followed by two voices in muted conversation. The front door buzzed. I pushed it open. Just before I stepped inside, I caught a flash of movement in the corner of my eye. I peered down the sidewalk but again saw nothing.

Perhaps it had been a reflection. Or a whirl of sleet. Or perhaps it had been a shiny blob. My scalp tingled with apprehension.

"What?" Meg asked.

"Probably nothing." I forced a cheerful tone. I did not want Meg bolting off when we were so close to reaching safety. We were bound together now. I would have to follow her if she ordered me to, and I did not fancy living in the alley with her forever. "Let's go up. We can't keep our hosts waiting."

After all I had done for Percy Jackson, I expected delight upon my arrival. A tearful welcome, a few burnt offerings, and a small festival in my honor would not have been inappropriate.

Instead, the young man swung open the apartment door and said, "Why?"

As usual, I was struck by his resemblance to his father, Poseidon. He had the same sea-green eyes, the same dark tousled hair, the same handsome features that could shift from humor to anger so easily. However, Percy Jackson did not favor his father's chosen garb of beach shorts and Hawaiian shirts. He was dressed in ragged jeans and a blue hoodie with the words AHS SWIM TEAM stitched across the front.

Meg inched back into the hallway, hiding behind me.

I tried for a smile. "Percy Jackson, my blessings upon you! I am in need of assistance."

Percy's eyes darted from me to Meg. "Who's your friend?"

"This is Meg McCaffrey," I said, "a demigod who must be taken to Camp Half-Blood. She rescued me from street thugs."

"Rescued . . ." Percy scanned my battered face. "You mean the 'beat-up teenager' look isn't just a disguise? Dude, what happened to you?"

"I may have mentioned the street thugs."

"But you're a god."

"About that . . . I *was* a god."

Percy blinked. *"Was?"*

"Also," I said, "I'm fairly certain we're being followed by malicious spirits."

If I didn't know how much Percy Jackson adored me, I would have sworn he was about to punch me in my already-broken nose.

He sighed. "Maybe you two should come inside."

4

Casa de Jackson
No gold-plated throne for guests
Seriously, dude?

ANOTHER THING I have never understood: How can you mortals live in such tiny places? Where is your pride? Your sense of style?

The Jackson apartment had no grand throne room, no colonnades, no terraces or banquet halls or even a thermal bath. It had a tiny living room with an attached kitchen and a single hallway leading to what I assumed were the bedrooms. The place was on the fifth floor, and while I wasn't so picky as to expect an elevator, I did find it odd there was no landing deck for flying chariots. What did they do when guests from the sky wanted to visit?

Standing behind the kitchen counter, making a smoothie, was a strikingly attractive mortal woman of about forty. Her long brown hair had a few gray streaks, but her bright eyes, quick smile, and festive tie-dyed sundress made her look younger.

As we entered, she turned off the blender and stepped out from behind the counter.

"Sacred Sibyl!" I cried. "Madam, there is something wrong with your midsection!"

The woman stopped, mystified, and looked down at her hugely swollen belly. "Well, I'm seven months pregnant."

I wanted to cry for her. Carrying such a weight didn't seem natural. My sister, Artemis, had experience with midwifery, but I had always found it one area of the healing arts best left to others. "How can you bear it?" I asked. "My mother, Leto, suffered through a long pregnancy, but only because Hera cursed her. Are you cursed?"

Percy stepped to my side. "Um, Apollo? She's not cursed. And can you not mention Hera?"

"You poor woman." I shook my head. "A goddess would never allow herself to be so encumbered. She would give birth as soon as she felt like it."

"That must be nice," the woman agreed.

Percy Jackson coughed. "So anyway. Mom, this is Apollo and his friend Meg. Guys, this is my mom."

The Mother of Jackson smiled and shook our hands. "Call me Sally."

Her eyes narrowed as she studied my busted nose. "Dear, that looks painful. What happened?"

I attempted to explain, but I choked on my words. I, the silver-tongued god of poetry, could not bring myself to describe my fall from grace to this kind woman.

I understood why Poseidon had been so smitten with her. Sally Jackson possessed just the right combination of compassion, strength, and beauty. She was one of those rare mortal women who could connect spiritually with a god as an equal—to be neither terrified of us nor greedy for what we can offer, but to provide us with true companionship.

If I had still been an immortal, I might have flirted

with her myself. But I was now a sixteen-year-old boy. My mortal form was working its way upon my state of mind. I saw Sally Jackson as a mom—a fact that both consternated and embarrassed me. I thought about how long it had been since I had called my own mother. I should probably take her to lunch when I got back to Olympus.

"I tell you what." Sally patted my shoulder. "Percy can help you get bandaged and cleaned up."

"I can?" asked Percy.

Sally gave him the slightest motherly eyebrow raise. "There's a first-aid kit in your bathroom, sweetheart. Apollo can take a shower, then wear your extra clothes. You two are about the same size."

"That," Percy said, "is truly depressing."

Sally cupped her hand under Meg's chin. Thankfully, Meg did not bite her. Sally's expression remained gentle and reassuring, but I could see the worry in her eyes. No doubt she was thinking, *Who dressed this poor girl like a traffic light?*

"I have some clothes that might fit you, dear," Sally said. "Pre-pregnancy clothes, of course. Let's get you cleaned up. Then we'll get you something to eat."

"I like food," Meg muttered.

Sally laughed. "Well, we have that in common. Percy, you take Apollo. We'll meet you back here in a while."

In short order, I was showered, bandaged, and dressed in Jacksonesque hand-me-downs. Percy left me alone in the bathroom to take care of all this myself, for which I was grateful. He offered me some ambrosia and nectar—food and drink of the gods—to heal my wounds, but I was not sure it would be safe to consume in my mortal state. I didn't want to self-combust, so I stuck with mortal first-aid supplies.

When I was done, I stared at my battered face in the bathroom mirror. Perhaps teenage angst had permeated the clothes, because I felt more like a sulky high schooler than ever. I thought how unfair it was that I was being punished, how lame my father was, how no one else in the history of time had ever experienced problems like mine.

Of course, all that was empirically true. No exaggeration was required.

At least my wounds seemed to be healing at a faster rate than a normal mortal's. The swelling in my nose had subsided. My ribs still ached, but I no longer felt as if someone were knitting a sweater inside my chest with hot needles.

Accelerated healing was the *least* Zeus could do for me. I was a god of medicinal arts, after all. Zeus probably just wanted me to get well quickly so I could endure more pain, but I was grateful nonetheless.

I wondered if I should start a small fire in Percy Jackson's sink, perhaps burn some bandages in thanks, but I decided that might strain the Jacksons' hospitality.

I examined the black T-shirt Percy had given me. Emblazoned on the front was Led Zeppelin's logo for their record label: winged Icarus falling from the sky. I had no problem with Led Zeppelin. I had inspired all their best songs. But I had a sneaking suspicion that Percy had given me this shirt as a joke—the fall from the sky. Yes, ha-ha. I didn't need to be a god of poetry to spot the metaphor. I decided not to comment on it. I wouldn't give him the satisfaction.

I took a deep breath. Then I did my usual motivational speech in the mirror: "You are gorgeous and people love you!"

I went out to face the world.

Percy was sitting on his bed, staring at the trail of blood droplets I had made across his carpet.

"Sorry about that," I said.

Percy spread his hands. "Actually, I was thinking about the last time I had a nosebleed."

"Oh . . ."

The memory came back to me, though hazy and incomplete. Athens. The Acropolis. We gods had battled side by side with Percy Jackson and his comrades. We defeated an army of giants, but a drop of Percy's blood hit the earth and awakened the Earth Mother Gaea, who had not been in a good mood.

That's when Zeus turned on me. He'd accused me of starting the whole thing, just because Gaea had duped one of my progeny, a boy named Octavian, into plunging the Roman and Greek demigod camps into a civil war that almost destroyed human civilization. I ask you: How was that my fault?

Regardless, Zeus had held *me* responsible for Octavian's delusions of grandeur. Zeus seemed to consider egotism a trait the boy had inherited from me. Which is ridiculous. I am much too self-aware to be egotistical.

"What happened to you, man?" Percy's voice stirred me from my reverie. "The war ended in August. It's January."

"It is?" I suppose the wintry weather should have been a clue, but I hadn't given it much thought.

"Last I saw you," Percy said, "Zeus was chewing you out at the Acropolis. Then *bam*—he vaporized you. Nobody's seen or heard from you for six months."

I tried to recall, but my memories of godhood were getting fuzzier rather than clearer. What had happened in the last six months? Had I been in some kind of stasis? Had Zeus taken that long to decide what to do with me? Perhaps there was a reason he'd waited until this moment to hurl me to earth.

Father's voice still rang in my ears: *Your fault. Your punishment.* My shame felt fresh and raw, as if the conversation had just happened, but I could not be sure.

After being alive for so many millennia, I had trouble keeping track of time even in the best of circumstances. I would hear a song on Spotify and think, Oh, that's new! Then I'd realize it was Mozart's Piano Concerto no. 20 in D Minor from two hundred years ago. Or I'd wonder why Herodotus the historian wasn't in my contacts list. Then I'd remember Herodotus didn't have a smartphone, because he had been dead since the Iron Age.

It's very irritating how quickly you mortals die.

"I—I don't know where I've been," I admitted. "I have some memory gaps."

Percy winced. "I hate memory gaps. Last year I lost an entire semester thanks to Hera."

"Ah, yes." I couldn't quite remember what Percy Jackson was talking about. During the war with Gaea, I had been focused mostly on my own fabulous exploits. But I suppose he and his friends had undergone a few minor hardships.

"Well, never fear," I said. "There are always new opportunities to win fame! That's why I've come to you for help!"

He gave me that confusing expression again: as if he wanted to kick me, when I was sure he must be struggling to contain his gratitude.

"Look, man—"

"Would you please refrain from calling me *man?*" I asked. "It is a painful reminder that I am a man."

"Okay . . . Apollo, I'm fine with driving you and Meg to camp if that's what you want. I never turn away a demigod who needs help—"

"Wonderful! Do you have something besides the Prius? A Maserati, perhaps? I'd settle for a Lamborghini."

"But," Percy continued, "I can't get involved in another Big Prophecy or whatever. I've made promises."

I stared at him, not quite comprehending. "Promises?"

Percy laced his fingers. They were long and nimble. He would have made an excellent musician. "I lost most of my junior year because of the war with Gaea. I've spent this entire fall playing catch-up with my classes. If I want to go to college with Annabeth next fall, I have to stay out of trouble and get my diploma."

"Annabeth." I tried to place the name. "She's the blond scary one?"

"That's her. I promised her *specifically* that I wouldn't get myself killed while she's gone."

"Gone?"

Percy waved vaguely toward the north. "She's in Boston for a few weeks. Some family emergency. The point is—"

"You're saying you cannot offer me your undivided service to restore me to my throne?"

"Um . . . yeah." He pointed at the bedroom doorway. "Besides, my mom's pregnant. I'm going to have a baby sister. I'd like to be around to get to know her."

"Well, I understand that. I remember when Artemis was born—"

"Aren't you twins?"

"I've always regarded her as my little sister."

Percy's mouth twitched. "Anyway, my mom's got that going on, and her first novel is going to be published this spring as well, so I'd like to stay alive long enough to—"

"Wonderful!" I said. "Remind her to burn the proper sacrifices. Calliope is quite touchy when novelists forget to thank her."

"Okay. But what I'm saying . . . I can't go off on another world-stomping quest. I can't do that to my family."

Percy glanced toward his window. On the sill was a potted plant with delicate silver leaves—possibly moonlace. "I've already given my mom enough heart attacks for one lifetime. She's just about forgiven me for disappearing last year, but I swore to her and Paul that I wouldn't do anything like that again."

"Paul?"

"My stepdad. He's at a teacher in-service today. He's a good guy."

"I see." In truth, I didn't see. I wanted to get back to talking about my problems. I was impatient with Percy for turning the conversation to himself. Sadly, I have found this sort of self-centeredness common among demigods.

"You *do* understand that I must find a way to return to Olympus," I said. "This will probably involve many harrowing trials with a high chance of death. Can you turn down such glory?"

"Yeah, I'm pretty sure I can. Sorry."

I pursed my lips. It always disappointed me when mortals put themselves first and failed to see the big picture—the importance of putting *me* first—but I had to remind myself that this young man had helped me out on many previous occasions. He had earned my goodwill.

"I understand," I said with incredible generosity. "You will at least escort us to Camp Half-Blood?"

"That I can do." Percy reached into his hoodie pocket and pulled out a ballpoint pen. For a moment I thought he wanted my autograph. I can't tell you how often that happens. Then I remembered the pen was the disguised form of his sword, Riptide.

He smiled, and some of that old demigod mischief twinkled in his eyes. "Let's see if Meg's ready for a field trip."

5

Seven-layer dip
Chocolate chip cookies in blue
I love this woman

SALLY JACKSON was a witch to rival Circe. She had transformed Meg from a street urchin into a shockingly pretty young girl. Meg's dark pageboy hair was glossy and brushed. Her round face was scrubbed clean of grime. Her cat-eye glasses had been polished so the rhinestones sparkled. She had evidently insisted on keeping her old red sneakers, but she wore new black leggings and a knee-length frock of shifting green hues.

Mrs. Jackson had figured out how to keep Meg's old look but tweak it to be more complementary. Meg now had an elfish springtime aura that reminded me very much of a dryad. In fact . . .

A sudden wave of emotion overwhelmed me. I choked back a sob.

Meg pouted. "Do I look that bad?"

"No, no," I managed. "It's just . . ."

I wanted to say: *You remind me of someone.* But I didn't dare open that line of conversation. Only two mortals *ever* had broken my heart. Even after so many centuries, I couldn't think of her, couldn't say her name without falling into despair.

Don't misunderstand me. I felt no attraction to Meg. I was sixteen (or four thousand plus, depending on how you looked at it). She was a very young twelve. But the way she appeared now, Meg McCaffrey might have been the daughter of my former love . . . if my former love had lived long enough to have children.

It was too painful. I looked away.

"Well," Sally Jackson said with forced cheerfulness, "how about I make some lunch while you three . . . talk."

She gave Percy a worried glance, then headed to the kitchen, her hands protectively over her pregnant belly.

Meg sat on the edge of the sofa. "Percy, your mom is so normal."

"Thanks, I guess." He picked up a stack of test preparation manuals from the coffee table and chucked them aside.

"I see you like to study," I said. "Well done."

Percy snorted. "I *hate* to study. I've been guaranteed admission with a full scholarship to New Rome University, but they're still requiring me to pass all my high school courses and score well on the SAT. Can you believe that? Not to mention I have to pass the DSTOMP."

"The what?" Meg asked.

"An exam for Roman demigods," I told her. "The Demigod Standard Test of Mad Powers."

Percy frowned. "That's what it stands for?"

"I should know. I wrote the music and poetry analysis sections."

"I will never forgive you for that," Percy said.

Meg swung her feet. "So you're really a demigod? Like me?"

"Afraid so." Percy sank into the armchair, leaving me to take the sofa next to Meg. "My dad is the godly one—Poseidon. What about your parents?"

Meg's legs went still. She studied her chewed cuticles, the matching crescent rings glinting on her middle fingers. "Never knew them . . . much."

Percy hesitated. "Foster home? Stepparents?"

I thought of a certain plant, the *Mimosa pudica*, which the god Pan created. As soon as its leaves are touched, the plant closes up defensively. Meg seemed to be playing mimosa, folding inward under Percy's questions.

Percy raised his hands. "Sorry. Didn't mean to pry." He gave me an inquisitive look. "So how did you guys meet?"

I told him the story. I may have exaggerated my brave defense against Cade and Mikey—just for narrative effect, you understand.

As I finished, Sally Jackson returned. She set down a bowl of tortilla chips and a casserole dish filled with elaborate dip in multicolored strata, like sedimentary rock.

"I'll be back with the sandwiches," she said. "But I had some leftover seven-layer dip."

"Yum." Percy dug in with a tortilla chip. "She's kinda famous for this, guys."

Sally ruffled his hair. "There's guacamole, sour cream, refried beans, salsa—"

"Seven layers?" I looked up in wonder. "You knew seven is my sacred number? You invented this for *me*?"

Sally wiped her hands on her apron. "Well, actually, I can't take credit—"

"You are too modest!" I tried some of the dip. It tasted almost as good as ambrosia nachos. "You will have immortal fame for this, Sally Jackson!"

"That's sweet." She pointed to the kitchen. "I'll be right back."

Soon we were plowing through turkey sandwiches, chips and dip, and banana smoothies. Meg ate like a chipmunk, shoving more food in her mouth than she could possibly chew. My belly was full. I had never been so happy. I had a strange desire to fire up an Xbox and play *Call of Duty*.

"Percy," I said, "your mom is awesome."

"I know, right?" He finished his smoothie. "So back to your story . . . you have to be Meg's servant now? You guys barely know each other."

"*Barely* is generous," I said. "Nevertheless, yes. My fate is now linked with young McCaffrey."

"We are *cooperating*," Meg said. She seemed to savor that word.

From his pocket, Percy fished his ballpoint pen. He tapped it thoughtfully against his knee. "And this whole turning-into-a-mortal thing . . . you've done it twice before?"

"Not by choice," I assured him. "The first time, we had a little rebellion in Olympus. We tried to overthrow Zeus."

Percy winced. "I'm guessing that didn't go well."

"I got most of the blame, naturally. Oh, and your father, Poseidon. We were both cast down to earth as mortals, forced to serve Laomedon, the king of Troy. He was a harsh master. He even refused to pay us for our work!"

Meg nearly choked on her sandwich. "I have to pay you?"

I had a terrifying image of Meg McCaffrey trying to pay me in bottle caps, marbles, and pieces of colored string.

"Never fear," I told her. "I won't be presenting you with a bill. But as I was saying, the second time I became mortal, Zeus got mad because I killed some of his Cyclopes."

Percy frowned. "Dude, not cool. My brother is a Cyclops."

"These were wicked Cyclopes! They made the lightning bolt that killed one of my sons!"

Meg bounced on the arm of the sofa. "Percy's brother is a Cyclops? That's crazy!"

I took a deep breath, trying to find my happy place. "At any rate, I was bound to Admetus, the king of Thessaly. He was a kind master. I liked him so much, I made all his cows have twin calves."

"Can I have baby cows?" Meg asked.

"Well, Meg," I said, "first you would have to have some mommy cows. You see—"

"Guys," Percy interrupted. "So, just to recap, you have to be Meg's servant for . . . ?"

"Some unknown amount of time," I said. "Probably a year. Possibly more."

"And during that time—"

"I will undoubtedly face many trials and hardships."

"Like getting me my cows," Meg said.

I gritted my teeth. "What those trials will be, I do not yet know. But if I suffer through them and prove I am worthy, Zeus will forgive me and allow me to become a god again."

Percy did not look convinced—probably because I did not sound convincing. I *had* to believe my mortal punishment was temporary, as it had been the last two times. Yet Zeus had created a strict rule for baseball and prison sentences: *Three strikes, you're out.* I could only hope this would not apply to me.

"I need time to get my bearings," I said. "Once we get to Camp Half-Blood, I can consult with Chiron. I can figure out which of my godly powers remain with me in this mortal form."

"If any," Percy said.

"Let's think positive."

Percy sat back in his armchair. "Any idea what kind of spirits are following you?"

"Shiny blobs," Meg said. "They were shiny and sort of . . . blobby."

Percy nodded gravely. "Those are the worst kind."

"It hardly matters," I said. "Whatever they are, we have to flee. Once we reach camp, the magical borders will protect me."

"And me?" Meg asked.

"Oh, yes. You, too."

Percy frowned. "Apollo, if you're really mortal, like, one hundred percent mortal, can you even get *in* to Camp Half-Blood?"

The seven-layer dip began to churn in my stomach. "Please don't say that. Of course I'll get in. I *have* to."

"But you could get hurt in battle now . . ." Percy mused. "Then again, maybe monsters would ignore you because you're not important?"

"Stop!" My hands trembled. Being a mortal was traumatic enough. The thought of being barred from camp, of being *unimportant* . . . No. That simply could not be.

"I'm sure I've retained some powers," I said. "I'm still gorgeous, for instance, if I could just get rid of this acne and lose some flab. I must have other abilities!"

Percy turned to Meg. "What about you? I hear you throw a mean garbage bag. Any other skills we should know about? Summoning lightning? Making toilets explode?"

Meg smiled hesitantly. "That's not a power."

"Sure it is," Percy said. "Some of the best demigods have gotten their start by blowing up toilets."

Meg giggled.

I did not like the way she was grinning at Percy. I didn't want the girl to develop a crush. We might never get out of here. As much as I enjoyed Sally Jackson's cooking—the divine smell of baking cookies was even now wafting from the kitchen—I needed to make haste to camp.

"Ahem." I rubbed my hands. "How soon can we leave?"

Percy glanced at the wall clock. "Right now, I guess. If you're being followed, I'd rather have monsters on our trail than sniffing around the apartment."

"Good man," I said.

Percy gestured with distaste at his test manuals. "I just have to be back tonight. Got a lot of studying. The first two times I took the SAT—ugh. If it wasn't for Annabeth helping me out—"

"Who's that?" Meg asked.

"My girlfriend."

Meg frowned. I was glad there were no garbage bags nearby for her to throw.

"So take a break!" I urged. "Your brain will be refreshed after an easy drive to Long Island."

"Huh," Percy said. "There's a lazy kind of logic to that. Okay. Let's do it."

He rose just as Sally Jackson walked in with a plate of fresh-baked chocolate chip cookies. For some reason, the cookies were blue, but they smelled heavenly—and I should know. I'm from heaven.

"Mom, don't freak," Percy said.

Sally sighed. "I hate it when you say that."

"I'm just going to take these two to camp. That's all. I'll be right back."

"I think I've heard that before."

"I *promise*."

Sally looked at me, then Meg. Her expression softened, her innate kindness perhaps overweighing her concern. "All right. Be careful. It was lovely meeting you both. Please try not to die."

Percy kissed her on the cheek. He reached for the cookies, but she moved the plate away.

"Oh, no," she said. "Apollo and Meg can have one, but I'm keeping the rest hostage until you're back safely. And hurry, dear. It would be a shame if Paul ate them all when he gets home."

Percy's expression turned grim. He faced us. "You hear that, guys? A batch of cookies is depending on me. If you get me killed on the way to camp, I am going be ticked off."

6

Aquaman driving
Couldn't possibly be worse
Oh, wait, now it is

MUCH TO MY DISAPPOINTMENT, the Jacksons did not have a spare bow or quiver to lend me.

"I suck at archery," Percy explained.

"Yes, but *I* don't," I said. "This is why you should always plan for *my* needs."

Sally lent Meg and me some proper winter fleece jackets, however. Mine was blue, with the word BLOFIS written inside the neckline. Perhaps that was an arcane ward against evil spirits. Hecate would have known. Sorcery really wasn't my thing.

Once we reached the Prius, Meg called shotgun, which was yet another example of my unfair existence. Gods do not ride in the back. I again suggested following them in a Maserati or a Lamborghini, but Percy admitted he had neither. The Prius was the only car his family owned.

I mean . . . wow. Just *wow*.

Sitting in the backseat, I quickly became carsick. I was used to driving my sun chariot across the sky, where every lane was the fast lane. I was not used to the Long Island

Expressway. Believe me, even at midday in the middle of January, there is nothing *express* about your expressways.

Percy braked and lurched forward. I sorely wished I could launch a fireball in front of us and melt cars to make way for our clearly more important journey.

"Doesn't your Prius have flamethrowers?" I demanded. "Lasers? At least some Hephaestian bumper blades? What sort of cheap economy vehicle is this?"

Percy glanced in the rearview mirror. "You have rides like that on Mount Olympus?"

"We don't have traffic jams," I said. "That, I can promise you."

Meg tugged at her crescent moon rings. Again I wondered if she had some connection to Artemis. The moon was my sister's symbol. Perhaps Artemis had sent Meg to look after me?

Yet that didn't seem right. Artemis had trouble sharing anything with me—demigods, arrows, nations, birthday parties. It's a twin thing. Also, Meg McCaffrey did not strike me as one of my sister's followers. Meg had another sort of aura . . . one I would have been able to recognize easily if I were a god. But, no. I had to rely on mortal intuition, which was like trying to pick up sewing needles while wearing oven mitts.

Meg turned and gazed out the rear windshield, probably checking for any shiny blobs pursuing us. "At least we're not being—"

"Don't say it," Percy warned.

Meg huffed. "You don't know what I was going to—"

"You were going to say, 'At least we're not being followed,'" Percy said. "That'll jinx us. Immediately we'll
notice that we *are* being followed. Then we'll end up in a
big battle that totals my family car and probably destroys
the whole freeway. Then we'll have to run all the way to
camp."

Meg's eyes widened. "You can tell the future?"

"Don't need to." Percy changed lanes to one that was
crawling slightly less slowly. "I've just done this a lot.
Besides"—he shot me an accusing look—"nobody can tell
the future anymore. The Oracle isn't working."

"What Oracle?" Meg asked.

Neither of us answered. For a moment, I was too stunned
to speak. And believe me, I have to be *very* stunned for that
to happen.

"It *still* isn't working?" I said in a small voice.

"You didn't know?" Percy asked. "I mean, sure, you've
been out of it for six months, but this happened on your
watch."

That was unjust. I had been busy hiding from Zeus's
wrath at the time, which was a perfectly legitimate excuse.
How was I to know that Gaea would take advantage of the
chaos of war and raise my oldest, greatest enemy from the
depths of Tartarus so he could take possession of his old lair
in the cave of Delphi and cut off the source of my prophetic
power?

Oh, yes, I hear you critics out there: *You're the god of
prophecy, Apollo. How could you* not *know that would happen?*

The next sound you hear will be me blowing you a giant
Meg-McCaffrey-quality raspberry.

I swallowed back the taste of fear and seven-layer dip. "I just . . . I assumed—I hoped this would be taken care of by now."

"You mean by demigods," Percy said, "going on a big quest to reclaim the Oracle of Delphi?"

"Exactly!" I knew Percy would understand. "I suppose Chiron just forgot. I'll remind him when we get to camp, and he can dispatch some of you talented fodder—I mean heroes—"

"Well, here's the thing," Percy said. "To go on a quest, we need a prophecy, right? Those are the rules. If there's no Oracle, there *are* no prophecies, so we're stuck in a—"

"A Catch-88." I sighed.

Meg threw a piece of lint at me. "It's a Catch-22."

"No," I explained patiently. "This is a Catch-88, which is four times as bad."

I felt as if I were floating in a warm bath and someone had pulled out the stopper. The water swirled around me, tugging me downward. Soon I would be left shivering and exposed, or else I would be sucked down the drain into the sewers of hopelessness. (Don't laugh. That's a perfectly fine metaphor. Also, when you're a god, you can get sucked down a drain quite easily—if you're caught off guard and relaxed, and you happen to change form at the wrong moment. Once I woke up in a sewage treatment facility in Biloxi, but that's another story.)

I was beginning to see what was in store for me during my mortal sojourn. The Oracle was held by hostile forces. My adversary lay coiled and waiting, growing stronger every day on the magical fumes of the Delphic caverns. And I was a weak mortal bound to an untrained demigod who threw garbage and chewed her cuticles.

No. Zeus could not *possibly* expect me to fix this. Not in my present condition.

And yet . . . *someone* had sent those thugs to intercept me in the alley. Someone had known where I would land.

Nobody can tell the future anymore, Percy had said.

But that wasn't quite true.

"Hey, you two." Meg hit us both with pieces of lint. Where was she finding this lint?

I realized I'd been ignoring her. It had felt good while it lasted.

"Yes, sorry, Meg," I said. "You see, the Oracle of Delphi is an ancient—"

"I don't care about that," she said. "There are three shiny blobs now."

"What?" Percy asked.

She pointed behind us. "Look."

Weaving through the traffic, closing in on us rapidly, were three glittery, vaguely humanoid apparitions—like billowing plumes from smoke grenades touched by King Midas.

"Just once I'd like an easy commute," Percy grumbled. "Everybody, hold on. We're going cross-country."

Percy's definition of *cross-country* was different from mine.

I envisioned crossing an actual countryside. Instead, Percy shot down the nearest exit ramp, wove across the parking lot of a shopping mall, then blasted through the drive-through of a Mexican restaurant without even ordering anything. We swerved into an industrial area of dilapidated warehouses, the smoking apparitions still closing in behind us.

My knuckles turned white on my seat belt's shoulder strap. "Is your plan to avoid a fight by dying in a traffic accident?" I demanded.

"Ha-ha." Percy yanked the wheel to the right. We sped north, the warehouses giving way to a hodgepodge of apartment buildings and abandoned strip malls. "I'm getting us to the beach. I fight better near water."

"Because Poseidon?" Meg asked, steadying herself against the door handle.

"Yep," Percy agreed. "That pretty much describes my entire life: *Because Poseidon.*"

Meg bounced up and down with excitement, which seemed pointless to me, since we were already bouncing quite a lot.

"You're gonna be like Aquaman?" she asked. "Get the fish to fight for you?"

"Thanks," Percy said. "I haven't heard enough Aquaman jokes for one lifetime."

"I wasn't joking!" Meg protested.

I glanced out the rear window. The three glittering plumes were still gaining. One of them passed through a middle-aged man crossing the street. The mortal pedestrian instantly collapsed.

"Ah, I know these spirits!" I cried. "They are . . . um . . ."

My brain clouded over.

"What?" Percy demanded. "They are what?"

"I've forgotten! I *hate* being mortal! Four thousand years

of knowledge, the secrets of the universe, a sea of wisdom—lost, because I can't contain it all in this teacup of a head!"

"Hold on!" Percy flew through a railroad crossing and the Prius went airborne. Meg yelped as her head hit the ceiling. Then she began giggling uncontrollably.

The landscape opened into actual countryside—fallow fields, dormant vineyards, orchards of bare fruit trees.

"Just another mile or so to the beach," Percy said. "Plus we're almost to the western edge of camp. We can do it. We can do it."

Actually, we couldn't. One of the shiny smoke clouds pulled a dirty trick, pluming from the pavement directly in front of us.

Instinctively, Percy swerved.

The Prius went off the road, straight through a barbed wire fence and into an orchard. Percy managed to avoid hitting any of the trees, but the car skidded in the icy mud and wedged itself between two trunks. Miraculously, the air bags did not deploy.

Percy popped his seat belt. "You guys okay?"

Meg shoved against her passenger-side door. "Won't open. Get me out of here!"

Percy tried his own door. It was firmly jammed against the side of a peach tree.

"Back here," I said. "Climb over!"

I kicked my door open and staggered out, my legs feeling like worn shock absorbers.

The three smoky figures had stopped at the edge of the orchard. Now they advanced slowly, taking on solid shapes.

They grew arms and legs. Their faces formed eyes and wide, hungry mouths.

I knew instinctively that I had dealt with these spirits before. I couldn't remember what they were, but I had dispelled them many times, swatting them into oblivion with no more effort than I would a swarm of gnats.

Unfortunately, I wasn't a god now. I was a panicky sixteen-year-old. My palms sweated. My teeth chattered. My only coherent thought was: *YIKES!*

Percy and Meg struggled to get out of the Prius. They needed time, which meant I had to run interference.

"STOP!" I bellowed at the spirits. "I am the god Apollo!"

To my pleasant surprise, the three spirits stopped. They hovered in place about forty feet away.

I heard Meg grunt as she tumbled out of the backseat. Percy scrambled after her.

I advanced toward the spirits, the frosty mud crunching under my shoes. My breath steamed in the cold air. I raised my hand in an ancient three-fingered gesture for warding off evil.

"Leave us or be destroyed!" I told the spirits. "BLOFIS!"

The smoky shapes trembled. My hopes lifted. I waited for them to dissipate or flee in terror.

Instead, they solidified into ghoulish corpses with yellow eyes. Their clothes were tattered rags, their limbs covered with gaping wounds and running sores.

"Oh, dear." My Adam's apple dropped into my chest like a billiard ball. "I remember now."

Percy and Meg stepped to either side of me. With a

metallic *shink*, Percy's pen grew into a blade of glowing Celestial bronze.

"Remember what?" he asked. "How to kill these things?"

"No," I said. "I remember what they are: *nosoi*, plague spirits. Also . . . they can't be killed."

7

Tag with plague spirits
You're it, and you're infectious
Have fun with that, LOL

"NOSOI?" PERCY PLANTED HIS FEET in a fighting stance. "You know, I keep thinking, *I have now killed every single thing in Greek mythology.* But the list never seems to end."

"You haven't killed me yet," I noted.

"Don't tempt me."

The three nosoi shuffled forward. Their cadaverous mouths gaped. Their tongues lolled. Their eyes glistened with a film of yellow mucus.

"These creatures are *not* myths," I said. "Of course, most things in those old myths are not myths. Except for that story about how I flayed the satyr Marsyas alive. That was a total lie."

Percy glanced at me. "You did *what?*"

"Guys." Meg picked up a dead tree branch. "Could we talk about that later?"

The middle plague spirit spoke. "Apollooooo . . ." His voice gurgled like a seal with bronchitis. "We have coooome to—"

"Let me stop you right there." I crossed my arms and feigned arrogant indifference. (Difficult for me, but I managed.) "You've come to take your revenge on me, eh?" I looked at my demigod friends. "You see, nosoi are the spirits of disease. Once I was born, spreading illnesses became part of my job. I use plague arrows to strike down naughty populations with smallpox, athlete's foot, that sort of thing."

"Gross," Meg said.

"Somebody's got to do it!" I said. "Better a god, regulated by the Council of Olympus and with the proper health permits, than a horde of uncontrolled spirits like *these*."

The spirit on the left gurgled. "We're trying to have a mooooment here. Stop interrupting! We wish to be free, uncontroooolled—"

"Yes, I know. You'll destroy me. Then you'll spread every known malady across the world. You've been wanting to do that ever since Pandora let you out of that jar. But you can't. I will strike you down!"

Perhaps you are wondering how I could act so confident and calm. In fact, I was terrified. My sixteen-year-old mortal instincts were screaming, *RUN!* My knees were knocking together, and my right eye had developed a nasty twitch. But the secret to dealing with plague spirits was to keep talking so as to appear in charge and unafraid. I trusted that this would allow my demigod companions time to come up with a clever plan to save me. I certainly *hoped* Meg and Percy were working on such a plan.

The spirit on the right bared his rotten teeth. "What will you strike us down with? Where is your booow?"

"It appears to be missing," I agreed. "But is it really? What if it's cleverly hidden under this Led Zeppelin T-shirt, and I am about to whip it out and shoot you all?"

The nosoi shuffled nervously.

"Yooou lie," said the one in the middle.

Percy cleared his throat. "Um, hey, Apollo . . ."

Finally! I thought.

"I know what you're going to say," I told him. "You and Meg have come up with a clever plan to hold off these spirits while I run away to camp. I hate to see you sacrifice yourselves, but—"

"That's not what I was going to say." Percy raised his blade. "I was going to ask what happens if I just slice and dice these mouth-breathers with Celestial bronze."

The middle spirit chortled, his yellow eyes gleaming. "A sword is such a small weapon. It does not have the pooooetry of a good epidemic."

"Stop right there!" I said. "You can't claim both my plagues *and* my poetry!"

"You are right," said the spirit. "Enough wooooords."

The three corpses shambled forward. I thrust out my arms, hoping to blast them to dust. Nothing happened.

"This is insufferable!" I complained. "How do demigods do it without an auto-win power?"

Meg jabbed her tree branch into the nearest spirit's chest. The branch stuck. Glittering smoke began swirling down the length of the wood.

"Let go!" I warned. "Don't let the nosoi touch you!"

Meg released the branch and scampered away.

Meanwhile, Percy Jackson charged into battle. He swung his sword, dodging the spirits' attempts to snare him, but his efforts were futile. Whenever his blade connected with the nosoi, their bodies simply dissolved into glittery mist, then resolidified.

A spirit lunged to grab him. From the ground, Meg scooped up a frozen black peach and threw it with such force it embedded itself in the spirit's forehead, knocking him down.

"We gotta run," Meg decided.

"Yeah." Percy backtracked toward us. "I like that idea."

I knew running would not help. If it were possible to run from disease spirits, the medieval Europeans would've put on their track shoes and escaped the Black Death. (And FYI, the Black Death was *not* my fault. I took one century off to lie around the beach in Cabo, and came back and found that the nosoi had gotten loose and a third of the continent was dead. *Gods*, I was so irritated.)

But I was too terrified to argue. Meg and Percy sprinted off through the orchard, and I followed.

Percy pointed to a line of hills about a mile ahead. "That's the western border of camp. If we can just get there . . ."

We passed an irrigation tank on a tractor-trailer. With a casual flick of his hand, Percy caused the side of the tank to rupture. A wall of water crashed into the three nosoi behind us.

"That was good." Meg grinned, skipping along in her new green dress. "We're going to make it!"

No, I thought, we're not.

My chest ached. Each breath was a ragged wheeze. I resented that these two demigods could carry on a conversation while running for their lives while I, the immortal Apollo, was reduced to gasping like a catfish.

"We can't—" I gulped. "They'll just—"

Before I could finish, three glittering pillars of smoke plumed from the ground in front of us. Two of the nosoi solidified into cadavers—one with a peach for a third eye, the other with a tree branch sticking out of his chest.

The third spirit . . . Well, Percy didn't see it in time. He ran straight into the plume of smoke.

"Don't breathe!" I warned him.

Percy's eyes bugged out as if to say, *Seriously?* He fell to his knees, clawing at his throat. As a son of Poseidon, he could probably breathe underwater, but holding one's breath for an indeterminate amount of time was a different matter altogether.

Meg picked up another withered peach from the field, but it would offer her little defense against the forces of darkness.

I tried to figure out how to help Percy—because I am all about helping—but the branch-impaled nosos charged at me. I turned and fled, running face-first into a tree. I'd like to tell you that was part of my plan, but even I, with all my poetic skill, cannot put a positive spin on it.

I found myself flat on my back, spots dancing in my eyes, the cadaverous visage of the plague spirit looming over me.

"Which fatal illness shall I use to kill the great Apolloooo?" the spirit gurgled. "Anthrax? Perhaps eboooola . . ."

"Hangnails," I suggested, trying to squirm away from my tormentor. "I live in fear of hangnails."

"I have the answer!" the spirit cried, rudely ignoring me. "Let's try this!"

He dissolved into smoke and settled over me like a glittering blanket.

8

Peaches in combat
I am hanging it up now
My brain exploded

I WILL NOT SAY my life passed before my eyes.

I wish it had. That would've taken several months, giving me time to figure out an escape plan.

Instead, my regrets passed before my eyes. Despite being a gloriously perfect being, I do have a few regrets. I remembered that day at Abbey Road Studios, when my envy led me to set rancor in the hearts of John and Paul and break up the Beatles. I remembered Achilles falling on the plains of Troy, cut down by an unworthy archer because of my wrath.

I saw Hyacinthus, his bronze shoulders and dark ringlets gleaming in the sunlight. Standing on the sideline of the discus field, he gave me a brilliant smile. *Even you can't throw that far,* he teased.

Watch me, I said. I threw the discus, then stared in horror as a gust of wind made it veer, inexplicably, toward Hyacinthus's handsome face.

And of course I saw *her*—the other love of my life—her fair skin transforming into bark, her hair sprouting green leaves, her eyes hardening into rivulets of sap.

Those memories brought back so much pain, you might think I would welcome the glittering plague mist descending over me.

Yet my new mortal self rebelled. I was too young to die! I hadn't even had my first kiss! (Yes, my godly catalogue of exes was filled with more beautiful people than a Kardashian party guest list, but none of that seemed real to me.)

If I'm being totally honest, I have to confess something else: all gods fear death, even when we are *not* encased in mortal forms.

That may seem silly. We are immortal. But as you've seen, immortality can be taken away. (In my case, *three stinking times*.)

Gods know about fading. They know about being forgotten over the centuries. The idea of ceasing to exist altogether terrifies us. In fact . . . well, Zeus would not like me sharing this information—and if you tell anyone I will deny I ever said it—but the truth is we gods are a little in awe of you mortals. You spend your whole lives knowing you will die. No matter how many friends and relatives you have, your puny existence will quickly be forgotten. How do you cope with it? Why are you not running around constantly screaming and pulling your hair out? Your bravery, I must admit, is quite admirable.

Now where was I?

Right. I was dying.

I rolled around in the mud, holding my breath. I tried to brush off the disease cloud, but it was not as easy as swatting a fly or an uppity mortal.

I caught a glimpse of Meg, playing a deadly game of tag

with the third nosos, trying to keep a peach tree between herself and the spirit. She yelled something to me, but her voice seemed tinny and far away.

Somewhere to my left, the ground shook. A miniature geyser erupted from the field. Percy crawled toward it desperately. He thrust his face in the water, washing away the smoke.

My eyesight began to dim.

Percy struggled to his feet. He ripped out the source of the geyser—an irrigation pipe—and turned the water on me.

Normally I do not like being doused. Every time I go camping with Artemis, she likes to wake me up with a bucket of ice-cold water. But in this case, I didn't mind.

The water disrupted the smoke, allowing me to roll away and gasp for air. Nearby, our two gaseous enemies re-formed as dripping wet corpses, their yellow eyes glowing with annoyance.

Meg yelled again. This time I understood her words. "GET DOWN!"

I found this inconsiderate, since I'd only just gotten up. All around the orchard, the frozen blackened remnants of the harvest were beginning to levitate.

Believe me, in four thousand years I have seen some strange things. I have seen the dreaming face of Ouranos etched in stars across the heavens, and the full fury of Typhon as he raged across the earth. I've seen men turn into snakes, ants turn into men, and otherwise rational people dance the macarena.

But never before had I seen an uprising of frozen fruit.

Percy and I hit the ground as peaches shot around

the orchard, ricocheting off trees like eight balls, ripping through the nosoi's cadaverous bodies. If I had been standing up, I would have been killed, but Meg simply stood there, unfazed and unhurt, as frozen dead fruit zinged around her.

All three nosoi collapsed, riddled with holes. Every piece of fruit dropped to the ground.

Percy looked up, his eyes red and puffy. "Whah jus happened?"

He sounded congested, which meant he hadn't completely escaped the effects of the plague cloud, but at least he wasn't dead. That was generally a good sign.

"I don't know," I admitted. "Meg, is it safe?"

She was staring in amazement at the carnage of fruit, mangled corpses, and broken tree limbs. "I—I'm not sure."

"How'd you do thah?" Percy snuffled.

Meg looked horrified. "I didn't! I just knew it would happen."

One of the cadavers began to stir. It got up, wobbling on its heavily perforated legs.

"But you *did* doooo it," the spirit growled. "Yooou are strong, child."

The other two corpses rose.

"Not strong enough," said the second nosos. "We will finish you now."

The third spirit bared his rotten teeth. "Your guardian would be sooooo disappointed."

Guardian? Perhaps the spirit meant me. When in doubt, I usually assumed the conversation was about me.

Meg looked as if she'd been punched in the gut. Her

face paled. Her arms trembled. She stamped her foot and yelled, "NO!"

More peaches swirled into the air. This time the fruit blurred together in a fructose dust devil, until standing in front of Meg was a creature like a pudgy human toddler wearing only a linen diaper. Protruding from his back were wings made of leafy branches. His babyish face might have been cute except for the glowing green eyes and pointy fangs. The creature snarled and snapped at the air.

"Oh, no." Percy shook his head. "I hate these things."

The three nosoi also did not look pleased. They edged away from the snarling baby.

"Wh-what is it?" Meg asked.

I stared at her in disbelief. She had to be the cause of this fruit-based strangeness, but she looked as shocked as we were. Unfortunately, if Meg didn't know how she had summoned this creature, she would not know how to make it go away, and like Percy Jackson, I was no fan of *karpoi*.

"It's a grain spirit," I said, trying to keep the panic out of my voice. "I've never seen a peach karpos before, but if it's as vicious as other types . . ."

I was about to say, *we're doomed*, but that seemed both obvious and depressing.

The peach baby turned toward the nosoi. For a moment, I feared he would make some hellish alliance—an axis of evil between illnesses and fruits.

The middle corpse, the one with the peach in his forehead, inched backward. "Do not interfere," he warned the karpos. "We will not allooow—"

The peach baby launched himself at the nosos and bit his head off.

That is not a figure of speech. The karpos's fanged mouth unhinged, expanding to an unbelievable circumference, then closed around the cadaver's head, and chomped it off in one bite.

Oh, dear . . . I hope you weren't eating dinner as you read that.

In a matter of seconds, the nosos had been torn to shreds and devoured.

Understandably, the other two nosoi retreated, but the karpos crouched and sprang. He landed on the second corpse and proceeded to rip it into plague-flavored Cream of Wheat.

The last spirit dissolved into glittering smoke and tried to fly away, but the peach baby spread his leafy wings and launched himself in pursuit. He opened his mouth and inhaled the sickness, snapping and swallowing until every wisp of smoke was gone.

He landed in front of Meg and belched. His green eyes gleamed. He did not appear even slightly sick, which I suppose wasn't surprising, since human diseases don't infect fruit trees. Instead, even after eating three whole nosoi, the little fellow looked hungry.

He howled and beat his small chest. "Peaches!"

Slowly, Percy raised his sword. His nose was still red and runny, and his face was puffy. "Meg, don move," he snuffled. "I'm gonna—"

"No!" she said. "Don't hurt him."

She put her hand tentatively on the creature's curly head. "You saved us," she told the karpos. "Thank you."

I started mentally preparing a list of herbal remedies for regenerating severed limbs, but to my surprise, the peach baby did not bite off Meg's hand. Instead he hugged Meg's leg and glared at us as if daring us to approach.

"Peaches," he growled.

"He likes you," Percy noted. "Um . . . why?"

"I don't know," Meg said. "Honestly, I didn't summon him!"

I was certain Meg *had* summoned him, intentionally or unintentionally. I also had some ideas now about her godly parentage, and some questions about this "guardian" that the spirits had mentioned, but I decided it would be better to interrogate her when she did not have a snarling carnivorous toddler wrapped around her leg.

"Well, whatever the case," I said, "we owe the karpos our lives. This brings to mind an expression I coined ages ago: *A peach a day keeps the plague spirits away!*"

Percy sneezed. "I thought it was apples and doctors."

The karpos hissed.

"Or peaches," Percy said. "Peaches work too."

"Peaches," agreed the karpos.

Percy wiped his nose. "Not criticizing, but why is he grooting?"

Meg frowned. "Grooting?"

"Yeah, like thah character in the movie . . . only saying one thing over and over."

"I'm afraid I haven't seen that movie," I said. "But this

karpos does seem to have a very . . . targeted vocabulary."

"Maybe Peaches is his name." Meg stroked the karpos's curly brown hair, which elicited a demonic purring from the creature's throat. "That's what I'll call him."

"Whoa, you are not adopting thah—" Percy sneezed with such force, another irrigation pipe exploded behind him, sending up a row of tiny geysers. "Ugh. Sick."

"You're lucky," I said. "Your trick with the water diluted the spirit's power. Instead of getting a deadly illness, you got a head cold."

"I hate head colds." His green irises looked like they were sinking in a sea of bloodshot. "Neither of you got sick?"

Meg shook her head.

"I have an excellent constitution," I said. "No doubt that's what saved me."

"And the fact thah I hosed the smoke off of you," Percy said.

"Well, yes."

Percy stared at me as if waiting for something. After an awkward moment, it occurred to me that if he was a god and I was a worshipper, he might expect gratitude.

"Ah . . . thank you," I said.

He nodded. "No problem."

I relaxed a little. If he had demanded a sacrifice, like a white bull or a fatted calf, I'm not sure what I would've done.

"Can we go now?" Meg asked.

"An excellent idea," I said. "Though I'm afraid Percy is in no condition—"

"I can drive you the rest of the way," he said. "If we can get my car out from between those trees. . . ." He glanced in that direction and his expression turned even more miserable. "Aw, Hades no. . . ."

A police cruiser was pulling over on the side of the road. I imagined the officers' eyes tracing the tire ruts in the mud, which led to the plowed-down fence and continued to the blue Toyota Prius wedged between two peach trees. The cruiser's roof lights flashed on.

"Great," Percy muttered. "If they tow the Prius, I'm dead. My mom and Paul *need* thah car."

"Go talk to the officers," I said. "You won't be any use to us anyway in your current state."

"Yeah, we'll be fine," Meg said. "You said the camp is right over those hills?"

"Right, but . . ." Percy scowled, probably trying to think straight through the effects of his cold. "Most people enter camp from the east, where Half-Blood Hill is. The western border is wilder—hills and woods, all heavily enchanted. If you're not careful, you can get lost. . . ." He sneezed again. "I'm still not even sure Apollo can get *in* if he's fully mortal."

"I'll get in." I tried to exude confidence. I had no alternative. If I was unable to enter Camp Half-Blood . . . No. I'd already been attacked twice on my first day as a mortal. There was no plan B that would keep me alive.

The police car's doors opened.

"Go," I urged Percy. "We'll find our way through the woods. You explain to the police that you're sick and you lost control of the car. They'll go easy on you."

Percy laughed. "Yeah. Cops love me almost as much as teachers do." He glanced at Meg. "You sure you're okay with the baby fruit demon?"

Peaches growled.

"All good," Meg promised. "Go home. Rest. Get lots of fluids."

Percy's mouth twitched. "You're telling a son of Poseidon to get lots of fluids? Okay, just try to survive until the weekend, will you? I'll come to camp and check on you guys if I can. Be careful and—CHOOOO!"

Muttering unhappily, he touched the cap of his pen to his sword, turning it back into a simple ballpoint. A wise precaution before approaching law enforcement. He trudged down the hill, sneezing and sniffling.

"Officer?" he called. "Sorry, I'm up here. Can you tell me where Manhattan is?"

Meg turned to me. "Ready?"

I was soaking wet and shivering. I was having the worst day in the history of days. I was stuck with a scary girl and an even scarier peach baby. I was by no means ready for anything. But I also desperately wanted to reach camp. I might find some friendly faces there—perhaps even jubilant worshippers who would bring me peeled grapes, Oreos, and other holy offerings.

"Sure," I said. "Let's go."

Peaches the karpos grunted. He gestured for us to follow, then scampered toward the hills. Maybe he knew the way. Maybe he just wanted to lead us to a grisly death.

Meg skipped after him, swinging from tree branches and cartwheeling through the mud as the mood took her.

You might've thought we'd just finished a nice picnic rather than a battle with plague-ridden cadavers.

I turned my face to the sky. "Are you sure, Zeus? It's not too late to tell me this was an elaborate prank and recall me to Olympus. I've learned my lesson. I promise."

The gray winter clouds did not respond. With a sigh, I jogged after Meg and her homicidal new minion.

9

A walk through the woods
Voices driving me bonkers
I hate spaghetti

I SIGHED WITH RELIEF. "This should be easy."

Granted, I'd said the same thing before I fought Poseidon in hand-to-hand combat, and that had *not* turned out to be easy. Nevertheless, our path into Camp Half-Blood looked straightforward enough. For starters, I was pleased I could *see* the camp, since it was normally shielded from mortal eyes. This boded well for me getting in.

From where we stood at the top of a hill, the entire valley spread out below us: roughly three square miles of woods, meadows, and strawberry fields bordered by Long Island Sound to the north and rolling hills on the other three sides. Just below us, a dense forest of evergreens covered the western third of the vale.

Beyond that, the buildings of Camp Half-Blood gleamed in the wintry light: the amphitheater, the sword-fighting stadium, the open-air dining pavilion with its white marble columns. A trireme floated in the canoe lake. Twenty cabins lined the central green where the communal hearth fire glowed cheerfully.

At the edge of the strawberry fields stood the Big House:

a four-story Victorian painted sky blue with white trim. My friend Chiron would be inside, probably having tea by the fireplace. I would find sanctuary at last.

My gaze rose to the far end of the valley. There, on the tallest hill, the Athena Parthenos shone in all its gold-and-alabaster glory. Once, the massive statue had graced the Parthenon in Greece. Now it presided over Camp Half-Blood, protecting the valley from intruders. Even from here I could feel its power, like the subsonic thrum of a mighty engine. Old Gray Eyes was on the lookout for threats, being her usual vigilant, no-fun, all-business self.

Personally, I would have installed a more interesting statue—of myself, for instance. Still, the panorama of Camp Half-Blood was an impressive sight. My mood always improved when I saw the place—a small reminder of the good old days when mortals knew how to build temples and do proper burnt sacrifices. Ah, everything was better in ancient Greece! Well, except for a few small improvements modern humans had made—the Internet, chocolate croissants, life expectancy.

Meg's mouth hung open. "How come I've never heard about this place? Do you need tickets?"

I chuckled. I always enjoyed the chance to enlighten a clueless mortal. "You see, Meg, magical borders camouflage the valley. From the outside, most humans would spy nothing here except boring farmland. If they approached, they would get turned around and find themselves wandering out again. Believe me, I tried to get a pizza delivered to camp once. It was quite annoying."

"You ordered a pizza?"

"Never mind," I said. "As for tickets . . . it's true the camp doesn't let in just anybody, but you're in luck. I know the management."

Peaches growled. He sniffed the ground, then chomped a mouthful of dirt and spit it out.

"He doesn't like the taste of this place," Meg said.

"Yes, well . . ." I frowned at the karpos. "Perhaps we can find him some potting soil or fertilizer when we arrive. I'll convince the demigods to let him in, but it would be helpful if he doesn't bite their heads off—at least not right away."

Peaches muttered something about peaches.

"Something doesn't feel right." Meg bit her nails. "Those woods . . . Percy said they were wild and enchanted and stuff."

I, too, felt as if something was amiss, but I chalked this up to my general dislike of forests. For reasons I'd rather not go into, I find them . . . uncomfortable places. Nevertheless, with our goal in sight, my usual optimism was returning.

"Don't worry," I assured Meg. "You're traveling with a god!"

"Ex-god."

"I wish you wouldn't keep harping on that. Anyway, the campers are very friendly. They'll welcome us with tears of joy. And wait until you see the orientation video!"

"The what?"

"I directed it myself! Now, come along. The woods can't be that bad."

———

The woods were that bad.

As soon as we entered their shadows, the trees seemed to crowd us. Trunks closed ranks, blocking old paths and opening new ones. Roots writhed across the forest floor, making an obstacle course of bumps, knots, and loops. It was like trying to walk across a giant bowl of spaghetti.

The thought of spaghetti made me hungry. It had only been a few hours since Sally Jackson's seven-layer dip and sandwiches, but my mortal stomach was already clenching and squelching for food. The sounds were quite annoying, especially while walking through dark scary woods. Even the karpos Peaches was starting to smell good to me, giving me visions of cobbler and ice cream.

As I said earlier, I was generally not a fan of the woods. I tried to convince myself that the trees were not watching me, scowling and whispering among themselves. They were just trees. Even if they had dryad spirits, those dryads couldn't possibly hold me responsible for what had happened thousands of years ago on a different continent.

Why not? I asked myself. *You still hold yourself responsible.*

I told myself to stuff a sock in it.

We hiked for hours . . . much longer than it should have taken to reach the Big House. Normally I could navigate by the sun—which shouldn't be a surprise, since I spent millennia driving it across the sky—but under the canopy of trees, the light was diffuse, the shadows confusing.

After we passed the same boulder for the third time, I stopped and admitted the obvious. "I have no idea where we are."

Meg plopped herself down onto a fallen log. In the green light, she looked more like a dryad than ever, though tree spirits do not often wear red sneakers and hand-me-down fleece jackets.

"Don't you have any wilderness skills?" she asked. "Reading moss on the sides of trees? Following tracks?"

"That's more my sister's thing," I said.

"Maybe Peaches can help." Meg turned to her karpos. "Hey, can you find us a way out of the woods?"

For the past few miles, the karpos had been muttering nervously, cutting his eyes from side to side. Now he sniffed the air, his nostrils quivering. He tilted his head.

His face flushed bright green. He emitted a distressed bark, then dissolved in a swirl of leaves.

Meg shot to her feet. "Where'd he go?"

I scanned the woods. I suspected Peaches had done the intelligent thing. He'd sensed danger approaching and abandoned us. I didn't want to suggest that to Meg, though. She'd already become quite fond of the karpos. (Ridiculous, getting attached to a small dangerous creature. Then again, we gods got attached to humans, so I had no room to criticize.)

"Perhaps he went scouting," I suggested. "Perhaps we should—"

APOLLO.

The voice reverberated in my head, as if someone had installed Bose speakers behind my eyes. It was not the voice of my conscience. My conscience was not female, and it was not that loud. Yet something about the woman's tone was eerily familiar.

"What's wrong?" Meg asked.

The air turned sickly sweet. The trees loomed over me like trigger hairs of a Venus flytrap.

A bead of sweat trickled down the side of my face.

"We can't stay here," I said. "Attend me, mortal."

"Excuse me?" Meg said.

"Uh, I mean come on!"

We ran, stumbling over tree roots, fleeing blindly through a maze of branches and boulders. We reached a clear stream over a bed of gravel. I barely slowed down. I waded in, sinking shin-deep into the ice-cold water.

The voice spoke again: *FIND ME*.

This time it was so loud, it stabbed through my forehead like a railroad spike. I stumbled, falling to my knees.

"Hey!" Meg gripped my arm. "Get up!"

"You didn't hear that?"

"Hear what?"

THE FALL OF THE SUN, the voice boomed. *THE FINAL VERSE*.

I collapsed face-first into the stream.

"Apollo!" Meg rolled me over, her voice tight with alarm. "Come on! I can't carry you!"

Yet she tried. She dragged me across the river, scolding me and cursing until, with her help, I managed to crawl to shore.

I lay on my back, staring wildly at the forest canopy. My soaked clothes were so cold they burned. My body trembled like an open E string on an electric bass.

Meg tugged off my wet winter coat. Her own coat was much too small for me, but she draped the warm dry fleece over my shoulders. "Keep yourself together," she ordered. "Don't go crazy on me."

My own laughter sounded brittle. "But I—I heard—"

THE FIRES WILL CONSUME ME. MAKE HASTE!

The voice splintered into a chorus of angry whispers. Shadows grew longer and darker. Steam rose from my clothes, smelling like the volcanic fumes of Delphi.

Part of me wanted to curl into a ball and die. Part of me wanted to get up and run wildly after the voices—to find their source—but I suspected that if I tried, my sanity would be lost forever.

Meg was saying something. She shook my shoulders. She put her face nose-to-nose with mine so my own derelict reflection stared back at me from the lenses of her cat-eye glasses. She slapped me, *hard*, and I managed to decipher her words: "GET UP!"

Somehow I did. Then I doubled over and retched.

I hadn't vomited in centuries. I'd forgotten how unpleasant it was.

The next thing I knew, we were staggering along, Meg bearing most of my weight. The voices whispered and argued, tearing off little pieces of my mind and carrying them away into the forest. Soon I wouldn't have much left.

There was no point. I might as well wander off into the forest and go insane. The idea struck me as funny. I began to giggle.

Meg forced me to keep walking. I couldn't understand her words, but her tone was insistent and stubborn, with just enough anger to outweigh her own terror.

In my fractured mental state, I thought the trees were

parting for us, grudgingly opening a path straight out of the woods. I saw a bonfire in the distance, and the open meadows of Camp Half-Blood.

It occurred to me that Meg was talking to the trees, telling them to get out of the way. The idea was ridiculous, and at the moment it seemed hilarious. Judging from the steam billowing from my clothes, I guessed I was running a fever of about a hundred and six.

I was laughing hysterically as we stumbled out of the forest, straight toward the campfire where a dozen teenagers sat making s'mores. When they saw us, they rose. In their jeans and winter coats, with assorted weapons at their sides, they were the dourest bunch of marshmallow roasters I had ever seen.

I grinned. "Oh, hi! I'm Apollo!"

My eyes rolled up in my head, and I passed out.

10

My bus is in flames
My son is older than me
Please, Zeus, make it stop

I DREAMED I WAS DRIVING the sun chariot across the sky. I had the top down in Maserati mode. I was cruising along, honking at jet planes to get out of my way, enjoying the smell of cold stratosphere, and bopping to my favorite jam: Alabama Shakes' "Rise to the Sun."

I was thinking about transforming the Spyder into a Google self-driving car. I wanted to get out my lute and play a scorching solo that would make Brittany Howard proud.

Then a woman appeared in my passenger seat. "You've got to hurry, man."

I almost jumped out of the sun.

My guest was dressed like a Libyan queen of old. (I should know. I dated a few of them.) Her gown swirled with red, black, and gold floral designs. Her long dark hair was crowned with a tiara that looked like a curved miniature ladder—two gold rails lined with rungs of silver. Her face was mature but stately, the way a benevolent queen should look.

So definitely not Hera, then. Besides, Hera would never smile at me so kindly. Also . . . this woman wore a large metal peace symbol around her neck, which did not seem like Hera's style.

Still, I felt I should know her. Despite the elder-hippie vibe, she was so attractive that I assumed we must be related.

"Who are you?" I asked.

Her eyes flashed a dangerous shade of gold, like a feline predator's. "Follow the voices."

A lump swelled in my throat. I tried to think straight, but my brain felt like it had been recently run through a Vitamix. "I heard you in the woods. . . . Were you—were you speaking a prophecy?"

"Find the gates." She grabbed my wrist. "You've gotta find them first, you dig?"

"But—"

The woman burst into flames. I pulled back my singed wrist and grabbed the wheel as the sun chariot plunged into a nosedive. The Maserati morphed into a school bus—a mode I only used when I had to transport a large number of people. Smoke filled the cabin.

Somewhere behind me, a nasal voice said, "By all means, find the gates."

I glanced in the rearview mirror. Through the smoke, I saw a portly man in a mauve suit. He lounged across the backseat, where the troublemakers normally sat. Hermes was fond of that seat—but this man was not Hermes.

He had a weak jawline, an overlarge nose, and a beard that wrapped around his double chin like a helmet strap. His hair was curly and dark like mine, except not as fashionably tousled or luxuriant. His lip curled as if he smelled something unpleasant. Perhaps it was the burning seats of the bus.

"Who are you?" I yelled, desperately trying to pull the chariot out of its dive. "Why are you on my bus?"

The man smiled, which made his face even uglier. "My own forefather does not recognize me? I'm hurt!"

I tried to place him. My cursed mortal brain was too small, too inflexible. It had jettisoned four thousand years of memories like so much ballast.

"I—I don't," I said. "I'm sorry."

The man laughed as flames licked at his purple sleeves. "You're not sorry *yet*, but you will be. Find me the gates. Lead me to the Oracle. I'll enjoy burning it down!"

Fire consumed me as the sun chariot careened toward the earth. I gripped the wheel and stared in horror as a massive bronze face loomed outside the windshield. It was the face of the man in purple, fashioned from an expanse of metal larger than my bus. As we hurtled toward it, the features shifted and became my own.

Then I woke, shivering and sweating.

"Easy." Someone's hand rested on my shoulder. "Don't try to sit up."

Naturally I tried to sit up.

My bedside attendant was a young man about my age— my *mortal* age—with shaggy blond hair and blue eyes. He wore doctor's scrubs with an open ski jacket, the words OKEMO MOUNTAIN stitched on the pocket. His face had a skier's tan. I felt I should know him. (I'd been having that sensation a lot since my fall from Olympus.)

I was lying in a cot in the middle of a cabin. On either

side, bunk beds lined the walls. Rough cedar beams ribbed the ceiling. The white plaster walls were bare except for a few hooks for coats and weapons.

It could have been a modest abode in almost any age— ancient Athens, medieval France, the farmlands of Iowa. It smelled of clean linen and dried sage. The only decorations were some flowerpots on the windowsill, where cheerful yellow blooms were thriving despite the cold weather outside.

"Those flowers . . ." My voice was hoarse, as if I'd inhaled the smoke from my dream. "Those are from Delos, my sacred island."

"Yep," said the young man. "They only grow in and around Cabin Seven—*your* cabin. Do you know who I am?"

I studied his face. The calmness of his eyes, the smile resting easily on his lips, the way his hair curled around his ears . . . I had a vague memory of a woman, an alt-country singer named Naomi Solace, whom I'd met in Austin. I blushed thinking about her even now. To my teenaged self, our romance felt like something that I'd watched in a movie a long ago time—a movie my parents wouldn't have allowed me to see.

But this boy was definitely Naomi's son.

Which meant he was *my* son too.

Which felt very, very strange.

"You're Will Solace," I said. "My, ah . . . erm—"

"Yeah," Will agreed. "It's awkward."

My frontal lobe did a one-eighty inside my skull. I listed sideways.

"Whoa, there." Will steadied me. "I tried to heal you, but honestly, I don't understand what's wrong. You've got blood, not ichor. You're recovering quickly from your injuries, but your vital signs are completely human."

"Don't remind me."

"Yeah, well . . ." He put his hand on my forehead and frowned in concentration. His fingers trembled slightly. "I didn't *know* any of that until I tried to give you nectar. Your lips started steaming. I almost killed you."

"Ah . . ." I ran my tongue across my bottom lip, which felt heavy and numb. I wondered if that explained my dream about smoke and fire. I hoped so. "I guess Meg forgot to tell you about my condition."

"I guess she did." Will took my wrist and checked my pulse. "You seem to be about my age, fifteen or so. Your heart rate is back to normal. Ribs are mending. Nose is swollen, but not broken."

"And I have acne," I lamented. "And flab."

Will tilted his head. "You're mortal, and *that's* what you're worried about?"

"You're right. I'm powerless. Weaker even than you puny demigods!"

"Gee, thanks. . . ."

I got the feeling that he almost said *Dad* but managed to stop himself.

It was difficult to think of this young man as my son. He was so poised, so unassuming, so free of acne. He also didn't appear to be awestruck in my presence. In fact, the corner of his mouth had started twitching.

"Are—are you amused?" I demanded.

Will shrugged. "Well, it's either find this funny or freak out. My dad, the god Apollo, is a fifteen-year-old—"

"*Sixteen,*" I corrected. "Let's go with sixteen."

"A sixteen-year-old mortal, lying in a cot in my cabin, and with all my healing arts—which I got from *you*—I still can't figure out how to fix you."

"There is no fixing this," I said miserably. "I am cast out of Olympus. My fate is tied to a girl named Meg. It could not be worse!"

Will laughed, which I thought took a great deal of gall. "Meg seems cool. She's already poked Connor Stoll in the eyes and kicked Sherman Yang in the crotch."

"She did *what?*"

"She'll get along just fine here. She's waiting for you outside—along with most of the campers." Will's smile faded. "Just so you're prepared, they're asking a lot of questions. Everybody is wondering if your arrival, your *mortal* situation, has anything to do with what's been going on at camp."

I frowned. "What has been going on at camp?"

The cabin door opened. Two more demigods stepped inside. One was a tall boy of about thirteen, his skin burnished bronze and his cornrows woven like DNA helixes. In his black wool peacoat and black jeans, he looked as if he'd stepped from the deck of an eighteenth-century whaling vessel. The other newcomer was a younger girl in olive camouflage. She had a full quiver on her shoulder, and her short ginger hair was dyed with a shock of bright green, which seemed to defeat the point of wearing camouflage.

I smiled, delighted that I actually remembered their names.

"Austin," I said. "And Kayla, isn't it?"

Rather than falling to their knees and blubbering gratefully, they gave each other a nervous glance.

"So it's really you," Kayla said.

Austin frowned. "Meg told us you were beaten up by a couple of thugs. She said you had no powers and you went hysterical out in the woods."

My mouth tasted like burnt school bus upholstery. "Meg talks too much."

"But you're mortal?" Kayla asked. "As in completely mortal? Does that mean I'm going to lose my archery skills? I can't even qualify for the Olympics until I'm sixteen!"

"And if I lose my music . . ." Austin shook his head. "No, man, that's wrong. My last video got, like, five hundred thousand views in a week. What am I supposed to do?"

It warmed my heart that my children had the right priorities: their skills, their images, their views on YouTube. Say what you will about gods being absentee parents; our children inherit many of our finest personality traits.

"My problems should not affect you," I promised. "If Zeus went around retroactively yanking my divine power out of all my descendants, half the medical schools in the country would be empty. The Rock and Roll Hall of Fame would disappear. The Tarot-card reading industry would collapse overnight!"

Austin's shoulders relaxed. "That's a relief."

"So if you die while you're mortal," Kayla said, "we won't disappear?"

"Guys," Will interrupted, "why don't you run to the Big House and tell Chiron that our . . . our *patient* is conscious. I'll bring him along in a minute. And, uh, see if you can disperse the crowd outside, okay? I don't want everybody rushing Apollo at once."

Kayla and Austin nodded sagely. As my children, they no doubt understood the importance of controlling the paparazzi.

As soon as they were gone, Will gave me an apologetic smile. "They're in shock. We all are. It'll take some time to get used to . . . whatever this is."

"You do not seem shocked," I said.

Will laughed under his breath. "I'm terrified. But one thing you learn as head counselor: you have to keep it together for everyone else. Let's get you on your feet."

It was not easy. I fell twice. My head spun, and my eyes felt as if they were being microwaved in their sockets. Recent dreams continued to churn in my brain like river silt, muddying my thoughts—the woman with the crown and the peace symbol, the man in the purple suit. *Lead me to the Oracle. I'll enjoy burning it down!*

The cabin began to feel stifling. I was anxious to get some fresh air.

One thing my sister, Artemis, and I agree on: every worthwhile pursuit is better outdoors than indoors. Music is best played under the dome of heaven. Poetry should be shared in the *agora*. Archery is definitely easier outside, as I can attest after that one time I tried target practice in my father's throne room. And driving the sun . . . well, that's not really an indoor sport either.

Leaning on Will for support, I stepped outside. Kayla and Austin had succeeded in shooing the crowd away. The only one waiting for me—oh, joy and happiness—was my young overlord, Meg, who had apparently now gained fame at camp as Crotchkicker McCaffrey.

She still wore Sally Jackson's hand-me-down green dress, though it was a bit dirtier now. Her leggings were ripped and torn. On her bicep, a line of butterfly bandages closed a nasty cut she must have gotten in the woods.

She took one look at me, scrunched up her face, and stuck out her tongue. "You look *yuck*."

"And you, Meg," I said, "are as charming as ever."

She adjusted her glasses until they were just crooked enough to be annoying. "Thought you were going to die."

"Glad to disappoint you."

"Nah." She shrugged. "You still owe me a year of service. We're bound, whether you like it or not!"

I sighed. It was ever so wonderful to be back in Meg's company.

"I suppose I should thank you. . . ." I had a hazy memory of my delirium in the forest, Meg carrying me along, the trees seeming to part before us. "How did you get us out of the woods?"

Her expression turned guarded. "Dunno. Luck." She jabbed a thumb at Will Solace. "From what he's been telling me, it's a good thing we got out before nightfall."

"Why?"

Will started to answer, then apparently thought better of it. "I should let Chiron explain. Come on."

I rarely visited Camp Half-Blood in winter. The last time had been three years ago, when a girl named Thalia Grace crash-landed my bus in the canoe lake.

I expected the camp to be sparsely populated. I knew

most demigods only came for the summer, leaving a small core of year-rounders during the school term—those who for various reasons found camp the only safe place they could live.

Still, I was struck by how few demigods I saw. If Cabin Seven was any indication, each god's cabin could hold beds for about twenty campers. That meant a maximum capacity of four hundred demigods—enough for several phalanxes or one really amazing yacht party.

Yet, as we walked across camp, I saw no more than a dozen people. In the fading light of sunset, a lone girl was scaling the climbing wall as lava flowed down either side. At the lake, a crew of three checked the rigging on the trireme.

Some campers had found reasons to be outside just so they could gawk at me. Over by the hearth, one young man sat polishing his shield, watching me in its reflective surface. Another fellow glared at me as he spliced barbed wire outside the Ares cabin. From the awkward way he walked, I assumed he was Sherman Yang of the recently kicked crotch.

In the doorway of the Hermes cabin, two girls giggled and whispered as I passed. Normally this sort of attention wouldn't have fazed me. My magnetism was understandably irresistible. But now my face burned. Me—the manly paragon of romance—reduced to a gawky, inexperienced boy!

I would have screamed at the heavens for this unfairness, but that would've been super-embarrassing.

We made our way through the fallow strawberry fields. Up on Half-Blood Hill, the Golden Fleece glinted in the lowest branch of a tall pine tree. Whiffs of steam rose from the head of Peleus, the guardian dragon coiled around the base of the trunk. Next to the tree, the Athena Parthenos looked angry red in the sunset. Or perhaps she just wasn't happy to see me. (Athena had never gotten over our little tiff during the Trojan War.)

Halfway down the hillside, I spotted the Oracle's cave, its entrance shrouded by thick burgundy curtains. The torches on either side stood unlit—usually a sign that my prophetess, Rachel Dare, was not in residence. I wasn't sure whether to be disappointed or relieved.

Even when she was not channeling prophecies, Rachel was a wise young lady. I had hoped to consult her about my problems. On the other hand, since her prophetic power had apparently stopped working (which I suppose in some *small* part was my fault), I wasn't sure Rachel would want to see me. She would expect explanations from her Main Man, and while I had invented *mansplaining* and was its foremost practitioner, I had no answers to give her.

The dream of the flaming bus stayed with me: the groovy crowned woman urging me to find the gates, the ugly mauve-suited man threatening to burn the Oracle.

Well . . . the cave was right there. I wasn't sure why the woman in the crown was having such trouble finding it, or why the ugly man would be so intent on burning its "gates," which amounted to nothing more than purple curtains.

Unless the dream was referring to something other than the Oracle of Delphi. . . .

I rubbed my throbbing temples. I kept reaching for memories that weren't there, trying to plunge into my vast lake of knowledge only to find it had been reduced to a kiddie pool. You simply can't do much with a kiddie pool brain.

On the porch of the Big House, a dark-haired young man was waiting for us. He wore faded black trousers, a Ramones T-shirt (bonus points for musical taste), and a black leather bomber jacket. At his side hung a Stygian iron sword.

"I remember you," I said. "Is it Nicholas, son of Hades?"

"Nico di Angelo." He studied me, his eyes sharp and colorless, like broken glass. "So it's true. You're completely mortal. There's an aura of death around you—a thick possibility of death."

Meg snorted. "Sounds like a weather forecast."

I did not find this amusing. Being face-to-face with a son of Hades, I recalled the many mortals I had sent to the Underworld with my plague arrows. It had always seemed like good clean fun—meting out richly deserved punishments for wicked deeds. Now, I began to understand the terror in my victims' eyes. I did not want an aura of death hanging over me. I definitely did not want to stand in judgment before Nico di Angelo's father.

Will put his hand on Nico's shoulder. "Nico, we need to have another talk about your people skills."

"Hey, I'm just stating the obvious. If this *is* Apollo, and he dies, we're all in trouble."

Will turned to me. "I apologize for my boyfriend."

Nico rolled his eyes. "Could you not—"

"Would you prefer *special guy?*" Will asked. "Or *significant other?*"

"Significant *annoyance*, in your case," Nico grumbled.

"Oh, I'll get you for that."

Meg wiped her dripping nose. "You guys fight a lot. I thought we were going to see a centaur."

"And here I am." The screen door opened. Chiron trotted out, ducking his head to avoid the doorframe.

From the waist up, he looked every bit the professor he often pretended to be in the mortal world. His brown wool jacket had patches on the elbows. His plaid dress shirt did not quite match his green tie. His beard was neatly trimmed, but his hair would have failed the tidiness inspection required for a proper rat's nest.

From the waist down, he was a white stallion.

My old friend smiled, though his eyes were stormy and distracted. "Apollo, it's good you are here. We need to talk about the disappearances."

11

Check your spam folder
The prophecies might be there
No? Well, I'm stumped. Bye

MEG GAWKED. "He—he really *is* a centaur."

"Well spotted," I said. "I suppose the lower body of a horse is what gave him away?"

She punched me in the arm.

"Chiron," I said, "this is Meg McCaffrey, my new master and wellspring of aggravation. You were saying something about disappearances?"

Chiron's tail flicked. His hooves clopped on the planks of the porch.

He was immortal, yet his visible age seemed to vary from century to century. I did not remember his whiskers ever being so gray, or the lines around his eyes so pronounced. Whatever was happening at camp must not have been helping his stress levels.

"Welcome, Meg." Chiron tried for a friendly tone, which I thought quite heroic, seeing as . . . well, *Meg*. "I understand you showed great bravery in the woods. You brought Apollo here despite many dangers. I'm glad to have you at Camp Half-Blood."

"Thanks," said Meg. "You're really tall. Don't you hit your head on light fixtures?"

Chiron chuckled. "Sometimes. If I want to be closer to human size, I have a magical wheelchair that allows me to compact my lower half into . . . Actually, that's not important now."

"Disappearances," I prompted. "What has disappeared?"

"Not *what*, but *who*," Chiron said. "Let's talk inside. Will, Nico, could you please tell the other campers we'll gather for dinner in one hour? I'll give everyone an update, then. In the meantime, no one should roam the camp alone. Use the buddy system."

"Understood." Will looked at Nico. "Will you be my buddy?"

"You are a dork," Nico announced.

The two of them strolled off bickering.

At this point, you may be wondering how I felt seeing my son with Nico di Angelo. I'll admit I did not understand Will's attraction to a child of Hades, but if the dark foreboding type was what made Will happy . . .

Oh. Perhaps some of you are wondering how I felt seeing him with a boyfriend rather than a girlfriend. If that's the case, *please*. We gods are not hung up about such things. I myself have had . . . let's see, thirty-three mortal girlfriends and eleven mortal boyfriends? I've lost count. My two greatest loves were, of course, Daphne and Hyacinthus, but when you're a god as popular as I am—

Hold on. Did I just tell you who I liked? I did, didn't I? Gods of Olympus, forget I mentioned their names! I am so embarrassed. Please don't say anything. In this mortal life, I've never been in love with *anyone*!

I am so confused.

Chiron led us into the living room, where comfy leather couches made a V facing the stone fireplace. Above the mantel, a stuffed leopard head was snoring contentedly.

"Is it alive?" Meg asked.

"Quite." Chiron trotted over to his wheelchair. "That's Seymour. If we speak quietly, we should be able to avoid waking him."

Meg immediately began exploring the living room. Knowing her, she was searching for small objects to throw at the leopard to wake him up.

Chiron settled into his wheelchair. He placed his rear legs into the false compartment of the seat, then backed up, magically compacting his equine hindquarters until he looked like a man sitting down. To complete the illusion, hinged front panels swung closed, giving him fake human legs. Normally those legs were fitted with slacks and loafers to augment his "professor" disguise, but today it seemed Chiron was going for a different look.

"That's new," I said.

Chiron glanced down at his shapely female mannequin legs, dressed in fishnet stockings and red sequined high heels. He sighed heavily. "I see the Hermes cabin have been watching *Rocky Horror Picture Show* again. I will have to have a chat with them."

Rocky Horror Picture Show brought back fond memories. I used to cosplay as Rocky at the midnight showings, because, naturally, the character's perfect physique was based on my own.

"Let me guess," I said. "Connor and Travis Stoll are the pranksters?"

From a nearby basket, Chiron grabbed a flannel blanket and spread it over his fake legs, though the ruby shoes still peeked out at the bottom. "Actually, Travis went off to college last autumn, which has mellowed Connor quite a bit."

Meg looked over from the old *Pac-Man* arcade game. "I poked that guy Connor in the eyes."

Chiron winced. "That's nice, dear. . . . At any rate, we have Julia Feingold and Alice Miyazawa now. They have taken up pranking duty. You'll meet them soon enough."

I recalled the girls who had been giggling at me from the Hermes cabin doorway. I felt myself blushing all over again.

Chiron gestured toward the couches. "Please sit."

Meg moved on from *Pac-Man* (having given the game twenty seconds of her time) and began literally climbing the wall. Dormant grapevines festooned the dining area— no doubt the work of my old friend Dionysus. Meg scaled one of the thicker trunks, trying to reach the Gorgon-hair chandelier.

"Ah, Meg," I said, "perhaps you should watch the orientation film while Chiron and I talk?"

"I know plenty," she said. "I talked to the campers while you were passed out. 'Safe place for modern demigods.' Blah, blah, blah."

"Oh, but the film is very good," I urged. "I shot it on a

tight budget in the 1950s, but some of the camera work was revolutionary. You should really—"

The grapevine peeled away from the wall. Meg crashed to the floor. She popped up completely unscathed, then spotted a platter of cookies on the sideboard. "Are those free?"

"Yes, child," Chiron said. "Bring the tea as well, would you?"

So we were stuck with Meg, who draped her legs over the couch's armrest, chomped on cookies, and threw crumbs at Seymour's snoring head whenever Chiron wasn't looking.

Chiron poured me a cup of Darjeeling. "I'm sorry Mr. D is not here to welcome you."

"Mr. Dee?" Meg asked.

"Dionysus," I explained. "The god of wine. Also the director of this camp."

Chiron handed me my tea. "After the battle with Gaea, I thought Mr. D might return to camp, but he never did. I hope he's all right."

The old centaur looked at me expectantly, but I had nothing to share. The last six months were a complete void; I had no idea what the other Olympians might be up to.

"I don't know anything," I admitted. I hadn't said those words very often in the last four millennia. They tasted bad. I sipped my tea, but that was no less bitter. "I'm a bit behind on the news. I was hoping you could fill me in."

Chiron did a poor job hiding his disappointment. "I see. . . ."

I realized he had been hoping for help and guidance—the

exact same things I needed from *him*. As a god, I was used to lesser beings relying on me—praying for this and pleading for that. But now that I was mortal, being relied upon was a little terrifying.

"So what is your crisis?" I asked. "You have the same look Cassandra had in Troy, or Jim Bowie at the Alamo—as if you're under siege."

Chiron did not dispute the comparison. He cupped his hands around his tea.

"You know that during the war with Gaea, the Oracle of Delphi stopped receiving prophecies. In fact, all known methods of divining the future suddenly failed."

"Because the original cave of Delphi was retaken," I said with a sigh, trying not to feel picked on.

Meg bounced a chocolate chip off Seymour the leopard's nose. "Oracle of Delphi. Percy mentioned that."

"Percy Jackson?" Chiron sat up. "Percy was with you?"

"For a time." I recounted our battle in the peach orchard and Percy's return to New York. "He said he would drive out this weekend if he could."

Chiron looked disheartened, as if my company alone wasn't good enough. Can you imagine?

"At any rate," he continued, "we hoped that once the war was over, the Oracle might start working again. When it did not . . . Rachel became concerned."

"Who's Rachel?" Meg asked.

"Rachel Dare," I said. "The Oracle."

"Thought the Oracle was a place."

"It is."

"Then Rachel is a place, and she stopped working?"

Had I still been a god, I would have turned her into a blue-belly lizard and released her into the wilderness never to be seen again. The thought soothed me.

"The original Delphi was a place in Greece," I told her. "A cavern filled with volcanic fumes, where people would come to receive guidance from my priestess, the Pythia."

"*Pythia.*" Meg giggled. "That's a funny word."

"Yes. Ha-ha. So the Oracle is both a place and a person. When the Greek gods relocated to America back in . . . what was it, Chiron, 1860?"

Chiron seesawed his hand. "More or less."

"I brought the Oracle here to continue speaking prophecies on my behalf. The power has passed down from priestess to priestess over the years. Rachel Dare is the present Oracle."

From the cookie platter, Meg plucked the only Oreo, which I had been hoping to have myself. "Mm-kay. Is it too late to watch that movie?"

"Yes," I snapped. "Now, the way I gained possession of the Oracle of Delphi in the first place was by killing this monster called Python who lived in the depths of the cavern."

"A python like the snake," Meg said.

"Yes and no. The snake species is named after Python the monster, who is also rather snaky, but who is much bigger and scarier and devours small girls who talk too much. At any rate, last August, while I was . . . indisposed, my ancient foe Python was released from Tartarus. He reclaimed the cave of Delphi. That's why the Oracle stopped working."

"But if the Oracle is in America now, why does it matter if some snake monster takes over its old cave?"

That was about the longest sentence I had yet heard her speak. She'd probably done it just to spite me.

"It's too much to explain," I said. "You'll just have to—"

"Meg." Chiron gave her one of his heroically tolerant smiles. "The original site of the Oracle is like the deepest taproot of a tree. The branches and leaves of prophecy may extend across the world, and Rachel Dare may be our loftiest branch, but if the taproot is strangled, the whole tree is endangered. With Python back in residence at his old lair, the spirit of the Oracle has been completely blocked."

"Oh." Meg made a face at me. "Why didn't you just say so?"

Before I could strangle her like the annoying taproot she was, Chiron refilled my teacup.

"The larger problem," he said, "is that we have no other source of prophecies."

"Who cares?" Meg asked. "So you don't know the future. Nobody knows the future."

"*Who cares?!*" I shouted. "Meg McCaffrey, prophecies are the catalysts for every important event—every quest or battle, disaster or miracle, birth or death. Prophecies don't simply foretell the future. They shape it! They *allow* the future to happen."

"I don't get it."

Chiron cleared his throat. "Imagine prophecies are flower seeds. With the right seeds, you can grow any garden you desire. Without seeds, no growth is possible."

"Oh." Meg nodded. "That would suck."

I found it strange that Meg, a street urchin and Dumpster warrior, would relate so well to garden metaphors, but Chiron was an excellent teacher. He had picked up on something about the girl . . . an impression that had been lurking in the back of my mind as well. I hoped I was wrong about what it meant, but with my luck, I would be right. I usually was.

"So where is Rachel Dare?" I asked. "Perhaps if I spoke with her . . . ?"

Chiron set down his tea. "Rachel planned to visit us during her winter vacation, but she never did. It might not mean anything. . . ."

I leaned forward. It was not unheard of for Rachel Dare to be late. She was artistic, unpredictable, impulsive, and rule-averse—all qualities I dearly admired. But it wasn't like her not to show up at all.

"Or?" I asked.

"Or it might be part of the larger problem," Chiron said. "Prophecies are not the only things that have failed. Travel and communication have become difficult in the last few months. We haven't heard from our friends at Camp Jupiter in weeks. No new demigods have arrived. Satyrs aren't reporting from the field. Iris messages no longer work."

"Iris what?" Meg asked.

"Two-way visions," I said. "A form of communication overseen by the rainbow goddess. Iris has always been flighty. . . ."

"Except that normal human communications are also on the fritz," Chiron said. "Of course, phones have always been dangerous for demigods—"

"Yeah, they attract monsters," Meg agreed. "I haven't used a phone in *forever*."

"A wise move," Chiron said. "But recently our phones have stopped working altogether. Mobile, landline, Internet . . . it doesn't seem to matter. Even the archaic form of communication known as *e-mail* is strangely unreliable. The messages simply don't arrive."

"Did you look in the junk folder?" I offered.

"I fear the problem is more complicated," Chiron said. "We have no communication with the outside world. We are alone and understaffed. You are the first newcomers in almost two months."

I frowned. "Percy Jackson mentioned nothing of this."

"I doubt Percy is even aware," Chiron said. "He's been busy with school. Winter is normally our quietest time. For a while, I was able to convince myself that the communication failures were nothing but an inconvenient happenstance. Then the disappearances started."

In the fireplace, a log slipped from the andiron. I may or may not have jumped in my seat.

"The disappearances, yes." I wiped drops of tea from my pants and tried to ignore Meg's snickering. "Tell me about those."

"Three in the last month," Chiron said. "First it was Cecil Markowitz from the Hermes cabin. One morning his bunk was simply empty. He didn't say anything about wanting to leave. No one saw him go. And in the past few weeks, no one has seen or heard from him."

"Children of Hermes do tend to sneak around," I offered.

"At first, that's what we thought," said Chiron. "But a

week later, Ellis Wakefield disappeared from the Ares cabin. Same story: empty bunk, no signs that he had either left on his own *or* was . . . ah, taken. Ellis was an impetuous young man. It was conceivable he might have charged off on some ill-advised adventure, but it made me uneasy. Then this morning we realized a third camper had vanished: Miranda Gardiner, head of the Demeter cabin. That was the worst news of all."

Meg swung her feet off the armrest. "Why is that the worst?"

"Miranda is one of our senior counselors," Chiron said. "She would never leave on her own without notice. She is too smart to be tricked away from camp, and too powerful to be forced. Yet something happened to her . . . something I can't explain."

The old centaur faced me. "Something is very wrong, Apollo. These problems may not be as alarming as the rise of Kronos or the awakening of Gaea, but in a way I find them even more unsettling, because I have never seen anything like this before."

I recalled my dream of the burning sun bus. I thought of the voices I'd heard in the woods, urging me to wander off and find their source.

"These demigods . . ." I said. "Before they disappeared, did they act unusual in any way? Did they report . . . hearing things?"

Chiron raised an eyebrow. "Not that I am aware of. Why?"

I was reluctant to say more. I didn't want to cause a panic without knowing what we were facing. When mortals panic, it can be an ugly scene, especially if they expect *me* to fix the problem.

Also, I will admit I felt a bit impatient. We had not yet addressed the most important issues—*mine*.

"It seems to me," I said, "that our first priority is to bend all the camp's resources to helping me regain my divine state. Then I can assist you with these other problems."

Chiron stroked his beard. "But what if the problems are connected, my friend? What if the only way to restore you to Olympus is by reclaiming the Oracle of Delphi, thus freeing the power of prophecy? What if Delphi is the key to it all?"

I had forgotten about Chiron's tendency to lay out obvious and logical conclusions that I tried to avoid thinking about. It was an infuriating habit.

"In my present state, that's impossible." I pointed at Meg. "Right now, my job is to serve this demigod, probably for a year. After I've done whatever tasks she assigns me, Zeus will judge that my sentence has been served, and I can once again become a god."

Meg pulled apart a Fig Newton. "I could order you to go to this Delphi place."

"No!" My voice cracked in midshriek. "You should assign me *easy* tasks—like starting a rock band, or just hanging out. Yes, hanging out is good."

Meg looked unconvinced. "Hanging out isn't a task."

"It is if you do it right. Camp Half-Blood can protect me while I hang out. After my year of servitude is up, I'll become a god. *Then* we can talk about how to restore Delphi."

Preferably, I thought, by ordering some demigods to undertake the quest for me.

"Apollo," Chiron said, "if demigods keep disappearing, we may not have a year. We may not have the strength to protect you. And, forgive me, but Delphi *is* your responsibility."

I tossed up my hands. "*I* wasn't the one who opened the Doors of Death and let Python out! Blame Gaea! Blame Zeus for his bad judgment! When the giants started to wake, I drew up a very clear *Twenty-Point Plan of Action to Protect Apollo and Also You Other Gods*, but he didn't even read it!"

Meg tossed half of her cookie at Seymour's head. "I still think it's your fault. Hey, look! He's awake!"

She said this as if the leopard had decided to wake up on his own rather than being beaned in the eye with a Fig Newton.

"*RARR*," Seymour complained.

Chiron wheeled his chair back from the table. "My dear, in that jar on the mantel, you'll find some Snausages. Why don't you feed him dinner? Apollo and I will wait on the porch."

We left Meg happily making three-point shots into Seymour's mouth with the treats.

Once Chiron and I reached the porch, he turned his wheelchair to face me. "She's an interesting demigod."

"*Interesting* is such a nonjudgmental term."

"She really summoned a karpos?"

"Well . . . the spirit appeared when she was in trouble. Whether she consciously summoned it, I don't know. She named him Peaches."

Chiron scratched his beard. "I have not seen a demigod with the power to summon grain spirits in a very long time. You know what it means?"

My feet began to quake. "I have my suspicions. I'm trying to stay positive."

"She guided you out of the woods," Chiron noted. "Without her—"

"Yes," I said. "Don't remind me."

It occurred to me that I'd seen that keen look in Chiron's eyes before—when he'd assessed Achilles's sword technique and Ajax's skill with a spear. It was the look of a seasoned coach scouting new talent. I'd never dreamed the centaur would look at *me* that way, as if I had something to prove to him, as if my mettle were untested. I felt so . . . so *objectified*.

"Tell me," Chiron said, "what did you hear in the woods?"

I silently cursed my big mouth. I should not have asked whether the missing demigods had heard anything strange.

I decided it was fruitless to hold back now. Chiron was more perceptive than your average horse-man. I told him what I'd experienced in the forest, and afterward in my dream.

His hands curled into his lap blanket. The bottom of it rose higher above his red sequined pumps. He looked about as worried as it is possible for a man to look while wearing fishnet stockings.

"We will have to warn the campers to stay away from the forest," he decided. "I do not understand what is happening, but I still maintain it *must* be connected to Delphi, and your present . . . ah, situation. The Oracle must be liberated from the monster Python. We must find a way."

I translated that easily enough: *I* must find a way.

Chiron must have read my desolate expression.

"Come, come, old friend," he said. "You have done it before. Perhaps you are not a god now, but the first time you killed Python it was no challenge at all! Hundreds of storybooks have praised the way you easily slew your enemy."

"Yes," I muttered. "Hundreds of storybooks."

I recalled some of those stories: I had killed Python without breaking a sweat. I flew to the mouth of the cave, called him out, unleashed an arrow, and *BOOM!*—one dead giant snake monster. I became Lord of Delphi, and we all lived happily ever after.

How did storytellers get the idea that I vanquished Python so quickly?

All right . . . possibly it's because I told them so. Still, the truth was rather different. For centuries after our battle, I had bad dreams about my old foe.

Now I was almost grateful for my imperfect memory. I could not recollect all of the nightmarish details of my fight with Python, but I *did* know he had been no pushover. I had needed all my godly strength, my divine powers, and the world's most deadly bow.

What chance would I have as a sixteen-year-old mortal with acne, hand-me-down clothes, and the nom de guerre Lester Papadopoulos? I was not going to charge off to Greece and get myself killed, thank you very much, especially not without my sun chariot or the ability to teleport. I'm sorry; gods do *not* fly commercial.

I tried to figure out how to explain this to Chiron in a calm, diplomatic way that did not involve stomping my feet or screaming. I was saved from the effort by the sound of a conch horn in the distance.

"That means dinner." The centaur forced a smile. "We will talk more later, eh? For now, let's celebrate your arrival."

12

Ode to a hot dog
With bug juice and tater chips
I got nothing, man

I WAS NOT IN THE MOOD TO CELEBRATE.

Especially sitting at a picnic table eating mortal food. With mortals.

The dining pavilion was pleasant enough. Even in winter, the camp's magical borders shielded us from the worst of the elements. Sitting outdoors in the warmth of the torches and braziers, I felt only slightly chilly. Long Island Sound glittered in the light of the moon. (Hello, Artemis. Don't bother to say hi.) On Half-Blood Hill, the Athena Parthenos glowed like the world's largest nightlight. Even the woods did not seem so creepy with the pine trees blanketed in soft silvery fog.

My dinner, however, was less than poetic. It consisted of hot dogs, potato chips, and a red liquid I was told was bug juice. I did not know why humans consumed bug juice, or from which type of bug it had been extracted, but it was the tastiest part of the meal, which was disconcerting.

I sat at the Apollo table with my children Austin, Kayla, and Will, plus Nico di Angelo. I could see no difference between my table and any of the other gods' tables. Mine should have been shinier and more elegant. It should have played music or recited poetry upon command. Instead it was just a slab of stone with benches on either side. I found the seating uncomfortable, though my offspring didn't seem to mind.

Austin and Kayla peppered me with questions about Olympus, the war with Gaea, and what it felt like to be a god and then a human. I knew they did not mean to be rude. As my children, they were inherently inclined to the utmost grace. However, their questions were painful reminders of my fallen status.

Besides, as the hours passed, I remembered less and less about my divine life. It was alarming how fast my cosmically perfect neurons had deteriorated. Once, each memory had been like a high-definition audio file. Now those recordings were on wax cylinders. And believe me, I remember wax cylinders. They did not last long in the sun chariot.

Will and Nico sat shoulder to shoulder, bantering good-naturedly. They were so cute together it made me feel desolate. It jogged my memories of those few short golden months I'd shared with Hyacinthus before the jealousy, before the horrible accident . . .

"Nico," I said at last, "shouldn't you be sitting at the Hades table?"

He shrugged. "Technically, yes. But if I sit alone at my table, strange things happen. Cracks open in the floor. Zombies crawl out and start roaming around. It's a mood disorder. I can't control it. That's what I told Chiron."

"And is it true?" I asked.

Nico smiled thinly. "I have a note from my doctor."

Will raised his hand. "I'm his doctor."

"Chiron decided it wasn't worth arguing about," Nico said. "As long as I sit at a table with other people, like . . . oh, these guys for instance . . . the zombies stay away. Everybody's happier."

Will nodded serenely. "It's the strangest thing. Not that Nico would ever misuse his powers to get what he wants."

"Of course not," Nico agreed.

I glanced across the dining pavilion. As per camp tradition, Meg had been placed with the children of Hermes, since her godly parentage had not yet been determined. Meg didn't seem to mind. She was busy re-creating the Coney Island Hot Dog Eating Contest all by herself. The other two girls, Julia and Alice, watched her with a mixture of fascination and horror.

Across the table from her sat an older skinny boy with curly brown hair—Connor Stoll, I deduced, though I'd never been able to tell him apart from his older brother, Travis. Despite the darkness, Connor wore sunglasses, no doubt to protect his eyes from a repeat poking. I also noted that he wisely kept his hands away from Meg's mouth.

In the entire pavilion, I counted nineteen campers. Most sat alone at their respective tables—Sherman Yang for Ares; a girl I did not know for Aphrodite; another girl for Demeter. At the Nike table, two dark-haired young ladies who were obviously twins conversed over a war map. Chiron himself, again in full centaur form, stood at the head table, sipping his bug juice as he chatted with two satyrs, but their mood was subdued. The goat-men kept glancing at me, then eating their silverware, as satyrs tend to do when nervous. Half a dozen gorgeous dryads moved between the tables, offering food and drink, but I was so preoccupied I couldn't fully appreciate their beauty. Even more tragic: I felt too embarrassed to flirt with them. What was *wrong* with me?

I studied the campers, hoping to spot some potential servants . . . I mean new friends. Gods always like to keep a few strong veteran demigods handy to throw into battle, send on dangerous quests, or pick the lint off our togas. Unfortunately, no one at dinner jumped out at me as a likely minion. I longed for a bigger pool of talent.

"Where are the . . . others?" I asked Will.

I wanted to say *the A-List*, but I thought that might be taken the wrong way.

Will took a bite of his pizza. "Were you looking for somebody in particular?"

"What about the ones who went on that quest with the boat?"

Will and Nico exchanged a look that might have meant, *Here we go.* I suppose they got asked a lot about the seven legendary demigods who had fought side by side with the gods against Gaea's giants. It pained me that I had not gotten to see those heroes again. After any major battle, I liked to get a group photo—along with exclusive rights to compose epic ballads about their exploits.

"Well," Nico started, "you saw Percy. He and Annabeth

are spending their senior year in New York. Hazel and Frank are at Camp Jupiter doing the Twelfth Legion thing."

"Ah, yes." I tried to bring up a clear mental picture of Camp Jupiter, the Roman enclave near Berkeley, California, but the details were hazy. I could only remember my conversations with Octavian, the way he'd turned my head with his flattery and promises. That stupid boy . . . it was his fault I was here.

A voice whispered in the back of my mind. This time I thought it might be my conscience: *Who was the stupid boy? It wasn't Octavian.*

"Shut up," I murmured.

"What?" Nico asked.

"Nothing. Continue."

"Jason and Piper are spending the school year in Los Angeles with Piper's dad. They took Coach Hedge, Mellie, and Little Chuck with them."

"Uh-huh." I did not know those last three names, so I decided they probably weren't important. "And the seventh hero . . . Leo Valdez?"

Nico raised his eyebrows. "You remember his name?"

"Of course! He invented the Valdezinator. Oh, what a musical instrument! I barely had time to master its major scales before Zeus zapped me at the Parthenon. If anyone could help me, it would be Leo Valdez."

Nico's expression tightened with annoyance. "Well, Leo isn't here. He died. Then he came back to life. And if I see him again, I'll kill him."

Will elbowed him. "No, you won't." He turned to me.

"During the fight with Gaea, Leo and his bronze dragon, Festus, disappeared in a midair fiery explosion."

I shivered. After so many centuries driving the sun chariot, the term *midair fiery explosion* did not sit well with me.

I tried to remember the last time I'd seen Leo Valdez on Delos, when he'd traded the Valdezinator for information. . . .

"He was looking for the physician's cure," I recalled, "the way to bring someone back from the dead. I suppose he planned all along to sacrifice himself?"

"Yep," Will said. "He got rid of Gaea in the explosion, but we all assumed he died too."

"Because he *did*," Nico said.

"Then, a few days later," Will continued, "this scroll came fluttering into camp on the wind. . . ."

"I still have it." Nico rummaged through the pockets of his bomber jacket. "I look at it whenever I want to get angry."

He produced a thick parchment scroll. As soon as he spread it on the table, a flickering hologram appeared above the surface: Leo Valdez, looking impish as usual with his dark wispy hair, his mischievous grin, and his diminutive stature. (Of course, the hologram was only three inches tall, but even in real life Leo was not much more imposing.) His jeans, blue work shirt, and tool belt were speckled with machine oil.

"Hey, guys!" Leo spread his arms for a hug. "Sorry to leave you like that. Bad news: I died. Good news: I got better! I had to go rescue Calypso. We're both fine now. We're taking Festus to—" The image guttered like a flame in a strong breeze, disrupting Leo's voice. "Back as soon as—" Static. "Cook tacos when—" More static. "*¡Vaya con queso!* Love ya!*" The image winked out.

"That's all we got," Nico complained. "And that was in August. We have no idea what he was planning, where he is now, or whether he's still safe. Jason and Piper spent most of September looking for him until Chiron finally insisted they go start their school year."

"Well," I said, "it sounds like Leo was planning to cook tacos. Perhaps that took longer than he anticipated. And *vaya con queso* . . . I believe he is admonishing us to *go with cheese*, which is always sound advice."

This did not seem to reassure Nico.

"I don't like being in the dark," he muttered.

An odd complaint for a child of Hades, but I understood what he meant. I, too, was curious to know the fate of Leo Valdez. Once upon a time, I could have divined his whereabouts as easily as you might check a Facebook timeline, but now I could only stare at the sky and wonder when a small impish demigod might appear with a bronze dragon and a plate of tacos.

And if Calypso was involved . . . that complicated things. The sorceress and I had a rocky history, but even *I* had to admit she was beguiling. If she'd captured Leo's heart, it was entirely possible he had gotten sidetracked. Odysseus spent seven years with her before returning home.

Whatever the case, it seemed unlikely that Valdez would be back in time to help me. My quest to master the Valdezinator's arpeggios would have to wait.

Kayla and Austin had been very quiet, following our

conversation with wonder and amazement. (My words have that effect on people.)

Now Kayla scooted toward me. "What did you guys talk about in the Big House? Chiron told you about the disappearances . . . ?"

"Yes." I tried to avoid looking in the direction of the woods. "We discussed the situation."

"And?" Austin spread his fingers on the table. "What's going on?"

I didn't want to talk about it. I didn't want them to see my fear.

I wished my head would stop pounding. On Olympus, headaches were so much easier to cure. Hephaestus simply split one's skull open and extracted whatever newborn god or goddess happened to be banging around in there. In the mortal world, my options were more limited.

"I need time to think about it," I said. "Perhaps in the morning I'll have some of my godly powers back."

Austin leaned forward. In the torchlight, his cornrows seemed to twist into new DNA patterns. "Is that how it works? Your strength comes back over time?"

"I—I think so." I tried to remember my years of servitude with Admetus and Laomedon, but I could barely conjure their names and faces. My contracting memory terrified me. It made each moment of the present balloon in size and importance, reminding me that time for mortals was limited.

"I have to get stronger," I decided. "I *must*."

Kayla squeezed my hand. Her archer's fingers were rough

and calloused. "It's okay, Apollo . . . Dad. We'll help you."

Austin nodded. "Kayla's right. We're in this together. If anybody gives you trouble, Kayla will shoot them. Then I'll curse them so bad they'll be speaking in rhyming couplets for weeks."

My eyes watered. Not so long ago—like this morning, for instance—the idea of these young demigods being able to help me would have struck me as ridiculous. Now their kindness moved me more than a hundred sacrificial bulls. I couldn't recall the last time someone had cared about me enough to curse my enemies with rhyming couplets.

"Thank you," I managed.

I could not add *my children*. It didn't seem right. These demigods were my protectors and my family, but for the present I could not think of myself as their father. A father should do more—a father should give more to his children than he takes. I have to admit that this was a novel idea for me. It made me feel even worse than before.

"Hey . . ." Will patted my shoulder. "It's not so bad. At least with everybody being on high alert, we might not have to do Harley's obstacle course tomorrow."

Kayla muttered an ancient Greek curse. If I had been a *proper* godly father, I would have washed her mouth out with olive oil.

"I forgot all about that," she said. "They'll *have* to cancel it, won't they?"

I frowned. "What obstacle course? Chiron mentioned nothing about this."

I wanted to object that my entire day had been an

obstacle course. Surely they couldn't expect me to do their camp activities as well. Before I could say as much, one of the satyrs blew a conch horn at the head table.

Chiron raised his arms for attention.

"Campers!" His voice filled the pavilion. He could be quite impressive when he wanted to be. "I have a few announcements, including news about tomorrow's three-legged death race!"

13

Three-legged death race
Five terrible syllables
Oh, gods. Please not Meg

IT WAS ALL HARLEY'S FAULT.

After addressing the disappearance of Miranda Gardiner—"As a precautionary measure, please stay away from the woods until we know more"—Chiron called forward the young son of Hephaestus to explain how the three-legged death race would work. It quickly became apparent that Harley had masterminded the whole project. And, really, the idea was so horrifying, it could only have sprung from the mind of an eight-year-old boy.

I confess I lost track of the specifics after he explained the exploding chain-saw Frisbees.

"And they'll be like, ZOOM!" He bounced up and down with excitement. "And then BUZZ! And POW!" He pantomimed all sorts of chaos with his hands. "You have to be really quick or you'll die, and it's awesome!"

The other campers grumbled and shifted on their benches.

Chiron raised his hand for silence. "Now, I know there were problems last time," he said, "but fortunately our healers in the Apollo cabin were able to reattach Paolo's arms."

At a table in back, a muscular teen boy rose and began ranting in what I thought was Portuguese. He wore a white tank top over his dark chest, and I could see faint white scars around the tops of his biceps. Cursing rapidly, he pointed at Harley, the Apollo cabin, and pretty much everyone else.

"Ah, thank you, Paolo," Chiron said, clearly baffled. "I'm glad you are feeling better."

Austin leaned toward me and whispered, "Paolo understands English okay, but he only speaks Portuguese. At least, that's what he claims. None of us can understand a word he says."

I didn't understand Portuguese either. Athena had been lecturing us for years about how Mount Olympus might migrate to Brazil someday, and we should all be prepared for the possibility. She'd even bought the gods Berlitz Portuguese DVDs for Saturnalia presents, but what does Athena know?

"Paolo seems agitated," I noted.

Will shrugged. "He's lucky he's a fast healer—son of Hebe, goddess of youth, and all that."

"You're staring," Nico noted.

"I am not," Will said. "I am merely assessing how well Paolo's arms are functioning after surgery."

"Hmph."

Paolo finally sat down. Chiron went through a long list of other injuries they had experienced during the first three-legged death race, all of which he hoped to avoid this time: second-degree burns, burst eardrums, a pulled groin, and two cases of chronic Irish step dancing.

The lone demigod at the Athena table raised his hand.

"Chiron, just going to throw this out there. . . . We've had three campers disappear. Is it really wise to be running a dangerous obstacle course?"

Chiron gave him a pained smile. "An excellent question, Malcolm, but this course will not take you into the woods, which we believe is the most hazardous area. The satyrs, dryads, and I will continue to investigate the disappearances. We will not rest until our missing campers are found. In the meantime, however, this three-legged race can foster important team-building skills. It also expands our understanding of the Labyrinth."

The word smacked me in the face like Ares's body odor. I turned to Austin. "The Labyrinth? As in *Daedalus's* Labyrinth?"

Austin nodded, his fingers worrying the ceramic camp beads around his neck. I had a sudden memory of his mother, Latricia—the way she used to fiddle with her cowry necklace when she lectured at Oberlin. Even *I* learned things from Latricia Lake's music theory class, though I had found her distractingly beautiful.

"During the war with Gaea," Austin said, "the maze reopened. We've been trying to map it ever since."

"That's impossible," I said. "Also insane. The Labyrinth is a malevolent sentient creation! It can't be mapped or trusted."

As usual, I could only draw on random bits and pieces of my memories, but I was fairly certain I spoke the truth. I remembered Daedalus. Back in the old days, the king of Crete had ordered him to build a maze to contain the monstrous Minotaur. But, oh no, a simple maze wasn't *good* enough for a brilliant inventor like Daedalus. He had to make his Labyrinth self-aware and self-expanding. Over the centuries, it had honeycombed under the planet's surface like an invasive root system.

Stupid brilliant inventors.

"It's different now," Austin told me. "Since Daedalus died . . . I don't know. It's hard to describe. Doesn't feel so evil. Not quite as deadly."

"Oh, that's hugely reassuring. So of course you decided to do three-legged races through it."

Will coughed. "The other thing, Dad . . . Nobody wants to disappoint Harley."

I glanced at the head table. Chiron was still holding forth about the virtues of team building while Harley bounced up and down. I could see why the other campers might adopt the boy as their unofficial mascot. He was a cute little pipsqueak, even if he was scarily buff for an eight-year-old. His grin was infectious. His enthusiasm seemed to lift the mood of the entire group. Still, I recognized the mad gleam in his eyes. It was the same look his father, Hephaestus, got whenever he invented some automaton that would later go berserk and start destroying cities.

"Also keep in mind," Chiron was saying, "that none of the unfortunate disappearances has been linked to the Labyrinth. Remain with your partner and you should be safe . . . at least, as safe as one can be in a three-legged death race."

"Yeah," Harley said. "Nobody has even *died* yet." He sounded disappointed, as if he wanted us to try harder.

"In the face of a crisis," Chiron said, "it's important to

stick to our regular activities. We must stay alert and in top condition. Our missing campers would expect no less from us. Now, as to the teams for the race, you will be allowed to choose your partner—"

There followed a sort of piranha attack of campers lunging toward each other to grab their preferred teammate. Before I could contemplate my options, Meg McCaffrey pointed at me from across the pavilion, her expression exactly like Uncle Sam's in the recruitment poster.

Of course, I thought. Why should my luck improve now?

Chiron struck his hoof against the floor. "All right, everyone, settle down! The race will be tomorrow afternoon. Thank you, Harley, for your hard work on the . . . um, various lethal surprises in store."

"BLAM!" Harley ran back to the Hephaestus table to join his older sister, Nyssa.

"This brings us to our other news," Chiron said. "As you may have heard, two special newcomers joined us today. First, please welcome the god Apollo!"

Normally this was my cue to stand up, spread my arms, and grin as radiant light shone around me. The adoring crowd would applaud and toss flowers and chocolate bonbons at my feet.

This time I received no applause—just nervous looks. I had a strange, uncharacteristic impulse to slide lower in my seat and pull my coat over my head. I restrained myself through heroic effort.

Chiron struggled to maintain his smile. "Now, I know this is unusual," he said, "but gods *do* become mortal from time to time. You should not be overly alarmed. Apollo's presence among us could be a good omen, a chance for us to . . ." He seemed to lose track of his own argument. "Ah . . . do something good. I'm sure the best course of action will become clear in time. For now, please make Apollo feel at home. Treat him as you would any other new camper."

At the Hermes table, Connor Stoll raised his hand. "Does that mean the Ares cabin should stick Apollo's head in a toilet?"

At the Ares table, Sherman Yang snorted. "We don't do that to everyone, Connor. Just the newbies who deserve it."

Sherman glanced at Meg, who was obliviously finishing her last hot dog. The wispy black whiskers at the sides of her mouth were now frosted with mustard.

Connor Stoll grinned back at Sherman—a conspiratorial look if ever I saw one. That's when I noticed the open backpack at Connor's feet. Peeking from the top was something that looked like a net.

The implication sank in: two boys whom Meg had humiliated, preparing for payback. I didn't have to be Nemesis to understand the allure of revenge. Still . . . I felt an odd desire to warn Meg.

I tried to catch her eye, but she remained focused on her dinner.

"Thank you, Sherman," Chiron continued. "It's good to know you won't be giving the god of archery a swirly. As for the rest of you, we will keep you posted on our guest's situation. I'm sending two of our finest satyrs, Millard and Herbert"—he gestured to the satyrs on his left—"to hand-deliver a message to Rachel Dare in New York. With any luck, she will be able to join us soon and help determine how we can best assist Apollo."

There was some grumbling about this. I caught the words *Oracle* and *prophecies*. At a nearby table, a girl muttered to herself in Italian: *The blind leading the blind.*

I glared at her, but the young lady was quite beautiful. She was perhaps two years older than I (mortally speaking), with dark pixie hair and devastatingly fierce almond eyes. I may have blushed.

I turned back to my tablemates. "Um . . . yes, satyrs. Why not send that other satyr, the friend of Percy's?"

"Grover?" Nico asked. "He's in California. The whole Council of Cloven Elders is out there, meeting about the drought."

"Oh." My spirits fell. I remembered Grover as being quite resourceful, but if he was dealing with California's natural disasters, he was unlikely to be back anytime in the next decade.

"Finally," Chiron said, "we welcome a new demigod to camp—Meg McCaffrey!"

She wiped her mouth and stood.

Next to her, Alice Miyazawa said, "Stand up, Meg."

Julia Feingold laughed.

At the Ares table, Sherman Yang rose. "Now *this* one—this one deserves a special welcome. What do you think, Connor?"

Connor reached into his backpack. "I think maybe the canoe lake."

I started to say, "Meg—"

Then all Hades broke loose.

Sherman Yang strode toward Meg. Connor Stoll pulled out a golden net and threw it over her head. Meg yelped and tried to squirm free, while some of the campers chanted, "Dunk—her! Dunk—her!" Chiron did his best to shout them down: "Now, demigods, wait a moment!"

A guttural howl interrupted the proceedings. From the top of the colonnade, a blur of chubby flesh, leafy wings, and linen diaper hurtled downward and landed on Sherman Yang's back, knocking him face-first into the stone floor. Peaches the karpos stood and wailed, beating his chest. His eyes glowed green with anger. He launched himself at Connor Stoll, locked his plump legs around the demigod's neck, and began pulling out Connor's hair with his claws.

"Get it off!" Connor wailed, thrashing blindly around the pavilion. "Get it off!"

Slowly the other demigods overcame their shock. Several drew swords.

"*C'è un karpos!*" yelled the Italian girl.

"Kill it!" said Alice Miyazawa.

"No!" I cried.

Normally such a command from me would've initiated a prison lockdown situation, with all the mortals dropping to their bellies to await my further orders. Alas, now I was a mere mortal with a squeaky adolescent voice.

I watched in horror as my own daughter Kayla nocked an arrow in her bow.

"Peaches, get off him!" Meg screamed. She untangled herself from the net, threw it down, then ran toward Connor.

The karpos hopped off Connor's neck. He landed at

Meg's feet, baring his fangs and hissing at the other campers who had formed a loose semicircle with weapons drawn.

"Meg, get out of the way," said Nico di Angelo. "That
thing is dangerous."

"No!" Meg's voice was shrill. "Don't kill him!"

Sherman Yang rolled over, groaning. His face looked
worse than it probably was—a gash on the forehead can
produce a shocking amount of blood—but the sight steeled
the resolve of the other campers. Kayla drew her bow. Julia
Feingold unsheathed a dagger.

"Wait!" I pleaded.

What happened next, a lesser mind could never have
processed.

Julia charged. Kayla shot her arrow.

Meg thrust out her hands and faint gold light flashed
between her fingers. Suddenly young McCaffrey was holding two swords—each a curved blade in the old Thracian
style, *siccae* made from Imperial gold. I had not seen such
weapons since the fall of the Rome. They seemed to have
appeared from nowhere, but my long experience with magic
items told me they must have been summoned from the
crescent rings Meg always wore.

Both her blades whirled. Meg simultaneously sliced
Kayla's arrow out of the air and disarmed Julia, sending her
dagger skittering across the floor.

"What the Hades?" Connor demanded. His hair had
been pulled out in chunks so he looked like an abused doll.
"Who *is* this kid?"

Peaches crouched at Meg's side, snarling, as Meg fended
off the confused and enraged demigods with her two swords.

My vision must have been better than the average mortal's, because I saw the glowing sign first—a light shining above Meg's head.

When I recognized the symbol, my heart turned to lead. I hated what I saw, but I thought I should point it out. "Look."

The others seemed confused. Then the glow became brighter: a holographic golden sickle with a few sheaves of wheat, rotating just above Meg McCaffrey.

A boy in the crowd gasped. "She's a communist!"

A girl who'd been sitting at Cabin Four's table gave him a disgusted sneer. "No, Damien, that's my *mom's* symbol." Her face went slack as the truth sank in. "Uh, which means . . . it's *her* mom's symbol."

My head spun. I did not want this knowledge. I did not want to serve a demigod with Meg's parentage. But now I understood the crescents on Meg's rings. They were not moons; they were sickle blades. As the only Olympian present, I felt I should make her title official.

"My friend is no longer unclaimed," I announced.

The other demigods knelt in respect, some more reluctantly than others.

"Ladies and gentlemen," I said, my voice as bitter as Chiron's tea, "please give it up for Meg McCaffrey, daughter of Demeter."

14

You've got to be kid—
Well, crud, what just happened there?
I ran out of syl—

NO ONE KNEW WHAT TO MAKE OF MEG.

I couldn't blame them.

The girl made even less sense to me now that I knew who her mother was.

I'd had my suspicions, yes, but I'd hoped to be proven wrong. Being right so much of the time was a terrible burden.

Why would I dread a child of Demeter?

Good question.

Over the past day, I had been doing my best to piece together my remembrances of the goddess. Once Demeter had been my favorite aunt. That first generation of gods could be a stuffy bunch (I'm looking at you, Hera, Hades, Dad), but Demeter had always been a kind and loving presence—except when she was destroying mankind through pestilence and famine, but everyone has their bad days.

Then I made the mistake of dating one of her daughters. I think her name was Chrysothemis, but you'll have to excuse me if I'm wrong. Even when I was a god, I had trouble remembering the names of all my exes. The young woman sang a harvest song at one of my Delphic festivals. Her voice was so beautiful, I fell in love. True, I fell in love with each year's winner and the runners-up, but what can I say? I'm a sucker for a melodious voice.

Demeter did not approve. Ever since her daughter Persephone had been kidnapped by Hades, she'd been a little touchy about her children dating gods.

At any rate, she and I had words. We reduced a few mountains to rubble. We laid waste to a few city-states. You know how family arguments can get. Finally we settled into an uneasy truce, but since then I'd made a point to steer clear of Demeter's children.

Now here I was—a servant to Meg McCaffrey, the most ragamuffin daughter of Demeter ever to swing a sickle.

I wondered who Meg's father had been to attract the attention of the goddess. Demeter rarely fell in love with mortals. Meg was unusually powerful, too. Most children of Demeter could do little more than make crops grow and keep bacterial fungi at bay. Dual-wielding golden blades and summoning karpoi—that was top-shelf stuff.

All of this went through my mind as Chiron dispersed the crowd, urging everyone to put away their weapons. Since head counselor Miranda Gardiner was missing, Chiron asked Billie Ng, the only other camper from Demeter, to escort Meg to Cabin Four. The two girls made a quick retreat, Peaches bouncing along excitedly behind them. Meg shot me a worried look.

Not sure what else to do, I gave her two thumbs-up. "See you tomorrow!"

She seemed less than encouraged as she disappeared in the darkness.

Will Solace tended to Sherman Yang's head injuries. Kayla and Austin stood over Connor, debating the need for a hair graft. This left me alone to make my way back to the Me cabin.

I lay on my sick cot in the middle of the room and stared at the ceiling beams. I thought again about what a depressingly simple, utterly mortal place this was. How did my children stand it? Why did they not keep a blazing altar, and decorate the walls with hammered gold reliefs celebrating my glory?

When I heard Will and the others coming back, I closed my eyes and pretended to be asleep. I could not face their questions or kindnesses, their attempts to make me feel at home when I clearly did not belong.

As they came in the door, they got quiet.

"Is he okay?" whispered Kayla.

Austin said, "Would you be, if you were him?"

A moment of silence.

"Try to get some sleep, guys," Will advised.

"This is crazy weird," Kayla said. "He looks so . . . human."

"We'll watch out for him," Austin said. "We're all he's got now."

I held back a sob. I couldn't bear their concern. Not being able to reassure them, or even disagree with them, made me feel very small.

A blanket was draped over me.

Will said, "Sleep well, Apollo."

Perhaps it was his persuasive voice, or the fact that I was more exhausted than I had been in centuries. Immediately, I drifted into unconsciousness.

Thank the remaining eleven Olympians, I had no dreams.

I woke in the morning feeling strangely refreshed. My chest no longer hurt. My nose no longer felt like a water balloon attached to my face. With the help of my offspring (*cabin mates*—I will call them cabin mates), I managed to master the arcane mysteries of the shower, the toilet, and the sink. The toothbrush was a shock. The last time I was mortal, there had been no such thing. And under-arm deodorant—what a ghastly idea that I should need enchanted salve to keep my armpits from producing stench!

When I was done with my morning ablutions and dressed in clean clothes from the camp store—sneakers, jeans, an orange Camp Half-Blood T-shirt, and a comfy winter coat of flannel wool—I felt almost optimistic. Perhaps I could survive this human experience.

I perked up even more when I discovered bacon.

Oh, gods—bacon! I promised myself that once I achieved immortality again, I would assemble the Nine Muses and together we would create an ode, a hymnal to the power of bacon, which would move the heavens to tears and cause rapture across the universe.

Bacon is good.

Yes—that may be the title of the song: "Bacon Is Good."

Seating for breakfast was less formal than dinner. We filled our trays at a buffet line and were allowed to sit wherever we wished. I found this delightful. (Oh, what a sad commentary on my new mortal mind that I, who once dictated the course of nations, should get excited about open seating.) I took my tray and found Meg, who was sitting by herself on the edge of the pavilion's retaining wall, dangling her feet over the side and watching the waves at the beach.

"How are you?" I asked.

Meg nibbled on a waffle. "Yeah. Great."

"You are a powerful demigod, daughter of Demeter."

"Mm-hm."

If I could trust my understanding of human responses, Meg did not seem thrilled.

"Your cabin mate, Billie . . . Is she nice?"

"Sure. All good."

"And Peaches?"

She looked at me sideways. "Disappeared overnight. Guess he only shows up when I'm in danger."

"Well, that's an appropriate time for him to show up."

"Ap-pro-pri-ate." Meg touched a waffle square for each syllable. "Sherman Yang had to get seven stitches."

I glanced over at Sherman, who sat at a safe distance across the pavilion, glaring daggers at Meg. A nasty red zig-zag ran down the side of his face.

"I wouldn't worry," I told Meg. "Ares's children like scars. Besides, Sherman wears the Frankenstein look rather well."

The corner of her mouth twitched, but her gaze remained far away. "Our cabin has a grass floor—like, *green* grass. There's a huge oak tree in the middle, holding up the ceiling."

"Is that bad?"

"I have allergies."

"Ah . . ." I tried to imagine the tree in her cabin. Once upon a time, Demeter had had a sacred grove of oaks. I remembered she'd gotten quite angry when a mortal prince tried to cut it down.

A sacred grove . . .

Suddenly the bacon in my stomach expanded, wrapping around my organs.

Meg gripped my arm. Her voice was a distant buzz. I only heard the last, most important word: "—Apollo?"

I stirred. "What?"

"You blanked out." She scowled. "I said your name six times."

"You did?"

"Yeah. Where did you go?"

I could not explain. I felt as if I'd been standing on the deck of a ship when an enormous, dark, and dangerous shape passed beneath the hull—a shape almost discernible, then simply gone.

"I—I don't know. Something about trees. . . ."

"Trees," Meg said.

"It's probably nothing."

It *wasn't* nothing. I couldn't shake the image from my dreams: the crowned woman urging me to find the gates. That woman wasn't Demeter—at least, I didn't think so. But the idea of sacred trees stirred a memory within me . . . something very old, even by *my* standards.

I didn't want to talk about this with Meg, not until I'd had time to reflect. She had enough to worry about. Besides, after last night, my new young master made me more apprehensive than ever.

I glanced at the rings on her middle fingers. "So yesterday . . . those swords. And don't do that thing."

Meg's eyebrows furrowed. "What thing?"

"That thing where you shut down and refuse to talk. Your face turns to cement."

She gave me a furious pout. "It does not. I've got swords. I fight with them. So what?"

"So it might have been nice to know that earlier, when we were in combat with plague spirits."

"You said it yourself: those spirits couldn't be killed."

"You're sidestepping." I knew this because it was a tactic I had mastered centuries ago. "The style you fight in, with two curved blades, is the style of a *dimachaerus*, a gladiator from the late Roman Empire. Even back then, it was rare—possibly the most difficult fighting style to master, and one of the most deadly."

Meg shrugged. It was an eloquent shrug, but it did not offer much in the way of explanation.

"Your swords are Imperial gold," I said. "That would indicate *Roman* training, and mark you as a good prospect for Camp Jupiter. Yet your mother is Demeter, the goddess in her Greek form, not Ceres."

"How do you know?"

"Aside from the fact that I was a god? Demeter claimed you here at Camp Half-Blood. That was no accident. Also, her older Greek form is much more powerful. You, Meg, are powerful."

Her expression turned so guarded I expected Peaches to hurtle from the sky and start pulling out chunks of my hair.

"I never met my mom," she said. "I didn't know who she was."

"Then where did you get the swords? Your father?"

Meg tore her waffle into tiny pieces. "No. . . . My step-dad raised me. He gave me these rings."

"Your stepfather. Your stepfather gave you rings that turn into Imperial golden swords. What sort of man—"

"A good man," she snapped.

I noted the steel in Meg's voice and let the subject rest. I sensed a great tragedy in her past. Also, I feared that if I pressed my questions, I might find those golden blades at my neck.

"I'm sorry," I said.

"Mm-hm." Meg tossed a piece of waffle into the air. Out of nowhere, one of the camp's cleaning harpies swooped down like a two-hundred-pound kamikaze chicken, snatched up the food, and flew away.

Meg continued as if nothing had happened. "Let's just get through today. We've got the race after lunch."

A shiver ran down my neck. The last thing I wanted was to be strapped to Meg McCaffrey in the Labyrinth, but I managed to avoid screaming.

"Don't worry about the race," I said. "I have a plan for how to win it."

She raised an eyebrow. "Yeah?"

"Or rather, I *will* have a plan by this afternoon. All I need is a little time—"

Behind us, the conch horn blew.

"Morning boot camp!" Sherman Yang bellowed. "Let's go, you special snowflakes! I want you all in tears by lunchtime!"

15

Practice makes perfect
Ha, ha, ha, I don't think so
Ignore my sobbing

I WISHED I HAD A DOCTOR'S NOTE. I wanted to be excused from PE.

Honestly, I will never understand you mortals. You try to maintain good physical shape with push-ups, sit-ups, five-mile runs, obstacle courses, and other hard work that involves sweating. All the while, you know it is a losing battle. Eventually your weak, limited-use bodies will deteriorate and fail, giving you wrinkles, sagging parts, and old-person breath.

It's horrific! If I want to change shape, or age, or gender, or species, I simply wish it to happen and—*ka-bam!*—I am a young, large, female three-toed sloth. No amount of push-ups will accomplish that. I simply don't see the logic in your constant struggles. Exercise is nothing more than a depressing reminder that one is not a god.

By the end of Sherman Yang's boot camp, I was gasping and drenched in sweat. My muscles felt like quivering columns of gelatinous dessert.

I did *not* feel like a special snowflake (though my

mother, Leto, always assured me I was one), and I was sorely tempted to accuse Sherman of not treating me as such.

I grumbled about this to Will. I asked where the old head counselor of Ares had gone. Clarisse La Rue I could at least charm with my dazzling smile. Alas, Will reported she was attending the University of Arizona. Oh, why does college have to happen to perfectly good people?

After the torture, I staggered back to my cabin and took another shower.

Showers are good. Perhaps not as good as bacon, but good.

My second morning session was painful for a different reason. I was assigned to music lessons in the amphitheater with a satyr named Woodrow.

Woodrow seemed nervous to have me join his little class. Perhaps he had heard the legend about my skinning the satyr Marsyas alive after he challenged me to a music contest. (As I said, the flaying part was *totally* untrue, but rumors do have amazing staying power, especially when I may have been guilty of spreading them.)

Using his panpipe, Woodrow reviewed the minor scales. Austin had no problem with these, even though he was challenging himself by playing the violin, which was not his instrument. Valentina Diaz, a daughter of Aphrodite, did her best to throttle a clarinet, producing sounds like a basset hound whimpering in a thunderstorm. Damien White, son of Nemesis, lived up to his namesake by wreaking vengeance on an acoustic guitar. He played with such force that he broke the D string.

"You killed it!" said Chiara Benvenuti. She was the pretty Italian girl I'd noticed the night before—a child of Tyche, goddess of good fortune. "I needed to use that guitar!"

"Shut up, Lucky," Damien muttered. "In the *real* world, accidents happen. Strings snap sometimes."

Chiara unleashed some rapid-fire Italian that I decided not to translate.

"May I?" I reached for the guitar.

Damien reluctantly handed it over. I leaned toward the guitar case by Woodrow's feet. The satyr leaped several inches into the air.

Austin laughed. "Relax, Woodrow. He's just getting another string."

I'll admit I found the satyr's reaction gratifying. If I could still scare satyrs, perhaps there was hope for me reclaiming some of my former glory. From here I could work my way up to scaring farm animals, then demigods, monsters, and minor deities.

In a matter of seconds, I had replaced the string. It felt good to do something so familiar and simple. I adjusted the pitch, but stopped when I realized Valentina was sobbing.

"That was so beautiful!" She wiped a tear from her cheek. "What was that song?"

I blinked. "It's called tuning."

"Yeah, Valentina, control yourself," Damien chided, though his eyes were red. "It wasn't *that* beautiful."

"No." Chiara sniffled. "It wasn't."

Only Austin seemed unaffected. His eyes shone with what looked like pride, though I didn't understand why he would feel that way.

I played a C minor scale. The B string was flat. It's *always* the B string. Three thousand years since I invented the guitar (during a wild party with the Hittites—long story), and I still couldn't figure out how to make a B string that stays in tune.

I ran through the other scales, delighted that I still remembered them.

"Now this is a Lydian progression," I said. "It starts on the fourth of the major scale. They say it's called Lydian after the old kingdom of Lydia, but actually, I named it for an old girlfriend of mine, Lydia. She was the fourth woman I dated that year, so . . ."

I looked up mid-arpeggio. Damien and Chiara were weeping in each other's arms, hitting each other weakly and cursing, "I hate you. I hate you."

Valentina lay on the amphitheater bench, silently shaking. Woodrow was pulling apart his panpipes.

"I'm worthless!" he sobbed. "Worthless!"

Even Austin had a tear in his eye. He gave me a thumbs-up.

I was thrilled that some of my old skill remained intact, but I imagined Chiron would be annoyed if I drove the entire music class into major depression.

I pulled the D string slightly sharp—a trick I used to use to keep my adoring fans from exploding in rapture at my concerts. (And I mean literally exploding. Some of those gigs at the Fillmore in the 1960s . . . well, I'll spare you the gruesome details.)

I strummed a chord that was intentionally out of tune. To me it sounded awful, but the campers stirred from their misery. They sat up, wiped their tears, and watched in fascination as I played a simple one-four-five progression.

"Yeah, man." Austin brought his violin to his chin and began to improvise. His resin bow danced across the strings. He and I locked eyes, and for a moment we were more than family. We became part of the music, communicating on a level only gods and musicians will ever understand.

Woodrow broke the spell.

"That's amazing," the satyr sobbed. "You two should be teaching the class. What was I thinking? Please don't flay me!"

"My dear satyr," I said, "I would never—"

Suddenly, my fingers spasmed. I dropped the guitar in surprise. The instrument tumbled down the stone steps of the amphitheater, clanging and *sproinging*.

Austin lowered his bow. "You okay?"

"I . . . yes, of course."

But I was not okay. For a few moments, I had experienced the bliss of my formerly easy talent. Yet, clearly, my new mortal fingers were not up to the task. My hand muscles were sore. Red lines dug into my finger pads where I had touched the fret board. I had overextended myself in other ways, too. My lungs felt shriveled, drained of oxygen, even though I had done no singing.

"I'm . . . tired," I said, dismayed.

"Well, yeah." Valentina nodded. "The way you were playing was *unreal*!"

"It's okay, Apollo," Austin said. "You'll get stronger. When demigods use their powers, especially at first, they get tired quickly."

"But I'm not . . ."

I couldn't finish the sentence. I wasn't a demigod. I wasn't a god. I wasn't even myself. How could I ever play music again, knowing that I was a flawed instrument? Each note would bring me nothing but pain and exhaustion. My B string would *never* be in tune.

My misery must have shown on my face.

Damien White balled his fists. "Don't you worry, Apollo. It's not your fault. I'll make that stupid guitar pay for this!"

I didn't try to stop him as he marched down the stairs. Part of me took perverse satisfaction in the way he stomped the guitar until it was reduced to kindling and wires.

Chiara huffed. "*Idiota!* Now I'll never get my turn!"

Woodrow winced. "Well, um . . . thanks, everyone! Good class!"

Archery was an even bigger travesty.

If I ever become a god again (no, not if; *when, when*), my first act will be to wipe the memories of everyone who saw me embarrass myself in that class. I hit one bull's-eye. *One*. The grouping on my other shots was abysmal. Two arrows actually hit *outside* the black ring at a mere one hundred yards. I threw down my bow and wept with shame.

Kayla was our class instructor, but her patience and kindness only made me feel worse. She scooped up my bow and offered it back to me.

"Apollo," she said, "those shots were fantastic. A little more practice and—"

"I'm the god of archery!" I wailed. "I don't practice!"

Next to me, the daughters of Nike snickered.

They had the insufferably appropriate names Holly and Laurel Victor. They reminded me of the gorgeous, ferociously athletic African nymphs Athena used to hang out with at Lake Tritonis.

"Hey, ex-god," Holly said, nocking an arrow, "practice is the only way to improve." She scored a seven on the red ring, but she did not seem at all discouraged.

"For *you*, maybe," I said. "You're a mortal!"

Her sister, Laurel, snorted. "So are you now. Suck it up. Winners don't complain." She shot her arrow, which landed next to her sister's but just inside the red ring. "That's why I'm better than Holly. She's always complaining."

"Yeah, right," Holly growled. "The only thing I complain about is how lame *you* are."

"Oh, yeah?" said Laurel. "Let's go. Right now. Best two out of three shots. The loser scrubs the toilets for a month."

"You're on!"

Just like that, they forgot about me. They definitely would've made excellent Tritonian nymphs.

Kayla took me by the arm and led me downrange. "Those two, I swear. We made them Nike co-counselors so they'd compete with each other. If we hadn't, they would've taken over the camp by now and proclaimed a dictatorship."

I suppose she was trying to cheer me up, but I was not consoled.

I stared at my fingers, now blistered from archery as well as sore from guitar. Impossible. Agonizing.

"I can't do this, Kayla," I muttered. "I'm too old to be sixteen again!"

Kayla cupped her hand over mine. Beneath the green

shock of her hair, she had a ginger complexion—like cream painted over copper, the auburn sheen peeking through in the freckles of her face and arms. She reminded me very much of her father, the Canadian archery coach Darren Knowles.

I mean her *other* father. And, yes, of course it's possible for a demigod child to spring from such a relationship. Why not? Zeus gave birth to Dionysus out of his own thigh. Athena once had a child who was created from a handkerchief. Why should such things surprise you? We gods are capable of infinite marvels.

Kayla took a deep breath, as if preparing for an important shot. "You can do it, Dad. You're already good. *Very* good. You've just got to adjust your expectations. Be patient; be brave. You'll get better."

I was tempted to laugh. How could I get used to being merely *good*? Why would I strain myself to get better when before I had been *divine*?

"No," I said bitterly. "No, it is too painful. I swear upon the River Styx—until I am a god again, I will not use a bow or a musical instrument!"

Go ahead and chide me. I know it was a foolish oath, spoken in a moment of misery and self-pity. And it was binding. An oath sworn on the River Styx can have terrible consequences if broken.

But I didn't care. Zeus had cursed me with mortality. I was not going to pretend that everything was normal. I would not be Apollo until I was *really* Apollo. For now, I was just a stupid young man named Lester Papadopoulos. Maybe I would waste my time on skills I didn't care about—like sword fighting or badminton—but I would *not* sully the memory of my once-perfect music and archery.

Kayla stared at me in horror. "Dad, you don't mean it."

"I do!"

"Take it back! You can't . . ." She glanced over my shoulder. "What is he doing?"

I followed her gaze.

Sherman Yang was walking slowly, trancelike, into the woods.

It would have been foolhardy to run after him, straight into the most dangerous part of camp.

So that's exactly what Kayla and I did.

We almost didn't make it. As soon as we reached the tree line, the forest darkened. The temperature dropped. The horizon stretched out as if bent through a magnifying glass.

A woman whispered in my ear. This time I knew the voice well. It had never stopped haunting me. *You did this to me. Come. Chase me again.*

Fear rolled through my stomach.

I imagined the branches turning to arms; the leaves undulated like green hands.

Daphne, I thought.

Even after so many centuries, the guilt was overwhelming. I could not look at a tree without thinking of her. Forests made me nervous. The life force of each tree seemed to bear down on me with righteous hatred, accusing me of so many crimes. . . . I wanted to fall to my knees. I wanted to beg forgiveness. But this was not the time.

I couldn't allow the woods to confuse me again. I would not let anyone else fall into its trap.

Kayla didn't seem affected. I grabbed her hand to make sure we stayed together. We only had to go a few steps, but it felt like a boot camp run before we reached Sherman Yang.

"Sherman." I grabbed his arm.

He tried to shake me off. Fortunately, he was sluggish and dazed, or I would have ended up with scars of my own. Kayla helped me turn him around.

His eyes twitched as if he were in some sort of half-conscious REM sleep. "No. Ellis. Got to find him. Miranda. My girl."

I glanced at Kayla for explanation.

"Ellis is from the Ares cabin," she said. "He's one of the missing."

"Yes, but Miranda, his girl?"

"Sherman and she started dating about a week ago."

"Ah."

Sherman struggled to free himself. "Find her."

"Miranda is right over here, my friend," I lied. "We'll take you there."

He stopped fighting. His eyes rolled until only the whites were visible. "Over . . . here?"

"Yes."

"Ellis?"

"Yes, it's me," I said. "I'm Ellis."

"I love you, man," Sherman sobbed.

Still, it took all our strength to lead him out of the trees. I was reminded of the time Hephaestus and I had to wrestle the god Hypnos back to bed after he sleepwalked into Artemis's private chambers on Mount Olympus. It's a wonder any of us escaped without silver arrows pincushioning our posteriors.

We led Sherman to the archery range. Between one step and the next, he blinked his eyes and became his normal self. He noticed our hands on his arms and shook us off.

"What is this?" he demanded.

"You were walking into the woods," I said.

He gave us his drill sergeant glower. "No, I wasn't."

Kayla reached for him, then obviously thought better about it. Archery would be difficult with broken fingers. "Sherman, you were in some kind of trance. You were muttering about Ellis and Miranda."

Along Sherman's cheek, his zigzag scar darkened to bronze. "I don't remember that."

"Although you didn't mention the other missing camper," I added helpfully. "Cecil?"

"Why would I mention Cecil?" Sherman growled. "I can't stand the guy. And why should I believe you?"

"The woods had you," I said. "The trees were pulling you in."

Sherman studied the forest, but the trees looked normal again. The lengthening shadows and swaying green hands were gone.

"Look," Sherman said, "I have a head injury, thanks to your annoying friend Meg. If I was acting strange, that's why."

Kayla frowned. "But—"

"Enough!" Sherman snapped. "If either of you mention this, I'll make you eat your quivers. I don't need people questioning my self-control. Besides, I've got the race to think about."

He brushed past us.

"Sherman," I called.

He turned, his fists clenched.

"The last thing you remember," I said, "before you found yourself with us . . . what were you thinking about?"

For a microsecond, the dazed look passed across his face again. "About Miranda and Ellis . . . like you said. I was thinking . . . I wanted to know where they were."

"You were asking a question, then." A blanket of dread settled over me. "You wanted information."

"I . . ."

At the dining pavilion, the conch horn blew.

Sherman's expression hardened. "Doesn't matter. Drop it. We've got lunch now. Then I'm going to destroy you all in the three-legged death race."

As threats went, I had heard worse, but Sherman made it sound intimidating enough. He marched off toward the pavilion.

Kayla turned to me. "What just happened?"

"I think I understand now," I said. "I know why those campers went missing."

16

Tied to McCaffrey

We might end up in Lima

Harley is evil

NOTE TO SELF: trying to reveal important information just before a three-legged death race is not a good idea.

No one would listen to me.

Despite last night's grumbling and complaining, the campers were now buzzing with excitement. They spent their lunch hour frantically cleaning weapons, lacing armor straps, and whispering among one another to form secret alliances. Many tried to convince Harley, the course architect, to share hints about the best strategies.

Harley loved the attention. By the end of lunch, his table was piled high with offerings (read: bribes)—chocolate bars, peanut butter cups, gummy bears, and Hot Wheels. Harley would have made an excellent god. He took the gifts, mumbled a few pleasantries, but told his worshippers nothing helpful.

I tried to speak with Chiron about the dangers of the woods, but he was so frantic with last-minute race preparations that I almost got trampled just standing near him. He trotted nervously around the pavilion with a team of satyr and dryad referees in tow, comparing maps and issuing orders.

"The teams will be almost impossible to track," he murmured, his face buried in a Labyrinth schematic. "And we don't have any coverage in grid D."

"But, Chiron," I said, "if I could just—"

"The test group this morning ended up in Peru," he told the satyrs. "We can't have that happen again."

"About the woods," I said.

"Yes, I'm sorry, Apollo. I understand you are concerned—"

"The woods are actually speaking," I said. "You remember the old—"

A dryad ran up to Chiron with her dress billowing smoke. "The flares are exploding!"

"Ye gods!" Chiron said. "Those were for emergencies!"

He galloped over my feet, followed by his mob of assistants.

And so it went. When one is a god, the world hangs on your every word. When one is sixteen . . . not so much.

I tried to talk to Harley, hoping he might postpone the race, but the boy brushed me off with a simple "Nah."

As was so often the case with Hephaestus's children, Harley was tinkering with some mechanical device, moving the springs and gears around. I didn't really care what it was, but I asked Harley about it, hoping to win the boy's goodwill.

"It's a beacon," he said, adjusting a knob. "For lost people."

"You mean the teams in the Labyrinth?"

"No. You guys are on your own. This is for Leo."

"Leo Valdez."

Harley squinted at the device. "Sometimes, if you can't find your way back, a beacon can help. Just got to find the right frequency."

"And . . . how long have you been working on this?"

"Since he disappeared. Now I gotta concentrate. Can't stop the race." He turned his back on me and walked off.

I stared after him in amazement. For six months, the boy had been working on a beacon to help his missing brother Leo. I wondered if anyone would work so hard to bring me back home to Olympus. I very much doubted it.

I stood forlornly in a corner of the pavilion and ate a sandwich. I watched the sun wane in the winter sky and I thought about my chariot, my poor horses stuck in their stables with no one to take them out for a ride.

Of course, even without my help, other forces would keep the cosmos chugging along. Many different belief systems powered the revolution of the planets and stars. Wolves would still chase Sol across the sky. Ra would continue his daily journey in his sun barque. Tonatiuh would keep running on his surplus blood from human sacrifices back in the Aztec days. And that other thing—science—would still generate gravity and quantum physics and whatever.

Nevertheless, I felt like I wasn't doing my part, standing around waiting for a three-legged race.

Even Kayla and Austin were too distracted to talk with me. Kayla had told Austin about our experience rescuing

Sherman Yang from the woods, but Austin was more interested in swabbing out his saxophone.

"We can tell Chiron at dinner," he mumbled with a reed in his mouth. "Nobody's going to listen until the race is over, and we'll be staying out of the woods anyway. Besides, if I can play the right tune in the Labyrinth . . ." He got a gleam in his eyes. "Ooh. Come here, Kayla. I have an idea."

He steered her away and left me alone again.

I understood Austin's enthusiasm, of course. His saxophone skills were so formidable, I was certain he would become the foremost jazz instrumentalist of his generation, and if you think it's easy to get half a million views on YouTube playing jazz saxophone, think again. Still, his musical career was not going to happen if the force in the woods destroyed us all.

As a last resort (a *very* last resort), I sought out Meg McCaffrey.

I spotted her at one of the braziers, talking with Julia Feingold and Alice Miyazawa. Or rather, the Hermes girls were talking while Meg devoured a cheeseburger. I marveled that Demeter—the queen of grains, fruits, and vegetables—could have a daughter who was such an unrepentant carnivore.

Then again, Persephone was the same way. You'll hear stories about the goddess of springtime being all sweetness and daffodils and nibbling on pomegranate seeds, but I'm telling you, that girl was frightening when she attacked a mound of pork spareribs.

I strode over to Meg's side. The Hermes girls stepped

back as if I were a snake handler. I found this reaction pleasing.

"Hello," I said. "What are we talking about?"

Meg wiped her mouth on the back of her hand. "These two wanna know our plans for the race."

"I'm sure they do." I plucked a small magnetic listening device from Meg's coat sleeve and tossed it back to Alice.

Alice smiled sheepishly. "Can't blame us for trying."

"No, of course not," I said. "In the same spirit, I hope you won't mind what I did to your shoes. Have a good race!"

The girls shuffled off nervously, checking the soles of their sneakers.

Meg looked at me with something resembling respect. "What did you do to them?"

"Nothing," I said. "Half the trick to being a god is knowing how to bluff."

She snorted. "So what's our top secret plan? Wait. Let me guess. You don't have one."

"You're learning. Honestly, I meant to come up with one, but I got sidetracked. We have a problem."

"Sure do." From her coat pocket, she pulled two loops of bronze, like resistance bands of braided metal. "You've seen these? They wrap around our legs. Once they're on, they *stay* on until the race is over. No way to get them off. I *hate* restraints."

"I agree." I was tempted to add *especially when I am tied to a small child named Meg*, but my natural diplomacy won out. "However, I was referring to a different problem."

I told her about the incident during archery, when Sherman had almost been lured into the forest.

Meg removed her cat-eye glasses. Without the lenses, her dark irises looked softer and warmer, like tiny plots of planting soil. "You think something in the woods is calling to people?"

"I think something in the woods is *answering* people. In ancient times, there was an Oracle—"

"Yeah, you told me. Delphi."

"No. Another Oracle, even older than Delphi. It involved trees. An entire grove of talking trees."

"Talking trees." Meg's mouth twitched. "What was that Oracle called?"

"I—I can't remember." I ground my teeth. "I *should* know. I should be able to tell you instantly! But the information . . . It's almost as if it is eluding me on purpose."

"That happens sometimes," Meg said. "You'll think of it."

"But it *never* happens to me! Stupid human brain! At any rate, I believe this grove is somewhere in those woods. I don't know how or why. The whispering voices, though . . . they are from this hidden Oracle. The sacred trees are trying to speak prophecies, reaching out to those with burning questions, luring them in."

Meg put her glasses back on. "You know that sounds crazy, right?"

I steadied my breathing. I had to remind myself that I was no longer a god. I had to put up with insults from mortals without being able to blast them to ashes.

"Just be on guard," I said.

"But the race doesn't even go through the woods."

"Nevertheless . . . we are not safe. If you can summon your friend Peaches, I would welcome his company."

"I told you, he sort of pops up when he feels like it. I can't—"

Chiron blew a hunting horn so loudly my vision doubled. Another pledge to myself: once I became a god again, I would descend upon this camp and take away all their horns.

"Demigods!" said the centaur. "Tie your legs together and follow me to your starting positions!"

We gathered in a meadow about a hundred yards from the Big House. Making it *that* far without a single life-threatening incident was a minor miracle. With my left leg bound to Meg's right, I felt the way I used to in Leto's womb just before my sister and I were born. And, yes, I remember that quite well. Artemis was always shoving me aside, elbowing me in the ribs and generally being a womb hog.

I said a silent prayer that if I got through this race alive, I would sacrifice a bull to myself and possibly even build myself a new temple. I am a sucker for bulls and temples.

The satyrs directed us to spread out across the meadow.

"Where is the starting line?" Holly Victor demanded, shoving her shoulder ahead of her sister's. "I want to be the closest."

"*I* want to be closest," Laurel corrected. "You can be *second* closest."

"Not to worry!" Woodrow the satyr sounded very worried. "We'll explain everything in a moment. As soon as I, um, know what to explain."

Will Solace sighed. He was, of course, tied to Nico. He

propped his elbow on Nico's shoulder as if the son of Hades were a convenient shelf. "I miss Grover. He used to organize things like this so well."

"I'd settle for Coach Hedge." Nico pushed Will's arm off. "Besides, don't talk about Grover too loudly. Juniper's right over there."

He pointed to one of the dryads—a pretty girl dressed in pale green.

"Grover's girlfriend," Will explained to me. "She misses him. A lot."

"Okay, everybody!" Woodrow shouted. "Spread out a little bit more, please! We want you to have plenty of room so, you know, if you die, you won't take down all the other teams too!"

Will sighed. "I am *so* excited."

He and Nico loped off. Julia and Alice from the Hermes cabin checked their shoes one more time, then glared at me. Connor Stoll was paired with Paolo Montes, the Brazilian son of Hebe, and neither of them seemed happy about it.

Perhaps Connor looked glum because his mangled scalp was covered in so much medicinal salve his head looked like it had been coughed up by a cat. Or perhaps he just missed his brother Travis.

As soon as Artemis and I were born, we couldn't *wait* to get some distance between us. We staked out our own territories and that was that. But I would've given anything to see her just then. I was sure Zeus had threatened her with severe punishment if she tried to help me during my time as a mortal, but she could have at least sent me a care package from Olympus—a decent toga, some magical acne cream, and maybe a dozen cranberry ambrosia scones from the Scylla Cafe. They made *excellent* scones.

I scanned the other teams. Kayla and Austin were bound together, looking like a deadly pair of street performers with her bow and his saxophone. Chiara, the cute girl from Tyche, was stuck with her nemesis, Damien White, son of . . . well, Nemesis. Billie Ng from Demeter was leg-tied with Valentina Diaz, who was hastily checking her makeup in the reflective surface of Billie's silver coat. Valentina didn't seem to notice that two twigs were sprouting from her hair like tiny deer antlers.

I decided the biggest threat would be Malcolm Pace. You can never be too careful with children of Athena. Surprisingly, though, he'd paired himself with Sherman Yang. That didn't seem like a natural partnership, unless Malcolm had some sort of plan. Those Athena children *always* had a plan. It rarely included letting me win.

The only demigods not participating were Harley and Nyssa, who had set up the course.

Once the satyrs judged we had all spread out sufficiently and our leg bindings had been double-checked, Harley clapped for our attention.

"Okay!" He bounced up and down eagerly, reminding me of the Roman children who used to cheer for executions at the Colosseum. "Here's the deal. Each team has to find three golden apples, then get back to this meadow alive."

Grumbling broke out among the demigods.

"Golden apples," I said. "I *hate* golden apples. They bring nothing but trouble."

Meg shrugged. "I like apples."

I remembered the rotten one she'd used to break Cade's nose in the alley. I wondered if perhaps she could use golden apples with the same deadly skill. Perhaps we stood a chance after all.

Laurel Victor raised her hand. "You mean the first team back wins?"

"*Any* team that gets back alive wins!" Harley said.

"That's ridiculous!" Holly said. "There can only be one winner. First team back wins!"

Harley shrugged. "Have it your way. My only rules are stay alive, and don't kill each other."

"*O quê?*" Paolo started complaining so loudly in Portuguese that Connor had to cover his left ear.

"Now, now!" Chiron called. His saddlebags were overflowing with extra first-aid kits and emergency flares. "We won't need any *help* making this a dangerous challenge. Let's have a good clean three-legged death race. And another thing, campers, given the problems our test group had this morning, please repeat after me: *Do not end up in Peru.*"

"Do not end up in Peru," everyone chanted.

Sherman Yang cracked his knuckles. "So where *is* the starting line?"

"There is no starting line," Harley said with glee. "You're all starting from right where you are."

The campers looked around in confusion. Suddenly the

meadow shook. Dark lines etched across the grass, forming a giant green checkerboard.

"Have fun!" Harley squealed.

The ground opened beneath our feet, and we fell into the Labyrinth.

17

Bowling balls of death
Rolling toward my enemies
I'll trade you problems

AT LEAST WE DID NOT LAND IN PERU.

My feet hit stone, jarring my ankles. We stumbled against a wall, but Meg provided me with a convenient cushion.

We found ourselves in a dark tunnel braced with oaken beams. The hole we'd fallen through was gone, replaced by an earthen ceiling. I saw no sign of the other teams, but from somewhere above I could vaguely hear Harley chanting, "Go! Go! Go!"

"When I get my powers back," I said, "I will turn Harley into a constellation called the Ankle Biter. At least constellations are silent."

Meg pointed down the corridor. "Look."

As my eyes adjusted, I realized the tunnel's dim light emanated from a glowing piece of fruit about thirty yards away.

"A golden apple," I said.

Meg lurched forward, pulling me with her.

"Wait!" I said. "There might be traps!"

As if to illustrate my point, Connor and Paolo emerged

from the darkness at the other end of the corridor. Paolo scooped up the golden apple and shouted, *"BRASIL!"*

Connor grinned at us. "Too slow, suckers!"

The ceiling opened above them, showering them with iron orbs the size of cantaloupes.

Connor yelped, "Run!"

He and Paolo executed an awkward one-eighty and hobbled away, hotly pursued by a rolling herd of cannon-balls with sparking fuses.

The sounds quickly faded. Without the glowing apple, we were left in total darkness.

"Great." Meg's voice echoed. "Now what?"

"I suggest we go the other direction."

That was easier said than done. Being blind seemed to bother Meg more than it did me. Thanks to my mortal body, I already felt crippled and deprived of my senses. Besides, I often relied on more than sight. Music required keen hearing. Archery required a sensitive touch and the ability to feel the direction of the wind. (Okay, sight was also helpful, but you get the idea.)

We shuffled ahead, our arms extended in front of us. I listened for suspicious clicks, snaps, or creaks that might indicate an incoming flock of explosions, but I suspected that if I *did* hear any warning signs, it would be too late.

Eventually Meg and I learned to walk with our bound legs in synchronicity. It wasn't easy. I had a flawless sense of rhythm. Meg was always a quarter beat slow or fast, which kept us veering left or right and running into walls.

We lumbered along for what might have been minutes or days. In the Labyrinth, time was deceptive.

I remembered what Austin had told me about the Labyrinth feeling different since the death of its creator. I was beginning to understand what he meant. The air seemed fresher, as if the maze hadn't been chewing up quite so many bodies. The walls didn't radiate the same malignant heat. As far as I could tell, they weren't oozing blood or slime, either, which was a definite improvement. In the old days, you couldn't take a step inside Daedalus's Labyrinth without sensing its all-consuming desire: *I will destroy your mind and your body.* Now the atmosphere was sleepier, the message not quite as virulent: *Hey, if you die in here, that's cool.*

"I never liked Daedalus," I muttered. "That old rascal didn't know when to stop. He always had to have the latest tech, the most recent updates. I *told* him not to make his maze self-aware. 'A.I. will destroy us, man,' I said. But noooo. He *had* to give the Labyrinth a malevolent consciousness."

"I don't know what you're talking about," Meg said. "But maybe you shouldn't bad-mouth the maze while we're inside it."

Once, I stopped when I heard the sound of Austin's saxophone. It was faint, echoing through so many corridors I couldn't pinpoint where it was coming from. Then it was gone. I hoped he and Kayla had found their three apples and escaped safely.

Finally, Meg and I reached a Y in the corridor. I could tell this from the flow of the air and the temperature differential against my face.

"Why'd we stop?" Meg asked.

"Shh." I listened intently.

From the right-hand corridor came a faint whining sound like a table saw. The left-hand corridor was quiet, but it exuded a faint odor that was unpleasantly familiar . . . not sulfur, exactly, but a vaporous mix of minerals from deep in the earth.

"I don't hear anything," Meg complained.

"A sawing noise to the right," I told her. "To the left, a bad smell."

"I choose the bad smell."

"Of course you do."

Meg blew me one of her trademark raspberries, then hobbled to the left, pulling me along with her.

The bronze bands around my leg began to chafe. I could feel Meg's pulse through her femoral artery, messing up my rhythm. Whenever I get nervous (which doesn't happen often), I like to hum a song to calm myself—usually Ravel's *Boléro* or the ancient Greek "Song of Seikilos." But with Meg's pulse throwing me off, the only tune I could conjure was the "Chicken Dance." That was not soothing.

We edged forward. The smell of volcanic fumes intensified. My pulse lost its perfect rhythm. My heart knocked against my chest with every *cluck, cluck, cluck, cluck* of the "Chicken Dance." I feared I knew where we were. I told myself it wasn't possible. We couldn't have walked halfway around the world. But this was the Labyrinth. Down here, distance was meaningless. The maze knew how to exploit its victims' weaknesses. Worse: it had a vicious sense of humor.

"I see light!" Meg said.

She was right. The absolute darkness had changed to

murky gray. Up ahead, the tunnel ended, joining with a narrow, lengthwise cavern like a volcanic vent. It looked as if a colossal claw had slashed across the corridor and left a wound in the earth. I had seen creatures with claws that big down in Tartarus. I did not fancy seeing them again.

"We should turn around," I said.

"That's stupid," Meg said. "Don't you see the golden glow? There's an apple in there."

All I saw were swirling plumes of ash and gas. "The glow could be lava," I said. "Or radiation. Or eyes. Glowing eyes are *never* good."

"It's an apple," Meg insisted. "I can smell apple."

"Oh, *now* you develop keen senses?"

Meg forged onward, giving me little choice but to go with. For a small girl, she was quite good at throwing her weight around. At the end of the tunnel, we found ourselves on a narrow ledge. The cliff wall opposite was only ten feet away, but the crevasse seemed to plunge downward forever. Perhaps a hundred feet above us, the jagged vent opened into a bigger chamber.

A painfully large ice cube seemed to be working its way down my throat. I had never seen this place from below, but I knew exactly where we were. We stood at the *omphalus*— the navel of the ancient world.

"You're shaking," Meg said.

I tried to cover her mouth with my hand, but she promptly bit it.

"Don't touch me," she snarled.

"*Please* be quiet."

"Why?"

"Because right above us—" My voice cracked. "Delphi. The chamber of the Oracle."

Meg's nose quivered like a rabbit's. "That's impossible."

"No, it's not," I whispered. "And if this is Delphi, that means . . ."

From overhead came a hiss so loud, it sounded as if the entire ocean had hit a frying pan and evaporated into a massive steam cloud. The ledge shook. Pebbles rained down. Above, a monstrous body slid across the crevasse, completely covering the opening. The smell of molting snakeskin seared my nostrils.

"Python." My voice was now an octave higher than Meg's. "He is here."

18

The Beast is calling
Tell him I'm not here. Let's hide
Where? In garbage. Natch

HAD I EVER BEEN SO TERRIFIED?

Perhaps when Typhon raged across the earth, scattering the gods before him. Perhaps when Gaea unleashed her giants to tear down Olympus. Or perhaps when I accidentally saw Ares naked in the gymnasium. That had been enough to turn my hair white for a century.

But I had been a god all of those times. Now I was a weak, tiny mortal cowering in the darkness. I could only pray my old enemy would not sense my presence. For once in my long glorious life, I wanted to be invisible.

Oh, why had the Labyrinth brought me here?

As soon as I thought this, I chided myself: Of *course* it would bring me where I least wanted to be. Austin had been wrong about the maze. It was still evil, designed to kill. It was just a little subtler about its homicides now.

Meg seemed oblivious to our danger. Even with an immortal monster a hundred feet above us, she had the nerve to stay on task. She elbowed me and pointed to a tiny ledge on the opposite wall, where a golden apple glowed cheerfully.

Had Harley *placed* it there? I couldn't imagine. More likely the boy had simply rolled golden apples down various corridors, trusting that they would find the most dangerous spots to roost. I was really starting to dislike that boy.

Meg whispered, "Easy jump."

I gave her a look that under different circumstances would've incinerated her. "Too dangerous."

"Apple," she hissed.

"Monster!" I hissed back.

"One."

"No!"

"Two."

"No!"

"Three." She jumped.

Which meant that I also jumped. We made the ledge, though our heels sent a spray of rubble into the chasm. Only my natural coordination and grace saved us from toppling backward to our deaths. Meg snatched up the apple.

Above us, the monster rumbled, "Who approaches?"

His voice . . . Gods above, I remembered that voice— deep and gruff, as if he breathed xenon rather than air. For all I knew, he did. Python could certainly *produce* his share of unhealthy gasses.

The monster shifted his weight. More gravel spilled into the crevasse.

I stood absolutely still, pressed against the cold face of the rock. My eardrums pulsed with every beat of my heart. I wished I could stop Meg from breathing. I wished I could stop the rhinestones on her eyeglasses from glittering.

Python had heard us. I prayed to all the gods that the monster would decide the noise was nothing. All he had to do was breathe down into the crevasse and he would kill us. There was no escaping his poisonous belch—not from this distance, not for a mortal.

Then, from the cavern above, came another voice, smaller and much closer to human. "Hello, my reptilian friend."

I nearly wept with relief. I had no idea who this newcomer was, or why he had been so foolish as to announce his presence to Python, but I always appreciated it when humans sacrificed themselves to save me. Common courtesy was not dead after all!

Python's harsh laugh shook my teeth. "Well, I was wondering if you would make the trip, Monsieur Beast."

"Don't call me that," the man snapped. "And the commute was quite easy now that the Labyrinth is back in service."

"I'm so pleased." Python's tone was dry as basalt.

I couldn't tell much about the man's voice, muffled as it was by several tons of reptile flesh, but he sounded calmer and more in control than I would have been talking to Python. I had heard the term *Beast* used to describe someone before, but as usual, my mortal brainpower failed me.

If only I'd been able to retain just the *important* information! Instead, I could tell you what I had for dessert the first time I dined with King Minos. (Spice cake.) I could tell you what color *chitons* the sons of Niobe were wearing when I slew them. (A very unflattering shade of orange.)

But I couldn't remember something as basic as whether this Beast was a wrestler, a movie star, or a politician. Possibly all three?

Next to me, in the glow of the apple, Meg seemed to have turned to bronze. Her eyes were wide with fear. A little late for that, but at least she was quiet. If I didn't know better, I might have thought the man's voice terrified her more than the monster's.

"So, Python," the man continued, "any prophetic words to share with me?"

"In time . . . my lord."

The last words were spoken with amusement, but I'm not sure anyone else would've recognized it. Aside from myself, few had been on the receiving end of Python's sarcasm and lived to tell the tale.

"I need more than your assurances," the man said. "Before we proceed, we must have *all* the Oracles under our control."

All the Oracles. Those words almost sent me off the cliff, but somehow I retained my balance.

"In time," Python said, "as we agreed. We have come this far by biding our time, yes? You did not reveal your hand when the Titans stormed New York. I did not march to war with Gaea's giants. We both realized the time for victory was not yet right. You must remain patient for a while longer."

"Don't lecture me, snake. While you slumbered, I built an empire. I have spent centuries—"

"Yes, yes." The monster exhaled, causing a tremor along

the cliff face. "And if you ever want your empire to come out of the shadows, you need to deliver on *your* side of the bargain first. When will you destroy Apollo?"

I stifled a yelp. I should not have been surprised that they were talking about me. For millennia, I had assumed that *everyone* talked about me all the time. I was so interesting they simply couldn't help it. But this business about destroying me—I didn't like that.

Meg looked more terrified than I'd ever seen her. I wanted to think she was worried for my sake, but I had a feeling she was equally concerned about herself. Again, those mixed-up demigod priorities.

The man stepped closer to the chasm. His voice became clearer and louder. "Don't worry about Apollo. He is exactly where I need him to be. He will serve our purpose, and once he is no longer useful . . ."

He did not bother finishing the statement. I was afraid it did not end with *we will give him a nice present and send him on his way.* With a chill, I recognized the voice from my dream. It was the nasal sneer of the man in the purple suit. I also had a feeling I'd heard him sing before, years and years ago, but that didn't make sense. . . . Why would I suffer through a concert given by an ugly purple-suited man who called himself the Beast? I was not even a *fan* of death metal polka!

Python shifted his bulk, showering us with more rubble. "And how exactly will you convince him to serve our purpose?"

The Beast chuckled. "I have well-placed help within

the camp who will steer Apollo toward us. Also, I have upped the stakes. Apollo will have no choice. He and the girl will open the gates."

A whiff of Python vapor floated across my nose— enough to make me dizzy, hopefully not enough to kill me.

"I trust you are right," said the monster. "Your judgment in the past has been . . . questionable. I wonder if you have chosen the right tools for this job. Have you learned from your past mistakes?"

The man snarled so deeply I could almost believe he was turning into a beast. I'd seen that happen enough times. Next to me, Meg whimpered.

"Listen here, you overgrown reptile," the man said, "my only mistake was not burning my enemies fast enough, often enough. I assure you, I am stronger than ever. My organization is everywhere. My colleagues stand ready. When we control all four Oracles, we will control fate itself!"

"And what a glorious day that will be." Python's voice was jagged with contempt. "But beforehand, you must destroy the *fifth* Oracle, yes? That is the only one I *cannot* control. You must set flame to the grove of—"

"Dodona," I said.

The word leaped unbidden from my mouth and echoed through the chasm. Of all the stupid times to retrieve a piece of information, of all the stupid times to say it aloud . . . oh, the body of Lester Papadopoulos was a terrible place to live.

Above us, the conversation stopped.

Meg hissed at me, "You idiot."

The Beast said, "What was that sound?"

Rather than answer, *Oh, that's just us*, we did something

even more foolish. One of us, Meg or me—personally, I blame her—must have slipped on a pebble. We toppled off the ledge and fell into the sulfurous clouds below.

SQUISH.

The Labyrinth most definitely had a sense of humor. Instead of allowing us to smash into a rock floor and die, the maze dropped us into a mound of wet, full garbage bags.

If you're keeping score, that was the *second* time since becoming mortal that I had crash-landed in garbage, which was two times more than any god should endure.

We tumbled down the pile in a frenzy of three-legged flailing. We landed at the bottom, covered with muck, but, miraculously, still alive.

Meg sat up, glazed in a layer of coffee grounds.

I pulled a banana peel off my head and flicked it aside. "Is there some reason you keep landing us in trash heaps?"

"Me? You're the one who lost his balance!" Meg wiped her face without much luck. In her other hand, she clutched the golden apple with trembling fingers.

"Are you all right?" I asked.

"Fine," she snapped.

Clearly that was not true. She looked as if she'd just gone through Hades's haunted house. (Pro tip: DO NOT.) Her face was pallid. She had bit her lip so hard, her teeth were pink with blood. I also detected the faint smell of urine, meaning one of us had gotten scared enough to lose bladder control, and I was seventy-five percent sure it wasn't me.

"That man upstairs," I said. "You recognized his voice?"

"Shut up. That's an order!"

I attempted to reply. To my consternation, I found that I couldn't. My voice had heeded Meg's command all on its own, which did not bode well. I decided to file away my questions about the Beast for later.

I scanned our surroundings. Garbage chutes lined the walls on all four sides of the dismal little basement. As I watched, another bag of refuse slid down the right-hand chute and hit the pile. The smell was so strong, it could have burned paint off the walls, if the gray cinder blocks had been painted. Still, it was better than smelling the fumes of Python. The only visible exit was a metal door marked with a biohazard sign.

"Where are we?" Meg asked.

I glared at her, waiting.

"You can talk now," she added.

"This is going to shock you," I said, "but it appears we are in a garbage room."

"But where?"

"Could be anywhere. The Labyrinth intersects with subterranean places all around the world."

"Like Delphi." Meg glowered at me as if our little Greek excursion had been my fault and not . . . well, only indirectly my fault.

"That was unexpected," I agreed. "We need to speak with Chiron."

"What is Dodona?"

"I—I'll explain it all later." I didn't want Meg to shut me up again. I also didn't want to talk about Dodona while trapped in the Labyrinth. My skin was crawling, and I didn't think it was just because I was covered in sticky soda syrup. "First, we need to get out of here."

Meg glanced behind me. "Well, it wasn't a total waste." She reached into the garbage and pulled out a second piece of glowing fruit. "Only one more apple to go."

"Perfect." The last thing I cared about was finishing Harley's ridiculous race, but at least it would get Meg moving. "Now, why don't we see what fabulous biohazards await us behind that door?"

19

They have gone missing?
No, no, no, no, no, no, no
No, et cetera

THE ONLY BIOHAZARDS we encountered were vegan cupcakes.

After navigating several torchlit corridors, we burst into a crowded modern bakery that, according to the menu board, had the dubious name THE LEVEL TEN VEGAN. Our garbage/volcanic gas stench quickly dispersed the customers, driving most toward the exit, and causing many non-dairy gluten-free baked goods to be trampled. We ducked behind the counter, charged through the kitchen doors, and found ourselves in a subterranean amphitheater that looked centuries old.

Tiers of stone seats ringed a sandy pit about the right size for a gladiator fight. Hanging from the ceiling were dozens of thick iron chains. I wondered what ghastly spectacles might have been staged here, but we didn't stay very long.

We limped out the opposite side, back into the Labyrinth's twisting corridors.

By this point, we had perfected the art of three-legged

running. Whenever I started to tire, I imagined Python behind us, spewing poisonous gas.

At last we turned a corner, and Meg shouted, "There!"

In the middle of the corridor sat a third golden apple.

This time I was too exhausted to care about traps. We loped forward until Meg scooped up the fruit.

In front of us, the ceiling lowered, forming a ramp. Fresh air filled my lungs. We climbed to the top, but instead of feeling elated, my insides turned as cold as the garbage juice on my skin. We were back in the woods.

"Not here," I muttered. "Gods, no."

Meg hopped us in a full circle. "Maybe it's a different forest." ·

But it wasn't. I could feel the resentful stare of the trees, the horizon stretching out in all directions. Voices began to whisper, waking to our presence.

"Hurry," I said.

As if on cue, the bands around our legs sprang loose. We ran.

Even with her arms full of apples, Meg was faster. She veered between trees, zigzagging left and right as if following a course only she could see. My legs ached and my chest burned, but I didn't dare fall behind.

Up ahead, flickering points of light resolved into torches. At last we burst out of the woods, right into a crowd of campers and satyrs.

Chiron galloped over. "Thank the gods!"

"You're welcome," I gasped, mostly out of habit. "Chiron . . . we have to talk."

In the torchlight, the centaur's face seemed carved from shadow. "Yes, we do, my friend. But first, I fear one more team is still missing . . . your children, Kayla and Austin."

Chiron forced us to take showers and change clothes. Otherwise I would have plunged straight back into the woods.

By the time I was done, Kayla and Austin still had not returned.

Chiron had sent search parties of dryads into the forest, on the assumption that they would be safe in their home territory, but he adamantly refused to let demigods join the hunt.

"We cannot risk anyone else," he said. "Kayla, Austin, and—and the other missing . . . They would not want that."

Five campers had now disappeared. I harbored no illusions that Kayla and Austin would return on their own. The Beast's words still echoed in my ears: *I have upped the stakes. Apollo will have no choice.*

Somehow he had targeted my children. He was inviting me to look for them, and to find the gates of this hidden Oracle. There was still so much I did not understand—how the ancient grove of Dodona had relocated here, what sort of "gates" it might have, why the Beast thought I could open them, and how he'd snared Austin and Kayla. But there was one thing I did know: the Beast was right. I had no choice. I had to find my children . . . my *friends.*

I would have ignored Chiron's warning and run into the forest except for Will's panicked shout: "Apollo, I need you!"

At the far end of the field, he had set up an impromptu hospital where half a dozen campers lay injured on stretchers. He was frantically tending to Paolo Montes while Nico held down the screaming patient.

I ran to Will's side and winced at what I saw.

Paolo had managed to get one of his legs sawed off.

"I got it reattached," Will told me, his voice shaky with exhaustion. His scrubs were speckled with blood. "I need somebody to keep him stable."

I pointed to the woods. "But—"

"I know!" Will snapped. "Don't you think I want to be out there searching too? We're shorthanded for healers. There's some salve and nectar in that pack. Go!"

I was stunned by his tone. I realized he was just as concerned about Kayla and Austin as I was. The only difference: Will knew his duty. He had to heal the injured first. And he needed my help.

"Y-yes," I said. "Yes, of course."

I grabbed the supply pack and took charge of Paolo, who had conveniently passed out from the pain.

Will changed his surgical gloves and glared at the woods. "We *will* find them. We *have* to."

Nico di Angelo gave him a canteen. "Drink. Right now, this is where you need to be."

I could tell the son of Hades was angry too. Around his feet, the grass steamed and withered.

Will sighed. "You're right. But that doesn't make me feel better. I have to set Valentina's broken arm now. You want to assist?"

"Sounds gruesome," Nico said. "Let's go."

I tended to Paolo Montes until I was sure he was out of danger, then asked two satyrs to carry his stretcher to the Hebe cabin.

I did what I could to nurse the others. Chiara had a mild concussion. Billie Ng had come down with a case of Irish step dancing. Holly and Laurel needed pieces of shrapnel removed from their backs, thanks to a close encounter with an exploding chain-saw Frisbee.

The Victor twins had placed in first, predictably, but they also demanded to know which of them had the *most* pieces of shrapnel extracted, so they could have bragging rights. I told them to be quiet or I would never allow them to wear laurel wreaths again. (As the guy who held the patent on laurel wreaths, that was my prerogative.)

I found my mortal healing skills were passable. Will Solace far outshone me, but that didn't bother me as much as my failures with archery and music had. I suppose I was used to being second in healing. My son Asclepius had become the god of medicine by the time he was fifteen, and I couldn't have been happier for him. It left me time for my other interests. Besides, it's every god's dream to have a child who grows up to be a doctor.

As I was washing up from the shrapnel extraction, Harley shuffled over, fiddling with his beacon device. His eyes were puffy from crying.

"It's my fault," he muttered. "I got them lost. I . . . I'm sorry."

He was shaking. I realized the little boy was terrified of what I might do.

For the past two days, I had yearned to cause fear in mortals again. My stomach had boiled with resentment and bitterness. I wanted someone to blame for my predicament, for the disappearances, for my own powerlessness to fix things.

Looking at Harley, my anger evaporated. I felt hollow, silly, ashamed of myself. Yes, me, Apollo . . . ashamed. Truly, it was an event so unprecedented, it should have ripped apart the cosmos.

"It's all right," I told him.

He sniffled. "The racecourse went into the woods. It shouldn't have done that. They got lost and . . . and—"

"Harley"—I placed my hands over his—"may I see your beacon?"

He blinked the tears away. I guess he was afraid I might smash his gadget, but he let me take it.

"I'm not an inventor," I said, turning the gears as gently as possible. "I don't have your father's skills. But I *do* know music. I believe automatons prefer a frequency of E at 329.6 hertz. It resonates best with Celestial bronze. If you adjust your signal—"

"Festus might hear it?" Harley's eyes widened. "Really?"

"I don't know," I admitted. "Just as you could not have known what the Labyrinth would do today. But that doesn't mean we should stop trying. Never stop inventing, son of Hephaestus."

I gave him back his beacon. For a count of three, Harley stared at me in disbelief. Then he hugged me so hard he nearly rebroke my ribs, and he dashed away.

I tended to the last of the injured while the harpies

cleaned the area, picking up bandages, torn clothing, and damaged weapons. They gathered the golden apples in a basket and promised to bake us some lovely glowing apple turnovers for breakfast.

At Chiron's urging, the remaining campers dispersed back to their cabins. He promised them we would determine what to do in the morning, but I had no intention of waiting.

As soon as we were alone, I turned to Chiron and Meg.

"I'm going after Kayla and Austin," I told them. "You can join me or not."

Chiron's expression tightened. "My friend, you're exhausted and unprepared. Go back to your cabin. It will serve no purpose—"

"No." I waved him off, as I once might have done when I was a god. The gesture probably looked petulant coming from a sixteen-year-old nobody, but I didn't care. "I have to do this."

The centaur lowered his head. "I should have listened to you before the race. You tried to warn me. What—what did you discover?"

The question stopped my momentum like a seat belt.

After rescuing Sherman Yang, after listening to Python in the Labyrinth, I had felt certain I knew the answers. I had remembered the name *Dodona*, the stories about talking trees . . .

Now my mind was once again a bowl of fuzzy mortal soup. I couldn't recall what I'd been so excited about, or what I had intended to do about it.

Perhaps exhaustion and stress had taken their toll. Or

maybe Zeus was manipulating my brain—allowing me tantalizing glimpses of the truth, then snatching them away, turning my aha! moments into huh? moments.

I howled in frustration. "I don't remember!"

Meg and Chiron exchanged nervous glances.

"You're not going," Meg told me firmly.

"*What?* You can't—"

"That's an order," she said. "No going into the woods until I say so."

The command sent a shudder from the base of my skull to my heels.

I dug my fingernails into my palms. "Meg McCaffrey, if my children die because you wouldn't let me—"

"Like Chiron said, you'd just get yourself killed. We'll wait for daylight."

I thought how satisfying it would be to drop Meg from the sun chariot at high noon. Then again, some small rational part of me realized she might be right. I was in no condition to launch a one-man rescue operation. That just made me angrier.

Chiron's tail swished from side to side. "Well, then . . . I will see you both in the morning. We *will* find a solution. I promise you that."

He gave me one last look, as if worried I might start running in circles and baying at the moon. Then he trotted back toward the Big House.

I scowled at Meg. "I'm staying out here tonight, in case Kayla and Austin come back. Unless you want to forbid me from doing that, *too*."

She only shrugged. Even her *shrugs* were annoying.

I stormed off to the Me cabin and grabbed a few supplies: a flashlight, two blankets, a canteen of water. As an after-thought, I took a few books from Will Solace's bookshelf. No surprise, he kept reference materials about me to share with new campers. I thought perhaps the books might help jog my memories. Failing that, they'd make good tinder for a fire.

When I returned to the edge of the woods, Meg was still there.

I hadn't expected her to keep vigil with me. Being Meg, she had apparently decided it would be the best way to irri-tate me.

She sat next to me on my blanket and began eating a golden apple, which she had hidden in her coat. Win-ter mist drifted through the trees. The night breeze rippled through the grass, making patterns like waves.

Under different circumstances, I might have written a poem about it. In my present state of mind, I could only have managed a funeral dirge, and I did not want to think about death.

I tried to stay mad at Meg, but I couldn't manage it. I supposed she'd had my best interests at heart . . . or at least, she wasn't ready to see her new godly servant get himself killed.

She didn't try to console me. She asked me no ques-tions. She amused herself by picking up small rocks and tossing them into the woods. That, I didn't mind. I happily would've given her a catapult if I had one.

As the night wore on, I read about myself in Will's books.

Normally this would have been a happy task. I am, after all, a fascinating subject. This time, however, I gained no satisfaction from my glorious exploits. They all seemed like exaggerations, lies, and . . . well, myths. Unfortunately, I found a chapter about Oracles. Those few pages stirred my memory, confirming my worst suspicions.

I was too angry to be terrified. I stared at the woods and dared the whispering voices to disturb me. I thought, Come on, then. Take me, too. The trees remained silent. Kayla and Austin did not return.

Toward dawn, it started to snow. Only then did Meg speak. "We should go inside."

"And abandon them?"

"Don't be stupid." Snow salted the hood of her winter coat. Her face was hidden except for the tip of her nose and the glint of rhinestones on her glasses. "You'll freeze out here."

I noticed she didn't complain about the cold herself. I wondered if she even felt uncomfortable, or if the power of Demeter kept her safe through the winter like a leafless tree or a dormant seed in the earth.

"They were my children." It hurt me to use the past tense, but Kayla and Austin felt irretrievably lost. "I should've done more to protect them. I should have antici-pated that my enemies would target them to hurt me."

Meg chucked another rock at the trees. "You've had a lot of children. You take the blame every time one of them gets in trouble?"

The answer was no. Over the millennia, I had barely managed to remember my children's names. If I sent them an occasional birthday card or a magic flute, I felt really good about myself. Sometimes I wouldn't realize one of them had died until decades later. During the French Revolution, I got worried about my boy Louis XIV, the Sun King, then went down to check on him and found out he had died seventy-five years earlier.

Now, though, I had a mortal conscience. My sense of guilt seemed to have expanded as my life span contracted. I couldn't explain that to Meg. She would never understand. She'd probably just throw a rock at me.

"It's my fault Python retook Delphi," I said. "If I had killed him the moment he reappeared, while I was still a god, he would never have become so powerful. He would never have made an alliance with this . . . this *Beast*."

Meg lowered her face.

"You know him," I guessed. "In the Labyrinth, when you heard the Beast's voice, you were terrified."

I was worried she might order me to shut up again. Instead, she silently traced the crescents on her gold rings.

"Meg, he wants to *destroy* me," I said. "Somehow, he's behind these disappearances. The more we understand about this man—"

"He lives in New York."

I waited. It was difficult to glean much information from the top of Meg's hood.

"All right," I said. "That narrows it down to eight and a half million people. What else?"

Meg picked at the calluses on her fingers. "If you're a demigod on the streets, you hear about the Beast. He takes people like me."

A snowflake melted on the back of my neck. "Takes people . . . why?"

"To train," Meg said. "To use like . . . servants, soldiers. I don't know."

"And you've met him."

"Please don't ask me—"

"Meg."

"He killed my dad."

Her words were quiet, but they hit me harder than a rock in the face. "Meg, I—I'm sorry. How . . . ?"

"I refused to work for him," she said. "My dad tried to . . ." She closed her fists. "I was really small. I hardly remember it. I got away. Otherwise, the Beast would've killed me, too. My stepdad took me in. He was good to me. You asked why he trained me to fight? Why he gave me the rings? He wanted me to be safe, to be able to protect myself."

"From the Beast."

Her hood dipped. "Being a good demigod, training hard . . . that's the only way to keep the Beast away. Now you know."

In fact, I had more questions than ever, but I sensed that Meg was in no mood for further sharing. I remembered her expression as we stood on that ledge under the chamber of Delphi—her look of absolute terror when she recognized the Beast's voice. Not all monsters were three-ton reptiles with poisonous breath. Many wore human faces.

I peered into the woods. Somewhere in there, five demigods were being used as bait, including two of my children. The Beast wanted me to search for them, and I would. But I would *not* let him use me.

I have well-placed help within the camp, the Beast had said. That bothered me.

I knew from experience that any demigod could be turned against Olympus. I had been at the banquet table when Tantalus tried to poison the gods by feeding us his chopped-up son in a stew. I'd watched as King Mithridates sided with the Persians and massacred every Roman in Anatolia. I'd witnessed Queen Clytemnestra turn homicidal, killing her husband Agamemnon just because he made one little human sacrifice to me. Demigods are an unpredictable bunch.

I glanced at Meg. I wondered if she could be lying to me—if she was some sort of spy. It seemed unlikely. She was too contrary, impetuous, and annoying to be an effective mole. Besides, she was technically my master. She could order me to do almost any task and I would have to obey. If she was out to destroy me, I was already as good as dead.

Perhaps Damien White . . . a son of Nemesis was a natural choice for backstabbing duty. Or Connor Stoll, Alice, or Julia . . . a child of Hermes had recently betrayed the gods by working for Kronos. They might do so again. Maybe that pretty Chiara, daughter of Tyche, was in league with the Beast. Children of luck were natural gamblers. The truth was, I had no idea.

The sky turned from black to gray. I became aware of a distant *thump, thump, thump*—a quick, relentless pulse that got louder and louder. At first, I feared it might be the blood in my head. Could human brains explode from too many worrisome thoughts? Then I realized the noise was mechanical, coming from the west. It was the distinctly modern sound of rotor blades cutting the air.

Meg lifted her head. "Is that a helicopter?"

I got to my feet.

The machine appeared—a dark red Bell 412 cutting north along the coastline. (Riding the skies as often as I do, I know my flying machines.) Painted on the helicopter's side was a bright green logo with the letters D.E.

Despite my misery, a small bit of hope kindled inside me. The satyrs Millard and Herbert must have succeeded in delivering their message.

"That," I told Meg, "is Rachel Elizabeth Dare. Let's go see what the Oracle of Delphi has to say."

20

Don't paint over gods
If you're redecorating
That's, like, common sense

RACHEL ELIZABETH DARE was one of my favorite mortals. As soon as she'd become the Oracle two summers ago, she'd brought new vigor and excitement to the job.

Of course, the previous Oracle had been a withered corpse, so perhaps the bar was low. Regardless, I was elated as the Dare Enterprises helicopter descended just beyond the eastern hills, outside the camp's boundary. I wondered what Rachel had told her father—a fabulously wealthy real estate magnate—to convince him she needed to borrow a helicopter. I knew Rachel could be quite convincing.

I jogged across the valley with Meg in tow. I could already imagine the way Rachel would look as she came over the summit: her frizzy red hair, her vivacious smile, her paint-spattered blouse, and jeans covered with doodles. I needed her humor, wisdom, and resilience. The Oracle would cheer us all up. Most importantly, she would cheer *me* up.

I was not prepared for the reality. (Which again, was a stunning surprise. Normally, reality prepares itself for *me*.)

Rachel met us on the hill near the entrance to her cave. Only later would I realize Chiron's two satyr messengers were not with her, and I would wonder what had happened to them.

Miss Dare looked thinner and older—less like a high school girl and more like a young farmer's wife from ancient times, weathered from hard work and gaunt from shortage of food. Her red hair had lost its vibrancy. It framed her face in a curtain of dark copper. Her freckles had faded to watermarks. Her green eyes did not sparkle. And she was wearing a dress—a white cotton frock with a white shawl, and a patina-green jacket. Rachel *never* wore dresses.

"Rachel?" I didn't trust myself to say any more. She was not the same person.

Then I remembered that I wasn't either.

She studied my new mortal form. Her shoulders slumped. "So it's true."

From below us came the voices of other campers. No doubt woken by the sound of the helicopter, they were emerging from their cabins and gathering at the base of the hill. None tried to climb toward us, though. Perhaps they sensed that all was not right.

The helicopter rose from behind Half-Blood Hill. It veered toward Long Island Sound, passing so close to the Athena Parthenos that I thought its landing skids might clip the goddess's winged helmet.

I turned to Meg. "Would you tell the others that Rachel needs some space? Fetch Chiron. He should come up. The rest should wait."

It wasn't like Meg to take orders from me. I half expected her to kick me. Instead, she glanced nervously at Rachel, turned, and trudged down the hill.

"A friend of yours?" Rachel asked.

"Long story."

"Yes," she said. "I have a story like that, too."

"Shall we talk in your cave?"

Rachel pursed her lips. "You won't like it. But yes, that's probably the safest place."

The cave was not as cozy as I remembered.

The sofas were overturned. The coffee table had a broken leg. The floor was strewn with easels and canvases. Even Rachel's tripod stool, the throne of prophecy itself, lay on its side on a pile of paint-splattered drop cloths.

Most disturbing was the state of the walls. Ever since taking up residence, Rachel had been painting them, like her cave-dwelling ancestors of old. She had spent hours on elaborate murals of events from the past, images from the future she'd seen in prophecies, favorite quotes from books and music, and abstract designs so good they would have given M. C. Escher vertigo. The art made the cave feel like a mixture of art studio, psychedelic hangout, and graffiti-covered highway underpass. I loved it.

But most of the images had been blotted out with a sloppy coat of white paint. Nearby, a roller was stuck in an encrusted tray. Clearly Rachel had defaced her own work months ago and hadn't been back since.

She waved listlessly at the wreckage. "I got frustrated."

"Your art . . ." I gaped at the field of white. "There was a lovely portrait of me—right there."

I get offended whenever art is damaged, especially if that art features me.

Rachel looked ashamed. "I—I thought a blank canvas might help me think." Her tone made it obvious that the whitewashing had accomplished nothing. I could have told her as much.

The two of us did our best to clean up. We hauled the sofas back into place to form a sitting area. Rachel left the tripod stool where it lay.

A few minutes later, Meg returned. Chiron followed in full centaur form, ducking his head to fit through the entrance. They found us sitting at the wobbly coffee table like civilized cave people, sharing lukewarm Arizona tea and stale crackers from the Oracle's larder.

"Rachel." Chiron sighed with relief. "Where are Millard and Herbert?"

She bowed her head. "They arrived at my house badly wounded. They . . . they didn't make it."

Perhaps it was the morning light behind him, but I fancied I could see new gray whiskers growing in Chiron's beard. The centaur trotted over and lowered himself to the ground, folding his legs underneath himself. Meg joined me on the couch.

Rachel leaned forward and steepled her fingers, as she did when she spoke a prophecy. I half hoped the spirit of Delphi would possess her, but there was no smoke, no hissing, no raspy voice of divine possession. It was a bit disappointing.

"You first," she told us. "Tell me what's been going on here."

We brought her up to speed on the disappearances and my misadventures with Meg. I explained about the three-legged race and our side trip to Delphi.

Chiron blanched. "I did not know this. You went to Delphi?"

Rachel stared at me in disbelief. "*The* Delphi. You saw Python and you . . ."

I got the feeling she wanted to say *and you didn't kill him?* But she restrained herself.

I felt like standing with my face against the wall. Perhaps Rachel could blot me out with white paint. Disappearing would've been less painful than facing my failures.

"At present," I said, "I cannot defeat Python. I am much too weak. And . . . well, the Catch-88."

Chiron sipped his Arizona tea. "Apollo means that we cannot send a quest without a prophecy, and we cannot get a prophecy without an Oracle."

Rachel stared at her overturned tripod stool. "And this man . . . the Beast. What do you know about him?"

"Not much." I explained what I had seen in my dream, and what Meg and I had overheard in the Labyrinth. "The Beast apparently has a reputation for snatching up young demigods in New York. Meg says . . ." I faltered when I saw her expression, clearly cautioning me to stay away from her personal history. "Um, she's had some experience with the Beast."

Chiron raised his brows. "Can you tell us anything that might help, dear?"

Meg sank into the sofa's cushions. "I've crossed paths with him. He's—he's scary. The memory is blurry."

"Blurry," Chiron repeated.

Meg became very interested in the cracker crumbs on her dress.

Rachel gave me a quizzical look. I shook my head, trying my best to impart a warning: *Trauma. Don't ask. Might get attacked by a peach baby.*

Rachel seemed to get the message. "That's all right, Meg," she said. "I have some information that may help."

She fished her phone from her coat pocket. "Don't touch this. You guys have probably figured it out, but phones are going even more haywire than usual around demigods. I'm not technically one of you, and even *I* can't place calls. I was able to take a couple of pictures, though." She turned the screen toward us. "Chiron, you recognize this place?"

The nighttime shot showed the upper floors of a glass residential tower. Judging from the background, it was somewhere in downtown Manhattan.

"That is the building you described last summer," Chiron said, "where you parleyed with the Romans."

"Yeah," Rachel said. "Something didn't feel right about that place. I got to thinking . . . how did the Romans take over such prime Manhattan real estate on such short notice? Who owns it? I tried to contact Reyna, to see if she could tell me anything, but—"

"Communication problems?" Chiron guessed.

"Exactly. I even sent physical mail to Camp Jupiter's drop box in Berkeley. No response. So I asked my dad's real estate lawyers to do some digging."

Meg peeked over the top of her glasses. "Your dad has lawyers? And a helicopter?"

"Several helicopters." Rachel sighed. "He's annoying. Anyway, that building is owned by a shell corporation, which is owned by another shell corporation, blah, blah, blah. The mother company is something called Triumvirate Holdings."

I felt a trickle like white paint rolling down my back. "*Triumvirate* . . ."

Meg made a sour face. "What does that mean?"

"A triumvirate is a ruling council of three," I said. "At least, that's what it meant in ancient Rome."

"Which is interesting," Rachel said, "because of this next shot." She tapped her screen. The new photo zoomed in on the building's penthouse terrace, where three shadowy figures stood talking together—men in business suits, illuminated only by the light from inside the apartment. I couldn't see their faces.

"These are the owners of Triumvirate Holdings," Rachel said. "Just getting this *one* picture wasn't easy." She blew a frizzy strand of hair out of her face. "I've spent the last two months investigating them, and I don't even know their names. I don't know where they live or where they came from. But I can tell you they own so much property and have so much money, they make my dad's company look like a kid's lemonade stand."

I stared at the picture of the three shadowy figures. I could almost imagine that the one on the left was the Beast. His slouching posture and the over-large shape of his head reminded me of the man in purple from my dream.

"The Beast said that his organization was everywhere," I recalled. "He mentioned he had colleagues."

Chiron's tail flicked, sending a paintbrush skidding across the cave floor. "Adult demigods? I can't imagine they would be Greek, but perhaps Roman? If they helped Octavian with his war—"

"Oh, they helped," Rachel said. "I found a paper trail—not much, but you remember those siege weapons Octavian built to destroy Camp Half-Blood?"

"No," said Meg.

I would have ignored her, but Rachel was a more generous soul.

She smiled patiently. "Sorry, Meg. You seem so at home here, I forgot you were new. Basically, the Roman demigods attacked this camp with giant catapulty things called onagers. It was all a big misunderstanding. Anyway, the weapons were paid for by Triumvirate Holdings."

Chiron frowned. "That is not good."

"I found something even more disturbing," Rachel continued. "You remember before that, during the Titan War, Luke Castellan mentioned he had backers in the mortal world? They had enough money to buy a cruise ship, helicopters, weapons. They even hired mortal mercenaries."

"Don't remember that, either," Meg said.

I rolled my eyes. "Meg, we can't stop and explain every major war to you! Luke Castellan was a child of Hermes. He betrayed this camp and allied himself with the Titans. They attacked New York. Big battle. I saved the day. Et cetera."

Chiron coughed. "At any rate, I do remember Luke

claiming that he had lots of supporters. We never found out exactly who they were."

"Now we know," Rachel said. "That cruise ship, the *Princess Andromeda*, was property of Triumvirate Holdings."

A cold sense of unease gripped me. I felt I should know something about this, but my mortal brain was betraying me again. I was more certain than ever that Zeus was toying with me, keeping my vision and memory limited. I remembered some assurances Octavian had given me, though—how easy it would be to win his little war, to raise new temples to me, how much support he had.

Rachel's phone screen went dark—much like my brain—but the grainy photo remained burned into my retinas.

"These men . . ." I picked up an empty tube of burnt sienna paint. "I'm afraid they are not modern demigods."

Rachel frowned. "You think they're ancient demigods who came through the Doors of Death—like Medea, or Midas? The thing is, Triumvirate Holdings has been around since way before Gaea started to wake. Decades, at least."

"Centuries," I said. "The Beast said that he'd been building his empire for centuries."

The cave became so silent, I imagined the hiss of Python, the soft exhale of fumes from deep in the earth. I wished we had some background music to drown it out . . . jazz or classical. I would have settled for death metal polka.

Rachel shook her head. "Then who—?"

"I don't know," I admitted. "But the Beast . . . in my dream, he called me his forefather. He assumed I would recognize him. And if my godly memory was intact, I think

I would. His demeanor, his accent, his facial structure—I have met him before, just not in modern times."

Meg had grown very quiet. I got the distinct impression she was trying to disappear into the couch cushions. Normally, this would not have bothered me, but after our experience in the Labyrinth, I felt guilty every time I mentioned the Beast. My pesky mortal conscience must have been acting up.

"The name Triumvirate . . ." I tapped my forehead, trying to shake loose information that was no longer there. "The last triumvirate I dealt with included Lepidus, Marc Antony, and my son, the *original* Octavian. A triumvirate is a very Roman concept . . . like patriotism, skullduggery, and assassination."

Chiron stroked his beard. "You think these men are ancient Romans? How is that possible? Hades is quite good at tracking down escaped spirits from the Underworld. He would not allow three men from ancient times to run amok in the modern world for centuries."

"Again, I do not know." Saying this so often offended my divine sensibilities. I decided that when I returned to Olympus, I would have to gargle the bad taste out of my mouth with Tabasco-flavored nectar. "But it seems these men have been plotting against us for a very long time. They funded Luke Castellan's war. They supplied aid to Camp Jupiter when the Romans attacked Camp Half-Blood. And despite those two wars, the Triumvirate is still out there— still plotting. What if this company is the root cause of . . . well, everything?"

Chiron looked at me as if I were digging his grave. "That is a very troubling thought. Could three men be so powerful?"

I spread my hands. "You've lived long enough to know, my friend. Gods, monsters, Titans . . . these are always dangerous. But the greatest threat to demigods has always been other demigods. Whoever this Triumvirate is, we must stop them before they take control of the Oracles."

Rachel sat up straight. "Excuse me? Oracles plural?"

"Ah . . . didn't I tell you about them when I was a god?"

Her eyes regained some of their dark green intensity. I feared she was envisioning ways she might inflict pain upon me with her art supplies.

"No," she said levelly, "you did not tell me about them."

"Oh . . . well, my mortal memory has been faulty, you see. I had to read some books in order to—"

"Oracles," she repeated. "Plural."

I took a deep breath. I wanted to assure her that those other Oracles didn't mean a thing to me! Rachel was special! Unfortunately, I doubted she was in a place where she could hear that right now. I decided it was best to speak plainly.

"In ancient times," I said, "there were many Oracles. Of course Delphi was the most famous, but there were four others of comparable power."

Chiron shook his head. "But those were destroyed ages ago."

"So I thought," I agreed. "Now I am not so sure. I believe Triumvirate Holdings wants to control *all* the ancient Oracles. And I believe the most ancient Oracle of all, the Grove of Dodona, is right here at Camp Half-Blood."

21

Up in my business
Always burning Oracles
Romans gonna hate

I WAS A DRAMATIC GOD.

I thought my last statement was a great line. I expected gasps, perhaps some organ music in the background. Maybe the lights would go out just before I could say more. Moments later, I would be found dead with a knife in my back. That would be exciting!

Wait. I'm mortal. Murder would kill me. Never mind.

At any rate, none of that happened. My three companions just stared at me.

"Four other Oracles," Rachel said. "You mean you have four other Pythias—"

"No, my dear. There is only one Pythia—*you*. Delphi is absolutely unique."

Rachel still looked like she wanted to jam a number ten bristle paintbrush up my nose. "So these other four *non-unique* Oracles . . ."

"Well, one was the Sybil of Cumae." I wiped the sweat off my palms. (Why did mortal palms sweat?) "You know, she wrote the Sibylline Books—those prophecies that Ella the harpy memorized."

Meg looked back and forth between us. "A harpy . . . like those chicken ladies who clean up after lunch?"

Chiron smiled. "Ella is a very special harpy, Meg. Years ago, she somehow came across a copy of the prophetic books, which we thought were burned before the Fall of Rome. Right now, our friends at Camp Jupiter are trying to reconstruct them based on Ella's recollections."

Rachel crossed her arms. "And the other three Oracles? I'm sure none of them was a beautiful young priestess whom you praised for her . . . what was it? . . . 'scintillating conversation'?"

"Ah . . ." I wasn't sure why, but it felt like my acne was turning into live insects and crawling across my face. "Well, according to my extensive research—"

"Some books he flipped through last night," Meg clarified.

"Ahem! There was an Oracle at Erythaea, and another at the Cave of Trophonius."

"Goodness," Chiron said. "I'd forgotten about those two."

I shrugged. I remembered almost nothing about them either. They had been some of my less successful prophetic franchises.

"And the fifth," I said, "was the Grove of Dodona."

"A grove," Meg said. "Like trees."

"Yes, Meg, like trees. Groves are typically composed of trees, rather than, say, Fudgsicles. Dodona was a stand of sacred oaks planted by the Mother Goddess in the first days of the world. They were ancient even when the Olympians were born."

"The Mother Goddess?" Rachel shivered in her patina jacket. "Please tell me you don't mean Gaea."

"No, thankfully. I mean Rhea, Queen of the Titans, the mother of the first generation of Olympian gods. Her sacred trees could actually speak. Sometimes they issued prophecies."

"The voices in the woods," Meg guessed.

"Exactly. I believe the Grove of Dodona has regrown itself here in the woods at camp. In my dreams, I saw a crowned woman imploring me to find her Oracle. I believe it was Rhea, though I still don't understand why she was wearing a peace symbol or using the term *dig it.*"

"A peace symbol?" Chiron asked.

"A large brass one," I confirmed.

Rachel drummed her fingers on the couch's armrest. "If Rhea is a Titan, isn't she evil?"

"Not all Titans were bad," I said. "Rhea was a gentle soul. She sided with the gods in their first great war. I think she wants us to succeed. She doesn't want her grove in the hands of our enemies."

Chiron's tail twitched. "My friend, Rhea has not been seen for millennia. Her grove was burned in the ancient times. Emperor Theodosius ordered the last oak cut down in—"

"I know." I got a stabbing pain right between my eyes, as I always did when someone mentioned Theodosius. I now recalled that the bully had closed all the ancient temples across the empire, basically evicting us Olympian gods. I used to have an archery target with his face on it. "Nevertheless, many things from the old days have survived or regenerated.

The Labyrinth has rebuilt itself. Why couldn't a grove of sacred trees spring up again right here in this valley?"

Meg pushed herself deeper into the cushions. "This is all weird." Leave it to the young McCaffrey to summarize our conversation so effectively. "So if the tree voices are sacred and stuff, why are they making people get lost?"

"For once, you ask a good question." I hoped such praise wouldn't go to Meg's head. "In the old days, the priests of Dodona would take care of the trees, pruning them, watering them, and channeling their voices by hanging wind chimes in their branches."

"How would that help?" Meg asked.

"I don't know. I'm not a tree priest. But with proper care, these trees could divine the future."

Rachel smoothed her skirt. "And without proper care?"

"The voices were unfocused," I said. "A wild choir of disharmony." I paused, quite pleased with that line. I was hoping someone might write it down for posterity, but no one did. "Untended, the grove could most definitely drive mortals to madness."

Chiron furrowed his brow. "So our missing campers are wandering in the trees, perhaps already insane from the voices."

"Or they're dead," Meg added.

"No." I could not abide that thought. "No, they are still alive. The Beast is using them, trying to bait me."

"How can you be sure?" Rachel asked. "And why? If Python already controls Delphi, why are these other Oracles so important?"

I gazed at the wall formerly graced by my picture. Alas,

no answers magically appeared in the whitewashed space. "I'm not sure. I believe our enemies want to cut us off from every possible source of prophecy. Without a way to see and direct our fates, we will wither and die—gods and mortals alike, anyone who opposes the Triumvirate."

Meg turned upside down on the sofa and kicked off her red shoes. "They're strangling our taproots." She wriggled her toes to demonstrate.

I looked back at Rachel, hoping she would excuse my street urchin overlord's bad manners. "As for why the Grove of Dodona is so important, Python mentioned that it was the one Oracle he could not control. I don't understand exactly why—perhaps because Dodona is the only Oracle that has no connection with me. Its power comes from Rhea. So if the grove is working, and it is free of Python's influence, and it is here at Camp Half-Blood—"

"It could provide us with prophecies." Chiron's eyes gleamed. "It could give us a chance against our enemies."

I gave Rachel an apologetic smile. "Of course, we'd rather have our beloved Oracle of Delphi working again. And we will, eventually. But for now, the Grove of Dodona could be our best hope."

Meg's hair swept the floor. Her face was now the color of one of my sacred cattle. "Aren't prophecies all twisted and mysterious and murky, and people die trying to escape them?"

"Meg," I said, "you can't trust those reviews on RateMyOracle.com. The hotness factor for the Sibyl of Cumae, for instance, is *completely* off. I remember *that* quite clearly."

Rachel put her chin on her fist. "Really? Do tell."

"Uh, what I meant to say: the Grove of Dodona is a benevolent force. It has helped heroes before. The masthead of the original *Argo*, for instance, was carved from a branch of the sacred trees. It could speak to the Argonauts and give them guidance."

"Mm." Chiron nodded. "And that's why our mysterious Beast wants the grove burned."

"Apparently," I said. "And that's why we have to save it."

Meg rolled backward off the couch. Her legs knocked over the three-legged coffee table, spilling our Arizona tea and crackers. "Oops."

I ground my mortal teeth, which would not last a year if I kept hanging around Meg. Rachel and Chiron wisely ignored my young friend's display of Megness.

"Apollo . . ." The old centaur watched a waterfall of tea trickling from the edge of the table. "If you are right about Dodona, how do we proceed? We are already shorthanded. If we send search teams into the woods, we have no guarantee they'll come back."

Meg brushed the hair out of her eyes. "We'll go. Just Apollo and me."

My tongue attempted to hide in the depths of my throat. "We—we will?"

"You said you gotta do a bunch of trials or whatever to prove you're worthy, right? This'll be the first one."

Part of me knew she was right, but the remnants of my godly self rebelled at the idea. I never did my own dirty work. I would rather have picked a nice group of heroes and sent them to their deaths—or, you know, glorious success.

Yet Rhea had been clear in my dream: finding the Oracle was my job. And thanks to the cruelty of Zeus, where I went, Meg went. For all I knew, Zeus was aware of the Beast and his plans, and he had sent me here specifically to deal with the situation . . . a thought that did not make me any more likely to get him a nice tie for Father's Day.

I also remembered the other part of my dream: the Beast in his mauve suit, encouraging me to find the Oracle so he could burn it down. There was still too much I didn't understand, but I had to act. Austin and Kayla were depending on me.

Rachel put her hand on my knee, which made me flinch. Surprisingly, she did not inflict any pain. Her gaze was more earnest than angry. "Apollo, you have to try. If we can get a glimpse of the future . . . well, it may be the only way to get things back to normal." She looked longingly at the blank walls of her cave. "I'd like to have a future again."

Chiron shifted his forelegs. "What do you need from us, old friend? How can we help?"

I glanced at Meg. Sadly, I could tell that we were in agreement. We were stuck with each other. We couldn't risk anyone else.

"Meg is right," I said. "We have to do this ourselves. We should leave immediately, but—"

"We've been up all night," Meg said. "We need some sleep."

Wonderful, I thought. Now Meg is finishing my sentences.

This time I could not argue with her logic. Despite my fervor to rush into the woods and save my children, I had to proceed cautiously. I could not mess up this rescue. And I was increasingly certain that the Beast would keep his captives alive for now. He needed them to lure me into his trap.

Chiron rose on his front hooves. "This evening, then. Rest and prepare, my heroes. I fear you will need all your strength and wits for what comes next."

22

Armed to the eyeballs:
A combat ukulele
Magic Brazil scarf

SUN GODS ARE NOT GOOD at sleeping during the day, but somehow I managed a fitful nap.

When I woke in the late afternoon, I found the camp in a state of agitation.

Kayla and Austin's disappearance had been the tipping point. The other campers were now so rattled, no one could maintain a normal schedule. I suppose a single demigod disappearing every few weeks felt like a normal casualty rate. But a pair of demigods disappearing in the middle of a camp-sanctioned activity—that meant no one was safe.

Word must have spread of our conference in the cave. The Victor twins had stuffed wads of cotton in their ears to foil the oracular voices. Julia and Alice had climbed to the top of the lava wall and were using binoculars to scan the woods, no doubt hoping to spot the Grove of Dodona, but I doubted they could see the trees for the forest.

Everywhere I went, people were unhappy to see me. Damien and Chiara sat together at the canoe dock, glowering in my direction. Sherman Yang waved me away when

I tried to talk with him. He was busy decorating the Ares cabin with frag grenades and brightly decorated claymores. If it had been Saturnalia, he definitely would have won the prize for most violent holiday decorations.

Even the Athena Parthenos stared down at me accusingly from the top of the hill as if to say, *This is all your fault*.

She was right. If I hadn't let Python take over Delphi, if I'd paid more attention to the other ancient Oracles, if I hadn't lost my divinity—

Stop it, Apollo, I scolded myself. *You're beautiful and everyone loves you.*

But it was becoming increasingly difficult to believe that. My father, Zeus, did not love me. The demigods at Camp Half-Blood did not love me. Python and the Beast and his comrades at Triumvirate Holdings did not love me. It was almost enough to make me question my self-worth.

No, no. That was crazy talk.

Chiron and Rachel were nowhere to be seen. Nyssa Barrera informed me that they were hoping against hope to use the camp's sole Internet connection, in Chiron's office, to access more information about Triumvirate Holdings. Harley was with them for tech support. They were presently on hold with Comcast customer service and might not emerge for hours, if indeed they survived the ordeal at all.

I found Meg at the armory, browsing for battle supplies. She had strapped a leather cuirass over her green dress and greaves over orange leggings, so she looked like a kindergartener reluctantly stuffed into combat gear by her parents.

"Perhaps a shield?" I suggested.

"Nuh-uh." She showed me her rings. "I always use two

swords. Plus I need a free hand for slapping when you act stupid."

I had the uncomfortable sense she was serious.

From the weapon rack, she pulled out a long bow and offered it to me.

I recoiled. "No."

"It's your best weapon. You're Apollo."

I swallowed back the tang of mortal bile. "I swore an oath. I'm not the god of archery or music anymore. I won't use a bow or a musical instrument until I can use them *properly*."

"Stupid oath." She didn't slap me, but she looked like she wanted to. "What will you do, just stand around and cheer while I fight?"

That had indeed been my plan, but now I felt silly admitting it. I scanned the weapon display and grabbed a sword. Even without drawing it, I could tell it would be too heavy and awkward for me to use, but I strapped the scabbard around my waist.

"There," I said. "Happy?"

Meg did not appear happy. Nevertheless, she returned the bow to its place.

"Fine," she said. "But you'd better have my back."

I had never understood that expression. It made me think of the KICK ME signs Artemis used to tape to my toga during festival days. Still, I nodded. "Your back shall be had."

We reached the edge of the woods and found a small going-away party waiting for us: Will and Nico, Paolo Montes, Malcolm Pace, and Billie Ng, all with grim faces.

"Be careful," Will told me. "And here."

Before I could object, he placed a ukulele in my hands.

I tried to give it back. "I can't. I made an oath—"

"Yeah, I know. That was stupid of you. But it's a combat ukulele. You can fight with it if you need to."

I looked more closely at the instrument. It was made from Celestial bronze—thin sheets of metal acid-etched to resemble the grain of blond oak wood. The instrument weighed next to nothing, yet I imagined it was almost indestructible.

"The work of Hephaestus?" I asked.

Will shook his head. "The work of Harley. He wanted you to have it. Just sling it over your back. For me and Harley. It'll make us both feel better."

I decided I was obliged to honor the request, though my possession of a ukulele had rarely made anyone feel better. Don't ask me why. When I was a god, I used to do an absolutely blistering ukulele version of "Satisfaction."

Nico handed me some ambrosia wrapped in a napkin.

"I can't eat this," I reminded him.

"It's not for you." He glanced at Meg, his eyes full of misgiving. I remembered that the son of Hades had his own ways of sensing the future—futures that involved the possibility of death. I shivered and tucked the ambrosia into my coat pocket. As aggravating as Meg could be, I was deeply unsettled by the idea that she might come to harm. I decided that I could not allow that to happen.

Malcolm was showing Meg a parchment map, pointing out various places in the woods that we should avoid. Paolo—looking completely healed from his leg surgery—stood next to him, carefully and earnestly providing Portuguese commentary that no one could understand.

When they were finished with the map, Billie Ng approached Meg.

Billie was a wisp of a girl. She compensated for her diminutive stature with the fashion sense of a K-Pop idol. Her winter coat was the color of aluminum foil. Her bobbed hair was aquamarine and her makeup gold. I completely approved. In fact, I thought I could rock that look myself if I could just get my acne under control.

Billie gave Meg a flashlight and a small packet of flower seeds.

"Just in case," Billie said.

Meg seemed quite overwhelmed. She gave Billie a fierce hug.

I didn't understand the purpose of the seeds, but it was comforting to know that in a dire emergency I could hit people with my ukulele while Meg planted geraniums.

Malcolm Pace gave me his parchment map. "When in doubt, veer to the right. That usually works in the woods, though I don't know why."

Paolo offered me a green-and-gold scarf—a bandana version of the Brazilian flag. He said something that, of course, I could not understand.

Nico smirked. "That's Paolo's good-luck bandana. I think he wants you to wear it. He believes it will make you invincible."

I found this dubious, since Paolo was prone to serious injury, but as a god, I had learned never to turn down offerings. "Thank you."

Paolo gripped my shoulders and kissed my cheeks. I may have blushed. He was quite handsome when he wasn't bleeding out from dismemberment.

I rested my hand on Will's shoulder. "Don't worry. We'll be back by dawn."

His mouth trembled ever so slightly. "How can you be sure?"

"I'm the sun god," I said, trying to muster more confidence than I felt. "I *always* return at dawn."

Of course it rained. Why would it not?

Up in Mount Olympus, Zeus must have been having a good laugh at my expense. Camp Half-Blood was supposed to be protected from severe weather, but no doubt my father had told Aeolus to pull out all the stops on his winds. My jilted ex-girlfriends among the air nymphs were probably enjoying their moment of payback.

The rain was just on the edge of sleet—liquid enough to soak my clothes, icy enough to slam against my exposed face like glass shards.

We stumbled along, lurching from tree to tree to find any shelter we could. Patches of old snow crunched under my feet. My ukulele got heavier as its sound hole filled with rain. Meg's flashlight beam cut across the storm like a cone of yellow static.

I led the way, not because I had any destination in mind, but because I was angry. I was tired of being cold and soaked. I was tired of being picked on. Mortals often talk about the whole world being against them, but that is ridiculous. Mortals aren't that important. In my case, the whole world really *was* against me. I refused to surrender to such abuse. I would do something about it! I just wasn't quite sure what.

From time to time we heard monsters in the distance—the roar of a drakon, the harmonized howl of a two-headed wolf—but nothing showed itself. On a night like this, any self-respecting monster would've remained in its lair, warm and cozy.

After what seemed like hours, Meg stifled a scream. I heroically leaped to her side, my hand on my sword. (I would have drawn it, but it was really heavy and got stuck in the scabbard.) At Meg's feet, wedged in the mud, was a glistening black shell the size of a boulder. It was cracked down the middle, the edges splattered with a foul gooey substance.

"I almost stepped on that." Meg covered her mouth as if she might be sick.

I inched closer. The shell was the crushed carapace of a giant insect. Nearby, camouflaged among the tree roots, lay one of the beast's dismembered legs.

"It's a *myrmeke*," I said. "Or it was."

Behind her rain-splattered glasses, Meg's eyes were impossible to read. "A *murr-murr-key?*"

"A giant ant. There must be a colony somewhere in the woods."

Meg gagged. "I hate bugs."

That made sense for a daughter of the agriculture goddess, but to me the dead ant didn't seem any grosser than the piles of garbage in which we often swam.

"Well, don't worry," I said. "This one is dead. Whatever killed it must've had powerful jaws to crack that shell."

"Not comforting. Are—are these things dangerous?"

I laughed. "Oh, yes. They range in size from as small as dogs to larger than grizzly bears. One time I watched a colony of myrmekes attack a Greek army in India. It was hilarious. They spit acid that can melt through bronze armor and—"

"Apollo."

My smile faded. I reminded myself I was no longer a spectator. These ants could kill us. Easily. And Meg was scared.

"Right," I said. "Well, the rain should keep the myrmekes in their tunnels. Just don't make yourself an attractive target. They like bright, shiny things."

"Like flashlights?"

"Um . . ."

Meg handed me the flashlight. "Lead on, Apollo."

I thought that was unfair, but we forged ahead.

After another hour or so (surely the woods weren't this big), the rain tapered off, leaving the ground steaming.

The air got warmer. The humidity approached bath-house levels. Thick white vapor curled off the tree branches.

"What's going on?" Meg wiped her face. "Feels like a tropical rain forest now."

I had no answer. Then, up ahead, I heard a massive flushing sound—like water being forced through pipes . . . or fissures.

I couldn't help but smile. "A geyser."

"A geyser," Meg repeated. "Like Old Faithful?"

"This is excellent news. Perhaps we can get directions. Our lost demigods might have even found sanctuary there!"

"With the geysers," Meg said.

"No, my ridiculous girl," I said. "With the geyser *gods*. Assuming they're in a good mood, this could be great."

"And if they're in a bad mood?"

"Then we'll cheer them up before they can boil us. Follow me!"

23

Scale of one to ten

How would you rate your demise?

Thanks for your input

WAS I RECKLESS to rush toward such volatile nature gods?

Please. Second-guessing myself is not in my nature. It's a trait I've never needed.

True, my memories about the *palikoi* were a little hazy. As I recalled, the geyser gods in ancient Sicily used to give refuge to runaway slaves, so they must be kindly spirits. Perhaps they would also give refuge to lost demigods, or at least notice when five of them wandered through their territory, muttering incoherently. Besides, I was Apollo! The palikoi would be honored to meet a major Olympian such as myself! The fact that geysers often blew their tops, spewing columns of scalding hot water hundreds of feet in the air, wasn't going to stop me from making some new fans . . . I mean *friends*.

The clearing opened before us like an oven door. A wall of heat billowed through the trees and washed over my face. I could feel my pores opening to drink in the moisture, which would hopefully help my spotty complexion.

The scene before us had no business being in a Long

Island winter. Glistening vines wreathed the tree branches. Tropical flowers bloomed from the forest floor. A red parrot sat on a banana tree heavy with green bunches.

In the midst of the glade stood two geysers—twin holes in the ground, ringed with a figure eight of gray mud pots. The craters bubbled and hissed, but they were not spewing at the moment. I decided to take that as a good omen.

Meg's boots squished in the mud. "Is it safe?"

"Definitely not," I said. "We'll need an offering. Perhaps your packet of seeds?"

Meg punched my arm. "Those are magic. For life-and-death emergencies. What about your ukulele? You're not going to play it anyway."

"A man of honor *never* surrenders his ukulele." I perked up. "But wait. You've given me an idea. I will offer the geyser gods a poem! I can still do that. It doesn't count as music."

Meg frowned. "Uh, I don't know if—"

"Don't be envious, Meg. I will make up a poem for you later. This will surely please the geyser gods!" I walked forward, spread my arms, and began to improvise:

> "Oh, geyser, my geyser,
> Let us spew then, you and I,
> Upon this midnight dreary, while we ponder
> Whose woods are these?
> For we have not gone gentle into this good night,
> But have wandered lonely as clouds.
> We seek to know for whom the bell tolls,
> So I hope, springs eternal,
> That the time has come to talk of many things!"

I don't wish to brag, but I thought it was rather good, even if I did recycle a few bits from my earlier works. Unlike my music and archery, my godly skills with poetry seemed to be completely intact.

I glanced at Meg, hoping to see shining admiration on her face. It was high time the girl started to appreciate me. Instead, her mouth hung open, aghast.

"What?" I demanded. "Did you fail poetry appreciation in school? That was first-rate stuff!"

Meg pointed toward the geysers. I realized she was not looking at me at all.

"Well," said a raspy voice, "you got my attention."

One of the palikoi hovered over his geyser. His lower half was nothing but steam. From the waist up, he was perhaps twice the size of a human, with muscular arms the color of caldera mud, chalk-white eyes, and hair like cappuccino foam, as if he had shampooed vigorously and left it sudsy. His massive chest was stuffed into a baby-blue polo shirt with a logo of trees embroidered on the chest pocket.

"O Great Palikos!" I said. "We beseech you—"

"What was that?" the spirit interrupted. "That stuff you were saying?"

"Poetry!" I said. "For you!"

He tapped his mud-gray chin. "No. That wasn't poetry."

I couldn't believe it. Did *no one* appreciate the beauty of language anymore? "My good spirit," I said. "Poetry doesn't have to rhyme, you know."

"I'm not talking about rhyming. I'm talking about getting your message across. We do a lot of market research, and that would *not* fly for our campaign. Now, the Oscar

Meyer Weiner song—*that* is poetry. The ad is fifty years old and people are still singing it. Do you think you could give us some poetry like that?"

I glanced at Meg to be sure I was not imagining this conversation.

"Listen here," I told the geyser god, "I've been the lord of poetry for four thousand years. I ought to know good poetry—"

The palikos waved his hands. "Let's start over. I'll run through our spiel, and maybe you can advise me. Hi, I'm Pete. Welcome to the Woods at Camp Half-Blood! Would you be willing to take a short customer satisfaction survey after this encounter? Your feedback is important."

"Um—"

"Great. Thanks."

Pete fished around in his vaporous region where his pockets would be. He produced a glossy brochure and began to read. "The Woods are your one-stop destination for . . . Hmm, it says *fun*. I thought we changed that to *exhilaration*. See, you've got to choose your words with care. If Paulie were here . . ." Pete sighed. "Well, he's better with the showmanship. Anyway, welcome to the Woods at Camp Half-Blood!"

"You already said that," I noted.

"Oh, right." Pete produced a red pen and began to edit.

"Hey." Meg shouldered past me. She had been speechless with awe for about twelve seconds, which must've been a new record. "Mr. Steamy Mud, have you seen any lost demigods?"

"Mr. Steamy Mud!" Pete slapped his brochure. "*That* is

effective branding! And great point about lost demigods. We can't have our guests wandering around aimlessly. We should be handing out maps at the entrance to the woods. So many wonderful things to see in here, and no one even knows about them. I'll talk to Paulie when he gets back."

Meg took off her fogged-up glasses. "Who's Paulie?"

Pete gestured at the second geyser. "My partner. Maybe we could add a map to this brochure if—"

"So *have* you seen any lost demigods?" I asked.

"What?" Pete tried to mark his brochure, but the steam had made it so soggy, his red pen went right through the paper. "Oh, no. Not recently. But we should have better signage. For instance, did you even know these geysers were here?"

"No," I admitted.

"Well, there you go! Double geysers—the only ones on Long Island!—and no one even knows about us. No outreach. No word-of-mouth. This is why we convinced the board of directors to hire us!"

Meg and I looked at each other. I could tell that for once we were on the same wavelength: utter confusion.

"Sorry," I said. "Are you telling me the forest has a board of directors?"

"Well, of course," Pete said. "The dryads, the other nature spirits, the sentient monsters . . . I mean, *somebody* has to think about property values and services and public relations. It wasn't easy getting the board to hire us for marketing, either. If we mess up this job . . . oh, man."

Meg squished her shoes in the mud. "Can we go? I don't understand what this guy's talking about."

"And that's the problem!" Pete moaned. "How do we write clear ad copy that conveys the right image of the Woods? For instance, palikoi like Paulie and me used to be famous! Major tourist destinations! People would come to us to make binding oaths. Runaway slaves would seek us out for shelter. We'd get sacrifices, offerings, prayers . . . It was great. Now, nothing."

I heaved a sigh. "I know how you feel."

"Guys," Meg said, "we're looking for missing demigods."

"Right," I agreed. "O, Great . . . Pete, do you have any idea where our lost friends might have gone? Perhaps you know of some secret locations within the woods?"

Pete's chalk-white eyes brightened. "Did you know the children of Hephaestus have a hidden workshop to the north called Bunker Nine?"

"I did, actually," I said.

"Oh." A puff of steam escaped Pete's left nostril. "Well, did you know the Labyrinth has rebuilt itself? There is an entrance right here in the woods—"

"We know," Meg said.

Pete looked crestfallen.

"But perhaps," I said, "that's because your marketing campaign is working."

"Do you think so?" Pete's foamy hair began to swirl. "Yes. Yes, that may be true! Did you happen to see our spotlights, too? Those were my idea."

"Spotlights?" Meg asked.

Twin beams of red light blasted from the geysers and swept across the sky. Lit from beneath, Pete looked like the world's scariest teller of ghost stories.

"Unfortunately, they attracted the wrong kind of attention." Pete sighed. "Paulie doesn't let me use them often. He suggested advertising on a blimp instead, or perhaps a giant inflatable King Kong—"

"That's cool," Meg interrupted. "But can you tell us anything about a secret grove with whispering trees?"

I had to admit, Meg was good at getting us back on topic. As a poet, I did not cultivate directness. But as an archer, I could appreciate the value of a straight shot.

"Oh." Pete floated lower in his cloud of steam, the spotlight turning him the color of cherry soda. "I'm not supposed to talk about the grove."

My once-godly ears tingled. I resisted the urge to scream, AHA! "Why can't you talk about the grove, Pete?"

The spirit fiddled with his soggy brochure. "Paulie said it would scare away tourists. 'Talk about the dragons,' he told me. 'Talk about the wolves and serpents and ancient killing machines. But don't mention the grove.'"

"Ancient killing machines?" Meg asked.

"Yeah," Pete said halfheartedly. "We're marketing them as fun family entertainment. But the grove . . . Paulie said that was our worst problem. The neighborhood isn't even zoned for an Oracle. Paulie went there to see if maybe we could relocate it, but—"

"He didn't come back," I guessed.

Pete nodded miserably. "How am I supposed to run the marketing campaign all by myself? Sure, I can use robo-calls for the phone surveys, but a lot of networking has to be done face-to-face, and Paulie was always better with that stuff." Pete's voice broke into a sad hiss. "I miss him."

"Maybe we could find him," Meg suggested, "and bring him back."

Pete shook his head. "Paulie made me promise not to follow him and not to tell anybody else where the grove is. He's pretty good at resisting those weird voices, but you guys wouldn't stand a chance."

I was tempted to agree. Finding ancient killing machines sounded much more reasonable. Then I pictured Kayla and Austin wandering through the ancient grove, slowly going mad. They needed me, which meant I needed their location.

"Sorry, Pete." I gave him my most critical stare—the one I used to crush aspiring singers during Broadway auditions. "I'm just not buying it."

Mud bubbled around Pete's caldera. "Wh-what do you mean?"

"I don't think this grove exists," I said. "And if it does, I don't think you know its location."

Pete's geyser rumbled. Steam swirled in his spotlight beam. "I—I *do* know! Of course it exists!"

"Oh, really? Then why aren't there billboards about it all over the place? And a dedicated Web site? Why haven't I seen a groveofdodona hashtag on social media?"

Pete glowered. "I suggested all that! Paulie shot me down!"

"So do some outreach!" I demanded. "Sell us on your product! Show us where this grove is!"

"I can't. The only entrance . . ." He glanced over my shoulder and his face went slack. "Ah, spew." His spotlights shut off.

I turned. Meg made a squelching sound even louder than her shoes in the mud.

It took a moment for my vision to adjust, but at the edge of the clearing stood three black ants the size of Sherman tanks.

"Pete," I said, trying to remain calm, "when you said your spotlights attracted the wrong kind of attention—"

"I meant the myrmekes," he said. "I hope this won't affect your online review of the Woods at Camp Half-Blood."

24

Breaking my promise
Spectacularly failing
I blame Neil Diamond

MYRMEKES SHOULD BE high on your list of monsters not to fight.

They attack in groups. They spit acid. Their pincers can snap through Celestial bronze.

Also, they are ugly.

The three soldier ants advanced, their ten-foot-long antennae waving and bobbing in a mesmerizing way, trying to distract me from the true danger of their mandibles.

Their beaked heads reminded me of chickens—chickens with dark flat eyes and black armored faces. Each of their six legs would have made a fine construction winch. Their oversize abdomens throbbed and pulsed like noses sniffing for food.

I silently cursed Zeus for inventing ants. The way I heard it, he got upset with some greedy man who was always stealing from his neighbors' crops, so Zeus turned him into the first ant—a species that does nothing but scavenge, steal, and breed. Ares liked to joke that if Zeus wanted such a species, he could've just left humans the way they were. I used to laugh. Now that I am one of you, I no longer find it funny.

The ants stepped toward us, their antennae twitching. I imagined their train of thought was something like *Shiny? Tasty? Defenseless?*

"No sudden movements," I told Meg, who did not seem inclined to move at all. In fact, she looked petrified.

"Oh, Pete?" I called. "How do you deal with myrmekes invading your territory?"

"By hiding," he said, and disappeared into the geyser.

"Not helpful," I grumbled.

"Can we dive in?" Meg asked.

"Only if you fancy boiling to death in a pit of scalding water."

The tank bugs clacked their mandibles and edged closer.

"I have an idea." I unslung my ukulele.

"I thought you swore not to play," Meg said.

"I did. But if I throw this shiny object to one side, the ants might—"

I was about to say *the ants might follow it and leave us alone.*

I neglected to consider that, in my hands, the ukulele made me look shinier and tastier. Before I could throw the instrument, the soldier ants surged toward us. I stumbled back, only remembering the geyser behind me when my shoulder blades began to blister, filling the air with Apollo-scented steam.

"Hey, bugs!" Meg's scimitars flashed in her hands, making her the new shiniest thing in the clearing.

Can we take a moment to appreciate that Meg did this

on purpose? Terrified of insects, she could have fled and left me to be devoured. Instead, she chose to risk her life by distracting three tank-size ants. Throwing garbage at street thugs was one thing. But this . . . this was an entirely new level of foolishness. If I lived, I might have to nominate Meg McCaffrey for Best Sacrifice at the next Demi Awards.

Two of the ants charged at Meg. The third stayed on me, though he turned his head long enough for me to sprint to one side.

Meg ran between her opponents, her golden blades severing a leg from each. Their mandibles snapped at empty air. The soldier bugs wobbled on their five remaining legs, tried to turn, and bonked heads.

Meanwhile, the third ant charged me. In a panic, I threw my combat ukulele. It bounced off the ant's forehead with a dissonant *twang*.

I tugged my sword free of its scabbard. I've always hated swords. Such inelegant weapons, and they require you to be in close combat. How unwise, when you can shoot your enemies with an arrow from across the world!

The ant spat acid, and I tried to swat away the goop.

Perhaps that wasn't the brightest idea. I often got sword fighting and tennis confused. At least some of the acid splattered the ant's eyes, which bought me a few seconds. I valiantly retreated, raising my sword only to find that the blade had been eaten away, leaving me nothing but a steaming hilt.

"Oh, Meg?" I called helplessly.

She was otherwise occupied. Her swords whirled in golden arcs of destruction, lopping off leg segments, slicing antennae. I had never seen a dimachaerus fight with such skill, and I had seen all the best gladiators in combat. Unfortunately, her blades only sparked off the ants' thick main carapaces. Glancing blows and dismemberment did not faze them at all. As good as Meg was, the ants had more legs, more weight, more ferocity, and slightly more acid-spitting ability.

My own opponent snapped at me. I managed to avoid its mandibles, but its armored face bashed the side of my head. I staggered and fell. One ear canal seemed to fill with molten iron.

My vision clouded. Across the clearing, the other ants flanked Meg, using their acid to herd her toward the woods. She dove behind a tree and came up with only one of her blades. She tried to stab the closest ant but was driven back by acid cross fire. Her leggings were smoking, peppered with holes. Her face was tight with pain.

"Peaches," I muttered to myself. "Where is that stupid diaper demon when we need him?"

The karpos did not appear. Perhaps the presence of the geyser gods or some other force in the woods kept him away. Perhaps the board of directors had a rule against pets.

The third ant loomed over me, its mandibles foaming with green saliva. Its breath smelled worse than Hephaestus's work shirts.

My next decision I could blame on my head injury. I could tell you I wasn't thinking clearly, but that isn't true. I was desperate. I was terrified. I wanted to help Meg. Mostly I wanted to save myself. I saw no other option, so I dove for my ukulele.

I know. I promised on the River Styx not to play music until I was a god once more. But even such a dire oath can seem unimportant when a giant ant is about to melt your face off.

I grabbed the instrument, rolled onto my back, and belted out "Sweet Caroline."

Even without my oath, I would only have done something like that in the most extreme emergency. When I sing that song, the chances of mutually assured destruction are too great. But I saw no other choice. I gave it my utmost effort, channeling all the saccharine schmaltz I could muster from the 1970s.

The giant ant shook its head. Its antennae quivered. I got to my feet as the monster crawled drunkenly toward me. I put my back to the geyser and launched into the chorus.

The *Dah! Dah! Dah!* did the trick. Blinded by disgust and rage, the ant charged. I rolled aside as the monster's momentum carried it forward, straight into the muddy cauldron.

Believe me, the only thing that smells *worse* than Hephaestus's work shirts is a myrmeke boiling in its own shell.

Somewhere behind me, Meg screamed. I turned in time to see her second sword fly from her hand. She collapsed as one of the myrmekes caught her in its mandibles.

"NO!" I shrieked.

The ant did not snap her in half. It simply held her— limp and unconscious.

"Meg!" I yelled again. I strummed the ukulele desperately. "Sweet Caroline!"

But my voice was gone. Defeating one ant had taken all my energy. (I don't think I have ever written a sadder sentence than that.) I tried to run to Meg's aid, but I stumbled and fell. The world turned pale yellow. I hunched on all fours and vomited.

I have a concussion, I thought, but I had no idea what to do about it. It seemed like ages since I had been a god of healing.

I may have lain in the mud for minutes or hours while my brain slowly gyrated inside my skull. By the time I managed to stand, the two ants were gone.

There was no sign of Meg McCaffrey.

25

I'm on a roll now
Boiling, burning, throwing up
Lions? Hey, why not?

I STUMBLED THROUGH the glade, shouting Meg's name. I knew it was pointless, but yelling felt good. I looked for signs of broken branches or trampled ground. Surely two tank-size ants would leave a trail I could follow. But I was not Artemis; I did not have my sister's skill with tracking. I had no idea which direction they'd taken my friend.

I retrieved Meg's swords from the mud. Instantly, they changed into gold rings—so small, so easily lost, like a mortal life. I may have cried. I tried to break my ridiculous combat ukulele, but the Celestial bronze instrument defied my attempts. Finally, I yanked off the A string, threaded it through Meg's rings, and tied them around my neck.

"Meg, I will find you," I muttered.

Her abduction was my fault. I was sure of this. By playing music and saving myself, I had broken my oath on the River Styx. Instead of punishing me directly, Zeus or the Fates or all the gods together had visited their wrath upon Meg McCaffrey.

How could I have been so foolish? Whenever I angered

the other gods, those closest to me were struck down. I'd lost Daphne because of one careless comment to Eros. I'd lost the beautiful Hyacinthus because of a quarrel with Zephyros. Now my broken oath would cost Meg her life.

No, I told myself. *I won't allow it.*

I was so nauseous, I could barely walk. Someone seemed to be inflating a balloon inside my brain. Yet I managed to stumble to the rim of Pete's geyser.

"Pete!" I shouted. "Show yourself, you cowardly telemarketer!"

Water shot skyward with a sound like the blast of an organ's lowest pipe. In the swirling steam, the palikos appeared, his mud-gray face hardening with anger.

"You call me a TELEMARKETER?" he demanded. "We run a full-service PR firm!"

I doubled over and vomited in his crater, which I thought an appropriate response.

"Stop that!" Pete complained.

"I need to find Meg." I wiped my mouth with a shaky hand. "What would the myrmekes do with her?"

"I don't know!"

"Tell me or I will *not* complete your customer service survey."

Pete gasped. "That's terrible! Your feedback is important!" He floated down to my side. "Oh, dear . . . your head doesn't look good. You've got a big gash on your scalp, and there's blood. That must be why you're not thinking clearly."

"I don't care!" I yelled, which only made the pounding in my head worse. "Where is the myrmekes' nest?"

Pete wrung his steamy hands. "Well, that's what we were talking about earlier. That's where Paulie went. The nest is the only entrance."

"To what?"

"To the Grove of Dodona."

My stomach solidified into a pack of ice, which was unfair, because I needed one for my head. "The ant nest . . . is the way to the grove?"

"Look, you need medical attention. I *told* Paulie we should have a first-aid station for visitors." He fished around in his nonexistent pockets. "Let me just mark the location of the Apollo cabin—"

"If you pull out a brochure," I warned, "I will make you eat it. Now, explain how the nest leads to the grove."

Pete's face turned yellow, or perhaps that was just my vision getting worse. "Paulie didn't tell me everything. There's this thicket of woods that's grown so dense, nobody can get in. I mean, even from above, the branches are like . . ." He laced his muddy fingers, then caused them to liquefy and melt into one another, which made his point quite well.

"Anyway"—he pulled his hands apart—"the grove is in there. It could have been slumbering for centuries. Nobody on the board of directors even knew about it. Then, all of a sudden, the trees started whispering. Paulie figured those darned ants must have burrowed into the grove from underneath, and that's what woke it up."

I tried to make sense of that. It was difficult with a swollen brain. "Which way is the nest?"

"North of here," Pete said. "Half a mile. But, man, you are in no shape—"

"I must! Meg needs me!"

Pete grabbed my arm. His grip was like a warm wet tourniquet. "She's got time. If they carried her off in one piece, that means she's not dead yet."

"She will be soon enough!"

"Nah. Before Paulie . . . before he disappeared, he went into that nest a few times looking for the tunnel to the grove. He told me those myrmekes like to goop up their victims and let them, um, ripen until they're soft enough for the hatchlings to eat."

I made an un-godlike squeak. If there had been anything left in my stomach, I would have lost it. "How long does she have?"

"Twenty-four hours, give or take. Then she'll start to . . . um, soften."

It was difficult to imagine Meg McCaffrey softening under any circumstances, but I pictured her alone and scared, encased in insect goop, tucked in some larder of carcasses in the ants' nest. For a girl who hated bugs— Oh, Demeter had been right to hate me and keep her children away from me. I was a terrible god!

"Go get some help," Pete urged. "The Apollo cabin can heal that head wound. You're not doing your friend any favors by charging after her and getting yourself killed."

"Why do you care what happens to us?"

The geyser god looked offended. "Visitor satisfaction is always our top priority! Besides, if you find Paulie while you're in there . . ."

I tried to stay angry at the palikos, but the loneliness and worry on his face mirrored my own feelings. "Did Paulie explain how to navigate the ants' nest?"

Pete shook his head. "Like I said, he didn't want me to follow him. The myrmekes are dangerous enough. And if those other guys are still wandering around—"

"Other guys?"

Pete frowned. "Didn't I mention that? Yeah. Paulie saw three humans, heavily armed. They were looking for the grove too."

My left leg started thumping nervously, as if it missed its three-legged race partner. "How did Paulie know what they were looking for?"

"He heard them talking in Latin."

"*Latin?* Were they campers?"

Pete spread his hands. "I—I don't think so. Paulie described them like they were adults. He said one of them was the leader. The other two addressed him as *imperator*."

The entire planet seemed to tilt. "Imperator."

"Yeah, you know, like in Rome—"

"Yes, I know." Suddenly, too many things made sense. Pieces of the puzzle flew together, forming one huge picture that smacked me in the face. The Beast . . . Triumvirate Holdings . . . adult demigods completely off the radar.

It was all I could do to avoid pitching forward into the geyser. Meg needed me more than ever. But I would have to do this right. I would have to be careful—even more careful than when I gave the fiery horses of the sun their yearly vaccinations.

"Pete," I said, "do you still oversee sacred oaths?"

"Well, yes, but—"

"Then hear my solemn oath!"

"Uh, the thing is, you've got this aura around you like you just *broke* a sacred oath, maybe one you swore on the River Styx? And if you break *another* oath with me—"

"I swear that I will save Meg McCaffrey. I will use every means at my disposal to bring her safely from the ants' lair, and this oath supersedes any previous oath I have made. This I swear upon your sacred and extremely hot waters!"

Pete winced. "Well, okay. It's done now. But keep in mind that if you don't keep that oath, if Meg dies, even if it's not your fault . . . you'll face the consequences."

"I am already cursed for breaking my earlier oath! What does it matter?"

"Yeah, but see, those River Styx oaths can take *years* to destroy you. They're like cancer. My oaths . . ." Pete shrugged. "If you break it, there's nothing I can do to stop your punishment. Wherever you are, a geyser will instantly blast through the ground at your feet and boil you alive."

"Ah . . ." I tried to stop my knees from knocking. "Yes, of course I knew that. I stand by my oath."

"You've got no choice now."

"Right. I think I'll—I'll go get healed."

I staggered off.

"Camp is the other direction," Pete said.

I changed course.

"Remember to complete our survey online!" Pete called after me. "Just curious, on a scale of one to ten, how would you rate your overall satisfaction with the Woods at Camp Half-Blood?"

I didn't reply. As I stumbled into the darkness, I was too busy contemplating, on a scale of one to ten, the pain I might have to endure in the near future.

I didn't have the strength to make it back to camp. The farther I walked, the clearer that became. My joints were pudding. I felt like a marionette, and as much as I'd enjoyed controlling mortals from above in the past, I did not relish being on the other end of the strings.

My defenses were at level zero. The smallest hellhound or dragon could have easily made a meal of the great Apollo. If an irritated badger had taken issue with me, I would have been doomed.

I leaned against a tree to catch my breath. The tree seemed to push me away, whispering in a voice I remembered so well: *Keep moving, Apollo. You can't rest here.*

"I loved you," I muttered.

Part of me knew I was delirious—imagining things only because of my concussion—but I swore I could see the face of my beloved Daphne rising from each tree trunk I passed, her features floating under the bark like a mirage of wood— her slightly crooked nose, her offset green eyes, those lips I had never kissed but never stopped dreaming of.

You loved every pretty girl, she scolded. *And every pretty boy, for that matter.*

"Not like you," I cried. "You were my first true love. Oh, Daphne!"

Wear my crown, she said. *And repent.*

I remembered chasing her—her lilac scent on the breeze, her lithe form flitting through the dappled light of the forest.

I pursued her for what seemed like years. Perhaps it was.

For centuries afterward, I blamed Eros.

In a moment of recklessness, I had ridiculed Eros's archery skills. Out of spite, he struck me with a golden arrow. He bent all my love toward the beautiful Daphne, but that was not the worst of it. He also struck Daphne's heart with a lead arrow, leeching all possible affection she might have had for me.

What people do not understand: Eros's arrows can't summon emotion from nothing. They can only cultivate potential that is already there. Daphne and I could have been a perfect pair. She was my true love. She could have loved me back. Yet thanks to Eros, my love-o-meter was cranked to one hundred percent, while Daphne's feelings turned to pure hate (which is, of course, only the flip side of love). Nothing is more tragic than loving someone to the depths of your soul and knowing they cannot and will not ever love you back.

The stories say I chased her on a whim, that she was just another pretty dress. The stories are wrong. When she begged Gaea to turn her into a laurel tree in order to escape me, part of my heart hardened into bark as well. I invented the laurel wreath to commemorate my failure—to punish myself for the fate of my greatest love. Every time some hero wins the laurels, I am reminded of the girl I can never win.

After Daphne, I swore I would never marry. Sometimes I claimed that was because I couldn't decide between the Nine Muses. A convenient story. The Nine Muses were my constant companions, all of them beautiful in their own way. But they never possessed my heart like Daphne did.

Only one other person ever affected me so deeply—the perfect Hyacinthus—and he, too, was taken from me.

All these thoughts rambled through my bruised brain. I staggered from tree to tree, leaning against them, grabbing their lowest branches like handrails.

You cannot die here, Daphne whispered. *You have work to do. You made an oath.*

Yes, my oath. Meg needed me. I had to . . .

I fell face forward in the icy mulch.

How long I lay there, I'm not sure.

A warm snout breathed in my ear. A rough tongue lapped my face. I thought I was dead and Cerberus had found me at the gates of the Underworld.

Then the beast pushed me over onto my back. Dark tree branches laced the sky. I was still in the forest. The golden visage of a lion appeared above me, his amber eyes beautiful and deadly. He licked my face, perhaps trying to decide if I would make a good supper.

"*Ptfh.*" I spat mane fur out of my mouth.

"Wake up," said a woman's voice, somewhere to my right. It wasn't Daphne, but it was vaguely familiar.

I managed to raise my head. Nearby, a second lion sat at the feet of a woman with tinted glasses and a silver-and-gold tiara in her braided hair. Her batik dress swirled with images of fern fronds. Her arms and hands were covered in henna tattoos. She looked different than she had in my dream, but I recognized her.

"Rhea," I croaked.

She inclined her head. "Peace, Apollo. I don't want to bum you out, but we need to talk."

26

Imperators here?
Gag me with a peace symbol
Not groovy, Mama

MY HEAD WOUND MUST have tasted like Wagyu beef.

The lion kept licking the side of my face, making my hair stickier and wetter. Strangely, this seemed to clear my thoughts. Perhaps lion saliva had curative properties. I guess I should have known that, being a god of healing, but you'll have to excuse me if I haven't done trial-and-error experiments with the drool of every single animal.

With difficulty, I sat up and faced the Titan queen.

Rhea leaned against the side of a VW safari van painted with swirling black frond designs like those on her dress. I seemed to recall that the black fern was one of Rhea's symbols, but I couldn't remember why. Among the gods, Rhea had always been something of a mystery. Even Zeus, who knew her best, did not often speak of her.

Her turret crown circled her brow like a glittering railroad track. When she looked down at me, her tinted glasses changed from orange to purple. A macramé belt cinched her waist, and on a chain around her neck hung her brass peace symbol.

She smiled. "Glad you're awake. I was worried, man."

I really wished people would stop calling me *man*. "Why are you . . . Where have you been all these centuries?"

"Upstate." She scratched her lion's ears. "After Woodstock, I stuck around, started a pottery studio."

"You . . . what?"

She tilted her head. "Was that last week or last millennium? I've lost track."

"I—I believe you're describing the 1960s. That was last century."

"Oh, bummer." Rhea sighed. "I get mixed up after so many years."

"I sympathize."

"After I left Kronos . . . well, that man was so square, you could cut yourself on his corners, you know what I mean? He was the ultimate 1950s dad—wanted us to be Ozzie and Harriet or Lucy and Ricky or something."

"He—he swallowed his children alive."

"Yeah." Rhea brushed her hair from her face. "That was some bad karma. Anyway, I left him. Back then divorce wasn't cool. You just didn't do it. But me! I burned my *apodesmos* and got liberated. I raised Zeus in a commune with a bunch of naiads and *kouretes*. Lots of wheat germ and nectar. The kid grew up with a strong Aquarian vibe."

I was fairly sure Rhea was misremembering her centuries, but I thought it would be impolite to keep pointing that out.

"You remind me of Iris," I said. "She went organic vegan several decades ago."

Rhea made a face—just a ripple of disapproval before

regaining her karmic balance. "Iris is a good soul. I dig her. But you know, these younger goddesses, they weren't around to fight the revolution. They don't get what it was like when your old man was eating your children and you couldn't get a real job and the Titan chauvinists just wanted you to stay home and cook and clean and have more Olympian babies. And speaking of Iris . . ."

Rhea touched her forehead. "Wait, were we speaking of Iris? Or did I just have a flashback?"

"I honestly don't know."

"Oh, I remember now. She's a messenger of the gods, right? Along with Hermes and that other groovy liberated chick . . . Joan of Arc?"

"Er, I'm not sure about that last one."

"Well, anyway, the communication lines are down, man. Nothing works. Rainbow messages, flying scrolls, Hermes Express . . . it's all going haywire."

"We know this. But we don't know why."

"It's them. They're doing it."

"Who?"

She glanced to either side. "The Man, man. Big Brother. The suits. The imperators."

I had been hoping she would say something else: giants, Titans, ancient killing machines, aliens. I would've rather tangled with Tartarus or Ouranos or Primordial Chaos itself. I had hoped Pete the geyser misunderstood what his brother told him about the imperator in the ants' nest.

Now that I had confirmation, I wanted to steal Rhea's safari van and drive to some commune far, far upstate.

"Triumvirate Holdings," I said.

"Yeah," Rhea agreed. "That's their new military-industrial complex. It's bumming me out in a big way."

The lion stopped licking my face, probably because my blood had turned bitter. "How is this possible? How have they come back?"

"They never went away," Rhea said. "They did it to themselves, you know. Wanted to make themselves gods. That never works out well. Ever since the old days they've been hiding out, influencing history from behind the curtains. They're stuck in a kind of twilight life. They can't die; they can't really live."

"But how could we not *know* about this?" I demanded. "We are gods!"

Rhea's laugh reminded me of a piglet with asthma. "Apollo, Grandson, beautiful child . . . Has being a god ever stopped someone from being stupid?"

She had a point. Not about me personally, of course, but the stories I could tell you about the *other* Olympians . . .

"The emperors of Rome." I tried to come to terms with the idea. "They can't *all* be immortal."

"No," Rhea said. "Just the worst of them, the most notorious. They live in human memory, man. That's what keeps them alive. Same as us, really. They're tied to the course of Western civilization, even though that whole concept is imperialist Eurocentric propaganda, man. Like my guru would tell you—"

"Rhea"—I put my hands against my throbbing temples—"can we stick to one problem at a time?"

"Yeah, okay. I didn't mean to blow your mind."

"But how can they affect our lines of communication? How can they be so powerful?"

"They've had centuries, Apollo. *Centuries*. All that time, plotting and making war, building up their capital-ist empire, waiting for this moment when you are mortal, when the Oracles are vulnerable for a hostile takeover. It's just evil. They have no chill whatsoever."

"I thought that was a more modern term."

"Evil?"

"No. *Chill*. Never mind. The Beast . . . he is the leader?"

"Afraid so. He's as twisted as the others, but he's the smartest and the most stable—in a sociopathic homicidal way. You know who he is—who he was, right?"

Unfortunately, I did. I remembered where I had seen his smirking ugly face. I could hear his nasal voice echo-ing through the arena, ordering the execution of hundreds while the crowds cheered. I wanted to ask Rhea who his two compatriots were in the Triumvirate, but I decided I could not bear the information at present. None of the options were good, and knowing their names might bring me more despair than I could handle.

"It's true, then," I said. "The other Oracles still exist. The emperors hold them all?"

"They're working on it. Python has Delphi—that's the biggest problem. But you won't have the strength to take him head-on. You've got to pry their fingers off the minor Oracles first, loosen their power. To do that, you need a new source of prophecy for this camp—an Oracle that is older and independent."

"Dodona," I said. "Your whispering grove."

"Right on," Rhea said. "I thought the grove was gone forever. But then—I don't know how—the oak trees regrew themselves in the heart of these woods. You have to find the grove and protect it."

"I'm working on that." I touched the sticky wound on the side of my face. "But my friend Meg—"

"Yeah. You had some setbacks. But there are always setbacks, Apollo. When Lizzy Stanton and I hosted the first women's rights convention in Woodstock—"

"I think you mean Seneca Falls?"

Rhea frowned. "Wasn't that in the '60s?"

"The '40s," I said. "The 1840s, if memory serves."

"So . . . Jimi Hendrix wasn't there?"

"Doubtful."

Rhea fiddled with her peace symbol. "Then who set that guitar on fire? Ah, never mind. The point is, you have to persevere. Sometimes change takes centuries."

"Except that I'm mortal now," I said. "I don't *have* centuries."

"But you have willpower," Rhea said. "You have mortal drive and urgency. Those are things the gods often lack."

At her side, her lion roared.

"I've gotta split," Rhea said. "If the imperators track me down—bad scene, man. I've been off the grid too long. I'm not going to get sucked into that patriarchal institutional oppression again. Just find Dodona. That's your first trial."

"And if the Beast finds the grove first?"

"Oh, he's already found the gates, but he'll never get through them without you and the girl."

"I—I don't understand."

"That's cool. Just breathe. Find your center. Enlighten-ment has to come from *within*."

It was very much like a line I would've given *my* wor-shippers. I was tempted to choke Rhea with her macramé belt, but I doubted I would have the strength. Also, she had two lions. "But what do I do? How do I save Meg?"

"First, get healed. Rest up. Then . . . well, how you save Meg is up to you. The journey is greater than the destina-tion, you know?"

She held out her hand. Draped on her fingers was a set of wind chimes—a collection of hollow brass tubes and medallions engraved with ancient Greek and Cretan sym-bols. "Hang these in the largest ancient oak. That will help you focus the voices of the Oracle. If you get a prophecy, groovy. It'll only be the beginning, but without Dodona, nothing else will be possible. The emperors will suffocate our future and divide up the world. Only when you have defeated Python can you reclaim your rightful place on Olympus. My kid, Zeus . . . he's got this whole 'tough love' disciplinarian hang-up, you dig? Taking back Delphi is the only way you're going to get on his good side."

"I—I was afraid you would say that."

"There's one other thing," she warned. "The Beast is planning some kind of attack on your camp. I don't know what it is, but it's going to be big. Like, even worse than napalm. You have to warn your friends."

The nearest lion nudged me. I wrapped my arms around his neck and allowed him to pull me to my feet. I managed to remain standing, but only because my legs locked up in complete fright. For the first time, I understood the trials that awaited me. I knew the enemies I must face. I would need more than wind chimes and enlightenment. I'd need a miracle. And as a god, I can tell you that those are never distributed lightly.

"Good luck, Apollo." The Titan queen placed the wind chimes in my hands. "I've got to check my kiln before my pots crack. Keep on trucking, and save those trees!"

The woods dissolved. I found myself standing in the central green at Camp Half-Blood, face-to-face with Chiara Benvenuti, who jumped back in alarm. "Apollo?"

I smiled. "Hey, girl." My eyes rolled up in my head and, for the second time that week, I charmingly passed out in front of her.

27

I apologize
For pretty much everything
Wow, I'm a good guy

"WAKE," SAID A VOICE.

I opened my eyes and saw a ghost—his face just as precious to me as Daphne's. I knew his copper skin, his kind smile, the dark curls of his hair, and those eyes as purple as senatorial robes.

"Hyacinthus," I sobbed. "I'm so sorry . . ."

He turned his face toward the sunlight, revealing the ugly dent above his left ear where the discus had struck him. My own wounded face throbbed in sympathy.

"Seek the caverns," he said. "Near the springs of blue. Oh, Apollo . . . your sanity will be taken away, but do not . . ."

His image faded and began to retreat. I rose from my sickbed. I rushed after him and grabbed his shoulders. "Do not *what*? Please don't leave me again!"

My vision cleared. I found myself by the window in Cabin Seven, holding a ceramic pot of purple and red hyacinths. Nearby, looking very concerned, Will and Nico stood as if ready to catch me.

"He's talking to the flowers," Nico noted. "Is that normal?"

"Apollo," Will said, "you had a concussion. I healed you, but—"

"These hyacinths," I demanded. "Have they always been here?"

Will frowned. "Honestly, I don't know where they came from, but . . ." He took the flowerpot from my hands and set it back on the windowsill. "Let's worry about you, okay?"

Usually that would've been excellent advice, but now I could only stare at the hyacinths and wonder if they were some sort of message. How cruel to see them—the flowers that I had created to honor my fallen love, with their plumes stained red like his blood or hued violet like his eyes. They bloomed so cheerfully in the window, reminding me of the joy I had lost.

Nico rested his hand on Will's shoulder. "Apollo, we were worried. Will was especially."

Seeing them together, supporting each other, made my heart feel even heavier. During my delirium, both of my great loves had visited me. Now, once again, I was devastatingly alone.

Still, I had a task to complete. A friend needed my help.

"Meg is in trouble," I said. "How long was I unconscious?"

Will and Nico glanced at each other.

"It's about noon now," Will said. "You showed up on the green around six this morning. When Meg didn't return with you, we wanted to search the woods for her, but Chiron wouldn't let us."

"Chiron was absolutely correct," I said. "I won't allow any others to put themselves at risk. But I must hurry. Meg has until tonight at the latest."

"Then what happens?" Nico asked.

I couldn't say it. I couldn't even *think* about it without losing my nerve. I looked down. Aside from Paolo's Brazilian-flag bandana and my ukulele-string necklace, I was wearing only my boxer shorts. My offensive flabbiness was on display for everyone to see, but I no longer cared about that. (Well, not much, anyway.) "I have to get dressed."

I staggered back to my cot. I fumbled through my meager supplies and found Percy Jackson's Led Zeppelin T-shirt. I tugged it on. It seemed more appropriate than ever.

Will hovered nearby. "Look, Apollo, I don't think you're back to a hundred percent."

"I'll be fine." I pulled on my jeans. "I have to save Meg."

"Let us help you," Nico said. "Tell us where she is and I can shadow-travel—"

"No!" I snapped. "No, you have to stay here and protect the camp."

Will's expression reminded me very much of his mother, Naomi—that look of trepidation she got just before she went onstage. "Protect the camp from what?"

"I—I'm not sure. You must tell Chiron the emperors have returned. Or rather, they never went away. They've been plotting, building their resources for centuries."

Nico's eyes glinted warily. "When you say emperors—"

"I mean the Roman ones."

Will stepped back. "You're saying the emperors of ancient Rome are alive? *How?* The Doors of Death?"

"No." I could barely speak through the taste of bile. "The emperors made themselves gods. They had their own temples and altars. They encouraged the people to worship them."

"But that was just propaganda," Nico said. "They weren't really divine."

I laughed mirthlessly. "Gods are sustained by worship, son of Hades. They continue to exist because of the collective memories of a culture. It's true for the Olympians; it's also true for the emperors. Somehow, the most powerful of them have survived. All these centuries, they have clung to half-life, hiding, waiting to reclaim their power."

Will shook his head. "That's impossible. How—?"

"I don't know!" I tried to steady my breathing. "Tell Rachel the men behind Triumvirate Holdings are former emperors of Rome. They've been plotting against us all this time, and we gods have been blind. *Blind.*"

I pulled on my coat. The ambrosia Nico had given me yesterday was still in the left pocket. In the right pocket, Rhea's wind chimes clanked, though I had no idea how they'd gotten there.

"The Beast is planning some sort of attack on the camp," I said. "I don't know what, and I don't know when, but tell Chiron you must be prepared. I have to go."

"Wait!" Will said as I reached the door. "Who is the Beast? Which emperor are we dealing with?"

"The worst of my descendants." My fingers dug into the doorframe. "The Christians called him the Beast because he burned them alive. Our enemy is Emperor Nero."

———

They must have been too stunned to follow me.

I ran toward the armory. Several campers gave me strange looks. Some called after me, offering help, but I ignored them. I could only think about Meg alone in the myrmekes' lair, and the visions I'd had of Daphne, Rhea, and Hyacinthus—all of them urging me onward, telling me to do the impossible in this inadequate mortal form.

When I reached the armory, I scanned the rack of bows. My hand trembling, I picked out the weapon Meg had tried to give me the day before. It was carved from mountain laurel wood. The bitter irony appealed to me.

I had sworn not to use a bow until I was a god again. But I had also sworn not to play music, and I had already broken that part of the oath in the most egregious, Neil-Diamondy way possible.

The curse of the River Styx could kill me in its slow cancerous way, or Zeus could strike me down. But my oath to save Meg McCaffrey had to come first.

I turned my face to the sky. "If you want to punish me, Father, be my guest, but have the courage to hurt *me* directly, not my mortal companion. BE A MAN!"

To my surprise, the skies remained silent. Lightning did not vaporize me. Perhaps Zeus was too taken aback to react, but I knew he would never overlook such an insult.

To Tartarus with him. I had work to do.

I grabbed a quiver and stuffed it with all the extra arrows I could find. Then I ran for the woods, Meg's two rings jangling on my makeshift necklace. Too late, I realized I had forgotten my combat ukulele, but I had no time to turn back. My singing voice would have to be enough.

I'm not sure how I found the nest.

Perhaps the forest simply allowed me to reach it, know-ing that I was marching to my death. I've found that when one is searching for danger, it's never hard to find.

Soon I was crouched behind a fallen tree, studying the myrmekes' lair in the clearing ahead. To call the place an anthill would be like calling Versailles Palace a single-family home. Earthen ramparts rose almost to the tops of the surrounding trees—a hundred feet at least. The circum-ference could have accommodated a Roman hippodrome. A steady stream of soldiers and drones swarmed in and out of the mound. Some carried fallen trees. One, inexplicably, was dragging a 1967 Chevy Impala.

How many ants would I be facing? I had no idea. After you reach the number *impossible*, there's no point in counting.

I nocked an arrow and stepped into the clearing.

When the nearest myrmeke spotted me, he dropped his Chevy. He watched me approach, his antennae bobbing. I ignored him and strolled past, heading for the nearest tun-nel entrance. That confused him even more.

Several other ants gathered to watch.

I've learned that if you act like you are supposed to be somewhere, most people (or ants) will not confront you. Normally, acting confident isn't a problem for me. Gods are allowed to be anywhere. It was a bit tougher for Lester Papadopoulos, dork teen extraordinaire, but I made it all the way to the nest without being challenged.

I plunged inside and began to sing.

This time I needed no ukulele. I needed no muse for

my inspiration. I remembered Daphne's face in the trees. I remembered Hyacinthus turning away, his death wound glistening on his scalp. My voice filled with anguish. I sang of heartbreak. Rather than collapsing under my own despair, I projected it outward.

The tunnels amplified my voice, carrying it through the nest, making the entire hill my musical instrument.

Each time I passed an ant, it curled its legs and touched its forehead to the floor, its antennae quivering from the vibrations of my voice.

Had I been a god, the song would have been stronger, but this was enough. I was impressed by how much sorrow a human voice could convey.

I wandered deeper into the hill. I had no idea where I was going until I spotted a geranium blooming from the tunnel floor.

My song faltered.

Meg. She must have regained consciousness. She had dropped one of her emergency seeds to leave me a trail. The geranium's purple flowers all faced a smaller tunnel leading off to the left.

"Clever girl," I said, choosing that tunnel.

A clattering sound alerted me to the approaching myrmeke.

I turned and raised my bow. Freed from the enchantment of my voice, the insect charged, its mouth foaming with acid. I drew and fired. The arrow embedded itself up to the fletching in the ant's forehead.

The creature dropped, its back legs twitching in death throes. I tried to retrieve my arrow, but the shaft snapped

THE HIDDEN ORACLE 255

in my hand, the broken end covered in steaming corrosive goo. So much for reusing ammunition.

I called, "MEG!"

The only answer was the clattering of more giant ants moving in my direction. I began to sing again. Now, though, I had higher hopes of finding Meg, which made it difficult to summon the proper amount of melancholy. The ants I encountered were no longer catatonic. They moved slowly and unsteadily, but they still attacked. I was forced to shoot one after another.

I passed a cave filled with glittering treasure, but I was not interested in shiny things at the moment. I kept moving.

At the next intersection, another geranium sprouted from the floor, all its flowers facing right. I turned that direction, calling Meg's name again, then returning to my song.

As my spirits lifted, my song became less effective and the ants more aggressive. After a dozen kills, my quiver was growing dangerously light.

I had to reach deeper into my feelings of despair. I had to get the blues, good and proper.

For the first time in four thousand years, I sang of my own faults.

I poured out my guilt about Daphne's death. My boastfulness, envy, and desire had caused her destruction. When she ran from me, I should have let her go. Instead, I chased her relentlessly. I wanted her, and I intended to have her. Because of that, I had left Daphne no choice. To escape me, she sacrificed her life and turned into a tree, leaving my heart scarred forever. . . . But it was *my* fault. I apologized in song. I begged Daphne's forgiveness.

I sang of Hyacinthus, the most handsome of men. The West Wind Zephyros had also loved him, but I refused to share even a moment of Hyacinthus's time. In my jealousy, I threatened Zephyros. I dared him, *dared* him to interfere.

I sang of the day Hyacinthus and I played discus in the fields, and how the West Wind blew my disc off course— right into the side of Hyacinthus's head.

To keep Hyacinthus in the sunlight where he belonged, I created hyacinth flowers from his blood. I held Zephyros accountable, but my own petty greed had caused Hyacinthus's death. I poured out my sorrow. I took all the blame.

I sang of my failures, my eternal heartbreak and loneliness. I was the worst of the gods, the most guilt-ridden and unfocused. I couldn't commit myself to one lover. I couldn't even choose what to be the god of. I kept shifting from one skill to another—distracted and dissatisfied.

My golden life was a sham. My coolness was pretense. My heart was a lump of petrified wood.

All around me, myrmekes collapsed. The nest itself trembled with grief.

I found a third geranium, then a fourth.

Finally, pausing between verses, I heard a small voice up ahead: the sound of a girl crying.

"Meg!" I gave up on my song and ran.

She lay in the middle of a cavernous food larder, just as I had imagined. Around her were stacked the carcasses of animals—cows, deer, horses—all sheathed in hardened goop and slowly decaying. The smell hit my nasal passages like an avalanche.

Meg was also enveloped, but she was fighting back with the power of geraniums. Patches of leaves sprouted from the thinnest parts of her cocoon. A frilly collar of flowers kept the goo away from her face. She had even managed to free one of her arms, thanks to an explosion of pink geraniums at her left armpit.

Her eyes were puffy from crying. I assumed she was frightened, possibly in pain, but when I knelt next to her, her first words were, "I'm so sorry."

I brushed a tear from the tip of her nose. "Why, dear Meg? You did nothing wrong. I failed *you*."

A sob caught in her throat. "You don't understand. That song you were singing. Oh, gods . . . Apollo, if I'd known—"

"Hush, now." My throat was so raw I could barely talk. The song had almost destroyed my voice. "You're just reacting to the grief in the music. Let's get you free."

I was considering how to do that when Meg's eyes widened. She made a whimpering sound.

The hairs on the nape of my neck came to attention. "There are ants behind me, aren't there?" I asked.

Meg nodded.

I turned as four of them entered the cavern. I reached for my quiver. I had one arrow left.

28

Parenting advice:

Mamas, don't let your larvae

Grow up to be ants

MEG THRASHED IN HER GOO CASE. "Get me out of here!"

"I don't have a blade!" My fingers crept to the ukulele string around my neck. "Actually I have *your* blades, I mean your rings—"

"You don't need to cut me out. When the ant dumped me here, I dropped the packet of seeds. It should be close."

She was right. I spotted the crumpled pouch near her feet.

I inched toward it, keeping one eye on the ants. They stood together at the entrance as if hesitant to come closer. Perhaps the trail of dead ants leading to this room had given them pause.

"Nice ants," I said. "Excellent calm ants."

I crouched and scooped up the packet. A quick glance inside told me half a dozen seeds remained. "Now what, Meg?"

"Throw them on the goo," Meg said.

I gestured to the geraniums bursting from her neck and armpit. "How many seeds did that?"

"One."

"Then this many will choke you to death. I've turned too many people I cared about into flowers, Meg. I won't—"

"JUST DO IT!"

The ants did not like her tone. They advanced, snapping their mandibles. I shook the geranium seeds over Meg's cocoon, then nocked my arrow. Killing one ant would do no good if the other three tore us apart, so I chose a different target. I shot the roof of the cavern, just above the ants' heads.

It was a desperate idea, but I'd had success bringing down buildings with arrows before. In 464 BCE, I caused an earthquake that wiped out most of Sparta by hitting a fault line at the right angle. (I never liked the Spartans much.)

This time, I had less luck. The arrow embedded itself in the packed earth with a dull *thunk*. The ants took another step forward, acid dripping from their mouths. Behind me, Meg struggled to free herself from her cocoon, which was now covered in a shag carpet of purple flowers.

She needed more time.

Out of ideas, I tugged my Brazilian-flag handkerchief from my neck and waved it like a maniac, trying to channel my inner Paolo.

"BACK, FOUL ANTS!" I yelled. "*BRASIL!*"

The ants wavered—perhaps because of the bright colors, or my voice, or my sudden insane confidence. While they hesitated, cracks spread across the roof from my arrow's impact site, and then thousands of tons of earth collapsed on top of the myrmekes.

When the dust cleared, half the room was gone, along with the ants.

I looked at my handkerchief. "I'll be Styxed. It *does* have magic power. I can never tell Paolo about this or he'll be insufferable."

"Over here!" Meg yelled.

I turned. Another myrmeke was crawling over a pile of carcasses—apparently from a second exit I had failed to notice behind the disgusting food stores.

Before I could think what to do, Meg roared and burst from her cage, spraying geraniums in every direction. She shouted, "My rings!"

I yanked them from my neck and tossed them through the air. As soon as Meg caught them, two golden scimitars flashed into her hands.

The myrmeke barely had time to think *Uh-oh* before Meg charged. She sliced off his armored head. His body collapsed in a steaming heap.

Meg turned to me. Her face was a tempest of guilt, misery, and bitterness. I was afraid she might use her swords on me.

"Apollo, I . . ." Her voice broke.

I supposed she was still suffering from the effects of my song. She was shaken to her core. I made a mental note never again to sing so honestly when a mortal might be listening.

"It's all right, Meg," I said. "I should be apologizing to you. I got you into this mess."

Meg shook her head. "You don't understand. I—"

An enraged shriek echoed through the chamber, shaking the compromised ceiling and raining clods of dirt on our heads. The tone of the scream reminded me of Hera whenever she stormed through the hallways of Olympus, yelling at me for leaving the godly toilet seat up.

"That's the queen ant," I guessed. "We need to leave."

Meg pointed her sword toward the room's only remaining exit. "But the sound came from there. We'll be walking in her direction."

"Exactly. So perhaps we should hold off on making amends with each other, eh? We might still get each other killed."

We found the queen ant.

Hooray.

All corridors must have led to the queen. They radiated from her chamber like spikes on a morning star. Her Majesty was three times the size of her largest soldiers—a towering mass of black chitin and barbed appendages, with diaphanous oval wings folded against her back. Her eyes were glassy swimming pools of onyx. Her abdomen was a pulsing translucent sac filled with glowing eggs. The sight of it made me regret ever inventing gel capsule medications.

Her swollen abdomen might slow her down in a fight, but she was so large, she could intercept us before we reached the nearest exit. Those mandibles would snap us in half like dried twigs.

"Meg," I said, "how do you feel about dual-wielding scimitars against this lady?"

Meg looked appalled. "She's a mother giving birth."

"Yes . . . and she's an insect, which you hate. And her children were ripening you up for dinner."

Meg frowned. "Still . . . I don't feel right about it."

The queen hissed—a dry spraying noise. I imagined she would have already hosed us down with acid if she weren't worried about the long-term effects of corrosives on her larvae. Queen ants can't be too careful these days.

"You have another idea?" I asked Meg. "Preferably one that does not involve dying?"

She pointed to a tunnel directly behind the queen's clutch of eggs. "We need to go that way. It leads to the grove."

"How can you be sure?"

Meg tilted her head. "Trees. It's like . . . I can hear them growing."

That reminded me of something the Muses once told me—how they could actually hear the ink drying on new pages of poetry. I suppose it made sense that a daughter of Demeter could hear the growth of plants. Also, it didn't surprise me that the tunnel we needed was the most dangerous one to reach.

"Sing," Meg told me. "Sing like you did before."

"I—I can't. My voice is almost gone."

Besides, I thought, I don't want to risk losing you again.

I had freed Meg, so perhaps I'd fulfilled my oath to Pete the geyser god. Still, by singing and practicing archery, I had broken my oath upon the River Styx not once but twice. More singing would only make me *more* of a scofflaw.

Whatever cosmic punishments awaited me, I did not want them to fall on Meg.

Her Majesty snapped at us—a warning shot, telling us to back off. A few feet closer and my head would have rolled in the dirt.

I burst into song—or rather, I did the best I could with the raspy voice that remained. I began to rap. I started with the rhythm *boom chicka chicka*. I busted out some footwork the Nine Muses and I had been working on just before the war with Gaea.

The queen arched her back. I don't think she had expected to be rapped to today.

I gave Meg a look that clearly meant *Help me out!*

She shook her head. Give the girl two swords and she was a maniac. Ask her to lay down a simple beat and she suddenly got stage fright.

Fine, I thought. I'll do it by myself.

I launched into "Dance" by Nas, which I have to say was one of the most moving odes to mothers that I ever inspired an artist to write. (You're welcome, Nas.) I took some liberties with the lyrics. I may have changed *angel* to *brood mother* and *woman* to *insect*. But the sentiment remained. I serenaded the pregnant queen, channeling my love for my own dear mother, Leto. When I sang that I could only wish to marry a woman (or insect) so fine someday, my heartbreak was real. I would never have such a partner. It was not in my destiny.

The queen's antennae quivered. Her head seesawed back and forth. Eggs kept extruding from her abdomen, which made it difficult for me to concentrate, but I persevered.

When I was done, I dropped to one knee and held up my arms in tribute, waiting for the queen's verdict. Either she would kill me or she would not. I was spent. I had poured everything into that song and could not rap another line.

Next to me, Meg stood very still, gripping her swords.

Her Majesty shuddered. She threw back her head and wailed—a sound more brokenhearted than angry.

She leaned down and gently nudged my chest, pushing me in the direction of the tunnel we needed.

"Thank you," I croaked. "I—I'm sorry about the ants I killed."

The queen purred and clicked, extruding a few more eggs as if to say, *Don't worry; I can always make more*.

I stroked the queen ant's forehead. "May I call you Mama?"

Her mouth frothed in a pleased sort of way.

"Apollo," Meg urged, "let's go before she changes her mind."

I was not sure Mama *would* change her mind. I got the feeling she had accepted my fealty and adopted us into her brood. But Meg was right; we needed to hurry. Mama watched as we edged around her clutch of eggs.

We plunged into the tunnel and saw the glow of daylight above us.

29

Nightmares of torches
And a man in purple clothes
But that's not the worst

I HAD NEVER BEEN SO HAPPY to see a killing field.

We emerged into a glade littered with bones. Most were from forest animals. A few appeared human. I guessed we had found the myrmekes' dumping site, and they apparently didn't get regular garbage pickup.

The clearing was hemmed with trees so thick and tangled that traveling through them would've been impossible. Over our heads, the branches wove together in a leafy dome that let in sunlight but not much else. Anyone flying above the forest would never have realized this open space existed under the canopy.

At the far end of the glade stood a row of objects like football tackle dummies—six white cocoons staked on tall wooden poles, flanking a pair of enormous oaks. Each tree was at least eighty feet tall. They had grown so close together that their massive trunks appeared to have fused. I had the distinct impression I was looking at a set of living doors.

"It's a gateway," I said. "To the Grove of Dodona."

Meg's blades retracted, once again becoming gold rings on her middle fingers. "Aren't we *in* the grove?"

"No . . ." I stared across the clearing at the white cocoon Popsicles. They were too far away to make out clearly, but something about them seemed familiar in an evil, unwelcome sort of way. I wanted to get closer. I also wanted to keep my distance.

"I think this is more of an antechamber," I said. "The grove itself is behind those trees."

Meg gazed warily across the field. "I don't hear any voices."

It was true. The forest was absolutely quiet. The trees seemed to be holding their breath.

"The grove knows we are here," I guessed. "It's waiting to see what we'll do."

"We'd better do something, then." Meg didn't sound any more excited than I was, but she marched forward, bones crunching under her feet.

I wished I had more than a bow, an empty quiver, and a hoarse voice to defend myself with, but I followed, trying not to trip over rib cages and deer antlers. About halfway across the glade, Meg let out a sharp exhale.

She was staring at the posts on either side of the tree gates.

At first I couldn't process what I was seeing. Each stake was about the height of a crucifix—the kind Romans used to set up along the roadside to advertise the fates of criminals. (Personally, I find modern billboards much more tasteful.) The upper half of each post was wrapped in thick lumpy wads of white cloth, and sticking out from the top of each cocoon was something that looked like a human head.

My stomach somersaulted. They *were* human heads. Arrayed in front of us were the missing demigods, all tightly bound. I watched, petrified, until I discerned the slightest expansions and contractions in the wrappings around their chests. They were still breathing. Unconscious, not dead. Thank the gods.

On the left were three teenagers I didn't know, though I assumed they must be Cecil, Ellis, and Miranda. On the right side was an emaciated man with gray skin and white hair—no doubt the geyser god Paulie. Next to him hung my children . . . Austin and Kayla.

I shook so violently, the bones around my feet clattered. I recognized the smell coming from the prisoners' wrappings—sulfur, oil, powdered lime, and liquid Greek fire, the most dangerous substance ever created. Rage and disgust fought in my throat, vying for the right to make me throw up.

"Oh, monstrous," I said. "We need to free them immediately."

"Wh-what's wrong with them?" Meg stammered.

I dared not put it into words. I had seen this form of execution once before, at the hands of the Beast, and I never wished to see it again.

I ran to Austin's stake. With all my strength I tried to push it over, but it wouldn't budge. The base was sunk too deep in the earth. I tore at the cloth bindings but only managed to coat my hands in sulfurous resin. The wadding was stickier and harder than myrmekes' goo.

"Meg, your swords!" I wasn't sure they would do any good either, but I could think of nothing else to try.

Then from above us came a familiar snarl.

The branches rustled. Peaches the karpos dropped from the canopy, landing with a somersault at Meg's feet. He looked like he'd been through quite an ordeal to get here. His arms were sliced up and dripping peach nectar. His legs were dotted with bruises. His diaper sagged dangerously.

"Thank the gods!" I said. That was not my usual reaction when I saw the grain spirit, but his teeth and claws might be just the things to free the demigods. "Meg, hurry! Order your friend to—"

"Apollo." Her voice was heavy. She pointed to the tunnel from which we'd come.

Emerging from the ants' nest were two of the largest humans I had ever seen. Each was seven feet tall and perhaps three hundred pounds of pure muscle stuffed into horsehide armor. Their blond hair glinted like silver floss. Jeweled rings glittered in their beards. Each man carried an oval shield and a spear, though I doubted they needed weapons to kill. They looked like they could crack open cannonballs with their bare hands.

I recognized them from their tattoos and the circular designs on their shields. Such warriors weren't easy to forget.

"Germani." Instinctively, I moved in front of Meg. The elite imperial bodyguards had been cold-blooded death reapers in ancient Rome. I doubted they'd gotten any sweeter over the centuries.

The two men glared at me. They had serpent tattoos curling around their necks, just like the ruffians who had jumped me in New York. The Germani parted, and their master climbed from the tunnel.

Nero hadn't changed much in one thousand nine hundred and some-odd years. He appeared to be no more than thirty, but it was a *hard* thirty, his face haggard and his belly distended from too much partying. His mouth was fixed in a permanent sneer. His curly hair extended into a wraparound neck beard. His chin was so weak, I was tempted to create a GoFundMe campaign to buy him a better jaw.

He tried to compensate for his ugliness with an expensive Italian suit of purple wool, his gray shirt open to display gold chains. His shoes were hand-tooled leather, not the sort of thing to wear while stomping around in an ant pile. Then again, Nero had always had expensive, impractical tastes. That was perhaps the only thing I admired about him.

"Emperor Nero," I said. "The Beast."

He curled his lip. "Nero will do. It's good to see you, my honored ancestor. I'm sorry I've been so lax about my offerings during the past few millennia, but"—he shrugged—"I haven't needed you. I've done rather well on my own."

My fists clenched. I wanted to strike down this potbellied emperor with a bolt of white-hot power, except that I had no bolts of white-hot power. I had no arrows. I had no singing voice left. Against Nero and his seven-foot-tall bodyguards, I had a Brazilian handkerchief, a packet of ambrosia, and some brass wind chimes.

"It's me you want," I said. "Cut these demigods down from their stakes. Let them leave with Meg. They've done nothing to you."

Nero chuckled. "I'll be happy to let them go once we've

come to an agreement. As for Meg . . ." He smiled at her. "How are you, my dear?"

Meg said nothing. Her face was as hard and gray as a geyser god's. At her feet, Peaches snarled and rustled his leafy wings.

One of Nero's guards said something in his ear.

The Emperor nodded. "Soon."

He turned his attention back to me. "But where are my manners? Allow me to introduce my right hand, Vincius, and my left hand, Garius."

The bodyguards pointed across to each other.

"Ah, sorry," Nero corrected. "My right hand, Garius, and my left hand, Vincius. Those are the Romanized versions of their Batavi names, which I can't pronounce. Usually I just call them Vince and Gary. Say hello, boys."

Vince and Gary glowered at me.

"They have serpent tattoos," I noted, "like those street thugs you sent to attack me."

Nero shrugged. "I have many servants. Cade and Mikey are quite low on the pay scale. Their only job was to rattle you a bit, welcome you to my city."

"*Your* city." I found it just like Nero to go claiming major metropolitan areas that clearly belonged to me. "And these two gentlemen . . . they are actually Germani from the ancient times? How?"

Nero made a snide little barking sound in the back of his nose. I'd forgotten how much I hated his laugh.

"Lord Apollo, please," he said. "Even before Gaea commandeered the Doors of Death, souls escaped from Erebos all the time. It was quite easy for a god-emperor such as myself to call back my followers."

"A god-emperor?" I growled. "You mean a delusional ex-emperor."

Nero arched his eyebrows. "What made *you* a god, Apollo . . . back when you were one? Wasn't it the power of your name, your sway over those who believed in you? I am no different." He glanced to his left. "Vince, fall on your spear, please."

Without hesitation, Vince planted the butt of his spear against the ground. He braced the point under his rib cage.

"Stop," Nero said. "I changed my mind."

Vince betrayed no relief. In fact, his eyes tightened with faint disappointment. He brought his spear back to his side.

Nero grinned at me. "You see? I hold the power of life and death over my worshippers, like any proper god should."

I felt like I'd swallowed some gel capsule larvae. "The Germani were always crazy, much like you."

Nero put his hand to his chest. "I'm hurt! My barbarian friends are loyal subjects of the Julian dynasty! And, of course, we are all descended from you, Lord Apollo."

I didn't need the reminder. I'd been so proud of my son, the original Octavian, later Caesar Augustus. After his death, his descendants became increasingly arrogant and unstable (which I blamed on their mortal DNA; they certainly didn't get those qualities from me). Nero had been the last of the Julian line. I had not wept when he died. Now here he was, as grotesque and chinless as ever.

Meg stood at my shoulder. "Wh-what do you want, Nero?"

Considering she was facing the man who killed her father, she sounded remarkably calm. I was grateful for her strength. It gave me hope to have a skilled dimachaerus and a ravenous peach baby at my side. Still, I did not like our odds against two Germani.

Nero's eyes gleamed. "Straight to the point. I've always admired that about you, Meg. Really, it's simple. You and Apollo will open the gates of Dodona for me. Then these six"—he gestured to the staked prisoners—"will be released."

I shook my head. "You'll destroy the grove. Then you'll kill us."

The emperor made that horrible bark again. "Not unless you force me to. I'm a reasonable god-emperor, Apollo! I'd much rather have the Grove of Dodona under my control if it can be managed, but I certainly can't allow *you* to use it. You had your chance at being the guardian of the Oracles. You failed miserably. Now it's my responsibility. Mine . . . and my partners'."

"The two other emperors," I said. "Who are they?"

Nero shrugged. "Good Romans—men who, like me, have the willpower to do what is needed."

"Triumvirates have never worked. They always lead to civil war."

He smiled as if that idea did not bother him. "The three of us have come to an agreement. We have divided up the new empire . . . by which I mean North America. Once we have the Oracles, we'll expand and do what Romans have always done best—conquer the world."

I could only stare at him. "You truly learned nothing from your previous reign."

"Oh, but I did! I've had centuries to reflect, plan, and prepare. Do you have any idea how annoying it is to be a god-emperor, unable to die but unable to fully live? There was a period of about three hundred years during the Middle Ages when my name was almost forgotten. I was little more than a mirage! Thank goodness for the Renaissance, when our Classical greatness was remembered. And then came the Internet. Oh, gods, I *love* the Internet! It is impossible for me to fade completely now. I am immortal on Wikipedia!"

I winced. I was now fully convinced of Nero's insanity. Wikipedia was always getting stuff wrong about me.

He rolled his hand. "Yes, yes. You think I am crazy. I could explain my plans and prove otherwise, but I have a lot on my plate today. I need you and Meg to open those gates. They've resisted my best efforts, but together you two can do it. Apollo, you have an affinity with Oracles. Meg has a way with trees. Get to it. Please and thank you."

"We would rather die," I said. "Wouldn't we, Meg?"

No response.

I glanced over. A silvery streak glistened on Meg's cheek. At first I thought one of her rhinestones had melted. Then I realized she was crying.

"Meg?"

Nero clasped his hands as if in prayer. "Oh, my. It seems we've had a slight miscommunication. You see, Apollo, Meg brought you here, just as I asked her to. Well done, my sweet."

Meg wiped her face. "I—I didn't mean . . ."

My heart compressed to the size of a pebble. "Meg, no. I can't believe—"

I reached for her. Peaches snarled and inserted himself between us. I realized the karpos was not here to protect us from Nero. He was defending Meg from *me*.

"Meg?" I said. "This man killed your father! He's a murderer!"

She stared at the ground. When she spoke, her voice was even more tortured than mine was when I sang in the anthill. "The *Beast* killed my father. This is Nero. He's—he's my stepfather."

I could not fully grasp this before Nero spread his arms.

"That's right, my darling," he said. "And you've done a wonderful job. Come to Papa."

30

I school McCaffrey
Yo, girl, your stepdad is wack
Why won't she listen?

I HAD BEEN BETRAYED BEFORE.

The memories came flooding back to me in a painful tide. Once, my former girlfriend Cyrene took up with Ares just to get back at me. Another time, Artemis shot me in the groin because I was flirting with her Hunters. In 1928, Alexander Fleming failed to give me credit for inspiring his discovery of penicillin. I mean, *ouch.* That stung.

But I couldn't remember *ever* being so wrong about someone as I had been about Meg. Well . . . at least not since Irving Berlin. *"Alexander's Ragtime Band"?* I remember telling him. *You'll never make it big with a corny song like that!*

"Meg, we are friends." My voice sounded petulant even to myself. "How could you do this to me?"

Meg looked down at her red sneakers—the primary-colored shoes of a traitor. "I tried to tell you, to warn you."

"She has a good heart." Nero smiled. "But, Apollo, you and Meg have been friends for just a few days—and only because I *asked* Meg to befriend you. I have been Meg's stepfather, protector, and caretaker for years. She is a member of the Imperial Household."

I stared at my beloved Dumpster waif. Yes, somehow over the past week she had become beloved to me. I could not imagine her as Imperial *anything*—definitely not as a part of Nero's entourage.

"I risked my life for you," I said in amazement. "And that actually *means* something, because I can die!"

Nero clapped politely. "We're all impressed, Apollo. Now, if you'd open the gates. They've defied me for too long."

I tried to glare at Meg, but my heart wasn't in it. I felt too hurt and vulnerable. We gods do not like feeling vulnerable. Besides, Meg wasn't even looking at me.

In a daze, I turned to the oak tree gates. I saw now that their fused trunks were marred from Nero's previous efforts—chain-saw scars, burn marks, bites from ax blades, even some bullet holes. All these had barely chipped the outer bark. The most damaged area was an inch-deep impression in the shape of a human hand, where the wood had bubbled and peeled away. I glanced at the unconscious face of Paulie the geyser god, strung up and bound with the five demigods.

"Nero, what have you done?"

"Oh, a number of things! We found a way into this antechamber weeks ago. The Labyrinth has a convenient opening in the myrmekes' nest. But getting through these gates—"

"You forced the palikos to help you?" I had to restrain myself from throwing my wind chimes at the emperor. "You used a nature spirit to destroy nature? Meg, how can you tolerate this?"

Peaches growled. For once I had the feeling that the grain spirit might be in agreement with me. Meg's expression was as closed up as the gates. She stared intently at the bones littering the field.

"Come now," Nero said. "Meg knows there are good nature spirits, and bad ones. This geyser god was annoying. He kept asking us to fill out surveys. Besides, he shouldn't have ventured so far from his source of power. He was quite easy to capture. His steam, as you can see, didn't do us much good anyway."

"And the five demigods?" I demanded. "Did you 'use' them, too?"

"Of course. I didn't plan on luring them here, but every time we attacked the gates, the grove started wailing. I suppose it was calling for help, and the demigods couldn't resist. The first to wander in was this one." He pointed to Cecil Markowitz. "The last two were your own children— Austin and Kayla, yes? They showed up after we forced Paulie to steam-broil the trees. I guess the grove was quite nervous about that attempt. We got two demigods for the price of one!"

I lost control. I let out a guttural howl and charged the emperor, intending to wring his hairy excuse for a neck. The Germani would have killed me before I ever got that far, but I was saved the indignity. I tripped over a human pelvis and belly-surfed through the bones.

"Apollo!" Meg ran toward me.

I rolled over and kicked at her like a fussy child. "I don't need *your* help! Don't you understand who your protector is? He's a monster! He's the emperor who—"

"Don't say it," Nero warned. "If you say 'who fiddled while Rome burned,' I will have Vince and Gary flay you for a set of hide armor. You know as well as I do, Apollo, we didn't *have* fiddles back then. And I did *not* start the Great Fire of Rome."

I struggled to my feet. "But you profited from it."

Facing Nero, I remembered all the tawdry details of his rule—the extravagance and cruelty that had made him so embarrassing to me, his forefather. Nero was that relative you never wanted to invite to Lupercalia dinner.

"Meg," I said, "your stepfather watched as seventy percent of Rome was destroyed. Tens of thousands died."

"I was thirty miles away in Antium!" Nero snarled. "I rushed back to the city and personally led the fire brigades!"

"Only when the fire threatened your palace."

Nero rolled his eyes. "I can't help it if I arrived just in time to save the most important building!"

Meg cupped her hands over her ears. "Stop arguing. Please."

I didn't stop. Talking seemed better than my other options, like helping Nero or dying.

"After the Great Fire," I told her, "instead of rebuilding the houses on Palatine Hill, Nero leveled the neighborhood and built a new palace—the Domus Aurea."

Nero got a dreamy look on his face. "Ah, yes . . . the House of Gold. It was beautiful, Meg! I had my own lake, three hundred rooms, frescoes of gold, mosaics done in pearls and diamonds—I could finally live like a human being!"

"You had the nerve to put a hundred-foot-tall bronze statue in your front lawn!" I said. "A statue of yourself as

Sol-Apollo, the sun god. In other words, you claimed to be *me*."

"Indeed," Nero agreed. "Even after I died, that statue lived on. I understand it became famous as the Colossus of Nero! They moved it to the gladiators' amphitheater and everyone began calling the theater after the statue—*the Colosseum*." Nero puffed up his chest. "Yes . . . the statue was the perfect choice."

His tone sounded even more sinister than usual.

"What are you talking about?" I demanded.

"Hmm? Oh, nothing." He checked his watch . . . a mauve-and-gold Rolex. "The point is, I had style! The people loved me!"

I shook my head. "They turned against you. The people of Rome were sure you'd started the Great Fire, so you scapegoated the Christians."

I was aware that this arguing was pointless. If Meg had hidden her true identity all this time, I doubted I could change her mind now. But perhaps I could stall long enough for the cavalry to arrive. If only I *had* a cavalry.

Nero waved dismissively. "But the Christians were terrorists, you see. Perhaps they didn't start the fire, but they were causing all sorts of other trouble. I recognized that before anyone else!"

"He fed them to the lions," I told Meg. "He burned them as human torches, the way he will burn these six."

Meg's face turned green. She gazed at the unconscious prisoners on the stakes. "Nero, you wouldn't—"

"They will be released," Nero promised, "as long as Apollo cooperates."

"Meg, you can't trust him," I said. "The last time he did this, he strung up Christians all over his backyard and burned them to illuminate his garden party. I was there. I remember the screaming."

Meg clutched her stomach.

"My dear, don't believe his stories!" Nero said. "That was just propaganda invented by my enemies."

Meg studied the face of Paulie the geyser god. "Nero . . . you didn't say anything about making them into torches."

"They won't burn," he said, straining to soften his voice. "It won't come to that. The Beast will not have to act."

"You see, Meg?" I wagged a finger at the emperor. "It's never a good sign when someone starts referring to himself in the third person. Zeus used to scold me about that constantly!"

Vince and Gary stepped forward, their knuckles whitening on their spears.

"I would be careful," Nero warned. "My Germani are sensitive about insults to the Imperial person. Now, as much as I love talking about myself, we're on a schedule." He checked his watch again. "You'll open the gates. Then Meg will see if she can use the trees to interpret the future. If so, wonderful! If not . . . well, we'll burn that bridge when we come to it."

"Meg," I said, "he's a madman."

At her feet, Peaches hissed protectively.

Meg's chin quivered. "Nero cared about me, Apollo. He gave me a home. He taught me to fight."

"You said he killed your father!"

"No!" She shook her head adamantly, a look of panic in her eyes. "No, that's not what I said. The *Beast* killed him."

"But—"

Nero snorted. "Oh, Apollo . . . you understand so little. Meg's father was weak. She doesn't even remember him. He couldn't protect her. *I* raised her. I kept her alive."

My heart sank even further. I did not understand everything Meg had been through, or what she was feeling now, but I knew Nero. I saw how easily he could have twisted a scared child's understanding of the world—a little girl all alone, yearning for safety and acceptance after her father's murder, even if that acceptance came from her father's killer. "Meg . . . I am so sorry."

Another tear traced her cheek.

"She doesn't NEED sympathy." Nero's voice turned as hard as bronze. "Now, my dear, if you would be so kind, open the gates. If Apollo objects, remind him that he is bound to follow your orders."

Meg swallowed. "Apollo, don't make it harder. Please . . . help me open the gates."

I shook my head. "Not by choice."

"Then I—I command you. Help me. Now."

31

Listen to the trees
The trees know what is up, yo
They know all the things

MEG'S RESOLVE may have been wavering, but Peaches's was not.

When I hesitated to follow Meg's orders, the grain spirit bared his fangs and hissed, "Peaches," as if that was a new torture technique.

"Fine," I told Meg, my voice turning bitter. The truth was, I had no choice. I could feel Meg's command sinking into my muscles, compelling me to obey.

I faced the fused oaks and put my hands against their trunks. I felt no oracular power within. I heard no voices—just heavy stubborn silence. The only message the trees seemed to be sending was: GO AWAY.

"If we do this," I told Meg, "Nero will destroy the grove."

"He won't."

"He has to. He can't control Dodona. Its power is too ancient. He can't let anyone else use it."

Meg placed her hands against the trees, just below mine. "Concentrate. Open them. Please. You don't want to anger the Beast."

She said this in a low voice—again speaking as if the

Beast was someone I had not yet met . . . a boogeyman lurking under the bed, not a man in a purple suit standing a few feet away.

I could not refuse Meg's orders, but perhaps I should have protested more vigorously. Meg might have backed down if I called her bluff. But then Nero or Peaches or the Germani would have just killed me. I will confess to you: I was afraid of dying. Courageously, nobly, handsomely afraid, true. But afraid nonetheless.

I closed my eyes. I sensed the trees' implacable resistance, their mistrust of outsiders. I knew that if I forced open these gates, the grove would be destroyed. Yet I reached out with all my willpower and sought the voice of prophecy, drawing it to me.

I thought of Rhea, Queen of the Titans, who had first planted this grove. Despite being a child of Gaea and Ouranos, despite being married to the cannibal king Kronos, Rhea had managed to cultivate wisdom and kindness. She had given birth to a new, better breed of immortals. (If I do say so myself.) She represented the best of the ancient times.

True, she had withdrawn from the world and started a pottery studio in Woodstock, but she still cared about Dodona. She had sent me here to open the grove, to share its power. She was not the kind of goddess who believed in closed gates or NO TRESPASSING signs. I began to hum softly "This Land Is Your Land."

The bark grew warm under my fingertips. The tree roots trembled.

I glanced at Meg. She was deep in concentration, leaning against the trunks as if trying to push them over.

Everything about her was familiar: her ratty pageboy hair, her glittering cat-eye glasses, her runny nose and chewed cuticles and faint scent of apple pie.

But she was someone I didn't know at all: stepdaughter to the immortal crazy Nero. A member of the Imperial Household. What did that even *mean*? I pictured the Brady Bunch in purple togas, lined up on the family staircase with Nero at the bottom in Alice's maid uniform. Having a vivid imagination is a terrible curse.

Unfortunately for the grove, Meg was also the daughter of Demeter. The trees responded to her power. The twin oaks rumbled. Their trunks began to move.

I wanted to stop, but I was caught up in the momentum. The grove seemed to be drawing on my power now. My hands stuck to the trees. The gates opened wider, forcibly spreading my arms. For a terrifying moment, I thought the trees might keep moving and rip me limb from limb. Then they stopped. The roots settled. The bark cooled and released me.

I stumbled back, exhausted. Meg remained, transfixed, in the newly opened gateway.

On the other side were . . . well, more trees. Despite the winter cold, the young oaks rose tall and green, growing in concentric circles around a slightly larger specimen in the center. Littering the ground were acorns glowing with a faint amber light. Around the grove stood a protective wall of trees even more formidable than the ones in the antechamber. Above, another tightly woven dome of branches guarded the place from aerial intruders.

Before I could warn her, Meg stepped across the

threshold. The voices exploded. Imagine forty nail guns firing into your brain from all directions at once. The words were babble, but they tore at my sanity, demanding my attention. I covered my ears. The noise just got louder and more persistent.

Peaches clawed frantically at the dirt, trying to bury his head. Vince and Gary writhed on the ground. Even the unconscious demigods thrashed and moaned on their stakes.

Nero reeled, his hand raised as if to block an intense light. "Meg, control the voices! Do it now!"

Meg didn't appear hurt by the noise, but she looked bewildered. "They're saying something . . ." She swept her hands through the air, pulling at invisible threads to untangle the pandemonium. "They're agitated. I can't— Wait . . ."

Suddenly the voices shut off, as if they'd made their point.

Meg turned toward Nero, her eyes wide. "It's true. The trees told me you mean to burn them."

The Germani groaned, half-conscious on the ground. Nero recovered more quickly. He raised a finger, admonishing, guiding. "Listen to me, Meg. I'd hoped the grove could be useful, but obviously it is fractured and confused. You can't believe what it says. It's the mouthpiece of a senile Titan queen. The grove must be razed. It's the only way, Meg. You understand that, don't you?"

He kicked Gary over onto his back and rifled through the bodyguard's pouches. Then Nero stood, triumphantly holding a box of matches.

"After the fire, we'll rebuild," he said. "It will be glorious!"

Meg stared at him as if noticing his horrendous neck beard for the first time. "Wh-what are you talking about?"

"He's going to burn and level Long Island," I said. "Then he'll make it his private domain, just like he did with Rome."

Nero laughed in exasperation. "Long Island is a mess anyway! No one will miss it. My new imperial complex will extend from Manhattan to Montauk—the greatest palace ever built! We'll have private rivers and lakes, one hundred miles of beachfront property, gardens big enough for their own zip codes. I'll build each member of my household a private skyscraper. Oh, Meg, imagine the parties we will have in our new Domus Aurea!"

The truth was a heavy thing. Meg's knees buckled under its weight.

"You can't." Her voice shook. "The woods— I'm the daughter of Demeter."

"You're *my* daughter," Nero corrected. "And I care for you deeply. Which is why you need to move aside. Quickly."

He set a match to the striking surface of the box. "As soon as I light these stakes, our human torches will send a wave of fire straight through that gateway. Nothing will be able to stop it. The entire forest will burn."

"Please!" Meg cried.

"Come along, dearest." Nero's frown hardened. "Apollo is of no use to us anymore. You don't want to wake the Beast, do you?"

He lit his match and stepped toward the nearest stake, where my son Austin was bound.

32

It takes a Village
People to protect your mind
"Y.M.C.A." Yeah

OH, THIS PART IS DIFFICULT TO TELL.

I am a natural storyteller. I have an infallible instinct for drama. I want to relate what *should* have happened: how I leaped forward shouting, "Nooooo!" and spun like an acrobat, knocking aside the lit match, then twisted in a series of blazing-fast Shaolin moves, cracking Nero's head and taking out his bodyguards before they could recover.

Ah, yes. That would have been perfect.

Alas, the truth constrains me.

Curse you, truth!

In fact, I spluttered something like, "Nuh-uh, dundoot!" I may have waved my Brazilian handkerchief with the hope that its magic would destroy my enemies.

The real hero was Peaches. The karpos must have sensed Meg's true feelings, or perhaps he just didn't like the idea of burning forests. He hurtled through the air, screaming his war cry (you guessed it), "Peaches!" He landed on Nero's arm, chomped the lit match from the emperor's hand, then landed a few feet away, wiping his tongue and crying, "Hat!

Hat!" (Which I assumed meant *hot* in the dialect of deciduous fruit.)

The scene might have been funny except that the Germani were now back on their feet, five demigods and a geyser spirit were still tied to highly flammable posts, and Nero still had a box of matches.

The emperor stared at his empty hand. "Meg . . . ?" His voice was as cold as an icicle. "What is the meaning of this?"

"P-Peaches, come here!" Meg's voice had turned brittle with fear.

The karpos bounded to her side. He hissed at me, Nero, and the Germani.

Meg took a shaky breath, clearly gathering her nerve. "Nero . . . Peaches is right. You—you can't burn these people alive."

Nero sighed. He looked at his bodyguards for moral support, but the Germani still appeared woozy. They were hitting the sides of their heads as if trying to clear water from their ears.

"Meg," said the emperor, "I am trying so hard to keep the Beast at bay. Why won't you help me? I know you are a good girl. I wouldn't have allowed you to roam around Manhattan so much on your own, playing the street waif, if I didn't know you could take care of yourself. But softness toward your enemies is not a virtue. You are my stepdaughter. Any of these demigods would kill you without hesitation given the chance."

"Meg, that's not true!" I said. "You've seen what Camp Half-Blood is like."

She studied me uneasily. "Even . . . even if it was true . . ." She turned to Nero. "You told me never to lower myself to my enemies' level."

"No, indeed." Nero's tone had frayed like a weathered rope. "We are better. We are stronger. We will build a glorious new world. But these nonsense-spewing trees stand in our way, Meg. Like any invasive weeds, they must be burned. And the only way to do that is with a true conflagration—flames stoked by blood. Let us do this together, and not involve the Beast, shall we?"

Finally, in my mind, something clicked. I remembered how my father used to punish me centuries ago, when I was a young god learning the ways of Olympus. Zeus used to say, *Don't get on the wrong side of my lightning bolts, boy.*

As if the lightning bolt had a mind of its own—as if Zeus had nothing to do with the punishments he meted out upon me.

Don't blame me, his tone implied. *It's the lightning bolt that seared every molecule in your body.* Many years later, when I killed the Cyclopes who made Zeus's lightning, it was no rash decision. I'd always *hated* those lightning bolts. It was easier than hating my father.

Nero took the same tone when he referred to himself as the Beast. He spoke of his anger and cruelty as if they were forces outside his control. If he flew into a rage . . . well, then he would hold *Meg* responsible.

The realization sickened me. Meg had been trained to regard her kindly stepfather Nero and the terrifying Beast as two separate people. I understood now why she preferred to spend her time in the alleys of New York. I understood why she had such quick mood changes, going from cartwheels to full shutdown in a matter of seconds. She never knew what might unleash the Beast.

She fixed her eyes on me. Her lips quivered. I could tell she wanted a way out—some eloquent argument that would mollify her stepfather and allow her to follow her conscience. But I was no longer a silver-tongued god. I could not outtalk an orator like Nero. And I would not play the Beast's blame game.

Instead, I took a page from Meg's book, which was always short and to the point.

"He's evil," I said. "You're good. You must make your own choice."

I could tell that this was not the news Meg wanted. Her mouth tightened. She drew back her shoulder blades as if preparing for a measles shot—something painful but necessary. She placed her hand on the karpos's curly scalp. "Peaches," she said in a small but firm voice, "get the matchbox."

The karpos sprang into action. Nero barely had time to blink before Peaches ripped the box from his hand and jumped back to Meg's side.

The Germani readied their spears. Nero raised his hand for restraint. He gave Meg a look that might have been heartbreak—if he had possessed a heart.

"I see you weren't ready for this assignment, my dear," he said. "It's my fault. Vince, Gary, detain Meg but don't hurt her. When we get home . . ." He shrugged, his expression full of regret. "As for Apollo and the little fruit demon, they will have to burn."

"No," Meg croaked. Then, at full volume, she shouted, "NO!" And the Grove of Dodona shouted with her.

The blast was so powerful, it knocked Nero and his guards off their feet. Peaches screamed and beat his head against the dirt.

This time, however, I was more prepared. As the trees' ear-splitting chorus reached its crescendo, I anchored my mind with the catchiest tune I could imagine. I hummed "Y.M.C.A.," which I used to perform with the Village People in my construction worker costume until the Indian chief and I got in a fight over— Never mind. That's not important.

"Meg!" I pulled the brass wind chimes from my pocket and tossed them to her. "Put these on the center tree! Y.M.C.A. Focus the grove's energy! Y.M.C.A."

I wasn't sure she could hear me. She raised the chimes and watched as they swayed and clanked, turning the noise from the trees into snatches of coherent speech: *Happiness approaches. The fall of the sun; the final verse. Would you like to hear our specials today?*

Meg's face went slack with surprise. She turned toward the grove and sprinted through the gateway. Peaches crawled after her, shaking his head.

I wanted to follow, but I couldn't leave Nero and his guards alone with six hostages. Still humming "Y.M.C.A.," I marched toward them.

The trees screamed louder than ever, but Nero rose to his knees. He pulled something from his coat pocket—a vial of liquid—and splashed it on the ground in front of him. I doubted that was a good thing, but I had more immediate concerns. Vince and Gary were getting up. Vince thrust his spear in my direction.

I was angry enough to be reckless. I grabbed the point of his weapon and yanked the spear up, smacking Vince under his chin. He fell, stunned, and I grabbed fistfuls of his hide armor.

He was easily twice my size. I didn't care. I lifted him off his feet. My arms sizzled with power. I felt invincibly strong—the way a god *should* feel. I had no idea why my strength had returned, but I decided this was not the moment to question my good luck. I spun Vince like a discus, tossing him skyward with such force that he punched a Germanus-shaped hole in the tree canopy and sailed out of sight.

Kudos to the Imperial Guard for having stupid amounts of courage. Despite my show of force, Gary charged me. With one hand, I snapped his spear. With the other, I punched a fist straight through his shield and hit his chest with enough might to fell a rhinoceros.

He collapsed in a heap.

I faced Nero. I could already feel my strength ebbing. My muscles were returning to their pathetic mortal flabbiness. I just hoped I'd have enough time to rip off Nero's head and stuff it down his mauve suit.

The emperor snarled. "You're a fool, Apollo. You *always* focus on the wrong thing." He glanced at his Rolex. "My wrecking crew will be here any minute. Once Camp Half-Blood is destroyed, I'll make it my new front lawn! Meanwhile, you'll be here . . . putting out fires."

From his vest pocket, he produced a silver cigarette lighter. Typical of Nero to keep several forms of fire-making close at hand. I looked at the glistening streaks of oil he had splashed on the ground. . . . Greek fire, of course.

"Don't," I said.

Nero grinned. "Good-bye, Apollo. Only eleven more Olympians to go."

He dropped the lighter.

I did not have the pleasure of tearing Nero's head off.

Could I have stopped him from fleeing? Possibly. But the flames were roaring between us, burning grass and bones, tree roots, and the earth itself. The blaze was too strong to stamp out, if Greek fire even *could* be stamped out, and it was rolling hungrily toward the six bound hostages.

I let Nero go. Somehow he hauled Gary to his feet and lugged the punch-drunk Germanus toward the ants' nest. Meanwhile, I ran to the stakes.

The closest was Austin's. I wrapped my arms around the base and pulled, completely disregarding proper heavy-lifting techniques. My muscles strained. My vision swam with the effort. I managed to raise the stake enough to topple it backward. Austin stirred and groaned.

I dragged him, cocoon and all, to the other side of the clearing, as far from the fire as possible. I would have brought him into the Grove of Dodona, but I had a feeling I wouldn't be doing him any favors by putting him in a dead-end clearing full of insane voices, in the direct path of approaching flames.

I ran back to the stakes. I repeated the process—uprooting Kayla, then Paulie the geyser god, then the others. By the time I pulled Miranda Gardiner to safety, the fire was a raging red tidal wave, only inches from the gates of the grove.

My divine strength was gone. Meg and Peaches were nowhere to be seen. I had bought a few minutes for the hostages, but the fire would eventually consume us all. I fell to my knees and sobbed.

"Help." I scanned the dark trees, tangled and foreboding. I did not expect any help. I was not even used to *asking* for help. I was Apollo. Mortals called to *me*! (Yes, occasionally I might have ordered demigods to run trivial errands for me, like starting wars or retrieving magic items from monsters' lairs, but those requests didn't count.)

"I can't do this alone." I imagined Daphne's face floating beneath the trunk of one tree, then another. Soon the woods would burn. I couldn't save them any more than I could save Meg or the lost demigods or myself. "I'm so sorry. Please . . . forgive me."

My head must have been spinning from smoke inhalation. I began to hallucinate. The shimmering forms of dryads emerged from their trees—a legion of Daphnes in green gossamer dresses. Their expressions were melancholy, as if they knew they were going to their deaths, yet they circled the fire. They raised their arms, and the earth erupted at their feet. A torrent of mud churned over the flames. The dryads drew the fire's heat into their bodies. Their skin charred black. Their faces hardened and cracked.

As soon as the last flames were snuffed out, the dryads crumbled to ash. I wished I could crumble with them. I wanted to cry, but the fire had seared all the moisture from my tear ducts. I had not asked for so many sacrifices. I had not expected it! I felt hollow, guilty, and ashamed.

Then it occurred to me how many times I *had* asked for sacrifices, how many heroes I had sent to their deaths. Had they been any less noble and courageous than these dryads? Yet I had felt no remorse when I sent them off on deadly tasks. I had used them and discarded them, laid waste to their lives to build my own glory. I was no less of a monster than Nero.

Wind blew through the clearing—an unseasonably warm gust that swirled up the ashes and carried them through the forest canopy into the sky. Only after the breeze calmed did I realize it must have been the West Wind, my old rival, offering me consolation. He had swept up the remains and taken them off to their next beautiful reincarnation. After all these centuries, Zephyros had accepted my apology.

I discovered I had some tears left after all.

Behind me, someone groaned. "Where am I?"

Austin was awake.

I crawled to his side, now weeping with relief, and kissed his face. "My beautiful son!"

He blinked at me in confusion. His cornrows were sprinkled with ashes like frost on a field. I suppose it took a moment for him to process why he was being fawned over by a grungy, half-deranged boy with acne.

"Ah, right . . . Apollo." He tried to move. "What the—?

Why am I wrapped in smelly bandages? Could you free me, maybe?"

I laughed hysterically, which I doubt helped Austin's peace of mind. I clawed at his bindings but made no progress. Then I remembered Gary's snapped spear. I retrieved the point and spent several minutes sawing Austin free.

Once pulled from the stake, he stumbled around, trying to shake the circulation back into his limbs. He took in the scene—the smoldering forest, the other prisoners. The Grove of Dodona had stopped its wild chorus of screaming. (When had that happened?) A radiant amber light now glowed from the gateway.

"What's going on?" Austin asked. "Also, where is my saxophone?"

Sensible questions. I wished I had sensible answers. All I knew was that Meg McCaffrey was still wandering in the grove, and I did not like the fact that the trees had gone silent.

I stared at my weak mortal arms. I wondered why I'd experienced a sudden surge of divine strength when facing the Germani. Had my emotions triggered it? Was it the first sign of my godly vigor returning for good? Or perhaps Zeus was just messing with me again—giving me a taste of my old power before yanking it away once more. *Remember this, kid? WELL, YOU CAN'T HAVE IT!*

I wished I could summon that strength again, but I would have to make do.

I handed Austin the broken spear. "Free the others. I'll be back."

Austin stared at me incredulously. "You're going in *there*? Is it safe?"

"I doubt it," I said.

Then I ran toward the Oracle.

3 3

Parting is sorrow
Nothing about it is sweet
Don't step on my face

THE TREES WERE using their inside voices.

As I stepped through the gateway, I realized they were still talking in conversational tones, babbling nonsensically like sleepwalkers at a cocktail party.

I scanned the grove. No sign of Meg. I called her name. The trees responded by raising their voices, driving me cross-eyed with dizziness.

I steadied myself on the nearest oak.

"Watch it, man," the tree said.

I lurched forward, the trees trading bits of verse as if playing a game of rhymes:

> *Caves of blue.*
> *Strike the hue.*
> *Westward, burning.*
> *Pages turning.*
> *Indiana.*
> *Ripe banana.*
> *Happiness approaches.*
> *Serpents and roaches.*

None of it made sense, but each line carried the weight of prophecy. I felt as if dozens of important statements, each vital to my survival, were being blended together, loaded in a shotgun, and fired at my face.

(Oh, that's a rather good image. I'll have to use it in a haiku.)

"Meg!" I called again.

Still no reply. The grove did not seem so large. How could she not hear me? How could I not see her?

I slogged along, humming a perfect A 440 hertz tone to keep myself focused. When I reached the second ring of trees, the oaks became more conversational.

"Hey, buddy, got a quarter?" one asked.

Another tried to tell me a joke about a penguin and a nun walking into a Shake Shack.

A third oak was giving its neighbor an infomercial sales pitch about a food processor. "And you won't believe what it does with pasta!"

"Wow!" said the other tree. "It makes pasta, too?"

"Fresh linguine in minutes!" the sales oak enthused.

I did not understand why an oak tree would want linguine, but I kept moving. I was afraid that if I listened too long, I would order the food processor for three easy installments of $39.99, and my sanity would be lost forever.

Finally, I reached the center of the grove. On the far side of the largest oak tree, Meg stood with her back to the trunk, her eyes closed tight. The wind chimes were still in her hand, but they hung forgotten at her side. The brass cylinders clanked, muted against her dress.

At her feet, Peaches rocked back and forth, giggling. "Apples? Peaches! Mangoes? Peaches!"

"Meg." I touched her shoulder.

She flinched. She focused on me as if I were a clever optical illusion. Her eyes simmered with fear. "It's too much," she said. "Too much."

The voices had her in their grip. It was bad enough for me to endure—like a hundred radio stations playing at once, forcibly splitting my brain into different channels. But I was used to prophecies. Meg, on the other hand, was a daughter of Demeter. The trees liked her. They were all trying to share with her, to get her attention at the same time. Soon they would permanently fracture her mind.

"The wind chimes," I said. "Hang them in the tree!"

I pointed to the lowest branch, well above our heads. Alone, neither of us could reach it, but if I gave Meg a boost . . .

Meg backed away, shaking her head. The voices of Dodona were so chaotic I wasn't sure she had heard me. If she had, she either didn't understand or didn't trust me.

I had to tamp down my feelings of betrayal. Meg was Nero's stepdaughter. She had been sent to lure me here, and our whole friendship was a lie. She had no right to mistrust *me*.

But I could not stay bitter. If I blamed her for the way Nero had twisted her emotions, I was no better than the Beast. Also, just because she had lied about being my friend did not mean I wasn't hers. She was in danger. I was not going to leave her to the madness of the grove's penguin jokes.

I crouched and laced my fingers to make a foothold. "Please."

To my left, Peaches rolled onto his back and wailed, "Linguine? Peaches!"

Meg grimaced. I could see from her eyes that she was deciding to cooperate with me—not because she trusted me, but because Peaches was suffering.

Just when I thought my feelings could not be hurt any worse. It was one thing to be betrayed. It was another thing to be considered less important than a diapered fruit spirit.

Nevertheless, I remained steady as Meg placed her left foot in my hands. With all my remaining strength, I hoisted her up. She stepped onto my shoulders, then planted one red sneaker on top of my head. I made a mental note to put a safety label on my scalp: WARNING, TOP STEP IS NOT FOR STANDING.

With my back against the oak, I could feel the voices of the grove coursing up its trunk and drumming through its bark. The central tree seemed to be one giant antenna for crazy talk.

My knees were about to buckle. Meg's treads were grinding into my forehead. The A 440 I had been humming rapidly deflated to a G sharp.

Finally, Meg tied the wind chimes to the branch. She jumped down as my legs collapsed, and we both ended up sprawled in the dirt.

The brass chimes swayed and clanged, picking notes out of the wind and making chords from the dissonance.

The grove hushed, as if the trees were listening and thinking, *Oooh, pretty.*

Then the ground trembled. The central oak shook with such energy, it rained acorns.

Meg got to her feet. She approached the tree and touched its trunk.

"Speak," she commanded.

A single voice boomed forth from the wind chimes, like a cheerleader screaming through a megaphone:

> *There once was a god named Apollo*
> *Who plunged in a cave blue and hollow*
> *Upon a three-seater*
> *The bronze fire-eater*
> *Was forced death and madness to swallow*

The wind chimes stilled. The grove settled into tranquility, as if satisfied with the death sentence it had given me.

Oh, the horror!

A sonnet I could have handled. A quatrain would have been cause for celebration. But only the deadliest prophecies are couched in the form of a limerick.

I stared at the wind chimes, hoping they would speak again and correct themselves. *Oops, our mistake! That prophecy was for a* different *Apollo!*

But my luck was not that good. I had been handed an edict worse than a thousand advertisements for pasta makers.

Peaches rose. He shook his head and hissed at the oak tree, which expressed my own sentiments perfectly. He hugged Meg's calf as if she were the only thing keeping him from falling off the world. The scene was almost sweet, except for the karpos's fangs and glowing eyes.

Meg regarded me warily. The lenses of her glasses were spiderwebbed with cracks.

"That prophecy," she said. "Did you understand it?"

I swallowed a mouthful of soot. "Perhaps. Some of it. We'll need to talk to Rachel—"

"There's no more *we*." Meg's tone was as acrid as the volcanic gas of Delphi. "Do what you need to do. That's my final order."

This hit me like a spear shaft to the chin, despite the fact that she had lied to me and betrayed me.

"Meg, you can't." I couldn't keep the shakiness out of my voice. "You claimed my service. Until my trials are over—"

"I release you."

"No!" I could not stand the idea of being abandoned. Not again. Not by this ragamuffin Dumpster queen whom I'd learned to care about so much. "You can't *possibly* believe in Nero now. You heard him explain his plans. He means to level this entire island! You saw what he tried to do to his hostages."

"He—he wouldn't have let them burn. He promised. He held back. You saw it. That wasn't the Beast."

My rib cage felt like an over-tightened harp. "Meg . . . Nero *is* the Beast. He killed your father."

"No! Nero is my stepfather. My dad . . . my dad unleashed the Beast. He made it angry."

"Meg—"

"Stop!" She covered her ears. "You don't know him. Nero is good to me. I can talk to him. I can make it okay."

Her denial was so complete, so irrational, I realized there was no way I could argue with her. She reminded me painfully of myself when I fell to earth—how I had refused to accept my new reality. Without Meg's help, I would've gotten myself killed. Now our roles were reversed.

I edged toward her, but Peaches's snarl stopped me in my tracks.

Meg backed away. "We're done."

"We can't be," I said. "We're bound, whether you like it or not."

It occurred to me that she'd said the exact same thing to me only a few days before.

She gave me one last look through her cracked lenses. I would have given anything for her to blow a raspberry. I wanted to walk the streets of Manhattan with her doing cartwheels in the intersections. I missed hobbling with her through the Labyrinth, our legs tied together. I would've settled for a good garbage fight in an alley. Instead, she turned and fled, with Peaches at her heels. It seemed to me that they dissolved into the trees, just the way Daphne had done long ago.

Above my head, a breeze made the wind chimes jingle. This time, no voices came from the trees. I didn't know how long Dodona would remain silent, but I didn't want to be here if the oaks decided to start telling jokes again.

I turned and saw something strange at my feet: an arrow with an oak shaft and green fletching.

There shouldn't have been an arrow. I hadn't brought any into the grove. But in my dazed state, I didn't question this. I did what any archer would do: I retrieved it, and returned it to my quiver.

34

Uber's got nothing

Lyft is weak. And taxis? Nah

My ride is da mom

AUSTIN HAD FREED THE OTHER PRISONERS.

They looked like they had been dipped in a vat of glue and cotton swabs, but otherwise they seemed remarkably undamaged. Ellis Wakefield staggered around with his fists clenched, looking for something to punch. Cecil Markowitz, son of Hermes, sat on the ground trying to clean his sneakers with a deer's thighbone. Austin—resourceful boy!—had produced a canteen of water and was washing the Greek fire off of Kayla's face. Miranda Gardiner, the head counselor of Demeter, knelt by the place where the dryads had sacrificed themselves. She wept silently.

Paulie the palikos floated toward me. Like his partner, Pete, his lower half was all steam. From the waist up he looked like a slimmer, more abused version of his geyser buddy. His mud skin was cracked like a parched riverbed. His face was withered, as if every bit of moisture had been squeezed out of him. Looking at the damage Nero had done to him, I added a few more items to a mental list I was preparing: *Ways to Torture an Emperor in the Fields of Punishment.*

"You saved me," Paulie said with amazement. "Bring it in!"

He threw his arms around me. His power was so diminished that his body heat did not kill me, but it did open up my sinuses quite well.

"You should get home," I said. "Pete is worried, and you need to regain your strength."

"Ah, man . . ." Paulie wiped a steaming tear from his face. "Yeah, I'm gone. But anything you ever need—a free steam cleaning, some PR work, a mud scrub, you name it."

As he dissolved into mist, I called after him. "And Paulie? I'd give the Woods at Camp Half-Blood a ten for customer satisfaction."

Paulie beamed with gratitude. He tried to hug me again, but he was already ninety percent steam. All I got was a humid waft of mud-scented air. Then he was gone.

The five demigods gathered around me.

Miranda looked past me at the Grove of Dodona. Her eyes were still puffy from crying, but she had beautiful irises the color of new foliage. "So, the voices I heard from that grove . . . It's really an Oracle? Those trees can give us prophecies?"

I shivered, thinking of the oak trees' limerick. "Perhaps."

"Can I see—?"

"No," I said. "Not until we understand the place better."

I had already lost one daughter of Demeter today. I didn't intend to lose another.

"I don't get it," Ellis grumbled. "You're Apollo? Like, *the* Apollo."

"I'm afraid so. It's a long story."

"Oh, gods . . ." Kayla scanned the clearing. "I thought I heard Meg's voice earlier. Did I dream that? Was she with you? Is she okay?"

The others looked at me for an explanation. Their expressions were so fragile and tentative, I decided I couldn't break down in front of them.

"She's . . . alive," I managed. "She had to leave."

"*What?*" Kayla asked. "Why?"

"Nero," I said. "She . . . she went after Nero."

"Hold up." Austin raised his fingers like goalposts. "When you say Nero . . ."

I did my best to explain how the mad emperor had captured them. They deserved to know. As I recounted the story, Nero's words kept replaying in my mind: *My wrecking crew will be here any minute. Once Camp Half-Blood is destroyed, I'll make it my new front lawn!*

I wanted to think this was just bluster. Nero had always loved threats and grandiose statements. Unlike me, he was a terrible poet. He used flowery language like . . . well, like every sentence was a pungent bouquet of metaphors. (Oh, that's another good one. Jotting that down.)

Why had he kept checking his watch? And what wrecking crew could he have been talking about? I had a flashback to my dream of the sun bus careening toward a giant bronze face.

I felt like I was free-falling again. Nero's plan became horribly clear. After dividing the few demigods defending the camp, he had meant to burn this grove. But that was only part of his attack. . . .

"Oh, gods," I said. "The Colossus."

The five demigods shifted uneasily.

"What Colossus?" Kayla asked. "You mean the Colossus of Rhodes?"

"No," I said. "The Colossus Neronis."

Cecil scratched his head. "The Colossus Neurotic?"

Ellis Wakefield snorted. "*You're* a Colossus Neurotic, Markowitz. Apollo's talking about the big replica of Nero that stood outside the amphitheater in Rome, right?"

"I'm afraid so," I said. "While we're standing here, Nero is going to try to destroy Camp Half-Blood. And the Colossus will be his wrecking crew."

Miranda flinched. "You mean a giant statue is about to stomp on *camp*? I thought the Colossus was destroyed centuries ago."

Ellis frowned. "Supposedly, so was the Athena Parthenos. Now it's sitting on top of Half-Blood Hill."

The others' expressions turned grim. When a child of Ares makes a valid point, you know the situation is serious.

"Speaking of Athena . . ." Austin picked some incendiary fluff off his shoulder. "Won't the statue protect us? I mean, that's what she's there for, right?"

"She will try," I guessed. "But you must understand, the Athena Parthenos draws her power from her followers. The more demigods under her care, the more formidable her magic. And right now—"

"The camp is practically empty," Miranda finished.

"Not only that," I said, "but the Athena Parthenos is roughly forty feet tall. If memory serves, Nero's Colossus was more than twice that."

Ellis grunted. "So they're not in the same weight class. It's an uneven match."

Cecil Markowitz stood a little straighter. "Guys . . . did you feel that?"

I thought he might be playing one of his Hermes pranks. Then the ground shook again, ever so slightly. From somewhere in the distance came a rumbling sound like a battleship scraping over a sandbar.

"Please tell me that was thunder," Kayla said.

Ellis cocked his head, listening. "It's a war machine. A big automaton wading ashore about half a klick from here. We need to get to camp right now."

No one argued with Ellis's assessment. I supposed he could distinguish between the sounds of war machines the same way I could pick out an off-tune violin in a Rachmaninoff symphony.

To their credit, the demigods rose to the challenge. Despite the fact that they'd been recently bound, doused in flammable substances, and staked like human tiki torches, they closed ranks and faced me with determination in their eyes.

"How do we get out of here?" Austin asked. "The myrmekes' lair?"

I felt suddenly suffocated, partly because I had five people looking at me as if I knew what to do. I didn't. In fact, if you want to know a secret, we gods usually don't. When confronted for answers, we usually say something Rhea-like: *You will have to find out for yourself!* Or *True wisdom must be earned!* But I didn't think that would fly in this situation.

Also, I had no desire to plunge back into the ants' nest.

Even if we made it through alive, it would take much too long. Then we would have to run perhaps half the length of the forest.

I stared at the Vince-shaped hole in the canopy. "I don't suppose any of you can fly?"

They shook their heads.

"I can cook," Cecil offered.

Ellis smacked him on the shoulder.

I looked back at the myrmekes' tunnel. The solution came to me like a voice whispering in my ear: *You know someone who can fly, stupid.*

It was a risky idea. Then again, rushing off to fight a giant automaton was also not the safest plan of action.

"I think there's a way," I said. "But I'll need your help."

Austin balled his fists. "Anything you need. We're ready to fight."

"Actually . . . I don't need you to fight. I need you to lay down a beat."

My next important discovery: Children of Hermes cannot rap. At all.

Bless his conniving little heart, Cecil Markowitz tried his best, but he kept throwing off my rhythm section with his spastic clapping and terrible air mic noises. After a few trial runs, I demoted him to dancer. His job would be to shimmy back and forth and wave his hands, which he did with the enthusiasm of a tent-revival preacher.

The others managed to keep up. They still looked like half-plucked, highly combustible chickens, but they bopped with the proper amount of soul.

I launched into "Dear Mama," my throat reinforced with water and cough drops from Kayla's belt pack. (Ingenious girl! Who brings cough drops on a three-legged death race?)

I sang directly into the mouth of the myrmekes' tunnel, trusting the acoustics to carry my message. We did not have to wait long. The earth began to rumble beneath our feet. I kept singing. I had warned my comrades not to stop laying down the righteous beat until the song was over.

Still, I almost lost it when the ground exploded. I had been watching the tunnel, but Mama did not use tunnels. She exited wherever she wanted—in this case, straight out of the earth twenty yards away, spraying dirt, grass, and small boulders in all directions. She scuttled forward, mandibles clacking, wings buzzing, dark Teflon eyes focused on me. Her abdomen was no longer swollen, so I assumed she had finished depositing her most recent batch of killer-ant larvae. I hoped this meant she would be in a good mood, not a hungry mood.

Behind her, two winged soldiers clambered out of the earth. I had not been expecting bonus ants. (Really, *bonus ants* is not a term most people would like to hear.) They flanked the queen, their antennae quivering.

I finished my ode, then dropped to one knee, spreading my arms as I had before.

"Mama," I said, "we need a ride."

My logic was this: Mothers were used to giving rides. With thousands upon thousands of offspring, I assumed the queen ant would be the ultimate soccer mom. And indeed, Mama grabbed me with her mandibles and tossed me over her head.

Despite what the demigods may tell you, I did not flail, scream, or land in a way that damaged my sensitive parts. I landed heroically, straddling the queen's neck, which was no larger than the back of an average warhorse. I shouted to my comrades, "Join me! It's perfectly safe!"

For some reason, they hesitated. The ants did not. The queen tossed Kayla just behind me. The soldier ants followed Mama's lead—snapping up two demigods each and throwing them aboard.

The three myrmekes revved their wings with a noise like radiator fan blades. Kayla grabbed my waist.

"Is this *really* safe?" she yelled.

"Perfectly!" I hoped I was right. "Perhaps even safer than the sun chariot!"

"Didn't the sun chariot almost destroy the world once?"

"Well, twice," I said. "Three times, if you count the day I let Thalia Grace drive, but —"

"Forget I asked!"

Mama launched herself into the sky. The canopy of twisted branches blocked our path, but Mama didn't pay any more attention to them than she had to the ton of solid earth she'd plowed through.

I yelled, "Duck!"

We flattened ourselves against Mama's armored head as she smashed through the trees, leaving a thousand wooden splinters embedded in my back. It felt so good to fly again, I didn't care. We soared above the woods and banked to the east.

For two or three seconds, I was exhilarated.

Then I heard the screaming from Camp Half-Blood.

35

Buck-naked statue
A Neurotic Colossus
Where art thy undies?

EVEN MY SUPERNATURAL POWERS of description fail me.

Imagine seeing yourself as a hundred-foot-tall bronze statue—a replica of your own magnificence, gleaming in the late afternoon light.

Now imagine that this ridiculously handsome statue is wading out of Long Island Sound onto the North Shore. In his hand is a ship's rudder—a blade the size of a stealth bomber, fixed to a fifty-foot-long pole—and Mr. Gorgeous is raising said rudder to smash the crud out of Camp Half-Blood.

This was the sight that greeted us as we flew in from the woods.

"How is that thing *alive?*" Kayla demanded. "What did Nero do—order it online?"

"The Triumvirate has vast resources," I told her. "They've had centuries to prepare. Once they reconstructed the statue, all they had to do was fill it with some animating magic—usually the harnessed life forces of wind or water spirits. I'm not sure. That's really more of Hephaestus's specialty."

"So how do we kill it?"

"I'm . . . I'm working on that."

All across the valley, campers screamed and ran for their weapons. Nico and Will were floundering in the lake, apparently having been capsized in the middle of a canoe ride. Chiron galloped through the dunes, harrying the Colossus with his arrows. Even by my standards, Chiron was a very fine archer. He targeted the statue's joints and seams, yet his shots did not seem to bother the automaton at all. Already dozens of missiles stuck from the Colossus's armpits and neck like unruly hair.

"More quivers!" Chiron shouted. "Quickly!"

Rachel Dare stumbled from the armory carrying half a dozen, and she ran to resupply him.

The Colossus brought down his rudder to smash the dining pavilion, but his blade bounced off the camp's magical barrier, sparking as if it had hit solid metal. Mr. Gorgeous took another step inland, but the barrier resisted him, pushing him back with the force of a wind tunnel.

On Half-Blood Hill, a silver aura surrounded the Athena Parthenos. I wasn't sure the demigods could see it, but every so often a beam of ultraviolet light shot from Athena's helmet like a search lamp, hitting the Colossus's chest and pushing back the invader. Next to her, in the tall pine tree, the Golden Fleece blazed with fiery energy. The dragon Peleus hissed and paced around the trunk, ready to defend his turf.

These were powerful forces, but I did not need godly sight to tell me that they would soon fail. The camp's defensive barriers were designed to turn away the occasional stray monster, to confuse mortals and prevent them from detecting the valley, and to provide a first line of defense against invading forces. A criminally beautiful hundred-foot-tall Celestial bronze giant was another thing entirely. Soon the Colossus would break through and destroy everything in its path.

"Apollo!" Kayla nudged me in the ribs. "What do we do?"

I stirred, again with the unpleasant realization that I was expected to have answers. My first instinct was to order a seasoned demigod to take charge. Wasn't it the weekend yet? Where was Percy Jackson? Or those Roman praetors Frank Zhang and Reyna Ramírez-Arellano? Yes, they would have done nicely.

My second instinct was to turn to Meg McCaffrey. How quickly I had grown used to her annoying yet strangely endearing presence! Alas, she was gone. Her absence felt like a Colossus stomping upon my heart. (This was an easy metaphor to summon, since the Colossus was presently stomping on a great many things.)

Flanking us on either side, the soldier ants flew in formation, awaiting the queen's orders. The demigods watched me anxiously, random bits of bandage fluff swirling from their bodies as we sped through the air.

I leaned forward and spoke to Mama in a soothing tone. "I know I cannot ask you to risk your life for us."

Mama hummed as if to say, *You're darn right!*

"Just give us one pass around that statue's head?" I asked. "Enough to distract it. Then set us down on the beach?"

She clicked her mandibles doubtfully.

"You're the best mama in the whole world," I added, "and you look lovely today."

That line always worked with Leto. It did the trick with Mama Ant, too. She twitched her antennae, perhaps sending a high-frequency signal to her soldiers, and all three ants banked hard to the right.

Below us, more campers joined the battle. Sherman Yang had harnessed two pegasi to a chariot and was now circling the statue's legs, while Julia and Alice threw electric javelins at the Colossus's knees. The missiles stuck in his joints, discharging tendrils of blue lightning, but the statue barely seemed to notice. Meanwhile, at his feet, Connor Stoll and Harley used twin flamethrowers to give the Colossus a molten pedicure, while the Nike twins manned a catapult, lobbing boulders at the Colossus's Celestial bronze crotch.

Malcolm Pace, a true child of Athena, was coordinating the attacks from a hastily organized command post on the green. He and Nyssa had spread war maps across a card table and were shouting targeting coordinates, while Chiara, Damien, Paolo, and Billie rushed to set up ballistae around the communal hearth.

Malcolm looked like the perfect battlefield commander, except for the fact that he'd forgotten his pants. His red briefs made quite a statement with his sword and leather cuirass.

Mama dove toward the Colossus, leaving my stomach at a higher altitude.

I had a moment to appreciate the statue's regal features, its metal brow rimmed with a spiky crown meant to represent the beams of the sun. The Colossus was supposed to be Nero as the sun god, but the emperor had wisely made the face resemble mine more closely than his. Only the line of its nose and its ghastly neck beard suggested Nero's trademark ugliness.

Also . . . did I mention that the hundred-foot statue was entirely nude? Well, of course it was. Gods are almost always depicted as nude, because we are flawless beings. Why would you cover up perfection? Still, it was a little disconcerting to see my buck-naked self stomping around, slamming a ship's rudder at Camp Half-Blood.

As we approached the Colossus, I bellowed loudly, "IMPOSTOR! I AM THE REAL APOLLO! YOU'RE UGLY!"

Oh, dear reader, it was hard to yell such words at my own handsome visage, but I did. Such was my courage.

The Colossus did not like being insulted. As Mama and her soldiers veered away, the statue swung its rudder upward.

Have you ever collided with a bomber? I had a sudden flashback to Dresden in 1945, when the planes were so thick in the air, I literally could not find a safe lane to drive in. The axle on the sun chariot was out of alignment for *weeks* after that.

I realized the ants were not fast enough fliers to escape the rudder's reach. I saw catastrophe approaching in slow motion. At the last possible moment, I yelled, "Dive!"

We plunged straight down. The rudder only clipped the ants' wings—but it was enough to send us spiraling toward the beach.

I was grateful for soft sand.

I ate quite a bit of it when we crash-landed.

By sheer luck, none of us died, though Kayla and Austin had to pull me to my feet.

"Are you okay?" Austin asked.

"Fine," I said. "We must hurry."

The Colossus stared down at us, perhaps trying to discern whether we were dying in agony yet or needed some additional pain. I had wanted to get his attention, and I had succeeded. Huzzah.

I glanced at Mama and her soldiers, who were shaking the sand off their carapaces. "Thank you. Now save yourselves. Fly!"

They did not need to be told twice. I suppose ants have a natural fear of large humanoids looming over them, about to squash them with a heavy foot. Mama and her guards buzzed into the sky.

Miranda looked after them. "I never thought I'd say this about bugs, but I'm going to miss those guys."

"Hey!" called Nico di Angelo. He and Will scrambled over the dunes, still dripping from their swim in the canoe lake.

"What's the plan?" Will seemed calm, but I knew him well enough by now to tell that inside he was as charged as a bare electrical wire.

BOOM.

The statue strode toward us. One more step, and it would be on top of us.

"Isn't there a control valve on its ankle?" Ellis asked. "If we can open it—"

"No," I said. "You're thinking of Talos. This is not Talos."

Nico brushed his dark wet hair from his forehead. "Then what?"

I had a lovely view of the Colossus's nose. Its nostrils were sealed with bronze . . . I supposed because Nero hadn't wanted his detractors trying to shoot arrows into his imperial noggin.

I yelped.

Kayla grabbed my arm. "Apollo, what's wrong?"

Arrows into the Colossus's head. Oh, gods, I had an idea that would never, ever work. However, it seemed better than our other option, which was to be crushed under a two-ton bronze foot.

"Will, Kayla, Austin," I said, "come with me."

"And Nico," said Nico. "I have a doctor's note."

"Fine!" I said. "Ellis, Cecil, Miranda—do whatever you can to keep the Colossus's attention."

The shadow of an enormous foot darkened the sand.

"Now!" I yelled. "Scatter!"

36

I love me some plague
When it's on the right arrow
Ka-bam! You dead, bro?

SCATTERING WAS THE EASY PART. They did that very well.

Miranda, Cecil, and Ellis ran in different directions, screaming insults at the Colossus and waving their arms. This bought the rest of us a few seconds as we sprinted for the dunes, but I suspected the Colossus would soon enough come after me. I was, after all, the most important and attractive target.

I pointed toward Sherman Yang's chariot, which was still circling the statue's legs in a vain attempt to electrocute its kneecaps. "We need to commandeer that chariot!"

"How?" Kayla asked.

I was about to admit I had no idea when Nico di Angelo grabbed Will's hand and stepped into my shadow. Both boys evaporated. I had forgotten about the power of shadow-traveling—the way children of the Underworld could step into one shadow and appear from another, sometimes hundreds of miles away. Hades used to love sneaking up on me that way and yelling, "HI!" just as I shot an arrow of death.

He found it amusing if I missed my target and accidentally wiped out the wrong city.

Austin shuddered. "I hate it when Nico disappears like that. What's our plan?"

"You two are my backup," I said. "If I miss, if I die . . . it will be up to you."

"Whoa, whoa," Kayla said. "What do you mean *if you miss?*"

I drew my last arrow—the one I'd found in the grove. "I'm going to shoot that gorgeous gargantuan in the ear."

Austin and Kayla exchanged looks, perhaps wondering if I'd finally cracked under the strain of being mortal.

"A plague arrow," I explained. "I'm going to enchant an arrow with sickness, then shoot it into the statue's ear. Its head is hollow. The ears are the only openings. The arrow should release enough disease to kill the Colossus's animating power . . . or at least to disable it."

"How do you know it will work?" Kayla asked.

"I don't, but—"

Our conversation was ruined by a sudden heavy downpour of Colossus foot. We darted inland, barely avoiding being flattened.

Behind us, Miranda shouted, "Hey, ugly!"

I knew she wasn't talking to me, but I glanced back anyway. She raised her arms, causing ropes of sea grass to spring from the dunes and wrap around the statue's ankles. The Colossus broke through them easily, but they annoyed him enough to be a distraction. Watching Miranda face the statue made me heartsick for Meg all over again.

Meanwhile, Ellis and Cecil stood on either side of the Colossus, throwing rocks at his shins. From the camp, a volley of flaming ballista projectiles exploded against Mr. Gorgeous's naked backside, which made me clench in sympathy.

"You were saying?" Austin asked.

"Right." I twirled the arrow between my fingers. "I know what you're thinking. I don't have godly powers. It's doubtful I'll be able to cook up the Black Death or the Spanish Flu. But still, if I can make the shot from close range, straight into its head, I might be able to do some damage."

"And . . . if you fail?" Kayla asked. I noticed her quiver was also empty.

"I won't have the strength to try twice. You'll have to make another pass. Find an arrow, try to summon some sickness, make the shot while Austin holds the chariot steady."

I realized this was an impossible request, but they accepted it with grim silence. I wasn't sure whether to feel grateful or guilty. Back when I was a god, I would've taken it for granted that mortals had faith in me. Now . . . I was asking my children to risk their lives again, and I was not at all sure my plan would work.

I caught a flash of movement in the sky. This time, instead of a Colossus foot, it was Sherman Yang's chariot, minus Sherman Yang. Will brought the pegasi in for a landing, then dragged out a half-conscious Nico di Angelo.

"Where are the others?" Kayla asked. "Sherman and the Hermes girls?"

Will rolled his eyes. "Nico convinced them to disembark."

As if on cue, I heard Sherman screaming from somewhere far in the distance, "I'll get you, di Angelo!"

"You guys go," Will told me. "The chariot is only designed for three, and after that shadow-travel, Nico is going to pass out any second."

"No, I'm not," Nico complained, then passed out.

Will caught him in a fireman's carry and took him away. "Good luck! I'm going to get the Lord of Darkness here some Gatorade!"

Austin hopped in first and took the reins. As soon as Kayla and I were aboard, we shot skyward, the pegasi swerving and banking around the Colossus with expert skill. I began to feel a glimmer of hope. We might be able to outmaneuver this giant hunk of good-looking bronze.

"Now," I said, "if I can just enchant this arrow with a nice plague."

The arrow shuddered from its fletching to its point.

THOU SHALT NOT, it told me.

I try to avoid weapons that talk. I find them rude and distracting. Once, Artemis had a bow that could cuss like a Phoenician sailor. Another time, in a Stockholm tavern, I met this god who was smoking hot, except his talking sword just would *not* shut up.

But I digress.

I asked the obvious question. "Did you just speak to me?"

The arrow quivered. (Oh, dear. That was a horrible pun. My apologies.) *YEA, VERILY. PRITHEE, SHOOTING IS NOT MY PURPOSE.*

His voice was definitely male, sonorous and grave, like a bad Shakespearean actor's.

"But you're an arrow," I said. "Shooting you is the whole point." (Ah, I really must watch those puns.)

"Guys, hang on!" Austin shouted.

The chariot plunged to avoid the Colossus's swinging rudder. Without Austin's warning, I would have been left in midair still arguing with my projectile.

"So you're made from Dodona oak," I guessed. "Is that why you talk?"

FORSOOTH, said the arrow.

"Apollo!" Kayla said. "I'm not sure why you're talking to that arrow, but—"

From our right came a reverberating *WHANG!* like a snapped power line hitting a metal roof. In a flash of silver light, the camp's magical barriers collapsed. The Colossus lurched forward and brought his foot down on the dining pavilion, smashing it to rubble like so many children's blocks.

"But that just happened," Kayla said with a sigh.

The Colossus raised his rudder in triumph. He marched inland, ignoring the campers who were running around his feet. Valentina Diaz launched a ballista missile into his groin. (Again, I had to wince in sympathy.) Harley and Connor Stoll kept blowtorching his feet, to no effect. Nyssa, Malcolm, and Chiron hastily ran a trip line of steel cable across the statue's path, but they would never have time to anchor it properly.

I turned to Kayla. "You can't hear this arrow talking?"

Judging from her wide eyes, I guessed the answer was, *No, and does hallucinating run in the family?*

"Never mind." I looked at the arrow. "What would you suggest, O Wise Missile of Dodona? My quiver is empty."

The arrow's point dipped toward the statue's left arm. *LO, THE ARMPIT DOTH HOLD THE ARROWS THOU NEEDEST!*

Kayla yelled, "Colossus is heading for the cabins!"

"Armpit!" I told Austin. "Flieth—er, fly for the armpit!"

That wasn't an order one heard much in combat, but Austin spurred the pegasi into a steep ascent. We buzzed the forest of arrows sticking out of the Colossus's arm seam, but I completely overestimated my mortal hand-eye coordination. I lunged for the shafts and came up empty.

Kayla was more agile. She snagged a fistful but screamed when she yanked them free.

I pulled her to safety. Her hand was bleeding badly, cut from the high-speed grab.

"I'm fine!" Kayla yelped. Her fingers were clenched, splattering drops of red all over the chariot's floor. "Take the arrows."

I did. I tugged the Brazilian-flag bandana from around my neck and gave it to her. "Bind your hand," I ordered. "There's some ambrosia in my coat pocket."

"Don't worry about me." Kayla's face was as green as her hair. "Make the shot! Hurry!"

I inspected the arrows. My heart sank. Only one of the missiles was unbroken, and its shaft was warped. It would be almost impossible to shoot.

I looked again at the talking arrow.

THOU SHALT NOT THINKEST ABOUT IT, he intoned. ENCHANT THOU THE WARPED ARROW!

I tried. I opened my mouth, but the proper words of enchantment were gone from my mind. As I feared, Lester Papadopoulos simply did not possess the power. "I can't!"

I SHALT ASSIST, promised the Arrow of Dodona. STARTEST THOU: "PLAGUEY, PLAGUEY, PLAGUEY."

"The enchantment does not start plaguey, plaguey, plaguey!"

"Who are you talking to?" Austin demanded.

"My arrow! I—I need more time."

"We don't have more time!" Kayla pointed with her wrapped bloody hand.

The Colossus was only a few steps away from the central green. I wasn't sure the demigods even realized how much danger they were in. The Colossus could do much more than just flatten buildings. If he destroyed the central hearth, the sacred shrine of Hestia, he would extinguish the very soul of the camp. The valley would be cursed and uninhabitable for generations. Camp Half-Blood would cease to exist.

I realized I had failed. My plan would take much too long, if I could even remember how to make a plague arrow. This was my punishment for breaking an oath on the River Styx.

Then, from somewhere above us, a voice yelled, "Hey, Bronze Butt!"

Over the Colossus's head, a cloud of darkness formed like a cartoon dialogue bubble. Out of the shadows dropped a furry black monster dog—a hellhound—and astride his back was a young man with a glowing bronze sword.

The weekend was here. Percy Jackson had arrived.

37

Hey, look! It's Percy
Least he could do was help out
Taught him everything

I WAS TOO SURPRISED TO SPEAK. Otherwise I would have warned Percy what was about to happen.

Hellhounds are not fond of heights. When startled, they respond in a predictable way. The moment Percy's faithful pet landed on top of the moving Colossus, she yelped and proceeded to wee-wee on said Colossus's head. The statue froze and looked up, no doubt wondering what was trickling down his imperial sideburns.

Percy leaped heroically from his mount and slipped in hellhound pee. He nearly slid off the statue's brow. "What the—Mrs. O'Leary, jeez!"

The hellhound bayed in apology. Austin flew our chariot to within shouting distance. "Percy!"

The son of Poseidon frowned across at us. "All right, who unleashed the giant bronze guy? Apollo, did you do this?"

"I am offended!" I cried. "I am only indirectly responsible for this! Also, I have a plan to fix it."

"Oh, yeah?" Percy glanced back at the destroyed dining pavilion. "How's that going?"

With my usual levelheadedness, I stayed focused on the greater good. "If you could please just keep this Colossus from stomping the camp's hearth, that would be helpful. I need a few more minutes to enchant this arrow."

I held up the talking arrow by mistake, then held up the bent arrow.

Percy sighed. "Of course you do."

Mrs. O'Leary barked in alarm. The Colossus was raising his hand to swat the trespassing tinkler.

Percy grabbed one of the crown's sunray spikes. He sliced it off at the base, then jabbed it into the Colossus's forehead. I doubted the Colossus could feel pain, but it staggered, apparently surprised to suddenly have grown a unicorn horn.

Percy sliced off another one. "Hey, ugly!" he called down. "You don't need all these pointy things, do you? I'm going to take one to the beach. Mrs. O'Leary, fetch!"

Percy tossed the spike like a javelin.

The hellhound barked excitedly. She leaped off the Colossus's head, vaporized into shadow, and reappeared on the ground, bounding after her new bronze stick.

Percy raised his eyebrows at me. "Well? Start enchanting!"

He jumped from the statue's head to its shoulder. Then he leaped to the shaft of the rudder and slid down it like a fire pole all the way to the ground. If I had been at my usual level of godly athletic skill, I could've done something like that in my sleep, of course, but I had to admit Percy Jackson was moderately impressive.

"Hey, Bronze Butt!" he yelled again. "Come get me!"

The Colossus obliged, slowly turning and following Percy toward the beach.

I began to chant, invoking my old powers as the god of plagues. This time, the words came to me. I didn't know why. Perhaps Percy's arrival had given me new faith. Perhaps I simply didn't think about it too much. I've found that thinking often interferes with doing. It's one of those lessons that gods learn early in their careers.

I felt an itchy sensation of sickness curling from my fingers and into the projectile. I spoke of my own awesomeness and the various horrible diseases I had visited upon wicked populations in the past, because . . . well, I'm awesome. I could feel the magic taking hold, despite the Arrow of Dodona whispering to me like an annoying Elizabethan stagehand, SAYEST THOU: "PLAGUEY, PLAGUEY, PLAGUEY!"

Below, more demigods joined the parade to the beach. They ran ahead of the Colossus, jeering at him, throwing things, and calling him Bronze Butt. They made jokes about his new horn. They laughed at the hellhound pee trickling down his face. Normally I have zero tolerance for bullying, especially when the victim looks like me, but since the Colossus was ten stories tall and destroying their camp, I suppose the campers' rudeness was understandable.

I finished chanting. Odious green mist now wreathed the arrow. It smelled faintly of fast-food deep fryers—a good sign that it carried some sort of horrible malady.

"I'm ready!" I told Austin. "Get me next to its ear!"

"You got it!" Austin turned to say something else, and a wisp of green fog passed under his nose. His eyes watered. His nose swelled and began to run. He scrunched up his face and sneezed so hard he collapsed. He lay on the floor of the chariot, groaning and twitching.

"My boy!" I wanted to grab his shoulders and check on him, but since I had an arrow in each hand, that was inadvisable.

FIE! TOO STRONG IS THY PLAGUE. The Dodona arrow hummed with annoyance. *THY CHANTING SUCKETH.*

"Oh, no, no, no," I said. "Kayla, be careful. Don't breathe—"

"ACHOO!" Kayla crumpled next to her brother.

"What have I done?" I wailed.

METHINKS THOU HAST BLOWN IT, said the Dodona arrow, my source of infinite wisdom. *MOREO'ER, HIE! TAKEST THOU THE REINS.*

"Why?"

You would think a god who drove a chariot on a daily basis would not need to ask such a question. In my defense, I was distraught about my children lying half-conscious at my feet. I didn't consider that no one was driving. Without anyone at the reins, the pegasi panicked. To avoid running into the huge bronze Colossus directly in their path, they dove toward the earth.

Somehow, I managed to react appropriately. (Three cheers for reacting appropriately!) I thrust both arrows into my quiver, grabbed the reins, and was able to level our descent just enough to prevent a crash landing. We bounced off a dune and swerved to a stop in front of Chiron and a group of demigods. Our entrance might have looked dramatic if the centrifugal force hadn't thrown Kayla, Austin, and me from the chariot.

Did I mention I was grateful for soft sand?

The pegasi took off, dragging the battered chariot into the sky and leaving us stranded.

Chiron galloped to our side, a cluster of demigods in his wake. Percy Jackson ran toward us from the surf while Mrs. O'Leary kept the Colossus occupied with a game of keep-away. I doubt that would hold the statue's interest very long, once he realized there was a group of targets right behind him, just perfect for stomping.

"The plague arrow is ready!" I announced. "We need to shoot it into the Colossus's ear!"

My audience did not seem to take this as good news. Then I realized my chariot was gone. My bow was still in the chariot. And Kayla and Austin were quite obviously infected with whatever disease I had conjured up.

"Are they contagious?" Cecil asked.

"No!" I said. "Well . . . probably not. It's the fumes from the arrow—"

Everyone backed away from me.

"Cecil," Chiron said, "you and Harley take Kayla and Austin to the Apollo cabin for healing."

"But they *are* the Apollo cabin," Harley complained. "Besides, my flamethrower—"

"You can play with your flamethrower later," Chiron

promised. "Run along. There's a good boy. The rest of you, do what you can to keep the Colossus at the water's edge. Percy and I will assist Apollo."

Chiron said the word *assist* as if it meant *slap upside the head with extreme prejudice*.

Once the crowd had dispersed, Chiron gave me his bow. "Make the shot."

I stared at the massive composite recursive, which probably had a draw weight of a hundred pounds. "This is meant for the strength of a centaur, not a teen mortal!"

"You created the arrow," he said. "Only you can shoot it without succumbing to the disease. Only you can hit such a target."

"From *here*? It's impossible! Where is that flying boy, Jason Grace?"

Percy wiped the sweat and sand from his neck. "We're fresh out of flying boys. And all the pegasi have stampeded."

"Perhaps if we got some harpies and some kite string . . ." I said.

"Apollo," Chiron said, "you must do this. You are the lord of archery and illness."

"I'm not lord of anything!" I wailed. "I'm a stupid ugly mortal teenager! I'm *nobody*!"

The self-pity just came pouring out. I thought for sure the earth would split in two when I called myself a *nobody*. The cosmos would stop turning. Percy and Chiron would rush to reassure me.

None of that happened. Percy and Chiron just stared at me grimly.

Percy put his hand on my shoulder. "You're Apollo. We

need you. You can do this. Besides, if you don't, I will personally throw you off the top of the Empire State Building."

This was exactly the pep talk I needed—just the sort of thing Zeus used to say to me before my soccer matches. I squared my shoulders. "Right."

"We'll try to draw him into the water," Percy said. "I've got the advantage there. Good luck."

Percy accepted Chiron's hand and leaped onto the centaur's back. Together they galloped into the surf, Percy waving his sword and calling out various bronze-butt-themed insults to the Colossus.

I ran down the beach until I had a line of sight on the statue's left ear.

Looking up at that regal profile, I did not see Nero. I saw myself—a monument to my own conceit. Nero's pride was no more than a reflection of mine. I was the bigger fool. I was exactly the sort of person who would construct a hundred-foot-tall naked statue of myself in my front yard.

I pulled the plague arrow from my quiver and nocked it in the bowstring.

The demigods were getting very good at scattering. They continued to harry the Colossus from both sides while Percy and Chiron galloped through the tide, Mrs. O'Leary romping at their heels with her new bronze stick.

"Yo, ugly!" Percy shouted. "Over here!"

The Colossus's next step displaced several tons of salt water and made a crater large enough to swallow a pickup truck.

The Arrow of Dodona rattled in my quiver. *RELEASE THY BREATH,* he advised. *DROPETH THY SHOULDER.*

"I *have* shot a bow before," I grumbled.

MINDETH THY RIGHT ELBOW, the arrow said.

"Shut up."

AND TELLEST NOT THINE ARROW TO SHUT UP.

I drew the bow. My muscles burned as if boiling water was being poured over my shoulders. The plague arrow did not make me pass out, but its fumes were disorienting. The warp of the shaft made my calculations impossible. The wind was against me. The arc of the shot would be much too high.

Yet I aimed, exhaled, and released the bowstring.

The arrow twirled as it rocketed upward, losing force and drifting too far to the right. My heart sank. Surely the curse of the River Styx would deny me any chance at success.

Just as the projectile reached its apex and was about to fall back to earth, a gust of wind caught it . . . perhaps Zephyros looking kindly on my pitiful attempt. The arrow sailed into the Colossus's ear canal and rattled in his head with a *clink, clink, clink* like a pachinko machine.

The Colossus halted. He stared at the horizon as if confused. He looked at the sky, then arched his back and lurched forward, making a sound like a tornado ripping off the roof of a warehouse. Because his face had no other open orifices, the pressure of his sneeze forced geysers of motor oil out his ears, spraying the dunes with environmentally unfriendly sludge.

Sherman, Julia, and Alice stumbled over to me, covered head to toe with sand and oil.

"I appreciate you freeing Miranda and Ellis," Sherman snarled, "but I'm going to kill you later for taking my chariot. What did you do to that Colossus? What kind of plague makes you sneeze?"

"I'm afraid I—I summoned a rather benign illness. I believe I have given the Colossus a case of hay fever."

You know that horrible pause when you're waiting for someone to sneeze? The statue arched his back again, and everyone on the beach cringed in anticipation. The Colossus inhaled several cubic acres of air through his ear canals, preparing for his next blast.

I imagined the nightmare scenarios: The Colossus would ear-sneeze Percy Jackson into Connecticut, never to be seen again. The Colossus would clear his head and then stomp all of us flat. Hay fever could make a person cranky. I knew this because I *invented* hay fever. Still, I had never intended it to be a killing affliction. I certainly never anticipated facing the wrath of a towering metal automaton with extreme seasonal allergies. I cursed my shortsightedness! I cursed my mortality!

What I had *not* considered was the damage our demigods had already done to the Colossus's metal joints—in particular, his neck.

The Colossus rocked forward with a mighty CHOOOOO! I flinched and almost missed the moment of truth when the statue's head achieved first-stage separation from his body. It hurtled over Long Island Sound, the face spinning in and out of view. It hit the water with a mighty WHOOSH and bobbed for a moment. Then the air *blooped* out of its neck hole and the gorgeous regal visage of yours truly sank beneath the waves.

The statue's decapitated body tilted and swayed. If it had fallen backward, it might have crushed even more of the camp. Instead, it toppled forward. Percy yelped a curse that would have made any Phoenician sailor proud. Chiron and he raced sideways to avoid being crushed while Mrs. O'Leary wisely dissolved into shadows. The Colossus hit the water, sending forty-foot tidal waves to port and starboard. I had never before seen a centaur hang hooves on a tubular crest, but Chiron acquitted himself well.

The roar of the statue's fall finally stopped echoing off the hills.

Next to me, Alice Miyazawa whistled. "Well, that de-escalated quickly."

Sherman Yang asked in a voice of childlike wonder: "What the Hades just happened?"

"I believe," I said, "the Colossus sneezed his head off."

38

After the sneezing
Healing peeps, parsing limericks
Worst God Award? Me

THE PLAGUE SPREAD.

That was the price of our victory: a massive outbreak of hay fever. By nightfall, most of the campers were dizzy, groggy, and heavily congested, though I was pleased that none of them sneezed their heads off, because we were running low on bandages and duct tape.

Will Solace and I spent the evening caring for the wounded. Will took the lead, which was fine with me; I was exhausted. Mostly I splinted arms, distributed cold medicine and tissues, and tried to keep Harley from stealing the infirmary's entire supply of smiley-face stickers, which he plastered all over his flamethrower. I was grateful for the distraction, since it kept me from thinking too much about the day's painful events.

Sherman Yang graciously agreed not to kill Nico for tossing him out of his chariot, or me for damaging it, though I had the feeling the son of Ares was keeping his options open for later.

Chiron provided healing poultices for the most extreme cases of hay fever. This included Chiara Benvenuti, whose good luck had, for once, abandoned her. Strangely enough, Damien White got sick right after he learned that Chiara was sick. The two had cots next to each other in the infirmary, which I found a little suspicious, even though they kept sniping at each other whenever they knew they were being watched.

Percy Jackson spent several hours recruiting whales and hippocampi to help him haul away the Colossus. He decided it would be easiest to tow it underwater to Poseidon's palace, where it could be repurposed as garden statuary. I was not sure how I felt about that. I imagined Poseidon would replace the statue's gorgeous face with his own weathered, bearded mien. Still, I wanted the Colossus gone, and I doubted it would have fit in the camp's recycling bins.

Thanks to Will's healing and a hot dinner, the demigods I had rescued from the woods quickly got back to full strength. (Paolo claimed it was because he waved a Brazilian-flag bandana over them, and I was not about to argue.)

As for the camp itself, the damage might have been much worse. The canoe dock could be rebuilt. The Colossus's footstep craters could be repurposed as convenient foxholes or koi ponds.

The dining pavilion was a total loss, but Nyssa and Harley were confident that Annabeth Chase could redesign the place next time she was here. With luck, it would be rebuilt in time for the summer.

The only other major damage was to the Demeter cabin. I had not realized it during the battle, but the Colossus had managed to step on it before turning around for the beach.

In retrospect, its path of destruction appeared almost purposeful, as if the automaton had waded ashore, stomped Cabin Four, and headed back out to sea.

Given what had happened with Meg McCaffrey, I had a hard time not seeing this as a bad omen. Miranda Gardiner and Billie Ng were given temporary bunks in the Hermes cabin, but for a long time that night they sat stunned among the smashed ruins as daisies popped up all around them from the cold winter ground.

Despite my exhaustion, I slept fitfully. I did not mind Kayla and Austin's constant sneezing, or Will's gentle snoring. I did not even mind the hyacinths blooming on the windowsill, filling the room with their melancholy perfume. But I could not stop thinking of the dryads raising their arms to the flames in the woods, and about Nero, and Meg. The Arrow of Dodona stayed silent, hanging in my quiver on the wall, but I suspected it would have more annoying Shakespearean advice soon. I did not relish what it might telleth me about my future.

At sunrise, I rose quietly, took my bow and quiver and combat ukulele, and hiked to the summit of Half-Blood Hill. The guardian dragon, Peleus, did not recognize me. When I came too close to the Golden Fleece, he hissed, so I had to sit some distance away at the foot of the Athena Parthenos.

I didn't mind not being recognized. At the moment, I did not *want* to be Apollo. All the destruction I saw below me . . . it was my fault. I had been blind and complacent. I had allowed the emperors of Rome, including one of my own descendants, to rise to power in the shadows. I had let my once-great network of Oracles collapse until even Delphi was lost. I had almost caused the death of Camp Half-Blood itself.

And Meg McCaffrey . . . Oh, Meg, where were you?

Do what you need to do, she had told me. *That's my final order.*

Her order had been vague enough to allow me to pursue her. After all, we were bound together now. What I *needed to do* was to find her. I wondered if Meg had phrased her order that way on purpose, or if that was just wishful thinking on my part.

I gazed up at the serene alabaster face of Athena. In real life, she didn't look so pale and aloof—well, not most of the time, anyway. I pondered why the sculptor, Phidias, had chosen to make her look so unapproachable, and whether Athena approved. We gods often debated how much humans could change our very nature simply by the way they pictured us or imagined us. During the eighteenth century, for instance, I could not escape the white powdered wig, no matter how hard I tried. Among immortals, our reliance on humans was an uncomfortable subject.

Perhaps I deserved my present form. After my carelessness and foolishness, perhaps humanity *should* see me as nothing but Lester Papadopoulos.

I heaved a sigh. "Athena, what would you do in my place? Something wise and practical, I suppose."

Athena offered no response. She stared calmly at the horizon, taking the long view, as always.

I didn't need the wisdom goddess to tell me what I must do. I should leave Camp Half-Blood immediately, before the campers woke. They had taken me in to protect me, and I had nearly gotten them all killed. I couldn't bear to endanger them any longer.

But, oh, how I wanted to stay with Will, Kayla, Austin—my mortal children. I wanted to help Harley put smiley faces on his flamethrower. I wanted to flirt with Chiara and steal her away from Damien . . . or perhaps steal Damien away from Chiara, I wasn't sure yet. I wanted to improve my music and archery through that strange activity known as *practice*. I wanted to have a home.

Leave, I told myself. *Hurry*.

Because I was a coward, I waited too long. Below me, the cabin lights flickered on. Campers emerged from their doorways. Sherman Yang began his morning stretches. Harley jogged around the green, holding his Leo Valdez beacon high with the hope it would finally work.

At last, a pair of familiar figures spotted me. They approached from different directions—the Big House and Cabin Three—hiking up the hill to see me: Rachel Dare and Percy Jackson.

"I know what you're thinking," Rachel said. "Don't do it."

I feigned surprise. "Can you read my mind, Miss Dare?"

"I don't need to. I know you, Lord Apollo."

A week ago, the idea would have made me laugh. A mortal could not *know* me. I had lived for four millennia. Merely looking upon my true form would have vaporized any human. Now, though, Rachel's words seemed perfectly reasonable. With Lester Papadopoulos, what you saw was what you got. There really wasn't much to know.

"Don't call me *Lord*," I sighed. "I am just a mortal teen. I do not belong at this camp."

Percy sat next to me. He squinted at the sunrise, the sea breeze tousling his hair. "Yeah, I used to think I didn't belong here either."

"It's not the same," I said. "You humans change and grow and mature. Gods do not."

Percy faced me. "You sure about that? You seem pretty different."

I think he meant that as a compliment, but I didn't find his words reassuring. If I was becoming more fully human, that was hardly a cause for celebration. True, I had mustered a few godly powers at important moments—a burst of divine strength against the Germani, a hay fever arrow against the Colossus—but I could not rely on those abilities. I didn't even understand how I had summoned them. The fact that I had limits, and that I couldn't be sure where those limits *were* . . . Well, that made me feel much more like Lester Papadopoulos than Apollo.

"The other Oracles must be found and secured," I said. "I cannot do that unless I leave Camp Half-Blood. And I cannot risk anyone else's life."

Rachel sat on my other side. "You sound certain. Did you get a prophecy from the grove?"

I shuddered. "I fear so."

Rachel cupped her hands on her knees. "Kayla said you

were talking to an arrow yesterday. I'm guessing it's wood from Dodona?"

"Wait," Percy said. "You found a talking arrow that gave you a prophecy?"

"Don't be silly," I said. "The arrow talks, but I got the prophecy from the grove itself. The Arrow of Dodona just gives random advice. He's quite annoying."

The arrow buzzed in my quiver.

"At any rate," I continued, "I must leave the camp. The Triumvirate means to possess all the ancient Oracles. I have to stop them. Once I have defeated the former emperors . . . only then will I be able to face my old enemy Python and free the Oracle of Delphi. After that . . . if I survive . . . perhaps Zeus will restore me to Olympus."

Rachel tugged at a strand of her hair. "You know it's too dangerous to do all that alone, right?"

"Listen to her," Percy urged. "Chiron told me about Nero and this weird holding company of his."

"I appreciate the offer of assistance, but—"

"Whoa." Percy held up his hands. "Just to be clear, I'm not offering to go with you. I still have to finish my senior year, pass my DSTOMP and my SAT, and avoid getting killed by my girlfriend. But I'm sure we can get you some other helpers."

"I'll go," Rachel said.

I shook my head. "My enemies would *love* to capture someone as dear to me as the priestess of Delphi. Besides, I need you and Miranda Gardiner to stay here and study the Grove of Dodona. For now, it is our only source of prophecy. And since our communication problems have not gone away, learning to use the grove's power is all the more critical."

Rachel tried to hide it, but I could see her disappointment in the lines around her mouth. "What about Meg?" she asked. "You'll try to find her, won't you?"

She might as well have plunged the Arrow of Dodona into my chest. I gazed at the woods—that hazy green expanse that had swallowed young McCaffrey. For a brief moment, I felt like Nero. I wanted to burn the whole place down.

"I will try," I said, "but Meg doesn't want to be found. She's under the influence of her stepfather."

Percy traced his finger across the Athena Parthenos's big toe. "I've lost too many people to bad influence: Ethan Nakamura, Luke Castellan . . . We almost lost Nico, too. . . ." He shook his head. "No. No more. You can't give up on Meg. You guys are bound together. Besides, she's one of the good guys."

"I've known many of the good guys," I said. "Most of them got turned into beasts, or statues, or—or trees. . . ." My voice broke.

Rachel put her hand over mine. "Things can turn out differently, Apollo. That's the nice thing about being human. We only have one life, but we can choose what kind of story it's going to be."

That seemed hopelessly optimistic. I had spent too many centuries watching the same patterns of behavior be repeated over and over, all by humans who thought they were being terribly clever and doing something that had never been done before. They thought they were crafting their own stories, but they were only tracing over the same old narratives, generation after generation.

Still . . . perhaps human persistence was an asset. They never seemed to give up hope. Every so often they *did* manage to surprise me. I never anticipated Alexander the Great, Robin Hood, or Billie Holiday. For that matter, I never anticipated Percy Jackson and Rachel Elizabeth Dare.

"I—I hope you're right," I said.

She patted my hand. "Tell me the prophecy you heard in the grove."

I took a shaky breath. I didn't want to speak the words. I was afraid they might wake the grove and drown us in a cacophony of prophecies, bad jokes, and infomercials. But I recited the lines:

> *"There once was a god named Apollo*
> *Who plunged in a cave blue and hollow*
> *Upon a three-seater*
> *The bronze fire-eater*
> *Was forced death and madness to swallow."*

Rachel covered her mouth. "A limerick?"

"I know!" I wailed. "I'm doomed!"

"Wait." Percy's eyes glittered. "Those lines . . . Do they mean what I think?"

"Well," I said, "I believe the blue cave refers to the Oracle of Trophonius. It was a . . . a very dangerous ancient Oracle."

"No," Percy said. "The *other* lines. *Three-seater, bronze fire-eater*, yadda yadda."

"Oh. I have no clue about those."

"Harley's beacon." Percy laughed, though I could not understand why he was so pleased. "He said you gave it a tuning adjustment? I guess that did the trick."

Rachel squinted at him. "Percy, what are you . . ." Her expression went slack. "Oh. *Oh.*"

"Were there any other lines?" Percy urged. "Like, except for the limerick?"

"Several," I admitted. "Just bits and pieces I didn't understand. *The fall of the sun; the final verse.* Um, *Indiana, banana. Happiness approaches.* Something about *pages burning.*"

Percy slapped his knee. "There you go. *Happiness approaches.* Happy is a name—well, the English version, anyway." He stood and scanned the horizon. His eyes fixed on something in the distance. A grin spread across his face. "Yep. Apollo, your escort is on the way."

I followed his gaze. Spiraling down from the clouds was a large winged creature that glinted of Celestial bronze. On its back were two human-size figures.

Their descent was silent, but in my mind a joyous fanfare of Valdezinator music proclaimed the good news.

Leo had returned.

39

Want to hit Leo?
That is understandable
Hunk Muffin earned it

THE DEMIGODS HAD TO TAKE NUMBERS.

Nico commandeered a dispenser from the snack bar and carried it around, yelling, "The line starts to the left! Orderly queue, guys!"

"Is this really necessary?" Leo asked.

"Yes," said Miranda Gardiner, who had drawn the first number. She punched Leo in the arm.

"Ow," said Leo.

"You're a jerk, and we all hate you," said Miranda. Then she hugged him and kissed his cheek. "If you ever disappear like that again, we'll line up to *kill you*."

"Okay, okay!"

Miranda had to move on, because the line was getting pretty long behind her. Percy and I sat at the picnic table with Leo and his companion—none other than the immortal sorceress Calypso. Even though Leo was the one getting punched by everyone in camp, I was reasonably sure he was the *least* uncomfortable one at the table.

When they first saw each other, Percy and Calypso had hugged awkwardly. I hadn't witnessed such a tense greeting since Patroclus met Achilles's war prize, Briseis. (Long story. Juicy gossip. Ask me later.) Calypso had never liked me, so she pointedly ignored me, but I kept waiting for her to yell "BOO!" and turn me into a tree frog. The suspense was killing me.

Percy hugged Leo and didn't even punch him. Still, the son of Poseidon looked disgruntled.

"I can't believe it," he said. "Six months—"

"I told you," Leo said. "We tried sending more holographic scrolls. We tried Iris messages, dream visions, phone calls. Nothing worked.— Ow! Hey, Alice, how you doing?— Anyway, we ran into one crisis after another."

Calypso nodded. "Albania was particularly difficult."

From down the line, Nico di Angelo yelled, "Please do not mention Albania! Okay, who's next, folks? One line."

Damien White punched Leo's arm and walked away grinning. I wasn't sure Damien even knew Leo. He simply couldn't turn down a chance to punch someone.

Leo rubbed his bicep. "Hey, no fair. That guy's getting back in the line. So, like I was saying, if Festus hadn't picked up on that homing beacon yesterday, we'd still be flying around, looking for a way out of the Sea of Monsters."

"Oh, I hate that place," Percy said. "There's this big Cyclops, Polyphemus—"

"I know, right?" Leo agreed. "What is up with that guy's *breath*?"

"Boys," Calypso said, "perhaps we should focus on the present?"

She did not look at me, but I got the impression she meant *this silly former god and his problems*.

"Yeah," Percy said. "So the communication issues . . . Rachel Dare thinks it's got something to do with this company, Triumvirate."

Rachel herself had gone to the Big House to fetch Chiron, but Percy did a reasonable job summarizing what she had found out about the emperors and their evil corporation. Of course, we didn't know very much. By the time six more people had punched Leo in the arm, Percy had brought Leo and Calypso up to speed.

Leo rubbed his new bruises. "Man, why does it not surprise me that modern corporations are run by zombie Roman emperors?"

"They are not zombies," I said. "And I'm not sure they run *all* corporations—"

Leo waved away my explanation. "But they're trying to take over the Oracles."

"Yes," I agreed.

"And that's bad."

"Very."

"So you need our help.— Ow! Hey, Sherman. Where'd you get the new scar, dude?"

While Sherman told Leo the story of Crotchkicker McCaffrey and the Demon Peach Baby, I glanced at Calypso.

She looked very different from what I remembered. Her hair was still long and caramel brown. Her almond-shaped eyes were still dark and intelligent. But now, instead of a *chiton* she wore modern jeans, a white blouse, and a shocking-pink ski jacket. She looked younger—about my mortal age. I wondered if she had been punished with mortality for leaving her enchanted island. If so, it didn't seem fair that she had retained her otherworldly beauty. She had neither flab nor acne.

As I watched, she stretched two fingers toward the opposite end of the picnic table, where a pitcher of lemonade sweated in the sunlight. I had seen her do this sort of thing before, willing her invisible aerial servants to whisk objects into her hands. This time, nothing happened.

A look of disappointment crossed her face. Then she realized I was watching. Her cheeks colored.

"Since leaving Ogygia, I have no powers," she admitted. "I am fully mortal. I keep hoping, but—"

"You want a drink?" Percy asked.

"I got it." Leo beat him to the pitcher.

I had not expected to feel sympathy for Calypso. We'd had harsh words in the past. A few millennia ago, I had opposed her petition for early release from Ogygia because of some . . . ah, drama between us. (Long story. Juicy gossip. Please *do not* ask me later.)

Still, as a fallen god, I understood how disconcerting it was to be without one's powers.

On the other hand, I was relieved. This meant she could not turn me into a tree frog or order her aerial servants to toss me off the Athena Parthenos.

"Here you go." Leo handed her a glass of lemonade. His expression seemed darker and more anxious, as if . . . Ah, of course. Leo had rescued Calypso from her prison island. In doing so, Calypso had lost her powers. Leo felt responsible.

Calypso smiled, though her eyes were still touched by melancholy. "Thank you, babe."

"*Babe?*" Percy asked.

Leo's expression brightened. "Yeah. She won't call me Hunk Muffin, though. I dunno why.— Ow!"

It was Harley's turn. The little boy punched Leo, then threw his arms around him and broke down sobbing.

"Hey, brother." Leo ruffled his hair and had the good sense to look ashamed. "You brought me home with that beacon of yours, H-Meister. You're a hero! You know I never would've left you hanging like that on purpose, don't you?"

Harley wailed and sniffled and nodded. Then he punched Leo again and ran away. Leo looked like he was about to get sick. Harley was quite strong.

"At any rate," Calypso said, "these problems with the Roman emperors—how can we help?"

I raised my eyebrows. "You *will* help me, then? Despite . . . ah, well, I always knew you were kindhearted and forgiving, Calypso. I meant to visit you at Ogygia more often—"

"Spare me." Calypso sipped her lemonade. "I'll help you if *Leo* decides to help you, and he seems to have some affection for you. Why, I can't imagine."

I let go of the breath I had been holding for . . . oh, an hour. "I'm grateful. Leo Valdez, you have always been a gentleman and a genius. After all, you created the Valdezinator."

Leo grinned. "I did, didn't I? I suppose that was pretty awesome. So where is this next Oracle you— Ow!"

Nyssa had made it to the front of the line. She slapped Leo, then berated him in rapid Spanish.

"Yeah, okay, okay." Leo rubbed his face. "Dang, *hermana*, I love you, too!"

He turned his attention back to me. "So this next Oracle, you said it was where?"

Percy tapped the picnic table. "Chiron and I were talking about this. He figures this triumvirate thingie . . . they probably divided America into three parts, with one emperor in charge of each. We know Nero is holed up in New York, so we're guessing this next Oracle is in the second dude's territory, maybe in the middle third of the U.S."

"Oh, the middle third of the U.S.!" Leo spread his arms. "Piece of torta, then. We'll just search the entire middle of the country!"

"Still with the sarcasm," Percy noted.

"Hey, man, I've sailed with the most sarcastic scalawags on the high seas."

The two gave each other a high five, though I did not quite understand why. I thought about a snippet of prophecy I'd heard in the grove: something about Indiana. It might be a place to start. . . .

The last person to come through the line was Chiron himself, pushed in his wheelchair by Rachel Dare. The old centaur gave Leo a warm, fatherly smile. "My boy, I am so pleased to have you back. And you freed Calypso, I see. Well done, and welcome, both of you!" Chiron spread his arms for a hug.

"Uh, thanks, Chiron." Leo leaned forward.

From underneath Chiron's lap blanket, his equine foreleg shot out and implanted a hoof in Leo's gut. Then, just as quickly, the leg disappeared. "Mr. Valdez," Chiron said in the same kindly tone, "if you ever pull a stunt like that again—"

"I got it, I got it!" Leo rubbed his stomach. "Dang, for a teacher, you got a heck of a high kick."

Rachel grinned and wheeled Chiron away. Calypso and Percy helped Leo to his feet.

"Yo, Nico," Leo called, "please tell me that's it for the physical abuse."

"For now." Nico smiled. "We're still trying to get in touch with the West Coast. You'll have a few dozen people out there who will definitely want to hit you."

Leo winced. "Yeah, that's something to look forward to. Well, I guess I'd better keep my strength up. Where do you guys eat lunch now that the Colossus stepped on the dining pavilion?"

Percy left that night just before dinner.

I expected a moving one-on-one farewell, during which he would ask my advice about test taking, being a hero, and living life in general. After he lent me his help in defeating the Colossus, it would have been the least I could do.

Instead, he seemed more interested in saying good-bye to Leo and Calypso. I wasn't part of their conversation, but the three of them seemed to reach some sort of mutual understanding. Percy and Leo embraced. Calypso even pecked Percy on the cheek. Then the son of Poseidon waded into Long Island Sound with his extremely large dog and they both disappeared underwater. Did Mrs. O'Leary swim? Did she travel through the shadows of whales? I did not know.

Like lunch, dinner was a casual affair. As darkness fell, we ate on picnic blankets around the hearth, which blazed with Hestia's warmth and kept away the winter chill. Festus the dragon sniffed around the perimeter of the cabins, occasionally blowing fire into the sky for no apparent reason.

"He got a little dinged up in Corsica," Leo explained. "Sometimes he spews randomly like that."

"He hasn't blowtorched anyone important yet," Calypso added, her eyebrow arched. "We'll see how he likes you."

Festus's red jewel eyes gleamed in the darkness. After driving the sun chariot for so long, I wasn't nervous about riding a metal dragon, but when I thought about what we'd be riding *toward*, geraniums bloomed in my stomach.

"I had planned to go alone," I told them. "The prophecy from Dodona speaks of the bronze fire-eater, but . . . it feels wrong for me to ask you to risk your lives. You have been through so much just to get here."

Calypso tilted her head. "Perhaps you *have* changed. That does not sound like the Apollo I remember. You definitely are not as handsome."

"I am still *quite* handsome," I protested. "I just need to clear up this acne."

She smirked. "So you haven't completely lost your big head."

"I beg your pardon?"

"Guys," Leo interrupted, "if we're going to travel together, let's try to keep it friendly." He pressed an ice pack to his bruised bicep. "Besides, we were planning to head west anyway. I got to find my peeps Jason and Piper and Frank and Hazel and . . . well, pretty much everybody at Camp Jupiter, I guess. It'll be fun."

"*Fun?*" I asked. "The Oracle of Trophonius will supposedly swallow me in death and madness. Even if I survive that, my other trials will no doubt be long, harrowing, and quite possibly fatal."

"Exactly," Leo said. "Fun. I don't know about calling the whole quest thing *Apollo's trials*, though. I think we should call it *Leo Valdez's Victory Lap World Tour*."

Calypso laughed and laced her fingers in Leo's. She may not have been immortal anymore, but she still had a grace and easiness about her that I could not fathom. Perhaps she missed her powers, but she seemed genuinely happy to be with Valdez—to be young and mortal, even if it meant she could die at any moment.

Unlike me, she had *chosen* to become mortal. She knew that leaving Ogygia was a risk, but she had done it willingly. I didn't know how she'd found the courage.

"Hey, man," Leo told me. "Don't look so glum. We'll find her."

I stirred. "What?"

"Your friend Meg. We'll find her. Don't worry."

A bubble of darkness burst inside me. For once, I hadn't been thinking of Meg. I'd been thinking about myself, and that made me feel guilty. Perhaps Calypso was right to question whether or not I'd changed.

I gazed at the silent forest. I remembered Meg dragging me to safety when I was cold and soaked and delirious. I remembered how fearlessly she fought the myrmekes, and how she'd ordered Peaches to extinguish the match when Nero wanted to burn his hostages, despite her fear of unleashing the Beast. I had to make her realize how evil Nero was. I had to find her. But how?

"Meg knows the prophecy," I said. "If she tells Nero, he will know our plans as well."

Calypso took a bite of her apple. "I missed the whole Roman Empire. How bad can one emperor be?"

"Bad," I assured her. "And he is allied with two others. We don't know which ones, but it's safe to assume they are equally cutthroat. They've had centuries to amass fortunes, acquire property, build armies . . . Who knows what they are capable of?"

"Eh," Leo said. "We took down Gaea in, like, forty seconds. This'll be easy squeezy."

I seemed to recall that the lead-up to the fight with Gaea had involved months of suffering and near misses with death. Leo, in fact, had died. I also wanted to remind him that the Triumvirate might well have orchestrated all our previous troubles with the Titans and giants, which would make them more powerful than anything Leo had ever faced.

I decided that mentioning these things might affect group morale.

"We'll succeed," Calypso said. "We must. So we will. I have been trapped on an island for thousands of years. I don't know how long this mortal life will be, but I intend to live fully and without fear."

"That's my mamacita," Leo said.

"What have I told you about calling me mamacita?"

Leo grinned sheepishly. "In the morning we'll start getting our supplies together. As soon as Festus gets a tune-up and an oil change, we'll be good to go."

I considered what supplies I would take with me. I had

depressingly little: some borrowed clothes, a bow, a ukulele, and an overly theatrical arrow.

But the real difficulty would be saying good-bye to Will, Austin, and Kayla. They had helped me so much, and they embraced me as family more than I had ever embraced *them*. Tears stung my eyes. Before I could start sobbing, Will Solace stepped into the light of the hearth. "Hey, everybody! We've started a bonfire in the amphitheater! Sing-along time. Come on!"

Groans were mixed in with the cheers, but most everyone got to their feet and ambled toward the bonfire now blazing in the distance, where Nico di Angelo stood silhouetted in the flames, preparing rows of marshmallows on what looked like femur bones.

"Aw, man." Leo winced. "I'm terrible at sing-alongs. I always clap and do the 'Old MacDonald' sounds at the wrong time. Can we skip this?"

"Oh, no." I rose to my feet, suddenly feeling better. Perhaps tomorrow I would weep and think about good-byes. Perhaps the day after that we would be flying toward our deaths. But tonight, I intended to enjoy my time with my family. What had Calypso said? *Live fully and without fear.* If she could do it, then so could the brilliant, fabulous Apollo. "Singing is good for the spirits. You should never miss an opportunity to sing."

Calypso smiled. "I can't believe I'm saying this, but for once I agree with Apollo. Come on, Leo. I'll teach you to harmonize."

Together, the three of us walked toward the sounds of laughter, music, and a warm, crackling fire.

GUIDE TO APOLLO-SPEAK

Achilles   the best fighter of the Greeks who besieged Troy in the Trojan War; extraordinarily strong, courageous, and loyal, he had only one weak spot: his heel

Admetus   the king of Pherae in Thessaly; Zeus punished Apollo by sending him to work for Admetus as a shepherd

Aeolus   the Greek god of the winds

Agamemnon   king of Mycenae; the leader of the Greeks in the Trojan War; courageous, but also arrogant and overly proud

agora   Greek for *gathering place*; a central outdoor spot for athletic, artistic, spiritual, and political life in ancient Greek city-states

Ajax   Greek hero with great strength and courage; fought in the Trojan War; used a large shield in battle

ambrosia   food of the gods; has healing powers

amphitheater   an oval or circular open-air space used for performances or sporting events, with spectator seating built in a semicircle around the stage

Aphrodite   the Greek goddess of love and beauty

apodesmos   a band of material that women in ancient Greece wore around the chest, particularly while participating in sports

Apollo   the Greek god of the sun, prophecy, music, and healing; the son of Zeus and Leto, and the twin of Artemis

Ares   the Greek god of war; the son of Zeus and Hera, and half brother to Athena

Argo   the ship used by a band of heroes who accompanied Jason on his quest to find the Golden Fleece

Argonauts   a band of heroes who sailed with Jason on the *Argo*, in search of the Golden Fleece

Artemis   the Greek goddess of the hunt and the moon; the daughter of Zeus and Leto, and the twin of Apollo

Asclepius   the god of medicine; son of Apollo; his temple was the healing center of ancient Greece

Athena   the Greek goddess of wisdom

Athena Parthenos   a giant statue of Athena; the most famous Greek statue of all time

ballista (ballistae, pl.)   a Roman missile siege weapon that launched a large projectile at a distant target

Batavi   an ancient tribe that lived in modern-day Germany; also an infantry unit in the Roman army with Germanic origins

Briseis   a princess captured by Achilles during the Trojan War, causing a feud between Achilles and Agamemnon that resulted in Achilles refusing to fight alongside the Greeks

Bunker Nine   a hidden workshop Leo Valdez discovered at Camp Half-Blood, filled with tools and weapons; it is at least two hundred years old and was used during the Demigod Civil War

Caesar Augustus   the founder and first emperor of the Roman Empire; adopted son and heir of Julius Caesar (*see also* Octavian)

Calliope   the muse of epic poetry; mother of several sons, including Orpheus

Calypso   the goddess nymph of the mythical island of Ogygia; a daughter of the Titan Atlas; she detained the hero Odysseus for many years

Camp Half-Blood   the training ground for Greek demi-gods, located in Long Island, New York

Camp Jupiter   the training ground for Roman demigods, located between the Oakland Hills and the Berkeley Hills, in California

Cassandra   the daughter of King Priam and Queen Hecuba; had the gift of prophecy, but was cursed by Apollo so that her predictions were never believed, including her warning about the Trojan Horse

catapult   a military machine used to hurl objects

Cave of Trophonius   a deep chasm home to the Oracle Trophonius; its extremely narrow entrance required a visitor to lie flat on his back before being sucked into the cave; called "The Cave of Nightmares" due to the terrifying accounts of its visitors

Celestial bronze   a rare metal deadly to monsters

centaur   a race of creatures that is half-human, half-horse

Ceres the Roman god of agriculture; Greek form: Demeter

Chiron a centaur; the camp activities director at Camp Half-Blood

chiton a Greek garment; a sleeveless piece of linen or wool secured at the shoulders by brooches and at the waist by a belt

Chrysothemis a daughter of Demeter who won Apollo's love during a music contest

Circe a Greek goddess of magic

Cloacina goddess of the Roman sewer system

Clytemnestra the daughter of the king and queen of Sparta; married and later murdered Agamemnon

Colosseum an elliptical amphitheater in the center of Rome, Italy, capable of seating fifty thousand spectators; used for gladiatorial contests and public spectacles such as mock sea battles, animal hunts, executions, re-enactments of famous battles, and dramas

Colossus Neronis (Colossus of Nero) a gigantic bronze statue of Emperor Nero; was later transformed into the sun god with the addition of a sunray crown

Cretan of the island of Crete

Crommyon a village in ancient Greece where a giant wild sow wreaked havoc before it was killed by Theseus

cuirass leather or metal armor consisting of a breastplate and backplate worn by Greek and Roman soldiers; often highly ornamented and designed to mimic muscles

Cyclops (Cyclopes, pl.) a member of a primordial race of giants, each with a single eye in the middle of his or her forehead

Cyrene a fierce huntress with whom Apollo fell in love after he saw her wrestle a lion; Apollo later transformed her into a nymph in order to extend her life

Daedalus a skilled craftsman who created the Labyrinth on Crete in which the Minotaur (part man, part bull) was kept

Daphne a beautiful naiad who attracted Apollo's attention; she was transformed into a laurel tree in order to escape him

Demeter the Greek goddess of agriculture; a daughter of the Titans Rhea and Kronos; Roman form: Ceres

dimachaerus a Roman gladiator trained to fight with two swords at once

Dionysus the Greek god of wine and revelry; the son of Zeus; activities director at Camp Half-Blood

Domus Aurea Emperor Nero's extravagant villa in the heart of ancient Rome, built after the Great Fire of Rome

Doors of Death the doorway to the House of Hades, located in Tartarus; doors have two sides—one in the mortal world, and one in the Underworld

drakon a gigantic yellow-and-green serpentlike monster, with frills around its neck, reptilian eyes, and huge talons; it spits poison

dryads tree nymphs

Erebos a place of darkness between earth and Hades

Eros the Greek god of love

Erythaea an island where the Cumaean Sibyl, a love interest of Apollo, originally lived before he convinced her to leave it by promising her a long life

Fields of Punishment the section of the Underworld where people who were evil during their lives are sent to face eternal punishment for their crimes after death

Gaea the Greek earth goddess; mother of Titans, giants, Cyclopes, and other monsters .

Germani (Germanus, sing.) tribal people who settled to the west of the Rhine river

Golden Fleece this hide from a gold-haired winged ram was a symbol of authority and kingship; it was guarded by a dragon and fire-breathing bulls; Jason was tasked with obtaining it, resulting in an epic quest

Gorgons three monstrous sisters (Stheno, Euryale, and Medusa) who have hair of living, venomous snakes; Medusa's eyes can turn the beholder to stone

Great Fire of Rome a devastating fire that took place in 64 CE, lasting for six days; rumors indicated that Nero started the fire to clear space for the building of his villa, Domus Aurea, but he blamed the Christian community for the disaster

greaves shin armor

Greek fire an incendiary weapon used in naval battles because it can continue burning in water

Grove of Dodona the site of the oldest Greek Oracle, second only to the Delphi; the rustling of trees in the grove provided answers to priests and priestesses who journeyed to the site

Hades the Greek god of death and riches; ruler of the Underworld

harpy a winged female creature that snatches things

Hebe   the Greek goddess of youth; daughter of Zeus and Hera

Hecate   goddess of magic and crossroads

Hephaestus   the Greek god of fire and crafts and of blacksmiths; the son of Zeus and Hera, and married to Aphrodite

Hera   the Greek goddess of marriage; Zeus's wife and sister

Hermes   Greek god of travelers; guide to spirits of the dead; god of communication

Herodotus   a Greek historian known as the "Father of History"

Hestia   Greek goddess of the hearth

hippocampi (hippocampus, sing.)   half-horse, half-fish creatures

hippodrome   an oval stadium for horse and chariot races in ancient Greece

Hittites   a group of people who lived in modern Turkey and Syria; often in conflict with Egyptians; known for their use of chariots as assault weapons

House of Hades   a place in the Underworld where Hades, the Greek god of death, and his wife, Persephone, rule over the souls of the departed

Hunters of Artemis   a group of maidens loyal to Artemis and gifted with hunting skills and eternal youth as long as they reject men for life

Hyacinthus   a Greek hero and Apollo's lover, who died while trying to impress Apollo with his discus skills

Hypnos   the Greek god of sleep

ichor   the golden fluid that is the blood of gods and immortals

imperator   a term for *commander* in the Roman Empire

Imperial gold   a rare metal deadly to monsters, consecrated at the Pantheon; its existence was a closely guarded secret of the emperors

Iris   the Greek goddess of the rainbow, and a messenger of the gods

Julian dynasty   the time period measured from the battle of Actium (31 BCE) to the death of Nero (68 CE)

karpoi (*karpos*, sing.)   grain spirits

kouretes   armored dancers who guarded the infant Zeus from his father, Kronos

Kronos   the youngest of the twelve Titans; the son of Ouranos and Gaea; the father of Zeus; he killed his father at his mother's bidding; Titan lord of fate, harvest, justice, and time; Roman form: Saturn

Labyrinth   an underground maze originally built on the island of Crete by the craftsman Daedalus to hold the Minotaur

Laomedon   a Trojan king whom Poseidon and Apollo were sent to serve after they offended Zeus

Lepidus   a Roman patrician and military commander who was in a triumvirate with Octavian and Marc Antony

Leto   mother of Artemis and Apollo with Zeus; goddess of motherhood

Lupercalia   a pastoral festival, observed on February 13 through 15, to avert evil spirits and purify the city, releasing health and fertility

Lydia   a province in ancient Rome; the double ax origi-
nated there, along with the use of coins and retail shops

Marc Antony   a Roman politician and general; part of the
triumvirate, with Lepidus and Octavian, who together
tracked down and defeated Caesar's killers; had an
enduring affair with Cleopatra

Marsyas   a satyr who lost to Apollo after challenging him
in a musical contest, which led to Marsyas being flayed
alive

Medea   a follower of Hecate and one of the great sorcer-
esses of the ancient world

Midas   a king with the power to transform anything he
touched to gold; he selected Marsyas as the winner
in the musical contest between Apollo and Marsyas,
resulting in Apollo giving Midas the ears of a donkey

Minos   king of Crete; son of Zeus; every year he made King
Aegus pick seven boys and seven girls to be sent to the
Labyrinth, where they would be eaten by the Minotaur;
after his death he became a judge in the Underworld

Minotaur   the half-man, half-bull son of King Minos of
Crete; the Minotaur was kept in the Labyrinth, where he
killed people who were sent in; he was finally defeated
by Theseus

Mithridates   king of Pontus and Armenia Minor in northern Anatolia (now Turkey) from about 120 to 63 BCE;
one of the Roman Republic's most formidable and
successful enemies, who engaged three of the prom-
inent generals from the late Roman Republic in the
Mithridatic Wars

Mount Olympus   home of the Twelve Olympians

myrmeke   a giant antlike creature that poisons and paralyzes its prey before eating it; known for protecting various metals, particularly gold

Nemesis   the Greek goddess of revenge

Nero   Roman emperor from 54 to 68 CE; the last in the Julian dynasty

New Rome   a community near Camp Jupiter where demigods can live together in peace, without interference from mortals or monsters

Nike   the Greek goddess of strength, speed, and victory

Nine Muses   Greek goddesses of literature, science, and the arts, who have inspired artists and writers for centuries

Niobe   daughter of Tantalus and Dione; suffered the loss of her six sons and six daughters, who were killed by Apollo and Artemis as a punishment for her pride

nosoi (*nosos*, sing.)   spirits of plague and disease

nymph   a female nature deity who animates nature

Octavian   the founder and first emperor of the Roman Empire; adopted son and heir of Julius Caesar (*see also* Caesar Augustus)

Odysseus   legendary Greek king of Ithaca and the hero of Homer's epic poem *The Odyssey*

Ogygia   the island home—and prison—of the nymph Calypso

omphalus   stones used to mark the center—or navel—of the world

Oracle of Delphi   a speaker of the prophecies of Apollo

Oracle of Trophonius   a Greek who was transformed into an Oracle after his death; located at the Cave of Trophonius; known for terrifying those who seek him

Ouranos   the Greek personification of the sky; father of the Titans

palikoi (*palikos*, sing.)   twin sons of Zeus and Thaleia; the gods of geysers and thermal springs

Pan   the Greek god of the wild; the son of Hermes

Pandora   the first human woman created by the gods; endowed with a unique gift from each; released evil into the world by opening a jar

Parthenon   a temple dedicated to the goddess Athena located at the Athenian Acropolis in Greece

Patroclus   son of Menoetius; he shared a deep friendship with Achilles after being raised alongside him; he was killed while fighting in the Trojan War

pegasus (pegasi, pl.)   a winged divine horse; sired by Poseidon, in his role as horse-god

Peleus   father of Achilles; his wedding to the sea-nymph Thetis was well attended by the gods, and a disagreement between them at the event eventually lead to the Trojan War; the guardian dragon at Camp Half-Blood is named after him

Persephone   the Greek queen of the Underworld; wife of Hades; daughter of Zeus and Demeter

phalanx (phalanxes, pl.)   a compact body of heavily armed troops

Phidias   a famous ancient Greek sculptor who created the Athena Parthenos and many others

Polyphemus the gigantic one-eyed son of Poseidon and Thoosa; one of the Cyclopes

Poseidon the Greek god of the sea; son of the Titans Kronos and Rhea, and brother of Zeus and Hades

praetor an elected Roman magistrate and commander of the army

Primordial Chaos the first thing ever to exist; a void from which the first gods were produced

Prometheus the Titan who created humans and gifted them with fire stolen from Mount Olympus

Pythia the name given to every Oracle of Delphi

Python a monstrous serpent that Gaea appointed to guard the Oracle at Delphi

Rhea Silvia the queen of the Titans, mother of Zeus

Riptide the name of Percy Jackson's sword; *Anaklusmos* in Greek

River Styx the river that forms the boundary between earth and the Underworld

Saturnalia an ancient Roman festival celebrating Saturn (Kronos)

satyr a Greek forest god, part goat and part man

shadow-travel a form of transportation that allows creatures of the Underworld and children of Hades to use shadows to leap to any desired place on earth or in the Underworld, although it makes the user extremely fatigued

Sibyl a prophetess

Sibylline Books a collection of prophecies in rhyme written in Greek; Tarquinius Superbus, a king of Rome, bought them from a prophetess and consulted them in times of great danger

siccae   a short curved sword used for battle in ancient Rome

Sparta   a city-state in ancient Greece with military dominance

Stygian iron   a magical metal, forged in the River Styx, capable of absorbing the very essence of monsters and injuring mortals, gods, Titans, and giants; has a significant effect on ghosts and creatures from the Underworld

Talos   a giant mechanical man made of bronze and used on Crete to guard its shoreline from invaders

Tantalus   According to legend, this king was such a good friend of the gods that he was allowed to dine at their table—until he spilled their secrets on earth; he was sent to the Underworld, where his curse was to be stuck in a pool of water under a fruit tree, but never be able to drink or eat

Tartarus   husband of Gaea; spirit of the abyss; father of the giants; a region of the Underworld

Theodosius   the last to rule over the united Roman Empire; known for closing all ancient temples across the empire

Thracian   of Thrace, a region centered on the modern borders of Bulgaria, Greece, and Turkey

Titan War   the epic ten-year battle between the Titans and the Olympians that resulted in the Olympians taking the throne

Titans   a race of powerful Greek deities, descendants of Gaea and Ouranos, that ruled during the Golden Age and were overthrown by a race of younger gods, the Olympians

trireme a Greek warship, having three tiers of oars on each side

triumvirate a political alliance formed by three parties

Trojan War According to legend, the Trojan War was waged against the city of Troy by the Achaeans (Greeks) after Paris of Troy took Helen from her husband, Menelaus, king of Sparta

Troy a Roman city situated in modern-day Turkey; site of the Trojan War

Tyche the Greek goddess of good fortune; daughter of Hermes and Aphrodite

Typhon the most terrifying Greek monster; father of many famous monsters, including Cerberus, the vicious multi-headed dog tasked with guarding the entrance to the Underworld

Underworld the kingdom of the dead, where souls go for eternity; ruled by Hades

Zephyros the Greek god of the West Wind

Zeus the Greek god of the sky and the king of the gods

Can't get enough of Apollo? Read the first chapter of
Book Two in the Trials of Apollo series,
THE DARK PROPHECY

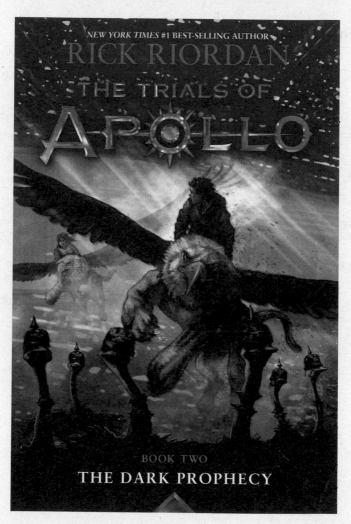

1

Lester (Apollo)
Still human; thanks for asking
Gods, I hate my life

WHEN OUR DRAGON declared war on Indiana, I knew it was going to be a bad day.

We'd been traveling west for six weeks, and Festus had never shown such hostility toward a state. New Jersey he ignored. Pennsylvania he seemed to enjoy, despite our battle with the Cyclopes of Pittsburgh. Ohio he tolerated, even after our encounter with Potina, the Roman goddess of childhood drinks, who pursued us in the form of a giant red pitcher emblazoned with a smiley face.

Yet for some reason, Festus decided he did not like Indiana. He landed on the cupola of the Indiana Statehouse, flapped his metallic wings, and blew a cone of fire that incinerated the state flag right off the flagpole.

"Whoa, buddy!" Leo Valdez pulled the dragon's reins. "We've talked about this. No blowtorching public monuments!"

Behind him on the dragon's spine, Calypso gripped Festus's scales for balance. "Could we *please* get to the ground? *Gently* this time?"

For a formerly immortal sorceress who once controlled air spirits, Calypso was not a fan of flying. Cold wind blew her chestnut hair into my face, making me blink and spit.

That's right, dear reader.

I, the most important passenger, the youth who had once been the glorious god Apollo, was forced to sit in the back of the dragon. Oh, the indignities I had suffered since Zeus stripped me of my divine powers! It wasn't enough that I was now a sixteen-year-old mortal with the ghastly alias Lester Papadopoulos. It wasn't enough that I had to toil upon the earth doing (ugh) heroic quests until I could find a way back into my father's good graces, or that I had a case of acne which simply *would not* respond to over-the-counter zit medicine. Despite my New York State junior driver's license, Leo Valdez didn't trust me to operate his aerial bronze steed!

Festus's claws scrabbled for a hold on the green copper dome, which was much too small for a dragon his size. I had a flashback to the time I installed a life-size statue of the muse Calliope on my sun chariot and the extra weight of the hood ornament made me nosedive into China and create the Gobi Desert.

Leo glanced back, his face streaked with soot. "Apollo, you sense anything?"

"Why is it *my* job to sense things? Just because I used to be a god of prophecy—"

"You're the one who's been having visions," Calypso reminded me. "You said your friend Meg would be here."

Just hearing Meg's name gave me a twinge of pain. "That doesn't mean I can pinpoint her location with my mind! Zeus has revoked my access to GPS!"

"GPS?" Calypso asked.

"Godly positioning systems."

"That's not a real thing!"

"Guys, cool it." Leo patted the dragon's neck. "Apollo, just try, will you? Does this look like the city you dreamed about or not?"

I scanned the horizon.

Indiana was flat country—highways crisscrossing scrubby

brown plains, shadows of winter clouds floating above urban sprawl. Around us rose a meager cluster of downtown high-rises—stacks of stone and glass like layered wedges of black and white licorice. (Not the yummy kind of licorice, either; the nasty variety that sits for eons in your stepmother's candy bowl on the coffee table. And, no, Hera, why would I be talking about you?)

After falling to earth in New York City, I found Indianapolis desolate and uninspiring, as if one proper New York neighborhood—Midtown, perhaps—had been stretched out to encompass the entire area of Manhattan, then relieved of two-thirds of its population and vigorously power-washed.

I could think of no reason why an evil triumvirate of ancient Roman emperors would take interest in such a location. Nor could I imagine why Meg McCaffrey would be sent here to capture me. Yet my visions had been clear. I had seen this skyline. I had heard my old enemy Nero give orders to Meg: *Go west. Capture Apollo before he can find the next Oracle. If you cannot bring him to me alive, kill him.*

The truly sad thing about this? Meg was one of my better friends. She also happened to be my demigod master, thanks to Zeus's twisted sense of humor. As long as I remained mortal, Meg could order me to do anything, even kill myself. . . . No. Better not to think of such possibilities.

I shifted in my metal seat. After so many weeks of travel, I was tired and saddle sore. I wanted to find a safe place to rest. *This* was not such a city. Something about the landscape below made me as restless as Festus.

Alas, I was sure this was where we were meant to be. Despite the danger, if I had a chance of seeing Meg McCaffrey again, of prying her away from her villainous stepfather's grasp, I had to try.

"This is the spot," I said. "Before this dome collapses under us, I suggest we get to the ground."

Calypso grumbled in ancient Minoan, "I already *said* that."

"Well, excuse me, sorceress!" I replied in the same language. "Perhaps if *you* had helpful visions, I'd listen to you more often!"

Calypso called me a few names that reminded me how colorful the Minoan language had been before it went extinct.

"Hey, you two," Leo said. "No ancient dialects. Spanish or English, please. Or Machine."

Festus creaked in agreement.

"It's okay, boy," Leo said. "I'm sure they didn't mean to exclude us. Now let's fly down to street level, huh?"

Festus's ruby eyes glowed. His metal teeth spun like drill bits. I imagined him thinking, *Illinois is sounding pretty good right about now.*

But he flapped his wings and leaped from the dome. We hurtled downward, landing in front of the statehouse with enough force to crack the sidewalk. My eyeballs jiggled like water balloons.

Festus whipped his head from side to side, steam curling from his nostrils.

I saw no immediate threats. Cars drove leisurely down West Washington Street. Pedestrians strolled by: a middle-aged woman in a flowery dress, a heavyset policeman carrying a paper coffee cup labeled CAFÉ PATACHOU, a clean-cut man in a blue seersucker suit.

The man in blue waved politely as he passed. "Morning."

"'Sup, dude," Leo called.

Calypso tilted her head. "Why was he so friendly? Does he not *see* that we're sitting atop a fifty-ton metal dragon?"

Leo grinned. "It's the Mist, babe—messes with mortal eyes. Makes monsters look like stray dogs. Makes swords look like umbrellas. Makes me look even more handsome than usual!"

Calypso jabbed her thumbs into Leo's kidneys.

"Ow!" he complained.

"I know what the Mist is, *Leonidas*—"

"Hey, I told you never to call me that."

"—but the Mist must be very strong here if it can hide a monster of Festus's size at such close range. Apollo, don't you find that a little odd?"

I studied the passing pedestrians.

True, I had seen places where the Mist was particularly heavy. At Troy, the sky above the battlefield had been so thick with gods you couldn't turn your chariot without running into another deity, yet the Trojans and Greeks saw only hints of our presence. At Three Mile Island in 1979, the mortals somehow failed to realize that their partial nuclear meltdown was caused by an epic chainsaw fight between Ares and Hephaestus. (As I recall, Hephaestus had insulted Ares's bell-bottom jeans.)

Still, I did not think heavy Mist was the problem here. Something about these locals bothered me. Their faces were too placid. Their dazed smiles reminded me of ancient Athenians just before the Dionysus Festival—everyone in a good mood, distracted, thinking about the drunken riots and debauchery to come.

"We should get out of the public eye," I suggested. "Perhaps—"

Festus stumbled, shaking like a wet dog. From inside his chest came a noise like a loose bicycle chain.

"Aw, not again," Leo said. "Everybody off!"

Calypso and I quickly dismounted.

Leo ran in front of Festus and held out his arms in a classic dragon-wrangler's stance. "Hey, buddy, it's fine! I'm just going to switch you off for a while, okay? A little downtime to—"

Festus projectile-vomited a column of flames that engulfed

Leo. Fortunately, Valdez was fireproof. His clothes were not. From what Leo had told me, he could generally prevent his outfits from burning up simply by concentrating. If he were caught by surprise, however, it didn't always work.

When the flames dissipated, Leo stood before us wearing nothing but his asbestos boxer shorts, his magical tool belt, and a pair of smoking, partially melted sneakers.

"Dang it!" he complained. "Festus, it's cold out here!"

The dragon stumbled. Leo lunged and flipped the lever behind the dragon's left foreleg. Festus began to collapse. His wings, limbs, neck, and tail contracted into his body, his bronze plates overlapping and folding inward. In a matter of seconds, our robotic friend had been reduced to a large bronze suitcase.

That should have been physically impossible, of course, but like any decent god, demigod, or engineer, Leo Valdez refused to be stopped by the laws of physics.

He scowled at his new piece of luggage. "Man . . . I *thought* I fixed his gyro-capacitor. Guess we're stuck here until I can find a machine shop."

Calypso grimaced. Her pink ski jacket glistened with condensation from our flight through the clouds. "And if we find such a shop, how long will it take to repair Festus?"

Leo shrugged. "Twelve hours? Fifteen?" He pushed a button on the side of the suitcase. A handle popped up. "Also, if we see a men's clothing store, that might be good."

I imagined walking into a T.J. Maxx, Leo in boxer shorts and melted sneakers, rolling a bronze suitcase behind him. I did not relish the idea.

Then, from the direction of the sidewalk, a voice called, "Hello!"

The woman in the flowery dress had returned. At least she *looked* like the same woman. Either that or lots of ladies in Indianapolis wore purple-and-yellow honeysuckle-pattern dresses and had 1950s bouffant hairstyles.

She smiled vacantly. "Beautiful morning!"

It was in fact a miserable morning—cold and cloudy with a smell of impending snow—but I felt it would be rude to ignore her completely.

I gave her a little parade wave—the sort of gesture I used to give my worshippers when they came to grovel at my altar. To me, the message was clear enough: *I see you, puny mortal; now run along. The gods are talking.*

The woman did not take the hint. She strolled forward and planted herself in front of us. She wasn't particularly large, but something about her proportions seemed off. Her shoulders were too wide for her head. Her chest and belly protruded in a lumpy mass, as if she'd stuffed a sack of mangos down the front of her dress. With her spindly arms and legs, she reminded me of some sort of giant beetle. If she ever tipped over, I doubted she could easily get back up.

"Oh, my!" She gripped her purse with both hands. "Aren't you children *cute!*"

Her lipstick and eye shadow were both a violent shade of purple. I wondered if she was getting enough oxygen to her brain.

"Madam," I said, "we are not children." I could have added that I was over four thousand years old, and Calypso was even older, but I decided not to get into that. "Now, if you'll excuse us, we have a suitcase to repair and my friend is in dire need of a pair of pants."

I tried to step around her. She blocked my path.

"You can't go yet, dear! We haven't welcomed you to Indiana!" From her purse, she drew a smartphone. The screen glowed as if a call were already in progress.

"It's him, all right," she said into the phone. "Everybody, come on over. Apollo is here!"

My lungs shriveled in my chest.

In the old days, I would have expected to be recognized as soon as I arrived in a town. *Of course* the locals would rush to welcome me. They would sing and dance and throw flowers. They would immediately begin constructing a new temple.

But as Lester Papadopoulos, I did not warrant such treatment. I looked nothing like my former glorious self. The idea that the Indianans might recognize me despite my tangled hair, acne, and flab was both insulting and terrifying. What if they erected a statue of me in my present form—a giant golden Lester in the center of their city? The other gods would never let me hear the end of it!

"Madam," I said, "I'm afraid you have mistaken me—"

"Don't be modest!" The woman tossed her phone and purse aside. She grabbed my forearm with the strength of a weight-lifter. "Our master will be delighted to have you in custody. And please call me Nanette."

Calypso charged. Either she wished to defend me (unlikely), or she was not a fan of the name Nanette. She punched the woman in the face.

This by itself did not surprise me. Having lost her immortal powers, Calypso was in the process of trying to master other skills. So far, she'd failed at swords, polearms, shurikens, whips, and improvisational comedy. (I sympathized with her frustration.) Today, she'd decided to try fisticuffs.

What surprised me was the loud CRACK her fist made against Nanette's face—the sound of finger bones breaking.

"Ow!" Calypso stumbled away, clutching her hand.

Nanette's head slid backward. She released me to try to grab her own face, but it was too late. Her head toppled off her shoulders. It clanged against the pavement and rolled sideways, the eyes still blinking, the purple lips twitching. Its base was smooth stainless steel. Attached to it were ragged strips of duct tape stuck with hair and bobby pins.

"Holy Hephaestus!" Leo ran to Calypso's side. "Lady, you broke my girlfriend's hand with your face. What *are* you, an automaton?"

"No, dear," said decapitated Nanette. Her muffled voice didn't come from the stainless-steel head on the sidewalk. It emanated from somewhere inside her dress. Just above her collar, where her neck used to be, an outcropping of fine blond hair was tangled with bobby pins. "And I must say, hitting me wasn't very polite."

Belatedly, I realized the metal head had been a disguise. Just as satyrs covered their hooves with human shoes, this creature passed for mortal by pretending to have a human face. Its voice came from its gut area, which meant . . .

My knees trembled.

"A *blemmyae*," I said.

Nanette chuckled. Her bulging midsection writhed under the honeysuckle cloth. She ripped open her blouse—something a polite Midwesterner would never think of doing—and revealed her true face.

Where a woman's brassiere would have been, two enormous bulging eyes blinked at me. From her sternum protruded a large shiny nose. Across her abdomen curled a hideous mouth—glistening orange lips, teeth like a spread of blank white playing cards.

"Yes, dear," the face said. "And I'm arresting you in the name of the Triumvirate!"

Up and down Washington Street, pleasant-looking pedestrians turned and began marching in our direction.

Can't get enough of heroes
battling monsters and mayhem?
You'll love The Kane Chronicles,
the *New York Times* #1 best-selling series
from Rick Riordan

THE
RED PYRAMID

WARNING

The following is a transcript of a digital recording. In certain places, the audio quality was poor, so some words and phrases represent the author's best guesses. Where possible, illustrations of important symbols mentioned in the recording have been added. Background noises such as scuffling, hitting, and cursing by the two speakers have not been transcribed. The author makes no claims for the authenticity of the recording. It seems impossible that the two young narrators are telling the truth, but you, the reader, must decide for yourself.

1. A Death at the Needle

WE ONLY HAVE A FEW HOURS, so listen carefully.

If you're hearing this story, you're already in danger. Sadie and I might be your only chance.

Go to the school. Find the locker. I won't tell you which school or which locker, because if you're the right person, you'll find it. The combination is 13/32/33. By the time you finish listening, you'll know what those numbers mean. Just remember the story we're about to tell you isn't complete yet. How it ends will depend on you.

The most important thing: when you open the package and find what's inside, *don't* keep it longer than a week. Sure, it'll be tempting. I mean, it will grant you almost unlimited power. But if you possess it too long, it will consume you. Learn its secrets quickly and pass it on. Hide it for the next person, the way Sadie and I did for you. Then be prepared for your life to get very interesting.

Okay, Sadie is telling me to stop stalling and get on with

the story. Fine. I guess it started in London, the night our dad blew up the British Museum.

My name is Carter Kane. I'm fourteen and my home is a suitcase.

You think I'm kidding? Since I was eight years old, my dad and I have traveled the world. I was born in L.A. but my dad's an archaeologist, so his work takes him all over. Mostly we go to Egypt, since that's his specialty. Go into a bookstore, find a book about Egypt, there's a pretty good chance it was written by Dr. Julius Kane. You want to know how Egyptians pulled the brains out of mummies, or built the pyramids, or cursed King Tut's tomb? My dad is your man. Of course, there are other reasons my dad moved around so much, but I didn't know his secret back then.

I didn't go to school. My dad homeschooled me, if you can call it "home" schooling when you don't have a home. He sort of taught me whatever he thought was important, so I learned a lot about Egypt and basketball stats and my dad's favorite musicians. I read a lot, too—pretty much anything I could get my hands on, from dad's history books to fantasy novels—because I spent a lot of time sitting around in hotels and airports and dig sites in foreign countries where I didn't know anybody. My dad was always telling me to put the book down and play some ball. You ever try to start a game of pick-up basketball in Aswan, Egypt? It's not easy.

Anyway, my dad trained me early to keep all my posses-sions in a single suitcase that fits in an airplane's overhead compartment. My dad packed the same way, except he was allowed an extra workbag for his archaeology tools. Rule number one: I was not allowed to look in his workbag. That's a rule I never broke until the day of the explosion.

It happened on Christmas Eve. We were in London for visitation day with my sister, Sadie.

See, Dad's only allowed two days a year with her—one in the winter, one in the summer—because our grandparents hate him. After our mom died, her parents (our grandparents) had this big court battle with Dad. After six lawyers, two fistfights, and a near fatal attack with a spatula (don't ask), they won the right to keep Sadie with them in England. She was only six, two years younger than me, and they couldn't keep us both—at least that was their excuse for not taking me. So Sadie was raised as a British schoolkid, and I traveled around with my dad. We only saw Sadie twice a year, which was fine with me.

[Shut up, Sadie. Yes—I'm getting to that part.]

So anyway, my dad and I had just flown into Heathrow after a couple of delays. It was a drizzly, cold afternoon. The whole taxi ride into the city, my dad seemed kind of nervous.

Now, my dad is a big guy. You wouldn't think anything could make him nervous. He has dark brown skin like mine, piercing brown eyes, a bald head, and a goatee, so he looks like a buff evil scientist. That afternoon he wore his cashmere winter coat and his best brown suit, the one he used for public lectures. Usually he exudes so much confidence that he dominates any room he walks into, but sometimes—like that afternoon—I saw another side to him that I didn't really understand. He kept looking over his shoulder like we were being hunted.

"Dad?" I said as we were getting off the A-40. "What's wrong?"

"No sign of them," he muttered. Then he must've realized he'd spoken aloud, because he looked at me kind of startled. "Nothing, Carter. Everything's fine."

Which bothered me because my dad's a terrible liar. I always knew when he was hiding something, but I also knew no amount of pestering would get the truth out of him. He was probably trying to protect me, though from what I didn't know. Sometimes I wondered if he had some dark secret in his past, some old enemy following him, maybe; but the idea seemed ridiculous. Dad was just an archaeologist.

The other thing that troubled me: Dad was clutching his workbag. Usually when he does that, it means we're in danger. Like the time gunmen stormed our hotel in Cairo. I heard shots coming from the lobby and ran downstairs to check on my dad. By the time I got there, he was just calmly zipping up his workbag while three unconscious gunmen hung by their feet from the chandelier, their robes falling over their heads so you could see their boxer shorts. Dad claimed not to have witnessed anything, and in the end the police blamed a freak chandelier malfunction.

Another time, we got caught in a riot in Paris. My dad found the nearest parked car, pushed me into the backseat, and told me to stay down. I pressed myself against the floorboards and kept my eyes shut tight. I could hear Dad in the driver's seat, rummaging in his bag, mumbling something to himself while the mob yelled and destroyed things outside. A few minutes later he told me it was safe to get up. Every other car on the block had been overturned and set on fire. Our car had been freshly washed and polished, and several twenty-euro notes had been tucked under the windshield wipers.

Anyway, I'd come to respect the bag. It was our good luck charm. But when my dad kept it close, it meant we were going to need good luck.

We drove through the city center, heading east toward my grandparents' flat. We passed the golden gates of Buckingham Palace, the big stone column in Trafalgar Square. London is a pretty cool place, but after you've traveled for so long, all cities start to blend together. Other kids I meet sometimes say, "Wow, you're so lucky you get to travel so much." But it's not like we spend our time sightseeing or have a lot of money to travel in style. We've stayed in some pretty rough places, and we hardly ever stay anywhere longer than a few days. Most of the time it feels like we're fugitives rather than tourists.

I mean, you wouldn't think my dad's work was dangerous. He does lectures on topics like "Can Egyptian Magic Really Kill You?" and "Favorite Punishments in the Egyptian Underworld" and other stuff most people wouldn't care about. But like I said, there's that other side to him. He's always very cautious, checking every hotel room before he lets me walk into it. He'll dart into a museum to see some artifacts, take a few notes, and rush out again like he's afraid to be caught on the security cameras.

One time when I was younger, we raced across the Charles de Gaulle airport to catch a last-minute flight, and Dad didn't relax until the plane was off the ground. I asked him point blank what he was running from, and he looked at me like I'd just pulled the pin out of a grenade. For a second I was scared he might actually tell me the truth. Then he said, "Carter, it's nothing." As if "nothing" were the most terrible thing in the world.

After that, I decided maybe it was better not to ask questions.

My grandparents, the Fausts, live in a housing development near Canary Wharf, right on the banks of the River Thames. The taxi let us off at the curb, and my dad asked the driver to wait.

We were halfway up the walk when Dad froze. He turned and looked behind us.

"What?" I asked.

Then I saw the man in the trench coat. He was across the street, leaning against a big dead tree. He was barrel shaped, with skin the color of roasted coffee. His coat and black pinstriped suit looked expensive. He had long braided hair and wore a black fedora pulled down low over his dark round glasses. He reminded me of a jazz musician, the kind my dad would always drag me to see in concert. Even though I couldn't see his eyes, I got the impression he was watching us. He might've been an old friend or colleague of Dad's. No matter where we went, Dad was always running into people he knew. But it did seem strange that the guy was waiting here, outside my grandparents'. And he didn't look happy.

"Carter," my dad said, "go on ahead."

"But—"

"Get your sister. I'll meet you back at the taxi."

He crossed the street toward the man in the trench coat, which left me with two choices: follow my dad and see what was going on, or do what I was told.

I decided on the slightly less dangerous path. I went to retrieve my sister.

Before I could even knock, Sadie opened the door.

"Late as usual," she said.

She was holding her cat, Muffin, who'd been a "going away" gift from Dad six years before. Muffin never seemed to get older or bigger. She had fuzzy yellow-and-black fur like a miniature leopard, alert yellow eyes, and pointy ears that were too tall for her head. A silver Egyptian pendant dangled from her collar. She didn't look anything like a muffin, but Sadie had been little when she named her, so I guess you have to cut her some slack.

Sadie hadn't changed much either since last summer.

[As I'm recording this, she's standing next to me, glaring, so I'd better be careful how I describe her.]

You would never guess she's my sister. First of all, she'd been living in England so long, she has a British accent. Second, she takes after our mom, who was white, so Sadie's skin is much lighter than mine. She has straight caramel-colored hair, not exactly blond but not brown, which she usually dyes with streaks of bright colors. That day it had red streaks down the left side. Her eyes are blue. I'm serious. *Blue* eyes, just like our mom's. She's only twelve, but she's exactly as tall as me, which is really annoying. She was chewing gum as usual, dressed for her day out with Dad in battered jeans, a leather jacket, and combat boots, like she was going to a concert and was hoping to stomp on some people. She had headphones dangling around her neck in case we bored her.

[Okay, she didn't hit me, so I guess I did an okay job of describing her.]

"Our plane was late," I told her.

She popped a bubble, rubbed Muffin's head, and tossed the cat inside. "Gran, going out!"

From somewhere in the house, Grandma Faust said something I couldn't make out, probably "Don't let them in!"

Sadie closed the door and regarded me as if I were a dead mouse her cat had just dragged in. "So, here you are again."

"Yep."

"Come on, then." She sighed. "Let's get on with it."

That's the way she was. No "Hi, how you been the last six months? So glad to see you!" or anything. But that was okay with me. When you only see each other twice a year, it's like you're distant cousins rather than siblings. We had absolutely nothing in common except our parents.

We trudged down the steps. I was thinking how she smelled like a combination of old people's house and bubble gum when she stopped so abruptly, I ran into her.

"Who's that?" she asked.

I'd almost forgotten about the dude in the trench coat. He and my dad were standing across the street next to the big tree, having what looked like a serious argument. Dad's back was turned so I couldn't see his face, but he gestured with his hands like he does when he's agitated. The other guy scowled and shook his head.

"Dunno," I said. "He was there when we pulled up."

"He looks familiar." Sadie frowned like she was trying to remember. "Come on."

"Dad wants us to wait in the cab," I said, even though I knew it was no use. Sadie was already on the move.

Instead of going straight across the street, she dashed up the sidewalk for half a block, ducking behind cars, then crossed to the opposite side and crouched under a stone wall. She started sneaking toward our dad. I didn't have much choice but to follow her example, even though it made me feel kind of stupid.

"Six years in England," I muttered, "and she thinks she's James Bond."

Sadie swatted me without looking back and kept creeping forward.

A couple more steps and we were right behind the big dead tree. I could hear my dad on the other side, saying, "—have to, Amos. You know it's the right thing."

"No," said the other man, who must've been Amos. His voice was deep and even—very insistent. His accent was American. "If I don't stop you, Julius, *they* will. The Per Ankh is shadowing you."

Sadie turned to me and mouthed the words "Per *what*?"

I shook my head, just as mystified. "Let's get out of here," I whispered, because I figured we'd be spotted any minute and get in serious trouble. Sadie, of course, ignored me.

"They don't know my plan," my father was saying. "By the time they figure it out—"

"And the children?" Amos asked. The hairs stood up on the back of my neck. "What about them?"

"I've made arrangements to protect them," my dad said. "Besides, if I don't do this, we're all in danger. Now, back off."

"I can't, Julius."

"Then it's a duel you want?" Dad's tone turned deadly serious. "You never could beat me, Amos."

I hadn't seen my dad get violent since the Great Spatula Incident, and I wasn't anxious to see a repeat of *that*, but the two men seemed to be edging toward a fight.

Before I could react, Sadie popped up and shouted, "Dad!"

He looked surprised when she tackle-hugged him, but not nearly as surprised as the other guy, Amos. He backed up so quickly, he tripped over his own trench coat.

He'd taken off his glasses. I couldn't help thinking that Sadie was right. He did look familiar—like a very distant memory.

"I—I must be going," he said. He straightened his fedora and lumbered down the road.

Our dad watched him go. He kept one arm protectively around Sadie and one hand inside the workbag slung over his shoulder. Finally, when Amos disappeared around the corner, Dad relaxed. He took his hand out of the bag and smiled at Sadie. "Hello, sweetheart."

Sadie pushed away from him and crossed her arms. "Oh, now it's *sweetheart*, is it? You're late. Visitation Day's nearly over! And what was that about? Who's Amos, and what's the Per Ankh?"

Dad stiffened. He glanced at me like he was wondering how much we'd overheard.

"It's nothing," he said, trying to sound upbeat. "I have a wonderful evening planned. Who'd like a private tour of the British Museum?"

Sadie slumped in the back of the taxi between Dad and me.

"I can't believe it," she grumbled. "One evening together, and you want to do research."

Dad tried for a smile. "Sweetheart, it'll be fun. The curator of the Egyptian collection personally invited—"

"Right, big surprise." Sadie blew a strand of red-streaked hair out of her face. "Christmas Eve, and we're going to see some moldy old relics from Egypt. Do you ever think about *anything* else?"

Dad didn't get mad. He never gets mad at Sadie. He just stared out the window at the darkening sky and the rain.

"Yes," he said quietly. "I do."

Whenever Dad got quiet like that and stared off into nowhere, I knew he was thinking about our mom. The last few months, it had been happening a lot. I'd walk into our hotel room and find him with his cell phone in his hands, Mom's picture smiling up at him from the screen—her hair tucked under a headscarf, her blue eyes startlingly bright against the desert backdrop.

Or we'd be at some dig site. I'd see Dad staring at the horizon, and I'd know he was remembering how he'd met her—two young scientists in the Valley of the Kings, on a dig to discover a lost tomb. Dad was an Egyptologist. Mom was an anthropologist looking for ancient DNA. He'd told me the story a thousand times.

Our taxi snaked its way along the banks of the Thames. Just past Waterloo Bridge, my dad tensed.

"Driver," he said. "Stop here a moment."

The cabbie pulled over on the Victoria Embankment.

"What is it, Dad?" I asked.

He got out of the cab like he hadn't heard me. When Sadie and I joined him on the sidewalk, he was staring up at Cleopatra's Needle.

In case you've never seen it: the Needle is an obelisk, not a needle, and it doesn't have anything to do with Cleopatra. I guess the British just thought the name sounded cool when they brought it to London. It's about seventy feet tall, which would've been really impressive back in Ancient Egypt, but on the Thames, with all the tall buildings around, it looks small and sad. You could drive right by it and not even realize you'd just passed something that was a thousand years older than the city of London.

"God." Sadie walked around in a frustrated circle. "Do we have to stop for *every* monument?"

My dad stared at the top of the obelisk. "I had to see it again," he murmured. "Where it happened…"

A freezing wind blew off the river. I wanted to get back in the cab, but my dad was really starting to worry me. I'd never seen him so distracted.

"What, Dad?" I asked. "What happened here?"

"The last place I saw her."

Sadie stopped pacing. She scowled at me uncertainly, then back at Dad. "Hang on. Do you mean Mum?"

Dad brushed Sadie's hair behind her ear, and she was so surprised, she didn't even push him away.

I felt like the rain had frozen me solid. Mom's death had always been a forbidden subject. I knew she'd died in an accident in London. I knew my grandparents blamed my dad. But no one would ever tell us the details. I'd given up asking my dad, partly because it made him so sad, partly because he absolutely refused to tell me anything. "When you're older" was all he would say, which was the most frustrating response ever.

"You're telling us she died here," I said. "At Cleopatra's Needle? What happened?"

He lowered his head.

"Dad!" Sadie protested. "I go past this *every* day, and you mean to say—all this time—and I didn't even *know*?"

"Do you still have your cat?" Dad asked her, which seemed like a really stupid question.

"Of course I've still got the cat!" she said. "What does that have to do with anything?"

"And your amulet?"

Sadie's hand went to her neck. When we were little, right before Sadie went to live with our grandparents, Dad had given us both Egyptian amulets. Mine was an Eye of Horus, which was a popular protection symbol in Ancient Egypt.

In fact my dad says the modern pharmacist's symbol, ℞, is a simplified version of the Eye of Horus, because medicine is supposed to protect you.

Anyway, I always wore my amulet under my shirt, but I figured Sadie would've lost hers or thrown it away.

To my surprise, she nodded. "'Course I have it, Dad, but don't change the subject. Gran's always going on about how you caused Mum's death. That's not true, is it?"

We waited. For once, Sadie and I wanted exactly the same thing—the truth.

"The night your mother died," my father started, "here at the Needle—"

A sudden flash illuminated the embankment. I turned, half blind, and just for a moment I glimpsed two figures: a tall pale man with a forked beard and wearing cream-colored robes, and a coppery-skinned girl in dark blue robes and a headscarf—the kind of clothes I'd seen hundreds of times in Egypt. They were just standing there side by side, not twenty feet away, watching us. Then the light faded. The figures melted into a fuzzy afterimage. When my eyes readjusted to the darkness, they were gone.

"Um…" Sadie said nervously. "Did you just see that?"

"Get in the cab," my dad said, pushing us toward the curb. "We're out of time."

From that point on, Dad clammed up.

"This isn't the place to talk," he said, glancing behind us. He'd promised the cabbie an extra ten pounds if he got us to the museum in under five minutes, and the cabbie was doing his best.

"Dad," I tried, "those people at the river—"

"And the other bloke, Amos," Sadie said. "Are they Egyptian police or something?"

"Look, both of you," Dad said, "I'm going to need your help tonight. I know it's hard, but you have to be patient. I'll explain everything, I promise, after we get to the museum. I'm going to make everything right again."

"What do you mean?" Sadie insisted. "Make *what* right?"

Dad's expression was more than sad. It was almost guilty. With a chill, I thought about what Sadie had said: about our grandparents blaming him for Mom's death. That *couldn't* be what he was talking about, could it?

The cabbie swerved onto Great Russell Street and screeched to a halt in front of the museum's main gates.

"Just follow my lead," Dad told us. "When we meet the curator, act normal."

I was thinking that Sadie never acted *normal*, but I decided not to say anything.

We climbed out of the cab. I got our luggage while Dad paid the driver with a big wad of cash. Then he did something strange. He threw a handful of small objects into the backseat—they looked like stones, but it was too dark for me to be sure. "Keep driving," he told the cabbie. "Take us to Chelsea."

That made no sense since we were already out of the cab, but the driver sped off. I glanced at Dad, then back at the cab, and before it turned the corner and disappeared in the dark, I caught a weird glimpse of three passengers in the backseat: a man and two kids.

I blinked. There was no way the cab could've picked up another fare so fast. "Dad—"

"London cabs don't stay empty very long," he said matter-of-factly. "Come along, kids."

He marched off through the wrought iron gates. For a second, Sadie and I hesitated.

"Carter, *what* is going on?"

I shook my head. "I'm not sure I want to know."

"Well, stay out here in the cold if you want, but *I'm* not leaving without an explanation." She turned and marched after our dad.

Looking back on it, I should've run. I should've dragged Sadie out of there and gotten as far away as possible. Instead I followed her through the gates.

Meet Magnus Chase and go on a
high-stakes adventure to Valhalla.

Read the first chapter of THE SWORD OF SUMMER,
the first book in the Magnus Chase and
the Gods of Asgard series.

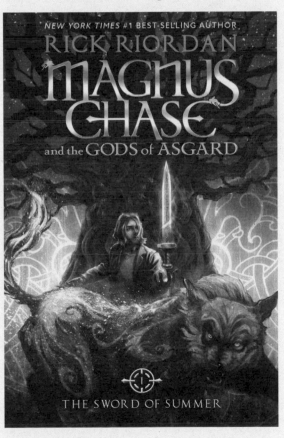

Good Morning!
You're Going to Die

YEAH, I KNOW. You guys are going to read about how I died in agony, and you're going be like, "Wow! That sounds cool, Magnus! Can I die in agony too?"

No. Just no.

Don't go jumping off any rooftops. Don't run into the highway or set yourself on fire. It doesn't work that way. You will not end up where I ended up.

Besides, you wouldn't want to deal with my situation. Unless you've got some crazy desire to see undead warriors hacking one another to pieces, swords flying up giants' noses, and dark elves in snappy outfits, you shouldn't even *think* about finding the wolf-headed doors.

My name is Magnus Chase. I'm sixteen years old. This is the story of how my life went downhill after I got myself killed.

My day started out normal enough. I was sleeping on the sidewalk under a bridge in the Public Garden when a guy kicked me awake and said, "They're after you."

By the way, I've been homeless for the past two years.

Some of you may think, *Aw, how sad.* Others may think, *Ha, ha, loser!* But if you saw me on the street, ninety-nine percent of you would walk right past like I'm invisible. You'd pray, *Don't let him ask me for money*. You'd wonder if I'm older than I look, because surely a teenager wouldn't be wrapped in a stinky old sleeping bag, stuck outside in the middle of a Boston winter. *Somebody should help that poor boy!*

Then you'd keep walking.

Whatever. I don't need your sympathy. I'm used to being laughed at. I'm definitely used to being ignored. Let's move on.

The bum who woke me was a guy called Blitz. As usual, he looked like he'd been running through a dirty hurricane. His wiry black hair was full of paper scraps and twigs. His face was the color of saddle leather, and was flecked with ice. His beard curled in all directions. Snow caked the bottom of his trench coat where it dragged around his feet—Blitz being about five feet five—and his eyes were so dilated, the irises were all pupil. His permanently alarmed expression made him look like he might start screaming any second.

I blinked the gunk out of my eyes. My mouth tasted like day-old hamburger. My sleeping bag was warm, and I really didn't want to get out of it.

"Who's after me?"

"Not sure." Blitz rubbed his nose, which had been broken so many times it zigzagged like a lightning bolt. "They're handing out flyers with your name and picture."

I cursed. Random police and park rangers I could deal with. Truant officers, community service volunteers, drunken college kids, addicts looking to roll somebody small and weak— all those would've been as easy to wake up to as pancakes and orange juice.

But when somebody knew my name and my face—that was

bad. That meant they were targeting me specifically. Maybe the folks at the shelter were mad at me for breaking their stereo. (Those Christmas carols had been driving me crazy.) Maybe a security camera caught that last bit of pickpocketing I did in the Theater District. (Hey, I needed money for pizza.) Or maybe, unlikely as it seemed, the police were still looking for me, wanting to ask questions about my mom's murder. . . .

I packed my stuff, which took about three seconds. The sleeping bag rolled up tight and fit in my backpack with my toothbrush and a change of socks and underwear. Except for the clothes on my back, that's all I owned. With the backpack over my shoulder and the hood of my jacket pulled low, I could blend in with pedestrian traffic pretty well. Boston was full of college kids. Some of them were even more scraggly and younger-looking than me.

I turned to Blitz. "Where'd you see these people with the flyers?"

"Beacon Street. They're coming this way. Middle-aged white guy and a teenage girl, probably his daughter."

I frowned. "That makes no sense. Who—"

"I don't know, kid, but I gotta go." Blitz squinted at the sunrise, which was turning the skyscraper windows orange. For reasons I'd never quite understood, Blitz hated the daylight. Maybe he was the world's shortest, stoutest homeless vampire. "You should go see Hearth. He's hanging out in Copley Square."

I tried not to feel irritated. The local street people jokingly called Hearth and Blitz my mom and dad because one or the other always seemed to be hovering around me.

"I appreciate it," I said. "I'll be fine."

Blitz chewed his thumbnail. "I dunno, kid. Not today. You gotta be extra careful."

"Why?"

He glanced over my shoulder. "They're coming."

I didn't see anybody. When I turned back, Blitz was gone.

I hated it when he did that. Just— *Poof.* The guy was like a ninja. A homeless vampire ninja.

Now I had a choice: go to Copley Square and hang out with Hearth, or head toward Beacon Street and try to spot the people who were looking for me.

Blitz's description of them made me curious. A middle-aged white guy and a teenage girl searching for me at sunrise on a bitter-cold morning. Why? Who were they?

I crept along the edge of the pond. Almost nobody took the lower trail under the bridge. I could hug the side of the hill and spot anyone approaching on the higher path without them seeing me.

Snow coated the ground. The sky was eye-achingly blue. The bare tree branches looked like they'd been dipped in glass. The wind cut through my layers of clothes, but I didn't mind the cold. My mom used to joke that I was half polar bear.

Dammit, Magnus, I chided myself.

After two years, my memories of her were still a minefield. I stumbled over one, and instantly my composure was blown to bits.

I tried to focus.

The man and the girl were coming this way. The man's sandy hair grew over his collar—not like an intentional style, but like he couldn't be bothered to cut it. His baffled expression reminded me of a substitute teacher's: *I know I was hit by a spit wad, but I have no idea where it came from.* His dress shoes were totally wrong for a Boston winter. His socks were different shades of brown. His tie looked like it had been tied while he spun around in total darkness.

The girl was definitely his daughter. Her hair was just as thick and wavy, though lighter blond. She was dressed more sensibly in snow boots, jeans, and a parka, with an orange T-shirt peeking out at the neckline. Her expression was more determined, angry. She gripped a sheaf of flyers like they were essays she'd been graded on unfairly.

If she was looking for me, I did not want to be found. She was scary.

I didn't recognize her or her dad, but something tugged at the back of my skull . . . like a magnet trying to pull out a very old memory.

Father and daughter stopped where the path forked. They looked around as if just now realizing they were standing in the middle of a deserted park at no-thank-you o'clock in the dead of winter.

"Unbelievable," said the girl. "I want to strangle him."

Assuming she meant me, I hunkered down a little more.

Her dad sighed. "We should probably avoid killing him. He *is* your uncle."

"But *two years?*" the girl demanded. "Dad, how could he not tell us for *two years?*"

"I can't explain Randolph's actions. I never could, Annabeth."

I inhaled so sharply, I was afraid they would hear me. A scab was ripped off my brain, exposing raw memories from when I was six years old.

Annabeth. Which meant the sandy-haired man was . . . *Uncle Frederick?*

I flashed back to the last family Thanksgiving we'd shared: Annabeth and me hiding in the library at Uncle Randolph's town house, playing with dominoes while the adults yelled at each other downstairs.

You're lucky you live with your momma. Annabeth stacked another domino on her miniature building. It was amazingly good, with columns in front like a temple. *I'm going to run away.*

I had no doubt she meant it. I was in awe of her confidence.

Then Uncle Frederick appeared in the doorway. His fists were clenched. His grim expression was at odds with the smiling reindeer on his sweater. *Annabeth, we're leaving.*

Annabeth looked at me. Her gray eyes were a little too fierce for a first grader's. *Be safe, Magnus.*

With a flick of her finger, she knocked over her domino temple.

That was the last time I'd seen her.

Afterward, my mom had been adamant: *We're staying away from your uncles. Especially Randolph. I won't give him what he wants. Ever.*

She wouldn't explain what Randolph wanted, or what she and Frederick and Randolph had argued about.

You have to trust me, Magnus. Being around them . . . it's too dangerous.

I trusted my mom. Even after her death, I hadn't had any contact with my relatives.

Now, suddenly, they were looking for me.

Randolph lived in town, but as far as I knew, Frederick and Annabeth still lived in Virginia. Yet here they were, passing out flyers with my name and photo on them. Where had they even *gotten* a photo of me?

My head buzzed so badly, I missed some of their conversation.

"—to find Magnus," Uncle Frederick was saying. He checked his smartphone. "Randolph is at the city shelter in the South End. He says no luck. We should try the youth shelter across the park."

"How do we even know Magnus is alive?" Annabeth asked miserably. "Missing for *two years*? He could be frozen in a ditch somewhere!"

Part of me was tempted to jump out of my hiding place and shout, *TA-DA!*

Even though it had been ten years since I'd seen Annabeth, I didn't like seeing her distressed. But after so long on the streets, I'd learned the hard way: you never walk into a situation until you understand what's going on.

"Randolph is sure Magnus is alive," said Uncle Frederick. "He's somewhere in Boston. If his life is truly in danger . . ."

They set off toward Charles Street, their voices carried away by the wind.

I was shivering now, but it wasn't from the cold. I wanted to run after Frederick, tackle him, and demand to hear what was going on. How did Randolph know I was still in town? Why were they looking for me? How was my life in danger now more than on any other day?

But I didn't follow them.

I remembered the last thing my mom ever told me. I'd been reluctant to use the fire escape, reluctant to leave her, but she'd gripped my arms and made me look at her. *Magnus, run. Hide. Don't trust anyone. I'll find you. Whatever you do, don't go to Randolph for help.*

Then, before I'd made it out the window, the door of our apartment had burst into splinters. Two pairs of glowing blue eyes had emerged from the darkness. . . .

I shook off the memory and watched Uncle Frederick and Annabeth walk away, veering east toward the Common.

Uncle Randolph . . . For some reason, he'd contacted Frederick and Annabeth. He'd gotten them to Boston. All this time, Frederick and Annabeth hadn't known that my mom was dead and I was missing. It seemed impossible, but if it were true, why would Randolph tell them about it now?

Without confronting him directly, I could think of only one way to get answers. His town house was in Back Bay, an easy walk from here. According to Frederick, Randolph wasn't home. He was somewhere in the South End, looking for me.

Since nothing started a day better than a little breaking and entering, I decided to pay his place a visit.